SCOTT M. SWAINE

FORGOTTEN MASTERS III

REPLY OF INTRIGUE

Primix Publishing
East Brunswick Office Evolution
1 Tower Center Boulevard, Ste 1510
East Brunswick, NJ 08816
www.primixpublishing.com
Phone: 1-800-538-5788

Published by Primix Publishing: 10/16/2024

ISBN: 979-8-89194-141-0(sc)
ISBN: 979-8-89194-256-1(hc)
ISBN: 979-8-89194-142-7(e)

Library of Congress Control Number: 2024905157

CONTENTS

Chapter 1
COMMENCEMENT

It was a new day in the city of Rolsklinde. The people meandered through the streets as they attended to their usual routines, largely unaware and uncaring of the affairs of the greater world outside their walls. Merchants hawked their local wares, what little they had for all the shortages of natural resources the city so often faced. Patrons attended the local taverns and inns, women took the duty of their household chores, and the children went to school.

A lone well-dressed man was making his way up the main avenue leading from the lower district of the city into the upper district. The upper district held many of the finer estate homes, the Governor's Manor, and the Academy of Arcana, where many young adults hoped to learn the intricacies of the magical arts. These buildings circled a large plaza, along with the main city temple and the city barracks, home of the local militia known as the Allegiance Guard.

The man seemed to be directed of purpose. He made a steady pace toward the plaza and turned off to the far side where the barracks building was found. He entered a large courtyard that often served as a training ground for new recruits. There were offices lining the right side, and turning to run along the rear of the yard. He pauses briefly to gain his bearings, and then continued straight across to the office of Captain Kholgard. When he arrives at the door, he knocks politely.

"Yes, come in," ushers the voice.

The man opens the door and confidently steps inside, closing the door behind him for privacy.

Captain Kholgard was sitting behind his desk reviewing a number of papers when the man entered. He looked up to see what was clearly a civilian, standing in the room, and waiting patiently for his turn.

"Yes, Citizen… What can we do for you?"

"Captain, I was sent to share a special meeting with you. I believe you were informed of this already by Lieutenant Carronel."

The Captain halted the casual review of his desk and turned to gaze determinedly at the man. The visitor was smartly dressed in a ruffled shirt and pants, which was not your typical commoner's clothing. Instead, it resembled the clothing of a wealthy merchant or a privileged administrator.

"The Lieutenant sent you? What's your name?"

"My name is Willit Sarens. I'm a former student from the academy, but now I'm working with His Lordship down there in the valley."

"You know, that's a line I thought I'd never hear in my lifetime," he chuckles. "And worse, that you might step into my office, and I would actually be expecting you."

"Yes Sir. Times sure do offer up their surprises on occasion."

"Come over and have a seat. What is it you need on this occasion?"

"It's my understanding Marelle sent you a note to expect me. It would seem we'll be working together on a number of…shall we say…special projects."

"Right, and it sounds like she's been coaching you, too."

"Yes, she gave me a number of important lessons. Before this, my only real service was to run out into the field and look at something, then run back to the academy just so the Dean could ignore whatever it was I was supposed to be reporting."

"Is that how they treat you over there? It's no wonder the academy never gave us much help, for all their blundering reports."

"To be honest, I didn't really know this until I was captured as a spy down there in Lord Thaelyn's camp. Marelle was there, and between the two of them, they started talking about stuff I had no prior knowledge of."

"What does that porker actually teach you in the academy?"

"How to be a good little lap dog…"

The Captain let out a bold laugh at the notion.

"All right, so what are we doing today?"

"This is my first time back in the city since my…" he coughs for emphasis, "…career change. I can't allow the Dean to see me, or else I'm sure there will be at least a few hells to pay, knowing him."

"Got it. Is this why you're dressed up like you're going to a temple ceremony?"

"Well, actually, I suppose you might say that. Most people would not normally expect to be seen like this, and certainly not someone like me."

"Don't you think you might stand out a little?"

"Stand out, maybe… Look like a former student from the academy, likely no. The Dean didn't regard us highly enough to understand which leg of our trousers to pull up first."

The Captain smiled brightly at the suggestion.

"You know, I think I like you, and that's saying something when we talk about you being from the academy."

"Anyway, I need to make contact with a friend of mine over there. We're close mates, and often think alike on a lot of things. But since I can't go in there myself, I need someone to drop a note with him to meet me outside."

"Ah, right. So, you're asking me for help?"

"Yes, if you could have one of your men dress up in plain clothes and deliver a note for me, that would be grand."

"In plain clothes?" he raises his brow.

"Yes. In case you haven't noticed lately, both the Dean's window, and the Governor's, face out onto the plaza, and I don't want them getting any crazy ideas about your guardsmen taking up an interest in mage studies."

"Clever…that little lady taught you well."

The Captain pulls out a scrap of paper and a pen to jot down a brief note.

"What's the name?"

"Jared Galwen. Be sure only he sees it, and if the Dean is present, we should abort and try again later."

"Right. And the message?"

"To meet me at the Ten Eagles in the lower district…"

"That's becoming a popular place lately. I've had a few of my own people browsing it with some of our other work."

"It's away from prying eyes, and as far as I've heard it, neither the Dean nor the Governor ever goes down there for any reason."

"Exactly right. When do you need this?"

"The sooner, the better. I need to establish myself with him."

"All right, I'll get my yard lieutenant on this. Are you going there now?"

"Yes, Sir!" he grins as he stands up from the chair.

The Captain nods as his guest leaves the building. He then struts over to the door to call in his Lieutenant from outside.

"Yes, Sir," the officer salutes as he arrives.

"I have an errand for you, Lieutenant. Listen up carefully…"

+ + + ◆ + + +

"Here it is, Your Grace, as requested."

"Ah, good, and thank you, Lady Amariyn. Now if we can just get our hands on the other one."

"Have you sent anyone down there yet?"

"Not as yet. Aerlie and I are still working on our briefings with our two spies. We finished the melds already, so they can speak the local tongue, and now it is just a matter of refining their acts to look and behave like Flame Elves."

"The whole affair sounds extremely delicate."

"Fortunately, our people come highly trained from all their academy courses, so they are capable of a wide variety of talents.

Although I will admit, on Tae'Eladar at least, we do not find ourselves with as much opportunity to practice this level of intrigue."

"For this point, I think you should consider yourselves blessed that you do not have any wars occurring on your world."

"Yes, but we have had our moments in the past."

"And you think the Daanen-Aryku will be able to work with these bottles? They're four centuries old, is it still possible to get anything out of them to test?"

"They were stored in what was essentially a cool dry area, by the descriptions. For you, a storage room, for Priestess Sehnisavain, the cellar of their temple, and the bottles were apparently sealed before being placed in their respective boxes. This could offer a few possibilities to preserve whatever still remained inside, within reason."

"I'm still a little at a loss to understand the ultimate purpose. We know it had to be the Suuden-Aryku that killed our trees with whatever poison these things held, and since they're enemies of this world regardless, why spend our time on this?"

"If the Governor of Rolsklinde is aligned with them, perhaps with the Dean at his side, I need a way to implicate him to expose his wrongdoings to the people. Having the Suuden-Aryku on his side complicates things for us, so we need to tip the balance as much as we can in our direction, and do so carefully so as not to spill anything prematurely."

"It makes me glad I am a priestess and not a soldier. I think all this intrigue would drive me mad after a while."

"It is most certainly a game for the thinking mind, and I will admit I am receiving a fair amount of exercise on this one."

Amariyn bows and leaves the room. She had been visiting with Thaelyn in the tactical office in the small settlement of Firstfall in the Badlands region. This began as a military foothold, where he had arrived due to a war against what was thought to be an orcish uprising of his home world, Tae'Eladar, but found it was actually an invasion from another one completely, which is where he found himself now, on Therinë.

His war against the orcs had been proceeding smoothly and

efficiently, as the orcs were generally a poor military power, with their only true threat potential being their excessively brutish manners and warmongering attitudes. But it was discovered they were actually a lesser faction in a much larger operation involving multiple members, some of which were invaders in this world.

This operation involved two other factions, one being the Flame Elves, who were a local society that had been corrupted and renamed by the dominating effect of a godlike being known as Sargeras. His kind were once thought to be long dead and forgotten, but the discovery of his movements escalated the severity of this war to new heights. The final member of this group was the Suuden-Aryku, a minion race Sargeras was using to play out his whims.

Thaelyn examined the box that Amariyn had delivered, which contained the bottle once used to poison their local Tree of Life. The tree was a sacred object in elven religion that once existed within a shrine in their city of Solinaia.

Priestess Sehnisavain and her people also had one, and it was also poisoned, supposedly by the same people and at the same time. The purpose was to try to break their spirits so that Sargeras could dominate them. In the case of her people, known originally as High Elves, he succeeded. But Thaelyn had recently liberated the Priestess and her two daughters, and now they were working together to fight back.

"General," Thaelyn begins. "Once we have the delivery from Kynesoth, we will need to send both of them to the Daanen-Aryku for study. I believe their advanced technology will be our best hope to find something."

"Of course, my Lord," he affirms. "And with a bit of good fortune, the two will match up, indicating to us that the substance must come from a common point of origin."

"Indeed. I would expect this to be the product of a much higher form of technology, not as much a natural poison or a product of a simpler form of alchemy. The Tree of Life can very often filter out such as these to cleanse itself. But if we are speaking of the Suuden-

Aryku, their science can perhaps produce synthetic substances, and I should think this would be rather dangerous for the tree."

"And I, for one, find it rather revolting that any sophisticated race worthy of their scientific achievements would stoop so low, if only for the possibility that they might also be under his control."

"It would seem he has been gathering up quite the menagerie of late. By the way, have we found anything new with our spies up in the dwarven enclave?"

"According to our most recent forays, they seem to represent your average dwarves in appearance, and most likely civilian, for their manner of dress. Our spies were able to sneak in under a cloak, and the dwarves did not seem to pay any mind to it, not that I would expect them to, as dwarves do not hold a practice to conduct spell-craft."

"Good. If they do not perform any sort of detection magic, we can have our people standing right over their shoulders and not be noticed. What sort of activities do we see thus far?"

"So far, our scouts are spending a fair amount of time just charting their tunnels. It would seem they have created a nice little maze up there. Initially, we have the forge Marelle spoke of during her visit, and it seems to be a busy center of work."

"Yes, the iron forge, which naturally brings us back to the Governor and his exclusive trade agreement, to which Rolsklinde does not seem to be receiving its fair share."

"Absolutely. There seems to be a fine amount of flow passing through, and it appears to be producing enough to supply the needs of that one city, and then some. But, if they are not actually receiving it, here is where we must assume the remainder is going to the Flame Elves and the orcs, although we haven't yet seen anyone picking up the supply in their storage lot."

"Very well," Thaelyn nods. "But it begs us to ask when they plan on doing this. What is their schedule? And then, the next question is what else they are doing up there. Do they have anything other than an iron forge, for example."

"To learn this, we will need to conduct much deeper surveys, but their tunnel system seems a little problematic. I think this is likely due to their long duration in that space and digging out so much material in this time."

"This could pose a few of its own problems, if that mountain is so heavily honeycombed by now."

"Yes, so we should apply some caution."

A nicely dressed man is seen crossing the plaza in the upper district of Rolsklinde, moving in the direction of the mage academy. He casually saunters through the door and into the main hall, where he sees a number of students in quiet study at tables and desks scattered around the room. Other students were browsing the bookcases, some of which were lining the walls and others freestanding on the far side of the room.

He pauses just inside the door, passing his glance around the assembly as if looking for something, but unsure what it was. He is noticed by several attending members, including a young woman with long blonde hair standing near one of the bookshelves. With no one else making any efforts to offer assistance, she decides to march over and see what he needs.

"Hello," she announces pleasantly. "Are you looking for something?"

"Ah, yes, my pardons," he begs politely. "I'm new on the job…a courier, you see."

"Oh, really! I was curious, because we don't usually see common visitors from off the street, and you don't look like a student, so I thought you might be lost. What do you need?"

"Yes, as it turns out, I'm supposed to be delivering a message, but unfortunately, I don't know the man I'm supposed to be delivering it to…at least not personally. Perhaps you can direct me?"

"I can certainly try. Do you have a name?"

"Yes, actually… Jared Galwen is the one."

"Ah, yes, I know him. In fact, he's a good friend of mine. I think he's, um…" she pauses to consider the course scheduling. "He's probably in his alchemy study right now. Can I offer to deliver this to him?"

"While that is very kind, my instructions are to deliver it to him personally."

"Oh, is this a private missive? Hmm, well, I think if we're quick, we might be able to sneak past the instructors. They can be rather picky about people poking their noses in the labs. We sometimes get these odd rumors going around that say they might be conducting secret experiments down there."

"Secret experiments?" he raises his brow. "What kind?"

"Well, it's mostly gossip in the hallways, but I've heard of people mysteriously vanishing in back alleys, and then some of the students tell of strange sounds coming up from the basement, which is where the alchemy labs are located. It's said we have a secret chamber down there that only the instructors know about, but they keep it locked, and sometimes you can hear moans coming out from behind the walls."

"You're kidding me!" he mutters nervously.

"In fact," she continues anxiously. "Some have even said the couriers that pass through, especially if they're not very well-known, can sometimes disappear without a trace! They just grab you and haul you off!"

The man's jaw drops as he gazes at her, aghast at the notion.

Several of the other students sitting at the tables had taken notice of the exchange by now, and they were all covering their mouths trying to hold back their laughter. The noise ushering up finally travelled across the room to the man, redirecting his attention to it. The woman finally relented and let out a bold giggle at her carefully played ruse.

The man studies her, and then the others, beginning to realize what was happening.

"Just a moment, young lady," he smirks. "What was all that about?"

"I'm simply teasing you…you know, the new guy."

"Oh, so you're one of those! Dear gods, you mages," he covers his eyes and shakes his head. "I didn't know you people actually had a sense of humor," he smiles.

"Really! Is that how the people outside see us?"

"Actually, there are a lot of ideas that float around, if you must know. But now, about this message I need to deliver."

"Right," she smiles. "And thanks for being such a good sport. Please, follow me and I'll lead you to Jared. He should be at one of the tables down there."

She leads the two of them through the room to a rear door that enters a hallway. They turn right and follow the corridor until it turns a corner. Partway along, they find a door leading down to the basement.

They pass through to find a large chamber with several pillars supporting the ceiling, and candelabras on tall stands spaced generously around the room. There were a series of alchemy tables along the walls with bottles and beakers for conducting experiments, jars of reagents, and other equipment, along with a collection of odd notes, papers, and reference books.

Several students were sharing their workspaces and performing class experiments, while a group of high-ranking instructors were conducting some research at a table in the far corner near a summoning circle drawn on the floor.

The young woman scanned the room to find Jared, landing her eyes on the instructors in the corner briefly, as if drawn to them for some curious reason, then continuing around to spy Jared at a table further along the wall adjacent to the door.

"There he is," she asserts and courses her way over to him. "Jared?" she calls quietly.

Jared was a mid-classman student wearing a typical deep red mage's robe with silver embroidery on the lapel, cuffs, and hemlines. He turns to the address.

"Tristeen, what are you doing here? I thought you were researching something in the library."

"I was, but we had a courier come in, and he's a bit raw, so I'm helping him out," she winks.

Jared studies her gesture, and then quickly glances at the man.

"You didn't play that one about the secret experiments…did you?"

"Who me?" she feigns innocence. "I'm a noble! I never play jokes like those on people."

"Oh, of course not…" he chuckles. "Well, why are you down here then?" he wonders while glancing at the visitor again.

"He's looking for you. Someone must like you today," she smiles sweetly.

"Me?"

"I have a private message to deliver," the man asserts. "Are you Jared Galwen?"

"Yes, I am. What is this about?"

"Here, this is for you…"

The man takes out a piece of paper from a vest pocket. It was neatly folded and sealed with a drop of wax. He hands it across.

Tristeen eyes the curiously official-looking document, but remains silent during the exchange.

"Who is it from?" Jared asks.

"My instructions are simply to deliver it directly into your hand. You are advised to read it in private, however," he glances sideways at the instructors across the way, who appeared deeply engrossed in their own research.

Both Jared and Tristeen took notice of the obvious gesture, and both felt a strange tang hit them.

"Do I owe you anything?" Jared asks.

"Oh no, it's fully taken care of. I'll take my leave now. I can find my own way out. Good day to you."

He offers a formal bow of the head and turns to leave, strutting away with a curiously erect posture for a simple courier.

Jared studies the note in his hand. He had never received anything with such a clearly professional appearance to it before. Such items like these were most often passed between people of higher stations, and he was not an important member of the academy, or anyone else of special mention within the city hierarchy.

"Tristeen, what do you think he meant by that?" he mutters distantly.

He quickly glanced at his experiment on the table. He wasn't conducting anything critical at the moment, so he moved his equipment off to the side to clear the workspace, and then made his way out of the room and into the hallway. Tristeen followed behind.

He stops midway in the corridor, checking around to ensure the area is clear of any passersby. He gazes into Tristeen's eyes, holding his stare for an extended moment.

"Do you want me to leave?" she asks. "I mean, if this is private, I don't want to intrude."

"Tristeen, no one in my family would send a note like this to me up here, and I don't know of anyone else who would take the time for it. And look at this..." he holds it up. "This is quality paper, not the sort of thing you would find in the lower district, and that's the only place where I might know people. And sealed with a wax stamp? Who would send ME a note so nicely folded and sealed with a wax stamp? And furthermore..." he quickly hushes himself as he turns towards the basement door and thumbs at it.

"Yeah, I get it," she admits. "Well, the only thing I can suggest is to read it and see. I'll turn my back if you like."

She steps off to the side and turns away from him, checking over her shoulder to make sure he is content with the scenario.

Jared took a brief moment before breaking the seal and opening the note. He held it close for a private review.

"What the bloody hell..." he wheezes silently.

Tristeen turned over her shoulder again just as he quickly crumpled the paper and stuffed it into a pocket. He appeared pale and speechless, and leaned back against the wall to catch his breath.

"Jared?" she ushers softly.

He remained silent for a moment longer, then abruptly turned to peek inside the basement, once again to check on those instructors in the corner. They were still deeply engrossed in whatever it was they were doing over there. He pulled back against the wall, and then anxiously turned to look down the corridor.

"Jared, what is it?" Tristeen urges. "You look like something bad happened."

"Bad? Oh no, um…" he flusters. "Tristeen, I need to go out for a bit. Can you cover for me?"

"Cover for you? What am I covering for?"

"It's just a wee trifle, you know. A message that I need to go meet someone, that's all."

"Oh really, and it has you jumping like a rat in a cathouse?"

"Well," he titters. "It's just that, um, it's a bit unexpected. Sorry, I guess I'm not used to receiving notes on such fine quality paper and sealed with wax stamps. This is a collector's item, you know!"

He attempts a disarming grin, even though he knew it wouldn't work on her. She eyes him suspiciously.

"Uh huh…especially after you crumpled it up so thoroughly," she intones flatly. "And how long am I supposed to be covering for you?"

"Um, I can't be sure, but I'll try not to take too long."

He smiles feebly and takes off down the hallway.

Tristeen stood there a few moments longer before turning and making her own way along the hallway. She caught a glimpse of him passing through the door into the main hall. She rushed up to it and further saw him exit out the front doors. She dashed up to the door to peek outside and spied him heading across the plaza at a hurried pace.

She glanced around the plaza. There were plenty of people moving around, attending to their usual chores, but none of them of any special importance, just average citizens. She steps outside and rushes across the plaza, ducking behind a building for cover as she starts tailing him through the city.

She suspected he was heading towards the lower district, judging by the roadways he was taking. She was not typically permitted by her family to travel that far from the Upper Ward, where the noble families made their homes, but on this occasion, she would risk it.

After all, she didn't answer to her mother for EVERY moment of her personal antics.

She played this game of pursuit all through the city until she saw him entering the Ten Eagles tavern. She was not surprised to see the trail lead here, as it was a popular place around town. But then, who would call him to meet here, and as such cause him to become so nervous?

She closed in on the building, sneaking up alongside and peeking in a window. Inside, she could see him wandering through the array of tables, as if looking for someone, then to locate a man sitting at a table near the rear of the establishment. Unfortunately for her, his back was turned. So she decided to take the plunge and step inside.

Jared found the man he was supposed to meet, edging his way around the table to see his face for confirmation. The young man was smartly dressed in a ruffled shirt and pants, resembling that of a highbrow merchant, rather than the man he thought he knew. He crept around the table to greet him.

"Willit?" he mutters cautiously.

"Jared!" he offers jovially. "Would you care to join me?"

"What in all the hells are you doing here? And what are these clothes?" he gestures with his hands. "And that note... What is this with Captain Kholgard now?"

"Maybe you'd like to sit and listen privately, rather than announce it to the rest of the city?"

Jared halts his tirade as he realizes the situation must be extremely sensitive, especially for the sequence of events that had been occurring lately between Thaelyn and his war effort, and the Dean with his questionable spy campaign for the Governor. He cautiously sits down on the opposite side of the table with his eyes intently focused on Willit's face, until he notices movement arriving just behind them.

"Uh oh..." he intones deeply.

"Yeah, uh oh," Tristeen mimics.

She stepped around to the other side to see who it was at the table. When she makes the connection, she nearly falls over backwards.

"Willit!" she whispers urgently and instantly takes up a chair.

"Tristeen, you shouldn't be here," he admits. "I don't want to get you in trouble with anyone, not your family for going places you shouldn't be going, or anyone else around here."

"Forget that! Willit, what happened to you? I thought you were captured in that camp down there. Did you escape, or did they simply let you go?"

"Neither. I'm working for them now, and as far as the two of you are concerned, you never saw me, understood?"

"Huh? What do you mean? What's going on? Why are you in here and…my goodness, you look nice in those clothes."

"Oh, this little thing?" he glances down at himself. "Yeah, I just tossed this on because I had nothing else to wear," he smirks.

"Willit, while I would really enjoy laughing at that remark, I'm more than just a little concerned over what's going on here."

"Yeah," Jared adds. "And what's this note from Captain Kholgard about?"

"Captain Kholgard?" Tristeen emits inquisitively. "Is that who sent the message?"

"Allegiance Guard paper, Tristeen, complete with his mark inside. It said to come down here…alone, by the way, and not to allow the Dean to know anything."

"Well, I can understand the part about the Dean. The Captain doesn't like him one bit."

"All right, listen," Willit begins. "Although my instructions are to make contact here, and my original intention was only to involve Jared, I guess we're stuck with this now."

"Why?" Tristeen wonders. "You don't trust me or something?"

"Tristeen, this is a serious affair, and I need to keep it discreet. I don't want to get you in trouble. You're a nice girl, and I like you, but this is dirty business we're talking about."

"And you think I can't handle a little dirty business?"

"That's not actually the point…"

"Right, the point is I come from a noble family and you're trying to protect me."

Willit sighs audibly, knowing her logic was often too precise to argue. She held a reputation for an exceptionally clear and deductive mind.

"All right, fine…" he relents. "I already know trying to argue with you is pointless. So, the two of you need to listen up close. From this moment, we're in this as a team, and no one is to know anything about me being here or what I'm doing. You want in, Tristeen? Fine, but there are rules to this game, and Jared, this means you too. I need your help here."

"Good," she affirms cheerfully. "So, what sort of game is it, and who's on the other side?"

"Gods' pity, you catch on quick. I'm working with Lord Thaelyn in that camp down there in the valley. After my capture, we had a little talk, and I learned a few things."

"What sort of things?"

"The sort they don't teach in the academy, or anywhere else around here."

"Willit, are we speaking about the general curriculum of the academy, or something else?"

"We're speaking about the toad that runs the place, he and the Governor, and how they corrupted our education system such that we don't know diddly about anything."

Tristeen gasps subtly and pulls back into her chair at the blatant mention, but briskly returns to the conversation.

"Willit, I had a talk once with the Captain up there, and he said a few things, although he couldn't give out a lot of details. But I was always under the impression these two were the leading authority figures in the city. And as they say, if you can't trust that…"

"Who can you trust?" he finishes. "Aye, that's a good one to go around the alleys and inns, just like the one about…for as long as anyone can remember…this or that."

"Uh oh, how do you mean that?"

"One thing at a time… As for whom to trust, at this point, it might as well be anyone other than the authority figures of this city. They, along with all their favorite catch phrases."

Tristeen felt her voice leave her at the mention, and for more than just the implied reason.

"Willit," Jared interjects. "What actually happened to you down there? Did they do something?"

"Yeah, they showed me what the world is like outside these walls we're never allowed to pass through. And the Dean lies through his over-polished teeth on all of it. So, listen up carefully."

He passes a casual glance around the room to see if anyone was paying attention, but the tavern was largely empty at this hour, and the few who were in attendance were busy in their own cups.

"First, forget everything you think you know about the world as it's taught to us in our schools. It's all just the Dean with his rubbish lessons to fill our heads with a lot of guff."

He pauses to study their faces. Neither of them was happy, especially Tristeen, who had traditionally given her trust to the Dean's wisdom.

"For that matter," he continues. "If either of you are temple-goers, forget that as well. It's more bunk, maybe even worse for the sort of tripe they dish out."

"I suppose this relates to those stories we get about the elves and such, right?" Tristeen muses. "This is what the Captain said once."

"Aye, so let's first start with our resource shortages. Everybody knows we have constant troubles with such like iron. We're supposed to have a trade deal with the dwarves up north for deliveries, but it always comes up short. The Governor uses the Dean as his negotiator, and no one else goes up there to make any contact with them, so it's an exclusive deal with them."

"Right," Jared admits. "I've heard where he goes up there for one thing or another on occasion."

"Good, next is we have these salvage operations going on in the valley. You've heard of those, right?"

"Yes," Jared nods.

"It's not very pleasant to think of, but yes," Tristeen adds.

"Pleasant or not, it's providing us with materials to supplement our other shortages, including iron."

"This stuff is said to be coming from his war with the orcs, I think, right?"

"Right, and he's doing a fine job on that side of it."

"Wow, for all I've heard of how tough those orcs are supposed to be, what does the battle scene actually look like if he's hauling back so much refuse from it?"

"Let's call it the spoils of war, rather than refuse. A lot of it might be trash, but there are a few good things we can salvage. As for the orcs, they're really not that tough, as it seems. That's one of the Dean's lies to give an excuse why we don't go out there, in addition to our shortages to supply us."

"Oh, how nice... So he tells us we have the shortages, and the orcs are supremely tough to fight, therefore we can't meet up to the challenge."

"I suppose I should also mention that His Lordship's army is actually very well outfitted. So, tough or not, his are much tougher."

"Well, all right, this would certainly make a difference."

"But the thing is, these orcs seem to have a lot of iron on them."

He pauses to let this sink in a moment.

"Willit," Tristeen wonders. "How can they NOT be so tough and yet have more iron than we do?"

"Obviously, they have a supply coming in, but they're not that good at working it. Orcs have a history more of scavenging or stealing, rather than making their own. Now, we know this war has been going on for four centuries in one form or another. But here's an interesting fact you won't find in your local library. We know the orcs originally came from Ruuki uy'Daan, same as the Daanen-Aryku, but the Daanen-Aryku used to have friendly relations with them before the orcs turned hostile and pushed them off their world and into ours. During this time, they were known to be more of a primitive tribal society that didn't work metal at all."

"So, how and where do they get this iron, or should I actually guess?"

"I think it becomes obvious it's from their relationship with the Suuden-Aryku. We learned from an informant that the Suuden-

Aryku deliver supplies to both the Flame Elves and the orcs, and the source is thought to be local, rather than imported from another world."

"So, the Suuden-Aryku have a local operation of some kind. They're supposed to be much more advanced, so they should be able to do this, right?"

"Oh, I'm sure of it, but they're probably not the ones actually doing the work. It might be another operation supplying the iron, and they act as a middleman to deliver it."

"All right, but you're losing me a little here. Who is making..." her voice cuts off sharply as a thought enters her mind.

"Before you finish, Tristeen, hear the rest of it, and then tell me what you think."

"All right, go on."

"Now, according to my information, which comes from certain members of the Guard, we haven't taken a direct hit on our walls for as long as anyone can remember."

"And there's that reference you made a moment ago."

"Aye. Unfortunately, it would seem the statement 'for as long as anyone can remember' doesn't carry any numbers to it, unless you talk to someone like Captain Kholgard and what he can recall during his personal lifetime."

"I see," she nods. "So, unless we have something to tell us precisely how long it's been, I'm going to guess you're suggesting the Dean and his backwards school lessons are applying some abstract notion here. And this relates as only for as long as someone can remember it, whoever that someone might be."

"Very good, no wonder you get so many honors for your group study projects."

"Thank you," she smiles. "But now, we need to ask how we can discover the real numbers. I wonder if there are any reference books that can help...something about the history of the city and whether we did or did not see an attack."

"I suppose you can try researching it, though I doubt you'll find anything if the Dean is burying so much of our history..."

"Burying it?"

"Aye, such that we don't know up from down about anything. Therefore, all these catch phrases. We don't even recall who our friends are, or where we came from."

"What do you mean, where we came from... Agh!" she covers her eyes and shakes her head. "Uh huh, and I walked right into that one."

The two men ushered up a tender chuckle at her reaction.

"Nice one, Tristeen," Willit smiles. "But I actually have an answer for you that'll knock those expensive shoes of yours halfway across the city."

"Oh dear, and are you going to tell me, or make me guess something for this part?"

"Let me work up to it."

"Yeah, something tells me I should've brought my notebook," she chuckles ironically.

"The Guard tells us that the Governor keeps them locked up in the city for little more than housecleaning work. On those very few occasions he let them out of their cages to help anyone, let's say the Daanen-Aryku, nothing really happened out there. They never saw any action, and all came home safe and happy."

"Well, that's certainly convenient. What about all those things out there that have been trying to kill us for so long? Oh wait, they never come up this far...for as long as anyone can remember..." she retorts sarcastically.

"Now, in the case of the Daanen-Aryku, we know they take hits on a fairly regular basis from the Suuden-Aryku. His Lordship made a pact with both the Night Elves and the Daanen-Aryku to offer support. He's got people out there by their ship reinforcing the Daanen-Aryku right now, since they seem to be the most vulnerable."

"Um, one moment... Why them and not the Night Elves?"

"The Night Elves haven't taken any hits for a long time, either. Half a century or so, as I hear it."

"Oh really! Wow, this is such a vigorous war we fight. No wonder the Captain was so peeved. He mentioned something about a purging effort, just to whittle things down and keep them there. Is this what we're talking about?"

"Basically. For the Night Elves, it's mostly orcs on their side, and like I said, they're not that much of a problem. The Night Elves might see a skirmish or two, but they can usually handle themselves. The Daanen-Aryku, on the other hand…they're in a bad way."

"How is that?"

"They've been hunted for thousands of years, and now they're down to the last of their kind."

"Whoa! That's definitely not something you hear in the world culture lectures. But how does this relate to the people saying they do strange things out there?"

"Strange to us, maybe, but if you're a couple million years more advanced, it wouldn't be so strange."

"Egads! A couple million years more advanced? Why didn't THAT get spread around a little!"

"Yeah, it might go along with the tripe that comes out of the temple. They'd rather badmouth them, instead of asking questions about who and what they really are. On a side note, it's also said the Daanen-Aryku have a few habits of taking their time with things. If it were us doing the work, knowing how people like us might like to move a bit faster, and if we had enough gumption to actually do it, we might be up there as well. But it's still a big jump ahead of us."

"Wonderful, so it's mostly just hype to induce fear and superstition against people who are higher than we."

"They're able to travel the stars above us. That ought to say something, if only anyone around here knew what it actually meant."

"Willit, wait a minute," Jared interjects. "What about those Night Elves, since we're on the topic of the temple and their bunk."

"Basically the same idea," he admits. "Fear tactics to divert our attention. Worse, they lock us inside these walls so we can't go out there and talk to anyone and actually learn something. So, it's what the schools say, meaning what the Dean tells them to say, and that's all. And the temple more likely works for the Governor and his attitude on things."

"Great gods, and I thought I hated the bastard before this."

"The elves have their religion, this much is true, but there's nothing unholy about it. In fact, it's probably more legit than what they feed you uptown. And for that matter, we probably had something similar, once upon a time. But this would likely be before the war when we were all mates together. Then, someone came along and spoiled it on us."

"Grand. Then what about the Flame Elves? The two elven races were supposed to be at war during all this time."

"Right, the Flame Elves," he clears his throat for emphasis. "That's a really interesting one. Let me come to that in just a moment. So, His Lordship has some people out there helping the Daanen-Aryku, but to keep things under wraps, he was working through the Guard and using costumes to disguise his troops as our people."

"Interesting, but why?"

"Tactics. To throw off the Suuden-Aryku as to who is actually out there, in case they hadn't noticed him yet, or weren't expecting him to get involved. And it is known we send people out on occasion."

"Ah," Tristeen asserts. "And since our people never get hit, this could provide the Daanen-Aryku with some peace?"

"While that's a fine idea, as I heard it, the part about the Guard never seeing any real action didn't come out until AFTER his people DID get hit. This was noticed by a member of the Guard currently stationed down there who was surprised that they were actually attacked this time."

"Uh oh…there goes our track record. So what happened?"

"His people killed the Suuden-Aryku raiding party."

Tristeen gaped at him with a long, blank stare before replying again.

"So, his people can actually kill Suuden-Aryku? I've heard they really ARE tough. Isn't this part true, at least?"

"Um…well, I suppose that really depends on how you look at it. We need to take this into context, so here it is. The Daanen-Aryku and the Suuden-Aryku are the same people, with the Daanen-Aryku running from Sargeras while the Suuden-Aryku became his servants.

They are a very highly advanced society, and use really powerful ranged weapons they call pulse plasma rifles."

"Yes, I think I've heard that mentioned before, and those are said to be really nasty."

"Aye, if you're on the receiving end of one. But this attack wasn't using those this time. They were using swords and plate armor, the kind you might see us using, but with this super-strong metal that our steel swords can't cut through."

"Wow, so what does this mean for the attack?"

"If it were our Guard members, they would've been cut to ribbons...probably literally."

"But these were his people, right?" Jared reflects. "And you said they killed the Suuden-Aryku, in this case."

"But Jared," Tristeen debates. "I see something wrong here already. If they were made to think these people were part of the Guard, and if this armor would essentially make them invulnerable to our steel swords... Willit, what about their swords...more of the same?"

"Aye, and it can rip right through steel."

"So, this would make a quick and easy kill, but this still doesn't make sense to me so far. They could do this with their rifle things, right?"

"Easily, unless you want to make a special demonstration for us little peeps who might need something down more on our level."

"Oh wonderful! So, is this supposed to be a show of some kind? But why do it like this, and why on this occasion?"

"This was a big question for them until recently when they found some new information to help them out with it. And it all seems to be centering on the Governor. Our troops were all sent by him, but he's not working with Thaelyn at all."

Now both listeners gasped and reeled back at the obvious insinuation.

Willit waited for one of them to return to the discussion. It was Tristeen who made the first attempt.

"Willit!" she whispers imperatively. "What are you trying to say here, precisely? My Dad and our friends already suspect he's holding that seat illegally, but this sounds like some sort of evidence."

"Aye, then listen to this. We don't get any attacks on our walls… ever. Our troops don't see any action…ever. We also see a lot of shortages in the city, along with those excuses not to go outside, and coincidentally, our enemies are swimming in iron."

"Dammit!" she screeches under her breath. "What then… He's selling our iron as protection from our alleged enemies?"

"And he keeps us pinned down inside our walls, with the Dean filling our heads with his rubbish about the outside world."

"And dammit again!" she curses.

"And I'm not even finished yet," he retorts smoothly.

"Willit, what else can you possibly drop on us?"

"Do you recall that informant I mentioned earlier?"

"Um, right, someone who informed about the iron going to the Flame Elves and orcs. What of it?"

"She's a Flame Elf," he states, and then reclines in his seat, folding his arms.

Tristeen wheezes audibly as her mouth falls open and her eyes grow wide. Jared was speechless and seemingly in a daze.

Willit waited a moment for them to recover, raising his brow and passing his glance inquisitively between them. He then leaned forward again.

"She's the High Priestess of their temple down there in Kynesoth, probably one of the last of their elders after this war basically killed them off down to their last city."

"Last city?!" Tristeen blurts. "But, what about all that talk of the elven war, all that stuff they did, and…well, you know."

"I would imagine most of it is true, within reason. There was a war, there was a lot of destruction, and they did burn everything they came across, and so on and so forth. BUT…" he emphasizes with a finger. "They did NOT join forces with anyone when the Daanen-Aryku came down with the Suuden-Aryku on their tails, and they did NOT even go willingly."

"Willit, wait," Jared submits. "Everything we learned about them tells us the two elven races started this war four hundred years ago. What was that about?"

"It was about a covert operation none of us was aware of that came to our world four centuries ago to disrupt our peace arrangement and break us up to weaken us as a whole. We're all apparently immigrants from Tae'Eladar...THAT is our history. But WE don't remember it. The Night Elves do, and even that Flame Elf recalled something, once we broke her out of her servitude to that Sargeras chap."

"Wonderful..." Tristeen groans.

"And of course, this is where that Lord Thaelyn comes from. Then, someone came along and fouled up the religions of the elves, which is apparently VERY important for them to maintain. In doing so, they basically broke them to pieces. The Night Elves managed to hold it together, but the High Elves, as they're supposed to be called, took a double hit on the damage and fell to Sargeras due to some sort of telepathic domination effect he laid down on them. The war is HIS doing, no one else's."

"And dammit, yet again!" Tristeen scorns emphatically. "I swear to you, just wait till I tell this to my father. He'll go nuts with it!"

"Tristeen, we're not supposed to be out there telling the whole world about this so far. We think there are spies watching us."

"All right, Willit, I understand, but my father and a couple of the others get into these debates constantly about how the Governor shouldn't be the Governor. If there is anyone we can trust, it's them, and I'm sure they'd love to hear this so we can put all these pieces together on how it got started. The Captain already told me about that man's prejudices, so this is simply another piece of it. Somewhere, HE had to get started as well. But now, what's the rest of it with these Flame...um...you said High Elves?"

"Yeah, now listen. His Lordship managed to...acquire...this informant by essentially stealing her away from their city using some really weird magic...don't even get me started on that," he chuckles. "Then, they found a way to convert her back to normal as a High Elf again, so she's basically as she should be now."

"Sargeras doesn't have his hands on her...or mind, or whatever it is, anymore?"

"That's right, she's free, and they're making plans to see about more. She told us a bunch of things about this war from her side, including how both the elven societies were made to blame each other and start fighting. This is how that blighter Sargeras apparently likes to work. He must've sent an agent of some kind to hit both sides and leave evidence behind to say the other one did it."

"Wow, that's simply nasty. You were right, Willit...very dirty business here."

"And we're still not finished. They were also used to launch a secret attack on the Daanen-Aryku, back there on Ruuki uy'Daan, to sabotage their ship, crashing it here intentionally."

"Incredible, so he's apparently gathering up everyone on this one world for some odd reason."

"It might seem that way. It might also interest you to know that they used them at one time to attack a world filled with dwarves."

He stopped again to check their reactions. The two listeners glanced at each other briefly before Tristeen returns back.

"Um, how is this significant?" she asks tentatively. "Other than for those dwarves up north."

"Those dwarves up north probably shouldn't be here. This world didn't have dwarves in it before they showed up...coincidentally four hundred years ago, and opened up trade with us for iron."

"You must be joking!" she shouts.

Her voice echoed around the room, and she quickly turned to see how many people might be responding to it. She flashed a casual grin and a flirtatious wave, sending the rest of the room back into their personal affairs before she returned to this one.

"So, what are we saying here? Sargeras finds a world full of dwarves...and what? I'm not sure if this follows naturally...they pick up a merchant caravan and set up shop here? That doesn't sound right."

"No it doesn't, and those dwarves don't act normal, like they're under a drug effect to keep them in line. This tells us he's got his hooks in them, much like the rest."

"Oh grand! And I wonder if this relates to our iron shortage, where the orcs and others are getting most of it. It sounds like some sort of labor camp."

"One thing I can tell you, this lady didn't hold any memory of dwarves before this and wasn't even aware of those we have now."

"But how is that possible if she was part of this group out there?"

"Apparently, Sargeras treats them as puppets, told to do things and not ask questions. Sound familiar? And they were never told."

"Oh, so we're not the only ones? That makes me feel MUCH better."

"Aye. And finally, the best one of all, although we don't have the full story on it yet. His Lordship is finding himself chasing a lot of conspiracies in this world. It's a mess out there," he shakes his head morosely.

"Gracious, Willit, what have we gotten ourselves into here? All right, go on."

"This one has to do with…da-da-da-dum…" he waves his hands theatrically. "The Plague!"

"You know, Willit, you're starting to scare me. Where are you getting all of this?"

"Marelle has been coaching me on my performance. She's good!"

"Marelle…Carronel? Haran's sister?"

"Aye, she's stationed down there working for the Captain. Anyway, the story goes the Flame Elves did this plague, right?"

"Right, so now you're going to tell me that's a lie too, I suppose. So, where is it actually coming from?"

"We don't know yet, but it goes without saying this High Elf, who is probably their topmost elder in the city, is none too pleased that her people, Flame Elves or otherwise, are being blamed for it. They're also upset that the Dean has been discovered to be in possession of stolen property."

"Stolen property, what kind?"

"Those mithril artifacts…"

"Oh great!" she moans. "And where did he steal them from?"

"Well, it's unlikely HE stole them. Remember, they've been in there for a long time."

"Right…" she nods.

"According to her, these are holy symbols stolen four centuries ago from Kynesoth as part of their elven religion, and the final reason they were taken by Sargeras. This is what pushed them over the edge."

Tristeen gasped and clamped her hands around her head, then screamed in outrage, once again drawing the attention of the room. She was stunned briefly, but then realized her outburst and quickly recomposed herself, spun around, and waved again.

"Sorry everyone," she calls into the room. "We're telling, um, ghost stories over here. Nothing special…"

She turned back to the discussion with a scowl on her face.

"Is this to say we are responsible for the whole thing up here? That man! And to think I actually looked up to him once, even if he was intolerable to deal with. But if this was four centuries ago, who actually did it? Do we know, or is it probably lost to time by now?"

"Probably lost to time, and it's questionable at this moment if he knows who the original owners are, but more than likely he does, especially if you consider his relationship with the Governor, and by association the Suuden-Aryku and whatever else is out there."

"So, clearly he holds a relationship of some kind, and we have a lot of backroom dealing going on here."

"Aye, you've got that much right."

"You know," Jared offers. "This sounds like it should carry a long history to it, if you think of how many deans and governors came before this. Those items have been with us since the beginning. Now, how do you suppose they got there? Someone steals them and they simply come wandering in through a door?"

"Oh, indeed!" Tristeen affirms. "And all the more reason to believe this could be part of some sort of hidden syndicate, like my dad and the others are suggesting recently. We didn't have a governor back in those days, it was originally a Council. Then HE comes in at just the right moment and takes over."

"How come? What changed to bring him in? Well, that is to say, a governor of any sort."

"The Plague, Jared, he's supposed to be our savior to put an end to it, but it didn't work out fully."

"Bloody hell! But this simply returns us back to that part now. If it's not the Flame Elves, and we get so much backtalk about this and that, who is really behind it, because this doesn't leave too many places to point fingers."

"Right, and I don't like the way this is turning out."

"Anyway," Willit resumes. "I suppose it goes without saying, the elves want these things back. It's a violation of their religion to let someone like the Dean play with them."

"Oh, surely, but how do we get them? Do we just march in there and demand he return them?"

"He'd never do that," Jared accedes. "He loves them too much. So unless someone knows where he keeps the key to that cabinet, we may have to wait on that for now."

"And what about the rest? Do we do anything at all?"

"His Lordship is taking this in steps, as he says," Willit affirms. "We can't tip the scales too much, too fast, for the apparent relationship the Governor has with the Suuden-Aryku. The last thing we need right now is them storming through the city to set things right. And we have a strong suspicion this could happen, too."

"Why?" she inquires tenuously. "And please go gently on this one."

"All right, try not to scream this time," he smiles mischievously. "This High Elf also told us the REAL reason we haven't had any attacks…for as long as anyone can remember…is because her people are under orders not to."

"Oh, well, all right, I suppose that would make sense, when you consider the other stuff with the iron and everything. How long has this been going on. Did she say?"

"They have some really long lifespans, it seems. And she's old enough to go back to the beginning, so there you have it."

"Dammit, so that means they NEVER attacked us."

"And I suppose this goes for the orcs as well, probably."

"Right, probably."

"All because we have someone on the inside managing us."

He pulls back in his chair again and crosses his arms with a contented grin, now bracing himself for the reaction.

Tristeen's voice catches in her throat with that last statement as she glares at his smug expression. May discretion be damned. This time, she jumps out of her chair and screams at the top of her lungs, stomping around in circles and spewing every curse word her refined, noble tongue could generate.

The two men exchanged glances as they watched the show.

"You did that intentionally," Jared relents. "Didn't you!"

"Yeah, it's so much fun watching her like this, don't you think?"

"Good thing we're on the other side of town from her folks. If they could hear this, she'd be washing her mouth out for a week."

"Are any of those actual real words she's using?"

"I don't know, I think she invents her own."

Tristeen continues for another few moments until she finally runs out of breath, then slowly returns to her seat, running her fingers through her hair trying to comb it back, and once again glancing around the room, as well as along the balconies upstairs, and some of the windows outside at all the people staring at her. Again, she smiles sweetly and waves while she searches for another excuse.

"Um, it was a little too quiet in here; so I uh, thought maybe we should liven things up a bit. You know, draw some more patrons inside."

She makes one more pass before returning a fierce scowl at Willit.

"You!" she scorns and jabs a finger at him. "All right, this definitely goes to my father and his circle. They need to hear this one, if nothing else."

"Just remember to keep it quiet until we can figure out a way to deal with it before it deals with each of us."

"Got it. Is there anything else? What are you actually doing here, and why did you call us...uh, him," she thumbs at Jared, "to meet you here?"

"The Dean was using us as spies on Lord Thaelyn to check up on him so they could plot against him."

"Plot AGAINST him?"

"Aye, he's making waves in a pond they don't want him making waves in. We have testimony from that High Priestess that her people were told to send an assassin to do him in, and it had to be by our spying to tell them when to do it. How do you like that for those people you're supposed to trust?"

Tristeen was agape at the statement, and Jared grimaced at the mention of it.

"Great gods!" she wheezes. "So those bastards are using us to try to kill someone?"

"Aye, and it probably doesn't stop there. So, he's turning it around now. I'm working as a spy for him up here. We need to find some evidence to show up the Governor and the Dean on some or all of this. For instance, that rogue Suuden-Aryku patrol was trying to tell our people not to play the hero out there."

"Because the Governor isn't the one to send it. After all, they're only supposed to clean up drunks, according to the Dean."

"Right. By now, they probably know it's actually him, since his men use magic out on the field...powerful stuff, too. Those of us in the academy couldn't match up to it in our wildest dreams. The strange part is they're not marching on him directly, even after that. Instead, they're sending hidden assassins rather than full-on attacks."

"I'm not sure if I follow this. If they're so far ahead of us, and with such weapons..."

"Aye, and so we figure the Governor is probably ordering them to hold back for some reason, like if he has something else on his mind."

"More of his backhanded style? But Willit, there is a difference between clearing out an invading force and taking out one man."

"You're right. Some of us feel he wants Thaelyn out of the way so these blokes can foul up yet another world. So we need to see what else is out there waiting for us. For this, I need Jared inside the academy to be my eyes and ears because I don't dare go in there myself. The Dean would surely hang me on a wall if he should see me coming home again."

"Right, I think I can understand that part."

"If you really want to help, Tristeen, do it quietly. Maybe do some research to see if the Dean has any secrets going on, or whatever."

"Secrets…" she contemplates briskly. "Wait, Jared, what are those instructors doing down in the basement lately? I've been noticing them hovering in that corner for a long while now."

"Aye, so have I," he affirms. "I think they're doing research on some kind of conjuring, or some such."

"A conjuring? Jared, I don't know if I like the sound of that just for the sound of it."

"Aye, and based on this here, neither do I. I was working one of the tables in there earlier and very carefully peeked over my shoulder to see what they were reading, and I saw a really strange book. It didn't look anything like the others we have on the shelves."

"A strange book…" she muses. "Describe it to me."

"Well, I couldn't get a very clear look at it, but the binding was smooth, and silvery in color…"

"Oh great, that one again…" she moans. "And the pages that don't look like paper?"

"A little on the shiny side, I think…but yeah."

"I've seen it. It's the Dean's, I think. He's pulled that one out a few times to gloat over. But now, if they're doing research with it, this isn't good."

"Why, what's inside?"

"I don't know where he got it, but it doesn't look normal, and if we're now talking about the Suuden-Aryku, that makes a little more sense. I saw it once and peeked inside when the Dean and his instructors stepped out for a break. It's got some weird stuff in there talking about something called the Outer Planes, and various locations and things that live there."

The two men glanced at each other, and then back at her.

"Tristeen," Jared intones warily. "If they're researching a conjuring, what can they be researching in this case?"

"Knowing the Dean as we do, you don't want to know."

The day was midway along when a collection of familiar faces came jumping through the gateway in the settlement of Firstfall. They were three individuals representing the local societies just arriving back from Tae'Eladar and the city of Bya'an Tamoranth, where they were attending a language course in Thaelyn's academy. This would allow them to become fluent in the language of Tae'Eladar, which was necessary for all their future interactions. The first two were female, a Night Elf and a human, and the third was a tall male Daanen'kai officer. They strolled across the settlement toward the tactical office to join Thaelyn and his officers for the daily review.

"Ah, Relissa and Marelle," Thaelyn announces pleasantly. "And Lieutenant Lapäli, I trust all is well with you this day?"

"Aye," Relissa responds chirpily. "This language bit is moving along so fast; I almost can't believe it. Only another month and we're done."

"Indeed, and then we can begin you on your full official training in the academy."

"That's the part I'm waiting for. I miss my little friends, so I'm hoping I can make some good progress, and maybe pick up a couple to carry with me."

"I actually hear this quite often from the ranger profession, where they feel a sense of emptiness without that small companion curled up on their shoulder."

"Do we have anything new, Your Lordship?" Marelle asks.

"We still have our scouts up in the dwarven enclave checking on their activities, but progress is slow for the complexity, and even the peril of navigating those tunnels. In addition, we are placing the final touches on our spies for our mission to Kynesoth and that bottle in the temple. We are still hoping to compare it with the one from Amariyn."

"Priestess Sehnisavain said it was in a basement, right? I wonder how easy it'll be to get to. Like, for instance, do they have any locked doors, or people who watch the place?"

"I am sure there are likely to be people working inside, but my greater concern is any repercussions regarding the disappearance of Priestess Sehnisavain. I doubt they would let that go without unleashing a few words."

"I don't think it's the words you need to worry about, my Lord," Relissa smirks. "But if we apply my idea about putting it on the orcs, that might work a bit to our favor."

"Indeed, but to do this, we need our spies inside to plant those seeds. Aside from that, we have those suggestions of the Governor, the Dean, their spies, and that assassin. If no one else is launching in our direction, this implies they are concocting another plan to take me out personally."

"Aye, and that's just another rub. He didn't want to help you in the war, tried bamboozling you with all his flunky talk, and now he's trying to kick you out of his little patsy game."

"And therefore, we should consider what HIS next move will be, as I suspect the others are being directed, or at least influenced by him in some way."

"Your Lordship," Lieutenant Lapäli asserts. "I'm trying to interpret your statement according to my own information on the Suuden-Aryku, and probably also the Flame Elves for this point. I'm having a hard time believing the Governor up there might hold such authority as to actually direct their operations."

"While this may be true, if he did NOT hold such authority, I think the situation would be quite different. Recall Priestess Sehnisavain's words. She said that I was interfering with something here. If we were so much of a bother, they should be making a full assault on our position, not sending a simple assassin. This represents a rather restrained attempt to clear an unwelcome interloper that is interfering in someone's plans during a time of war."

"And let's not forget," Marelle considers. "That assassin was wearing adamantium, as well as that rogue Suuden-Aryku patrol."

"Indeed, and this further complicates matters. I can understand if they would send a cloaked assassin, this much is clear. I can also understand if that assassin might wear such as mithril or adamantium, as these are desirable materials for a number of reasons, not the least of which being they are lightweight and durable. The question becomes, would a Suuden'kai High Commander do such a thing? And then, why would he do this when he holds so much superior firepower that he could simply blast us off the face of the planet with a single command."

"I will admit," the Lieutenant responds. "This would not make any sense to me, not if you consider his methods where our own people are concerned, and all the times they attacked us. This is contrary to their known behavior."

"Then there is clearly another factor affecting their known behavior in this case, leaving us with little else but the possibility of the Governor and whatever role he plays."

"But Your Lordship, I must still object to this suggestion for another reason. Why would High Commander Geilv submit himself to someone else's authority at all? The position of a High Commander is the highest rank in our military hierarchy. No one else, save possibly for the Council of Elders, holds a higher position of authority. So, unless he is intentionally submitting himself to the authority of another person, and worse, someone who is outside his ranks, as the Governor would seem to be, then…"

"Padriyl," Marelle interjects. "You ask why the High Commander might submit himself to someone else's authority, but didn't your entire society submit themselves to Sargeras? He's not part of your society, not native to your world, but apparently, he owns the place now. So I say, whoever HE assigns the role becomes the new boss."

"Oh great, but yes, you do have a point. But the governor of that city up there? That seems like a weak assignment to me."

"Maybe, unless it relates to him managing things for someone. If we're saying he holds something special here, what can it be? Your Lordship, what happened on that day the Governor came down here to meet with you? For instance, you said he tried charging you money for squatting on this land, and also asking for gifts before he signed up with you in any kind of deal."

"Yes," Thaelyn reflects. "His famous suggestion of joining forces to purge, as he calls it, the villains of the world. But he was not speaking of the orcs or Flame Elves, in this case. And he wanted me to hand over as much of our military hardware as he could carry home."

"Did he show any kind of recognition of what it was? What I mean to say is, before all this, I didn't have a flippin' clue what mithril or adamantium were. How did he appear?"

"Hmm…"

Thaelyn pauses as he recalls his conversation with the Governor and Dean on that first day, where they arrived in their coach and began their debates on the local politics.

"He did seem to recognize it was better than your average steel. And this does pose an interesting question. Unless you know what it is, metal is still metal, even if it does tend to stand out for its enchantments."

"Then I'll put it to you that he knows something the rest of us do not. If Haran knew of mithril in his academy, but adamantium was barely a fable, how would anyone else know what it is? And yet, here is someone who apparently not only knows what it is, but has a secret stash somewhere."

"Yes, good… But now we need a link. On that first day, he made what could be interpreted as a threat relating to my intrusion in the local affairs. He phrased it as a suggestion of unknown and potentially dire perils that lay in wait for the unwary."

"Nice guy. We should hire him as a local tour guide," she chuckles. "But if you think he's in charge, and we say he's using backhanded methods, like an assassin, don't you think that might be a futile effort after the Suuden-Aryku thing out by the Naarg uy'Sodrad? Your people laid those troopers out flat. And presumably, if you outfit your men with adamantium, and you likely wear it as well, I might say using an assassin wouldn't necessarily work…well, not unless she got a lucky hit."

"This is true. Clearly, it was a feeble attempt, but maybe he was hoping for that lucky hit. She was cloaked, after all, and had I been a normal man, it might have worked."

"Ah hah! That's the key, I'll bet!" Marelle grins.

"Jiggers, Marelle," Relissa moans. "You look a wee bit like he's rubbing off on you now."

"Hey, I'm trying to learn a few lessons here. I recall Haran saying the Dean referred to you as a simple man, and Aerlie as your simple woman. So, this has to be part of the link. They cannot know who you are underneath that shiny exterior, so a cloaked assassin might be all that's needed."

"Nicely done…" he affirms. "But the overriding question is still why we are not seeing a large-scale assault to finish the process. And then, why ONLY that assassin to begin with?"

Thaelyn leaned back in his chair to consider once more his conversation with the Governor.

"He and the Dean came down here first thing in the morning, so this must have been an attempt to be the first in meeting with me, before any others, and in the hope of trying to persuade me to follow his corruption. In the absence of that…ah yes, he was most certainly displeased with my noble, law-abiding stature."

"I'll bet that carries a clue," Marelle argues. "If he can get rid of you personally, he can try corrupting the rest somehow."

"This is a very clever proposal, and it fits nicely with how things seem to be elsewhere around here. We are laying into the orcs rather heavily, and the word from Priestess Sehnisavain is the Suuden'kai are shedding them off as a form of punishment for drawing my attention. We have not made any direct movements on anyone else; therefore, they may not regard us as an immediate threat, thus allowing time for them to study us, and using clandestine methods to remove me personally."

"And here's another bit," Relissa adds. "Those Suuden-Aryku are still laying into the Daanen-Aryku, even after that one hit gone wrong. You said once it could be to put on a show, like to say nothing has changed."

"Indeed!" he asserts with a finger for emphasis. "They are playing a game on us to stall for time."

"And wasting a lot of people along the way," Marelle winces. "You're taking them all down, right?"

"We are, and yet they still come at us. If I were that High Commander of theirs, I would be asking myself why I am sending so many men to their deaths. This might then reflect on our position here. It is clear he is holding back."

"Unless…" Marelle mutters distantly with a tiny smile curling on her lips. "They see you cleaning up all their patrols out by the Naarg uy'Sodrad, and know you're dangerous to come up against face-to-face. So, a frontal assault probably isn't a good idea."

"Yes, this holds merit. Our shield mages are proving quite effective against their weapons, and our other methods are making life hard on them. Furthermore, this inherent weakness of theirs to injury due to this artificial lifeform may cause them to desire to keep their distance."

"Right, a simple bow and arrow will do the trick. So, even at range, you're still dangerous."

"But let us not forget, we have that potential for an orbital strike."

"I know, but they're not using it, which is further evidence of holding back, and like Padriyl said, a Suuden'kai High Commander might not choose to simply hold back like that. Not after taking so many other losses, assuming HE was the one making decisions. That orbital thing might be the BEST way to remove you, but he's not using it."

"Cu'Nar's pity, Marelle," Padriyl relents. "But I have to agree with you. This would not only go against their history, but simple military logic."

"And this tells me he IS under some form of external control. Now, are we saying someone is controlling him, or simply advising him behind some clandestine action. We had an assassin, but you once said this might be beneath the Suuden'kai mentality, for all their other choices. Also, to use adamantium, and for that matter swords and plate armor, is also against their normal habits. That rogue attack was a demonstration, as much as anything, but why not simply use rifles…unless someone is playing with us?"

"Playing?" Thaelyn leans forward again.

"That's what they've been doing with the Daanen-Aryku for so long. Now they could be doing it to you."

"Yes…" he muses pensively. "Sargeras…he might certainly find it entertaining. To draw it out slowly and corrupt us like he did everyone else here."

"Buggers to that, I say!" Relissa yips. "If they think you to be anything normal, they're in for a big disappointment."

"Absolutely, and this is where our best tactical advantage could be. So far, they are underestimating me, and studying us for our weaknesses. The Dean's spies, for example…watching my movements so the Governor could order that assassin. If this is the case, then we are once again speaking of a scheme to remove me personally, rather than my army, if we are so inconveniently interfering with their plans."

"But I don't think he'll be sending any more spies down here," Relissa offers. "Not with those towers up and running."

"This is also true, so he would likely try something else, and at this moment, I would think it should involve isolating me elsewhere for the best effect."

"Jiggers… But another thing that hits me. Even if he did make a full run at you here, you've got your army all over the bleedin' place by now. Trying to remove that would be a bit of a job by now, wouldn't it?"

"It would, and likely along the way, word would spread in some form or another that would invoke our people to begin to evac…"

His voice cuts off as a thought comes to him. He furrows his brow as he consolidates the image.

"Indeed!" he intones thoughtfully. "This might be a potential cause for concern."

"What?" Relissa leans in to listen.

"Portals, my dear fellows… We are to them as those orcs were to us. I recall now when he doubted my capacity to pose a threat of any kind, adamantium or otherwise. But when I told him I had a full world behind me with millions of soldiers in reserve, he quickly stifled his rebuttal. Further, that those people were entirely devoted to me and would rush to my aid with but a single word. This may be our link; he is afraid to invoke that response. If just one mage should escape to Tae'Eladar, the remainder of my army would return to avenge whatever these heathens did to us. And they would not relent until the last of them was destroyed."

"Jiggers..." Relissa moans intensely. "When you put it that way..."

"But consider for a moment, regardless of how you state it. Unlike what you may have had in this world, where they laid a covert plan to disrupt things for you, mine is well-organized and prosperous. I remember I made mention of this, and that I brought it together by my own hand, so this too would indicate I am not one to be trifled with. Therefore, he knows I hold more resources than he is willing to invoke in proper warfare. And with our obvious display thus far for our effectiveness in battle, he is afraid, holding back artificially to see about an opening. Thus, he is hoping instead to dismantle my rule, and therefore my own machinations."

"Weakening you and your people on Tae'Eladar," Marelle concludes. "Much like they did to us here, I might add. So he's trying to make small hits rather than bigger ones. Even if he did hit you from above, it wouldn't be the end of you. More would come."

"My Lord," the General considers. "While this is certainly a fine amount of reasoning, should we be concerned about Tae'Eladar in all this? If he should desire to dismantle all that you have created, we should also consider this. If they know enough to find us by using these orcs on a covert mission, could they also send the Suuden-Aryku in their ships for a raid using these bombardment weapons?"

"Holy Jiggers!" Relissa yips. "General, that's not a nice thought you just had there."

"Indeed, it is not," Thaelyn agrees. "But it is a valid one. They made secret attempts in this world; therefore, they might do the same there. I think a little insurance is in order. While I am here, perhaps I can speak with Adalon and inform her of this potential. She can serve to watch the local front for us."

"Who is Adalon?" Marelle wonders.

"She is an old and dear friend of mine. We go back some distance together, and she certainly has her ways about her. She would also have a few contacts, I should think, to assist her in keeping a vigil."

"All right, sounds good enough. We have her watch our backs while we move forward. Nice and secure. Now what? We need to move against these people somehow."

"We must try to keep them off-balance for as long as this holds up. In the meantime, we should see about dismantling a few of their local machinations…weaken them as they would wish to weaken us."

"All right, what's up with those dwarves? We can start with that."

"So far, our scouts are still trying to chart their way through those tunnels. It would seem the dwarves have hollowed out a fair portion of that mountain up there during this time."

"That sounds like a lot of work."

"And it leaves the situation in a precarious state for the inherent stability of what remains. Take out too much, and you could have a cave-in."

"Ouch, that's not good."

"We will need to allow more time to analyze that one. Then we have the Dean and these mithril symbols, but to make an advance on that would likely require a direct approach, and I do not wish to expose ourselves just yet. Instead, we should continue with the orcs, and plan against the Flame Elves, but here we have another potential concern."

"What's that?"

"I would wish to make all efforts to redeem them, but to do so would require taking them into our possession. And to take them into our possession is to advance on their position. But to advance on their position is to announce our intentions to everyone else, and this again exposes us."

"It sounds like you just defeated your own statement."

"Perhaps…perhaps not… Recall Priestess Sehnisavain and her

two daughters. Also, those scouts we picked up once. We were able to redeem them using a dryad's touch, or else the tree directly. If Sargeras's only control is these songs to drive them to obey, I wonder if we can override them by other means. He used covert methods to take them away from us, so can we use our own to take them back?"

"Uh oh…someone's going to be a little upset for that," she grins.

"Essentially, there are two ways to do this, either a direct assault or a covert method. My impression is that these Flame Elves may be regarded as an asset."

"Just for the sake of argument," Marelle inquires. "Why do you think this?"

"A number of reasons come to mind. Firstly, with all proper respect to those involved, I think the matter of the orcs being regarded as expendable may be reasonable, as they are not as sophisticated as the elves, and therefore their usefulness is limited. The elves were used on at least a few occasions where stealth and guile were involved. They also hold their magical qualities, which are surely more advanced than the orcs, and their tempers, despite the behavior of dear young Mynae when we were interrogating her, are much better restrained by compare."

"All right, I suppose it works so far."

"We should probably include the fact that neither the Night Elves nor the humans have come under attack in this time, so could he be holding them in reserve?"

"If so, that fills me with so much joy," she frowns.

"Therefore, with the Flame Elves, if we use a direct assault, it should involve taking the entire city intact. It must be fast, it must be silent, and it must be over and done before anyone notices."

"You don't ask for much, do you? How would you plan something like this?"

"It would call for a nighttime raid, certainly. But the details would need to be carefully worked out with a thorough study of the place. We also have their outposts. I must ask myself how they would respond if a few of those should go missing," he chuckles deviously.

"My Lord," the General offers. "If they are regarded as an asset, my thoughts are the Suuden-Aryku might not wish to spend them against us. Our army would easily outnumber them. This alone makes the idea futile. Therefore, disturbing those outposts might cause them to withdraw back to the city for protection."

"An excellent thought, General. But then we have the covert method. We will be inserting spies soon. I wonder what opportunities might present themselves once we are inside. If we can abduct a few more of their ranking authority figures, convert them, and then reinsert them..."

"Jiggers, my Lord," Relissa chuckles. "That would be a wicked twist."

"For this, we must stay alert and move gently to feel our way around. Your idea of claiming the Priestess being abducted by orcs could provide an open door for our own bit of espionage."

"I'm going to love to see how this plays out," Marelle smiles. "The Governor is doing it to us, now we do it to those Flame Elves."

"And we take one element of this war force out of play. But now, the next item on the list is Rolsklinde. Marelle, I recall you mentioned recently that your mother was suffering from this plague up there in the city, correct?"

"Yes, I got a note passed through the Captain that she's, um..." she sighs woefully. "It was from my Aunt Tania, and my mom is basically dying."

"I am very sorry to hear that, but I think we should go up there and see what we can do about it."

"There's no cure, at least not that any of us know about, so I don't think there's anything you can do to help her. No one ever recovers from it. Once it hits, that's the end."

"Perhaps, but if it was described as a curse by the Flame Elves, and yet Sehnisavain denies any knowledge of it, and furthermore that it only hits when you exceed age fifty, this is much too mechanical. And if the Suuden-Aryku have a presence in the city, I want to know if they could be responsible."

"Do you think they could be infecting us with something?"

"Almost anything is possible at this point. And so, I am going to send a few of our priests up there to investigate for me. Where is she located at this time?"

"At my aunt's house in the lower district."

"All right, I will send you on an investigation with my people for a preliminary review. We will involve those same priests I used during that inquest with the Flame Elf scouts. They speak the local tongue, so they can make the examination. But you will need to play the investigator to lead them around. Can you do this?"

"Absolutely! And it might help me take something back for what those bastards took from me, meaning my dad, and then my mom, to say nothing of everyone else up there."

"Good. General, call in our people and let us begin. I wish to find an answer to this and see how we can prevent any more."

+ + ◆ + +

"Ah, Tristeen!" Josef calls as his daughter arrives on the terrace of their home. "I'm so glad you came in just now."

"I just got out of my classes, although I barely had the patience to actually finish them today, and then ran home to see all of you."

She eagerly sat down with the group, which included her father and two others who came together quite often for discussions and debate on the city politics and other intellectual matters. She was carrying a notebook and held it anxiously in her lap.

"I learned something today that'll drive you wild," she states.

"Really! Well, we also found something, so which of us should go first?"

"You found something? What was it?"

"Indeed, we have, or at least we think we have. Seth has been rummaging around his cellar for the past several days trying to locate some of his ancestors' old journals and memoirs. We were waiting for you to join us before delving into it, since it was you who began directing us at some sort of a conspiracy taking the Governor's seat."

"Right..." she rolls her eyes audaciously. "Um, about that... I may have come up with the idea, and it was actually Abraim who suggested the conspiracy by a hidden party, and while I'm sure he's right, we have a new little problem."

"A new one? Oh grand… Well, what is it?"

"Let's go first things first. What did you find? This might actually affect my part."

"Well, Tristeen," Abraim submits. "Over the past few days, we have felt much more confident in our opinions on this matter. So much, in fact, that we have been spreading some quiet rumors and gossip through the streets on it. The people need to know. Whoever he is, we want him to start feeling the pressure."

"That's dangerous, Abraim. If he's part of some kind of syndicate, they won't take well to our rabble-rousing. And even worse for what I learned. But go on."

"Worse? What do you mean?"

"Well, to put it simply, if they hold any muscle on their side, we will need to coordinate with some of our own before going too deep, so we should probably take this cautiously."

"I see, and you do hold a point, I suppose. Still, I think most people do not pay as much attention to these things as they should."

"Yes, you're probably right. All we ever see is a lot of rhetoric and other nonsense to keep them dumbed down."

"And ultimately, we do need to bring this into resolution. We were thinking this is precisely the reason for spreading the rumors among the public. If the people begin to feel the injustice, we could form the foundations of an insurrection. Even if he is part of a secret organization, they cannot stop a full rebellion."

"Oh dear…" she winces. "We may want to reconsider that perspective in a moment. What else?"

"Tristeen, dear," Josef wonders. "What's wrong?"

"Dad, I learned something from a friend today that blew my mind…or what was left of it after everything else he said. But please, let's hear the rest of this first. What did you find, Seth?"

The three men all glared at each other, and then at Tristeen for her agitated poise and manners, suddenly feeling a bit nervous for the implications, but Seth continued with his presentation, anyway.

"All right, listen carefully," he begins. "I found some old memoirs in a chest tucked away deep in the cellar of our home. These were left behind by one of my ancestors, who kept records of the odd occurrences happening during the early days of the war. As you all know, the position of a single governor first appeared four centuries ago, at approximately the same time as the start of the elven war. Before this, our city was once ruled by a council of statesmen who were members of our own families. Then, quite suddenly, it changed, and afterwards we had a single governor replacing the lot of them. According to the notes in these journals, this also coincided with the appearance of this horrible plague we now endure."

"Ah yes!" Abraim declares. "This plague has been with us for so long, I think many of us cannot remember precisely when it first appeared, except that it was described as some manner of curse set upon us by the Flame Elves."

Tristeen drops her head and covers her eyes in a moment of anxiety at the suggestion, but she keeps her silence. The reaction didn't go unnoticed by the others, causing them to pause in their statements.

"Tristeen?" Josef ushers softly. "Are you alright?"

She looks up at him with begging eyes and nods.

"What did you find in those books, Seth?" she asks. "Did they say anything about it?"

"In a manner, yes..." he replies cautiously. "My ancestor made it a practice to record the progression of the disease during his lifetime. I found several books detailing how it first arrived and how it spread through the populace in those early years. But there is a curious detail which places a note of suspicion in my mind. Perhaps, with all these other insults we had to contend with by the Governor and his claim to rule, I am simply formulating excuses, but I will bring this up for your consideration."

Seth picks up a set of papers he had sitting on the table next to him. He begins shuffling through them and pulls out one from the stack.

"The papers I have here are some notes I made to summarize what

I found in the journals. It starts out as the old Council becoming mysteriously ill with a strange new disease. They succumbed to it rather quickly, complaining of severe headaches and memory loss. We now know this to be the plague that still haunts us, but it was unknown to them at the time."

"Right," Abraim considers. "I seem to recall this from the stories passed down."

"During this period, a strange man came amongst us, declaring we had been afflicted with a curse set down by the Flame Elves. He claimed he understood the nature of their magic, presumably by some earlier study he made, and could protect us, but he needed the power of authority within the city to command the necessary resources to prepare this protective magical aura. For this reason, he also needed the full cooperation of both the mage academy and the temple."

"A likely excuse!" Josef decrees. "Give me your loyalty, and I'll protect you from the Big Bad Elves."

"Really!" Tristeen muses. "That's actually interesting…totally preposterous, but interesting. So, it involves the academy, which means the Dean…that fits nicely. And then the temple, which would involve the priests…how convenient."

"Convenient?" Seth wonders. "You mean, relating to this new thing you found?"

"Well, who is it that most often decries the Night Elves and Daanen-Aryku with the Governor's prejudices? If Captain Kholgard says we're actually supposed to be friends, but everyone hates them for these ugly rumors, where does that leave us?"

"She's right," Abraim notes. "This would do well to isolate us during this time, when in fact we should be working together. And worse, they keep us boxed inside these walls. That's a nice little conspiracy circle there."

"But it also suggests this began a long time ago. So, what else happened?"

"At first," Seth continues. "The Council and their families refused, naturally. But then, the disease began to spread through more of the population, and the people were panicking. The noble families soon found themselves under pressure to relent, and so the Council was disbanded, and the Governorship established."

"Fear tactics," Josef concludes.

"Yeah, makes perfect sense," Tristeen affirms. "Regardless of where the plague actually came from or why it's here, this sounds like someone was manipulating the situation. What happened after that?"

"According to this," Seth resumes. "The notes seem to progress over a few decades until my ancestor finally took ill and passed on. But they suggest the new governor began controlling the affairs of the mage academy and the temple in an attempt to stave off the effects of this curse. He was never completely successful at bringing it to a full halt, but he did manage to stabilize it so that it would not spread rampantly throughout the city's population, limiting itself to only those of the upper age group we see now. The reason for this, as it was described, is due to the Flame Elves maintaining it on their end, so it was a never-ending battle."

"And no doubt," Josef huffs, "this applies the justification for his continued rule, or at least that of his successors."

"Very neat and clean," Tristeen nods. "But why doesn't anyone remember this? Actually, why am I asking that question...I know the answer," she titters.

"You do?" Josef inquires.

"I would imagine," Seth responds. "It might be due in part to so much confusion and hysteria that occurred in those early days, compounded by the sudden loss of so many who remembered the times prior to this, that we lost some of this knowledge. Since that time, our history, as I recall it during my childhood years in school, does not cover it in such a manner as what we have here."

"Right..." Tristeen states flatly. "Because of the Dean and his graduate students...who become our future teachers."

"His graduate students?" Josef muses.

"Dad, surely you know the teachers in our schools are actually his graduates."

"Well, yes, I understood this already, but what do you mean?"

"Recall what we spoke of last time. Control of information. He works for the Governor, and the Governor seems to like to control things, like us going outside for any reason to talk to people."

"Right."

"We have that propaganda he keeps spewing out, and also the schools. And the Dean, for as much of a spineless worm as he might be, governs what, if anything, they teach in there. And he does this through his proxies, his graduate students. He teaches them, they teach us…what he teaches them to teach us."

"Egads! Are you saying what I think you're saying?"

"That's right. If we don't remember anything, it's more likely because he erased it on us, denying us to know our own history by now."

"Blast!" Abraim scorns. "And I thought he was a worm before this. That simply gives him too much credit."

"Oh, this is minor compared to the rest of it," Tristeen shrugs. "This much we can probably correct, if only we can get those people to behave normally, and stop licking his shoes every day."

"Where did you hear this, Tristeen?" Josef urges. "This is a rather serious accusation, so we need to have some way of demonstrating it."

"Demonstrate?" she asserts and points at Seth's papers. "Who owns the academy? And why don't we see any of this in school?"

"But Tristeen," Seth interjects. "The Dean of today did not hold his position during my youth. So, are you saying ALL the Deans are a part of this conspiracy? Every man who ever sat in that chair?"

"For that matter," Abraim wonders. "What about the priests? You said he demanded BOTH the academy and the temple."

"This is clearly part of that conspiracy circle," Tristeen affirms. "All of it, and probably from the beginning. Therefore, most of our history has probably been either erased or fabricated to suit their needs. This would also explain those favorite catch phrases they keep shoving down our throats to keep us in line."

"Catch phrases?"

"Oh yes! Like the one about our city authority. If you can't trust them… What is it?"

"Dear gods, but yes. Who can you trust?"

"There is no one else!" Seth grumbles. "Not if they own everything!"

Tristeen continues, "Then we get these horrid rumors about our neighbors, telling us to stay at home and don't bother helping them with anything, not even to talk to them."

"Incredible…" Abraim moans. "And therefore, even if they had something to say, we wouldn't listen."

"That's a very clever game they played," Seth affirms. "They hit us from both sides, just to cover everything. Don't go out and talk to people, they're all bad, and so you won't listen to it anyway. And OUR leaders are always right."

"As for where I got it…" Tristeen submits.

She now begins to reference her notebook to recall her earlier conversation with Willit.

"First, I have a couple of friends from the academy. We'll just use first names for now…Jared and Willit. Both of them were being used by the Dean for his so-called scouting runs into the valley, but better to say spy runs for what they were actually doing. Neither the Governor nor the Dean like those people who arrived down there."

"I recall you mentioned this last time," Abraim accedes.

"Yeah, but to the point where they used our spy runs to send an assassin to try to kill that Lord Thaelyn guy."

"What?!" he shouts. "Great gods, and THAT surely is criminal."

"It also demonstrates some of the muscle they own, so be careful up here."

"Yes, I suppose that does put a slight damper on things."

"Now, during this time, Willit was captured in their camp, being a spy working for someone who is being declared a criminal in Lord Thaelyn's eyes, if only for the reason of sending spies to report on his activities when neither the Dean nor the Governor have any real interest in participating. Therefore, these spy activities are being described as hostile acts by an unfriendly foreign power."

"That does not sound very good for that poor young man," Seth moans.

"As for Willit, he's not the one to worry about. Lord Thaelyn is apparently a much more considerate individual than you might expect. Willit is working for HIM now," she smirks.

The three men all glanced at each other as she continued.

"Willit sent a note to Jared at the academy to call him into a private meeting. I followed along out of curiosity, at least as much for the strange manner in which the note arrived as to what Jared's reaction was to it."

"Why is that?" Seth wonders.

"It was apparently sent by Captain Kholgard on Allegiance Guard paper, very neat and proper, and with a wax stamp on it. He's very professional," she smiles. "It was to inform him to meet Willit at the Ten Eagles downtown."

"Really!"

"Eh, Tristeen," Josef raises his brow. "Does this mean you travelled all the way down there as well?"

"Yes, Dad, so don't tell Mom, or I'll have to listen to her ranting for the rest of the month. I can take care of myself in that place."

"All right, dear," he smiles.

"One of the things I learned that you probably won't hear in the Dean's custom-made school lessons is we're not native to this world at all. All of us, and I mean ALL of us, including both elven societies, are originally immigrants from Lord Thaelyn's world, which is called Tae'Eladar. Our cousins are still there, and we're a split from that world from probably thousands of years ago. The elves still recall this, but apparently, we do not."

"Well now," Abraim shakes his head. "Isn't that lovely..."

"This is a small thing for now, but it further tells me we're not supposed to be so isolated. Next is these orcs. You're aware of the name Sargeras, right?"

"Yes, I've heard this bandied about a few times."

"He's apparently been much more active in things than any of us could imagine. For one, these orcs...he apparently owned them from a LONG time ago. According to Lord Thaelyn, his reason for being here is a recent invasion of some kind starting a war on his world. Therefore, he's here now, chasing them back to ours. But apparently, this is not the beginning. Those orcs initially arrived there, thousands of years ago, as part of a migration effort from… places unknown…" she waves her hands theatrically. "Now we have this new invasion, and this time with a name attached. Coincidence? Probably not…"

"This is beginning to sound like yet another conspiracy of some sort."

"Then we have the Daanen-Aryku and the Suuden-Aryku, who, by the way, are the same society, with the only real difference being Sargeras. The Suuden-Aryku follow him, the Daanen-Aryku are running from him."

"Well, that's certainly nice, and again something you don't hear in the daily gossip."

"And for many thousands of years too…"

"Egads, for so long?" he winces.

"Yeah, I learned once from another friend of mine that these people have really long lifespans. So, they're being chased from one world to another during this time, until they came to this last one called Ruuki uy'Daan, where these orcs live. Again, coincidence? At this point, it sounds planned."

"Indeed, who was driving that ship of theirs?"

"Good question. They were friends initially, but then the orcs turned coat on them and attacked, probably because of Sargeras, or maybe the Suuden-Aryku, whoever it is that gives the orders, told them to do so."

"And this is when they came here to our world, right?"

"Right, when they crashed in the eastern plains, because their ship was actually sabotaged and brought here intentionally."

"Sabotaged! By whom, the orcs?" Josef wonders. "I always heard they were a rather brutish group."

"They are, but they're basically described as a primitive tribal society, not even capable of working metal without outside help."

"Interesting, but then who was it that sabotaged the Daanen-Aryku ship?"

"Flame Elves..."

"What?!" he shouts. "How did they do that? They didn't join until after they...um, arrived. Tristeen, what is it you learned today?"

"They were a part of it from the very beginning, a covert plan that stole them away."

"Stole them away from what?"

"Well, from their own minds, really, along with our mutual alliance. Sargeras is said to be an immensely powerful entity of some kind, by the stories I hear. Telepathic, meaning he can apparently dominate a person, turning their mind into putty that he can make perform whatever he wants them to do. And they were his first conquest in this world four centuries ago."

"What about the war between the two elven societies?" Seth asks.

"The Suuden-Aryku must've sent an agent of some kind down here to corrupt their religion and break them apart...in fact, to break ALL of us apart. We were all friendly with each other, and these two others cooperated in their religious beliefs. Then, one day, something bad happens and bam! You have war. What WE don't know is the two elven societies were both hit, and evidence left behind to implicate each other."

"That's a whole other conspiracy there!" Seth blurts.

"This is simply nasty," Abraim moans.

"This may also be where that new governor comes in," Tristeen continues. "He tells us all these stories, and not to go outside anymore, isolating us so we never learn the truth. So, now we have the war. The Flame Elves were once called High Elves, and apparently much nicer than they are now. They also had a bunch of holy artifacts in one of their temples. These were stolen as part of this conspiracy. The Night Elves got hit with only one part of this, but the High Elves got hit twice, and this caused them to break down so far that Sargeras could get inside and take over."

"Blast! Again..." Abraim growls.

"Tristeen," Josef implores. "Is ALL of this from that friend of yours?"

"Yeah, he got the full story, or at least what we have so far. Lord

Thaelyn is doing more to unravel things than any of us could ever imagine."

"He must be a very intelligent man."

"Intelligent…maybe also to say determined…and certainly NOT controlled by anyone," she giggles. "Now, generally speaking, the Dean sends his spies out to presumably report on what's happening out there. This is then supposed to be shared with the Guard to help protect the city. Unfortunately, most of it goes in the trash, as it's considered irrelevant."

"Irrelevant?" Abraim retorts abrasively. "The defense of the city is irrelevant?"

"Yeah, this is where Lord Thaelyn is calling both the Governor and the Dean criminals, and for everything HE is discovering about them, to say nothing of what you think of it."

"Oh, grand…suddenly I'm sorry about speaking of passing rumors."

"Yeah, and you're not going to like the rest of it, so hold on tight. Our official reason for the Guard not going outside is due to the supply shortages, right?"

"Yes."

"Meaning, we can't supply ourselves well enough to fight those really tough orcs out there that are flooding all across the land, but never up to our walls."

"Eh, excuse me? How do you mean that?"

"This is another of their favorite catch phrases. Surely you know how most people talk around here. 'For as long as anyone can remember, blah-blah-blah…' Right? It's another of those things they shove at us to keep us in line."

"Uh huh, and I'm getting visions now. So, did you hear it differently?"

"The whole thing is subjective. The statement itself is entirely abstract, and also entirely dependent on whom you talk to, how old they are, and what they actually experienced in their lifetime, therefore what they can remember. There are no real numbers involved. And our history is otherwise wiped so no one can remember anything else."

"Wonderful. And you're right. So, what is the final answer in all this?"

"We were probably NEVER attacked directly on our walls."

"Never?" he intones sharply. "But what is all this talk about a war of any kind?"

"Yeah, this would be another good one. And it would also be subjective. Whose war? The elves are said to be at war. The Flame Elves are said to have destroyed everything out there, eventually joined by the orcs and the Suuden-Aryku when they made their official arrival. The Dean loves to place blame on THEM for the war, describing them in such a way as to make them appear as villains. And then we have the Governor and his prejudices. But if the TRUE villains are associated with agents of Sargeras, the rest are pawns in a really big game."

"Incredible," Seth asserts. "So, this Sargeras seems mostly intent on going around and making trouble for others."

"And diverting the blame, and further to lock us up so we can't talk to people, leaving us with only hearsay and bigotry filling our ears, keeping us docile and afraid."

"That is simply sinister."

"And devious," Abraim groans.

"Now, we don't have all the details yet," Tristeen admits. "After all, this war isn't over, and we might yet find more hidden secrets. But what we have now is already bad. Lord Thaelyn has apparently been conducting his own investigations. We have the Flame Elves, to which he captured one for interrogation and discovered their history. Now he's out to see about redeeming them away from Sargeras."

"That sounds quite noble of him."

"He sounds like a guy with some very high standards. He's also discovered a number of other dealings we aren't aware of up here. This is where we need to be discreet, because the Governor is in some very deep and very dirty business, and we do NOT want him to think we're starting a rebellion, because his 'friends' aren't the sort you want to meet. We'll let Lord Thaelyn deal with it. He's got an army on his side."

"So, this is where you're getting those reactions you had earlier," Abraim recalls. "This muscle we need has to be on the scale of a professional army. Grand…just grand."

"I know. Now, about our shortages…we've all heard about the issue of iron, right?"

"Yes."

"The Governor uses the Dean to negotiate with the dwarves. This is fairly common knowledge for those of us who observe it. The dwarves deliver a wagon every so often to the north gate, but there's never enough to meet our demands. Therefore, our shortages, and therefore, the Guard is never allowed to make any serious movements. Have you heard of the salvaging operations in the valley?"

"I think I heard a few words on that," Abraim admits. "I've heard of new supplies of iron coming in from it as well, and this has actually gone to reduce our shortfalls somewhat. What about it?"

"Thank Lord Thaelyn for it. This is his gift to us. He's fighting off all those really tough orcs who are swarming all across the land."

"By the sound of it," Josef reflects. "The man must be spending a great many of his own along the way."

"Not really. He's actually doing quite well with it so far. Willit tells us his army is actually very well outfitted. So, those really tough orcs aren't flooding the land anymore. His supremely tough soldiers are doing it instead!" she giggles.

"Gracious," Josef murmurs. "He must have some very fine equipment, I suppose."

"I have this other friend, a really close one that I haven't seen for a while because he got into an argument with the Dean, and then got expelled." She lowers her head.

"I'm sorry to hear that, my dear," Josef offers. "What was the argument about?"

"He made first contact with those people on one of his spy runs to the valley. He came back to report this world-shaking news to the Dean, and at first the Dean laughed at him, which isn't so unusual. And then, when he tried pushing the issue, where this truly amazing discovery should be broadcast all over the city, they got into an argument where the Dean said it's to be shelved, and no one is to know about it. The Guard is only supposed to clean up drunks from the streets, and the rest of us shouldn't bother with it, as it's none of our concern."

"I swear to you," Abraim spurns. "For this point alone, I'm tempted to storm that building and drag him out by the ears."

"I was standing outside the door when it happened, and I listened to the exchange. I heard words mentioned, some of which are almost mythical to me."

"Eh, my dear," Josef hesitates inquisitively. "What words are these, hmm?" he raises an eyebrow.

"Not THOSE kinds, Dad." She closes her eyes and shakes her head bemusedly. "Although they came close a few times. No, these are names of things I know of from some of the studies we have at the academy. One of them is a metal called mithril."

"What's that?"

"It's said not to be found here, but it's a strange metal that's supposed to be much stronger than steel, and very magical in nature. We have some specimens in the academy, which we have recently learned are actually that stolen property from the High Elves."

"High Elves...um..."

"Now called Flame Elves..."

"Ah yes."

"These are those holy artifacts they once held, and what finished them for Sargeras to take over."

"Wait a moment! These are INSIDE the academy?"

"Yeah, and the Dean keeps them under lock and key at most times."

"Are we trying to say he stole them?"

"We can't," Seth corrects. "This would've been four hundred years ago, right? If this is what caused the elves to be stolen away from us, it had to be that blasted Sargeras doing the deed with his hidden agents."

"But if THEY stole them," Josef charges. "What are they doing in OUR academy with OUR Dean, unless HE is also involved with them?"

"But HE is also owned by the Governor!" Abraim asserts. "Which would now implicate HIM. Especially if HE is the one who first started turning our noses up at the rest."

"Anyway," Tristeen continues. "It seems Lord Thaelyn uses this in his military, along with another metal of a similar nature called adamantium. So, those orcs probably don't stand a chance with all their rich iron supplies…which they're not supposed to have."

She pauses to let that settle for a moment. The three men took notice of her lapse to analyze the suggestion.

"Tristeen," Abraim wonders. "What do you mean by that?"

"All those really tough orcs that were flooding the land aren't really all that tough. They're not that good at using iron. And besides, that statement is just more propaganda to excuse us from doing anything about it."

"Blast!"

"I probably should've guessed that one," Seth relents. "By her repeated use of the term."

"Indeed, and I think we need to watch her a little more closely," Abraim grins.

"But anyway," Tristeen adds. "They seem to have a lot, and so they must be getting it from somewhere. Which means a supplier, which means the Suuden-Aryku, right?"

"Right…"

"Wrong."

"Wrong?"

"Well, right AND wrong."

"Tristeen…" he intones warily. "Which is it, right or wrong?"

"Both, or maybe neither, depending on where you stand and how you look at it."

"All right, so where are we to understand the first part?"

"Right is to say the Suuden-Aryku are providing this to both the

Flame Elves and the orcs. Wrong is they're not making it themselves; they only deliver it."

"All right, so far, so good… And to the next?"

"To the next, we need to change the subject briefly. The Guard is sometimes sent out to offer support aid to our alleged friends."

"Alleged friends?"

"Yeah, you recall the Governor and his delightful perspective on things."

"Oh, but of course, how could I forget?"

"The Night Elves seem to be doing well enough, but the Daanen-Aryku take hits from the Suuden-Aryku quite often. The Guard has been known to go out there on special occasions to play nice and make it look like we're actually helping them."

"Yes, this is rather curious. We describe them as this or that unpleasantness, but we send out people to protect them from harm."

"Sounds like a contradiction in terms," Seth offers. "And clearly a ploy, but for what purpose…simply to play nice?"

"Probably," Tristeen accedes. "And on each of these occasions, they came home without incident. Nothing ever happened out there to make it look like a war was occurring."

"Indeed, and why is this?"

"Let me move to the next part, and then you'll see. Lord Thaelyn learned about this practice, so he started sending his own people out there in disguise as Guard members, hoping to carry an illusion in the eyes of the Suuden-Aryku, so they wouldn't know who it is they're actually fighting."

"Ah, very good. Play a little ruse on them."

"And they took an attack almost immediately."

"Uh oh…"

"This was clearly a show of force on the part of the Suuden-Aryku. They used swords on this occasion, which they aren't known to use at all, and wore armor made from more of this adamantium, which our steel swords can't hurt."

"Ouch! This doesn't sound good. How did he fare on this occasion?"

"If these were actual Guard members out there, they'd be stew meat by now. But Lord Thaelyn's men were able to kill THEM instead."

"Gracious, so how do we describe this if it sounds like the same material?"

"I think we can describe it as his men being better trained."

"Well, thank goodness for that," Josef sighs.

"And no wonder all those really tough orcs are falling so quickly," Abraim smirks.

"Now…" Tristeen makes ready for her finale. "Here's the really important part. Lord Thaelyn is not working with the Governor, as the Governor doesn't want to work with him, right? Whenever the Governor sent our people out, nothing happened. But on this one occasion, where Lord Thaelyn sent his people out, disguised as ours, they take an attack. The difference…it wasn't sent by the Governor."

All three men reeled back in their chairs when she finished that portion, but she wasn't done yet.

"AND…" she continues pertly. "If you consider we never took a direct hit on our walls, AND if you consider the Guard is never allowed to go outside due to all of our shortages, AND if you consider such things as orcs, who don't make their own iron, but have tons of it in fresh supply…what do you get?"

Now she leans back to watch the show.

The three men gaze at each other for their mutual impressions. Slowly, their faces each turned aghast.

"That Man!" Abraim screams.

"Both of them, I would say!" Josef surges. "So, we have OUR shortages, but the enemy has plenty of goods in their pockets!"

"And we get the lovely peace and freedom of no attacks on our walls or against the obligatory Guard deployment to our alleged friends."

"And this implicates the Governor in foul play on a grand scale," Seth admits. "But what do we do with it? Are we saying he made peace with these Suuden-Aryku for NOT attacking us if we hand over all our iron?"

"If so," Josef argues. "His 'friends' are the Suuden-Aryku themselves!"

"Everybody, one moment," Tristeen interjects. "We're still not finished."

"Dear gods, Tristeen," Abraim relents. "There's more?"

"Probably more still than what I have here. Personally, from what I understand of these Suuden-Aryku, I think iron probably doesn't hold as much value to them. They can probably get this anywhere. Those dwarves up there look like they're under a control effect, which means Sargeras has his hooks in them also. And they're apparently not native to this world any more than we are. According to this elf, she never heard of dwarves on THIS world before, but she does know the name from Sargeras attacking a full world of them once."

"Oh, wonderful…"

"My personal suspicion is I think they and these otherwise mythical metals are related, because if it's said we don't have them here, they have to come from somewhere, and this opens a new door for us, especially if the Suuden-Aryku were once seen wearing it."

"You have a good point there. So, maybe they did actually find something here."

"That would certainly offer up value," Seth suggests. "The iron could only be supplemental for the local races to use."

"And finally," Tristeen concludes. "Recall the Flame Elf that Lord Thaelyn liberated? She tells us her people are under orders not to attack us at all, and this probably applies to the orcs as well. Further, they are NOT responsible for this plague, which means, if Seth's notes are correct, we have yet another agent inside here. And I say this because she tells us we're being managed by someone."

"Unbelievable!" Abraim shrieks! "This is worse than any syndicate! This is a foreign spy!"

"And a most insidious one at that," Seth accedes. "But how do we describe the apparent lack of a transition from one to another during these four centuries?"

"Likely they replace him from the outside somehow, sight unseen by any of us."

"This is where my friends and I come in," Tristeen advises. "We're joining forces to do a little digging inside the academy to find more evidence, and maybe to discover anything else they're doing out there."

"Tristeen," Josef cautions. "This is serious business here. You said it yourself; these people are simply nasty."

"I know, Dad, but I'm just as qualified to research this as anyone. Lord Thaelyn needs people on the inside, which means us, and so far, they don't know we exist."

Chapter 2

WHAT LIES BENEATH

"Are you feeling any better now, Lieutenant?" shouts the driver. "Um…" Marelle responds nervously. "Well, I suppose I have to answer yes, within reason. I mean, I'm not really that raw when riding a mount. I've ridden horses plenty of times, but, um…" she peers over the side at the view below. "Dear gods, don't turn us upside-down."

The two of them were part of a team flying from Firstfall up to Rolsklinde on gryphons. Marelle and the gryphon driver were in the lead of a small flight of the animals currently passing over the mountain range at the north end of the valley, soon to cross over into the plains region where the city was located.

Naturally, Marelle was not accustomed to flying, and being out in the open, as it was for riding atop an animal high above the land, the view was both breathtaking and alarming to the uninitiated.

She scanned the horizon to all sides of her. This would represent her first time to view the world from above, and regardless of her fret, she could not help but to admire the sights and the simple sensation of unbound freedom.

"But you know," she considers. "Other than for the long drop, once you get used to it, it's not so bad."

"Indeed, we're well accustomed to this form of travel back home.

But even though we might be raised on it, that first time can still be a tad worrying."

"It's amazing what you people can do over there. I've been trying to pay attention to it. His Lordship once said that all things can be understood if you only set yourself to learn."

"Aye! Those are likely the finest words you'll ever hear."

The mountains below passed by serenely, and now they were coming into view of the southern watch tower for the Allegiance Guard. Marelle cautiously leaned over to look down at the tower, which seemed so small from up here, and the men standing around outside, apparently in conversation.

"Oh, so that's what they do with their time out here," she smirks. "Just standing around chatting... I may have to send a note to the Captain on that," she grins.

In a few moments time, the city came into sight underneath them. She gazed at it, panning her view across the wide stretch of buildings surrounded by the thickly fortified wall. She could see whole districts at a glance from up here, along with the roads and avenues connecting the lower and upper sections.

"It's so humbling to see it like this," she murmurs to herself.

"Lieutenant," the driver asks. "Where do we go, once we cross the walls?"

"Turn off to the left along that wide avenue," she stretches out an arm to point at a prominent street coming into view. "We're going into the southwest neighborhood over there."

"Right to that!"

He angles the gryphon to the west as they cross overhead in the skies above the city.

Many of the people on the ground were simply attending to their common chores, running errands, and visiting the local markets. They were not accustomed to looking up in the sky at anything in particular. Then one man happens to catch a glimpse of something out of the corner of his eye. Naturally, he turns to look at it, at first not sure what it was he was seeing. He places a hand over his brow to shield his eyes as he tries to focus on it.

"'Ere now," he exclaims to another passerby. "What's that up there? Are those birds?"

The other man halts and looks up to follow the first one's direction.

"That's not any bird I ever saw before. Look at it! It's got four legs to it!"

"Aye! And they've got people riding atop! By the gods!"

The increasing level of their voices drew even more attention. Now a small gathering was staring up at the flight of strange creatures passing overhead.

"What in all the hells are they?" shouts one person.

"Not just that," responds another. "But who are those people riding them?"

"Where did they come from?" calls another one.

"I just now saw them come up from, uh... Bloody hell, can they be from the valley down there?"

"You mean those new people?"

"Aye, there's been a lot of talk lately of them helping us with the war and supplying us with new goods."

"Right, I've heard of that, even though some of it isn't much for new material, but I won't cry over it."

"But why are they coming up here now?" shouts another onlooker. "And on flying beasties as well!"

"Where are they going?"

"Uh..." another citizen responds as he follows the gryphons and their apparent flight path. "They look to be heading off to the western boroughs."

"Why out there?"

"Why are you asking me?" he shouts.

"Well, let's follow along and see!"

Now the assembly, which had grown exponentially by now, starts a mass charge to follow the airborne travelers.

Marelle had been looking down at the people below, and she could see many of them looking back up at them by now. When she noticed a large group of bodies start moving along underneath, she knew the scene was going to be chaotic by the time they set down.

"Um, we're making a scene up here. Did you know that?"

"Aye," the driver responds. "The thought came across a while back, starting with His Lordship. He suggested this would make a grand show in their skies, and we could use this to draw their notice that there is indeed a world out there worth learning about."

"Clever guy," she smiles.

They continued along to the west until a large residential section came into view. The movements of the crowds on the ground drew even more people as they took notice of the mad rush. They kept at a distance behind the flight of winged creatures, not knowing if they wanted to get too close or where they would come down.

"All right," Marelle points again over the driver's shoulder. "Down there, that row of houses."

"Aye, right then…"

He raises his hand for the others in the group and signals a sweeping motion to descend to the ground. He then gives a command to the animal to begin its descent. The people on the ground slowed as they saw the large creatures apparently coming in for a landing.

"Dear gods!" shouts one man. "Those bloody beasts are huge!"

"Aye to that!" affirms another. "And if they can carry two people, you'd better believe they'd have to be strong buggers as well."

"I wouldn't want to be on the receiving end of those claws!" asserts another onlooker. "They look sturdy enough to rip a man to shreds, they do!"

The gryphons descend in a gradual sweep for a smooth landing, and Marelle ducks low in her saddle to cushion the force. They flap vigorously just as they touch down and settle neatly on the ground, then walk the rest of the way.

"Over there, that one," she points to one of the nearby homes.

The people kept a cautious distance at first, but when they saw the gryphon riders were aiming towards one of the local homes, several of them carefully moved up to within speaking range.

"You up there," shouts one of them. "Eh, my pardons, but what's all this about?"

Marelle turned to the address, being the leader of this expedition inside the city, and the primary one charged to interact with the locals.

"We're visiting this house over here. My family lives there."

"Bloody hell, ma'am! You came all this way riding one of these beasties just to say hello to your kinfolk?"

"Why not!" she affirms eagerly. "Beats all the hells out of riding a horse. These things don't stop at walls or rough terrain. Also, it's a chance to get a feel for flying. Those people down in the valley have some wonderful things to teach us if anyone around here is willing enough to open their ears and listen."

"Eh, wait now. What do you mean by that?"

The gryphons were coming to a stop by now, and Marelle and her driver were preparing to dismount. She unbuckled her harness and unclamped her legs from the special stirrups so she could free herself from the saddle. The gryphon laid itself down for ease of access, and she slid off the side.

"Sir..." she responds. "I live here. I serve the Allegiance Guard, so I know how people are in this city, and one thing I'm sure of is they are sorely lacking the will to ask questions about anything outside these walls. If it doesn't involve who spilled their beer on their temple finest, or what mistress is sleeping with what john, you simply don't care. Well, there's a world out there, and like it or not, we're all a part of it, walls or no walls."

"Ma'am, I never said anything about any of that."

"I know, but we're all like this, to some degree or another. And the reason for it is largely the leftover bashing we get in school to stop asking questions about those important things we're supposed to be asking about."

"Aye," responds another pedestrian. "I'm with you there. I still recall a wee bit of that."

"Exactly, and you can thank the Dean for it, because the teachers that were bashing you were once his students. Therefore, he is the one controlling our education...or lack of it."

"The lack of it?"

"Yes...the lack of it, as they don't teach us the first thing about what's really going on out there…only what he wants you to know, and therefore the bashing over asking those questions. He's got a god complex that doesn't want you to know anything beyond the rhetoric he and the Governor invent."

"Great gods, so that's the reason, is it? But why is that? They're supposed to be the city authority serving to protect us. And if you can't trust that…"

"Oh!" she raises her hand. "Don't even say it. Who can you trust, right? This is also part of that bashing, to take their word over anything else, and to…trust it."

"Bloody hell, now that just ties it."

"I know. When I finally learned of it, I blew my top. Like I said, I work for the Guard, and I've been out there. We've learned a few things about them that make them suspicious in our eyes of wrongdoing. They are both suspected of several questionable acts, and so far, we think this is just the beginning. The trouble is, they are also suspected to be in cahoots with the real enemies out there, and it's not those people they keep blaming for our troubles."

"Wait!" shouts a woman. "When you say, not those people they keep blaming for something. Are you saying the elves?"

"Them and the Daanen-Aryku, more rhetoric to divert our attention. So listen up close, but also keep it quiet. We probably made a scene for half the city just now. We did this for a reason, to pull your attention away from all the bunk they feed you in school and the temple. You can spread the word if you like, but you also need to spread the word to hush up, because if the wrong ears hear about it, they might call on their real friends to hush things up their way, get it?"

"Aye, sure," she relents. "But what do we do about all this?"

"We're already doing it, but the people are in a delicate situation. Let's not give those bastards reason to foul up our lives any more than they already have."

"But ma'am," offers the first man again. "How the bloody hell long has this been going on? The Dean, the Governor…"

"Apparently, much longer than any of us care to imagine. That famous expression, 'for as long as I can remember…this and that…' is their invention just to keep us under their thumbs such that we can't remember anything outside our own lifetimes."

"Blast!" he shouts. "So, that's where those beastly words come from!"

"Right, but just keep it to yourselves for now. We're working the problem, but from an angle they hopefully won't be expecting."

Marelle now turns to join a group of priests who were riding along in the flight. They assembled outside the house.

"All right, a quick refresh," she announces. "I'm told each of you is able to speak our language, correct?"

"Yes, Lieutenant," the lead priest nods. "If you may recall, we were present in that tribunal His Lordship conducted on those Flame Elf prisoners inside E.D."

"Good, although I believe you were wearing hoods at the time, and I have to admit, I wasn't paying as much attention to your faces."

"That's quite alright," he smiles politely.

She turns and leads them up to the house.

By this time, the commotion outside had called the attention of the residents of the home, who were standing in the doorway and watching the affair on the street. A middle-aged woman and her eldest daughter, both dressed in simple work clothes and stained from the daily household chores, watched as Marelle made her way up to the house.

"Marelle?" the woman emits cautiously. "What's going on here?"

"Marelle!" the elder girl gushes excitedly. "What are those things?" she points at the gryphons. "Is this something new for the Guard?"

"Not quite," she responds as she glances over her shoulder. "These belong to His Lordship down there in the valley. We're just using them to come up for a visit. Aunt Tania, I got your note about Mom, so I'm stopping by to pay my respects."

"Ah, good, and I'm so sorry, Marelle, but you know how this plague is."

"I know. I've been trying to prepare myself for this for a long time, but it just doesn't work. I still remember when it hit Dad."

"But who are all these people, and why bring so many up here just to visit a dying woman?"

"Some of these people are priests. His Lordship down there in the valley is very curious about this plague and why we have it, so he sent them up here to investigate."

"But Marelle!" Tania urges. "We all know it's a plague by the Flame Elves. You didn't tell him that?"

"Yes, I explained the whole thing. Now we're conducting an investigation to learn the details, and to see if there's anything we can do about it. So far, we've been discovering a lot of peculiar conflicts in these stories."

"Conflicts? But this comes to us from the priests, and surely, they would know better."

"What they know or don't know isn't the question here. Our knowledge was never able to solve it, so maybe Thaelyn's people might offer some new ideas. These people want to examine her for this illness. Maybe we can find something wrong, or else bring her somewhere for another opinion."

"All right, Marelle, I suppose I can't argue with you. Come on in, she's in the bedroom."

Tania leads the group into the house.

The gathering of citizens outside still clustered around the gryphons, many of them studying the curious creatures, but keeping a distance due to the fierce appearance of the animals. Some of the onlookers were beginning to break off and return to their former tasks, leaving the results of this occasion to spread around for later discussion and gossip.

Tania brought Marelle into a room to the rear of the house, followed by the priests who were carrying medical bags. They found an elder woman lying motionless on a bed and wrapped in a blanket. Marelle gazed at her longingly.

"Mom..." she whispers silently and sighs.

She then turns to the lead priest and begins speaking in the Tae'Eladaran language.

"We'll use this language for now, as my aunt is very devout in her beliefs, and very stubborn to convince otherwise."

"Is she now," he chuckles softly.

"This is my mom," she directs to the bed. "And by the looks of her, she's apparently well into this illness. As far as we are told here in the city, this is a curse brought to us by the Flame Elves, but we already know the Flame Elves aren't responsible. Priestess Sehnisavain says she's never even heard of it before this. And since we know there is a connection of some kind between the Governor and the Suuden-Aryku, we're suspecting this might have origins outside our world, especially if you consider, as His Lordship likes to say, this is simply too mechanical."

"Indeed, and just to make a quick review, can we go over the symptoms again?"

"Sure. It hits sometime after we turn fifty, although it seems to vary by a few years. The victim first suffers from bad headaches, then progresses to memory loss to the point where they can't remember anything at all. They can no longer take care of themselves and basically turn into what you see here. Not long after, they die."

"Very good, and my deepest sorrows for your grief."

"Yeah, it's hard, because we all know it's coming for us. It's our eventual fate. Although, if you look at my aunt here, she and others keep praying to our...gods...that they'll find salvation one day."

Marelle steps out of the way and the priests position themselves around the bed. They set down their bags and open them to reveal a myriad of tools, as well as belts containing a variety of vials filled with various medicinal agents.

Both Tania and her daughter watched with skepticism and some small amount of intrigue at the unusually professional appearance of these people. They did not look anything like the priests of their own temple, nor did they behave like them.

The priests pulled the blankets away from the woman and began a systematic examination of her body, pulling open her clothing to study the skin underneath. Two of them began with the upper torso and arms, while the third checked her legs and feet.

The elder girl moved in close to Marelle to get her attention.

"Marelle," she whispers. "What are they doing? I mean, I know what they're doing…I think, but um…well, what are they doing?"

Marelle turns a passing grin, though very slight, at the girl's curious statement.

"Leesa, they're trying to understand why she's sick."

"Yeah, I get that part, but, well, for instance, why are they looking at her feet, when it should be her head that's making trouble for us?"

"Oh, that…" she chuckles softly. "I'm told their medical practice is probably a lot more advanced than ours. I don't know the full details of it, I'm still learning a lot of things, but we think something happened here that made her sick, and it's not a curse of any kind."

"Not a curse? But they all say it is. What about the priests? My Mom spends a lot of time up there, you know. They tell her all sorts of things."

"Yes, I know, and they also tend to beat it into you, so you stop asking why this or that is the only thing to listen to. This might also be the reason for your statement that they 'all' say this, as the word 'all' is limited to those people you are so often told to trust. What about you, Leesa? Do you listen to them as much as she does?"

"Um…" she dithers as she ponders the statement, then glances briefly at her mother. "Well, she drags me along all the time…"

"Leesa!" Tania snaps. "You should know better than to talk like that! The worship we make at the temple is the only thing that keeps us safe inside these walls."

"Tania," Marelle asserts. "With respect…you're my aunt, and I love you, but shut up. If my mom is dying, she was never safe from anything. It still got to her, just like everyone else, including Dad, and with no exceptions. That is not what I call safe, and…for as long as anyone can remember…it has always been this way. There is something wrong here, especially if you think we are safe just because someone tells you it's so, but it still happens. So, I'm not listening to those people we're told to listen to anymore until they can provide proof of what they're talking about. And that…" she points at the woman in the bed, "...is not proof of being safe. Now, Leesa, you were saying?"

"Yeah, um..." she mumbles cautiously as she passes a glance between the two women. "Well, we go up there and the priests say a bunch of stuff, but I'm not as much interested in hearing it. I think it's partly because I listen to you and Haran about all the things you see and do, and so I'm wondering what's really going on out there. People say we haven't had an attack for as long as anyone can remember, so I'm asking myself, where is this big bad war we're supposed to be afraid of, and all those Flame Elves, if no one can remember anything."

"Do you want to know the answer to it?"

"Well, yeah. I mean, I've been up on the walls a bunch of times, even though the guards tell me I shouldn't be playing up there, but I look out in the fields, and I don't see anything like a war."

"That's because the guards keep us safe in here," Tania proclaims.

"Mom, the guards tell me they haven't seen anything...for as long as they can remember. Do you know how many times I hear those words? It gets tiring after a while. What are they keeping us safe from if they haven't ever seen anything and can't remember the last time anyone ever did?"

"I'm sure it's just because of our strong defense that those heathens don't dare come close to us."

"Oh, they don't come close, but the Flame Elves can get inside and make us sick?"

"This is a curse, Leesa! And curses don't stop at walls!"

"All right, so where are the Flame Elves making this curse if the guards never actually saw one within range of the city to make a curse at us?"

"Ooh! Leesa, I don't understand you sometimes. The priests say this curse creeps along the land and seeps into our city every night. How do you stop something like that?"

"Well, let's see. My first thought is to go out there and find them, then...oh, I don't know...make them stop?" she chuckles ironically.

The girl's statement also incurs a spontaneous round of soft laughter amongst the priests as they quietly listened in.

"Oh really!" Tania gushes. "And do you think you can do this?"

"Well, the guards on the walls aren't. They tell me they're not even allowed to go out there unless they actually see something coming this way. How do you make something stop if you never go out there and do anything…for as long as anyone can ever remember?"

"This simply means those horrid Flame Elves are doing this somewhere out there at one of their unholy sacrificial altars. You do know they have those, don't you?"

"Oh, of course," she feigns submission. "Because the priests tell us, right?"

"Right!"

"And yet the guards don't ever get instructions to…go out…and do something about it? Whether right outside the walls or miles away, it's still going out and putting an end to it. And we're told to listen to this tripe and keep on praying for some miracle, not actual people doing any actual work. You know, Mom, I think I'm taking Marelle's side on this one. There is something wrong here. How do we know what's out there if we don't have any proof? Those priests don't go out there, or do they?"

"Leesa, they don't need to go out there. They have holy guidance to teach them! And you don't go around questioning that!"

"Oh, drat it all, that's right!" she huffs sarcastically and stomps a foot. "Holy guidance. Which still doesn't answer the one about why the Guard, who are supposed to be protecting us, don't actually do anything. You know, this means one of two things should happen. Either those priests, with their 'holy sight'…" she flutters her fingers, "…should point the way for the guards to jump on those Flame Elves, so we can be done with it, finally. Or else the guards should go out and scour the land themselves. And if all this has been going on… for as long as anyone can remember…and some of us are pretty old by now to remember things, I think that's enough time to get up off your bum and do something. Don't you think?"

"Um… Well…"

"Ah hah! Got you!" she playfully jabs a finger at her. "Because if praying to a god to do the deed results in this," she waves a hand at the woman in the bed, "I'd say it didn't work in her case, and all those others from around the city. And I think a good many of them did pray to those gods for help, but didn't get it."

"Woohoo, Leesa!" Marelle applauds. "Not a bad bit of deduction."

"Aye! Finally, I broke that bit. Which means, regardless of the priests saying something, the Guard is being told not to do anything about it. Not unless they see something coming right up to our walls. And this comes right back to what you said. Something is wrong with all of this. We are not safe, no matter how much praying we make, as no one is doing anything physical about it, not even those gods we pray to. So, Marelle, what do you think we should be doing about it?"

"One thing is for sure; I think I'd like to go up there and start asking those priests a few questions. If the Guard has orders not to go outside, for any reason at all, this is bad for us inside here and whatever this plague actually is."

"Madam, if I may briefly," the lead priest interjects to Tania. "Your daughter here does hold a valid point, if to put this into logical thinking. You do have such as logical thinking in this fair city, do you not?"

"Um, well..." Tania asserts politely. "I'm just a simple woman, perhaps not as refined as some."

"Be that as it may, still, you have a mind, and that mind should be capable of independent thought, despite what anyone else might say to you. Unfortunately, that statement...for as long as anyone can remember...seems to be a popular deterrent to prevent that mind from actually thinking. You cannot remember what is outside your personal experience. But what about your mother, or your grandmother, other than what they personally can recall, and then share with you. What about the history of this city, and what anyone else might experience, then to record for future generations to remember?"

"I can't be sure what to say about that. I mean, we have our schools. Don't they teach us everything there is to know?"

"I suppose this is largely subjective. What is it you are supposed to know, and by whose opinion should you know of it, especially if they are filling you with such statements as, 'for as long as you can remember…' and leave it at that. For instance, do they teach you what happened a century ago? Two centuries ago? Four centuries? A full millennium? Do they teach you where you originally came from, that you first built this city? Do they teach you where any of the other races came from that they built theirs?"

"Whoa! Please! No, I don't recall any of that, and I must wonder why it would be so important to begin with."

"Ah, so any history, outside what you might personally know, is now irrelevant. Therefore, those people you are supposed to listen to in your schools become the one and only authority to teach you whatever they want you to know, and the rest doesn't matter."

"He's got you, Mom," Leesa nods.

"Your schools tend to demand absolute compliance with their instruction, and your mind, with its ability to think independently, is being stifled. Therefore, you cannot remember anything outside your personal experience, and stop asking questions about the rest, as they do not permit this. This then lends itself to manifest with such an indifferent attitude that you no longer care."

"Oh, dear…" Tania moans.

"Furthermore, if you cannot remember anything outside your own lifetime, and lose all interest in it to begin with, your schools, which are supposed to be teaching you the history of the world, no longer have anything to teach. Your attitude would deny whatever you once learned to be recorded for anyone else to learn. Therefore, you, perhaps also your mother, your grandmother, and who knows how many others, with any and all of their personal experiences, are lost. This now makes you susceptible to any of those individuals who represent themselves as your instructors to give you whatever it is they want you to know. And this is made worse with that one phrase about remembering things which will stifle your ambitions to want more."

"But… They…"

"Yes, 'they' can now invent anything 'they' desire and claim it to be real. After all, how would you know the difference, if your personal memories don't cover the distance, and your schools are not recording anything that came before your time? What's more, your indifference does not permit you to pursue any proof to demonstrate their words. Therefore, it all becomes hearsay, and not necessarily the kind sort."

"All right, I believe I see your point."

"And what is even worse," he asserts with a finger. "I must agree with this young lady here. If you are being offended by someone, curse or otherwise, your Guard should be sent out to deal with it before it brings any more harm. It is really that simple. Life should be regarded as more precious than that. What sort of arrangement do you have here where your authority figures allow the people to suffer a plague, or anything else that takes lives, and never take affirmative action to resolve it?"

"But good Sir," Tania pleads. "We offer our worship, along with our priests, every day for deliverance and protection, and I am fully committed to this as the only way to resolve this problem."

"But I beg to differ. The only way...as opposed to what, physically going out there to find the cretins who perform this and put a proper end to it? Like this young lady said, is your god doing this instead? How long does it take for your gods, or even your city guard, or anyone else around here, to realize any course of action to be taken?"

"Um..." she hesitates.

"He's got you again, Mom," Leesa affirms. "That's exactly what I was saying. What good is prayer, if no one, including our gods, goes out there to actually do something about it. We've been at this...for as long as anyone can remember...and it hasn't changed anything."

"Indeed," the priest asserts. "For instance, do your priests promise to go out there and stop it themselves? Clearly, your Guard is not doing it, especially if they have orders to stay at home and wait for something to come here instead. And if you are praying so hard, and for so long to your gods, they do not seem to be resolving it either. And this too for a long period of time. I should think gods would not require as much. Surely, they ought to be able to stop this. After all, these are simply elves...mortal creatures who do not compare to gods."

"Yes," Tania nods. "I suppose that does sound like a contradiction. But could it be they also have gods…of some kind…and um…"

"A conflict between the two? I suppose you could argue this. This might then need to come down to either your god winning over theirs, or theirs winning over yours. But this also leads us to an ultimate conclusion from our perspective down here. If your god wins, huzzah for him, and keep on praying. But if their god wins, you might need to find yourselves another god who holds greater power to get the job done."

"Oops!"

"That's a good one," Leesa nods.

"Madam," the priest continues. "We are, as much, law enforcers as we are anything else. Such as this plague of yours, whatever the cause, would be regarded as a crime. If you have such a thing as law enforcement here, it should go into action to resolve it. But if it is not, I would further suggest that is also a crime. Inaction to solve a crime is as much an offence as the crime itself."

"Uh oh!" Leesa yips. "Does this mean the Guard is in trouble here?"

"I would rather say the one to blame here is whoever gives that order to intentionally stay at home."

"But that would be, um…who, Marelle?"

"It would have to go up to the Governor, at this point," she replies. "And we already suspect him of a few things."

"But Marelle," Tania blurts. "He's the top authority in the city, and if you…"

"Hold on!" she interrupts. "If you're about to say, if you can't trust that…blah blah, keep it. That's another of their favorite sayings to stifle that mind of yours. They are the ones who feed you all the rubbish in school, which you cannot trust. Therefore, the ones you are supposed to be trusting are the ones you should not be trusting. It's a conspiracy, and we already have several things on our side we're investigating to see how far it goes."

The priest returned to his work, leaving Tania in a fluster for the inflammatory statements. Both Marelle and Leesa felt a mote of satisfaction at the victorious conclusion.

"Wow," Leesa mumbles, as she watches. "Now that is a priest I could listen to. So, Marelle, you want to go up and talk to ours, huh? Can I come along? I'd love to hear this one."

"Leesa, while I'm pleased with your support, the people we're dealing with have some powerful friends behind them, and those friends aren't the sort of people you want to play games with on the walls."

"But Marelle, if nothing ever comes up to our walls, what are we supposed to be afraid of out there?"

"First is the reason why they don't come up to our walls, and it has nothing to do with the city defense. They have orders not to, and by those same people who are keeping us boxed inside here. So, regardless of what your mother thinks of our guard keeping the city safe, they mostly snooze for a lack of anything else to do. And part of this relates to what's inside here with us, and the relationships they share to those outside."

"Relationships? In here? You mean inside the city?"

"Yeah, at least some of which keeps feeding us all these lines. None of it seems to be by accident. And all of it has been going on…for as long as any of us can remember…"

Marelle glares at Tania a moment before returning to the priests and the woman on the bed.

"Have you found anything yet?" she asks.

"Lieutenant," reports the lead member. "So far, we've examined the full length of this woman's body for anything we might normally be expecting, such as common injuries like cuts and bruises, or bites and stings. These might be expected as your more traditional cause, but there are none here. Then we considered potential injections of something into the body."

"Injections? What do you mean?"

"Do you know what I mean when I use the word injection?"

"Well, um…actually, not really. Not the way you people likely use the term."

"All right, let me explain, as you may not have this here. Lady Aerlie has aided us tremendously over the years to improve our medical procedures and capacity. In the past few centuries, we have seen some fine advances in how we conduct the healing arts, and not simply for the advances in the divine component, but also technology to apply medicines and to conduct surgical procedures. One such is to use a tool like this…"

He brings his bag around and rummages through it, pulling out an odd device. It was long enough to fit neatly across the palms of both hands and appeared as a slender cylindrical shape with a shiny little button on one end and a short hollow cavity in the upper section where one might place a cartridge. The working end appeared as a tube with a slot for a longer cartridge, and terminated in a ring.

Marelle gazed at it curiously and stepped closer for a better view.

"Ouch, I'm not so sure I would want someone to come at me with one of those, medical or not."

He turns it over to look inside the open end at the bottom. She saw a metal plate recessed within the tube with several tiny holes in it.

"Do you see these holes here? Just inside is an injector array, with several thin needles set into it. It's loaded on a spring to keep it inside until one might place a small vial in this chamber here," he points at the lower slot. "The vials are interchangeable, as is the needle array, to clean and sterilize the item. This up here," he now points at the upper slot, "is to place a small cartridge of compressed air. When assembled, one can fill it with virtually any sort of medicine you might need for the occasion. You place it against the skin, press this button on top, and the air will propel a plunger to push the medicine out from the vial, through the needles, which are hollow by the way, and quickly into the body. It's a fast and very convenient way to deliver medicine into a body as needed."

Leesa studied the item uncertainly.

"Does it hurt when you use it?" she asks.

"There is a minor pinch," he explains. "But it is usually over and done before you know it."

"Uh huh…"

"Wow, that's actually not so bad," Marelle nods. "So, are you saying you're looking for evidence of something like this now?"

"Yes," he accedes. "The marks left behind would not last long, but if this illness is recent, we might see something. Our trouble is we do not so far."

"Meaning, if it was something like this, it wasn't recent, or maybe not like this at all. Great, what else can we think of?"

The priests continued to pour over the body of the woman and discussing ideas amongst themselves.

"Could it be a foreign body of some sort?" asks one of them. "Something that may have invaded her and lodged inside?"

"There were no obvious injuries," considers the third one. "If she was hit by something, we should see a point of impact or penetration."

"Wait," interjects the lead member. "If it was recent, we should see it. What if this is a slow poison of some kind, and she was hit by it at some earlier moment?"

"Then are we speaking of a foreign body lodged inside, or a poison delivered by an injection? If it occurred a while ago, we would no longer see the point of injection."

"Granted…then let us see about foreign bodies. Lieutenant, do you know of any occasion where your people might feel any sort of sensation of injury or discomfort before this illness comes to you?"

"I don't think I've ever heard mention of it," Marelle ponders.

"If this is occurring at such a precise moment in their lives," the second priest mentions. "My guess would be this is being delivered at a scheduled occasion."

"Blast!" the lead member scorns subtly. "And if we are speaking of conspiracies in this city, this does not bode well at all! What if she could've been called in for a meeting, or some otherwise innocent occasion, and then blindsided by something?"

"That would be sinister," the third priest growls.

"Um…" Marelle interjects. "Can any of you tell me if you can see what's actually wrong with her inside there?"

"Yes, I can," the lead member offers. "But it is not at all pleasant, and I did not wish to disturb you for it," he pauses as he glances at Leesa. "Or your family..."

Marelle looks briefly at Leesa and Tania before returning to the priests and speaking in the Tae'Eladaran language again.

"All right, I understand, but I think I need to know, nice or not. After all, she's my mother and I want to know what's killing her."

"Hey!" Leesa protests as she gapes at her. "That's not fair!"

"Leesa, I'm sorry, but let me make the decision. I don't want to give you nightmares."

"Nightmares..." she huffs. "I think I'm old enough by now..." she grumbles.

"Very well," the priest returns. "But brace yourself. Most of her body appears normal for her age, although lying here for so long, and apparently in a deteriorating condition, her body is showing signs of distress. However, you mentioned her condition involves headaches and memory loss, and this clearly relates to the brain."

He pauses to take a deep breath and glance at the others before continuing.

"We are seeing a great amount of damage of the tissue inside, as if her brain is degrading into something...um..." he winces and gazes at her morosely. "It resembles something like a partially digested soup."

Marelle grimaces strongly at the revolting suggestion. She turned away and closed her eyes as she struggled to contain herself.

Tania and Leesa both observed the reaction and glanced at each other. Then Leesa urgently taps on Marelle's shoulder, raising her brow inquisitively.

"Well?" she asks imperatively. "What is it? I think I'm old enough not to have nightmares any more...I think."

"Leesa..." she sighs. "All right, I'll try to put this gently. Her brain is deteriorating badly, such that it doesn't really resemble a brain anymore."

"I don't really know what a brain is supposed to look like anyway, but can you tell me what it's turning into?"

"This is the part to give nightmares. We'll just say it's decomposing into something like soup."

"Yuk! All right, I get it, and that sounds really bad. But now, what's causing it?"

"They're going to check to see if anything got inside her to cause this."

"How do they do that?"

"These people, so I've learned, have something they call Healer's Sight, which is a divine gift from their gods that lets them literally see inside the body. They can use this to check for illness and injury of internal organs, muscles, broken bones, and other things."

"Wow, that sounds like a powerful gift. Do our priests have this?"

"Given everything we just argued about a moment ago, I seriously have my doubts. In fact, given what I know of their gods," she points assertively at the priests, "I'm asking myself if we have any true gods at all."

"Marelle!" Tania snaps urgently. "How can you say that? Do you have any idea what you're talking about?"

"Actually, yes. At this point, I do. Notice I used the words, true gods. There's a difference. True gods are physical beings who perform physical work, unlike ours. Therefore, Aunt Tania, right now, I know more about what I'm talking about than anything you have to offer, or those priests up north. Not the least of which is because I actually go out there and look at things, including those awful Flame Elves, the similarly awful Night Elves, those strange and undesirable Daanen-Aryku, and everything else those people say are doing so many bad things. First, the elves, all of them, are supposed to be worshiping a body of gods that is far more legitimate than anything we can claim. When they ask for help, they get it. And when they talk to them, those gods talk back…to everyone, not just priests. So, there's never any question they're real and paying attention to things."

"Huh?" she winces.

"Second, the Daanen-Aryku are a society of such fantastically high wisdom that we might look like bugs compared to them. So, if it seems strange, it's because we don't have any flippin' idea what we are looking at. And the only reason we think so many bad things is once again due to those people we are told to trust, but in fact should not be trusted. We are locked inside these walls for a reason, Tania, and told not go out there and exercise our ability to think. It is also the reason nothing comes up here, so we don't get any funny ideas of talking to them to learn the truth."

"Gods be blessed…" Leesa moans. "So, that's the deal, ay?"

"And all this is thanks to our lovely governor and his prejudices. No doubt, they all work for him."

Tania felt stifled at the lengthy assertion. She simply scowled at Marelle and turned away, crossing her arms as she simmered.

The priests continued the examination, checking the woman's arms and legs, her abdomen, and working their way up the torso, until one of them makes a finding.

"Here! Look here!"

He points to a location on the woman's right shoulder in the well above the clavicle. The others move in to take a look.

"Gods' pity!" exclaims the second one. "What is that thing?"

"I'll tell you this much," replies the third. "It's definitely not supposed to be in there."

"Aye, but look at that. Are those legs, or some other projection?"

"Legs?!" Marelle shouts. "There's something alive inside there?"

"At ease, Lieutenant," the lead member offers. "This doesn't look like a living item, but rather a device of some sort. One moment…"

He takes another look, this time examining the skin above the site.

"Yes, see here…" he directs to the others. "This tiny scarring, this is an incision mark."

"Just barely, to be sure," remarks the third. "And by the looks of it, this must have been at a much earlier moment."

"Yes, this is fully healed and showing signs of aging, along with the rest of it."

"What are you people talking about?" Marelle pleads.

"Lieutenant, I think we found it, or at least it certainly qualifies as a potential cause. We see a very small incision here on her shoulder, and beneath that is a device that seems to be lodged just inside."

"And the legs?"

"My guess tells me they are to hold it in place, a bit like an anchor. They are very evenly spaced around the item."

"And this is what's making us sick? But what is it, can you tell? And how did it get there in the first place?"

"This would represent a technology we are not familiar with, and clearly it cannot come from any of you, so this leaves us with very few other choices."

"If this has been here for so long," the second priest considers. "I must ask myself how long exactly. When did she first receive it?"

"Aye," the third one affirms. "And this surely isn't the sort of thing you simply pick up by accident. She would need to undergo some manner of procedure for it, I should think."

"Gods above, you're right! You would need to sit still for this one. Maybe that blindsided bit we mentioned was right!"

"Could it be she received it while asleep in bed one night?" the lead member wonders.

"If so," the second one ponders. "Someone would need to sneak in, and then likely place her into a deeper sleep before attending to it. I think this offers too many complications. Too much potential for discovery, especially if this is applied to the full population."

"The full..." the third one mutters urgently. "Bloody hell!"

The priest pulls away from the woman on the bed and marches briskly over to Marelle.

"Lieutenant, if you will permit me..."

He proceeds to examine Marelle's shoulder at the same location. Marelle suddenly feels a quiver run through her for the obvious implications.

"You people are simply scary," she whispers. "But better you than the ones who did this."

The priest studies her shoulder a moment, and then turns to the others.

"She has it."

"Blast, and blast again!" the lead member scorns. "All right, we must be looking at some procedure of application here. Lieutenant, if you please, how old are you, and how old is this woman here?" he gestures at the bed.

"I'm thirty-two, and my mom is fifty-two."

"Very good, so if we are to say you receive this at a predictable moment, and at your age, you already have it. What about this woman here?" he gestures at Tania.

"Aunt Tania, you're thirty-nine now, right?"

"Yes…" she relents tersely.

The priest now makes a brief examination of Tania's shoulder, then Leesa's. He nods on both occasions.

"And, young lady," he asks. "How old are you?"

"Seventeen," Leesa responds meekly.

"This is looking bad," Marelle surmises.

"I simply do not understand what you people are talking about," Tania groans.

"Tania, at this point, I really don't blame you. Not for the slipshod education we get in school. But suffice it to say, you need to be here personally to stick this thing inside the body. That means the enemy is inside the city."

She perks up and turns abruptly to Marelle with a heavy frown.

"Are you saying those horrid Flame Elves are somewhere among us in here? Gods be blessed, they must be hiding in some dark alley, casting their awful spells at us from behind our backs."

"By the Gods! Tania, didn't you hear these people just now? It's a device…and object, not a spell…and of the sort we can't make in this world. That means it's not from this world. And you need to be physically in contact with them to get it. It requires a surgical procedure, and you need to SIT DOWN for it!" she shouts. "Someone needs to cut a hole in you, stick this inside, close up the hole, and you walk away. Now, when in your lifetime, for as long as you can remember, did you ever do that?!"

"Are you now taunting me with those words?"

"I think I might need to, in order to push it through that overly devout skull of yours and emphasize why we are made to use them in the first place. What this says is, this is not a curse. The Flame

Elves deny any knowledge of it. We know this because we asked one. And needless to say, she's a little upset that we're blaming her people for our misfortune. So, I would advise you to shut your yapper about priests, gods, and curses. It's all lies. Everyone has it, and apparently long before it actually makes us sick. I have it, you have it, even Leesa has it, and she's only seventeen!"

Tania turned to glare worriedly at her daughter.

"Then, where does it come from?" she emits softly.

"This is a good question, and perhaps the best one to ask right now."

"If this is consistent throughout," the lead priest reflects. "We are looking at a population stemming, perhaps, from childhood and up."

"Such heathens!" the second priest spurns. "They would do this to children!"

"Aye, but let's keep our calm. Now that we know of it, we need to find the cause. Do we have any other children in the local vicinity we could examine?"

"Um…" Marelle pauses to think. "Tania has three others, but I think they would be in school right now."

"I say we march over there and make a survey," the second priest states. "We need to know how far this goes, and if the younger ones are in school at this hour, this is the only way to discover it."

"Where is this school, Lieutenant?" the lead member inquires.

Marelle pauses to consider this, and then turns to Leesa for the answer. The girl takes notice of the stare and straightens up to respond.

"The kids go to the one over on Humbar Lane. Do you remember where that is?"

"Yeah," Marelle nods. "I remember it from my own time there. So, now we need to find the lower limit, and then figure out how it happens."

"And for this, you need the other kids. Do we wait for them to come home, or go to them?"

"We need to do this now since we need to file a report and decide what to do about it. If this is a conspiracy, we need to know who is behind it, and put a stop to it before anyone else gets hurt."

"A conspiracy?" Tania mumbles. "But, if it requires people to do this, and it's not from around here…then who?"

"This is one of the things we need an answer for. The source simply must be from outside this world. This gives us only one option, but they can't be the ones inside the city actually doing it."

"Um, just for the sake of asking, why not?"

"Well, I think they would tend to stand out…" Marelle pauses briefly, and then begins giggling impulsively.

"What are you laughing at?" Leesa wonders.

"Standing out…they're really tall people."

"Uh huh…" she grins. "All right, so I'll ask again. Can I come with you?"

Marelle smiles and lets out a soft laugh, shaking her head incredulously.

"Leesa, you're going to drive your mother mad one day, same as I did mine."

"She already does that," Tania sighs. "Go ahead, take her. It'll give her something to do, she so hates housework."

"All right, but stay close and do as I say. I'm still a lieutenant in the Guard, remember?"

"Yes, Ma'am!" the girl yips eagerly.

Marelle returns to address the priests.

"All right, here's the deal. The school is on Humbar Lane, which is two streets over. We have Cayn, at fourteen years, Branden at ten, and Shana at seven. Let's hope this works for us."

"Fourteen through seven," the second priest muses. "That's quite a spread. Under these conditions, I might suggest we make a full run through all of them. If this is a school with such a range of ages, the broader selection might serve to better narrow it down."

"It would," the lead member agrees.

"All right, whatever you think," Marelle admits. "Follow me."

The priests all nod and pack up, once again wrapping the woman in her blanket for safekeeping until they return.

Marelle now leads the entourage out of the house and into the street. They form a parade of individuals marching with a determined stance through the streets towards the school.

The people outside had largely dispersed by now, with only a few diehards holding on to see what might happen next with the strange visitors. They watched as the group emerged from the modest home and began strutting across town.

"Lieutenant," the lead priest begins. "I am strongly of the opinion that we should take that woman to the Daanen-Aryku for a proper review. My understanding is they ought to have the wisdom to identify what this device is and what purpose it may serve."

"It's affecting only the neural tissues," the second man offers. "Nothing else. That's mighty precise, if you ask me."

"Aye, but can a poison do that?" the third man considers. "I should think, in that case, it would hit much more than just the brain."

"Likely so. I think just about anything, a toxin, a poison, anything within our knowledge books, wouldn't be so precise."

"Right, but then, you just gave direction to your own question. Anything in OUR books, but this is more likely the Suuden-Aryku, and they must have some very different books."

"And further that it takes so long to hit in the first place, especially if to give it to them as children, and only to see it take hold at age fifty."

"Aye," the lead member agrees. "But you know what I think. If this is a device made by the Suuden-Aryku, I'll bet they're able to squeeze a tiny clock into it somehow."

"Hey, now there you go! And then have it tick off the years."

"That's a lot of years to tick off," the third one admits. "The next thing we should ask ourselves is why…simply to give cause to place blame on someone for something?"

"Sounds as good as anything else coming out of this place," the lead member suggests.

They continued along the streets until they came upon a quaint one-room schoolhouse. Marelle looked up at the building as they approached, recalling her own childhood where she once attended classes here. She leads them up to the door and steps inside.

There were several teachers in session with a large number of children of different ages arranged into groups. When Marelle and her party arrived inside, it drew everyone's attention. Most of the children stopped what they were doing to gawk at the priests in their ornate robes, and the headmaster of the schoolhouse got up from his desk to meet the visitors.

"Yes, eh…" he examines Marelle's uniform for her rank insignia. "Lieutenant. Is there something I can do for you?"

"Yes," she begins politely. "Very simply, we are conducting a health survey. These priests desire to examine the children to ensure they are not ill in any way…you know, to prevent outbreaks."

"Outbreaks? What kind of outbreak? Is there something going around?"

"Essentially, yes, but we're hoping to contain it before it hits anyone else. And naturally, we are concerned for the children. But we'll try to do this as quickly as possible so as not to disrupt your class too much," she smiles charmingly.

"Eh, right. Well, Lieutenant, this looks very official," he pauses to study the priests in their robes of an otherwise alien fashion design. "These are priests, you say? They don't look like the ones we have up in the temple."

"They're a special group working on this health survey. Therefore, the different colors."

"Oh, right. Well then, how do you want to go about this?"

"What if we line them up in nice little rows and process them one-by-one? I think it'll go along quickly enough."

The schoolmaster goes up to the class and calls his instructors to attention. Together, they assemble the children and line them up in rows for each of the priests to examine. Marelle stands off to one side, along with Leesa, to supervise.

"Leesa," Marelle whispers privately. "Help me with their ages, will you? We're looking for the youngest one that seems to have this thing."

"And this'll give us an idea of when we get it, right?"

"Within reason… After that, we'll need to take Mom to some friends to find out what that thing is, and then what to do about it."

"What friends, those people in the valley again?"

"Actually, in this case, the Daanen-Aryku."

Leesa frowned discreetly at Marelle for the suggestion, before softening her expression as she reflected on the earlier arguments.

"Um, Marelle, just how do you think they can help? What was all that talk earlier?"

"The Daanen-Aryku are a society of scientists and scholars, and they are well above us on a lot of things. If this thing is actually from the Suuden-Aryku, which is the most likely source, the Daanen-Aryku might be able to identify what it is and what it does."

"So, you think the Suuden-Aryku are putting this inside our bodies? But how?"

"That's one question we still need to answer. Like I said, they would stand out too much if to do it themselves. So, it must be someone local, and that's bad."

"All right, but let me ask you this. Relating to the priests and everything they say about the elves and Daanen-Aryku, which you were screaming at Mom not to listen to, can you tell me something, even if she doesn't like to hear it?"

Marelle gazed at the girl briefly as she composed her thoughts on the subject.

"Fine, but for now, keep this to yourself. We have enemies here in the city with us, and we can't let them know we're catching on to them just yet. And if they're associated with the Suuden-Aryku, we certainly don't want them getting any ideas, either."

"Got it..." she nods.

"First, we've found out the Governor is in league with the Suuden-Aryku, and the Dean is his lapdog holding stolen goods that apparently played a role in starting this war."

"Oops! That's bad news already."

"The Governor came down to the valley shortly after those people arrived. He played a very bad ruse on them, hoping to cheat trinkets and treasures for himself, and refused to play nice when they offered to join forces to fight this war."

"And that's also not nice."

"The Dean fills our heads in school with all his guff of a false history and lessons of the world around us, and no doubt the priests do the same from their post, all probably at the demand of the Governor to keep us in our place."

"And that's another bad thing! Great gods, who do we trust anymore? This is just like you said up there."

"Lord Thaelyn in the valley is your best choice for now," Marelle affirms. "We're supposed to be fighting this war, but we're not even allowed to go outside. Our friends are being treated like enemies due to all this guff, and the real enemies are robbing us blind with these so-called supply shortages."

"And then that one! I swear, Marelle, how did all this get so twisted up on us?"

"That's just one more question to answer. And part of it involves those famous expressions to further confound things. So far, we've got a few people working quietly trying to find out."

"Who? Or am I allowed to know if it's some big secret?"

"It's a secret, you can be sure of that. We do not want them discovering we're learning what they're doing."

"Well, Marelle, if we're all in trouble here, I don't want to just sit around waiting for another plague, or a real attack or something. I want to help somehow. Is there anything I can do?"

"Leesa, I don't want you to get hurt by any of this…"

"Marelle! I've got something inside my shoulder, so I think I'm already hurt. I'm seventeen by now, so I'm old enough to make my own say, aren't I?"

"And your mother? What do you think she'll have to say about it?"

"Nothing good, like always…so where do I get started?" she grins daringly.

Marelle studies the girl's face and smiles softly, shaking her head.

"Dammit, Leesa, you really are a spitting image of me when I was your age. All right, but keep it under wraps. Go see Captain Kholgard at the barracks and tell him I sent you. Have him arrange a horse for you and come down to the valley. I'll work with you there."

The children were lining up, and the priests were processing them in sequential order. Both Marelle and Leesa took mental notes of their ages until they began to see a pattern emerge. By the time they finished the full attendance, they had a clear impression of their result.

The priests stepped back, and Marelle met with the schoolmaster again.

"Eh, Lieutenant," he announces. "I'm a little confused. What is this about? They only looked at one shoulder. Why?"

Marelle glared sternly at the man, suddenly making him feel very small.

"What," he protests. "Did I do something wrong?"

"Priest, check this man. I'm curious about something."

The lead priest moves around and approaches the schoolmaster, then reaches for his lapel to pull open a space to examine the man's shoulder.

"Interesting. He has it as well."

"He does?" Marelle intones curiously. "Well, what do you know. They're not completely immune after all. I guess Acolyte Sarens was right."

"Are you thinking it might be these instructors?" the second priest wonders.

"It's an idea, but I think also prone to those complications you mentioned. It's too easily discovered by observers. I'm simply curious about him as he's a former student from the mage academy, and that associates him with the Dean."

"If he has it," the third priest considers. "He must've been a victim of another individual, perhaps not associated with the Dean."

"At least not directly," the second one accedes.

"All right," Marelle concludes. "So, our numbers narrow it down to the age of twelve."

"And bloody wicked at that, to go so young." the lead priest affirms.

"Right, so now we need to figure out where and when. What do you recommend next?"

"Before I go any further with it," he responds. "I would wish to report to His Lordship and gain his opinion first."

"Sounds reasonable, and then take this to the Daanen-Aryku for a better idea of what it is."

"Right, I would agree. And then we need to make an assessment of what to do about it."

Marelle nods and starts directing the assembly out of the building.

"Eh, Lieutenant..." the schoolmaster announces.

She turns to face him as the priests file out onto the street again.

"Can you tell me what this is about? What do I have? And what is this mention of the Daanen-Aryku, and so on?"

"These people are priests serving Lord Thaelyn in the valley. And they hold more knowledge than anyone around here about a number of things. They're concerned about us for our health."

"Really! Well, I'm gratified for that, but I don't feel ill, nor have I seen any of these children exhibiting anything. Can you tell me what this illness is about?"

Marelle glared intently at him, enough to make him feel uncomfortable, if only for the implications of her temperament.

"Lieutenant," he infers tenderly. "Did I do something wrong here? I'm simply a schoolteacher, doing the best I can to conduct my work."

"You're a former student of the academy, meaning the Dean. That doesn't place you very high in my book."

"Well, I'm sorry, but it's a choice I once made in the hopes of finding work for myself. I had higher hopes for it, but once I got there, it didn't pan out like I expected."

"Oh, so you're actually not happy with the lousy education you received up there?"

"Honestly? Yes. And then there were all the times I had to kiss the Dean's backside."

"All right, I'll pull back a little on you. My brother was once a student up there, and none of us in the Guard like the Dean or his lackeys, for how they treat anyone else around here."

"Lieutenant, I never treated anyone so badly that I deserve to be treated like this. But I do understand your position."

"All right, I'm sorry. I'm simply upset over a lot of things. Are we speaking of Dean Malorn here?"

"No, I graduated a few years before his predecessor retired, Dean Sobahn. But he was generally the same. A few of the others came from Malorn, however," he glances around the room.

"I see. Anyway, this relates to the Plague. I'm investigating where it actually comes from and why we have it. His Lordship thinks it's not a curse, neither is it by the Flame Elves. He says it's too mechanical, and so far, we've discovered a strange device of some kind under the skin on our right shoulders. It's not supposed to be there, and we think everyone in the city is getting them, starting with our children at twelve years."

"What?" he grimaces. "How is that possible?"

He turns to examine his shoulder as he waits for her response.

"That's why I'm conducting this investigation. It would seem none of us, so far, is exempt to this assault, and this is what I'm going to call it, an assault by someone putting something inside our bodies that ultimately kills us later in life. And there's only one place something like this can come from. The trouble is how it gets in there in the first place."

"Where do you think it comes from?"

"This looks like a technological device, but you need the right kind of science to make it. This goes beyond our people, and has to be an enemy force, like the Suuden-Aryku."

"But what about the curse everyone talks about?"

"Those priests up north seem to like to spread a lot of tripe from what I'm assuming to be the Governor. He's known to us to hold a lot of deep prejudices over just about everyone and everything out there. No doubt, this would justify the curse."

"Priests..." he muses briskly. "But wait! You said twelve? That's... um, that's when we have the Festival of Passage!"

Marelle's face frowns deeply as the connection is instantly made in her mind. Leesa was standing next to her and instinctively turned to her shoulder, placing a hand on it in reminiscence of the event.

"Bloody hell, you're right!" Marelle growls quietly. "Now that's a fine way to treat the people! Blindsided, they said. Aye, and in plain sight! Those blasted priests promise us this divine protection, when in fact they're the ones doing it! Ooh! Just you wait till I get up there."

"Yeah, good luck with that. But then what? If you say the Governor is doing all the advertising…"

"Right, and his lapdog the Dean with our schools," she pauses to consider her next action. "Yeah, this is going to end here and now! I'll tell you what. I'm taking charge here. You want to play the role of filling our young minds with the wisdom of our people? Then you start doing it right, you and all the others."

He glares at her firmly, then passes his glance around the room at the other instructors.

"Lieutenant, you don't hold that sort of authority. He's the topmost man to hold authority in our education system, just under the Governor himself."

"Bully to that!" she protests. "Both are suspected of illegal workings, so in my book, and that of Captain Kholgard, neither is duly regarded to hold any proper authority at all. And we all know the stuff you teach here doesn't teach anything anyway. Now, do you want to keep your job? Then you'll start listening to me. If he tells you to do something, you'll simply smile and say, 'Yes Sir, anything you say, Sir,' and then report directly to the Captain for his instructions until the situation is brought under control. Got it?"

"Can you actually do that? What illegal workings? I don't understand."

"They're associated with the enemy out there, which is why no one around here has enough brains to know up from down. And at this point in time, we can't let them know we're wise to it. So, here are your new instructions. Gather up the other instructors, all of them, everywhere, and hold a meeting to share this quietly. Then start teaching our kids right."

"But Lieutenant, even if I did as you say, these books are all that we have to teach with. You talk about up and down, but using what?"

Marelle looked around the room at the bookshelves as she pondered the situation. She strolls over to one of the groups and their instructor, and picks up a nearby schoolbook to examine it.

"I remember this from my own childhood," she muses.

The headmaster follows her.

"Yeah," he sighs. "They don't give us anything new unless something wears out so badly, it falls apart."

"That's not good. Things change every so often. People do things, sometimes learn stuff, but no one ever writes it down?"

"Not in these books."

"Great. All right, I'll see if I can get some new material for you. For now, just keep it under control."

She smiles softly and pats him on the shoulder, then turns to leave.

She joins the others outside and pulls out a trans-com from her pocket. She was issued one just before leaving the settlement, and Thaelyn instructed her on how to use it, so she could call in on what they discovered. She brings up the iconic pad, and selects one to make a call, then a directory listing for Thaelyn's unit.

A chirping ring sounds out from the unit on the table in the tactical office in Firstfall. Thaelyn picks it up.

"This is Thaelyn,"

"Your Lordship, this is Marelle, we have some information for you. Suffice it to say, we have a problem up here, and my dander is burning up right now."

"This surely does not surprise me. What is it this time?"

"First, let me pass you to the priests to hear their side."

She hands over the unit to the lead priest in the group. He studies the curious item before bringing it up to his ear.

"My Lord, are you there?"

"Yes, Priest Garrain, do we have anything?"

"Indeed, we do, my Lord, and it is rather unpleasant."

"I was expecting as much, what is it?"

"Firstly, we examined the woman. She is entirely unaware of her surroundings and appears near to death by now. We can see a large amount of deterioration of her neural tissue, to the point where we might describe it as decomposing. The remainder of her body seems fairly normal for her age, save for the distress that might come about due to her lack of ability to attend to herself."

"This is rather disparaging. Can you determine a potential cause?"

"Yes, we found what appears to be a device of some sort implanted just below the skin on the right shoulder, apparently the result of a surgical procedure by the appearance of a tiny scar left behind. We have discussed the possibility of this being a procedural event that might occur at some predictable moment, due to, as you say, the curiously mechanical nature of the illness, and we made a rather startling discovery."

"Indeed, and what is that now?"

"We began with those in attendance to test a theory that it is occurring to the full population of the city. The Lieutenant here has one in her shoulder, along with two others in the house, one of whom was as young as seventeen years."

"Powers behold," he mutters. "This is occurring to them at such a young age?"

"Worse, my Lord. The Lieutenant here assisted us in continuing this experiment to see just how young it goes. Her family has three other children, currently in school. This led us to conduct a general survey of the student body to find a more precise number. As a result, our findings show it is consistently appearing in those of age twelve and above."

As Thaelyn listened to the report, he felt a moment of rage shoot through him.

"Blasphemy!" he shouts and pounds his fist on the table, much to the surprise of the other officers in the room. "They spread such as lies and fables, and deny the free investigation of the truth, then to send assassins and otherwise describe our efforts to rid their world of these villains as an unwelcome inconvenience! And yet they assault their own children! Where do we stand at this time?"

"My Lord, at present, our thoughts are that it could be a device with a clock timer that ticks off to an appropriate moment before releasing this agent into the body. How does this sound to you?"

"This sounds entirely plausible, and a most excellent suggestion on your part, although it would need to be a rather extraordinary timing mechanism to stretch for so long a period. But then, we must ask what is inside, precisely. And even though this sort of technology would require a rather high level of expertise in the medical sciences, I would still desire a study to provide us with our physical evidence for presentation."

"Which would then take us to the Daanen-Aryku, correct?"

"Yes, do this, and then report back to me. We will proceed from there."

"Very good, my Lord, we will attend to this promptly. Eh, Lieutenant, did you have anything else to report? You spent an extended moment in conversation with that man."

"Yes," she affirms.

She holds out her hand to take back the unit and brings it up to her ear.

"Your Lordship, I was in conversation with the school headmaster a moment ago, and we shared a revelation together."

"Indeed, is this one of those you describe as filling your heads with so much rubbish?"

"Yes, but we came to an understanding. Much like with Haran and Acolyte Sarens, it seems we have additional people who are not satisfied with their own education."

"How intriguing," he muses.

"Therefore, I'm taking charge of things here. I gave him an ultimatum to ignore the Dean from this moment forward, and report instead to Captain Kholgard, and only look like he's playing nice for the Dean. We need to find a way to update their books with new information, and bring our education system under new management, but quietly. Those things date back to my own childhood, and look nearly as old by now."

"Indeed. Very well, if you feel you can keep it under control. What was this revelation?"

"When I mentioned this is occurring at twelve years, he made an association. First, you need to know our priests tell all sorts of wild stories for just about everything out there. Sacrifices and blood rituals, unholy rites, errant deeds...you name it, someone did it."

"Just like your Governor."

"Yes, exactly, and naturally, this includes the Flame Elves for this horrible curse. I think a lot of people around here listen to them more than anything else."

"This is already a problem, but how does it relate?"

"You're not going to like this one. They also hold a yearly event we call the Festival of Passage, which is mandated by the temple for all children of twelve years to receive a blessing to protect them from this really awful Flame Elf curse."

Thaelyn felt another surge of rage rush through him.

"Unbelievable!" he roars. "And what is worse, they dare call themselves priests!"

"And this also implicates them to be associated with the others."

"Indeed! It would seem that Governor has a tidy little operation running up there. Very well, take your mother to the Daanen-Aryku and attend to that for now. I will need to think very carefully about the rest."

"All right, I'll call you when we have a result."

They end the link, and she stows the unit in her pocket again.

"And I thought they were heathens before," the second priest mumbles under his breath.

"Aye, I agree fully," the lead member admits. "But for now, we need to attend to the rest."

"Right," Marelle directs. "Back up to the house."

They begin another quick march up to the house again. The curious manners of their conduct were drawing a lot of eyes and causing many to ask questions about what they were doing. The activity was becoming the most exciting event in recent history in this corner of town.

"Marelle?" Leesa wonders. "Um, you said this could relate to the Governor, right?"

"Yeah."

"Which one? Because this curse has be going on for...um... well, you know."

Marelle suddenly halts as the association hits. She is quickly followed by the priests who all stop in their tracks along with her, and they all glare at the girl.

"Great gods, lass," declares the third priest. "Four centuries worth? This dates back a little beyond where this one fellow could reach."

"Yeah," Marelle scorns. "So much for simple prejudices. This is an organized scheme. It must be another of those covert things His Lordship was speaking of once. That Priestess Sehnisavain said something about a council at one time, and then suddenly we have a governor coming into it."

They continued along until they arrived at the house again. The gryphons were still sitting outside, along with their respective drivers, all contentedly enjoying the warm sun and cool breezes.

"We need the stretcher," the lead priest orders.

The other two turn towards the gryphons and remove a stretcher that was attached to one of the animals. This animal was configured as a type of flying ambulance. The stretcher was part of an assembly, running along its back on a cushioned mounting track, that offered a shock absorbing ride for the passenger.

The people gathered in the streets once again, watching and waiting. This was a very unusual procedure for them to observe, and they studied it carefully. Some of them were trying to speculate what was happening, but most simply waited.

The priests took the stretcher inside the house and back into the bedroom.

"Marelle," Tania interrupts as they pass by. "What is going on here?"

"We're taking Mom to some people to make a proper study of that thing inside her shoulder. We think we know where it's coming from, and right now I'm ready to bust a few heads, and then some, but I'm going to wait for my orders first."

"Really…um, so what is it?"

"Tania, right now, I think I should wait until we have some confirmation. What we have here is serious, but also speculative. We need to know what's inside and how it relates to anything. But it feels like a knife in the back for what it represents, and the people doing it are a nasty group."

"Oh, dear…"

The priests approach the bed and remove the elder woman from her blanket wrapper, then secure her firmly in the stretcher with safety straps. They then take her outside and attach the stretcher to the gryphon.

"What in all the hells are they doing there?" mutters one onlooker.

"Loading someone up?" notes another.

"Is that a sick woman they have there?" observes a third one.

"Aye, and look at her face. She looks like she's got the Plague!"

The collected assembly ushers up a moan and steps back a pace.

"But where are they going with her?"

"I can't say for sure, for that one, but I'll tell you one thing. I don't think I'd want to be tied down like that on the back of one of those beasties, with or without any wits about me."

Marelle studied the priests and this peculiar arrangement of transportation. She found herself marveling at the sight, but also shared some of the other opinions going around.

"All right, Lieutenant," the lead priest asserts. "We're all ready."

"Good…" she affirms and turns to Leesa. "We need to go now. I'll let you know what we find out. Keep the faith, and not the one they sell at the temple."

Marelle now joins the team mounting up on the gryphons. The ambulance gryphon didn't include a driver, as the stretcher took up the full space of the creature's back.

The driver on Marelle's ride led the charge again, calling to the rest, including the ambulance gryphon to follow. They lined up along the street, with the intent to use it as a runway.

"Clear the way, people," Marelle shouts to the assembled crowds.

"Oi! Right then," returns one of the onlookers. "Everyone! Clear the street, or you'll get your bum trampled, I'll bet!" he laughs boldly.

The crowd parts ways, and the lead driver takes off in a dash. The creatures follow in a long line, building up speed, and then flapping furiously to gain lift. The ambulance gryphon followed suit, with its passenger held firmly in place on its shock-absorbed mounting.

The flight took to the air again, and the people on the ground gawked at the majestic display. They made a steep incline to gain altitude while heading off to the east.

"All right lads," the lead driver shouts. "Form up while I link with our charge."

He maneuvers his mount alongside the carrier and pulls out a long lance-like staff from a slot at his side. He begins casting a chant on it while aiming at a rod extending forward from the other gryphon's collar. A thin line of energy formed between them, creating a kind of virtual tow link, since the other gryphon didn't have its own driver. He then arranged the group in a V pattern, with himself in front and the carrier in the middle.

The other drivers each pulled out similar staffs and cast their own chants to link with his, and each one placed their staffs into mounting slots of the gryphon collars. The lead driver now begins a new chant to envelop the full flight in a series of transport spheres in preparation of bringing them into high-speed transit.

The people on the ground were once again following the troupe in the sky, trying to guess where they might be off to next. It wouldn't last long, though, as the flight of otherworldly creatures formed up and flashed away in a streak across the sky, followed by a soft clapping of thunder on the ground.

Marelle marveled at the extraordinary experiences she had during this time. Her initial fear of flying was now being replaced by the sheer awe of power to travel in ways unrestricted by the traditional burdens.

The landscape passed by rapidly below her, and it didn't take long for them to see the hulking form of the Daanen-Aryku citadel coming into view. The Naarg uy'Sodrad, the ship once used by the Daanen'kai refugees to travel between worlds, was half buried in a hill after it crashed into the countryside.

The flight leader brought the gryphons out of their supersonic travel and began their descent. Several Daanen'kai troopers were on patrol, along with some of the Order troops, when the booming of the shock wave hit them. They all turned to observe the animals coming in for a landing. A smaller watch guard near the ship carefully made its approach as the flight settled on the ground.

"In all the nether-space…" the guard leader shouts as he studies the odd creatures. "Who are you? Are you part of His Lordship's people?"

"Yes," Marelle responds. "We have a medical issue that needs your attention."

"A medical issue," he returns as he glances across the assembly, soon to settle on the ambulance. "That's absolutely incredible! You can use these creatures for that?"

"They can apparently do a lot of things over there."

"Amazing… All right, so what's the problem here?"

"This is my mother back here. She, and just about everyone else in our city, is subject to a plague that's been going on probably since this war got started. It's probably another of our local conspiracies we've been discovering, but that's another issue. We found a device hidden under the skin on her right shoulder. We need to know what it is, and this is where you come in. Do you think you can help us?"

"A device, like an implant? How in the name of the cu'Nar did she get that?" he closes his eyes and shakes his head. "Right, so I guess that's the question here. We'll need to bring her inside."

He makes a cursory pass around the local fields.

"I would recommend we bring you all inside and out of sight. If you go through there…" he points to what appears to be a tunnel entrance in the hillside. "That leads to our vehicle hangar, which is partway alongside the ship. Go in there and settle yourselves. I'll call someone over to assist."

Marelle nods and passes the instructions to the others, and they form a caravan leading into the tunnel.

They travelled along the neatly dug-out passageway for some distance, due largely to the immense size of the Naarg uy'Sodrad, until they came to what was clearly a large hangar door leading into a broad chamber with several vehicles parked in their stalls. They entered inside and settled the gryphons into place just as they saw a medical team coming through a doorway in the rear of the compartment to meet them.

"Greetings and welcome to the Naarg uy'Sodrad," calls the lead member of the medical team. "I'm Med-tech Ankhia Tad'vaal. What do we have here?"

"Greetings, Med-tech, I'm Lieutenant Marelle Carronel of the Allegiance Guard. What we have is a mystery that's driving most of us up the wall. We need your help to find a way back down from it."

"All right, but what is it? I got word of some mysterious implant that's causing some kind of plague. Is this a contagion, or something else?"

"A contagion? No, I wouldn't call it that. Murder, yes, I'd definitely call it that. Behind me is my mother, although this is beside the point for now, as we all seem to have it. These people are priests and medical experts from Tae'Eladar, and we've discovered something in her right shoulder. It's a device where we think it might be set to a clock and given to us at around age twelve, based on our investigation of a school full of children."

"Twelve?" she winces. "And for humans, that's very young."

"Right, and this clock seems to tick off after we pass fifty. It's been with us since probably the beginning of the war, and likely another covert plot by the Suuden-Aryku, or whoever it is that keeps doing this to us. How do you like that for treatment?"

"Dear cu'Nar, and I thought we had it bad. All right, bring her over here," she motions to a hover-gurney.

The people dismount and unfasten the patient from her mounting, then transfer her to the gurney and set her down. The group then proceeds through the door and along the corridors to a transport chute station, where they take a car deeper into the vessel to the medical ward.

The Daanen'kai interns move the woman onto one of the examination beds while Ankhia prepares a scanning platform mounted on an arm on a track in the ceiling. Marelle watches intently, both in fascination and a little trepidation, of the technological wonders around her.

Ankhia begins programming a standard scan on the patient, causing a wide beam to project from the emitter as the arm makes a slow pass across the length of the patient. An image came up on the monitor over her head with several color-highlighted areas to indicate the woman's current medical condition. She studied the image and a statistical readout along the side.

"Cu'Nar's pity, look at that," she mumbles to herself.

"What do you see?" Marelle asks.

"You said this is your mother?"

"Yeah. I already know she's dying, and her brain is turning into soup in there, so don't try holding back. Just tell me."

"That's a good analysis…I'm impressed. Is that from these people here?"

"Yeah, they've got a few skills of their own."

"Really! I must admit, I'm a little surprised they could come to these conclusions when this is a technology that should be well outside their level of understanding."

"From what I've seen, all I can say is don't underestimate them."

"I've heard of poor Tanjhira and her troubles, so I guess it's my turn now. All right, what I'm looking at here are multiple developing conditions across her body, but I'm going to suggest most of them are collateral with the decomposition of her neural membranes. How long has she been in this condition?"

"It started a little over two weeks ago. It begins as a headache, then goes to memory loss, until they end up like this, and then death."

"A nice little progression…which goes along with what I'm seeing inside the cranium. But the real question, I suppose, is what's causing it. You said there's an implant in the right shoulder. Hmm, yes, here it is…" she points at the image in the shoulder region. "Let me make a detail scan of that."

She reprograms the scan for an enlarged image of the shoulder. Marelle braces herself for what she might see, recalling the description of something with leg-like projections. The arm makes another pass, this time focusing only on the shoulder, and the image changes with a new display of a circular body with six short prongs sticking out at regular intervals.

"Well, they were right," Marelle relents. "It's ugly, whatever it is."

"I would agree, but if you are thinking in terms of something like a bug, those aren't actually legs, those are anchoring hooks."

"Yeah, these people already mentioned that, but it doesn't help matters much by looking at it. Now, a few questions… What is it, what does it do, and although it's probably obvious, where does it come from?"

"All right, right off the top, this would resemble a medical implant, by any normal definition I can offer. We use technology similar to this, but this design is different. By the size and shape, I might suggest it to be a dispenser node, which means it would contain some kind of drug that it would dispense into the body over time."

"All right, so it had something inside, then opened up and let it out once the clock ticked down. What was it and how does it work?"

"One moment…"

Ankhia programs yet another scanning beam, this time a narrow focus beam directly into the implant to conduct an analysis of the contents. She studies the readout as it appears on the monitor.

"First off, I see organic compounds, which could be a solution or a gel to contain something. But then, here…" she points at the screen. "Genetic coding! Dear cu'Nar, we have something alive in here, like a bacterium or a virus! And the computer doesn't recognize it, either!"

"Are you expecting it would?" she chuckles ironically. "This is probably by the Suuden-Aryku, and knowing them as we do, they probably made this custom for us."

"You're probably closer to the truth than you might realize, but I'd still like to make a careful study to see if I can decode this information. Now, if this was placed inside a dispenser node, and then given to this woman…did you say it's affecting your full city population?"

"Yeah, I have one inside me, and we're pretty sure everyone from twelve and up has it."

Ankhia turned to look mournfully at Marelle.

"We need to get those out as soon as possible. You say it activates at age fifty?"

"Sometime after that, give or take a few years."

"That's probably a programming variation to offer a little bit of play with the numbers."

"Whatever… We have a big problem if our full population has these."

"This would require a surgical procedure to install. Although it's small, so it wouldn't necessarily require a major operation."

"Yeah, we think we know where it might be coming from, and that's just one more thing getting on my nerves now."

"What is that?"

"We have a yearly service that our wonderful priests put on, and every kid at this age is required to attend. They put a ceremonial thing around the neck and hold it in place on the shoulders. Next thing you know, you feel pain on the one side. They say this is a test to bear up against to show your strength in the face of all the horrible dangers that never come up against our walls."

"Wow, you have such fabulous people over there. So this ceremonial item you describe might be the implantation device. How do you plan on proceeding with this?"

"I'll need to report back to His Lordship first and let him decide the best course of action. If these priests are in league with the others, we have a circle of very bad people in control of our city."

Chapter 3

COUNTERMEASURES

A team of scouts was making routine forays into the dwarven enclave north of the city of Rolsklinde. Their purpose was largely to chart the tunnel system and discover what the dwarves were doing inside. Along the way, they had been taking notice of a number of anomalies regarding the occupants and their behaviors. They were now exiting outside the front entrance to take a break and convene for a review of their observations.

"Buggers, that place is a wreck!" relents one scout.

"Aye," affirms another one. "If they're not careful, all those holes they're digging will bring what's left of the mountain down on them."

"I'll say one thing," the third one admits. "This doesn't look like a proper settlement to me. The sleep chamber barely has a few mats on the floor, and the feasting hall is little more than a bunch of tables and benches."

"Did you see the kitchen?" the first one asks. "Not much to speak of there. A few chopping blocks and a big stewpot..."

"I peeked inside there once...didn't like the look or the smell of it, whatever it is."

"What about that farming chamber?" the second scout asks. "Did anyone dare take a look at it?"

"I saw it, but I recall it was surveyed once already. What of it?"

"I'll show you. Follow me."

The three of them cast cloaking enchantments on themselves and return inside for another look. They followed a series of tunnels leading up to the first furnace room, which is where Marelle once made her initial attempt at a diplomatic meeting, then continued along through another series into a large feasting hall lined with rows of tables and benches. They turned off to the right through a doorway into a kitchen area, where a pair of dwarves were chopping some meat and carving out the undersides of a fresh batch of mushrooms to put into a stewpot.

The scout points at the scene from within his cloak, knowing that the others in the profession carried glyphs on their bodies as part of their training to permit them to see each other while invisible to the outside world. He used a form of silent language with his hands to indicate the mushrooms on the table, and then to follow into the next chamber.

They entered what was clearly a large cavern that appeared to be expertly sculpted with a high ceiling and broad floor. There was a storeroom on one side stocked with sacks of grain and bales of straw. Offset from that was a large pen filled with some unknown breed of animal vaguely resembling sheep. Beyond the pen was a masonry wall which seemed to seal off this segment of the cavern. Set into the wall was an oblong metal hatch, and mounted just to the side was a metal cabinet.

The scout waves to the others for a moment of pause. He ducks back through the door into the kitchen for another look, then returns promptly and dispels his cloak. The other two followed suit.

"Taking a wee bit of a chance, aren't you?" whispers the first scout. "What if someone should come this way and see us?"

"I don't think they'd react to it even if they did. You recall when Captain Hagmaert was said to describe them as being in some kind of stupor? Well, I think he's right. They don't talk or do anything else you would expect from normal people. But now, look at this."

He leads them up to the wall and the hatch-like door.

"This here doesn't look like any dwarven work I might ever see, not unless these dwarves have come a long way in their engineering sciences."

"Right, I see it. And this door is a bit too unique for the rest of it. There are no obvious levers or knobs for opening it, which means it must use another method, and powered in some way, and this speaks of the Suuden-Aryku. See here, this button..." he points to a small panel on the side. "It's lit up from the inside, and that means power."

"Aye, and there's a window set in the door. Take a look."

The other two scouts step up to peek through a small window set into the upper portion of the door. Through the window, they see another large chamber. It appeared rougher and more natural than the neatly chiseled one they were in. It was dimly lit with a luminescent glow from lichens on the surrounding walls. The floor descended several steps from the entrance, and the sides of the cavern were moist from trickles of water running down the rocks, and edged by thin patches of ice.

The two scouts gazed in awe and trepidation at the strange alien sight. On the floor was a broad farming area filled with an odd variety of mushrooms. The caps were a dark taupe with an odd bluish-violet phosphor glow spotting the upper skin. The shape was irregular and broad, and it sat atop a long stem. A strangely opaque mist flowed across the room, apparently being emitted from a large machine on the far wall.

"Bloody hell, lads!" retorts the third scout quietly. "I don't think I want to spend an evening for dinner in this place! What is this here? It looks like it's neatly sealed off from the rest."

"This door looks like it might be airtight," suggests the second scout. "And this is already bad. It reminds me of the Sarrukhan time capsule in a way."

"Aye, you're right, that same sort of hermetic seal."

"And here, look at this..."

He steps over to the cabinet mounted on the wall just to the side. He opens it to reveal a set of masks with a pair of cylindrical filters attached to their sides.

"I can't say I'm fully up on their technology," he continues. "But this looks a bit like a filter for the air, a touch like what we have in some of our bigger industries back home where they raise a lot of dust. But if we're not talking dust in this case, it's the air itself, and that means those things can't be local."

"Then where did this come from and how did it get here? This has to be Suuden-Aryku, for sure. Dwarves breathe the same as we do, as far as I can tell," he chuckles.

"Right, so who wants to take the plunge and step inside with me?" he grins tenderly.

"You actually want to go inside?" the first one intones warily.

"If these dwarves are doing it, it must be safe within reason, at least for a short bit," he pauses to glance through the window again. "I see liquid water, but also a bit of ice there on the rocks. It may be cold, but if we don't stay long, we can step in for a quick peek."

"What's this little room here?" the first one asks of a small chamber just inside the door.

"Some kind of antechamber, by the looks of it," the third one considers. "I see another panel there with buttons."

"Probably for a transition between the two," the second scout offers. "If the air inside is bad for us out here, this probably swaps it as you go to-and-fro."

"Makes good sense to me, and therefore the reason for the masks. You put them on before you go inside, step into this little room, hit the button, and then proceed ahead. Then repeat in reverse order on your way out. A fine little setup."

The second scout directs the group away from the door and pulls out a set of masks from the cabinet to pass around. They all carefully examined the masks to learn how they might be applied, and then placed them over their faces, securing them tightly with straps around the head. They checked each other to ensure a tight fit.

"Right, now, lads!" the second scout announces enthusiastically. "We're travelling to a bright new world here. Cheerio!"

The other two glared at him, and then at each other as the man presses the button to open the door. The door slides into the wall to reveal a smallish chamber with walls resembling a clear glasslike substance, allowing them to see through to the farming chamber. The three of them step inside.

The scout turns and finds another button just inside the door to close it. He hits that and then turns to the other panel on the transparent door. This one had two buttons separated by a pair of vertical light bars.

"This is a fine one. See here," he points at the light bars. "One of these is fully alight, and the other one is not. So, if we are to suggest these buttons swap it over, then this other one should do the trick for us."

He presses the second button and together they wait. In an instant, they feel a sudden rush of air around them. The first light bar begins to drop while the other one rises, and with the changing of the atmosphere, they feel the temperature drop dramatically. This continues for several moments until the environment stabilizes and the second door opens automatically. They step into the other room.

"Is everyone breathing well enough?" he offers.

"Aye, I'm fine," the first one admits.

"Here as well," the third scout nods in agreement. "It's definitely cold in here, though," he adds. "And now that we're here, what do you suggest?"

The scouts study the surroundings, bending low to take a closer look at the mushrooms and the farming surface. One of them tries to move closer to the cooling unit on the rear wall.

"This couldn't be dwarven make," he suggests. "I see writing that isn't Dwarvish. It actually looks a bit more like that new study they're putting together right now for the Daanen-Aryku language."

"And that's essentially the same as the Suuden-Aryku, as far as I know," the first one submits. "They're all basically the same lot from Azgarén, if you don't count the manners."

"Aye, and look here," the second one points. "These little barrels..."

They gathered around to study a set of two barrels. They were dark red with stenciling on the side, suggesting an identifying mark and brief notation. Each container was just large enough to fit nicely in both arms. The lids were removed, revealing one to be empty, and the other only a third full, with a silvery gray powder inside.

"What do you think, lads?" the second scout inquires. "My best would say it's for the farm, maybe something to add to the soil. See this scoop here?"

"Aye, I'll agree to that," the first one affirms. "So, they set this up to grow something not of this world, needing some uniquely special conditions, not the least of which is air we can't breathe, and then something for the soil. Now what?"

"I'll tell you what I think," the third one relents. "His Lordship will take a grand liking to this one. And I'll bet he'll want us to take samples for the Daanen-Aryku to study and see what's inside. If this is what's making these buggers behave like zombies, he'll need to know about it."

+++◆+++

A pair of elven priests were on their way along a road through a wooded section of hillside. The scenery was peaceful, with lush trees and other wilderness foliage. The journey could easily represent a pleasant outing to enjoy the fresh air, but on this occasion, they were seemingly returning from a patrol outpost. They were heading in the direction of the Flame Elf city of Kynesoth.

The road was old and largely abandoned, mostly dirt by now, with only a few pave stones scattered here and there. It was a remnant of a civilization that had mostly vanished over the centuries, leaving the natural environment to retake what once belonged to it.

The western gates of the city could be seen in the distance. The city itself was a large, well-developed urban establishment fortified within a high stone wall. There were guard towers connected by walkways along the top, and patrols crisscrossing between them.

The two priests strolled along the road until they came within range of the city gates, when a voice rang out from one of the towers above.

"Halt! Who goes there?"

"We are servants of our Lord, returning from the southern watch point to perform a service in His name. Do you wish to question this?"

"It's my duty to question those who approach this gate. What service is this?"

"One to which we were called upon to perform, and this directed us to travel all this distance to attend, but not to be hindered by a mere tower guard. Beyond that, we are not directed to advertise it to the world around us. Perhaps you would wish for him to bring his own explanation down upon you? You served your role, and you questioned us. But as you can clearly see, we are not orcs, nor anything else unexpected to be seen on this road. Now, allow us to finish what we were called upon to do."

The tower guard pauses in contemplation. He didn't want to get in trouble by his superiors for neglecting his duties at the gate, but he further didn't want to get in trouble with the priests, because that would translate to getting in trouble with Sargeras.

"I do not wish to offend," he replies. "We are under orders by the First Deacon to maintain a high level of alert after the strange disappearance of an important official. As for you, you may pass. Be on with your duties."

"Well stated, you have performed your service fairly."

The tower guard calls the others to open the gate and the two priests enter inside. They followed a main avenue that travelled straight through the city to the eastern gate on the opposite side, but they did not intend to go that far. Their objective was the main city temple.

They walked along the road, mostly keeping their eyes forward on their objective, but discreetly glancing side-to-side at the local citizens who were attending their various tasks. The city resembled any other populated center for the activities occurring. There were workshops and marketplaces, schools and academies, and people travelling along the roads from place to place.

Very few people paid any real attention to a pair of priests travelling on the road at this time of day. Their presence could be explained by any number of reasons, from emerging out of their homes and going to work, to travelling from work back home or to any other location, depending on where they might be seen at that moment.

They continued forward until they eventually saw the large temple structure a few streets ahead. They made their way up to it determinedly, as if they had important work waiting for them. As they arrived at the front door, they paused to glance at the local traffic and other activities, then to glance at each other and nod subtly before opening the door and stepping inside in a carefully rehearsed poise.

The temple was spacious inside, with a high cathedral ceiling, rows of pillars lining the sides, statuaries and paintings, and lots of pews. A broad dais could be seen on the other side, with a podium and an altar against the wall in the background. The rear wall was curved with many alcoves interspaced along its length, apparently once used for religious icons, but now vacant. And along the sides were doors leading into chambers deeper within the building.

They moved forward, expecting at least one of the resident priests to take notice and move to intercept, possibly to ask a few questions. They would no doubt represent unfamiliar faces in this place, at least insofar as what was normal to be seen. They made their approach to the dais, and as expected, drew the attention of a local priestess.

"You! I do not believe I have seen you here before. Who are you and what are you doing here?"

The first of the priests stepped forward to speak.

"We were called here to serve our Lord. He did not inform you?"

"Called here?" she muses. "No, I did not hear his songs speak to me of this."

"Then he must not consider you with such a need to know of our reasons, or else he would have shared it with you."

"You would suggest him to dismiss me as unworthy?"

She was a younger priestess, and the man expected her to protest, so he stood there stoically defying her dispute and staring at her unwaveringly.

"Unworthy? This is not for me to say. As for us, we heard his songs, and we answered to such demand as to travel all the way from the southern watch point. This is no small gesture to deliver in His name."

"Indeed," she relents softly. "But it disturbs me that I might not know of it. I have served faithfully in my time. I would expect more by now."

"Perhaps, but then, ours is a particularly sensitive demand. This may carry its own definition. Also our point of origin might afford a suggestion, as we might represent an impartial body, as opposed to those so closely positioned in this place."

"Interesting. Then what reason is it that you were called here?"

"The reason carries multiple roles for us. We heard whispers of an elder member of our beloved temple gone missing. Is this correct?"

"Yes, we do not know where she is. It was High Priestess Sehnisavain. Our last word was she had been seen walking the streets with her two daughters, Tyshalis and Rhyvanith. A guard saw them pass through one of the gates and turn off into the woods."

"Indeed, this is also my understanding. And then they vanished. This is unfortunate, and also the reason for us to investigate. But to do this, we must ensure no other incidents occur to make trouble for us. Those invaders are insidious. Have you heard of the failure of the orcs?"

"I have. But those miserable brutes were not of much use, anyway. They just barely served to harass the Night Elves to the north, and even at that, they did very little actual harm."

"But it is precisely for this reason we must keep a close watch. The invaders used tactics of stealth and surprise on them. We cannot allow ourselves to fall victim to the same. Therefore, we have been instructed to perform a ritual that we believe will offer a protective ward to improve our security."

"Really! How will this ritual be performed? Do you require assistance?"

"We may call upon a few here and there to assist, but for now, we must locate a relic that is said to be in storage."

"What relic?"

"It is said to be very old. We will know it when we see it. An image was given to us of what to look for. By the way, with the High Priestess gone missing, who will replace her...you, perhaps?"

"No, I'm not high enough in rank. More than likely, it will be Ilothonna, her First Deacon. I'm Kerali, her Second Deacon."

"Ah, but of course..." he nods. "And yet, if you would wish to assist us in locating this relic, you may follow. We suspect it will be buried somewhat by now."

"Of course, this way," she directs calmly. "The storeroom is in the basement."

The priestess steps around the dais to the door along the side. The two men glance at each other, then continue their gaze briskly around the rest of the room, which was empty at this time. It would seem the people of this city didn't spend as much time sitting in prayer as an average citizen would, instead receiving Sargeras's songs directly inside their minds.

They followed the priestess as she passed through the door and along a hallway up to another door. She pulled out a key and unlocked it, then beckoned them to step inside. The three of them descended a set of stairs into a basement lined with shelves and filled with many boxes and sacks of various sizes.

"How does this item appear?" she asks.

"Firstly, it is in a box of about this size," he gestures with his hands a size a little larger than a shoebox and square. "It would likely be very dusty by now, so the original color might not show through well."

"We have a lot of boxes here. This may take some time."

"This is true, so let us begin."

One of the men moves forward, followed by the priestess, while the other takes another side. They begin searching the shelves and moving stacks of boxes to investigate what was underneath.

"Oh, this is curious. What do we have over here?"

The priestess finds herself drawn by the statement as he points at some containers on the floor. As she bends down for a closer look, the man discreetly waves to the other one. The second man steps up behind the priestess to make a quick gesture with his hand, waving his palm with two fingers extended in a clockwise circle behind her head, then sliding it downward, as if to pull down a blind.

The woman never knew what hit her. She let out a muted groan and collapsed to the floor in a deep sleep.

"You're simply not nice!" the first man chides teasingly.

"Hey, you told me to do it!" the second one retorts.

"Yes, but you're a priest…an actual one, that is. Are you supposed to be doing this sort of thing to unsuspecting citizens?"

"It's all in the delicate Measure of Balance, my son," he grins. "Normally, we use that over the face, but technically, it doesn't matter which side of the head it's on. Now, send her off quickly before we have any more 'assistants' come down here."

The first man pulls out a rune stone and casts the enchantment for a portal. The rune glows in its traditional manner with a ring around it, and he touches it to the fallen priestess. She vanishes in a flash.

"Good," the priest asserts. "We'll let the druids handle her from this point. The tree will take care of her redemption for us."

"Right, so now, where is that box for Sehnisavain…"

The two of them now begin their search in earnest for the box containing the bottle used to kill the High Elf Tree of Life.

✦✦✦✦✦

"My Lord, we seem to have a delivery out here," Captain Hagmaert announces through the door of the tactical office at Firstfall.

"What kind?"

"Looks like a Flame Elf took a rather unfortunate hit. Knocked her right out!" he laughs.

"Oh, did it now. I suppose this means our spies have arrived. Good, this is promising. I wonder if we can perform a little of our own espionage against our friends out there."

"That would be a fine one; turn it right around on them."

Thaelyn was in a meeting with Relissa and Marelle, along with the other officers.

"Jiggers, my Lord," Relissa mutters. "So, we've got peeps on the inside of Kynesoth now. I never would've guessed I'd see the day for that one."

"You simply need a well-coordinated team with good skills and a bit of daring."

"Aye, try to find one of those around here, though. They had us over a barrel, good and tight. Now what?"

"Their primary goal for now is to find that bottle. Once done, we are going to make a few tests to see if we can interfere with their command structure."

"But Your Lordship," Marelle considers. "This could get complicated. If we start making too much noise, wouldn't someone get a little curious after a while?"

"While this is certainly possible, we must consider what Sehnisavain said during our interview. She said Sargeras uses these songs as a driving force, but it is the Suuden-Aryku to actually deliver the instructions for them to follow. This tells me Sargeras is NOT in direct control of their actions, but rather they follow a more traditional chain of command, with the threat of punishment, or fear tactics, as we mentioned once, to keep them under control."

"Right, so he delivers these songs to keep them entranced, and then threatens them to keep them in line. Such a wonderful god we have here."

"Aye, like everything else," Relissa admits.

"And this means he's not using them quite the same as you did in that demonstration with Captain Hagmaert, when you were trying to teach me about this thing called clairvoyance."

"Correct," Thaelyn affirms. "At least within reason... If they are using a more traditional command structure, modified by this so-called divine influence to reinforce their obedience, we may find ourselves with a few curious opportunities."

"Like if to use this divine suggestion, maybe along with a few of their own threats to 'encourage' their compliance," she snickers.

"You could potentially undermine his control methods. But then, what about the Suuden-Aryku in this equation?"

"The Priestess mentioned she used a trans-com with this High Commander Geilv, and he might also send an officer to deliver goods on occasion. But she also mentioned she had two assistants working alongside of her."

"So, we need to work on them next."

"We dare not return Sehnisavain back to her former post, at least not yet. But if we can convert those assistants efficiently enough, they might not be as easily noticed if we return them back as new agents."

"Buggers!" Relissa snaps. "So, we're snatching up bodies, converting them, and sending them back to snatch up more bodies. That gives me a few wiggles for sure!"

"But we also need alibis to go around, so we must move cautiously. And if we can deliver falsehoods to the Suuden-Aryku, no one will know the better."

"And this gives us the freedom to play a few tricks," Marelle nods. "Not a bad bit of espionage. I might even say this is a weak spot in Sargeras's control methods."

"Indeed, and this does bring up a curious mention."

"What's that?"

"We know that the High Elves suffered a form of pain due to the loss of their Tree of Life, and this, combined with the theft of their holy symbols, caused them to fall into such despair that Sargeras could get inside and take possession. But if this control effect is only limited to a coercive influence, not to actively dominate their minds or manipulate their bodies as puppets on a string, this means his strength of control is in fact rather weak."

"All right, and this is despite the fact that Mynae claimed it to be so powerful during that interrogation of yours."

"Propaganda, I would suspect...we are seeing a large volume of that circulating around, and this further influences my opinion of his weakness. He is using falsehoods and misinformation to manipulate his subjects at least as much as anything else. If he were so all-powerful, he would simply play a full domination effect, or portray himself as a true god and earn their sincere loyalty. That would certainly encourage compliance and deny us such ease to convert them back."

"That's an interesting idea."

"But now consider this. The Primordials were alleged to be very powerful beings, regardless of how this one is behaving. And yet, if his best effort is to apply only a meager coercive effect to motivate these elves, and if we suggest this to be a weakness, I have a suspicion of where that weakness may originate."

"All right, this should be good. What is it?"

"The Daanen-Aryku tell us that he arrived on their home world offering this promise of great power in exchange for some form of service. Whatever the reason for this request, he needed the Suuden-Aryku to perform this on his behalf. Sehnisavain also tells of a path he is following, using the Suuden-Aryku, as it would seem, to journey on this path. This then suggests this path to be outside his capacity, or maybe outside his desire to travel personally."

"That doesn't sound good, actually…either of those."

"Indeed. If we say it is outside his desire, this might correlate with his preference to remain hidden from the Estelar. And if it passes through Tae'Eladar, it will likely pass right under their noses."

"Yes, that's reasonable."

"But whether this, or if it is simply outside his capacity, it might also mean something else. His long absence, perhaps in slumber, or some other condition where he was inactive for a long period, might have left him in a weakened state."

"Ah, now I think I see where you're going with this. So, in this weakened state, he might not have as much capacity for the full domination effect, and therefore, the elves can be so easily turned back."

"And further, if we consider range. He is very literally a universe away from us, if we say he is still on the Suuden-Aryku home world. That is a long range, even for a god to reach. Furthermore, he is attempting to spread himself over a quantity of numbers, which complicates matters even more."

"Gods' pity, I could learn more from you than with an army of scholars and priests back home, assuming any of them would actually teach anything useful."

Thaelyn smiles and moves to another set of papers on the table for the next session.

"Now, moving on to the dwarven enclave, thus far we have charted a labyrinth of tunnels, and our own dwarven experts are suggesting the mountain may be close to collapsing in on itself if we do not bring this into proper alignment soon. One suggestion is to carve a new tunnel through a segment of otherwise untouched strata, carefully shoring it up to ensure its integrity, and then close off the rest."

"Is there anything inside worth keeping?" Marelle wonders. "Other than an iron forge?"

"Indeed, there is, as it turns out, and this raises even more questions. You might find it interesting to know that you can find adamantium in this world, and likely mithril as well, as they tend to go together."

Marelle's face went blank at the suggestion. Her mouth fell open, and she stared at him in shock.

"We have it here after all?!" she yelps. "And those bastards lied to us yet again! Not that it actually surprises me."

"Firstly, our estimates for the output of that iron forge seem adequate to supply the Flame Elves and the orcs with at least a fair amount of material. And with so little going to you, we cannot discount the possibility that the rest is going to them. But the question still remains as to how it is being delivered, and for this we may need to continue our observations to see who picks it up."

"Meaning, for instance, the Suuden-Aryku."

"Next is an adamantium forge deep underground, as well as a large storage depot where they are apparently stockpiling what our scouts are describing as mountains of ingots."

"Mountains?! As in, something-that-reaches-over-your-head sort of mountains?"

"Indeed, and this is puzzling, as it raises a number of curious questions as to why they are stockpiling so many ingots, rather than any other kind of finished good."

"Ingots… Well, what can you do with ingots? You could make something else out of them later, couldn't you?"

"You could, but then we must ask, what are they making, and who is making it? If we consider the Suuden-Aryku are not likely capable of working adamantium directly, due to the nature of the material and their lack of background in the magical arts, we must instead suggest it to be the dwarves working it. But unless we suggest these dwarves to be such a highly advanced society, their best would be the more traditional wares we might be familiar with here, meaning armor and weapons."

"Like those we saw on the rogue Suuden'kai team and that Flame Elf assassin."

"Correct, and this fits nicely with the thought. But this also defies what we see in our interactions out by the Naarg uy'Sodrad, as the rest of the Suuden'kai troops do not seem to be using this, nor did our Flame Elf informants reveal anything from their side."

"So this leaves us empty-handed, unless the Suuden-Aryku are saving it for something else."

"And this alone is enough to make me worry, when we consider the size of these stockpiles, and how long this might have been occurring. This could be only one of many such volumes."

"And over the course of four centuries since they apparently first arrived," she muses. "What about the dwarves themselves? Do we have anything new on them?"

"Our observations continue to suggest they are under a potent effect, and it seems consistent. There have been no visitations by anyone to deliver anything into their hands, so we must then assume they are administering themselves as part of this control effect."

"Jiggers!" Relissa yips. "That's nasty. You put them under once and give them orders to do it to themselves from there."

"Yes, and this is very troubling. But a self-perpetuating effect requires a supply. Therefore, we must identify what it is they are using and remove it from them. Beyond this, they do not speak or interact in any common form, as normal people would. They simply work, eat, sleep, eat, and work again, in that order. Also, the enclave itself appears to be rather austere for any kind of proper settlement. Finally, and this is perhaps the most curious feature…" he grins faintly. "There are no casks of ale or any other spirited libation to be found anywhere."

"Um, all right," Marelle muses warmly. "I suppose I need to ask this, not that I need to ask for the simple reason of having a nice mug of beer on hand once in a while, but um…why?"

"Dwarves are notorious for their love of ale. No proper dwarf would go a day without a good full pint or more at the end of his work shift. In fact, this does not bear a resemblance to a proper community, more like a work camp for the arrangement. With this in mind, I recently gave them instructions to begin a survey of the population count to test a theory."

"What kind of theory?"

"So far, by the appearance of it, the population seems to be entirely male."

"Jiggers," Relissa moans. "So, we're talking about a slave camp, and made worse for this mind control drug effect. Now I suppose we'll need to help them next. But this one would be a bugaboo to work if the Suuden-Aryku are using them to mine adamantium and pick it up on occasion. We can't just go in there and haul them out without someone noticing."

"This is true, and at this moment, I think it would be impractical for us to try replacing them with our own in hopes of impersonating the original crew, especially if the Suuden-Aryku are familiar with the members from their previous interactions. Then we have the issue of language in case they use a native form we are not otherwise familiar with."

"So, what then? We leave them for later?"

"We may need to for now until we can resolve the larger issues. We need to expel the Suuden-Aryku from this world."

"That may not be easy," Padriyl offers as he listened in. "I doubt they will so quickly just pick up and leave. They never demonstrated such tendencies to let go of anything in the past."

"Perhaps, but I am also noticing a lessening of their frequency of attack out near the Naarg uy'Sodrad. It would seem they are realizing our potential and holding back to preserve their numbers."

"Agreed, and this also doesn't fit with their patterns unless, like you said earlier, there is another factor at play on this occasion."

"Like the Governor?" Marelle wonders.

"At this point," Thaelyn considers. "I would wager it could be either-or. I would think futility would still represent itself as futility after a while. With or without any control influences, they should still see the trends in front of them and choose alternate methods, or simply halt the wasteful loss. The only deviating factor here might be to ask how valuable the Suuden-Aryku are to Sargeras that he would wish to spend them so frivolously as he has with everything else. If the attacks are lessening, I might wager they are more valuable than most others."

"This is a good conclusion," Padriyl nods. "But at the same time, it also makes me ask what sort of alternative he might consider, if not simply to halt completely."

"Indeed!" he chuckles. "Now, Marelle, according to your captain, he is assigning someone to a new office to begin coordinating these schoolmasters of yours. It would seem you made a solid impression with that one you spoke to yesterday. Captain Kholgard tells us he had a meeting with several of them thus far, and will coordinate their own covert missions to defy the Dean and begin teaching a more appropriate curriculum in their classes. This will not translate into anything useful in the immediate term, but it is a start."

"At least those kids will have a chance now," she relents.

"We will see about providing new books after a careful study of what you have now and what we can do to provide better subject matter. I am thinking of the Night Elves and their schools. If we make a tender assumption that you all shared similar studies once upon a time, perhaps we can borrow something from them."

"That's a good idea!"

"Then we have Acolyte Sarens and his team. He reports that he made contact with not one, but two of his friends up there, and will be assigning them to various tasks. He further reports that the Dean has some of his top instructors working on a project in their basement...something relating to a conjuring, and this is suspect from the beginning."

"A conjuring? That doesn't sound good, not that I fully understand what it is, but Haran tried to teach me a little from his studies."

"Yes, this is a mystery. He says they do not often perform such rituals, and these people were seen reading from a very strange book that came out of the Dean's private collection. This brings serious concern to my mind for the implications of what the Dean is looking for and why."

"My Lord," the General offers. "If he and the Governor are so closely connected, and they both desire you out of the way, could this be related to another attempt at you?"

"If so, it would represent an act of desperation on their part, depending on what they bring forth. Rather than have the Suuden'kai commander out there simply blast us into oblivion, he would instead attempt to bring something into this realm that should not otherwise be here...and for what, another assassination attempt?"

"It does seem a bit like overkill for the effort alone."

"I must ask myself of the integrity of these men and their faculties. This could bring a fair amount of collateral damage if let loose rampantly in the city."

Thaelyn allows his mind to drift off to that first meeting he had with the Governor and the words mentioned along the way.

"Yes..." he muses silently. "This is where we were starting to argue. I am trying to recall the sequencing of our statements here. He had just laid down his proposal of a joint venture if we handed over our fine military hardware, and I argued our policy of not interfering with a foreign society's natural growth. He took offence of this, and... ah yes, my suggestion of creating an imbalance of capacity. Then I described myself as a man of law and justice, and that I prefer to investigate things, rather than take any one man's opinions."

"Ouch!" Marelle winces. "I'm sure he loved that one."

"Oh, to be sure, he had a few words for it," he smiles discreetly. "Here is also where I believe I stated I would join sides with whomever was worthy of my support, including those people he so fervently despised."

"Oh! Naturally!" she titters. "And now, he wants you out of the way so badly, he'll conjure up something big and hairy to do his work for him, since he can't do it any other way."

"Aye!" Relissa yips. "And bloody well take half the city with him!"

"And perhaps also to satisfy his lust for power," Thaelyn agrees. "Claiming this world to be so dangerous when the true dangers are from his own workings. This brings us around to the next point in these reports, and it seems to fit nicely with the rest."

He returns briefly to review his notes.

"Acolyte Sarens says one of his friends belongs to a noble family, and apparently her father holds a circle of debate on city politics and such."

"I'll bet I know who that is," Marelle nods. "The only noble to attend the academy, Tristeen Macaid."

"'Ere now!" Relissa perks up. "I know that name. Haran would talk about her every time he got into one of his moods."

"Yeah, so this could be interesting. Does she have anything to say so far?"

"According to this," Thaelyn smiles. "She was apparently in discussion with this circle where one of them found some old journal notes about the government that came before. It was a council of statesmen composed of members of the noble families."

"Blast!" Marelle blurts. "So, Sehnisavain was right when she mentioned this during our meeting."

"Apparently, this is part of that forgotten history of yours, and likely covered up by the Dean and his predecessors."

"Wonderful. And this reminds me of what Leesa said during our investigation. So, how did it turn over to a single governor?"

"Oh yes, Marelle," he grins. "You will surely like this one. As the story goes, a stranger arrived with the initial reports of this plague curse by the Flame Elves, so it must have been shortly after the High Elves were taken. He offered a convenient curative solution, but naturally, in order to achieve it, he would need power of authority over the mage academy and the temple, as well as the city in general."

"Bloody hell!" Relissa shouts. "That's a fine way to take control of things."

"Indeed, and apparently it succeeded, as the people were seemingly taking ill at random. But this curative solution only reduced it to the elder members with the excuse of this being a kind of tug-of-war between the two."

"Sounds like a good way to keep his position of authority," Marelle relents.

"So, it would seem he built this empire based on false information and other mischief, and his successors apparently maintained it this way. I find it fascinating, however, that he might find so many others during this time to corrupt as his later assigns."

"He had to offer them something…something big, I would think."

"Perhaps. This could also point to an organization of some sort, something like a thieves' guild, or a syndicate to perpetuate these actions. But at this moment I think it is moot. We must now dig away at his foundations."

"Good, I'm all for it, but where do we start? We have the teachers doing their part, but that won't show any results for years. What we need is to get inside the temple and replace those priests with our own, then start spreading a few new rumors around."

"This is a fine idea, but I would first like to know how closely the Dean and the Governor pay attention to their temple services. If they hold such faith of the priests doing their job that they do not need to peek in on them from time to time, we might find our opportunity. Perhaps we can find a way to excuse ourselves as…oh, say with new inductees to replace a retiring set."

"I like that one. But who will replace them, more of your people? You'll need to prepare more operatives for that."

"And so it is…" he leans back and sighs. "Although, I am reminded again of those priests that aided you with your investigation of that implant."

"Those guys are getting some good exercise!" she snickers. "Perfect, but we might also need another mage for the runes."

Tristeen was attending her alchemy study in the basement labs of the academy. She had taken up space at a table on the far side of the room, just across the corner from where the team of instructors still gathered in a tight cluster near the conjuring circle. She was mostly pretending to work on her studies, and occasionally turned to glance discreetly over her shoulder to see if she could catch anything being said by the instructors.

She had one of her textbooks laid out on the table and was pouring over a formula that required several reagents. There was a cabinet behind her with a wide assortment of bottles and jars inside, commonly used by the students to store dry ingredients such as powders and herbs. She stepped across to it and began peering inside, as if looking for something to fill a need for her work.

The instructors mumbled intently to themselves over the particulars of a sensitive application of runic drawings in the circle. She was able to hear some of their conversation and decided to try a test.

"You've been there for a long while," she muses casually. "Are you preparing some new lesson for the classes?"

One of the instructors turned his gaze around at the girl, clearly annoyed that someone would disturb their studies. But when he saw it was Tristeen, a noble heiress, he softened his approach somewhat to that of an unconcerned dismissal.

"Eh…this is clearly for the higher classmen. It involves some very complex procedures and, eh…we are simply arranging it into a proper context for our lectures."

"Ah, for the higher classmen…of course! Will we see any sort of demonstration?"

"A demonstration?" he glances abruptly at the others in the group. "Well, this is not for demonstration. These rituals are simply too potent to demonstrate for casual observation."

"Ah, but you hope to eventually prepare this for a class study for the higher students?"

"It is still under review, and there are many details to go over before we come to that."

"I see. But gracious, if it's so potent that it can't be demonstrated for a casual display, what would the higher students actually do with it? Oh, wait, I think I understand. Yes, of course, I should've seen this before. I'll bet this is going to be used as a powerful new weapon to fight all our enemies out there. I mean, we all know the Suuden-Aryku, along with those awful Flame Elves and the orcs have been threatening our world…for as long as anyone can remember…and the terrible shortages we face in the city are so severe that the Guard can't conduct any serious outward movements to fight back! So it all comes down to us, right?" she smiles sweetly.

The instructor glared at her, at least as much for her intrusion into his affairs, as for the excessively verbose statement over details he really didn't care about, and neither was it his intention to concern himself with anything outside the walls. The students were expected to only involve themselves with the details of their studies and whatever the Dean dictated.

"Eh, Acolyte Macaid, this really isn't of any special interest to you. What we are studying here is a private issue for a future application at the Dean's discretion, nothing more."

"Ah, naturally. The Dean's discretion…" she deliberates. "But of course. And he does know best what this city needs. After all, I've heard all sorts of stories about orcs rampaging across the land, even though no one can ever recall them coming up to our walls directly. And then we have the Flame Elves, also said to be rampaging across the land, and coincidentally, never coming up to our walls…for as long as anyone can remember. But that doesn't change the fact that they're still out there. My goodness, after all, we have this terrible plague affecting us, and that surely is a threat, if nothing else is, because it's inside our walls. And if the Guard can't go out there to fight our obvious enemies who are giving this to us in the first place, then surely it falls to those of us here in the academy to do our part to protect our homes and save our people. Isn't that right, Master?"

Again, she smiles innocently and promptly turns back to her desk to finish her experiment, leaving the man speechless for her cleverly disguised outburst.

Jared was at his usual table on the other side of the room when he took notice of her vociferous presentation, which was clearly intended to draw the attention of everyone in the room to point out a series of obvious flaws and conflicting arguments in the practice of the academy. He smiled at the performance and then returned to his work.

Later in the day, when the class had finished, they convened at a table in the main hall. As usual, there were other students in study and a few browsing the shelves searching for research books.

"Tristeen, that was a bit risky, don't you think?" Jared whispers privately.

"No, not as risky as to come right out and tell them they're licking the boots of a traitor to the city. But I want to start putting a little pressure on them. Not a lot, mind you…just enough to let them know there are details out there that can be brought together to form suppositions with clear reasoning, not this rubbish they're trying to shove at us. And then, I want to get the other students in on it. If we rise up collectively, the Dean will lose power."

"But do we actually want to do this? We're trying to keep a low profile here."

"A low profile…as if to say we don't know the Dean and the Governor are as crooked as a crank handle…yes. But I think whatever those people are doing down there, it's not good…not for us and not for the city. A lecture for the higher classmen? Pshaw! Why do the higher classmen suddenly warrant the finer points of a conjuring that is so potent, they don't dare make a demonstration of it? They don't even teach US anything useful, even as middle classmen! Best case scenario, I can throw a bit of ice on the ground and light a piece of kindling for a fireplace. And this is the grand benefit of magic around here, most of it spent in the alchemy lab trying not to blow the place up."

"All right, so let's say you're right. What can we do about it? We don't want to start anything that could get us in trouble with the Dean."

"No, not directly…" she admits. "Clearly, we can't let him know what we know, but we should start letting on with the other students what we know so that they know it as well. What if he should try one of his crazy experiments on us next?"

"You're not going to play that 'experiment in the basement' joke on me, are you?"

"No…" she pauses in deep thought. "But you know, Jared, you just gave me an idea. Eventually, he and the Governor are going to become aware of the city turning against them. Now, what do you think they'll do about that?"

"Likely call in these friends of theirs to clean up…"

"Right. And what about us? Where will we be at that time?"

"Who do you mean, Tristeen? Us, as to say you and me, or us like…"

"The full student body, Jared…" she cautions. "The way he treats us, he wants us to behave as his servants, licking his shoes like all the rest. We need to stop doing this. One way or another, we cannot allow him to think he owns us. And if the day should ever come when he thinks he no longer controls us, knowing how he and the Governor like to keep things under their thumbs, and just like with Haran getting expelled, we might no longer hold any value. But simple expulsion might not be their preferred choice, especially if we're making noise. If they're willing to call up something too dangerous for a casual demonstration, and if it relates to anything they have in mind to actually use on someone, that represents a murderous intent. We need to be ready for that."

✦✦✦✦✦

The guards at the north gate of Firstfall stood a vigilant watch. In the distance, they began to make out a rider on horseback coming in. The rider appeared as a young female in commoner's clothing. She rode up to the line of guards and they motioned her to stop. The girl complied and tried speaking to them.

"Excuse me, do you understand me?"

The guards did not respond verbally, but instead responded with a shaking of the head and a wave of the hand, suggesting a pause in the conversation.

"Great," she mumbles to herself. "How am I supposed to get anywhere with people who don't speak the language?"

The guards make a cursory inspection and motion for her to dismount. Then, one guard takes the horse around to a hitching post on the side while another waves for her to follow as he leads her up to the tactical office for a meeting. As they pass through the quaint little square in the center of the settlement, she takes notice of all the people and shops that had opened up during this time.

"This place looks like a small village or something," she remarks privately. "What are you people actually doing down here? I thought you were fighting a war, not building a city."

They approach the door, and he brings her inside.

"My Lord, we have a visitor," he announces. "I think this may be the lass the Lieutenant mentioned earlier."

"Indeed, and thank you. I will take it from here."

The guard salutes and leaves the room.

Leesa suddenly felt rather timid in this place. It was one thing when she went up to the barracks in the city to speak with Captain Kholgard about the horse. But it was another thing entirely to be out in the wilds in the middle of a town that wasn't otherwise supposed to be here, owned by people who were not from this world, and fighting a war said to be so dangerous, the people of the city were never allowed to go outside.

She studied the people at the table, moving from Thaelyn to the General, then to what she interpreted to be a Night Elf, at least by the coloring of the skin, and a Daanen-Aryku by his towering shape. Finally, behind him, she sees a familiar face sitting at the table.

She cautiously steps forward into the room.

"And who do we have here?" Thaelyn asks jovially. "A young lady from the city, perchance?"

"I, um… Yeah. My name is Leesa Gobbard," she peeks around at Marelle. "I'm her cousin from up in the city. She told me to come here and see if I could help in any way."

"Indeed, Marelle did tell us about you. She says you tend to follow in her footsteps somewhat," he smiles gently. "Very well then, come forward and let us see what we can do together. I am Lord Thaelyn, by the way," he begins directing with gestures around the table. "And this here is General Gabarleine, Lieutenant Lapäli, and over here is Relissa Moonshimmer. These tend to be our most important officers relating to our current affairs."

"Wow, you're an actual Lord?" she mumbles nervously, and then fumbles, trying to recall her culturing on how to curtsey.

Thaelyn smiles at the girl's obvious youthful innocence before continuing.

"Truly a charming example… Now, you should know that before you can find any proper application for yourself, you will need to undergo some amount of education in the world affairs. If you are like most of the citizens of your city, you are likely to be just as underprivileged as the rest for the true nature of the concerns facing us."

"Right, Marelle told me a little bit, and I was following along when she was doing that investigation about these things in our shoulders. By the way, is there anything we can do to fix that?"

"Indeed, there is, and in fact Marelle has already seen to it in her example. We are also scheduling her brother, Haran, for his procedure. We have two choices, the Daanen-Aryku or our own. Either will suffice, but the item in question will need to come out."

"And how do you do that, or should I even ask?" she glances at her shoulder and lifts a hand to it.

"It is a surgical procedure, to be sure, but a small one, fortunately."

"Oh, that's good, I suppose. But, um, does it hurt? I guess it probably doesn't matter if I want the bleedin' thing out. But you know…"

"In either case, we have ways to anesthetize the body, so you do not feel anything. You should not worry about that."

"Good, that makes me feel a little better. But now, what can I actually do to help? I know I'm young, but I'm sure I'm old enough to do something."

"At this time, we have a few operatives in the city already. We will need to consider carefully where we can place you, but you must remember the first rule here is discretion. Whatever role you play, you must play it well. Our opponents cannot know who you are outside what we want them to know. Working as a spy is not an easy role. It requires a quick mind, a clever guise, and sometimes a bit of daring."

"All right, where do we start?"

"Marelle, I believe you have another apprentice to train."

"Right," she affirms. "Leesa, come with me and I'll show you around."

The two of them join and move outside where Marelle begins introducing the girl to a variety of people and their stories of the war.

Chapter 4

UNDERMINING ADVANCE

The morning review was brief today. The war on the orcish front was moving forward on schedule, and a forward team of scouts had reported something of interest coming into view for the next advance. A follow-up report was anticipated to arrive later in the day.

Thaelyn sat in his chair in the tactical office studying a report they received the previous afternoon from the scouts watching the dwarves. He seemed deep in contemplation, and the General was becoming curious as to his silence.

"My Lord, you seem lost in thought this morn. Would you care to share it?"

"My apologies, General, I am simply reminiscing over all the great achievements we have accomplished in our history together. And then, when I look at this, I find myself impressed by the result. Although this may seem like a small mention on the surface, it can be interpreted as a sign of our direction."

"Indeed, and what might that be?"

"This is the report we received yesterday from our investigation of the dwarves and that farm of theirs. In our modern day, our society understands the application of electricity and the use of mechanisms to perform some of our work, so I suppose it is a simple matter to interpret a doorway operated by a button switch, as opposed to a knob or a lever, especially if to consider our opponents are the Suuden-Aryku, who are themselves a very highly technical society."

"Of course…"

"But then, to properly understand and navigate their way through an airlock and into a chamber with an entirely alien environment to it, using filtration masks to allow them to breathe in that space… this requires inspiration. How would you know of such a thing as a chamber to transition between two distinct atmospheres if you come from a society that has never travelled to such places with alien environments?"

The General grins, and then laughs as he listens to the suggestion.

"Yes, my Lord, and I think we owe it largely to you and your inspired teachings."

"Oh, General, I think I cannot take credit for this example. I may allow myself some acclaim for my direction, but in truth, it is the people who did most of the work. I merely pointed a finger here and there."

"I would still argue that without your finger-pointing, and perhaps that of Adalon as well, we would not be where we are today. And so this direction you speak of…does this give you any new insight as to where we might find ourselves in the years to come?"

"It certainly does provide some curious perspectives. But then I am also considering this war and where it might ultimately lead us, and what we may learn along the way. This, in itself, may change many things."

"Yes, I might have to agree. If our intention is to carry ourselves to new worlds to find Sargeras, we may need to learn many new secrets, if only to provide for ourselves to meet up to this challenge."

Thaelyn sighs and nods silently as he sets the paper down on the table and brings his attention back to the matters at hand.

"All right," he begins. "Aerlie and I are working on a new set of operatives, four this time. We will again involve those same three priests from Marelle's investigation. They already speak the language, so we might as well take advantage of this."

"Naturally."

"The final one will need to be a mage, and therefore we need to conduct another meld to share the language in his case. But one new meld is not too much to ask, I think."

"Better than to do all of them," he smiles.

"He can serve to manage our transport needs using runes, maybe also as a sort of secretary, to assist in managing our affairs on this side."

"Very good."

"This procedure is likely to be delicate, but our spies up there have managed to discover a few things by casually engaging some of those who are close to the Governor in a bit of small talk. The messengers he uses say he has never been seen outside his manor."

"And therefore," the General muses. "He would not necessarily be checking on the operations of his lessers, at least not personally. But this is also strange, my Lord. If he never goes outside, where does he actually live…inside the manor proper? But then, I find it interesting that he lives alone with no family or other relations. And so, I must ask myself, does he not hold any sort of social life…a female companion at the very least?"

"The information we have thus far suggests no, which is a rather curious premise. One would think if he were to pass his reign down to a successor, either he needs to train someone, or else provide an heir. So, unless we are to suggest he is part of an organization where they secretly install a new operative to replace him, the transition is vague to say the least."

"And if he does not go outside at any moment, what is this organization and how do they interact?"

"This is true. And at the same time, if one were to suggest an organization providing a replacement from time to time, someone would take notice."

"Including taking notice of him leaving, whether he should retire from his position, or at least to be carried out on a stretcher if he should fall ill to something."

"This sounds rather devious," Thaelyn ponders. "Unless we are to say they use a back door, and under the cover of darkness."

"That does sound sinister."

"We should continue investigating this to see if we can follow a historical path, perhaps to say any witnesses or employees who may have seen something. It might lead us to a potential source. Anyway, these new operatives will serve to replace their existing priests in their temple. We will give those people a taste of a true religion, and put an end to this blasphemy of their so-called curse."

"This will not give us a complete solution until we can remove those implant devices."

"Correct, and we will attend to this once we establish our own operations and dismantle his."

"Will we be performing this operation ourselves inside that temple?"

"I suppose we could once we stabilize the occupation. We can proceed from there after we have a few of our own procedures in place. But we must also be sure to keep it quiet. Even though the Governor may not make any visits, we still have the Dean, and those two seem very closely associated."

"Yes, that Dean is representing himself to be something of a right hand to the Governor. He might be the one to maintain many of these other operations on his behalf."

"If this is the case, our people will need to create some very elaborate excuses to keep him placated."

The morning progressed to midday, and the meeting took on additional members to share in the review. Relissa, Marelle, and Lieutenant Lapäli had finished their classes for the day and were coming up to date on the reports.

"Your Lordship," Padriyl submits. "My Commander tells me he has received those two bottles from the elven trees, and they are currently under examination in the labs. Although he is a bit skeptical if they may find anything at all, he informs me that he'll let you know as soon as they learn something."

"Good, Lieutenant. Even though we already believe they were left there by agents relating to Sargeras, it would be nice to know if the contents are such as to narrow our focus to those whom we believe to be responsible for its manufacture."

"Your Lordship," Marelle offers. "I'm looking over this report about the dwarves and this farm of theirs. I don't know much about mushrooms and drugs of any kind, at least not outside what we might have with our herbalists in the city. But if these mushrooms are providing a drug effect, it would have to be very strong to put them into such a daze like what we saw that day."

"Indeed. I have conferred with Aerlie on this, as she tends to specialize in this field of study. This would represent an especially potent effect if to render them to such a state where you could make your attempt at interaction, and they did not even notice you in the room. It might even go so far as to create a hypnotic effect, and this suggests a highly psychoactive ingredient."

"Whatever that is…" she smiles sheepishly.

"It is a drug that can affect your mood and behavior, perhaps placing you into an altered state of mind. The trouble is, as far as any examples we might find commonly available in nature, this might not be as effective unless it is highly refined. Some plants might possess this, but in their natural condition, they may only provide a hallucinogenic effect, making you feel perhaps light-headed and dizzy."

"Not like this. So, how do we explain these mushrooms?"

"Yes, here we have a problem. We already have a concern for their alien origin, and then this fertilizer that was found, which might only serve to exacerbate the situation. We do not know this species of fungus, so the parameters are outside our understanding. I have ordered samples to be taken and studied by the Daanen-Aryku to see what we are working with, but I am also concerned about any other effects these mushrooms might inflict. Drugs of any kind often induce side effects, and this causes me some worry for their health up there. And some mushrooms can be toxic, as well as hold other detrimental effects."

"Great," she slouches to the table and shakes her head. "So, not only do we need to help them with the drug, but we may also need to help them if they're poisoned. And probably not just those here in this world."

"It's so bloody unbelievable," Relissa reflects. "They hit their world, finally take over, and bring a bunch of them here to mine adamantium for them…maybe also iron to make a good show for the rest, and fill up their heads with so much fluff, they don't know up from down."

"And we can't really do anything about it, at least not yet, until we clean house a little from all the rest."

"Speaking of cleaning house, Marelle," Thaelyn asserts. "I am considering placing your cousin as a new attendant in the Governor's Manor. We are going to see if we can replace one of his former messengers with our own."

"One of his former messengers?" she ushers cautiously. "Um, what happened, or is going to happen, to the former one?"

"Oh, that…yes," he grins. "He will be receiving a change of occupation."

"Oh dear…"

"Ah, but come now, Marelle," he relates heartily. "One should not spend their entire life dedicated to a single role. One needs a bit of diversity now and then."

"Right, and what new role will he be taking?" she raises her brow.

"One that will carry him to exotic locations and meet with exciting new people. From there, he will likely need some time to acclimate in order to find a temporary position for himself, at least until this unfortunate issue of war is resolved."

"Uh huh…"

"But, for as much as I dislike the idea of kidnapping someone, the issue of security carries its own demands, and we cannot have him interfering with our efforts to preserve lives on a larger scale."

"Right, I understand. I just wouldn't want to be the guy with a bag being thrown over his head in a dark alley."

"To be honest, I think we would not use the bag approach. More than likely, as it was in Kynesoth, he will have an unfortunate encounter with one of our priests."

"Jiggers!" Relissa snaps. "I think I'm staying away from your temples!" she chuckles.

✦✦◆✦✦

"Priest Cydulean, what are you saying here?" ushers the Flame Elf priestess. "How do we explain the loss of Sehnisavain if not as an attack by the invaders?"

"Priestess Ilothonna," replies the first visiting priest. "The invaders are to the north. We came from the south, as part of our last assignment. We were given instructions to investigate. Our Lord, as you know, paid very close attention to her, and his last known recollection placed her on the roadways leading west of the city. We were told to investigate, as he no longer heard the songs of her mind reaching up to him."

"I am surprised our Lord would speak to you before speaking to me. After all, I am her First Deacon."

"I feel he was protecting you from coming into the same as what came to her. We would certainly not wish to lose two of you. We, on the other hand, were much more convenient to make a more efficient survey."

"And what did you find?" she asks.

"So far, our findings are incomplete, but they lead to strong suggestions. It would seem the High Priestess and her two daughters were indeed the victims of foul play, but the scene did not appear as an attack by the invaders."

"How do you mean? If not the invaders, then who...or what?"

"We conducted a careful search of the woods, which led us on a trail where we eventually found a scene of a skirmish. While we did not find any bodies, we did notice artifacts that might have belonged to the High Priestess and her two daughters."

"But no bodies? This does actually sound like those invaders to me, based on the reports I heard once of their attacks on the orcs."

"Yes, but with one important difference. Those invaders are said to have been very clean and left no trace of their actions as a tactic to confuse the orcs. This scene was sloppy by compare."

"Sloppy! Then what was it, an attack by wild animals?"

"Wild animals..." he chuckles ironically. "Wild, perhaps... Animalistic, perhaps... But we think it was not animals. This actually bore more of an intelligent purpose. We found some other artifacts that suggested orcs."

"Orcs!" she shouts. "Why would they attack us? They're supposed to be allies, as unpleasant as that may sound for their manners."

"This is indeed a good question, and one that we also asked."

Ilothonna turns and hangs her head in remembrance.

"I grieve deeply for this," she mourns. "Tyshalis and Rhyvanith were quite young, and I weep for the loss of my sister. Do you think they're dead?"

"This gave the appearance of a raid of some sort, and traditionally, orcs are not known to take prisoners. But this one appeared different. We did not see any evidence of killings, such as bloodstains."

"No evidence..." she considers optimistically. "So, this might suggest they were taken as captive rather than killed outright. And if this is the case, we need to find them before those heathenish curs cause any serious harm!"

"And this certainly places the orcs at odds with us now," suggests the other visiting priest. "Especially in light of our investigation."

"But Priest Sumisal," she demands. "What were they doing out there in the first place? The High Priestess, the orcs... Those beasts were supposed to be partners with us and the Suuden-Aryku."

"Supposed to be, yes. We have a couple of thoughts on this. First, this may be a rogue band, so anything could be possible with that. The orcs seem to have a penchant for mischief. They may be getting bored out there with nothing else to do. They are not allowed to attack the human city, same as we, and they seem to have occupied a broad space. Those in the further regions may be looking for a little excitement. We are aware that those up north, at one time, would make occasional skirmishes on the Night Elf city, but those further away might not be in a convenient location for it. However, they may be in a convenient location for us."

"Intolerable!" she huffs. "So, in the absence of anything else to do, they might make skirmish attacks on us simply for the fun of it?"

"Possibly. I would agree with your feelings on the matter, but these are, after all, orcs. However, while this may be a potential for concern, we had another, even more serious one, arise. One to which we might actually expect by now, and so should you, if I may, despite your attitude that we are…supposed to be…allies."

"Supposed to be?"

"Indeed. If you would permit me these words, ours seems to be a rather arrogant attitude in this regard, as if to say we hold such an overriding position of authority, and with such impunity for our actions, that they should regard us as allies despite anything else. And yet, we are not coming to their aid in this time of need. Would allies do this?"

"Uh oh… Yes, I see it. They are disgruntled. And our attitude suggests they don't dare do this, when in fact they might feel entitled to it by now."

"We have these orders to essentially shed them off, due perhaps to their role in drawing so much unwanted attention."

"Meaning those invaders up there."

"Correct. It is known to us that they served whatever purpose they were intended to serve, and they no longer hold value. This is not a polite attitude for…allies…to hold for each other."

"I suppose you are right."

"Furthermore, the shedding off is being described as a form of punishment for attracting this attention. Now, if they should ever realize any part of this, they will likely desire a little retaliation for being discarded, do you think?"

"Then this would represent a revenge attack!" she surges.

"It might, but at the same time, we must also ask how this relates to the High Priestess. This is where we are asking some of these questions, and therefore, the reason for this investigation."

"What is this investigation actually about? Can you tell me?"

"The details are very tender," Cydulean offers. "We have a special long-range expedition out there right now, using some very carefully trained scouts performing a survey to gather what we hope to be informational detail that might otherwise have been unavailable to us by other means."

"That sounds serious. What is it relating to?"

"Before we go into that," Sumisal responds. "Let us first speak of the orcs. I think it is prudent to cover ourselves in the event they are planning anything on any of our other positions. This might have been a mere convenience attack if they happened to cross paths."

"Oh, but of course! They might have more out there and they're testing our defenses."

"Indeed. Our last information tells us these invaders have driven the orcs a considerable distance away from us by now. But this also brings its own concern. We could possibly say this is a coincidence that they crossed paths, but if this is a band of orcs, rogue or otherwise, they are making a determined effort to circle around the lines to find us."

"Yes! I would agree. This is entirely too coincidental for my taste. They cannot attack the city proper, and they are falling fast due to those invaders, so instead they found a soft target right at that most inconvenient moment, hoping for a little revenge. We surely cannot allow this to go unpunished!"

"Absolutely. Our outpost has not seen anything pass through our immediate area, and I do not recall any reports from anywhere else…at least not recently…"

"Not recently?"

"Well, there was an odd mention of a small scouting party gone missing."

"Yes, I recall something about this, and also from the south. So this might suggest a circle maneuver from down there, and likely trying to avoid the outposts directly, instead hitting the softer targets."

"This is reasonable. So this must be coming from another location, and probably very cleverly concealed. I might even say this is as much an act of desperation to hide it so determinedly."

"You may be right. So, what do we do about it?"

"A careful search would be a good place to start. We have several outposts in our surrounding area. Perhaps we could give our people a bit of exercise…they have nothing else to do but walk in circles," he chuckles softly. "Maybe we can uncover something, assuming it is still in the area."

"Still in the area…" she muses. "But what if they left the area, maybe taking Sehnisavain and the girls as hostages?"

"This could pose a problem, and it also offers a complication that could relate to our investigation."

"What?" she gasps. "How?"

"First, I think, regardless of this possibility, we should cover ourselves. It could be another matter altogether, and we would be remiss in our duties to jump to conclusions."

"Oh, but yes, of course…"

"For instance, if we sent a few long-range scouts to the south to investigate any movements, but be mindful to stay at a distance from the invaders and their front lines. They seem entirely too well-organized to take chances against. We should spy on the activities of the orcs from afar, maybe to see if they have any rogue teams attempting to evade or otherwise circle around us."

"And if we should see anything?"

"Naturally, we would wish to see about the transport of hostages, but surely our people can take down a few orcs. What do you think? And again, we do not wish to expose ourselves unnecessarily. Let us keep mostly to a stealth approach for now."

"Yes, of course," she affirms. "But it would seem like we might be taking our own front against the orcs…essentially to go out helping those invaders," she sighs. "I wonder what the High Commander would say about this. He has not given any new orders so far, although I will need to report this to him."

"May I recommend we delay that for now," Cydulean offers.

"Delay? Why should I delay reporting to the High Commander the loss of our most important member, and such a turn of events that we are now at war with the orcs?"

"Personally," Sumisal responds. "I have my doubts he would be at all surprised about the orcs and their reactions."

"Yes, you may be right."

"As for the High Commander," Cydulean continues. "This is where an important part of our investigation comes in, but again, the details are sensitive and very fragmented so far. Therefore, that special team we have out there in the field. And in fact, we are going to need to establish ourselves here for a time with an office, to which we can collect our reports and pursue additional inquiries."

"An office...um, well..." she glances around trying to visualize what's available.

"What about the one used by the High Priestess? As we said earlier, we are special assigns working on her behalf, even if our position is a very private one. And in her absence, that office would serve well as a temporary base until we can correct this situation."

"Well, it's not the normal procedure to offer it up like this, but alright. Follow me. I'll show you where it is."

Ilothonna now leads the two visiting priests to the office once used by Priestess Sehnisavain. Once inside, she briefly shows them around.

"Very good," Cydulean affirms. "Now, we must first organize ourselves by arranging meetings with our military commanders to scout the area, and also to see about the nearest orcish encampments."

"Agreed, and if we see anything moving around out there, surely we will wish to engage, especially if we can find any hostages."

"I would further desire to cover ourselves to the south. It is the only conceivable direction they could be coming from at this point."

"Absolutely, maybe to send out a few additional patrols to cover more area."

"Good. And perhaps, if we can find an opportune moment to make a few of our own hits, maybe we could try jabbing at them from the side. We can take a lesson or two from those invaders along the way."

Ilothonna gazed into his eyes with a small, contented smile.

"Really, are we now taking lessons from our enemies?"

"Why not?" he shrugs. "It served them so well, and so it will serve us now. But our strikes against the orcs must be silent and swift. I do not suggest we go so far as to destroy entire camps…we do not have as large a force as the invaders to allow this method. Ours will be smaller skirmish attacks to inflict confusion and disarray. We will launch quick volleys and pull back, and not give them time for reprisals. And we will repeat this from different vantages to keep them off-balance."

"Sounds like a clever plan."

"But now, as for the investigation… Keeping in mind, the details are not all in, but one primary question is why the High Priestess was out there to begin with. If she was out there for a reason, we must understand what that reason was. And then, could it be the orcs simply got in the way?"

"Uh oh…that coincidence you mentioned?"

"Perhaps…or perhaps not… As I said, we have a special team out there trying to locate our evidence. We were originally investigating these invaders, and certain inconsistencies of their actions."

"Can you explain these inconsistencies briefly?"

"I suppose this could be explained in two directions, ours and theirs. They seem focused on the orcs. If this is their only concern, I think they should have no other interest whatsoever toward anything else, including us…"

"Oops…" she mutters softly. "Um, we were told recently to send an assassin out there not long ago. Could that do something?"

"It could!" he asserts strongly. "And probably not a wise course. Not with that massive army they have out there. And what? We do not see them marching on us for the favor of it? This would surely complicate that notion of inconsistencies."

"Yes, it would."

"They are also described as unwanted in our world, and the orcs are accused of bringing them here to apparently interfere with something. Whatever it is they are interfering with, it does not seem to involve us, so why are we so concerned about it? And this also includes the Suuden-Aryku, who are also apparently not taking any direct action."

"Yes, this might stand out."

"But now, with the High Priestess involved, we must wonder if there is more to it, as if to say she received special instruction to serve a purpose uniquely demanding of some special qualification she possessed."

"Really! That's an interesting perspective. Why would you think she has any special qualification?"

"The only real suggestion I can offer at this time is due to her tenure, maybe also her age, and what knowledge she possesses from her lifetime experiences."

"Maybe..." she considers distantly.

"Here is where this attack might cause a complication. Was it really a revenge attack, or could it hold a deeper meaning? Especially when you consider the target in question...no less than the High Priestess. Her loss seems all too convenient in my mind."

"Convenient?" Ilothonna grimaces at the suggestion. "How do you mean convenient?"

"Again, we are a special taskforce secretly assigned under the High Priestess, and most recently, to investigate these invaders."

"Right, even though the High Commander gave us instructions that we are not to attack them."

"It is in part because we are told not to attack them," he intones emphatically. "Here is where we have these inconsistencies occurring around us, and they seem to be compounding now."

"Compounding!" she winces.

"And thus the reason we began asking questions. This is something that has been building up for quite some time. But it was not until recently when these elements began to hit a critical threshold that we sprang into action."

He turns and begins pacing around the room as he composes his thoughts.

"You must understand, this is to be held confidential until we can determine the meaning of it."

"Right, you have my attention."

"We should consider these details. I will allow you to draw your own conclusion to see if it matches mine. First, we are not permitted to attack the human city to the north, correct?"

"Yes."

"It has been this way since the beginning, and the reason given to us is to say there is someone inside who is managing it."

"I have heard this as well, from Sehnisavain, by the way."

"Yes, good. At the same time, we are told not to attack the Night Elf city up there, either."

"Yes, so it seems, and this has often puzzled me."

"Naturally, as they tell us we are supposed to be at war with them. But how do you fight a war if you are not actually fighting?"

"Yes! And this is what I hear quite often from our younger members, who are so impatient with their orders."

"Indeed, young ambition…" he nods. "Next, she was instructed at one time to prepare a group of special operatives to carry a device given to us by the Suuden-Aryku, and to follow along with a group of orcs as they were searching for the next step our Lord is pursuing for some sort of ancient portal. Are you aware of this?"

"Yes, and I actually helped her with that."

"All right, and presumably they were successful. However, somewhere along the way, those same orcs created trouble for the local societies of that world, and this is what brought these new invaders back to us."

"Right, and this is why the Suuden-Aryku are shedding off the orcs, because of this mention of punishing them for the error."

"However, this is where it gets interesting. Just like with the cities up north, we are not permitted to attack them."

"Yes, that massive army we would not otherwise wish to tangle with."

"This may be true, and I also heard it said they were studying them for any weaknesses. But it still does not set well in my mind. We are not attacking them, and neither are the Suuden-Aryku, who surely hold enough power to do something."

"Yes. So, is there a reason for this?"

"We believe there is, but here is where one of those inconsistencies falls into place. Let me ask you this question. Have you travelled up there in recent times, or heard of anyone else travelling up there?"

"Not I…" she shakes her head. "Other than for the assassin, um… We had a number of scouts peeking over the mountains a few times."

"And have you heard of what happened up there when those people arrived?"

"I've heard stories of black clouds, rumbling noises, and a lot of other nonsense, but we generally have instructions to keep away entirely, due to all those soldiers they have patrolling the area. The place is said to be swarming with them."

"Yes, I suppose it might be by now. So, I guess you have no idea what the place looks like at present, correct?"

"Huh?" she puzzles. "We are speaking of the Badlands, right? It's supposed to be a desert wasteland, although I do recall someone ranting about trees or some such," she laughs half-mindedly.

"Right," he smiles jestingly. "And that desert waste has been out there for perhaps a very long time, but no longer," his expression turns serious. "If you heard reports of trees, it means that desert wasteland is no more."

Ilothonna's sarcasm instantly faded, and her face went blank. She glared at him for the seemingly impossible suggestion.

"What do you mean by that?" she asks softly.

"The entire valley has been transformed into woodlands and meadows. This means, whatever forces they unleashed up there, their army is not the only thing to be afraid of. But here is where we are wondering about the rest of it. And if the High Priestess was getting involved, there must be a link we were previously unaware of."

"Really!" she emits enthusiastically.

"This might also account for one of those inconsistencies," Sumisal notes. "If they were so offended by your assassin, I think this city would be a burning waste by now."

"Oops!"

Cydulean continues, "Our taskforce has been operating very quietly for…well, let us simply say, for a long time. We've been watching and waiting for the evidence to appear to give us our leads to follow up on these inconsistencies we've been monitoring for so long, and like I said, it was not until these new invaders arrived when we found what we were hoping to be our opportunity. That team we have out there right now is conducting a search to identify and confirm one or more of these suspicions, and I hope to see them return safely to bring back what we so desire to make our conclusions."

He turns and begins pacing the other way as he continues his thoughts.

"Our initial suspicion comes from this long duration of war we are supposed to be fighting. When we first received word of their arrival, but then told not to attack while we had the chance, this alerted us to something very peculiar that required answers. So we managed to infiltrate a scout to spy on them from afar. This was largely before they settled into the region, and we knew to take advantage of this quickly."

"Good, and what did you see?"

"Initially, we saw a lot of soldiers laying claim to the ground they were standing on, which is to be expected. They were also hastily importing materials to build an outpost of some sort, which is also to be expected."

"Yes, this makes good sense."

"Not long after that, we happened to catch notice of arrivals in the area. Carriages, one of which we identified as belonging to the humans, and sometime later, others for the Night Elves and the Daanen-Aryku."

"Uh oh…but what does this mean? They're making contact with our enemies, which should make them more of an enemy, right?"

"You might think so, but recall those inconsistencies. We are not allowed to attack anyone up there. If Rolsklinde is being managed by someone, this suggests they are on the same side as us, especially if we have orders not to attack. But strangely, we still regard them, in one form or another, as enemies. This is a contradiction."

"Yes, it is," she affirms.

"Now, how do we apply this to the city of Solinaia? In contrast to Rolsklinde, where we have word of someone managing it, the order is again not to attack."

"Yes, and I suppose I should admit, I have wondered about this on a few occasions."

"There are a few whispers that suggest our Lord has plans for them," Sumisal offers. "Maybe not unlike what he had for our own people. But is this to say they are enemies up to the point when he takes this action? And why so long to wait for it?"

"Um...hmm..."

"But in the case of these invaders," Cydulean continues. "They are also said to be enemies, and also where we are told not to attack them, but we do go out with an assassination attempt, even though it was very unwise to do so. And yet..." he emphasizes with a finger. "By this time, it should be fairly obvious where it came from. Ilothonna, this would amount to a clear act of war. I find it unlikely they could not know of us by now. And yet, again, do we see them marching in our direction."

"No," she states firmly. "And this ought to invoke something, unless we say they're so weak..." her voice halts as she reconsiders.

"I would be very careful with that word 'weak', Priestess," Sumisal suggests. "If they hold the power to turn a desert waste into a forested wilderness, and are currently marching across the land, conquering it away from anything that once stood there, even if it is only orcs, I think the only thing that is 'weak' here is the word itself. We already know they use portals for many of their actions. We do not even teach this amongst our own."

"Yes, you are absolutely right. Forgive me, it is an old habit. And look at us, one lonely city out here in the face of that."

"Indeed!"

"Therefore," Cydulean continues. "We have this link we are previously unaware of. They are holding back, and rather strongly, especially if they know we sent an assassin out there. This brings us back to these visits by the others and what words were exchanged, then to ask what relationship they hold now, and how this reflects on us, assassin or otherwise. And finally, we need to return to the High Priestess. She was called away only after that assassin incident, correct?"

Ilothonna abruptly turns to meet his eyes.

"Yes, she was…" she muses tenderly.

"Something has happened, and it involves this link. Now, Ilothonna, ask yourself how those orcs fit into it. She was abducted so conveniently at the time she was following this strange link. Was it coincidence, or was it planned? And is someone trying to hide something from us?"

Ilothonna glared at him for the controversial statement. In her mind, it was forming a picture, but at the same time, she was also experiencing an internal conflict of motivations. Her conscious intuition was fighting the songs of Sargeras to obey, and it was starting to show in her face. Her breathing quickened, and her skin was flushing.

"Priest Cydulean, can you please give me a hint on what this link could be about? Do we know anything, even a starting point?"

"Some of this could be described as speculation, but if we are told not to attack, and this is not simply for the numbers involved, could it involve something else? They met with representatives of the other races. If they are reaching out to them, they clearly have an opinion of some sort driving them. Might they have had an opinion of us down here? Might they still have an opinion, and might Sehnisavain have suspected something, therefore, she felt a calling of some sort? Might this opinion be the reason they are holding back, even in the face of…oh, let us describe it briefly as our impudent action of sending an assassin up there."

"Impudent?" she blurts.

"Yes, because it was a foolish thing to do, numbers or otherwise."

"I, uh…" she cocks her head reflexively as her internal conflicts increase. "Yes, foolish, surely that. Impudent? Maybe so. It was unwise. They could probably crush us for the favor of it. And worse, we felt so, um…arrogantly empowered to do it."

"Absolutely, Ilothonna," Sumisal nods. "I think that statement is very appropriate, especially if you involve that habit of yours, and so many others, to describe everything else out there as weak."

"Oh, yes! One city, this is all we have. The humans may only have one, and the Night Elves as well, so we could maybe claim something for those, but these people…" she shakes her head. "They are simply frightening."

"We have that scout we sent out there once," Cydulean remarks. "She reported a very strange occurrence. I cannot be entirely sure how it plays out, but it certainly stood out in the report. They apparently planted a tree. Now, I realize this might not seem like much, but subsequent sightings, which are few by now, have seen people resembling elves clustered around it, as if it holds a unique purpose."

"Elves?!" she shouts. "They have elves over there?"

"Yes, how interesting that they seem to have elves among them. And by the way, there are also apparently humans in that lot. And this is from another world? How strange. We have orcs, but they are known to come from another world, and this might be native for them. We have the Suuden-Aryku, and also from a world where they might be native. But here we are in this world, us here, and then to find another world with more of the same?"

"Um, yes, I suppose I might have to agree. This is to say, another world, and another race of beings who would be…should be different from us, I suppose?"

"The pattern seems to lead in this direction, and I suppose it makes sense. This now becomes one of those questions, possibly a cause for those opinions of theirs…now that they are here. And then this tree, which seems to be a center of religious focus."

"They're worshipping a tree?" she winces.

"I might normally agree with you over the audacity of the idea, but the practice seems to stand out as if the thing holds some special value. And if this tree holds such potency, I wonder how it relates to what happened in the valley itself."

Ilothonna gasps and draws back from the statement. She muddles the suggestion privately.

"If this could be the source of their power..." she muses. "It would represent a tremendous level of authority over the forces of nature. Yes, maybe this could be something to get down on your knees and pray to. Another world, another race...or something else native to it, and in this case very powerful, enough to alter the land around it. Wow."

"It might. Now, a few of those questions. I am envisioning something specific here, so try to follow along."

"All right, go on."

"The orcs come from a world which seems to be exclusively populated by orcs. The Suuden-Aryku the same for their kind. But look at us here. This world seems to have not one, not even two, but three completely different races. And this is to suggest the Night Elves, though they are still called elves, are different from us."

"Um, wait. That reference...they are still called elves."

"Yes, we call ourselves elves. They also call themselves elves, though their features appear different than ours. What does this say? Is this to say they so coincidentally use the same race name as we do?"

"Uh..." she flusters. "Coincidentally?"

"And now we see what we call invaders arriving. Humans, who appear the same as our own examples up north. Coincidence? If we suggest each world should have something different, this is a remarkable coincidence. We also have yet another..." he waves a finger for emphasis, "...example of elves. They also appear different, but still elvish in appearance."

"Yet another? As if to say they could be another form?"

"It might appear that way. If we can have two examples of people who call themselves elves, could there be more? But this one arrived along with the humans from another world completely. And this now makes us wonder why? Do they hold a relation to us?"

"A relation!" she shouts. "And therefore that idea of an opinion, I suppose, and everything else that follows."

"This would now make good sense for them reaching out to the others," Sumisal admits. "Although it might also suggest they hold something similar for us here, if only we were friendly enough to do so."

"Oh! My dearest apologies that we are not..." her voice cuts out abruptly. "Um...yes," she emits more softly. "I think I see a picture developing."

"Yes, and in fact, with this suggestion in mind, one might even ask, if to look at it from the other side, they might be surprised to find US here, if theirs could be regarded in a similar fashion."

"Oh wow, that would be an interesting discovery. And so, naturally, they might be curious; therefore, to send out people to make contact...to whomever might be friendly enough to actually talk to them. Ugh. And we sent an assassin. Oh yes! This is surely a fine way to say hello."

"You are absolutely right, Ilothonna," Sumisal nods.

"This could therefore be part of the mystery," Cydulean infers. "And here is where the High Priestess comes in. Did she know of something? Did she feel something, and therefore this need to go outside the walls to investigate? And then, was she discovered and taken away by someone who did not want the rest of us to know."

"Whoa!" Ilothonna blasts. "How do you mean that?"

"I can only come back to that suggestion of someone interfering with something."

"Interfering...but who, in this case? Because if they're simply trying to reach out to familiar faces for some extraordinary discovery that might not otherwise be expected..."

"Yes, interfering. They are 'interfering' with something. But what about those orcs we apparently sent into their world on that mission? Could that not be called interfering with something?"

"And worse!" Sumisal adds. "Our impudence...our arrogance...

to think we hold a right to do it in the first place. That was their world, after all. What were we interfering with that brought them back here to investigate, then to make this extraordinary discovery of more like them living here. Surely, if any of us could hold any ancestral wisdom, like one such as Sehnisavain, they might find it interesting to learn. Unfortunately, many of us are too young to recall those days. And it would seem that part of our history is conveniently absent to remind us."

"Absent!" she growls.

"Yes. Where is that library we should probably have, with all our ancestral books and tomes, depicting the long history we no doubt have in this world. Surely, our history must extend longer than the few or several centuries we can actually recall from our verbal references, which seem to be the only references we have by now."

"I Swear!!" she screams.

Ilothonna grimaced for the implications. The conflict in her mind was growing, and her face was flinching.

"And so," Cydulean concludes. "They are said to be interfering with something. This is said by…someone…who didn't like them coming back after we…interfered…with their world. And this, if I dare say, is compounded by our impudence to think we have a right to do it at all, then to argue for the repercussions we are likely deserving of by now. They appear as both humans and elves, of one form or another, who are clearly allied together, as opposed to any of us here. And they hold an interest in reaching out to those of us who are willing to speak. But the reasoning for this might demand someone with such time-honored wisdom that it predates the apparent lack of our libraries to remind the rest of us."

"Oh yes, such convenience, Priest Cydulean!" she groans. "And now what?"

"I think this is all we can say for now," he admits. "At least until that expedition returns."

Midafternoon comes to Firstfall, and a message arrives from a much-anticipated scouting report. Sightings had been made recently of a rather substantial orcish camp with an oddly glowing feature at its center. A reconnaissance mission was dispatched under stealth to investigate.

"My Lord, here we are," the General announces. "Just as we were hoping."

"What is it, General?"

"That camp our people are observing, less than a day's march from our front lines. According to our calculations, this would be several hundred miles distant from our location, but so far, the first to be discovered. It has an exit portal, and our people say they observed a number of orcish reinforcements entering into view from it."

Thaelyn takes the paper and studies it briefly.

"One!" he declares. "And how many more after this, I wonder. We still have a long way to go before we meet the southern reach."

"So we actually found one," Marelle muses distantly.

"All right, my Lord," Relissa ponders. "Now that we found it, what do we do about it?"

"First," he responds. "I would like to take a close look at it. Do we have a rune?"

"Yes, here," the General adds. "It came bundled with the report."

Thaelyn takes the rune and studies it briefly as he considers his next move.

"I will make a brief visit to this location to examine the terrain and the details of the camp. This report suggests the camp is of a larger size than the others we have seen, not that it surprises me. We will decide how best to go about this on my return."

"My Lord!" Relissa snaps. "You're going alone?"

"Relissa... Surely, by now, you should know me well enough to understand that a group of orcs are of no great concern to me. Besides, this rune will take me to a reasonably safe location outside the camp, where I can find a suitable vantage point for my observations. I should not be there long enough for anyone to take notice."

"Well then, Your Lordship," Marelle proposes. "If that's the case, certainly you wouldn't mind a couple of tag-alongs to join you. I, for one, am very curious to see what this looks like first-hand. I promise I'll be good…" she smirks.

"Me too…" Relissa asserts. "In all my years of scouting, I've never seen a portal like this before. I'd really like to know how they're getting into our world."

"All right, I suppose there is no harm in this. Very well then, come along with me."

He takes down a bag that was hanging on a wall and places some scopes into it that were sitting on a table nearby. He then hangs it over his shoulder and leads the other two outside, where he casts an enchantment on the rune to engage the portal energies. One by one, they each leave the camp.

They arrived on a gently rolling prairie. Tall grasses dominate a landscape of broad fields and small knolls. A short distance to the north appears to be piles of rubble arranged in what might have once been the outlay of a village or small town. To the west could be seen plumes of smoke, the clear signs of current habitation, rising over a gradual slope that terminated in a pit on its southern end.

"That would be our mark, over there," Thaelyn points to the smoke. "Keep your heads low. There may be patrols out here that our scouts may have missed."

They begin moving in the direction of the smoke plumes, cautiously climbing the leeward side of the knoll. As they reach the top, a wide sprawl of orcish tents and huts comes into view on the other side.

"Stop here. We will use the scopes and observe from this point."

He takes the bag off his shoulder and opens it, pulling out scopes for each of them. Through the scopes, they observe the large settlement. It was not as large as the one once seen in the Badlands, but still of substantial enough size to require some tactical consideration. Among the structures, they can see the forms of many thousands of orcs milling about.

"That's a big camp, Your Lordship," Marelle admits. "That could qualify for a small city, in my books."

"Not as big as the bugger he took out in the Badlands, though, Marelle," Relissa jests. "What do you think, my Lord? I'm guessing a couple of ten great on this one."

"Your guesses are doing well, Relissa. I would agree, perhaps around twenty thousand or so. But the worst of it is that portal. Do you see it? There between those large structures."

Between two large buildings was a glowing aperture hovering within a circle of stones. Through the scope, one could just make out a faint image of an unknown land depicted within the circular shape.

"Fascinating," Marelle mutters. "If I understand this correctly, that image we're looking at is from the other side?"

"Correct. That would be the origin of this group. And if these orcs originate from Ruuki uy'Daan, this is what it looks like, or at least some small part of it."

"Is there any way of closing that thing?"

"Yes, but not from this side, unfortunately. You need to be at the source in order to shut down a portal. And herein lies our greatest problem. We currently have no way to go to Ruuki uy'Daan to close these features and prevent more incursions of orcs from passing through."

"So, what do we do about this? If we can't close it, they'll just keep coming through. We'll never get rid of them!"

"Patience, Marelle. For the moment, we must take this space and hold it. I have been anticipating this discovery for some time now. We will establish a permanent camp here with high security. Any new orcs passing through the portal will be cut down the instant they arrive. It will be a most unpleasant welcome, but it will keep them from rebuilding a force in this area."

"And how long do you think you can keep that up? It'll be a non-stop battle almost every day for…well, forever, unless you have some new trick up your sleeve."

"Oh, I always try to keep a few tricks up my sleeve, and right now I am thinking of one that stands nearly eight feet tall, has blue skin, horns and a tail, but she is far from ready for a mission like this."

"Jiggers!" Relissa moans. "Are you talking about Kaliya?"

"She has already been to Ruuki uy'Daan, and she was able to carry a physical object from there back to us. However, this was at least as much of a fluke as it was a predetermined intent. By her descriptions, she barely understood what she was doing at that moment."

"And how does this help us?" Marelle wonders.

"For this, we need to conduct a few experiments to see how far she can go with it. At the very least, if she can travel there at all, she could perhaps carry something with her to enable others to follow. But she needs proper training to develop this skill, and for this, I will need to consult with a friend of mine up in Sigil. She works there, and she should hold more experience in this skill than what I have."

"Must be nice to have friends like those."

"Indeed, it is," he smiles. "But this may have to wait until some of her other priorities come to completion. She has enough work ahead of her as it is."

"Aye, the poor girl," Relissa agrees.

Thaelyn surveys the surrounding terrain around the settlement. The open space was a blend of grassy fields and a few low-rising knolls. Somewhere off to the north of their position was the front line of his army pushing into the region. There were no significant features to offer shelter or obstruction to the settlement, so the advance ought to proceed smoothly.

"Very well," he states. "I believe we have enough here. We should return and make our plans. I wish to take this as soon as possible."

Thaelyn backs away down the knoll, with Relissa and Marelle at his side. When the settlement is out of view, they rise up and begin walking away. Then Thaelyn halts unexpectedly.

Relissa is first to notice this, with her quick elven senses picking up on his increasingly familiar habits. She stops suddenly with her head twitching over to watch him. She instinctively drops her posture into the grass for concealment.

Marelle, being slightly less accustomed to Thaelyn's signals, and not as quick with her reflexes, notices Relissa's reaction and impulsively drops to the ground in a squatted kneel.

"Buggers!" Relissa whispers gently.

"Yeah, and again I don't have a weapon with me," Marelle grieves likewise.

"Both of you stay here," Thaelyn orders in a hushed voice. "I will take care of this."

He begins sprinting down the knoll and then turns to the south. Relissa and Marelle both watch closely as a group of six orcs come into view from the area of the pit at the far end of the knoll.

"Dammit!" Marelle mumbles. "He's taking six of them?"

"Easy does it, girl," Relissa reassures. "He knows what he's doing, I hope."

Thaelyn reaches the flat expanse at the bottom of the knoll. He stops and raises his right hand high in the air. A bright flash of light issues out from it. The clearly visible display quickly drew the patrol's attention to what appeared to be a lone man standing in the field. They instantly charge to attack.

Thaelyn briskly jabs a hand at them, sending a swarm of a half-dozen small fiery projectiles shooting out at one of the orcs and puncturing him in multiple areas. He yowls in pain and falls to the ground. Thaelyn then flings the other hand out, and another set flies off to strike a second orc, also bringing it down. The remaining orcs continue to rush towards him.

Thaelyn now extends his right arm at full length to his side, with his hand open and ready. An instant later, his greatsword jumps out of its sheath on his back, spins in the air, and snaps into his hand.

"Gods be blessed," Marelle whispers. "I wish my sword would do that."

The orcs are nearly on top of him when he swings his left hand in an arcing motion, sending one of them hurtling into the air, backflipping several times and falling to the ground some distance away to the side, stunned and disoriented. He follows this by lurching forward at the center of the remaining three orcs, ramming it with his left shoulder and knocking it fiercely to the ground. He twists and brings his sword downward in a powerful backhanded slice, cutting neatly through the next orc at midsection. Both pieces fall to the ground immobile.

Marelle's eyes were bulging at the rapid execution of his moves. Relissa kept low as she watched, being no less impressed by the efficiency of the assault.

The final orc in the group turns in an attempt to make his first strike, but Thaelyn counters with an upward side kick to the chest, knocking it over backwards. He quickly inverts his sword and jabs it straight down into the chest of the orc under his feet.

In this time, the orc he sent flying off to the side was just starting to pull himself to his feet again.

Thaelyn makes a quick twirl of his sword to remove any residue and stows it back into its sheath. As he returns his sword, he steps over to the nearby orc, who is still struggling to return upright after the kick. Thaelyn grabs it by the neck and lifts it with one arm, then swings it over his head and slams it hard into the ground. He then brings a powerful fist jab into the creature's chest, shattering bone and exploding its heart. Blood spews from its mouth as it spends its last breath.

Marelle continued to watch the fight, feeling awestruck at the ease and expediency in the sequence of kills.

"Relissa," she muses. "I've never been in battle myself. And those stories we kept hearing about orcs always said these things don't die as easily...at least not by our hands."

"Aye, maybe... But then, how many of those stories can you actually trust?"

"Right."

"Also, that bugger of a sword he's carrying isn't your usual steel, and he's not your usual guardsman, either. How many of you can use magic?"

"I think even Haran isn't that good, and he's the one who was supposed to be studying it," she chuckles ironically.

Thaelyn casually steps over the body of his most recent kill, seemingly ignoring the imminent danger as the last orc, the one tossed aside telekinetically, begins rushing forward again. The orc lifts his club high as he approaches from Thaelyn's blind side, making ready to bring it down hard against him. As he comes within reach,

Thaelyn quickly evades by ducking to one side and delivering a harsh kidney jab. The orc recoils from the blow and stumbles.

"Ouch!" Marelle whispers and winces sympathetically.

Thaelyn makes a reverse spin to deliver a hard elbow slam into the orc's brow, knocking it back a step. He follows with another spin and a sidekick to the head.

"How in all the hells is he making those moves?" Marelle exclaims. "He's wearing plate, or at least partial plate. Even in chain, I don't have that kind of mobility."

"Aye, that's a good one. But then, that's not your usual armor, either. He's also able to weave complex magic in that, and Haran once said you can't do that in anything more than a cloth robe. As for those moves, have you ever seen fighting like that before?"

"Never. Sword and shield, that's all they teach us. This kicking and jabbing…I don't even know what that is. When wearing our armor, we just can't move like that."

The orc is staggered from the martial assault. It drops to its knees as Thaelyn steps in. He wraps his hands around its head and twists harshly, breaking its neck. The creature slumps to the ground.

Thaelyn strolls away from the carnage to reunite with the others. He pulls out a small kerchief from a slot in his belt to wipe his hands.

"We should go now," he proclaims calmly. "I will issue directives to prepare an attack immediately."

Relissa and Marelle jog down the slope to meet him. They look around at the scene one last time. Their faces are a portrait of shock and awe.

"And you teach this in your academy?" Marelle murmurs softly.

"The telekinesis is one thing I cannot teach. You are either born with it, or it is blessed upon you by the Gods. But the rest I can teach."

He returns the kerchief and pulls out a return rune to begin casting the enchantment on it. A moment later, they are back in Firstfall.

The group proceeds back inside the tactical office. General Gabarleine looks up at the arrivals and sees blood stains and the disheveled appearance of Thaelyn's attire.

"Did my Lord see a bit of excitement out there?" he asks jestingly.

"Just barely enough to get the heart pumping, General," Thaelyn replies with a smile.

The General lets out a soft chuckle before continuing.

"And what is your opinion of the tactics we might use in this case, my Lord?"

"I want you to instruct a group of mages to head out there immediately and mark way-lines out of sight on the flanking sides of the settlement. You will then prepare three additional brigades for transport into those locations. The attack will begin with the advance of the division from the north, and as they draw the bulk of the settlement's attention, the other three will move in from the sides and rear, crushing them."

"Very good, my Lord, I'll get to work on this right away."

"In the meantime, General, I think I will take my leave for a while to tidy up."

"As you wish, my Lord..."

"High Priestess," the younger cleric grumbles. "I still cannot understand what happened here. You vanish from the city, disappear into the woods, and then reappear here with these invaders. And you actually thank them for it?"

"Kerali..." Sehnisavain urges. "You only just recently awoke from your episode, so you still need time to understand they are not the enemy...he is! The one who stole us away from our true gods to begin with. The trouble is you are too young even to know the truth of it. And this is made worse as we were commanded by that heathen to destroy all our history. I was there when our sacred Tree of Life was killed. I thought it was the Night Elves, but it was not. Theirs was also killed, and they had evidence in their hands that suggested we were responsible, when we were not."

"So, you are saying someone else killed these trees, and then stole these holy symbols from our temple, just so we could be taken by Sargeras to be used as what, his servants?"

"Yes. This is what he does. If you will not follow him willingly, he takes you by force. And we would never follow such a beast like that willingly! And to make matters worse, we have also been blamed for another act we are not responsible for, and that is a plague afflicting the humans of Rolsklinde. He is making us the fools on top of defiling us with his blasphemy."

"And what of these people? We were told they were invaders..."

"Yes, so we were told. And I suppose, in a manner of speaking, they are. But they are also our brethren from the original world we all came from. We are not native to Therinë. Our ancestors once migrated there from Tae'Eladar, and our ancestral kin are still here, all of us, both elves and humans. We simply became lost after our long journey. But I doubt any of that really matters to him, not if they do not also serve his wants. These people are called invaders who are interfering with something...no doubt interfering with his hidden interests."

"And so, what is he actually hoping to do here? We sent that assassin once, right?"

"Yes, hoping to take away their leader. Most likely, he is hoping to corrupt and pervert yet another world with his villainy. The way it sounds to me, that creature giving us our orders would prefer to toy with them, as he seems to be doing with everything else."

"Uh huh, that figures."

"But rather than destroy us for the favor of that assassin, these people want to redeem us for our betrayal of our old gods."

"Well, that certainly sounds righteous of them. No disrespect, but if we're so responsible for everything we did back home, I would think everyone would want to destroy us for the favor of that!"

"Maybe, if it were not for us being dominated by that beast."

Sehnisavain found her hands full trying to reacquaint her newest charge with the missing knowledge of their ancestral origins. The younger priestess was still suffering from her disorientation after waking up in Firstfall with the druids. She is the one who had been abducted from the basement of the temple in Kynesoth, thanks to the two agents who were sent to find the bottle for Sehnisavain. Like most of the Flame Elves in the modern day, she had been born into this predicament, and as such, she was not privileged to know of the High Elves' culture or history.

On this occasion, Sehnisavain had brought her to the temple in Bya'an Tamoranth to show her the icons of the elven pantheon, collectively known as the Seldarine.

"See here," she points to the array of icons. "These are the gods our ancestors once worshipped. They are specific to our people since our earliest days. We once had some of this back home, at least until he came along and forced us to defile everything."

"Is this where all those empty alcoves come from in the temple?"

"Yes. And now it falls to us to take back what was taken from us. Our history, our culture, everything we once cherished. That monster who ruined our lives is not even supposed to exist! These gods you see around us," she waves her hands around the dais at the full assembly of deific icons and statues. "They are known as the Estelar, a society of gods that destroyed the others because they were found to be committing atrocities on lesser lifeforms...and it seems Sargeras is still doing it."

"But if they destroyed the others, why is Sargeras still alive?"

"Likely because he managed to escape capture, which means not only is he a criminal, but a fugitive from the law."

"Law? These gods here are some sort of law enforcement?"

"The gods are essentially a society of people, much like us in many ways, but much older, such that people like us might see them as gods, in a literal sense of the word. The way I understand it, they rule all of Creation in the modern day. And yes, they do have a form of law, or at least a policy of conduct, not unlike any other who holds certain values and principles. Just because they're gods doesn't give them free license to do whatever they please."

"Wow, now there's a concept."

"It is a common error on the part of people like us to think the gods should be immune to the repercussions of their actions, no matter what those actions might be. His kind had their chance, but failed to demonstrate their responsibility and respect for other forms of life. The Estelar simply did what they felt was necessary to bring justice for those who were made victim."

"All right. But if they're some kind of law enforcement, why don't they do something about him and what he's doing to us?"

"I'm sure they will once they find him. But he's been hiding during this time, and very cleverly evading them."

"But if he's hiding…" she muddles the meaning. "How could he come here and bother us? Where is he actually hiding?"

"We think he is taking up residence on the home world where the Suuden-Aryku live. The story from the Daanen-Aryku tells us he arrived there once, long ago, and fooled them into thinking he would offer great wisdom and power in exchange for their service. Now we see they are also transformed into his slaves."

"Slaves…" she mumbles silently. "And they command us in his name? Making us more of his slaves… And what about the orcs?"

"More than likely, as these people tell us, since they seem to know a few things about orcs from their history, they probably worship him as a god and choose to follow voluntarily."

"That sounds almost as bad, maybe even worse. If they chose this voluntarily, they will not so easily break away from it."

"Correct. Now, understand, Kerali, these people have not attacked us directly because they feel they can help us. For all of their numbers, I doubt our walls would hold them back, and our people number too few to resist for long. And yet, they have not made any movements against us out of their respect for us as High Elves…what we are born to be, not as the Flame Elves he made us into."

"And am I supposed to be thankful for this? Remember, High Priestess, I was tricked into assisting them in the basement, and the next thing I know, I wake up here with all these strange people around me."

"Yes, well," she chuckles softly. "You may need to forgive them for that. First, they needed to get inside there to find a bottle for me, and second, they wanted to bring additional people out to convert and use as agents to help the rest. It's either that, or simply raid the entire city and capture everyone at once, but this would likely stand out if anyone is watching."

"I see. And no doubt, if they all behave as I am right now, they'll have their hands full trying to convince us of who we truly are. Ugh."

"Right. That bottle is necessary to test a theory. I once found it by our old tree, and took it as evidence that the Night Elves were responsible for killing it. But they also have a similar bottle of High Elf design, and this was found with their tree. This means a third party was responsible, not either of us."

"Maybe I don't fully understand the reason here. If we know someone did this…"

"Knowing it by theory, and having evidence to demonstrate to the people, are two different things."

"Ah, so they're trying to get something to show us…right, something to show a bunch of people who might not want to listen to begin with," she chuckles ironically.

"Kerali, the hardest part in all this is to make our people understand who we really are. It was all we ever had to worship the trees and our holy symbols. We come from a world where these items were our entire existence. Then he steals them away and tries to convince us that we do not need them, instead to follow his songs, and if that does not work, to threaten us with his punishment. Is that the sort of god you really want to worship?"

The younger priestess gazes wistfully at the elder one, and then peruses the arrangement of icons lined up in their alcoves. She sighs deeply.

"So, which of these am I supposed to start with, if this is what I'm actually supposed to be worshipping?"

"We will begin with the Protector. He is the leader of the Seldarine."

Chapter 5

REPATRIATION

"Tristeen, what is actually going on here? This is starting to sound crazy."

"Sara, there's nothing crazier around here than what's been going on in this city for the past four hundred years. It's only now that we're starting to learn of it."

"And why only now? Four hundred years is a long time for no one to notice this."

"Yes, you're right, and it's shameful in a way. But, when you consider the people who have been keeping it from us in the first place, it starts to make sense."

"You mean the Dean and the Governor? But you're saying this has been going on for four hundred years. They can't be that old."

"Sara, you're missing the point. They're only the most recent in what's probably a long line of them."

Tristeen was in conversation with a group of students in the main hall of the academy, trying to keep their voices down, but nevertheless having a heated discussion. She had been slowly trying to inform the student body in batches, so as not to draw attention from any of the instructors or the Dean of her activities.

"Wait a moment, both of you," another student interjects. "If we're saying there's a long line of them, where are they coming from?"

"Jon," Tristeen responds. "It started four centuries ago when a man of unknown origin came to the city and demanded to be made governor, or else he would let our people fall victim to some mysterious new illness that was hitting us at random."

"But it was said this was a curse of the Flame Elves, right?"

"It's always been described that way, but it's no curse, and it's not the Flame Elves doing it. The Flame Elves were the first victims in this world. That monster, Sargeras, apparently found us much earlier than we ever knew about. They were attacked by a covert plot to break them of their religious beliefs and weaken them so Sargeras could take them as his servants. The Night Elves were also hit, but managed to hold on."

"Then what was the war between the elves?" Sara asks.

"A lie to make us think they started it."

"A lie! By whom?"

"Probably that same man, or whoever he's associated with, that came and demanded the Governor's chair, then made up these stories about the plague and who knows what else. It's all part of a plot to break up our alliance and isolate us so we could each be subjugated under their authority in one form or another. It's a sinister game, and we're made the fools for it by people who came in behind our backs with superior knowledge and superior capacity to play these games on little people who don't know any better."

"Oh grand. Then what is it that's actually killing us? Because I know there are people dying…you can't lie about something like that when your grandmum is lying on the bed staring up at the ceiling with glassy eyes."

"Put your fingers up here on your right shoulder," she demonstrates with hers. "Gently press down in this area… Do you feel something hard underneath there?"

The others in the group follow her example and feel around for the small implant under the skin.

"That's what causes the illness. It's not a curse, it's a device placed just under the skin as a surgical procedure."

"A surgical procedure!" Sara yips quietly. "How did that happen? I don't remember anything like that."

"My friends have been making an investigation and found out it's a device that contains a substance that causes the plague illness. It's apparently on a clock timer to open up and let it loose in our bodies when we hit fifty-something. The Flame Elves don't have anything like this. They're no more advanced in their science than we are, probably. This is high science, the type of thing you might find in a society that can travel outside our world. And if it started four hundred years ago, it wasn't the Daanen-Aryku. So, who else is out there making trouble for us?"

"But if you're suggesting the Suuden-Aryku in all this, how do we get it? I still don't recall anything."

"That man who came to us four hundred years ago demanded control of the academy and the temple as part of this solution, as he called it, to control the plague. After that, it was only controlled to the point of keeping it to our elder members, but never fully resolved. Now think for a moment… What is it the priests of the temple are supposed to be doing that they say protects us from this awful plague?"

The others in the group pause to consider the suggestion until finally they come to the realization.

"Bloody hell, Tris," Jon relents. "You're talking about the Festival, aren't you?"

"There you go, Jon. That thing they put around the neck that hurts on the right shoulder, but we're all supposed to hold very still for it. And they keep it there for a while, as part of this so-called test they talk about. It's likely a device of some kind that puts this thing in there to begin with."

She pauses to gauge their expressions, then briefly glances around the room to see if anyone else was paying attention.

"Now," she continues. "If you consider that man who came to us in the beginning, who demanded the academy, the temple, and the Governor's chair, and then starts poisoning us with this plague, just to keep up the image. Then we have people like the Dean that force us to lick his shoes every day, not to ask questions or try to learn anything about the world outside these walls, when I happen to know for a fact there's a lot to be learned, and most of it doesn't correlate with what's in these books over here," she thumbs at the rows of shelving behind her. "Then to consider how the Governor has no apparent interest in fighting this war, despite the fact that our people are dying of something called a curse by our enemies. How does this add up to you so far?"

"Badly, to be sure."

"We have the priests that make the people believe if we pray hard enough to our gods, we'll be saved. Well, has anyone ever been saved? Is the curse dead after four hundred years of praying for protection? It's a sorry sight to see the people out there not able to put it together when it should be so obvious. And further evidence of our inability to actually put it together…little people, and at this point with a very poor education, no thanks to the Dean and his students playing our teachers."

"Aye," Sara admits mournfully. "She's got us on that one."

"I'll give you two excuses for it. Listen to these words. For as long as I can remember…blah blah. And then, in reference to our city authority, if you can't trust them…blah blah on that side."

"Who can you trust…" she relents. "Great gods, Tris, I get it. They feed this to us almost every day until we're ready to burst from it."

"And finally, what are those instructors doing downstairs right now? They said it's for the higher classmen for a future lesson, but too dangerous to be demonstrated. How do you define something that's too dangerous to use, and yet safe enough to teach someone in an academy that barely teaches you how to mix two beakers of reagents without spilling them?"

Her listeners were riveted by now, glancing around at each other for their reactions.

"And this is where we stand right now," Tristeen wraps up. "The Dean is a crook. The Governor is a bigger crook. Both are apparently in league with those enemies we're supposed to be fighting out there but aren't. And we are simple stooges expected to follow orders without question. Well, I'm not doing it anymore, and neither should you."

She finishes by leaning back in her chair and folding her arms.

The others in the group again glance at each other, and then to the other tables of students who were engaged in their studies.

"All right, Tris," Sara offers. "So, what are we supposed to do about this? If the Dean hears even one word of it, ye gods, he'll blow the lid right off that noggin of his for sure! And that's got nothing to say about what he'll do to the rest of us!"

"Aye, and then the Governor," Jon adds. "If he's friendly to those bloody Suuden-Aryku out there, and if HE gets one word of this, blowing the lid off will be the least of our worries."

"I'm expecting that business downstairs to result in something nasty," Tristeen suggests. "I can't see how or why the Dean would have them do anything just for the fun of it. Not with this much effort. They're up to something. So, we need to spread the word to the rest of the student body not to trust anything he says or does from this point. If he tells us to 'stand here'..." she points figuratively at the floor. "That's trouble. If he tells us to 'drink this'..." she again gestures figuratively with a hand holding a vial. "That's also trouble. And if he tells us to shut up and do as we're told, we need to band together and say, 'No sir, not this time'..."

"Um, Tris..." Jon hesitates. "Not that I want to argue with you on that, but what do you think his reaction might be to it?"

"Not a good one," Sara considers guardedly. "You can be sure of that!"

"Look," Tristeen submits. "I figure it's better to make our stand and walk away, rather than become some unfortunate victim of his games. Even without these games, he would still demand us to lick his shoes and never do anything to improve the situation in this city. Which do you prefer?"

"Well, she's got a point on that one," Jon admits. "That much is certain, if you consider the plague, at the very least."

"Aye, I suppose it is," Sara affirms. "This plague is still killing people, and if it's not actually a curse, we need to be doing something about it, and we aren't."

"Even if it was a curse, we should still do something about it. The Guard doesn't go out there, so who's up for putting a stop to it, I say!"

"All right," Tristeen concludes. "So we're in agreement. Keep your eyes open, and let me know if you hear anything."

A time of celebration was coming to the people of Solinaia. The Night Elves had been planning this for many days since Amariyn delivered the official news to Thaelyn that they desired to reunite with the people of Tae'Eladar. Preparations have been underway, with people laying out decorations and setting up tables and chairs in plazas and parks in anticipation of the ceremony to swear in the city as a new prefecture to the kingdom.

The morning ritual in the tactical office in Firstfall was put off for this occasion, having been rescheduled for later in the day. The language classes for Relissa and her friends had also been rescheduled to make room for this event. Other plans were being organized to allow leave time for some of the troops to participate in the festivities on a rotating basis, as well as arrangements being made for citizens of Tae'Eladar who might wish to attend.

Thaelyn, Aerlie, and a delegation of other officials from Bya'an Tamoranth gathered in Firstfall, making ready to transport to the vicinity of Solinaia. The other officials included several members of the Tae'Eladaran High Council who would oversee the political assimilation of the city and its people, and representatives of the merchant and craftsman guilds, who would begin work on converting the city's economic structure and industrial services, bringing the city up to Tae'Eladaran standards.

Relissa and her friends, along with Sehnisavain and her two daughters, had joined the group by now, although the elder priestess was nervous about going to Solinaia after the tragic history her people shared. Still, she owed it to her longtime friend, Amariyn, and Aerlie assisted by donating a set of formal dresses to the elven guests.

"If we are all assembled," Thaelyn announces. "Then we should be on our way. The people are waiting."

A mage opens a portal aperture, and the entourage passes through. They arrive outside the city and make their way to the hidden entrance, as they did once before.

"My Lord," Relissa mentions. "You should be making up some new runes for this, ay? I mean, we don't need to be having you pop up out here from now on."

"Indeed, we will have some of our mages make a visit to attend to this inside the city, at least as an interim until we can build a proper gateway."

They pass through the gate and into the city, coursing their way along the pathways and lanes leading through the lower portion towards the Council district. Along the way, the local citizens begin to follow them, gathering up into a large procession marching through the city. As they arrive in the square outside the Council building, they are greeted by Councilmembers Amariyn and Throdeth, among others.

"Greetings, Your Grace!" Amariyn praises. "We are all so thrilled at your visit."

"As am I, Lady Amariyn. It is a joyous occasion for all of us. Here with me are members of my Council, as well as guild masters, to see you off to a good start in your new lives, once the details of the swearing in are complete."

"Excellent," Throdeth exclaims. "We've made arrangements for the people to gather outside here in the square. Although with so many citizens in our fair city, they are very likely to fill up every available space in sight of you. We believe it would be most convenient for them to see you if you were to stand up here on the Council building steps."

"This would seem fair enough, Councilman. Then we should begin arranging ourselves and allow the people to find their places."

The delegation moves off to the side to make room on the steps for Thaelyn to make his presentation. The people gather in the square, coming in from all sides. The platforms and walkways on the upper levels fill with even more spectators.

Thaelyn takes up his position on the front step of the Elven Council building. He turns to face the large gathering in the square. Every corner was packed with bodies. The people were pulled in so tightly, there was barely room to breathe. The crowd continued stretching along the lanes leading away from the square and out of sight.

He waits a few moments longer for the people to settle into their places and come to order, then begins speaking boldly in a prominent voice.

"We have gathered here on this day for a most joyous occasion, where the people of Solinaia, who have been detached from their Brothers and Sisters for nigh as long as any would dare to remember, now find themselves returned to their ancestral kin and the links they did once find broken."

He pauses to observe their faces before continuing.

"Though lost for a good measure of time, you did persevere in the face of many trials, some of which did test your resolve and those of your fellows near to the point of no return. From this, you now find yourselves reborn, with fresh opportunities and new frontiers to cross, with new challenges and new discoveries to test yourselves against, and from this you will gain new strength. And at your side, we will stand, as you will stand beside us."

A rousing praise gushes up from the assembly as he closes his statement. Thaelyn pans his gaze around the plaza, as the crowds cheer and wave their hands in the air. Finally, he brings them back into order.

"It is an honor, a privilege, and a pleasure when we can invite new citizens amongst us. A pleasure that I must admit we have not seen for some measure of time, as our world has already found itself complete. But here we stand on a new world, a place I must similarly admit I did not expect to find myself for a fair amount of time until our people might be ready to travel thusly in the due course of our own discoveries. But this war we find ourselves drawn into has brought with it a number of abbreviated admissions."

He glances around at his delegation briefly as he prepares to finish.

"I will consider us fortunate for a number of reasons. For one, that we found members of our lost people who so desperately needed our help and support. For another, that we now find ourselves with opportunities to learn and discover that which might not have come to us by other means. Knowledge is a precious commodity, and as we stand here and cast our eyes skyward, we see more out there than we could possibly imagine. And though this war may have cost us dearly, we shall not let them pass in vain. We shall move forward in their honor and step into a future with high expectations and rewards."

Another rousing cheer flies up, with more waving hands and whistles.

"And so it must come to pass!"

Thaelyn now turns to the General, who was holding his sword ceremoniously. He draws it out, taking it in both hands and raising it up over his head for all to see, then inverting it and setting it to stand on end in a knight's repose. He raises his right hand and holds it up to the audience.

"We who are the people of Tae'Eladar, do decree that we hold stewardship of our own. We who are the people of Tae'Eladar, do decree that we hold fast to the principles of the Societies of the Estelar and their teachings, that the doctrines of the Measure of Balance will guide us and our actions for all those we may encounter in our travels. And to this end, we do offer this oath to those who would join with us on the journey of life and the path of enlightenment."

He pauses once more to offer a brief respite.

"Be you here, who are assembled, admitting to my call?"

A collective cry wells up from the audience, a resounding wave of voices, all speaking as one.

"Aye!"

"Be you here, who are assembled, admitting to my grace?"

"Aye!"

"Be you here, who are assembled, admitting to my service?"

"Aye!"

"Be it known, for the Council of the Night Elves has petitioned, by the will of the people of Solinaia, that they and thee shall come to the side of mine own. Is this, in truth, your plea?"

"Aye!"

"Be it known, for with this mandate, you who are assembled would become citizens of my domain, to serve as my subjects, to bequeath unto me your duty and your promise to the fulfillment of our combined destiny, to the glory of the kingdom. Is this, in truth, your plea?"

"Aye!"

"Be there a man or woman present who would not declare this so, let them speak now!"

Silence fills the air. Thaelyn glances around briskly to check their faces.

"So be it! As the Gods above shall pay witness, let these words be borne across the realms! From this day forward, it shall be known that the people of Solinaia, as will their children and heirs, are welcomed into my arms as they are welcomed into my kingdom."

"Huzzah!"

An uproarious cry of cheering and applause rises from around the plaza. Echoes and shouts of joy filled the streets. From the upper levels of the city, people threw down flowers and ornamental sprigs of pine and mint. Several musicians emerge with flutes and lyres, and begin playing to the merriment of the people. Food and drink flow freely out the doors of the taverns and inns, and dancing ensues in the streets.

Thaelyn returned his sword to its sheath and strolled out into the plaza to meet with his new subjects. A barmaid passes nearby carrying a load of mugs, passing them out as she goes along. He calls her over and takes one for himself, then raises it up to the crowd and brings it to his lips. The crowd lets out another cheer as the people offer up their own mugs to share their first drink with their new Lord.

✦✦✦

That evening, in the city of Rolsklinde, a gentle knocking is heard on the door of the Governor's office.

"Yes, enter," the Governor calls.

The door opens and Dean Malorn steps inside with a morbid look on his face. He walks silently over to the Governor's desk, where he stands and waits.

The Governor had his attention directed out the window to observe the setting sun. He did not notice the Dean's disdainful countenance at first. The room remains silent a moment longer until the Governor, perturbed by the excessive lull, turns to look at his visitor.

"Dean, what is it?" he asks, feeling a growing sense of doom. "What has happened that disturbs you so?"

"I have just endured the return of a scout from Solinaia," the Dean declares flatly. "The Night Elves have offered their fealty to Thaelyn. The city has been sworn in and declared as a new province to his kingdom."

"I was afraid of this," the Governor admits. "But it means nothing, do you hear? Nothing changes! We take Thaelyn down, and the rest will fall after him."

"As you decide, my Lord."

"What is the status of your little…project?"

"We are progressing, but to find the right one has not been easy. One does not simply go about this as if to ask directions at a street corner. The lesser ones are often unwilling to cooperate without sufficient incentive, as they tend to be more afraid of their uppers than they are of us. However, I believe we finally found what we're looking for. But conjuring forth a creature of this kind is a very delicate procedure. The preparations to call it out will need to be very precise."

"I am well aware of that, Dean, but the longer we delay, the more influence Thaelyn develops in this world. I wish to see him fall as soon as possible…maybe also to find a way into that delightful little paradise of his and have a few of my own pleasures with it," he chuckles coarsely as his mind drifts off. "It sounds as if those peons have been busy over there since…" he cuts his voice off as he recalls his visitor. "That will be all, Dean. You may go."

"Yes, my Lord, and I will give this project my full attention," he replies promptly.

As the day's events came to a close for the delegation, they returned to Firstfall. Haran and Sehnisavain continued back home to Bya'an Tamoranth, along with most of the delegation visiting the new district, while Thaelyn and the other officers conducted a brief meeting to review the day's military affairs.

The multi-point attack on the orcish camp containing the portal was an unqualified success. The orcs were annihilated, and the camp was captured. The division of troops moving down from the north had occupied the space and will hold it until a proper base could be built with a permanent garrison.

The end of the day comes with no new developments.

In the morning, life returns to its usual pattern. The meeting in the tactical office progresses well until a tonal announcement is heard coming from Thaelyn's trans-com unit. Thaelyn picks it up to answer the call.

"This is Thaelyn."

"Greetings, Your Lordship, this is Commander Nazég. I have some preliminary details that I thought you might find interesting on those samples."

"Ah, good, Commander. What do we have so far?"

"First and foremost, we were successful in extracting viable samples from each of those bottles. I must admit, I was a bit skeptical at first, believing we might be dealing with organic compounds that would've degraded too greatly over the years to make an effective test. However, the two samples do appear to be one and the same substance."

"As I suspected, which leads us to believe these two events may have been caused by the same perpetrators. But now we must determine who those perpetrators are, even though we have sufficient cause to believe it may involve the Suuden-Aryku."

"Well, Your Lordship, I don't think you'll need to worry about that much longer. We were able to identify a component in this substance which our scientists believe may be the primary catalytic ingredient, at least as far as plant life is concerned. However, I've heard a few details about these Trees of Life, and this causes me to wonder how they may react to it. But if they share any of the basic cellular structure with the more traditional forms of vegetation, this will certainly cause them a good bit of suffering."

"And what might that be, Commander?"

"The compound has the potential to cause a systemic plasmolysis reaction, which is to say the protoplasm inside the cell shrinks away from the cell wall due to the loss of water by means of osmosis. In severe cases, this can cause the condition of cytorrhysis, or the collapse of the cell, and a withering effect of the plant. If it is not corrected, it can cause severe damage and possibly the death of the plant."

"And this would certainly fit the descriptions we have heard from the experiences of the people who were caring for the trees. But now, Commander... Could this be the work of a mage alchemist in a society such as what we have in this world dating back four centuries ago?"

"I doubt it. This would require an advanced medical lab. The molecule we discovered was synthetic, and very reactive. It could not have been made by any society on this world that we know about. I must admit that we have the technology to create a substance such as this, but then so do the Suuden-Aryku. And since this occurred before we arrived, this leaves us with only one possibility."

"And so, Commander, we must look to the Suuden-Aryku as the likely culprits in this affair, at least insofar as they must be the ones to produce it. But whether they actually applied it is another thing, and for this, we need to consider Priestess Sehnisavain's report of someone in Rolsklinde, along with our spies and the tale of this stranger who came upon them with the original stories of this plague of theirs."

"This one simply ties my horns in knots. Someone spent some time on this, this much you can be sure of."

"And when we consider those elven holy symbols, we have one more piece of a puzzle with some rather unpleasant implications."

"So it would seem. Our next topic would be those mushrooms. We made a few very disturbing discoveries relating to those."

"Oh, and what is that now?"

"First, they do contain a potent psychoactive compound. Ankhia admits she doesn't know anything about dwarven physiology to give you an accurate depiction, but if they're anything like humans, this would certainly do the trick for the descriptions you gave of their behavior."

"They do share many physical qualities together."

"All right, but then we come to the bad part. Those mushrooms are laced with heavy metals, and we think they pick this up from the soil, and maybe due to that fertilizer. This seems to be part of their growth cycle, as they're based on an alien biochemistry. This would then accumulate in the body over time, likely causing a deterioration of their health until they eventually die."

"How long; can you estimate for us?"

"Once again, she has to reflect on her lack of proper knowledge of dwarven physiology to give us an accurate number. But in the case of a human, she's estimating six to eight months, if they're eating this in that stew of theirs every day."

"I see. Dwarves, in my experience, tend to have sturdier builds than your average human. They also make their homes largely underground, so they tend to hold a certain resistance to such elements, at least to some small degree. Therefore, if we add perhaps fifty percent to that number, we find ourselves with the better part of a year, and not counting what time this particular group has already spent up there."

"That sounds bad, especially if they've already been up there a while. This also suggests they're not the first."

"Indeed, and we will need to see about this soon. And this leaves us with the final question of how they first arrived and what happened to the rest of them on that world Sehnisavain mentioned once."

"I don't envy you for figuring this one out. And if all this funnels back down to someone in Rolsklinde managing the affair, along with the Suuden-Aryku providing for it, I would suggest caution if you should ever wish to make a visit."

"Thank you, Commander. We will be watching this very closely."

"Of course... Good day to you."

Thaelyn ends the link and replaces the unit in its holster.

"This is very disturbing, General," he reflects. "And getting worse..."

"Indeed, my Lord, one might ask what we have stepped into here in this world."

"Someone's mastermind plan to make trouble. And now we must unravel it. So, let us speak of the return of our three young High Elf scouts..."

✦

"Master Cydulean, we will need to find a more efficient way in which to conduct this."

"I realize that, Sumisal, but until we can secure a broader foundation here, we need to make do with what we have."

"Granted. Very well, our attendant is supposed to be ready today, so go ahead and check on it. I'll hold things for us up here."

"Right, I'll be back shortly."

The two men were in discussion in Sehnisavain's office in the temple in Kynesoth, after having established themselves as specialist priests in the eyes of the Flame Elves. Cydulean, who was actually a Master mage from the Order academy, gets up from the desk and marches out of the room. He turns down a hallway, which is part of a private area of the temple leading behind the dais platform in the auditorium hall. He follows it around to the door leading into the basement and pulls out a key to unlock it.

He checks to ensure no one is watching before entering and closing the door behind him. He lights a series of sconces on the walls as he proceeds deeper into the room toward a far corner that is secluded from view. There he finds a small basket on the floor with a rolled-up note inside. He picks it up and pulls apart a small string that ties it closed, then unfurls it and begins to read.

"Good, she's ready," he mutters privately.

He pulls out a pen to cross out the existing message and writes a new one, reusing the same piece of paper for a return note. When he is finished, he ties it closed and pulls out a rune from his pocket to cast a portal enchantment on it. When the rune is ready, he takes the note and drops it onto the rune to send it away. He then moves the basket out of the way in anticipation of another delivery…a larger one this time. Finally, he steps back and waits.

Several moments pass, and the room is silent. The basement was not frequented very often, so he held confidence in his security to conduct his work down here. He mulled the thought that once they established a more secure environment, they might move the portal arrival zone out of the basement and into one of the other rooms for convenience.

A few more moments pass, and the stillness is broken by a sudden flash arriving in the corner of the room where the note was found. But this time, a body appeared out of the ball of light.

"Welcome home, Priestess," he offers gently.

The female Flame Elf convert wobbled slightly on her arrival, not being accustomed to this form of transit.

"Such a curious way to travel," she emits softly.

She pauses briefly to gain her bearings before stepping out of the corner. She stares at the man in front of her.

"You…" she sighs. "I still remember that little trick you and your friend pulled on me down here. Where is he, by the way?"

"We're using Sehnisavain's office for the moment to conduct our work."

"Can I trust you will not be playing any more of these pranks on me?" she smiles tenderly.

"On this occasion, Priestess, we are now working together. With apologies, it was necessary to remove you as you were a witness to our arrival, and we had to decide what to do about it. Also, you could be useful if we could make you understand the greater burdens we face. As a close associate to the High Priestess, you carry value."

"I suppose I should be thankful for that, but just out of curiosity, what if I did not hold this position?"

"Likely, you would still be useful to some degree, just not to the point of being able to interact with the others as you do."

"All right, I suppose that's reasonable. Now, perhaps we should make a proper introduction. Which one are you? You must be the mage, right?"

"Yes, Master Cydulean, although I'm to be addressed as Priest Cydulean in front of the others. My partner is an actual priest. His name is Sumisal."

"And you're both High Elves, which allows you to move among us so easily. Very clever, you certainly fooled me."

The man smiles pleasantly.

"If it helps any, we are all the same people, and on Tae'Eladar at least, very close family to one another. But now, Priestess Kerali, if you will follow me. Oh, and remember, if anyone asks about your extended absence, you were at home trying to recover from your grief over the loss of the High Priestess after our arrival and the report you received from it. Do you live with anyone, such as family members?"

"I may sometimes stay with my parents when I am not occupying my quarters here. I have not chosen a partner for myself, as I don't quite feel ready for that yet."

"All right, we'll need to find a cover for that as well, if it should ever come up."

The two of them make their way out of the basement and into the hallway, once again locking the door and returning to their office. On their arrival, the Priestess meets with the other operative.

"Ah, Priestess," he announces pleasantly. "I trust you are feeling better after your little, eh...spell?" he grins.

She rolls her eyes at him and nods, acknowledging the moment of humor he brought to the occasion.

"Yes, Priest Sumisal, but I hope not to experience such a rush of weariness again if you please. This one left me with some rather strange dreams lingering."

"Of course, then we should be on with our work."

"Where are we at present with our unfortunate situation of the High Priestess? I heard it was the dastardly work of those orcs. Is that correct?"

"Indeed, and a most disturbing turn this is. We thought we were allies with them, but it would seem their dismissal has left them with a few errant motivations."

"And our people, what are we doing about it?"

"Priestess Ilothonna has sent word to our outposts to make a few surveys to see where they may be coming from. However, we are also playing out an inquiry as to why Sehnisavain was out there in the first place. It has been decided that she was seeking a most unusual tree, and our suspicions are that this tree is found in that camp to the north of us, in the possession of those invaders we coincidentally have orders not to attack. We find it curious that the orcs attacked at this specific moment, and against this specific target, when she was apparently trying to reach that tree."

"Really!" Kerali muses in her gesture of roleplay.

Midday had come to Firstfall, and along with it was the arrival of Relissa and her group from their language classes. They joined Thaelyn and the General in the tactical office.

"Marelle," Thaelyn announces. "We have work for you."

"I was expecting as much. Leesa is ready, as best we can manage for now. I sent her up there early this morning to meet with Acolyte

Sarens. They should be waiting for us to install the other part of this operation."

"Good, and this is where you come in. We have our people waiting outside. One of them is a mage, so he will provide transport. Be discreet, Lieutenant, this much I think is the most important."

"Absolutely, Your Lordship. And I can't express enough how much I feel about finding a solution to this one particular problem," she bows, and returns outside.

She finds a group composed of several men, each dressed in casual attire and carrying large shoulder bags, almost as if they were travelling on a weekend getaway with their overnight luggage. They joined together with a local mage holding a rune to Rolsklinde. He enchants it and sends the group away.

They arrived in front of the south gate to the city. From there, they enter through the gates, and Marelle leads them to the Ten Eagles tavern, where she waves to call Willit and Leesa over to join them. Together, they travel along the avenues to the plaza in the upper district. But Marelle stops the entourage just before entering the plaza proper.

"Up there," she points discreetly to a large building on the right. "That's the Governor's Manor, and that window upstairs is his office. It looks right out onto the plaza, so if he should happen to be looking outside, he can see just about everything out here. And over there," she points across the way to the academy. "Upstairs there in the corner on the left, that's the Dean's office, and with basically the same view. So, we need to be careful of those two."

She turns left and leads the group into the plaza. Nearby was the temple, while the barracks were on the far end. The assembly casually saunters along until they reach the temple doors, and then enter inside. They step forward along a central aisle, passing by several rows of pews. The building was empty at this time of day. There were only two resident priests managing the religious affairs. They take notice of the new arrivals and come out to meet them.

"Ah, come in, good citizens!" the first priest calls soothingly. "Do you wish to offer yourselves in worship, or perhaps there is another service you desire?"

Marelle halts her team and eyes the two men carefully, while casually glancing around the room to ensure they were alone. They both appeared mature, where one was clearly a middle-aged man, no different from any other she might have seen before. The other one, however... She stared at him, for his clearly elderly features did not resemble any other man she might have seen before...at least not in this city.

"You know," she begins. "I have to admit, I don't visit the temple very often, but you sure look like you've been around a while. How old are you?"

The elder priest frowns and glances briefly at his partner before returning his reply.

"My dear young lady, I am simply a servant of our blessed gods, given this great gift to serve our people for as long as they desire me. I do not count my years by such trivial values."

"Really, then you must be very fortunate, especially when you consider this terrible plague we suffer so often."

"Yes, these are indeed hard times, and it is precisely for this reason that I dedicate myself to the devotion of our gods that we might one day find our salvation."

"This is actually a very interesting topic here. I'm also looking to help our people find salvation, so maybe together we can actually discover what it is. What do you think?"

"Uh..." he hesitates. "But what do you mean? That is to say, we offer our prayers every day to our gods that they will deliver us from this horrid curse by those unclean elves. What else can we possibly do when their wretched magic defiles our streets each night, and our people cannot find the freedom to live their lives fully?"

"Well, as an officer in the Allegiance Guard, one thing that comes to mind is to find what actually causes this plague and put an end to it."

"Ah, but of course, I see your direction. Unfortunately, those accursed elves seethe it into the open land from their unholy altars and blood sacrifices. We can never know precisely where they are to find them. Therefore, it is all we can do to give ourselves to our gods that they will guide us and protect us."

"You know, I was speaking to a relative recently about this. We do this sometimes," she smiles sweetly. "And this same topic came up, and she felt that you, with your Holy Sight, ought to know a few things. Isn't this true?"

"Oh, that!" he chuckles softly. "Yes, our gods may try to inform us of this from time to time, but those horrid elves keep changing their methods on us, such that it becomes very difficult to narrow our focus on them."

"Wow, those elves must be simply awful!" she feigns.

"Indeed, they are," he nods solemnly.

"Such that not even gods can find them? I mean, wow, gods are...well, gods! How can you hide from that?"

"Um..." he perks up uncertainly.

"And at the same time," she continues unabated. "It's the duty of the Guard to protect the city from so many errant deeds, don't you think? And yet, they never receive instruction to actually go out there, find those unholy altars, and destroy them. Such a pity," she shakes her head.

"Oh, but of course, I have heard of this as well," he consoles. "It surely must have to do with all those shortages we suffer."

"Absolutely! That story goes all around the city. But you know, I would think, as someone who works for the Guard, the lives of our people would be a little more important than a simple shortage of something like iron. I mean, lives are lives, and what is iron, but a material thing. Right?"

"Well, yes, I suppose this would certainly hold reason."

"And yet, my brother...he used to attend the academy over here," she glances over her shoulder and out the door. "One time, he was talking to the Dean...or maybe I should say arguing with him..." she chuckles. "Anyway, the Dean gave the impression that the Guard isn't actually supposed to do anything at all except pick up drunks off the street. Can you imagine that?" she feigns surprise.

"Really! My goodness, that would be a bit of a surprise. But surely there must be a misinterpretation somewhere."

"Oh, I suppose we could say that. I mean, after all, he's part of the city authority, and as they say, if you can't trust that…" she shrugs.

"Indeed! How true it is."

"And so, we're not going to trust them anymore," she returns flatly. "I'm a law enforcer, and this curse, or whatever it is, is killing people. Last I heard, that's called murder, and I intend to put a stop to it."

"Oh… Um…" he frowns solemnly and glances at his partner. "How do you mean? I mean, if the gods say…"

"My orders come from a chain of command that is much closer to home…my Captain. And his orders also come from a chain of command that is much closer to home…that guy in the building over here…" she thumbs in the general direction of the Governor's Manor. "And those orders say to go pick up drunks, not fight for the lives of our people. And these are those authority figures we're supposed to trust…with our lives."

"Oh, dear."

"Therefore, we are no longer listening to them and their catch phrases to trust things that don't work, like those gods of yours, who, as gods, should have more than enough power to smite everything out there to ashes, if they truly wanted to. After all, these are gods, aren't they? And this is what gods are supposed to do, especially if you pray for your life against such awful, horrible, and unholy things like the High Elves out there that were corrupted by Sargeras four hundred years ago behind all our backs."

"Huh? Wait a moment. High Elves, what are those? And what do you mean, four hundred years ago?"

"Otherwise known in the modern day as Flame Elves, and this is the result of a secret arrival to take them away from us way back in the beginning. And everything since then is just a lot of storytelling."

"And just how do you know this, young lady?"

"Oh! I'm sorry, I forgot to mention I'm working for Lord Thaelyn down there in the valley…" her voice becomes more serious, "…who does not trust our authority figures, and who does investigate things," she affirms sternly. "And he takes it all the way up to finding those answers you and your gods seem incapable of giving anyone else, including us in the Guard so we can do the job we're supposed to be doing…saving lives. And he found out they were stolen away when those creeps came in behind our backs and corrupted their real religion, and further spoiled the alliance we all shared at the time."

"A real religion?" he balks. "And an alliance?"

"Then, Sargeras used them in a campaign to wipe just about everything else out there, joined eventually by the rest with their… official…arrival, three and a half centuries ago, up to the point of our last cities, then to stop, pinning us down and holding us in place for some ulterior motive. I mean, after all, four hundred years. If they really wanted us dead, we would be dead by now. But this hasn't happened."

"Uh huh…you think so?"

"The Suuden-Aryku hold the capacity with their advanced weapons to blast whole cities right off the map. Does that say something to you? But instead, all this resulted in simply erasing our history so no one can remember anything…for as long as they can remember, and filling our heads with false promises to keep on praying, while each and every one of our friends and relatives falls victim to something you and your gods couldn't find even if your life depended on it. But then again…wait. This brings me back to the beginning. You look like you've managed to escape from that life-threatening plague that's killing the rest of us. Good gracious!" she feigns again. "If your gods were so successful in your case, why couldn't they share this with the rest of us? How old did you say you were again?"

"Me?" he protests. "No, as I said, I do not measure such a trivial thing as the years of my life in the service of our gods."

"Right. In other words, you don't bother counting anymore, because you don't have a timeclock ticking down on you, like the rest of us. Then I'll put it to you another way…" she turns to the lead member of her troupe. "Priest, check his shoulder. Let's see how his 'god' allowed him to live so long."

"Huh?" the elder priest retorts. "Wait a moment!" he steps back from the suggestion. "You can't do that!"

"Oh really?" she grins mischievously. "Why would you suddenly be so offended that we simply want to look at your shoulder, Priest!" she spurns. "Like I said, this plague is murder, and I want to know why your…gods…didn't give us a solution after four hundred years of howling up to them."

"This is ridiculous! You can't just come in here and interrogate me!"

"Interrogate? After you poison us with your lies? No, interrogation is not what I have in mind. I'm here to arrest you."

Now she turns serious.

"Restrain these two men and check their shoulders," she orders.

The group now rushes forward to catch the two priests. They grab the men's arms and hold them tight, while one priest begins examining the elder man's shoulder.

"Very curious," he offers. "This man is without his implant. And it looks as though it was removed intentionally. See here…" he points at a clear scarring. "This is the incision, and what appears to be marks from stitching. Not a very clean job, I might add."

"Not clean, in what way?"

"Well, by the standards we have back home, this is sloppy work."

"Really! So these priests aren't even as good at performing health care as your average farmhand on a sick horse?"

"That's a good way of putting it."

"Just what is it you're talking about?" the elder priest demands.

The lead priest of Marelle's troupe now examines the other man's shoulder. He turns and nods.

"This one as well… Both are missing their implants and showing scars from the work."

"How old would you say this man is, if to judge by the standards of your people back home?"

"I might say he's a good early to mid-sixties."

"How interesting…" she muses openly. "I guess all his prayers were finally answered. Too bad it doesn't work that way for the rest of us. So, in a city where no one survives past their early fifties, this guy manages to make sixty all because of his beloved gods who can't find those nasty elves and their altars. Incredible…"

"You people are mad!" the elder man argues. "Just who do you think you are?"

"I'm that salvation you mentioned earlier," Marelle responds confidently. "Though not sent by your gods," she snaps. "These men here are real priests, who worship real gods, actual ones who do like to see progress on occasion, and may even get personally involved, if the situation demands it."

"What?" he winces.

"Yes, there are beings out there who are immensely old, and people like us might call them gods. They might even offer guidance on occasion, and something like this plague would seriously burn their bum for the criminal offense. I have no doubt, if they were running the show up there, they would either give us the precise directions to find those unholy altars, or else they would simply do it themselves. And we wouldn't be here talking about it four centuries later."

"You can't be serious!"

"Furthermore, these are the very same gods those elves used to follow until Sargeras showed up and turned their minds inside-out. And likely the same gods we worshipped here before you arrived and turned our minds inside-out, along with those other authority figures we are intimidated into trusting."

"Oh! Intimidated, is it? And do you think your gods can do any better?"

"Priest, if you actually know who Sargeras is, he's a god alright, but from a dead society after our gods killed the rest. That is who they are. So, you might want to stifle your attitude, as I would imagine, in a few more years, you'll see it for yourself. Oh, what a joy it will be to see the look on your face."

"Uh huh…"

"Do you see these people here?" she points at the other priests.

"These are humans, much like you and me, but not from this world. They come from another world entirely, which is the same one our people once came from. Therefore…more humans, as well as elves, as well as those gods we are supposed to be following, as this is where it all started, part of that lost history we aren't allowed to remember, so those authority figures can keep us under their thumbs with such wonderful catch phrases and storytelling, and orders to only pick up drunks, not do anything useful."

The man pauses to glance around at the others as she continues.

"And all this while you poison our children at that Festival of yours with devices inside our shoulders…the real cause of the plague. So much for your gods. As for us, we're not listening to them anymore. We're taking this into our own hands, which we probably should've done a long time ago, had it not been for you and yours denying us asking those questions. It took an unwelcome intruder to our lands, according to that governor over there, to open our eyes to it."

"And just what do you think you can do about any of that? Do you think you can fight them and turn them away?"

"I guess you don't pay much mind to the daily gossip from outside those walls you never allow us to pass through. Lord Thaelyn, down there in the valley, is wiping the land clean from all that unholy… whatever. And when he's finished out there, he intends to come up here and do the same for that city authority. He has a huge army, and a full world to provide for him. He's cleared a large number of those orcs by now, and got the rest on the run. Those Suuden-Aryku are taking heavy losses and finally realizing to keep away. And as for those Flame Elves, well, let's just say they won't be conducting any more unholy whatever from this moment. They're apparently down to their last city, much like the rest of us, and that city won't stand a chance once he turns his sights on it."

"You must be kidding me!"

"Kidding? You know, if you think I'm kidding, it could just as easily be due to our complete lack of knowing of anything beyond…

for as long as we can remember…and what a world that actually does teach things can actually do with it. What do you say to that?"

"Well…um…"

"Yeah, it hurts a little, especially if you sent an unwanted intrusion into that world to make trouble for them, and they come back here to find you! Wow, what a surprise that might be. A world of intelligent people who actually take the time to solve mysteries and fight all the bad things out there. And this, I might also add, is because of the lessons they receive from their gods…law enforcers and such who do, in fact, demand results. Right, Priest Garrain?"

"Absolutely, Lieutenant," he nods. "And therefore, dear Sir," he directs at the elder priest. "As one of our gods specializes in law and justice, virtually every citizen back home is a deputized agent to serve that cause. If any of your authority figures were to visit us there, they would find a very hostile environment to practice their deeds."

"Wonderful," he moans.

Marelle now turns to her troupe to give her orders.

"Priest Garrain, I'm not even sure if we have the right sorts of laws on the books to cover something like this, other than outright murder, and I would like to make this look good. We may need to combine a few things to do this. Can you offer something?"

"I could offer a multitude of thoughts," he muses. "Naturally, we have murder, but in this case, we have one called protracted homicide. It means to offer a longer term or a delay in timing, such as with a slow poison or something similar."

"Great!"

"Aside from that, we can offer slander and defamation of character; further to involve impersonating the clergy," he glares at the false priests. "Also, such as conspiracy to commit murder, in association with whoever provided these elements. We might then add malicious mischief and public endangerment if we consider their acts while doing the deed, and most importantly, assault with a dangerous device and a deadly substance. I might even throw in misleading claims for all their excuses of this curse."

"Wow, not bad," she giggles. "That should put them away for

the rest of their god-protected lives. But now, we need to remove these people quietly. My first thought is to hand them over to my captain. Leesa, go over there and quietly have him bring out a posse of men to haul these two away. Just remember the windows up there and whoever might be looking outside."

The girl nods and dashes off to her task.

"As for the rest of you, we're taking over the operation of this temple. I want our priests to get themselves ready. As for the two of you," she directs at the former priests. "Where is that thing you were using at the Festival? I want to take a close look at it."

"Why should I cooperate with you?" the elder man retorts abrasively.

Marelle steps up and slams her knee firmly into his groin, causing him to buckle over in extreme pain.

"Because even at sixty, it would seem you still have those things dangling between your legs. Now, unless you want another demonstration, you will start cooperating."

A short while later, across the way from the temple and inside the Governor's Manor, was the Governor's secretary in his office on one side of the foyer. His duties usually revolved around the administrative management and assignment of directives to other offices around town. Sitting at a side desk was his assistant, who would often run errands and take up chores involving most of the footwork.

A pleasant-mannered young lady with long auburn hair strolls into the office. She was wearing a white blouse and a dark blue pleated full-length skirt, with a matching vest. She steps into the room with a confident attitude and waits patiently. The man looks up from his paperwork with a curious gaze as he addresses her.

"Eh, yes, citizen, how can I help you?"

"Yes, I was sent over here by the priests in the temple. We're conducting a health survey, and they have an urgent need for your assistant to make a visit. There's a concern about something that seems to be going around lately."

"A health survey? What do you mean? Do we have some manner of illness spreading now?"

"We've been taking notice of a few isolated cases, and the study is still in its early stages, but we surely don't want it to get out of hand, now do we?" she smiles sweetly. "They're simply trying to catch it before it goes too far, and they desire to ensure those in the most important positions are examined first to prevent any disruptions of our services."

"Oh, well, if you say so. Do they require me for any reason?"

"Do you leave this office very often? It's mostly regarded to be affecting those who spend a lot of time outdoors, like runners and other messengers."

"Oh, well, no. I spend almost all my time in here, so if that's the case..."

"Right, as I thought. Then I just need to borrow this man here," she motions to the assistant. "It's my understanding he does most of the errands, right?"

"Yes, actually."

"Good, then come along," she waves to the younger man.

The two of them leave the office and exit the building, then travel across the plaza to the temple.

"Sit down here," she instructs.

The man takes up a seat while a priest in an unusually ornate robe approaches from the platform at the head of the room. Another man followed in a more professional outfit, and the assistant studied them for the strange attire.

"Are you new here?" he asks. "I don't recognize you from my last visit."

"Ah, indeed," the priest affirms calmly. "We are newly inducted to the service, and already we find ourselves immersed in a number of important matters. How have you been feeling of late? Have you experienced any dizziness, fatigue...fainting spells?"

"Um, no..."

The priest leans in and holds his left hand in front of the man's face.

"Here, follow my fingers. How many do you see?"

"I see two of them sticking up."

"Most excellent, now follow them around..."

The priest makes a clockwise circle around the man's face, followed by opening his palm and passing it straight down. The man tries to follow, but soon slumps to the bench, unconscious.

"Hmm, how tragic," the priest relents. "He does suffer from fainting spells," he grins.

"That's a neat trick," Leesa mentions. "Can you teach me that? My little sister sometimes has trouble sleeping at night. This would save me and my mom a lot of headaches."

"Indeed, many young mothers say the same. We actually do hold lessons at our temple in B.T."

The priest motions for his partner to come over and take care of the unfortunate man on the bench. He pulls out a rune, enchants it, and sends the former assistant on his way.

"All right, Leesa," the priest offers. "It's your game now. Play it well."

"Yeah, time for me to live up to my cousin's level of standards."

The girl now departs for her own exercise. She had been coached by both Marelle and Aerlie in her manners and poise, so she could carry herself in this game. She returns to the Governor's Manor and the secretary's office.

"Excuse me," she announces with a gentle knock on the door.

The secretary looks up from his desk to see the neatly dressed young lady again standing in the doorway.

"Yes? How is he?"

"He was feeling a bit dizzy as it turns out. In fact, once he got over there, my goodness, he just passed right out on us!"

"Oh no! Will he be alright? His service in this office was rather important. I often have a need for a runner to make errands and deliver messages, especially for the Governor who demands his orders to be delivered to the various offices around town."

"Oh dear," she feigns. "Well, I guess this is to be expected. I'll tell you what. I'm not busy right now, so what if I could fill in for him until he feels better? I believe he will be sent home for a while to recover. My service often leaves me with extra time on my hands, and if it turns out that you need my help on a more regular basis, I can request a temporary transfer until something else comes along," she smiles innocently.

"Hmm, well..." he examines her for her age and appearance. "You look a bit young..."

"Why thank you!" she interjects pertly. "My friends always said I'll probably be the talk of the town for my appearance alone. I do try to take good care of myself, you know."

"Um, well, yes," he chuckles anxiously for her apparent buoyancy. "It certainly appears that way. And you look so nice in that dress. Are you perchance from the Upper Ward?"

"Well, I tend not to brag too much, even though I know a lot of the families up there do..."

"Right, so I've heard. And what's your name, Miss?"

"Simply call me Leesa. We don't usually trouble ourselves with the rest...you know; because we're all so close."

"Jared? Can we talk?"

Tristeen was approaching her friend at one of the tables in the main hall at the academy. They had both been released from their classroom lessons and were now engaged in free study time. It was usually during this period when they might get together to discuss their private issues.

"Tristeen! I was hoping you would stop by just now."

"Right, I figured we needed to sit a moment. Have you seen that circle they're drawing down there in the basement?"

"Yeah, I peeked over at it when I was down there for my alchemy study. What do you think about it?"

"What do I think?" she whispers urgently. "I'll tell you what I think...a study course for the higher classmen? Balderdash! Those glyphs they're inscribing aren't for any simple conjuring I could ever imagine. No wonder it's not for demonstration. Whatever they're hoping to bring out of that must be extremely dangerous. There's not one tiny gap between them. It's a solid warding circle. I may not know much about conjuring, but the talk we get tells me you don't draw glyphs that complex and that tight together unless whatever you're hoping to call out is powerful enough to rip this whole building apart!"

She halts her tirade as she carefully pans her gaze around the room to ensure no one is paying any special attention to her, even though a few eyes are turning in her direction for the wording.

"Well, Tristeen," Jared relents. "The next question we should be asking is why. What purpose does this serve? Is the Dean looking for something? Is he hoping to gain new knowledge, or maybe a potent artifact?"

"I suppose anything is possible, knowing him like we do. It's rumored that conjuring up something big like this could be used to ransom something out of it."

"That sounds dangerous simply for the implications. Are we speaking of conjuring up a demon? I wouldn't even want to try something like that, potent artifact or no."

"We should get this to Willit so he can report it in. And then warn the rest in here to pay very close attention to what those maniacs are doing. If this thing should get loose, we need to put as much distance between us as possible."

"But Tristeen, this also implies something. If it gets loose, how do we stop it?"

"Jared, if it gets loose, I don't think we can stop anything, not with our poor skills in magic. Do you think a little fireball, or a trickle of ice would do anything to it?"

"I honestly don't know, but maybe you're right. The trouble here is, if not us then who?"

"Let's just play it by ear and see," she rubs her cheek worriedly. "Maybe we're overreacting. I mean, even the Dean shouldn't want something like this to get out of control. It would be just as much a threat to him as any other. More than likely, he has some demand for it."

"Either way, this sounds bad," he sighs. "It basically means he's losing his mind and gone mad for power."

✦✦✦

The guards watching the walls of Kynesoth held vigil over the roadways leading off into the woods, as well as the surrounding countryside. Typically, nothing ever occurred out there. No hostile forces were ever seen approaching the city, no invading armies, and no war parties…nothing. The watch was actually a bit boring, but the guards held their duties with high regard.

Along the roadway from the west comes a trio of wayward scouts. It was a small party consisting of a young priestess, an even younger mage, and a youthful male archer. They hurried along the road almost as if they were being chased, even though there were no others in sight. As they approached the gate, the guards called out the traditional announcement.

"Halt. Who goes there?"

"We are a scouting patrol returning from an extended mission," shouts the priestess. "We were on special assignment from Priest Cydulean, who should be expecting our return. We carry vital information he requested. You must open the gate at once that we may fulfill our service."

"What mission was this? Where did you come from?"

"Sir, it is a secret expedition he ordered, and not one to discuss with a tower guard. It contains sensitive information to be delivered only to his counsel. If you need more than this, you should discuss it with him, but I doubt he would be pleased with you holding us back in this matter."

"I… It's my job to guard this gate!" he relents with a sigh.

"Fine, and you did it well, but now let us finish ours."

"Right. Then let them through!" he shouts to the gate crew.

The guards open the gate, and the team enters, only to hurry their way along towards the temple.

When they arrived, they rushed inside and up to the altar platform. Priestess Kerali was attending to the altar and the alcoves, cleaning and dusting them, even though they were not necessarily dirty or had anything noteworthy to clean. It was mostly just to occupy time and to make it look as though she had a duty to perform. She quickly took notice of the three individuals arriving on the platform who were out of breath.

"You look like you ran the full distance from wherever it was you just came from. Who are you?"

"We are a special mission returning to meet with Priest Cydulean," the young priestess replies. "We carry vital information that needs to be reported to him directly."

Priestess Kerali knew instantly that any reference made to Priest Cydulean was part of the secret plan by Thaelyn to rescue the High Elves of Kynesoth. She curled a tiny smile on her lips, and briefly glanced around at the empty room before returning to her roleplay.

"Yes, last I saw, he was in session with Priestess Ilothonna. Is this so important that we must disturb him?"

"Yes, especially so..."

"I see. Then we should not delay ourselves. Follow me."

The Priestess led the young troupe off the platform and through to the offices in the rear.

Inside Sehnisavain's office, a meeting was taking place. A military officer was reporting on the situation outside.

"So far, we are unsure where these orcs are coming from," he informs the group. "The invaders seem to have pushed them back a great distance from their highest marks, even well past our own borders with the beasts."

"Could this be a rogue party that circled around them?" Cydulean asks.

"If it is, they would need to have travelled a great distance to find us."

"That suggests desperation in my mind," Sumisal considers.

"Maybe, unless…" Cydulean muses intriguingly.

"What are you thinking, Cydulean?"

"If they no longer share such close proximity to us, this raiding party must be from another source. On that can reach us efficiently enough to give them access."

"Another source?" Sumisal wonders. "But what other source, if not one of their own camps?"

"A source that holds the ability to move overland by great distances and very quickly."

"But wait, are we speaking of horses, perhaps? I think our people would know if a band of horses was passing by."

"Do orcs actually use horses?" Ilothonna inquires.

"Not to my knowledge," Cydulean replies. "I'm actually thinking of something different, and this also fits with my suspicions from before."

"Your suspicions again," she relents. "I'm still trying to recover from your previous statements regarding those people in the valley, and all those coincidences and such."

"Yes, and then we have that. Furthermore, that Sehnisavain was out there, and then taken away by something unseen, and likely for a reason. I wonder if this could be a part of it."

"All right, how so?"

"We are not aware of orcs ever using horses. Although I suppose this could always change…after all, people can learn things, right?"

"Yes, I suppose so."

"But like Sumisal said, a band of horses might tend to stand out. Their sounds, the disturbance on the land…"

"Yes."

"I might also suggest their tracks," the officer includes.

"Oh, indeed, and our people would surely know to look for those! And as such, I need to think outside the norm. Whatever the means of their arrival, as well as their apparent ease of departure, it was not by land."

"Not by land!" Ilothonna shouts. "But that could only lead to one other conclusion."

"And thus the reason for the untimely disappearance of the High Priestess, right when she was trying to gain knowledge from people we are not intended to trust."

"Huh? What do you mean?"

At this moment, Priestess Kerali appears at the door with her visitors. The commotion of their arrival draws the attention of the people inside, who all turn to look at the new faces. The two priests glance at each other and nod silently.

"All right, Captain," Cydulean announces to the officer. "That is all for now. Continue your scouting as best you can. Try to locate the nearest orcish camp of any kind, whether to the south, the southwest, maybe even the southeast, in case they are trying to circle around our rearguard."

The officer bows and promptly leaves the room.

"Kerali," Ilothonna directs. "Who are these people and why bring them in here?"

"They are private couriers for Priest Cydulean," she replies.

"Ah, at last," he croons. "I was almost ready to lose hope of your safe return."

Ilothonna steps out of the way as Cydulean motions the trio of scouts to come forward.

"Priest Cydulean," she submits. "Do you wish for me to leave while you carry your conversation?"

"No, stay, Ilothonna," he offers. "You are as much a part of these proceedings as the rest. Your participation is important."

"As you wish," she nods.

"Now, as to the three of you," he redirects at the scouting party. "What do you have to report?"

"Priest Cydulean," responds the young priestess. "As you can see, we just now returned from our extended tour. It was a difficult one, but I believe we accomplished our goal."

Ilothonna found herself curiously drawn to interrupt the report to inquire about this tour.

"Eh, excuse me, if I may. Who exactly are you and where were you travelling?"

"Oh, of course…my apologies, First Deacon. My name is Curate Eilihel Moonglow, this is Adept Mynae Silverwind, and Huntsman Kethron Whisperwood," she motions to the others. "We are part of the Archpriest's special forces team, previously assigned to a post south of the city…"

"Archpriest!" Ilothonna screeches abruptly and glares at Cydulean.

"Oh," she emits casually. "You were not informed of this as yet? My apologies, but yes. Ours is a very special service branch."

"I wasn't even aware we had such a position!"

"Ours is a very secretive level of service," Cydulean notes smoothly. "Knowledge of it tends to go on a need-to-know basis, and with respect, Ilothonna, you did not need to know before this. We are a hidden function that parallels the High Priestess. It began in the early days, and in part due to a number of curious anomalies we were observing at the time, which raised certain questions along the way. Since then, our sect has been performing a level of secret surveillance over our internal security, as well as a system of checks and balances to ensure the integrity of our ranks. We also keep a close eye on our allegiances to make sure they keep to their word."

"Are you speaking of the Suuden-Aryku in this case?"

"Them, or anyone else we are supposed to be aligned with, as one can never be too sure of anything in a world so heavily devastated as ours. And who is it that did this devastation?"

"I, uh… Well, wait, our history tells us of this war, and we actually participated in it to a large extent."

"Indeed, we did, and we spent a great many of our people along the way…and to do what? Recall that earlier conversation. First, we might want to ask ourselves what purpose it serves to wipe the full population of this world down to the last city of each, then simply to stop. It might also serve us to ask why we apparently have no surviving history to teach our younger generations about what came before. This is to say, we destroyed everything only to forget it ever existed."

"Oh, wow."

"And then we have our attitudes that we held full authority to do it at all, and the impunity not to carry any blame for it. This made matters even worse."

"Oops!"

"And furthermore, to declare everything else out there as weak, when we are no better for what is left of us."

"Ack! All right, you got me. I'll keep my mouth shut."

"Combine all this, and it is enough to make a few of us wonder why it had to be done. Unfortunately, many of us did not ask these questions at a time when it might carry value. And then, what about the war in that world said to be populated by dwarves?"

"A war with dwarves? What are dwarves?"

"You do not even know of them?"

"No, when did this occur?"

"Perhaps you are simply too young to know of it, which coincidentally complicates matters."

"Complicates?"

"Yes, a part of that history we are apparently made to forget. If we do not even recall that which we did in the service of our Lord, where is the wisdom of doing anything at all if we are made to forget what we did soon after?"

"Oh no, that doesn't sound good. And for multiple reasons."

"Indeed, and I might say this is suspect for the implications. If not for those of us who were present at the time to witness it, it would cease to exist in our memories altogether!"

"What happened during this war?"

"It was apparently an important element of our service, but it cost a great many lives. Very simply, I would say, to hide it from our people is tantamount to keeping vital information away from us that would otherwise teach our people, if nothing else, why we are reduced to one surviving city out of what used to be a nation!"

Ilothonna drew back, aghast at the notion.

"This particular war occurred nearly four centuries ago," he continues. "Shortly after our Lord came and lifted us up. The issue here is a great many of us were called to service, but none ever came back from it. There was no explanation as to why, other than to say the battle was bloody, and we never received word as to the end result. We were simply expected to serve and die for our Lord, or so it was said."

"So it was said…by whom?"

"Those alleged allies that give us our orders…"

"What?!" she shouts. "So, what is it you're actually trying to say here?"

"Let us keep our calm, Ilothonna. I would wish to keep that decision until after I have heard from my scouts."

Cydulean now turns to the scouting party and prepares to debrief his charges.

"As you were saying, Curate…your mission?"

"Yes," Eilihel begins. "According to instruction, we travelled to investigate those invaders to the north and what relationship we believe they have with the city of Rolsklinde, among others. As you know, we received a report of delegations meeting in secret to discuss what we thought might be an alliance."

"With the various races up north…"

"Yes. There were apparently three coaches of various descriptions arriving. The first, we believe, was the humans."

"Good, and what do we know of that one?"

"It would seem the meeting resulted in an unfavorable conclusion with the leader of that city which, as you were suspecting, is that one said to be managing them on behalf of the Suuden-Aryku."

"An unfavorable conclusion?"

"Yes, by the posturing and apparent shouting overheard by the original scouts, it sounded like arguing, followed by a hasty withdraw of the carriage."

"That does indeed sound unfavorable," Sumisal notes. "But then, how do we explain those deliveries of supplies?"

"Deliveries of supplies!" Ilothonna interjects. "What deliveries?"

"Yes, our scouts have reported a large depot that has been forming in the northern region of the valley. We suspect this is due to their war with the orcs and the spoils left behind."

"Spoils left behind from orcs?" she winces. "What possible value would any of that hold?"

Sumisal simply shrugs as Cydulean continues.

"Curate?" he directs. "Did you get a look at it?"

"Yes," Eilihel continues. "Our observations report there is indeed a large volume of what is essentially rubbish in there…you know, bits of broken timbers, hides, some odd crates, maybe with food supplies, and such. Some of it might hold value if you are a craftsman with the right skills. But we were also able to take notice of stockpiles of iron, which is certainly of some value."

"Iron, very well," Ilothonna admits. "That could serve some potential."

"Yes, and it would seem there is a sizeable quantity being taken away."

"We are aware the Suuden-Aryku were delivering supplies to them on occasion, so this would not surprise me. But why is it important here?"

"It is being recovered by people from the city, not the invaders in the valley."

"Wait," she flusters. "I think I missed something here. The people in the city are taking this after the invaders bring it back… and yet they failed to negotiate any sort of alliance?"

"This was indeed very curious, and so we were forced to continue our investigation. Mynae was able to provide us with invisibility cover, while Kethron aided in supporting our needs out there in the wilds."

"That's a nice little troupe you have there."

"Yes, very efficient to our needs. But we were deep into territory that we have traditionally been told is off-limits to us due to our instructions not to approach the human city."

"Meaning to say, you were up there near Rolsklinde at this point in time."

"Very close to it, yes. We saw regular caravans of wagons coming and going. But we chose not to enter the city proper at that time, instead to see about the other delegations. This led us further to the east, within range of sighting the Daanen-Aryku territory and that ship of theirs…or what's left of it. We needed to see if there was any obvious evidence of interaction between them."

"I understand, and the result?"

"Our observations tell us they seem to be reinforcing the Daanen-Aryku against the Suuden-Aryku."

"Reinforcing!" she retorts intensely. "Then this would represent a successful alliance, would it not?"

"It would, but curiously, we at first saw them using disguises as Allegiance Guard from Rolsklinde."

"Huh? Why?"

"Some of our old scouting reports told us of the occasional tours of Guard members going out on rare occasions to offer aid to them."

"And this is from Rolsklinde, under the management of that one individual, who is supposed to be on our side and against the others?"

"Yes! How very curious. But our opinions suggest it might be just a show to defer attention."

"Uh huh… He puts on a show of aid, when in fact he's not supposed to be doing anything at all. Well, maybe it's just to conceal himself."

"Maybe."

"And what result are they having? Are they actually attacking the Suuden-Aryku?"

"So far, it looks mostly defensive, but very effective for the apparent results."

"Effective?!" she shouts. "The Suuden-Aryku are said to be a very potent force, for their weapons and other devices. How is it possible these invaders can defeat them?"

"One thing we observed is the extensive use of magic, which the Suuden-Aryku do not seem capable of repelling. Also, it would seem, for all they are said to possess in other areas, simple bows and arrows, as well as swords, are cutting them down quite efficiently."

"Incredible! Then I suppose these invaders should be considered a great threat to us if they ever did turn our way."

"It would surely seem that way, and not only for their numbers.

They were seen making extensive use of portals to launch out against the orcs. This is how they apparently hit them blindsided."

"Portals, yes…" Ilothonna muses. "If they could create even one of those in our vicinity, it would mean trouble."

"And this would therefore negate any potential value of our outposts," Sumisal adds. "And even the city walls themselves!"

Ilothonna jerks her gaze up to meet him. The clear implications were dire in her mind.

"Curate," Cydulean continues. "What about that camp of theirs?"

"Yes, and then there is that camp, if you can call it that…" she rolls her eyes for emphasis.

Ilothonna turns to study the young priestess, desiring to prompt her to finish her statement, but holding back.

"That camp…" Eilihel relates. "In the time since they have arrived, it has grown into nothing less than a village! It is also making trade with what we have seen to be new farming activities to the north, also from that city."

"And again," Ilothonna asks. "You say this is without any form of alliance?"

"It seems apparent that the agent inside the city did not make an alliance. If he did, his other allegiances are not following in kind. So, if he is true to his own, he should not be doing so."

"All right, this makes sense. But how is it we see this out there?"

"We are drawing from a number of observations. He makes a show of support for the others, which might mean he falsifies his intentions to those who observe. If he does this inside the city as well, and since he is said to be managing them, it might be an unfavorable condition. We could overhear such words as fulfilling shortages of goods in their city. If he is so badly managing things, those people probably made a few of their own choices."

"Oh, how nice. This is as much a rebellion against his practices."

"Also, we see more of this over near Solinaia, where they are also apparently building new farms and making trade. This leads us to believe there is a discrepancy in what we have been told of these relations, and the so-called trouble these invaders are supposed to be making here."

"Oh no, and this might relate to our earlier debate. Right, Priest Cydulean?"

"It could very easily," he nods. "If we are related in some way, they found former members of a much larger society here in our world. And if we look at them, all of them allied together, that world might represent a parent society to ours, especially if we cannot recall our history to remember how we came to be here. They called for these delegations, and regardless of that one managing Rolsklinde, the people apparently saw value in what these people had to offer."

Sumisal lets out a modest chuckle as he listens. Ilothonna glares at him.

"Yes," he muses ironically. "And we call them weak. Well, I think this is changing now."

"Thank you, Priest Sumisal," she retorts. "But yes, you may have a point. This might also reverse some of that damage we caused once."

"But this also brings us back to that statement of interfering with something," Cydulean reflects. "And I believe it was the Suuden-Aryku who used this term. But if this all started when we interfered in something on their world, this is a simple repercussion to that. We sent orcs to a place they were not desired and did so with apparently all the arrogance and rampant belief in our impunity when it was clearly not warranted."

"Oh dear. And someone is upset, but not learning their lesson on the topic."

"Oh, absolutely, Ilothonna. I think anyone could see that, if only they opened their eyes to it. This means someone amongst the hierarchy is demonstrating a considerable lack of proper judgment if they are unwilling to accept responsibility for their actions, and instead blaming it on someone else."

"Exactly. Therefore, if we speak of that agent, or the Suuden-Aryku, whoever it is using these words, these invaders are interfering with something they are trying to accomplish here. For this, we need to consider what they are trying to accomplish that could be interfered with. Um, well, other than this 'surprise' visit by more of the same as our own people, which might be unexpected, I would think…or would it?"

"I might suggest it could be unexpected. Unless these people make it a habit to travel to other worlds and set up colonies."

"Possibly. But if we say it was unexpected in our case."

"If it was unexpected, then it is something else occurring here that they are interfering with. One obvious thing could be the oppression we see occurring around us."

"Oppression? I'm not…sure…" she flusters.

"Yes. Let us examine the individual components. We can say the orcs were likely a threat to the Night Elves. They are down to their last city, and it halted to keep them there…that ulterior motive, whatever it is. This is now oppression."

"Worse, Cydulean," Sumisal adds. "This is a purging effort, to actually take it down, then the oppression to hold it there."

"Indeed, good point."

"Ugh!" Ilothonna screeches. "Purging! That's not a simple war, that's the intentional destruction of things for nothing more than to destroy something!"

"It is," he admits. "And so we could easily say the Night Elves are simply showing appreciation for removing those creatures off their doorsteps."

"All right, this makes sense."

"The Daanen-Aryku are apparently longtime enemies of the Suuden-Aryku, so supporting them could also win favor."

"It could, I suppose. I don't know as much about their history, but offering a defense would speak for itself. And the humans? Allowing them to rummage through those rubbish heaps, probably for iron, would be beneficial. Therefore, to earn favor with the people, even if that agent is unhappy about it."

"And this would certainly represent a detrimental form of management," Sumisal offers.

"It does!" Cydulean affirms. "And that is surely a form of interference. Further, if you consider, they are able to move outside their walls to conduct farming, much the same as the Night Elves. I do not recall this in the past."

"They are rediscovering their freedom..." Ilothonna considers deeply. "And wait...but then, that would mean... But how would this relate to a war of any kind?"

"A war better described as a purging effort, followed by oppression?" Sumisal suggests. "Four centuries, we see this world devastated down to the last few cities, then to stop cold, only to oppress whatever remains. Interference? Yes, that would be interference, if to disrupt that."

"Then our purpose was never to attack?" she grimaces. "We tear down this world to the last few cities and then leave it to those who oppress. The orcs were oppressing the Night Elves, the Suuden-Aryku were oppressing the Daanen-Aryku, and doing so for centuries after they arrived here, and that agent may be oppressing the humans inside their own walls."

"Indeed, this does not build a pretty picture. This is no war in the proper sense of it. It seems more to maintain them for some ulterior motive. Even us, who are told we are at war, but where we never go out and fight. This only keeps us on edge, wondering..."

"Right. And what about us?" she inquires urgently.

"Yes," Cydulean conjectures thoughtfully. "What about us... We're down to the last of our cities after we assisted in wiping everything else out of existence for them to oppress what remains. We behaved like butchers slaughtering animals, spending most of our population in the process, and even more on that war with the dwarves, with no definable result. What about us? Yes, and what about that special mission using the orcs? They make trouble, bring it back here to us, but along the way, those people take up sides to...interfere...with the oppression in this world, bringing benefit to everyone other than those who caused it. What about us? After all, it's OUR world, not the orcs and not the Suuden-Aryku. What about us...all of us, Ilothonna?"

The distressed elder woman gazed at Cydulean wistfully as she began to assemble the pieces.

"Priest Cydulean," she emits worriedly. "Are we actually saying we were used?"

"One way to answer that is to say this world was supposed to be fully populated at one time…or at least mostly so. Now it is not. Worse, those of us who caused it then lost our history to recall the occasion."

"And further," Sumisal offers. "To demonstrate such arrogance and this impudent belief that we were entitled to all that we did, even though we were also made to forget half of it."

"Oh yes! That one stings."

Ilothonna found herself passing her gaze between the two of them as if in a ping-pong match while they debated the issue, with her nerves growing increasingly tense along the way.

Cydulean continues, "Who is to blame here? Us, for one, the orcs for another…but they don't belong here, and neither do the Suuden-Aryku. If you want to be technical about it, they're both invaders, much like these others, and regardless of who they serve. So the question is why they would want this world destroyed in the first place. The only direction for me right now is to go back and ask why Sehnisavain was wandering around outside the safety of the walls. And then, we might need to reflect on that tree again. Curate, did you learn anything about those Night Elves along the way?"

"Oh yes, Priest Cydulean," Eilihel responds emphatically. "And even more! Admittedly, it was very difficult to infiltrate their city, but we had Mynae use a cloak, and she was able to collect our information."

"Hold!" Ilothonna demands. "Inside their city? You actually went inside the city of Solinaia?"

"Yes, First Deacon," Mynae offers. "Unlike around here, they don't seem to practice as much detection magic as we do. I guess they feel pretty confident with their natural camouflage of forested growth."

"Um, wait, I don't quite understand what you mean. I've never been up that way to see it myself."

"Oh, my apologies. Their home city is nestled within a dense forest cover, and apparently, they use this as a form of natural concealment to hide where it actually is. You need to be right on top of it, and perfectly in-line to a secret entrance to find a way in. This, as opposed to ours which is clearly visible for miles around."

"Oh! Really! How interesting. All right, continue."

"When we began to suspect the potential power of this tree in the invader's camp, and then their suspected alliance with Solinaia, we had to ask ourselves if the Night Elves might find value in it. The one in that camp is surrounded by elves quite often, so if it holds such value to elves in general, do the Night Elves have one in their city we could use for comparison, and what role does it hold for them?"

"Good. And what did you discover?"

"Initially, we did not see one in their city, so we figured they did not have one previously."

"Not previously. Interesting."

"But as we returned later, just to recheck our observations, we found they apparently got a new one. A young sapling, much the same as what we see in that camp."

"Ah, and so, do we see an effect of any kind?"

"Well, once we were able to get close enough for our own observation. The streets were packed side to side leading up to it. So, if this is an effect, the whole city wanted to see it and offer whatever respect they give to these things."

Ilothonna gasped, and her eyes bulged at the notion.

"This also suggests a form of knowledge," Eilihel admits. "If they know what it is at all, and the full city wanted to pay respect to it...or whatever, they all know what it is, and this simply has to date back to an earlier form of reckoning."

"Historical, perhaps?" she whispers.

"Oh, I'm pretty sure of it, especially for what we saw later, on another return visit."

"Another one? Just how many are you making up there?"

"Enough to determine this effect, or maybe the relationship over time, to see if there is any form of progression."

"A progression. This is clever. And your result?"

"Initially," Mynae asserts. "I suppose we could say the general ambiance was sullen, like they were just barely living their lives in a bleak environment of depression. And while I think we could possibly attribute some of this to that condition of being oppressed, it seemed to run deeper than simply being boxed up inside their city."

"All right, so could this relate to why we say they are weak?"

"Maybe so. But this doesn't make a lot of sense. First Deacon, we are told that our people once felt a terrible pain of loss, and this is when our Lord came to us to relieve this pain. We are also told the Night Elves are weak for this same reason. Am I right?"

"Yes, these are the lessons we learn. How does this relate to your observations?"

"Well, one thing that comes to mind is to ask what caused the pain in the first place. We apparently felt this pain, but are we saying they felt it as well? And then, they were run down to their last city, only to suggest He has some ulterior motive for what remains. But this still doesn't answer if they felt this pain for the same reason as ours, or is there something else we are missing."

"Um, this is a curious notion, but I suppose you do have a point."

"Whatever the case may be, this tree seems to have corrected it. That next visit, after the tree arrived, saw them perked up and behaving much more like people living pleasant lives. We could surely account for some of this as the orcs being driven away, but this new worship, and a constant flow of it, seems to be empowering them in strange ways. Like they are newly alive."

"And this might relate to that pain, being weak, and this restored them. I see."

"I wonder if this associates in any way with our earlier statements of a relationship," Cydulean notes. "Historical knowledge? From where? The full population knew of these things, which means it is a racial thing, not professional. For instance, to say only limited to a priesthood or some such."

"Likely so," Eilihel nods. "And also not limited to only one society of elves, but perhaps multiple."

"Not…limited…" Ilothonna groans as she lays her hands against her temples to hold back a developing headache.

The elder priestess's face went blank. Even though Sargeras's songs still rushed through her mind, she was becoming dizzy from all these incompatible interpretations.

"If this is the case," Cydulean offers. "Then I must wonder what we might find for ourselves. We do not recall a history here of anything. And it seems none of us are allowed to remember, given how much they buried, or otherwise deny us to ask about."

"Not allowed!" Ilothonna shouts. "Something beneficial to elves, racially known to perhaps all of us, and we're not allowed to recall it?"

"Indeed, Ilothonna," Sumisal adds. "And this naturally begs us to ask where it comes from. Where do we receive all these stories we are told? Where do we receive our attitudes of impunity to destroy things simply for someone to oppress? For instance, are they handed down to us by our ancient ancestors? We have no libraries to teach us. Are they given to us by our immediate forefathers? All we have there is largely more of the same as we speak about within our own."

"That verbal recollection, the only thing that seems to remain. Dammit! I'm starting to hate that. We lost something. Something important, I'll bet."

"And this is starting to narrow it down to that which may be given to us by outsiders. If it is said we once felt this pain of loss, and the suggestion points to a similarity with the Night Elves and their alleged weakness, this may be something that relates to elves in general. And likely it was global."

"Global!" she gushes. "Something to hit that big nation we once had? Ooh!" she scorns.

"Yes. This doesn't sound good for a lot of reasons. And this tree seems to offer a restorative effect, as well as some form of religious significance…hmm…but then… Wait a moment. Of course!"

"What?" Ilothonna wonders.

"Curate, you said you made one more visit up there, right?"

"Yes, Priest Sumisal," she nods. "This came sometime after. We wanted to see how things appeared after the initial dust settled."

"Ah, good. And did you find anything interesting?"

"Oh, we did! Once again, Mynae was able to collect a few whispers here and there, at least until she saw something strange occurring. Mynae?"

"I'm barely able to interpret what I saw," she admits delicately. "Changes of some kind. New things, like construction. And strangers visiting the place, humans, but I don't think they were from Rolsklinde. These had to be more of those newcomers."

"Oh dear," Ilothonna moans. "What are they doing up there now? Could you hear what they said?"

"It was strange in the beginning, but eventually I pulled together enough to understand they have joined the kingdom of that other world, essentially returning to their ancient home."

Ilothonna drew back, aghast at the idea. She clamped her hands around her head and screamed, falling back against the wall.

Eilihel and her team watched, and felt a small note of mischief at seeing the poor woman's fret, but they had to keep their composure. Cydulean and Sumisal also felt a little of their own, but now they had to nail it home.

"Indeed, Curate," Sumisal nods contentedly. "And this might fall in with my thoughts a moment ago. Cydulean? How do you interpret this?"

"Interesting for the informational content. Disturbing for the implications. And also distressing for our own position along the way, where we are and how we got here."

"How we got here?" Ilothonna whimpers.

"A relationship. This might confirm it for us. These are our own people, but from some forgotten parent society our ancestors likely broke away from to form a new colony. Perhaps also forgotten by them as well, if we say it was so long ago, they lost contact with us,"

"Or we them," Sumisal offers.

"Yes, either way, we became separated. This could account for their behavior on their first arrival. They discovered us and reached out to those who would listen. But if any of them explained who we were at the time, which I'm sure was likely the case, especially if you consider the condition of this world, this might exclude us… because we are not a friendly body in this world."

"Not after everything we did to it," Ilothonna winces.

"As for me," Sumisal explains. "If you want to inflict a form of pain, rob away something important. And if that thing you rob away offers this sort of fulfillment, it would surely cause pain. And if it affects elves of any kind, ours might have been included. But this does demand an explanation of why."

"Blast it!" she shouts. "Are you kidding me, Priest Sumisal. Do you actually need to ask that question? Our history is gone. We don't even remember where we came from or how we got to this point, unless someone happened to be alive back then. And then a global wipe of something important to all elves? That sounds like a deliberate assault. Unless you want to tell me, we experienced a disaster of some kind to kill off a bunch of trees we don't seem to remember, but the Night Elves do recall this…"

"Yes, Ilothonna, this would tend to stand out. Further, if we suggest the loss of our history is intentional. A disaster that killed a bunch of odd trees? But did it also burn down all our libraries and such which held all our ancestral wisdom, and yet so conveniently left everything else intact that we could continue on as we are?"

"Yes! This is sabotage! Pure and simple! And who is responsible?"

"Indeed, at this moment, there are not too many directions to point fingers. Neither the orcs nor the Suuden-Aryku were present in our world at that time. And if they are the only 'invaders' who are foreign to us, it had to be something else. For this, I will give you one more thing to groan over. If you want to impose a religion of any sort, custom-made for your purpose, you will first need to remove any and all previous ones, plus whatever other knowledge might conflict with your custom example."

The woman was clearly distressed by now, and getting worse. She glares intensely at the man for his statement.

"You mean to say…" she gasps.

Cydulean paused in clear contemplation of this scenario. He begins pacing around his desk.

"You once mentioned we were used. This appears highly probable, and in a very devious and despicable manner. Then people arrive out of nowhere and offer at least some of us here solutions. And they are described as interfering with something."

"Interfering with that reason we are being used."

"But this also smells of a conspiracy," Sumisal advises. "A stolen religion? We spend our people like water to clean this world for someone to arrive and oppress whatever remained. To what end, I don't know, because they keep us all on edge with stories of a war no one ever fights. One thing is for sure; I do not wish to see the end result if it calls for whatever remains of us to give ourselves up to it."

"Absolutely!" she yelps.

"And then we have Sehnisavain. If she knew of this, but was then abducted, who could be responsible for this? Orcs perhaps, maybe to leave evidence to distract us, but then assisted by the Suuden-Aryku? And who do they follow, Ilothonna? There can be only one name here, and he sits behind all of it."

"Him! Then we're saying he doesn't want us to know, so that he..." her voice trails off.

"...Can manage us," he finishes. "Just like that agent is managing the humans, and we could also say, in a roundabout manner, the others are...managing...everything else. Then the invaders arrive and spoil everything for them. Oh yes, they are surely interfering with something. This whole scenario is a disaster, and we were a part of it, all thanks to him. And yet, we don't even know the full extent of it if our memories are so badly restricted."

Ilothonna can't take any more. She grabs her head and screams in fury.

"Sargeras, you monster!" she wails. "Why are you here? Leave us alone, and get out of my head, you horrid demonic beast!"

Sumisal sighs heavily as the woman undergoes her breakdown.

Cydulean watches, silently admitting the argument was essentially won. This not only proved a point that they could win this battle without taking military action, instead forcing her free will to take back control. Although, he silently asked himself if it would've been easier to just hit her over the head and drag her out, rather than struggle with all this. He stepped up and wrapped an arm around her to comfort the woman in her moment of suffering.

"Someone started something by sending those orcs out on that mission," he declares. "Whatever the reason for that mission, the orcs came back with something unexpected and undesired by the ones demanding it."

Ilothonna pulls her head up to respond.

"Unexpected…by them, at least. But I'll bet the Night Elves remember something, if they also recall those trees. And then, these people don't attack us, even if we send an assassin. They must also remember something, and likely it relates to who we are…or were, before all this happened. And they instead take the battle to those who started the whole thing. Who are these people that fight other people's wars?"

"That's a really interesting question to ask. And it might further relate to the idea of a parent society, if we can be described as children under that."

"Oh, please, I'm a wreck already. No more."

"This clearly requires a closer examination of that tree," Sumisal offers. "It could hold many answers for us, but we are not going to learn anything unless we can get close enough to see it."

"Oh dear," Ilothonna rebukes nervously. "Priest Sumisal, what are you saying? That we go into their camp now? After everything else is said and done?"

"Well, they haven't come down here as yet. So, if we say they know something, either they are biding their time for some reason, or we should make our own move. I seriously doubt there is any reason for them to hold back if they wanted to launch a military strike on us down here. They could've done that a long time ago."

"It may be the only way," Cydulean nods. "Consider this, Ilothonna. Sehnisavain was out there trying to investigate something, perhaps this very same tree. She came from a time before the war… before Sargeras, so she must have possessed knowledge from that earlier moment. This could include a former religion."

"Great... I wish I could've been alive back then, but I was born too late. So, what then?"

"My only advice for you is to seek those answers we are being kept away from. If this is what Sehnisavain was trying to do, you must follow as her next-in-line."

"But what if more orcs come and attack again? Or the Suuden-Aryku..."

"The previous ones were probably sent because she was being so closely monitored at the time. Perhaps she made the mistake of giving a report to the High Commander, or some other reference, and this informed them as to her intentions. We will not make that same mistake."

"All right, I agree. I will not report to the High Commander again...certainly not until I have a firm answer to all of this and know where we stand on it."

"Excellent," he nods, and glances at Eilihel and her team. "We will send you out on horseback, in this case. I will have my scouts accompany you to ensure your safe arrival. I cannot be sure of the reason for this, but apparently Sehnisavain was not riding a horse."

"Actually, I do not recall her travelling much at all, and certainly not on horseback...a carriage sometimes, but not directly on horseback."

"This is certainly a viable answer. Then we should attend to this quickly, before anything else occurs. We will prepare a team of our best horses to leave in the morning."

Thaelyn was just arriving in the tactical office in Firstfall for the morning review.

"My Lord," the General announces. "We have word from Kynesoth."

"We do? And what word is that?"

"Our careful play has yielded results. The Priestess Ilothonna, First Deacon to High Priestess Sehnisavain, is preparing to ride out of the city in the hopes of understanding the inner workings of the mystery of our occupation."

"How interesting," Thaelyn muses. "And also very promising. This simply exemplifies the nature of this link they share with Sargeras, that it can be weakened with only a careful play of words. This is good. Perhaps we can use this to good effect with the remainder of their population. This reminds me, we should check with Priestess Rumoren about that new life-seed we ordered a while back. We will need it if we should hope to give them back a little piece of themselves to aid in their redemption."

"Will you be participating on this occasion?" the General asks. "I would think we should keep ourselves to a low profile on this matter, in case the Suuden-Aryku are observing us. If they should notice you, or any other large envoy travelling down there, it might tip them off that we are attempting to steal their Flame Elves away from them."

"Indeed, and at the same time, we must play this out carefully within the city, no matter how we attend to it, so that we can accomplish our goal and redeem them before the Suuden-Aryku decide to carry them away outside our reach. If the Suuden-Aryku do consider them a valuable tool, we need to rob them of this value. This will ultimately weaken their position, and whatever future use they may have planned."

"But the natural question is how we might perform this without first making a large display of it, and second by protecting ourselves and the High Elves from any repercussions."

"We will need to provide a rapid evacuation plan, likely using mages and portal runes, and drawing the full population through to safety, probably to Tae'Eladar in this case."

"Very good. This takes care of them. Now, how do you think the Suuden-Aryku will react to their disappearance?" the General grins mildly.

"For the moment, I think this may depend largely on how they learn of it. If we can deliver false information through to that High Commander of theirs, we could buy ourselves some time. But in the end, they will probably not be very happy, if they do actually wish to keep them for anything."

"How do you feel today, Ilothonna?" Kerali asks.

"Not much better. I didn't sleep much last night, if at all. I was awake most of the night trying to shut out those songs, but they just keep nagging at me, trying to take me back. It reminds me of when I was young and first heard them. Now I understand what it was. He was forcing his way in back then, and he's doing it again even now."

"I'm sorry for you, but you're not the only one. We all suffered for it. You must now be our salvation. Go, find our answer, and bring it home for us."

"I will," she affirms. "Kerali, you will need to attend to things here in my absence."

"What if the High Commander should call us on that trans-com? What should I say?"

"The High Priestess is resting at home, and I am occupied with an important task…oh, let's say on the other side of town to give an excuse, and you will simply take a message for whatever it is he tells us to do. We'll hope this is enough to keep him until I return."

"All right, let's hope we don't have any surprises along the way. Good luck, Ilothonna."

The Priestess was saddling up on her horse, along with Eilihel and her team, in preparation for a careful, but quick, ride north to the valley to investigate the scene and whatever they hoped to learn of the so-called invaders. Cydulean and Sumisal were staying behind to assist Kerali in managing the affairs of the temple and the city in her absence.

The riders departed from the stables near the western gate, passing through the gate and angling northward. The roadways leading between the cities had long since degraded into dusty trails, some of which were overgrown with vegetation by now, so the ride was mostly overland by whatever means they could muster.

They would maintain a hastened rate of travel, if only to avoid anyone taking notice of them until they might find themselves inside the valley. Once on the other side of the hilly terrain that separated them, they might feel a slight sense of safety, not so much from the invaders, but from the zone of control they maintained from anything else out there.

They crossed fields and rolling hills which climbed higher out of their local territory, keeping a close eye for anything that might be moving other than themselves. It was a warm sunny day with gentle breezes, and the ride actually seemed pleasant for the fresh air and country fragrances.

As midmorning approached, they arrived at the crest of the range of hills separating them from the valley. Ilothonna slowed the group to examine the valley that lay in front of them, with its green pastures and wooded glens. She stared at it in awe.

"Unbelievable," she whispers. "When I was young, I recall my lessons of the local surroundings, and this was described as the Badlands, correct?"

"Yes, it was," Eilihel smiles discreetly. "And still is, I suppose."

"And the Badlands was described as a dry, desert wasteland."

"That's how the stories go, at least."

"But how? What am I looking at right now?"

"This is apparently their work. Do not ask me how, but they did this."

"They hold such power?" she wheezes. "It stretches as far as I can see."

"This is clearly the result of something big. That's all I can say."

"And someone doesn't want us learning of it? Yes, I suppose to learn of this might put a crimp on someone's plans for us."

She coaxes her horse to begin down the slope, followed by Eilihel and the others. They reach the flat prairie at the bottom and kick themselves into a fast trot, hoping to make up for the time it took to go over the rougher terrain on the other side.

"Curate," Ilothonna shouts. "What else can you tell me of these people? We really have no idea what opinion they have of us, friend or foe, despite their lack of aggression in our direction. Surely, they must know of us, and probably that we are associated with the Suuden-Aryku."

"I would imagine they know a lot about us by now. They have been associating with the humans of Rolsklinde, the Night Elves, and the Daanen-Aryku, so one or another of those would likely have told the story by now."

"This doesn't necessarily sound good for a peaceful meeting, especially after that assassin we sent. I have doubts they will be friendly to us. I want you to stay close to me and let me do the talking. We should be ready if we must try to escape, although if they are so powerful, I must ask myself how far we would get."

They sped along the plains, crossing the grassy fields, and dodging among the wooded glens. The fragrances of the valley seemed even more alive than the hillside terrain of their home.

"Do you smell that?" Ilothonna utters warmly. "Have you ever smelled anything like that before?"

Eilihel simply smiled. She was riding behind Ilothonna, so the elder priestess didn't see it, but Eilihel glanced at Mynae as the scouting team understood the nature of the living essences rising up from the valley.

They continued along, feeling motivated to hurry forward. Soon, they began to catch a glimpse of the village ahead. At first, it was only peeking through the trees, but as it came into fuller view, Ilothonna felt a sudden urge to halt. Her inherent uncertainty at seeing what was still considered an unknown invading force was playing on her mind.

She and the others stood stationary on the grassy field just barely in view of the settlement, a team of four horse riders, standing at a distance and studying the strangely foreign bustle of activity ahead. She glanced at her escort, hoping to find support and the courage to continue forward. Eilihel gazes back at her and nods gently.

Ilothonna returns to the scene ahead and coaxes the animal to walk the rest of the way in, preferring to take the final advance slow and easy in order to test the waters before jumping in completely.

"My Lord," shouts a guard into the tactical office. "We have riders coming up from the south, four of them."

"Indeed, are we expecting any guests from that direction?" he jests.

Thaelyn gets up from the table and strolls over to the doorway. He stops and peers outside towards the southern gate.

"We will treat them as with any other visitor. Have the guards at the gate allow them in after the customary review. Keep our people in a relaxed posture. We do not wish to frighten or otherwise disturb them unnecessarily."

"Aye!" the guard replies and rushes off.

"My Lord," the General begins as he joins Thaelyn at the door. "This is a moment of truth we see here. If this works out well for us, we will have solved one of our fronts without any battle at all."

"Yes, and what a pleasant outcome that would be. But we must still proceed carefully."

Ilothonna studied the activity in the settlement as they continued their slow approach. She watched with bated breath as the guards at the gate took notice of their imminent arrival.

"Slow and easy," she mutters softly. "Take it slow."

As they moved closer, she started to feel something strange inside her. She instinctively brought a hand up to her forehead.

"Do you feel that...anyone? I feel a little strange."

"Could it be the stress of being out here?" Eilihel responds innocently. "Remember how you felt yesterday."

"Yes, but this is different, I think."

"Maybe... Wait, could it be that tree?"

"The tree...is it doing something to us?"

"Well, if you consider they treat it like a holy item, and if we suggest this to mean it holds power of some sort. And then to say it might be specific to elves in some way. Perhaps this is a proximity thing, and we're feeling that power by now."

"Do we continue or turn back?"

"Our purpose is to learn, is it not? If we turn back, we will learn nothing."

"Yes, you're right, I'm just feeling..." she flusters. "It's confusing me."

"If I may," Mynae offers. "A thought comes to me. You are fighting Sargeras's songs right now. If he wants you so badly, and our purpose is to find that tree right now..."

"But of course!" she emits faintly. "That monster wants us to go back home. We have to push forward...to escape from him..."

"And this simply reinforces the idea. That pain of loss. What if it relates to the tree?"

"The tree? But I don't understand how a tree...a simple tree... or is it so simple..."

The four riders had finally come to the gate, and the guards waved them to a halt, where they began the customary inspection.

"They're checking us," Ilothonna states cautiously. "All right, I suppose this should be expected. Village or no, it still seems largely military by all these soldiers around here."

The guards finish their review and then wave to the riders to dismount. Ilothonna was feeling rather vulnerable at this moment, but she forced herself to comply. Eilihel and the others followed suit and joined by her side.

"Excuse me, guard," Ilothonna tries speaking to them.

The guard waves his hand and speaks in an unknown language to the elves, then parts an opening and waves them to enter inside the gate.

"They don't speak our language," Ilothonna notes. "This is going to be hard. How do we speak to them if we don't share a common tongue?"

"Someone must know it," Eilihel suggests. "If they're able to speak to the others up north, someone must've learned."

"All right, then we must find that person...but how?"

"I would hazard to guess they'll find us soon," Mynae offers.

The four elves strolled along slowly through the village. Many eyes were on them, making Ilothonna feel even more nervous. She was now deep inside a camp of invaders, and surrounded on all sides by a lot of strange people, many of whom were soldiers. And to top it all off, she was feeling even dizzier. She raised both hands to her forehead and felt herself wobbling a bit. Eilihel came to her side to support her.

"You don't feel that as much as I do," she notes of the younger priestess.

"I feel many things right now, but perhaps your age and your time spent in service has conditioned you with a stronger sense of his songs. If the tree is conflicting with that, then you might feel it a bit more than I in my young service."

"Conflicting…such an interesting term to use…"

"I suppose so. If this tree represents something we lost, and he replaced it with his own, I might suspect the two would conflict."

Ilothonna paused in contemplation of the younger priestess's words. It was beginning to make sense to her. She looked around the village to find the tree they were speaking of, and found a large circle filled with several tan-skinned elves in strange organic coverings, standing near a young sapling.

"There…" she mumbles and points feebly. "Are we allowed to just walk up to it?"

"I don't see anyone trying to stop us."

The group ambles forward, with Ilothonna leading the way, though just barely.

Thaelyn watched from the doorway of the tactical office as the Priestess and her entourage moved in the direction of the tree. He decides now is the time to make his greeting. He steps out into view and makes a casual approach.

Ilothonna and the others quickly took notice of the tall nobleman in his ornate armor and royal attire, coming in for a meeting.

"Good greetings to you, visitors," he announces pleasantly. "My name is Lord Thaelyn. May I know the pleasure of your acquaintance?"

Ilothonna stares into his golden eyes. She studies the unusual color, almost becoming lost in it.

"I'm, uh… I'm…" she tries to shake off her dizziness. "Please forgive me. I'm feeling, um, a little disoriented right now. You speak our language. Good... I was becoming worried over..." she feels another swoon, "...over who we were supposed to speak to here. My name is Priestess Ilothonna, First Deacon to... Well, it might not matter anymore, we've lost her. But, um, before I continue, I need to ask..."

She feels another wobble coming on and pauses to catch her breath as she was feeling even more disoriented as time passed.

"You do not appear well, Priestess," Thaelyn observes. "Perhaps you should sit down. Where did you just now come from? We do not normally see visitors coming up from our south."

"No, I suppose not. We're, um...we're from the city of Kynesoth."

"Kynesoth? How curious..." he feigns innocently. "We are told of that particular city belonging to a society that calls itself Flame Elves, as unpleasant as that name sounds to our ears."

"It sounds unpleasant to you?"

"Well, I should say it does. We have many societies of elves in our world, and they take a variety of names for themselves, but this one defies their usual manner for the conventions."

"Really! What other names do they have?"

"Well now, let us see..." he surveys the camp conspicuously. "We have seven main clans of elves. They are all part of a mother race we describe as Tel'Quessir. Their clan names often depict certain qualities of their appearances or preferential modes of living. For instance, we have Wood Elves, like those over by the tree," he casually points at the circle. "We have a pair that have been known to take different names over the years, some call them the Gold and Silver, for their approximate skin tones, and others describe them as the Sun and Moon clans, as a form of colloquialism for their habitats."

"That's strange. How do the habitats differ?"

"The Sun Elves prefer hot arid regions, while the Moon Elves take colder, perhaps even icy regions. It is largely a form of diversification to distribute their population over a broader area."

"Really!"

"Then, we have one that is apparently a distant relative to the Night Elves here in this world..."

"What?" she blurts. "You have Night Elves in your world?"

"Well, we do not use that name for the body we have back home. They actually take another name, but they stem from the same ancestral kin, once known as a clan called the Ssri."

"Ancestral kin? But is that to say the Night Elves originally came from your world?"

"Yes, they did. It was a time of migration for many of the elven races, although those of us on our world did not know of this continued migration of your societies. We only learned of this once we arrived here."

"Wait! Our society? Us? My people also came from your world? When was this?"

"This would count on the order of, oh…many thousands of years ago. We had a discussion once with one of them that referenced a local historical event on our side, and this helped us to orient the timing."

"Oh! Really! So we can reference a historical thing on your side, and this would simply confirm a point of origin for us on this side? How typical!" she intones firmly. "And here we don't even recall what we did a few centuries ago."

"We have seen a number of occasions of lost history occurring here, so this would not surprise me."

"I doubt it could be anything as bad as ours. What name do we use over there?"

"Your kind is known as the Cala clan, commonly known as High Elves. And in fact, the Night Elves tell us you continued to use this name right up until this Sargeras took you into his possession."

"Took us…into…possession…" she mumbles and begins toppling over.

Eilihel had been trying to support her, but now Mynae came up on the other side. Thaelyn also leaned in to offer assistance.

"Priestess, you are not at all well," he mentions subtly. "I do think you should sit down."

"That tree…" she murmurs. "We heard of it here…scouts… And the Night Elves…home…"

"You are referring to the sacred Tree of Life, I presume. Yes, this is a sacred item for all elves."

"All elves? What is it?"

"You do not know what the Tree of Life is?"

"No…never heard that name… But we were talking…back home…trying to understand…" she shakes her head to refocus herself. "These people here are scouts, just returned from a long run, trying to learn something. They managed to observe a few things, and we were putting together a few pieces. You say it holds meaning to all elves, meaning us too?"

"It should. It is an ancestral part of elven tradition, sacred to all elves and part of their heritage from your ancient home world, where your kind originated. It is a link to the natural world around you. Your kind holds a rather unique bond with nature, and the tree is the essence that binds you. Without it, you tend to feel lost, perhaps even empty. This is how we found the Night Elves, by the way, so we replaced their tree for them."

"Replaced it? What happened to the previous one?"

"It was killed four centuries ago, when we believe agents of Sargeras first arrived in this world."

Now Ilothonna collapses fully to the ground and starts wailing loudly. Her panicked screams filled the settlement.

"That monster!" she shouts. "Of course! And this simply confirms it! How despicable! What else can you tell me about this? You first arrived here, made contact with the others…um…"

"They told us about you, naturally. This long war, the destruction. Every elven city apparently had these trees once upon a time, it is part of your ancestral traditions, which you apparently maintained during this time."

"Every city? Meaning us as well. Yes, naturally, and so we have that pain of loss hitting us. But why do you behave as you do with us? You don't attack, not even after we sent an assassin up here. Um…I mean…well, you do know of that, right? We're told it came in, but was killed."

"Oh yes, we know of it. It was a bit surprising, but we already knew of Sargeras by then, and suspected you were likely taken by him. Your kind would not likely follow one such as he willingly. Elves have their own pantheon of gods, and clearly, he would want to violate that and replace it with his."

"Oh! We have our own native gods as well? Yes. This would add insult to injury, I'm sure."

"More than you might think. Therefore, we suspected the assassin was engineered, and not necessarily by you. As such, we held back, hoping to find another way around it."

"I see. Then I beg you to help me now," she blubbers. "His voice is in my head, and I can't get it out!"

"Yes, this is what we were worried about. It's a form of telepathic domination. Such a creature as he might try using this. Come, you need to visit the tree. It will heal you. It can restore your sense of harmony again, and shut his wailings out."

Thaelyn and the others picked Ilothonna off the ground and began walking her to the tree. Her feet dragged along as Thaelyn and Eilihel pulled her across to the circle. Several druids came to assist further to carry the woman inside the circle.

As soon as Ilothonna felt the ground under her, she began to feel the sensation of the spiritual energies wafting up into her body. She buckled to the ground from the unexpected rippling effect of the nurturing embrace.

"What's happening to me?"

"Priestess," Thaelyn responds calmly. "Although this tree is still quite young, the energies it possesses are quite potent. It carries a powerful healing aura. This circle is regarded as holy ground by elven traditions. Within this space, you can feel the spirit of the tree itself. And yes, before you say it, this one does have a spirit. This is why it is regarded as sacred to all elves, no matter who you are or where you come from."

"How is that possible…a tree?"

"It is not a simple tree, as you may find in so many other places. It is a remnant of your ancient home world. It is said that all things there can feel one another through these spiritual links. Furthermore, if it is suddenly taken away from you, as if to say killed, you would feel a deep spiritual loss and a form of pain. And apparently, four centuries ago, someone came along in this world and did exactly this…to all your elven cities, as each of them had one present."

"All of us? And so, that pain…it was him, wasn't it!" she blasts feebly. "He did this intentionally! And then he destroyed our history, so we don't even remember."

"That would certainly be an effective way to replace yours with his," he nods. "Here…" he points at the trunk. "If you touch the tree itself, you will feel its presence, and then you will understand. It will reunite you back to where you belong, like all elves should be. The Night Elves already found theirs, and everyone back home enjoys the same."

Ilothonna cranes her head around to look at the tree. The druids had brought her within arm's reach. She struggled to reach forward and touch it. Her hand trembled as she stretched it at length, finally laying her fingers on the trunk. She held it there, and a soft whispering came into her mind, soothing her thoughts and replacing the songs of Sargeras with the gentle melodies of nature. She felt sleepy and sagged to the ground.

Thaelyn sighed deeply after watching her retreat into her recuperative sleep.

"Well, that went well enough, I suppose. But I do hope the others can be brought around without as much discomfort."

"I would tend to think otherwise, Your Lordship," Eilihel admits. "We might see many more like this."

"Then we have much work ahead of us. But at least this is a start, a proof of concept."

Chapter 6

REDIRECTED INTENTS

It is later in the day when Ilothonna awakens from her slumber. She feels groggy and somewhat disoriented, but the experience was not as severe as with the others during their turn. Her memories are already beginning to return when she hears a soft voice speaking to her.

"Priestess?"

She pulls herself up into a reclining position and blinks several times, trying to focus on the shape of a young priestess sitting in front of her.

"Curate, is that you?"

"Yes, Priestess," Eilihel responds calmly. "How do you feel?"

"I feel… I'm not quite sure. I feel rested, a little sluggish… My mind seems to be spinning, but it's getting better."

Ilothonna glances around cautiously at the other people in her immediate view, including several druids. She finds herself struggling to recall where she was and why she was here.

"We're in that camp, which is more like a village, as I recall."

"Yes, Priestess, we're still here. You are just now waking up by the tree. It's healed you. You're back to being a High Elf again…

or perhaps I should say for the first time, since I doubt you would know what it was to begin with."

"Why do you say that?"

"Because, like most of us, you were born into a society governed by the songs of that beast named Sargeras, and he made our people into what we now call Flame Elves."

"Flame Elves…High Elves, right… I'm starting to remember a conversation with someone. Our people…"

"We come from their world, originally. Our early ancestors, along with the Night Elves, and a band of humans, migrated to this world long ago, and then became lost, it would seem. It was all we had to form our own society and try to keep our memories alive of our heritage and ancient traditions. Then he came along and ruined it."

"Why?"

"The 'why' is a bit uncertain, other than to say he likes playing with small creatures like us as toys. He seems to have a larger motive, however, and this is a bit troubling, when you look at where we are, and what could be ahead of him."

"And why is that?"

"We have come to at least one conclusion, and that is he seems to be using this world as a jumping off point, collecting his playthings all in one basket before moving ahead. And where he seems to be moving, for whatever crazy reason, is in the direction of that secret mission by those orcs. This, in itself, cannot be a good thing, as we are told he originally came from there, and has enemies who live there now."

"Right, that would be a bad thing, I think. It might suggest a motive against them. Either that, or a suicide move," she chuckles.

"Absolutely!" she smiles softly. "Meanwhile, he is known as a tyrant and a monster that holds very little regard for life on our scale. Do you recall our discussions back in the temple about the war and our role in it?"

"Um, I remember orcs, then Suuden-Aryku, conflicts of our orders, these invaders supporting the others…the Night Elves and a tree…something about managing us…yes, and spending our people on so many wars that we're down to the last."

"Good, you remember. But now, Priestess, I need to confess something to you, and I wish you to hear me out before yelling at me, and arguing that I did something wrong."

"All right, I'm listening. What is it?"

"First, I'm not a special agent working for an archpriest in some secret service no one knows about. In truth, there really is no such thing as an archpriest in our service. This was a small lie to give an excuse for what we needed to accomplish down there."

"And what is it you're trying to accomplish?"

"We're trying to save our people from that monster and his songs."

Ilothonna stares at the younger priestess for a moment, only now beginning to realize she no longer heard his songs in her mind, and instead felt a strangely serene sensation of fulfillment that ran much deeper than his songs ever did. She glances down at herself and raises a hand to examine it, then briefly studies the tree again before returning to Eilihel.

"What actually happened to me, Curate? Why do I feel this way, can you explain?"

"I could, but perhaps I should allow another to explain, as she comes from a time before Sargeras, and carries our old history with her."

"And who is that?"

Eilihel now points over Ilothonna's shoulder. The Priestess finds herself impulsively following the direction, thereby turning to look behind her. For a moment, she couldn't be sure if she could believe her eyes, but the moment broke almost as quickly as it set in.

"Sehnisavain!" she shouts.

Ilothonna lurches forward and embraces the elder woman in a tight hug.

"My dearest sister, I thought you were dead. What happened? Let me look at you. Are you injured?" she glances along the woman's length to examine her. "What about those orcs, did they harm you?

And wait, what are you doing here? Did these people rescue you somehow?"

"Ilothonna," she smiles softly. "Will you allow me a moment to actually speak? First, you need to understand a few things about what is truly occurring here. There were never any orcs. I was brought up here by the tree."

"The tree?" she takes another look at it. "How do you mean that?"

"Surely by now, you understand the tree is not just another stick of wood. This one holds a very special kind of spirit called a dryad. But this tree is very young, so the spirit is comparatively weak. These people around us are druids, priests of nature, and specifically aligned to speak to the spirit. They combined their songs with that of the spirit to lure me out of the city and up here for cleansing."

"Cleansing?"

"Yes, this is how I might describe it, for lack of a better way. I was once a caretaker of a shrine we had in our city with a tree like this. Ours was a fully mature grove with the mother tree and six daughters, and they gave our people the fulfillment of our ancestral origins. All the elven cities had this, both the High Elves and the Night Elves. Then, four centuries ago, someone came and killed all of them, stealing away from us that which made us who we were."

"The loss..." Ilothonna muses.

"At the same time, we also held a set of holy symbols representing our true gods, the gods of the elven nations known as the Seldarine, and these were stolen from us. These two events occurred at the same time and caused our people to fall into such despair that Sargeras and his blasphemous songs could take control of us."

"The pain, and then his...alleged...rescue," her face begins to flush. "So, what you're saying is he robbed us in order to take control of us, and spend our people like water under a bridge to fight his wars?"

"And not simply that, but his kind are ancient enemies to those like our ancestral gods."

"They're ancient enemies?!" she shrieks. "How insufferable! And what about the Suuden-Aryku?"

"The Daanen-Aryku were once part of that society. They tell us he apparently came to their world and promised some great power in return for their service. The Daanen-Aryku escaped in the hopes of evading him, but the rest apparently accepted this offer, and we believe he turned them into some manner of servant race."

"And they now issue his commands to the rest of us," she scorns. "Spending us to serve his sacrilegious designs."

Ilothonna turns around to glare at Eilihel, and then the others in her team who were all gathered around the tree.

"What was this you were saying about a little lie to save our people?"

"Priest Cydulean and Priest Sumisal are secret agents from Lord Thaelyn," Eilihel replies. "Cydulean is actually a high-ranking mage in his military Order, and Sumisal is one of his priests. They are both High Elves from his world, sent to infiltrate our city and try to gain some leverage to bring us out of Sargeras's management. As for our roles," she glances at Mynae and Kethron. "We were indeed stationed at an outpost south of our city, but we are simple scouts that were patrolling our immediate area, nothing more."

"Then how did you come to be here?"

"We were captured. It was a surprise hit. They took us with hardly any trouble, by the sound of it. That assassin you sent drew their attention. They were avoiding a fight with us, hoping to deal with the orcs first, and then moving to us later. Lord Thaelyn knew that as High Elves, we should not behave as we did as Flame Elves. He did not wish to attack us outright, instead to find the reason for our betrayal to our true gods. The assassin simply prompted him to take action sooner rather than later, since it was obvious you were taking action against him."

"I recall something about him and that assassin…not engineered by us, and looking for another way around it. And he took his fight elsewhere. He must be a very savvy individual to understand all this."

"We could easily say that with the rest of our people as part of his nation, he might feel an obligation to see us returned, much like the Night Elves. Beyond that, he is also a Child of those same gods we are meant to worship."

Ilothonna gaped at the suggestion. Her mouth fell open and she let out a long wheeze.

"Are you actually serious with that statement?"

"Yes, his kind is known as Celestials, half something like us, and half Estelar, which is the name of this society of gods."

"Estelar…and these gods are enemies to Sargeras?"

"He and his kind, yes… They were once known as Primordials. The Estelar found them conducting such atrocities as what we're seeing here, and they were punished. Destroyed, mostly, but Sargeras apparently escaped. Now Thaelyn is hunting him."

"Oh, dear… And what about us, our people, he wants to help us, right?"

"He does," Eilihel nods. "And did from the beginning, but he needed to understand us first. Our team was captured and interrogated to understand why we serve Sargeras, for as much as we had to offer. Then he went after Sehnisavain, once he had a name to go by, and used the tree in her case since she was so deeply buried inside the city. Rather than sending his own spies to simply abduct her, he used the tree to call her out. He then used his spies to deliver a ruse placing the blame on the orcs for her disappearance. This would spark a careful controversy about who our friends and enemies are out there."

"Incredible. This guy is dangerous even without a military."

"Kerali was also abducted, using a portal rune to evacuate her from the basement, then returned later after she had been cleansed, and now she works for him as well."

"Really!" she winces. "This is frightening. He's able to steal people away, and then send them back with a new purpose? No wonder someone describes him as interfering with something. But how does he hope to do the rest?"

"There were two general possibilities in discussion. A military movement to conquer our city, which I think, for these people, would not be too difficult. But it would probably make a mess, and the Suuden-Aryku would likely take notice. We didn't want that. The other is more discreet, to see if we could invoke the people to realize the nature of the situation and fight these songs. If Sargeras's influence can be broken by the power of free will, much like in your example, and if even for a brief time, we could redeem the people, and no one will know a thing."

"That…is very clever," she muses thoughtfully. "Although mine was quite a struggle."

"Maybe, but it gives us a chance to redeem ourselves, I think. And you are living proof of it. We had to test this theory, and you became our test subject. I hope you're not angry, but you did serve a very important role for us…all our people."

"Really! Hmm, well, under these conditions, I will refrain from the yelling and arguing of wrongdoing. In fact, between all of you, that was a very complex game you played. But now, what about the Suuden-Aryku? How would we manage converting away from Sargeras and no longer following their instructions?"

"Until this war is fully resolved," Sehnisavain surmises. "We will need to play a game on them from this point."

"And this, um, Lord Thaelyn? No one seems to be attacking him around here. Do we know why? Could it be because he's half god?"

"He is not letting on who he is in this world, other than what is apparent, and keeping the rest a secret in the face of his enemies. But one possible reason for no attacks is because his people make such extensive use of portals. So attacking him would be futile, as more would come. And these people apparently do not take no for an answer."

"Whoops! Yes, that would be a problem."

"Rather, I suspect it may be that creature…" she grimaces. "The one who gives so many of these orders is playing a game on him. If we reflect on this aspect of playing with toys, he may consider Lord Thaelyn as one of them. I heard recently of something occurring up in Rolsklinde which could be his next move in the making, but I dare not think of what it could be. Meanwhile, as for our people, we will need his help, and we should offer ourselves to his service to assist."

"Good, then I'll help you. I just need you to tell me what to do."

Ilothonna pauses as she collects her thoughts. She glances fondly again at her sister, but then another thought comes to her, and she begins looking around the settlement.

"By the way, Sehnisavain, where are the girls?"

"Oh, yes, Tyshalis and Rhyvanith are both in their world, in their home city of Bya'an Tamoranth. They are taking up studies with Lady Aerlie on our culture and religion."

"Are they alright? Who is this Lady Aerlie?"

"They are both doing well, but the poor young things have so much to learn. That beast not only stole our people, but he also denied us to maintain any of our native heritage and wisdom. As for Lady Aerlie, she is Lord Thaelyn's wife and queen."

"Queen...?" she gasps. "Meaning to say he is a king? We sent an assassin to kill a king?!" she shrieks.

"Of the full world of Tae'Eladar..." Sehnisavain adds.

"Of an entire world?!" she screeches. "In the name of...um...in the name of... What name should I be using here?"

Sehnisavain smiles amusingly.

"I might recommend calling out the Protector for this one."

"Good, thanks. In the name of the Protector...whoever that is... what did those orcs bring back to us?"

"Our salvation..."

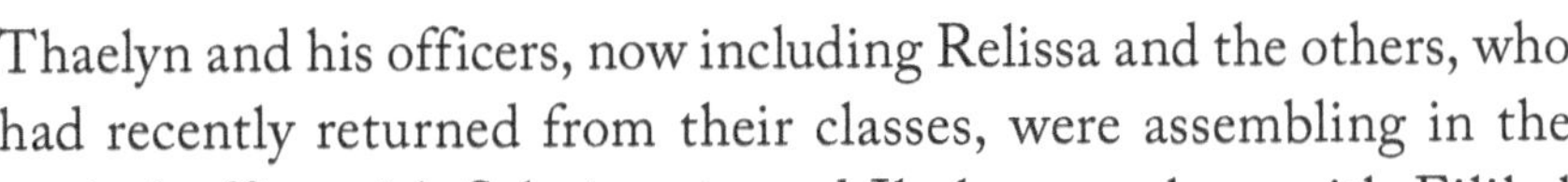

Thaelyn and his officers, now including Relissa and the others, who had recently returned from their classes, were assembling in the tactical office with Sehnisavain and Ilothonna, along with Eilihel and her team.

"So, you are her sister?" Thaelyn asks.

"Yes, Your Grace," Ilothonna submits politely. "But younger by a century."

"And yet you were still born after Sargeras arrived."

"Yes, I believe it was not long after."

"It is rather interesting to learn of these timelines, but also disturbing for the ramifications."

"Aye," Relissa accedes. "You're real lucky to have each other after all this, but it's a crying shame you didn't get a chance to know who you're supposed to be."

"Yes, I understand," Ilothonna admits. "Most of our surviving population is probably in this condition by now. I think my sister is the only remaining elder member that still recalls our society that came before."

"Indeed," Thaelyn continues. "And therefore, her memories become invaluable. I wonder if you might still hold any written documentation."

"I know we have a number of old boxes in the basement," Sehnisavain recalls. "There might be something in there. We used to have a library, but unfortunately it was razed after we were taken and driven to remove our old identity."

"This in itself is tragic. Knowledge is a valuable commodity, and I am sure you had a lot of it."

"Yes, I do recall many historical records of our arrival and the time we spent here. I spoke to Amariyn about this once, and she said her husband is a historian. The library they have up there probably holds many of the same records. We did try to share this, to the best of my knowledge."

"Good, if we have this much, it can help to correct for the loss."

"It's more than what we have," Marelle relents. "This much is for sure, after the Governor and the Dean had their way with us."

"Perhaps we can see about distributing some of this for better coverage."

"When I was speaking to Amariyn," Sehnisavain reflects. "I was trying to refresh myself on some of our old history, as part of my own rehabilitation. She mentioned the first of what apparently turned out to be five Crown Wars in your world. My goodness, what history we had over there!"

"Yes, there were many such moments occurring between the nations."

"Her husband became curious about this, and he began a careful review to cross-reference these moments between their library and yours. She tells me he had every old book in the room piled up on the floor and every table," she chuckles.

"Aye!" Relissa smiles. "That's my Dah!"

"She mentioned a finding in an old journal made by one of the early expeditioners. These are apparently the last few notes we have on the history carried from Sein'amar to this world. It documents their travels using some sort of portal created by a most unusual form of relic."

"Oh? This is interesting," Thaelyn notes. "Aerlie and I were once asking about this. How did your people find their way to this world? First, you are in a different universe. How might you even find such a place to aim a portal at?"

"I personally wouldn't know the mechanics of something like that, but according to Amariyn, this old journal spoke of a cave in a northern range of mountains. Inside, they found a stone carving, like an archway to a door, but simply embedded in a wall and surrounded by strange runic glyphs."

"An archway to a door..." he muses. "This might resemble an archaic runic portal aperture. I wonder where it could be located."

"The journal went on to say the expedition leader had found an artifact of some sort that caused it to come alive."

"Really!"

"Great gods," the General intones. "That one must be truly ancient in its design, and likely by a much higher power."

"Indeed, but what is it doing on Tae'Eladar?"

"Do you recognize this depiction?" Sehnisavain wonders.

"Those of us amongst the Outer Planes might refer to such devices as doors in places like Sigil and other locations out there. They often require what we call keys, which could be an item or a gesture, a spoken word, or some such, to activate them. But I find it highly unusual to find one in a world like Tae'Eladar, so now I must wonder how it got there and who built it."

"Interesting... Well, whatever the case, the expedition included the original team members, which were representatives of each of our races here, along with many caravans of goods, to help establish us in our new homes. The man who wrote this said they were motivated by this inspirational leader who came to them speaking of fresh new lands to escape from the tragedy of our recent war, as well as the new arrival of what he called man-beasts in the land."

"Man-beasts? This is a curious term. What could he be describing here?"

"My Lord," the General offers. "Maybe if we were to reflect on our own history a moment to see what might fit this description. This was around the time of the first Crown War, correct? How long ago was that?"

"It would have been, oh…" he leans back and reflects on the old Tae'Eladaran history, "…very nearly ten millennia by now, I think. We had the arrival of several of the elven societies by then. And I believe the dwarves were present…"

As they collectively pondered the idea, the General suddenly had a flash.

"Oh dear…and… Great Gods!" he gushes. "An arrival! The orcs! That first invasion!"

Thaelyn instantly perked up at the mention. He glared urgently at the General before returning to Sehnisavain. The rest of the group took quick notice of this association.

"Oh jiggers," Relissa moans. "Here we go again. And you said ten millennia?"

"Indeed!" Thaelyn groans. "I do not like this, General. And how, in all Creation, did a band of wayward travelers find their way to a world we are now standing on, due again to those very same orcs?"

"My Lord," he offers. "This could not be any sort of coincidence here. And I am also reminded of the Daanen-Aryku right now. They made that so-called wild jump to this region, did they not?"

"They did, but are we now saying that strange portal that should not otherwise be on Tae'Eladar was placed there intentionally to lead these people here for some later purpose?"

"Flaming Buggers!" Relissa shouts. "We were planted here on

purpose?! Gods above, this world is becoming a mighty unfriendly place to live."

"Well..." Marelle emits distantly. "This would explain why everyone is gathering around here lately. Sargeras must be using it as a jumping off point and making a lot of long-term plans for it."

"This man, the leader of that expedition," Thaelyn muses. "What became of him? Who was he, where did he come from, where did he ultimately go, and what was this key he used? We need to see about that portal and make a close inspection of it. But if this was yet another agent of Sargeras, he must have known of this world as well, and further of Tae'Eladar to deliver those orcs and to build that portal. And these people would be his future focus for whatever purpose he has here."

"This further implies their inherent value," the General suggests.

"And naturally, this further demands us to take that value away from him."

The sudden tensions had drawn the two High Elves closer to the table as they oversaw the conversation.

"Your Grace," Sehnisavain begins. "If that creature has such desires for us, even back then, this cannot be good for whatever purpose he ultimately holds for your world, or whatever else is around it. We should remember those orcs and that mission."

"Yes, and this clearly must represent his purpose for returning. Meanwhile, we must undermine his capacity here, and this brings us back to the remainder of your people."

"Um, right," Ilothonna interjects. "So, how do you suggest giving aid to our people if he holds so much interest over us?"

"First and foremost," he asserts. "We have been preparing a life-seed for you. This will replenish your shrine with a new tree. But before we can proceed with this, we need to prepare the soil. The Night Elves had to do the same, and they spent a fair amount of time digging out and replacing the old soil from the previous tree with fresh filling. Now it is your turn."

"All right, I'm sure we can do this."

"I might further recommend we expedite this somewhat, as we

have a full city of people that need to be redeemed, and I feel time is against us if the Suuden-Aryku should desire to put you to another task. I would imagine, as we press forward in our war efforts, they will become increasingly impatient with our involvement…or perhaps I should say our interference, as Sehnisavain once described it, with their operations."

"What do you think they might do, under those conditions?"

"This is a good question. We have not come under any direct attack, and for this we are suspecting they are either studying us for our methods, or perhaps fearful of us for our tactics, including our use of portals. This could be the reason for your assassination attempt to remove me as the primary influence of our military, and possibly to disrupt my rule for other forms of espionage. We think they may be preparing another attempt up in Rolsklinde, but so far, we are unsure of what to expect out of it."

"Just out of curiosity," Ilothonna reflects while cautiously glancing at Eilihel. "Would any such attempt as this be a serious concern for you…um, you know, because of…" she briskly rolls her eyes up and raises her brow intriguingly.

Thaelyn senses her meaning and grins pleasantly.

"If made by mortal hands, likely not… I have had more than any man's share of that during my lifetime on Tae'Eladar while we worked to bring the various nations together. And I have seen even more by even greater foes in my time back home in the Outer Planar regions."

"I'm not actually familiar with that reference, but I'll guess by the things said before that I probably don't want to know," she chuckles weakly.

"Indeed!" he smiles. "Now, as for the Suuden-Aryku, we have considered the prospect that they might be saving the last of you for some purpose. They are not spending you on any outward attacks, save for that one assassin, and it could very well be that you might hold value for other objectives. For instance, the Suuden-Aryku do not seem to be familiar with the practice of magic, but you would. This in itself is value."

"Under these circumstances, would you have us join you in your war efforts? I, for one, would love to get back at them for all the suffering they caused us."

"You and perhaps a great many others, but this is not a wise course of action at this time, for reasons not the least of which being your small numbers. I would much prefer to protect you and remove you from their reach. The Suuden-Aryku are likely just another minion race. It is Sargeras we must focus on. The rest are merely standing in our way. But given their reckless behavior, and the devastation we are seeing in this world, I do not wish to see any more loss."

"I understand," she sighs. "All right, so our first goal is to redeem our people. Then what? If we are to be removed from their reach, where do we go?"

"I will offer temporary occupancy on Tae'Eladar, at least until we can secure the situation here. The practice we have observed so far with Sargeras, and his minions, seems to be to destroy whatever they do not wish to control, and reduce the rest down to that which is easily managed. Rolsklinde, for example, with the Governor who is presumably managing it on behalf of the Suuden-Aryku, and your people reduced down to your last city. Solinaia is essentially the same idea, though they do not seem to have anyone so closely managing it."

"They're keeping it in reserve after us, probably."

"Perhaps, but no longer, as they have joined us in our kingdom by now, so whatever plan Sargeras had for it will now have to go through me."

"I heard something about this," Ilothonna muses thoughtfully. "Eilihel and her team. But we're on a completely different world from you."

"I keep my doors open for all those who can follow our principles and cultural beliefs. And at this point, it should not be limited to distance."

"And you also have High Elves in that, right?"

"All the elven races of Tae'Eladar are included, save for one which tends to be very hostile."

"Which one is that?"

"The cousins of the Night Elves, known as Drow. They became violent in our early history, also due to those Crown Wars, and turned against the rest. Since then, they have been driven into their own pockets and have been smoldering ever since. One day, I suppose we will need to find a solution to this, but they tend not to listen to any form of exchange."

"How interesting, but if the Night Elves could join, how would you feel about our people?"

"Yours would be welcome, but you will also need to undergo a considerable amount of rehabilitation to understand the history of your society."

"Right, of course…"

"But for now, our work demands us to return you back to your people, along with Sehnisavain, and begin preparing your shrine. You will have your work cut out for you in directing your people back into a proper alignment, and once the tree is planted, you will begin a systematic redemption process. I can loan you our druidic high priestess and some number of her attendants to assist. But we must move as quickly as we can to have your people ready before the Suuden-Aryku get any new ideas for you."

"And especially that creature who describes himself as their leader," Sehnisavain scorns. "He is the worst of it."

"Perhaps, but let us keep ourselves to what is within our reach for now."

Thaelyn gets up from the table and directs the group outside. He calls the druidic high priestess and relates his instructions. He also sends word for additional horses to be delivered from Tae'Eladar.

"Sehnisavain, can you ride a horse?" he asks.

"I cannot ever recall riding one before," she replies. "Most of my travels tend to be in a carriage around town. In fact, I've not been outside the walls since all this began."

"Do you think you could do so on this one occasion? Sending a horse down there would be much easier than a carriage."

"If I must… Just make sure it's a gentle one."

"Very good. Here is how we will proceed," Thaelyn announces

to the group. "We have a portal exit point down there in a wooded glen not far from the western gate of the city. It is secluded, out of view of the city proper, and we have been using this for many of our operations. We will send your entire party through to arrive there promptly, rather than travelling the full distance from here."

"Sending us through on horseback?" Ilothonna retorts.

"Yes, our portals can be used on virtually any body. The only stipulation is your horses are not conditioned for this mode of transport, so you will need to coddle them on your way out, then to move away from the arrival zone to allow for the next. Be prompt about it, as we tend to use a timing system for sending our people through."

He pauses to survey the assembled gathering, which now involved several druids.

"Priestess Sehnisavain, your rank will come into play here. You will need to enforce the idea of a peaceful envoy coming with you to aid your people. Any guards or others that might take offence to strangers will need to be quelled."

"Yes, I understand," she replies. "My authority in our city carries a fair amount of weight. This should not be a problem."

"We already have our agents inside your temple. Master Cydulean will assist further with the transportation of people and goods as necessary to deliver into this equation. This may include replacement soil for your shrine, to expedite the restoration process. We can bag it up and send it through for you."

As Thaelyn conducted his review, a disturbance was occurring off to the side. It brought the attention of the group to the arrival of several stablemen, followed by several horses jumping through portals into the settlement.

Ilothonna gazed at the clean manners and calm demeanor of the animals as they arrived in view, behaving as if this was a common activity to suddenly appear out of nowhere.

"You people must be very advanced in your ways," she mutters.

"We have been using these ways for many centuries," Thaelyn smiles. "Now, those of you without horses previously will use these instead. Sehnisavain, this includes you. Our horses are very well behaved when passing through a portal. Then, when you arrive, you will lead this entourage into your city and begin your work."

"All right, I believe I'm ready," she checks herself carefully, further examining her priestly robe. "This attire I'm wearing isn't exactly proper for riding a horse."

"Perhaps, but for now, you may need to make do."

He begins directing the assembly to load up onto their mounts, with Ilothonna and Eilihel assisting Sehnisavain with hers. He then calls up a mage with the rune to their destination.

"We will send our people through first, since they are more experienced, and then the rest will follow after. Ours will be able to assist you to arrange yourselves on arrival."

He directs the mage to take a position some distance away, and the man begins conjuring the portal as a projected aperture hovering in space. Ilothonna watched as the swirling circular apparition formed in thin air.

"So that's what it looks like," she muses silently.

One by one, the druids line up and coax their horses into a trot, advancing confidently on the aperture and leaping through the swirling vortex, vanishing from view.

Ilothonna studied their actions, suddenly feeling a little nervous about her own travel.

The mage cancelled the apparition and recast for secondary transport. In this mode, he came up to Sehnisavain and stroked her horse on the neck a few times, speaking a few command words into its ear. The horse nickered softly, and he touched the rune to its shoulder, sending the horse and its rider away. He then moves to the others, allowing a generous timing effect to permit the horses to move out of the way on the other side before sending the next.

On the roadway just outside the city of Kynesoth, a large group of people appeared on horseback. The guards on the walls watching the surrounding fields took immediate notice of the gathering and called in additional members from the streets below for backup. The watchman on the tower studies the arriving troupe and takes notice of a few familiar faces. Nevertheless, he calls out in his traditional manner.

"Halt! Who goes there?"

"Guard," Sehnisavain announces boldly. "Surely, it is not necessary to use those words every time you see people out here."

"Um, well, these are the rules I need to follow, High Priestess. It's my job, you know."

"Very well, if this is how you like it, then know I am the High Priestess Sehnisavain Deepglade, and you will display your proper manners in my presence!"

"But yes...I mean, I didn't mean anything inappropriate..."

"So be it. And with me is my First Deacon, Priestess Ilothonna, some number of our scouts, and a diplomatic entourage here to assist our people in their time of need."

"A diplomatic... But I thought you were... Where did you just come from?"

"A pilgrimage to find the truth of the world we live in. And now, we have important work to attend. Therefore, you will come down off that wall and open this gate at once."

"Me? But my duty..."

"Your duty is being reassigned. We are calling an assembly at the temple. Your participation is required."

"But wait, who are these others? A diplomatic party? Whose diplomatic party?"

"People who represent our ancient history, which we were cursed to forget, and who have come to remind us of who we really are. Now open this gate!"

A tonal ring sounds off from the drawer of Governor Dramon's desk. It was a familiar announcement from his personal trans-com. He opens the drawer to retrieve it and answers the call.

"Yes, Commander, what do we have today?"

"I have a status update," responds the flat, emotionless voice.

"Of course, and how are your efforts progressing?"

"We still take persistent losses near the Nazég vessel. The reinforcing troops continue to make use of abnormal procedures."

"Commander, how is it that your highly trained and supremely advanced soldiers are being cut down by those simpletons? Granted, they might have adamantium armor, but are you still deploying troops with pulse rifles?"

"Affirmative."

"Then why are your troops, which are equipped with pulse rifles, being brought low by his troops using swords?"

"His troops also use weapons resembling bows and arrows."

"Oh, but of course, I forgot…" he feigns ignorance. "And yet, you can't seem to kill any of those bowmen with your pulse rifles? What about those new shields of yours?"

"They are only marginally effective to absorb the hits. That ammunition of theirs seems to apply a destructive force on the material. In some cases, it is melting the shield body, and in others, it appears as a corrosive force to degrade them until they are useless."

"Interesting…" he muses thoughtfully. "This would indeed represent a problem. Those bows must be a work of art. Well, perhaps we can further augment ourselves with more experience. But still, rifles versus bows? This should tilt things in our favor. Are you able to inflict any damage on them?"

"Negative. They are deploying some form of defensive shield that repels our rifle fire."

"What?!" he screams. "Commander, are we speaking of a physical barrier of some sort, like a traditional shield you hold in your hand?"

"Uncertain. It does appear to be held in their hand, but it does not appear physical. Instead, it appears as a creation of their abnormal abilities."

"Magic again! But how in all Creation can a bunch of finger-wigglers put up a shield to repel pulse plasma fire?"

"Unknown, but it seems impenetrable."

"Blast!" he scorns. "These people must've progressed far in their studies since my last observation. Is there anything else?"

"Affirmative. They are also deploying entities of an unnatural characteristic."

"Entities?" he raises his brow. "Wait, when you say unnatural, can you be more precise?"

"The definition defies a scientific explanation. These entities seem to possess partial intelligence and directed purpose, but they are not organic in nature."

"All right, then what are they made of, can you tell?"

"Our reports say they appear to be made of inanimate substances. We have observed what resembles water, fire, and earthen materials."

"Ah! But of course! I understand. These are described as elementals, Commander, and I suppose it is to be expected if they're using such highly skilled mages out there. These entities may not be as susceptible to your weapons, so you are advised to maintain caution, perhaps simply to keep away from them."

The Governor pauses to consider these new aspects.

"He's got some fine talent out there," he surmises. "Commander, this is becoming problematic. If these people hold such an effective shield construct that it can repel your weapon's fire, we have a serious problem. I will have you pull back and disengage the Daanen-Aryku. There is no further point in attempting any more attacks for as long as he's out there. What about that camp of his? I believe you mentioned something about a wall around it, correct?"

"Affirmative."

"Are we speaking of perhaps a stone wall or a wooden palisade?"

"Negative. It resembles that same shield technology."

"Argh!" he roars and pounds his desk. "They created a form of physical technology as well? Incredible, and intolerable," he fumes. "They have indeed come far...too far for such small creatures."

"Marshal, do we attack their base?"

"Negative, Commander. First, if they're using a physical technology for this shield, as well as a conjured form that can be deployed on their troops, this means they have an effective means of defending against any form of ground or aerial attack."

"What about an orbital strike?"

"While the thought amuses me, I must once again address the issue of these portals. For as long as they hold any ability to return to this world, we need to consider a more subversive way to address this. We have a plan currently underway here. I will wait to see what sort of results it brings and then go from there. In the meantime… hmm, I wonder if our delightful little Flame Elves could be of some value," he ponders a moment. "No, maybe not. Not if he has so many mages out there with so many elaborate skills. All right, for now, you will go on standby."

"Affirmative."

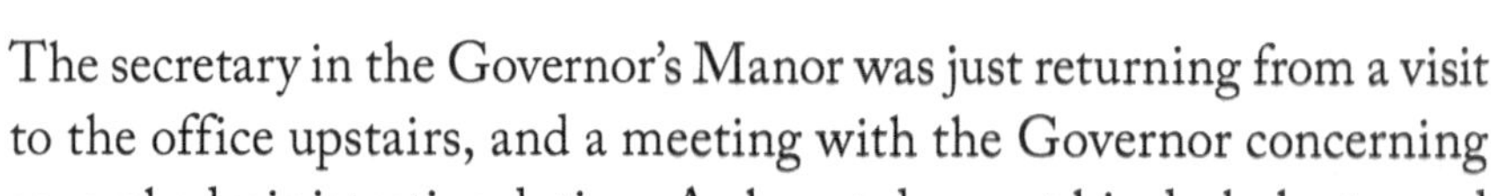

The secretary in the Governor's Manor was just returning from a visit to the office upstairs, and a meeting with the Governor concerning several administrative duties. As he sat down at his desk, he turned to his temporary assistant across the way.

"Leesa, the Governor has an errand to run…do you mind?"

"Oh, not at all," she replies cheerily. "What does he need?"

"It is a simple thing, and one he does quite often. He needs you to run over to the academy and call the Dean into a meeting up in his office."

"Of course, right away."

She jumps out of her seat and rushes out of the room, leaving the building and hurrying over to the academy. Upon entering the main hall, she pauses to gain her bearings. She had never actually visited inside the academy before, and suddenly found herself asking where she needed to go to find the Dean's office.

Tristeen was studying at one of the tables, but she was also keeping a close eye on the local affairs, especially in light of the recent events occurring in the basement and their obvious implications. She happened to take notice of the young auburn-haired girl entering the room and appearing a little lost, so she gets up to investigate.

"Hello?" she announces. "You're a new face, and very nicely

dressed for anyone who might just be walking around out there!" she gazes admiringly at the girl's clothes.

Leesa impulsively glanced at her professional-appearing white blouse and matching blue skirt and vest, feeling very confident in her presentation.

"Oh, why thank you. Yes, I'm a temporary assistant in the Governor's Manor, as his usual runner is on leave. I was sent to call the Dean into a meeting, but I'm not actually sure where his office is."

"Oh, him..." Tristeen huffs quietly. "Yes, you'll need to go through that door back there..." she points to the rear of the room, "...turn right and take the stairs, then turn left to the end of the hall."

"I guess by your reaction, you don't hold much regard for him?"

"Oh, never mind me. I have a few issues with his management techniques."

"Maybe this is something we could talk about one day?"

"Us?" Tristeen hesitates as she mulls her obligations to her spy connections. "Um, well, this probably wouldn't be of much interest to someone working inside the Governor's Manor. These are two different institutions, you know."

"Maybe so, but the Dean and the Governor seem to hold a close relationship. Maybe there's something we could share...you know, a little girl talk," she smiles harmlessly.

Tristeen studied her carefully for her manners, and again for her clothing, then recalling Willit and his uncanny appearance.

"You mean you might actually want to talk about the Governor and his...um, I mean the Dean?"

"That's interesting," she muses. "His...what?"

Now Tristeen was becoming curious as to this young lady's origins, as well as her manners, which seemed to hint at something.

"You said you're a temporary assistant. When did you start work?"

"Oh, not long ago. His former assistant felt a little under-the-weather, and is currently taking some unexpected time off."

"Former assistant...and unexpected time off? Why do I get the impression he didn't simply choose to take this time off?"

"Well, choosing is a relative term here. He fell unconscious while the priests in the temple were examining him for a strange new illness they claimed was going around."

"Wait. A strange new illness they claimed was going around? And what is it if not an illness going around?"

"Oh, it's truly tragic. So far, it's only a few isolated cases of people in certain positions who are conveniently…ahem…" she feigns a cough to clear her throat. "My pardons," she smiles impishly. "I mean, coincidentally falling ill, and therefore need to be replaced, at least temporarily, by others like me who just so happen to be available to take up the slack."

"Uh huh…" Tristeen nods and grins reflexively. "You know, you sound like a guy I know."

"Really! But I'll bet a girl like you probably knows a lot of nice guys. With hair like that, you can't possibly be from the lower district…can you?"

Tristeen was now very curious about this girl. She glances quickly around the hall and takes the girl by the arm to lead her into a corner for a private conversation.

"Who in all the hells are you?" she whispers urgently. "You're dropping a lot of clues here. You can't be a simple replacement runner. Not in those clothes! You look like you could pass for a noble, but I am a noble, and I would know if you're one of us."

"Naturally," Leesa smiles softly. "You must be Tristeen. I heard about you up here from Willit Sarens. I'm another part of our little spy operation, but you didn't hear that from me."

"Oh, but of course! But who are you now?"

"Just call me Leesa. And as far as you know, I'm just a young girl trying to make her way, and for those who don't know the noble families as much, I could be one of you."

"Oh, really!" she chuckles. "Well, be careful if you should happen to pass by my house, or else my mom will drag you inside for one of her famous tea parties."

"Oh? Is it fun?"

"Fun is a relative term, much like this former assistant you mentioned taking time off," she grins. "So, what role are you supposed to be playing?"

"We shouldn't talk too much about that. My cousin has been coaching me on my performance, so I need to make this look good. I was installed as a runner in the Governor's Manor to replace the other one."

"And what actually happened to the other one?"

"The priests over there…new ones, also installed to replace the older set. We've figured out who is really responsible for the Plague, and it comes down to them and the Festival we're all told is so good for us."

"Oh, bloody hell!" she spurns under her breath. "I swear to you… And does this involve that thing under the skin?"

"Aye, it does! That's what the bleedin' collar does to us with all that pain. It slips a tiny bugger of a thingy inside there with a kind of clock timer on it to open up at fifty or so years and make us sick. And it can't be from anything other than the Suuden-Aryku for the design of it."

"Figures! If you can't trust the authority around here…"

"Aye, and buggers to that, I say! Anyway, I'm working for my cousin to check the happenings inside the Manor, and what that blighter might be doing to us next."

"Your cousin? Who is that?"

"Marelle Carronel. She's a member of the Guard."

"Marelle again! That lady sure is getting busy out there."

"Aye! And we're expecting things to get worse before they get better, but I shouldn't spend any more time here. I'm supposed to call the Dean to a meeting."

"Right, and knowing him, he doesn't like to be late. All right, on with you then…and it was good meeting you."

They break up with Leesa continuing through the rear door to the hallway, then up the stairs and onward to the Dean's office. She knocks softly before entering.

"Yes?" he responds. "Who are you, young lady?" he asks casually as he studies her appearance.

"I'm a new assistant for the Governor. He sent me over to call you into a meeting in his office."

"Ah! Very good… You're new? What happened to the other fellow?"

"He is taking time away to rest after an unfortunate spell he experienced."

"Really…" he emits nonchalantly.

The Dean sets aside a stack of papers he was reviewing and rises from his desk. He begins on his way out the door, with Leesa following close behind. He glances at her again as the two of them stroll along the hallway to the stairs.

"You appear very nice in that dress. Might you be from one of the noble families?"

"Oh, but Dean…" she responds innocently. "This little thing? Does it show so much?"

"Indeed!" he chuckles. "We see so few of those wandering about outside the Upper Ward. In fact, we have one attending our studies here. I wonder, have you ever considered taking up classes?"

"Well, the thought may have crossed my mind on a few occasions, but my mother tends to argue that such things are not for a cultured young lady to engage in."

"Oh! But then why are you working as a runner in the Governor's office?"

"Because I tend not to listen to my mother as much."

The Dean laughed buoyantly at her clever repartee as they continued out of the building.

The two of them hurried across the plaza and into the Governor's Manor, where Leesa offered a parting wave and returned to the secretary's office. But she doesn't return to her desk immediately. Instead, she stops just inside the door and discreetly turns to watch the Dean as he continues upstairs, then knocks on the Governor's door before entering.

"My Lord, you called for me?" he announces politely.

"Yes Dean," the Governor grumbles. "We have a problem with those people in the valley."

"Of course, my Lord, I'm sure we knew of that already. What is it this time?"

"My contacts tell me not only are they still romping around in the vicinity of the Naarg uy'Sodrad, but they're also consistently destroying the Suuden-Aryku patrols. And not simply with their bows and arrows, but also with conjured elementals and some form of shield that blocks the Suuden'kai weapons."

"Incredible! Such things exist to block those weapons?"

"On their world, it would seem so. We need to deal with that man quickly so I can prepare some countermeasures against those who follow him. What is the report on your efforts at the academy? I trust you are very nearly ready by now, hmm?"

"Yes, my Lord, we are just putting the finishing touches on the circle. We need to be absolutely sure the glyphs are perfect in order to contain the creature..."

"Dean, containing it really isn't my greatest concern. Summoning it is the only thing that interests me at the moment. Very well, see to it as best you can. Then we need to bring him to us, away from his camp and his guards. I will prepare a note to be delivered to his camp. We will send it by way of a courier...perhaps you could dress one of your students to serve this role, as it would seem my usual runner has taken ill."

"Of course, that seems easy enough. I can call on one of our spies who was visiting the region previously. He knows the way well enough. Is there anything else?"

"Yes, actually, it occurs to me we have not checked on the miners for a while. Perhaps you could attend to this."

"Ah yes! But of course, and it would seem to me they should be ready for more of that dressing agent for their farms."

"Indeed, and we have a few new canisters in the basement. I will have you attend to this first thing tomorrow morning to give you time for the trip."

"Very well, my Lord, I'll prepare a wagon and have it ready on the morrow."

"Excellent, that is all, Dean."

The Dean bows politely and turns to leave.

Leesa had quietly snuck upstairs to listen in on the exchange. When she heard the parting words, she quickly dashed to the end of the hall and ducked inside a storage closet, closing the door to a crack, just enough to see the Dean exit the office and back down the stairs. She then came out of hiding and quietly returned to her desk.

✦✦✦✦✦

A large assembly of elves was gathering in front of the temple in Kynesoth. Sehnisavain was standing on the steps overlooking the affair, along with Ilothonna and Kerali, and their foreign delegation of druids. The two agents, Cydulean and Sumisal, were also attending, but mostly standing in the background.

"My fellow citizens!" Sehnisavain shouts boldly to the crowd. "I know many of you have pondered the mystery of my absence, and some have said it might be orcs, or some other foul deed that took me away. But in truth, I was called away to seek out an answer to a desperate need. I undertook a pilgrimage to follow this path, and at the end, I found what I was searching for. Now I have returned to share this with the rest of you."

She pauses to glance at the visiting delegation.

"I sought to discover the nature of the world around us, and to answer a series of questions that have plagued our authority leaders for some time since the arrival of these newcomers in the valley to the north. What I learned along the way was not only disturbing to my mind but also revolting to my senses. It brought back memories of a time that was forgotten by our people. A time that was critically important to us, but then stolen away. And since that time, we were denied remembering it, denied our ancestral teachings, our history, our culture, our moral values, and our high standards of nobility… our very identity of who we are supposed to be as a people. Instead, we became this…" she waves a hand around the masses and the city in general.

A hushed murmuring ushered up from the crowd as they tried to reconcile her meaning.

"None of you who are alive today would know of this, as none of you were ever given these teachings to learn from. Our libraries were burned, our books destroyed, and our schools restricted in their lessons. But I came from a time before all this began, and I may be the only one who still remembers. What we are today is not what we were meant to be once upon a time."

She paused to glance at their faces before continuing.

"Four hundred years ago, our world went to war. The reasons for this may be lost to many of us, only to say we are at war and therefore we must be ready to fight. But no one has fought anything for so long that most of us might think the war is not a war. Instead, it is simply a condition to disturb us into thinking we are imminent to come under attack. We destroyed the greater part of this world…a world that was once at peace and friendly to one another. We became aggressors! We became tyrants! We became the murderers of innocent people! And for what reason? Did any of them do ill to us? The simple answer is no."

Again, the crowd whispered privately as they still tried to interpret her direction.

"A crime was committed against us, this much we know. But that crime was not by any of them. And yet, in the beginning, some of us were made to think it was so. Since then, we have destroyed our world, our home, and they who were once our friends and neighbors. It is no wonder how they who remain might wish us dead, and for good reason. But we did this because we were told to do this! Forced into it by heathens who hold no regard for our history, our culture, or our native manners. And this becomes the crime."

The murmuring grew louder as they began to realize the meaning of her words.

"Now we see these new arrivals in the lands to the north. They are described to us as undesirable, but we are told not to attack, the same as we are told not to attack the last remaining city of the Night Elves, and that of the humans. We destroy everything down to the last, but keep them for…what reason? Is this a reason by our own choosing? No. It is a reason by they who gave us the order to do so. And it is probably for a very similar reason that we are being kept inside our own city walls and not sent out to do anything else. We are servants, and not in a kind manner of speaking. Not when it demands the blood of innocents, and the restraint of even more innocents. Here is where one might use the word slaves."

The voices in the plaza rise briskly as they begin to feel a mote of injustice.

"These newcomers in the valley to the north seem strange to us. We might ask, where did they come from, and why are they here…why are they described as undesirable. The answer to that is they are not under the same authority that made us slaves. I have personally heard them described as interfering with our local affairs. Yes! Interfering with someone oppressing the rest of us into slavery? I might find that offensive if I were the one doing it."

The crowd now rose up in a shout, with several fists waving in protest.

"They came here because we sent an invasion of orcs into their world. Those orcs stirred up trouble, and that trouble followed them back here. They defended their homes, nothing more, and this authority calls them undesirable for the pleasure of it. Now, here they are, discovering us in our respective prisons, oppressed through slavery. We have learned they made peace with the Night Elves, and began assaulting the orcs on their doorsteps, driving them away and liberating those unfortunate people. We learned they sided with the Daanen-Aryku, and bolstered their defense against the Suuden-Aryku, protecting them and liberating them from their oppression. And this is called undesirable. And then we have the human city…"

She pauses again to judge their reactions.

"I am aware the city of Rolsklinde is supposed to be managed by someone who is friendly with the Suuden-Aryku. These newcomers tried to negotiate an agreement with him, but it failed, as he does not want to cooperate with them. But the people of that city held differing ideas, as his management of the city is failing to treat them politely. Therefore, an agreement was made with them to bring aid to their benefit. And this too is undesirable. Undesirable to those who want to oppress and control the rest of us. And for this, we might wish to point our fingers at the Suuden-Aryku, as they seem to be the largest player in this game. But they are not."

The crowd suddenly went silent at this contradiction, and hushing sounds were heard as they waited for her to continue.

"Remember, my good people. This started four centuries ago, and they had not yet arrived, but someone else did, and this is where the original crime was committed against the people of this world… all of them!" she shouts. "And ours were the first to fall victim to it, turning us into what some might call monsters who murdered the rest. And even worse, we are taught to scorn the rest with our arrogance and bigotry that we held a right to do this, when in fact, it is they who made us do this who carry this blame."

This revelation was starting to burn many of the people with shame and revulsion. It was also beginning to conflict with the songs of Sargeras, which were still trying to maintain control.

"In this very place, our most exalted temple, our people once worshiped a selection of gods native to all the Elven nations, not only ours here, but the Night Elves as well. And in this place, we once held a set of our most holy icons representing the last remaining artifacts of our ancient religion, a part of our identity of being elves. We would trade these between the cities, including the Night Elf cities, as we all shared in this. This should give you an idea of how close we once were. But not only that, in this square, just in front here, was a shrine to another holy artifact. It was a part of our ancient heritage, from a place that we, as elves, originally came from. This world is not our first home. We once migrated here from another one, and we brought these things with us."

A soft cooing of oohs and ahs ushered up from the crowd.

"In our ancient home, our kind was very highly devoted to the essences of nature, and the spiritual harmony of life. This is yet another offence to us, that we would go out and harm so much of it, as this is not our true nature. But it IS what became of us after this horrid crime turned our senses upside-down on us. And as a symbol of this harmony, our kind once gave itself to the friendship of a very unique form of life. A tree, but not just any tree, as you might find in the woodlands. This one held a spirit of its own, a living mind we would commune with."

The assembled people all gazed at each other over the seemingly absurd notion of speaking to a tree.

"Yes, I can see it in you," she continues. "I might expect this if you only think of a tree to be useful as firewood. But not this one. Our kind worshipped it, as it brought us strength, unity, and peace of mind and spirit. It linked all living things, that we might all feel the serenity of nature. And we had one here in the city, as did all the Elven cities, both ours and the Night Elves…at least until this crime took them away four centuries ago, and burned our very souls for the loss. This became that legendary pain we suffered."

A sudden whooshing of voices gushed up from the masses as this revelation hit home.

"And who do you think came to our rescue with his songs, but He who then told us to defile our very nature and destroy everything else around us!" she screeches.

Now the crowd rose up in shouts and more fist waving, and this time with enough fury to fight back the songs trying to hold them down.

Cydulean and Sumisal both glanced at each other and raised their brows for the sudden outbreak.

Sehnisavain continues, "Sargeras! His name stands behind all of this. He is the only true enemy here. The orcs do not belong here. They are invaders! The Suuden-Aryku do not belong here. They are invaders! This world was ours, along with the Night Elves and the humans. We are the only ones who belong here. But then he came, and he brought the others with him. He defiled our once peaceful world, turning each of us against the others, and brought what was once a proud civilization into complete ruin. Then he oppresses the remainder, and likely to keep us as slaves to be used elsewhere at his whims. Well, my fellow citizens, I say, no more!!"

The crowds roar in bold agreement, shouting and whistling in support of her statement. Sehnisavain raises a hand to draw their attention again.

"This brings us back to those people up north…who are they, where do they come from, why are they here. Well, as it turns out, that monster was trying to make trouble for yet another world out there, and how curious it is that this one is the very same world we first came out of! Those people are our people…the original ones that spawned our ancestors!"

A sudden rush of gasps and whines poured out from the assembly, and now their voices rumbled with soft discussion over the implications.

"We are told not to attack them, and yet that creature who seems to hold the authority of this invading force calls them undesirable and interfering with his schemes. No doubt, as he made trouble for them, he was likely not expecting a return from it," she chuckles. "It would seem our blessed kin, and others on that world, have made a proud achievement in this time, uniting their world as one. From this, they found such strength that I doubt even Sargeras himself could oppose it! And here they are, doing exactly that. And this is where we stand now. They learned of what we did out there. But they also learned of our misery. They held every reason to bring justice for all those who were killed senselessly…all that which we committed under his name. But they did not do this. Instead, they chose not to attack us, but rather to offer aid to remove us from his blasphemy, and return us to our old ways."

The crowd now emits a surge of cries and whimpers, but also intermixed with howls and wails, as they now found themselves fighting the songs more than ever.

"Our people have a name…a true name. We are not Flame Elves. This is his creation, as he made us his slaves to burn everything in sight. How typical!" she huffs. "Our kind is part of a larger body of elven nations, known as the Tel'Quessir. In our ancestral tongue, ours is a clan once called the Cala'Quessir, High Elves. Our kin on that other world still uses this name, and they are proud of it. They still worship the old gods, and they are proud of that too. But now, if you want to know something of particular revulsion, listen to this! Our old gods, known to us as the Seldarine, are enemies to such like Sargeras. He is not even supposed to be alive, much less offending the children of the true gods!" she shrieks.

This made the crowd go wild. Screams and roars echoed through the streets at the clear outrage that someone would steal them away from their ancestral bindings and force them to commit so many vile deeds. Shouts and hollers resounded from the assembly at the downfall of Sargeras and his insane methods.

Sehnisavain knew this final blow would hit hard, but she needed to rouse them up so vigorously that when she laid the final bombshell on them, it would overwhelm Sargeras's songs completely with so much rage and anguish at what he had done. The people needed to blast his songs out of their minds.

"Four centuries ago," Sehnisavain resumes. "Secret agents of Sargeras arrived here and spoiled our peace with the other races. They stole our sacred holy symbols, defiling our ancestral religion, and perverting our souls with his songs to fill the space left behind. Recall your youth when you first heard him. He does not care if you want him or not. All he cares about is you are a body he can control, by force, if necessary."

The crowd roars in agreement.

"And then he tells us to destroy everything else in our world, spending our once great population on so much folly because it is simply easier for his other servants, the Suuden-Aryku, to manage us for the smaller counts. That is the only reason for our war."

The crowds again roared in outrage, even louder this time. They were nearly ready to rampage out the gates by now, but Sehnisavain knew she had to keep them under control.

"But hear me out!" she shouts. "As we must also understand, we are not the only ones. Our kind does not simply go out and bring reckless destruction without proper authority of mind. He may have corrupted our people once, but we believe he also corrupted the Suuden-Aryku on their world. They are made to do things we believe they do not control themselves. He seems to be controlling them, and by means appropriate to their nature. He uses lies and false promises to control his minions, and he uses devices for those who do not otherwise listen. Once, we were told to send a part of our population to another world to do battle with another society, one called dwarves. We spent a great many of our people on it, but with no word as to our result. I have recently come to understand some of those same dwarves have been found in our world, a world they are not native to, and under an effect to control their minds while they slave away in a mine to the north, serving him, no doubt, and whatever new whims he has for himself."

The crowds settle back a bit as they begin to realize the severity of these machinations.

"This seems to be where we receive our iron, but this is not their primary purpose, as they were found to be mining something else, even more precious. A metal we were not even aware of existing in this world before now, but he seems to want this, and in large quantity. We do not know why, but surely it cannot be a good thing."

She pauses to glance at the druids behind her, who were patiently waiting their turn.

"In the valley to the north…the Badlands, as so many of us call them, those newcomers came here as part of the defense of their home from these orcs we sent. They found us, and they found him behind all these crimes, and they have dedicated themselves to correcting the wrongdoings of this world. Their leader is a man of unquestioned principles and righteous decree. Their purpose is law and justice, to serve any who might be wronged by anyone else, and this would include even such as a god, if he should so dare to offend people like us!"

The crowds reverberate with moans of awe and wonder.

"And with him, he brought to our world this same sacred object that we once held dear to us right here in our city. A new Tree of Life, planted in his camp up there. He also bestowed one of these to the Night Elves, to restore them back to their ancestral roots and to heal their pain from the loss they once suffered. And here he offers the same to us!"

She now turns and waves at the druids behind her.

"These people are part of a diplomatic envoy to help us in our time of need, to restore our spiritual sanity. As a people, we are not strong enough to fight any longer, even though I feel many of you would desire this. We are too few, and our enemies too strong, and too far away. First, we must heal ourselves, and as we do this, those others up there will seek their own ways to find our enemies, and bring this justice on our behalf. We should ally ourselves with them, and offer our support, and they will support us in return. As for Sargeras, we may still hear his blasphemous songs in our minds, but now we must shut them out! And to do this, they have come to give us back what he stole from us!"

An uprising of cheers rings out, but the sounds are tempered by the conflict with the influence still being generated by Sargeras's songs. Now the people are enraged and determined to overcome this by forcing themselves to defy the effect.

"Good people of Kynesoth," Sehnisavain urges as she tries to refocus their attention. "We have work to do, and it must be done quickly if we are to free ourselves from his grip. We once held a shrine to our old faith, right here in the plaza. This is where our old tree once stood, and we must clear the way for a new one. These people behind me are priests called druids, and they specialize in this work. They do not speak our language, and unfortunately, most of you do not speak theirs. This is yet another sacrilege forced upon us to deny us the privilege even to learn our ancestral tongue. So I will say to you now, bring any tools you can find. Let us begin to pry up these pave stones and open the land once more. We need to dig out the old vestiges of the poison that once killed our tree, and replace it with fresh clean soil to provide a healthy beginning for our future!"

The crowds now cry out and begin dashing off in all directions to find shovels and picks. Some rush off to bring in wagons to haul away the debris, while others simply go to work using their bare hands.

Leesa was just getting off work for the day. She left the Governor's Manor and made a determined line to the lower district. Her destination was the Ten Eagles tavern where she had in mind to meet with her contact. She rushed along briskly through the street, largely ignoring the stares from the other travelers for her oddly extravagant manner of dress.

When she finally arrived at her destination, she casually entered inside and began meandering towards the back where Willit often made his meetings. But before she could make her goal, a half-drunk patron approached her from the side.

"Hey there, little lady," he slurs through his inebriation. "I don't think I've seen you here before. Such a pretty little one, too… You must work upstairs, right? Ooh, I'd like to see what you've got cooking underneath all that."

Leesa turns to find the man half staggering as he advanced on her.

"No, I'm not someone who works upstairs," she replies coolly. "Those girls are all upstairs already. I'm here on other business."

"Well, I could still make it worth your while. I've got the coin, and you sure got the goods!"

He reaches out and takes her by one arm, then tries pulling her in lasciviously.

At first, she simply tried pulling away, but as she realized his drunken determination, she responded keenly by spinning around and landing a solid elbow slam to his jaw. This caused him to reflexively let go of her arm. She followed with a swivel on her heel, and a knee in the groin, and finished by clasping her hands and delivering a heavy smash to his temple, knocking him fully to the ground.

"I'm on official business," she states firmly. "My cousin serves the Guard, and I serve her. And she taught me a few things about how to deal with men like you."

Now she turns and saunters over to the table to sit with Willit.

Like most of the patrons at this moment, his attention was drawn to the disturbance of the unassuming young lady in her professional dress laying out the drunken assailant.

"Gods' pity, Leesa. I hope I never meet you in a dark alley," he chuckles.

She simply smiles and begins her report.

"Willit, we have a little problem. Or maybe I should say His Lordship has the problem."

"All right, what is it?"

"The Governor held a meeting with the Dean today. I tried listening in and heard them talk about the trouble he's making out by the Naarg uy'Sodrad, which the Governor doesn't seem at all happy about, and how he wants to deal with him, and anyone else who follows him."

"Nice guy. We have someone who actually knows how to fight a war, and he wants to put a stop to it."

"They started talking about something the Dean is supposed to be doing in his academy."

"Probably that conjuring…"

"I heard words talking about a circle, and glyphs being perfect to contain something."

"Exactly, a conjuring for something big and nasty, and the circle needs warding glyphs to contain it safely."

"Well, I think the Governor doesn't really care about the containing part, only the summoning part."

"Oh, how nice of him to care so much for the safety of the city… Anything else?"

"Yeah, he said something about writing a note to bring him up here and away from his guards."

"Yes, and this is what we were concerned about. It must be a little surprise, and the Governor wants to isolate His Lordship to make him vulnerable. Combine this with the lack of interest in containing it, and it means he hopes to set it loose, probably 'accidentally' and let it make a little trouble. I'll be sure to pass this along. Did you hear anything else?"

"I heard them talking a bit about the dwarves, and the Dean is supposed to go up there tomorrow morning to check on them."

"All right, this is another thing. He's got some of his scouts up there watching the place, and waiting to see if anyone goes in to pick up all that metal they're mining. Maybe now we'll see who comes for it."

"Good. Willit, I'm a little scared now. That thing they're hoping to conjure. What should I do if I see it coming my way?"

"Run."

Chapter 7

UNEXPECTED REBUKE

"My Lord, I'm just on my way out to check on the dwarves. Do you have any last-minute instructions?"

"No, Dean, not at this time. Go about your work and let me know the condition of the stores up there. It should be full again, and then some, for all my distractions around here."

"Of course… I'll report in once I return."

The Dean was making an obligatory visit to the Governor's office before his trip north to the dwarven enclave. This was one of his routine duties, and included a general survey of the situation, as well as occasionally delivering supplies.

On this day, he needed to bring with him a wagon full of materials to resupply the dwarves. Leesa was at her desk when he came in, and as he came back downstairs, she decided to see if she could involve herself to any degree.

"Dean? Do you need any assistance?"

"Oh, no thank you, young lady. I just need to pick up a few things from the basement here."

"I was noticing you driving a wagon out there. Are you travelling today?"

"Ah, yes, I need to make a quick trip up to the dwarves as part of our, uh, trade relationship."

"Oh, really! I've often wondered what sort of trade we make with them. I've heard we receive iron from them, although it seems such a shame that it doesn't last long. Still, I often wondered what it is we trade in exchange for it."

"Oh, well, you really don't need to concern yourself with that. The Governor makes these deals where we exchange a few goods in return for their iron…them being all the way up there, they often don't have access to a few important items."

"Ah, so that's it…" she peeks out the front window at the wagon sitting outside. "I see some bales of hay, a couple bags of something, and you said you need to get something out of the basement. Can I help?"

"Well, I uh…" he glances at her prim attire.

"Oh please," she refutes. "You don't need to worry about me being a noble who doesn't know how to do a little work. Even though my mother always groaned about her little girl doing manual labor, I actually enjoy getting my hands dirty on occasion," she smiles brightly.

"Really! You must bring her a lot of joy for all your wayward behavior. Very well, if you would simply give me a hand with a couple of things I need to pull out of there, it would save me the extra trip."

She follows him down a short hallway to a door. He pulls out a key from a vest pocket and unlocks it, then leads the two of them down a set of stairs, lighting a lantern on the wall as they go.

"This here," he points to a series of barrel-like objects. "We need two of them. They're a bit heavy, though."

Leesa steps in and confidently squats down to tilt one canister slightly to the side so she can slip a hand underneath for support. She keeps her back straight and uses her legs to bring it up neatly. It was a familiar habit from so much of her commoner's life in the lower district, and it clearly signaled experience at lifting heavy objects.

However, the Dean studied her, expecting her to be some frilly young lady who might simply try bending at the waist, and then struggling with her back muscles to bring herself upright again.

He found himself impressed, but also a little surprised, that she performed the maneuver so expertly.

"Indeed, you do seem to know a few things about manual labor," he mentions casually.

Leesa took notice of his glare, and began to realize she was following her old habits from her labors at home, so she quickly thought of an excuse.

"I would sometimes sneak away and look for odd jobs without my mom knowing," she admits with a wink. "A girl can learn a few things that way, you know."

"Clever, and a bit devious, as well."

The two of them carried their loads back up the stairs. Leesa took note of the design of the canister. The color was dark red, and it seemed composed of an unknown material, hard but subtly flexible, and sealed with a lid. She also took note of some kind of writing, but the lettering seemed alien to her. They carried the canisters outside and loaded them on the wagon.

"Is there anything else?" she asks.

"That will be all, thank you. Oh, would you mind locking that door for me? The Governor likes to keep it that way. He has a number of items down there he doesn't want just anyone poking around."

"Oh, certainly! How long do you expect to be gone, by the way?"

"The trip usually takes the better part of the day, going up and coming back. And I'll need to report to him once I return…eh, you know, to keep him informed of our negotiations."

"Naturally," she nods. "Then perhaps I will see you again."

Leesa smiles politely and returns inside, while the Dean sets himself into place on the driver's box and whistles at the horses to proceed forward.

She watches him through the window as he pulls away out of view, then turns once again to go back to the basement. She examines the door, which had a key lock on the outside and the locking latch on the inside. She peeked inside for another look, then quickly glanced down the hall to make sure no one was coming before she went down the stairs again.

She began nosing around several boxes found on a series of shelves. She pulled out an oddly unusual device from a concealed pocket under her belt. The item was unusual for her origins, but not for those she worked for. She was equipped with a trans-com, which included a built-in camera feature, and now she was taking pictures of everything she found down there.

After several long moments of photographing the contents of the Governor's private stash, she came back upstairs, cautiously peeking through the door, and then locking it behind her before returning to her duty.

✦✦✦

Across the way, inside the temple, the priests were preparing for their first day on the job, and it wasn't expected to be an easy one. The temple was filling up with parishioners for the first time after coming under new management.

"Just who are you and where did you come from?" shouts one member.

"My name is Priest Hernan Garrain," explains the head clergyman. "We are the newly inducted ministry of this temple. The previous membership was found to be conducting criminal acts, to say nothing of their heretical practices and false morals."

"Criminal acts?" complains another patron. "And false morals? How do you mean this?"

Leesa's mother, Tania, was in attendance today, and her surprise at seeing these priests again, to say nothing of them apparently taking up occupancy in her favorite temple, was quickly raising her ire.

"I remember you from that time you were visiting our home. What are you doing here now?"

"Ah, Madam Gobbard, how nice to see you again. With respect, Tania, we are taking charge of your preposterous religion and preparing to give you a proper education, as opposed to that nonsense you were receiving from those imposters you had in here previously."

"Imposters! They were priests! You don't go around questioning something like that. They carry divine power to teach us!"

"Tania, if I were to dress up as a member of your Allegiance Guard over there and begin parading around like I owned the place, does this make me an Allegiance Guard? And further, does this allow me to dictate to you how to live your life? No it does not. Your priests were not priests, only dressed for the occasion and filling you with a lot of lies about your alleged gods."

"Alleged gods?" she shouts.

"Yes! Alleged! Those gods, after four hundred years of you praying to them, could not once actually save you from your troubles. Real gods would be a bit more efficient than that. This is made worse by your Guard members, the ones who hold the physical authority to actually do the work, are actually under orders not to do any work, despite your gods and whatever divine power you claim they were providing to do it with. So, not only are your priests and their gods false, your political authority, that which you are forced to…trust… so often, are precisely the wrong ones to trust. And worse is they shove these expressions down your throats, and deny you to question anything after that."

This lengthy deluge of accusations caused the full assembly to rise up with moans and cries, until he begins again.

"This is repeated in your schools, by the way, which is controlled by your Dean over there, and he is part of this authority you are made to trust implicitly, if only because…if you can't trust that…" he shrugs. "And at this moment, the only thing right in that statement is that you have no one else to trust around here, as they own everything. Well, no longer. We are here now to remove that restraining collar they once placed upon you. And since we are not restricted by their rules, we will apply ourselves to correct the situation. Meaning to say, you will now learn what they are hiding from you."

"Hiding?" she retracts subtly.

He turns to the rest of the assembly as he continues.

"We are real priests, who worship real gods, the kind where if you speak to them, you hear a response, and if you ask them for something, they will deliver it into your hands. And our gods teach real lessons, the sort that make you grow and learn, not hide behind walls pretending the world outside does not exist. Therefore, Tania, while I admire your dedication, simply proclaiming someone to have any form of 'right' to do something, if for no other reason than because they appear official to you, does not justify you, as a responsible citizen, to ignore the greater observable events of the world around you. And after four centuries of observable events, it is truly a shame that none of you opened your eyes wide enough to actually pay attention."

He pauses to glance around at the assembled patrons.

"For example, unlike your priests and their divine authority, we discovered what this plague of yours was truly about. Remember our visit to your house? Therefore, you should first learn to count, where after four centuries of begging your priests and their gods to deliver you, none of them succeeded. Second, you should learn to watch, as every citizen you were hoping to find salvation for has suffered this illness, without exception. This alone should cause you to question those priests and their divine...whatever...that they even know what they are talking about."

"I uh..."

"And yet," he asserts with a finger. "In one day, we who are not so fervently dedicated to your gods, and who do not follow such extraordinary wisdom as to trust people who are so questionably trustworthy, not only found the cause of your illness, but we also found out who was responsible."

"But, um..." she ducks her head. "This doesn't quite answer why you're in here now, unless..."

"...Unless your priests were involved, yes," he nods assertively. "I would imagine, much like in your schools, they deny you to question anything because they batter you with all their rhetoric of all-powerful gods who simply should not be questioned under any circumstances. Therefore, we have arrested those priests on multiple charges, not the least of which being murder by means of delivering a deadly substance into your bodies and claiming they were protecting you from something outside your view, all in the name of your false gods."

"Just one moment here!" shouts another listener. "What are you talking about up there?"

"We are priests in the service of Lord Thaelyn, King of Tae'Eladar. You may have heard of us by now as having essentially taken over the Badlands valley to the south. You may also know of us for our efforts to fight your war, which none of you seem to be doing, and bringing back a considerable volume of salvageable resources for your citizens to use as supplements for your local shortages. We are also responsible for opening up your freedoms to move outside your walls, and perhaps a number of other privileges your own authority figures seem to have neglected to offer during these past several centuries."

"You've lost me. What does any of this have to do with our priests?"

"In short, we are speaking of a conspiracy to keep you under their thumbs, these authority leaders of yours. This is made worse by forcing you to bow down to them as all-powerful wise men who are not to be questioned. Now, allow me to explain in greater detail. As priests in the service of our Lord and King, we are also part of his military Order. Our military is dedicated to law and justice, much like others might worship a religion, and we do not stop at walls to enforce the greater principles of our...faith."

"Wow..."

"As such, we are just as much law enforcers as we are holy men and caregivers of our people back home. Your Governor refused to cooperate with us to fight this war you all claim is outside your walls. But your Captain Kholgard, over at the barracks, had other ideas, as he personally hates your governor. Especially, as he calls it, the man going behind his back to conduct questionable dealings."

The priest pauses as he begins pacing across the dais.

"When we first arrived, our Lord Thaelyn called upon representatives of the local races. The friendly ones, that is, for a political conference to decide how to fight this war. You people claim your world has been under siege for four hundred years, and your population cut down to the last of your cities. And yet, even though we might represent a deciding force now arriving in this world, where we could possibly turn this around for you, he instead chose to demand gold and treasures out of us for our unwelcome intrusion into his private garden, as he was very clearly not interested in fighting anything, and seemed quite content to blame all your woes on someone else."

The crowd ushered up a series of moans at this obvious fault.

"Therefore, we made a deal with your Captain Kholgard behind your Governor's back to assist your city and your people against what are clearly your enemies out there, regardless of your Governor's wishes, or lack thereof, to participate. But we are discovering, not all of your enemies are...out there," he points a finger figuratively outwards of the city.

"Does this mean the priests in here?" the man asks. "You said they were arrested, but what did they do?"

"They were arrested for several things combined. First, we have slander and defamation of character of your friends and neighbors, meaning the Night Elves and the Daanen-Aryku, both of whom were made to believe by your Governor and his own political falsehoods that you were supposed to be their friends and allies. But you were made to believe they were horrors from beyond. How is this possible? Very simply, you are not permitted to ask questions or travel outside the walls to speak to them. Are you even aware that before this tragic war began, all the native races were partners in friendship? Probably not. Thank your schools for that. It seems a large portion of your history went missing at one time, and you are now denied asking questions about it."

"Grand..."

"Next are a number of lesser charges of malicious conduct relating to the local people. This might include so many of the stories to dissuade your attention from the greater facts that were clearly circling around you. But you, with this denial to ask questions, failed to see them. Further, the threat of your gods, as such all-powerful creatures that surely cannot be wrong, denying you to ask about that, either. If your gods were so all-powerful, your Guard should have received orders to march out there, find your enemies, destroy their altars, and be finished with it, and perhaps centuries ago, shortly after it started. And yet, you didn't even take notice of the passage of this great length of time, and so many lives lost along the way."

"In other words, what you're saying is we're all a bunch of flaming dolts who can't open our eyes wide enough to see the folly of it. Grand again."

"Indeed. That other famous saying…for as long as I can remember… Well, I suppose it doesn't matter, as your schools don't teach you anything to begin with."

"Uh huh…"

"But now, let us see about the next one. The worst of it is this…"

He turns to the altar behind him where he finds a metal box, which they pulled out earlier from a storeroom in a rearward portion of the temple. Then, he opens it to produce a ceremonial collar with a short cape. He holds it up for display.

"Do you recognize this item?"

The assembly emits a series of oohs when they see the artifact, which was traditionally depicted as a holy relic.

"Where have you seen this before? Can anyone tell me?"

Several hands go up and voices ring out.

"That's from the Festival of Passage," shouts a woman. "The ceremonial collar they used to bless our children and protect us from the plague."

"Indeed, so it is said. But curiously, for all the former priests claimed of its protective powers, none of you ever questioned the fact that it never worked. Each member of this society still fell ill from it, consistently and perpetually. To the thinking mind, this ought to be a clearly questionable concern as to why you keep praying to it, and for four hundred years. But it would seem your priests maintained such tight control over your thinking minds that you no longer made the attempt."

The murmurs now descended into moans.

The priest turns the item over to the underside and displays this to the audience. The underside was a translucent plastic shell. Although the details were too small for many of the followers to make out at distance, the priest demonstrated by pointing at a series of small holes and a retractable door where one could just make out machine parts inside.

"See here, the underside, which I doubt any of you were ever permitted to see before. This is no holy relic, and neither is it a sacred item. It is a machine with a specific purpose, and built by someone with an exceptionally high degree of scientific wherewithal, especially in the medical studies."

Priest Garrain again returns to the altar, which he was using as a type of evidence table, and picks up another box. This was an elongated plastic storage box, biologically sealed, and with a large quantity of small objects inside. He now holds this up for display.

"Inside this box is a supply of smallish metal objects described as medical implants, also created by that society with the very high degree of medical study. Inside each is a substance deemed extremely dangerous to the body, in this case the brain. They are inserted, one by one, into this device, and the device laid on the shoulders of an unsuspecting victim, in this case your twelve-year-old children."

The assembly let out a sudden rush of groans and wails.

"The implants include a tiny clocklike mechanism to tick off when you arrive at fifty years or thereabouts, before it opens up."

The priest returns to the altar, setting down the box and picking up another item he had waiting. He now holds up a small transparent case with the implant device once taken out of Marelle during her procedure at the Naarg uy'Sodrad. It had been packaged in a bio-containment cube.

"Look here," he states boldly. "Although this may be unpleasant to the eyes to look upon, this is not a creature. It is one of those implants, in this case found inside the body of one person, but then removed and packaged here for study. It has a number of prongs to anchor it in place inside the body, and the central portion is a well to hold the substance to poison you."

He paces across the dais, holding up the items for display to the crowd.

"The collar device has a button to push to engage its functioning, where a series of small needles pop out and administer a fast-acting drug into the skin of your right shoulder. This has the effect of numbing the skin for the next procedure, where a door opens up to reveal a series of surgical instruments designed to cut a small incision, insert the implant just under the skin, and then seal it up with another substance to quickly heal the injury. If you gently feel around your right shoulder, you will find the result."

The assembly all turn to investigate their shoulders, carefully feeling around the area until they find a lump under the skin. This caused even more moans and cries as they made the discovery.

"What makes this even worse," the priest continues, "is it was disguised as anything other than a traditional medical device, even by the standards of those people who might normally build such things. This is a clear and intentional effort to fool you into thinking it is something else, and made worse by the simple fact that your society isn't advanced enough to recognize it in the first place."

He returns to set the items back on the altar before continuing.

"This is your so-called blessing to protect you from those awful Flame Elves out there and their vicious curse none of you ever tried to put a final end to. All you ever did was listen to your priests and their wailings about gods doing the work for you."

"All right," calls one man. "I think we get it. You don't need to rub it in."

"I think I do need to rub it in, as you allowed this to continue for so incredibly long without question. You must carry responsibility for yourself, as well as your children, your friends, and your neighbors in this world, but you are not. You have a militia in this city. Why did you not demand them to go out there and put an end to it when your gods apparently failed, even after one year, to say nothing of four hundred?"

The assembly emitted a painful moaning as they were forced to realize this failing.

"But indeed, now we must continue, as there is more to this crisis than just this."

"More?" he shouts.

"Yes, a fair amount of it, to be sure. Your priests are not the only criminals here. One of them was estimated to be well older than possible for the average lifespans of people in this city, representing a man well into his sixties, by the estimates we might make of our people back home, who habitually reach that age and more."

The audience ushers up another series of oohs.

"Further, they seemed to know about the devices in their shoulders. They knew of it enough to remove their own, thus allowing them to avoid this plague in their own bodies. But clearly, they forgot to explain this to anyone else…except, I suppose, their successors. So, this is not just the recent priests, as it represents all of them since the beginning of this war, and the curse you describe. But now, we must examine how it got started."

He again paces across the dais.

"I cannot be sure about those of you here, or any of the other families in this city, but the noble families are said to have maintained a series of journals of their history and city affairs. They apparently felt it was their duty to do so, due to a most curious and disturbing event that took place once."

He pauses as he prepares to engage in this next lecture.

"Once upon a time, all the societies of this world were at peace, and mutually dependent on each other for your combined survival. The Flame Elves, as you call them now, were once called High Elves. And they, along with the Night Elves, shared a religion together of their true gods…a religion I suspect you might have also shared, to some extent, if you managed to maintain anything from your ancient origins."

"Ancient origins?" calls another man.

"Yes, another part of your missing history. All of you in this world, save for the Daanen-Aryku, are immigrants from our world of Tae'Eladar. We have the remainder of your population on our side. Our people worship a society of beings we call the Estelar, although I doubt you would know this name here, even if you did have any proper knowledge of the true gods, as we made a few advances on our side. And unlike your priests and their fantasies, our gods are real, they are measurable, and if you ask one for help, you will get it," he asserts firmly. "But this is another thing. The elves have their pantheon, and the humans have theirs. Assuming you kept your devotions on your arrival, you might have continued this, at least until this holocaust occurred and destroyed everything your people built together."

He begins pacing again.

"Are you familiar with the name Sargeras? He is an exceptionally powerful creature on the scale of a god. He is the one truly responsible for all of this, along with his agents, who secretly arrived in this world four centuries ago. The High Elves were his first victims. He destroyed their religious association to break them and then took possession of them forcefully to make them his slaves. Everything they did after that was a product of his domination of their minds. The Night Elves carry a history where they had a holy item in their possession, as part of their native religion. We also discovered that the High Elves had the same, and this was in each of their cities. These were taken away, and this crime left evidence pointing at each other as the ones responsible. This represents a conspiracy to start a war by false means."

The crowd let out another moan as they considered this new revelation.

"You here are made to think they started the war, and destroying everything else, largely due to someone here inside your city, and likely also an agent of Sargeras, turning you away from their plight, and defiling their names with such blasphemies as calling them unholy and sacrilegious. And the man doing this is your own Governor."

This caused a rush of loud groans, but before anyone could question it, the priest was speaking again.

"Four hundred years ago, your noble families recorded the history of these events. Your city was once ruled by a council of statesmen taken from those same noble families. Then the war starts, and people start taking ill from something unknown. A man comes along, declaring himself capable of protecting you from this awful curse of the Flame Elves. But he demands to be made Governor, with full control of the city, the academy…" he points out the door and across the plaza, "…and the temple…" he waves a hand around the room. "This is your conspiracy. He did not deserve the role, and neither was he legitimately performing any service for you. He robbed you through blackmail and coercion."

"Great gods…" moans one follower.

"His priests became your oppressors, forcing you to feel the pain of this war, even inside these walls, but never to go out there and correct it. His dean became the dictator of your education system. His students were made to teach you as children only what he felt was necessary to keep you under control. You were denied asking questions, denied going outside to learn the truth of anything, and denied seeking justice against the crimes of this war."

"Then why is he still in that bloody office of his!" shouts a man. "I'm guessing by all this he's still out there, not in a prison somewhere, ay?"

"He is still there because you are all made to…trust…him, as your authority figure."

"Oh great. Me and my bloody mouth for simply speaking it."

"Yes, but here we have yet another problem. Allow me to continue. The Governor of today is likely only the most recent, as we suspect he is part of something bigger, like a criminal syndicate, replacing their elder members with fresh ones outside your view. We are still investigating this so far. But it goes even farther, and now outside the walls."

"Uh oh…" he mumbles. "How far outside?"

"To begin with, you have your supply shortages of iron in this city. The dwarves up north do not seem to be fully supplying your needs, and it is said your Governor has an exclusive agreement. Therefore, why are you not receiving all the iron they produce? The reason, that material you are salvaging down in the valley. It came from the orcs. We have information that says the Suuden-Aryku provide supplies to them, as well as the Flame Elves, and it is believed to be a local supply. Those dwarves up there are indeed producing a fair amount, but you are not receiving it."

This caused a loud rumbling amongst the crowd.

"We have scouts up there watching the dwarves," the priest continues. "First, they do not appear to be behaving naturally. Instead, they appear to be behaving as if under a control effect, and we think it is a potent drug to make them follow directions without thought or question. This means someone is controlling them, and it has to be the Suuden-Aryku for this point. They are also producing more than just iron, and you are not even aware of it. And this means the iron is likely just a secondary product, and the more precious metals are going to the Suuden-Aryku."

"Bloody hell, man!" shouts a woman. "Are you saying he's selling us out?"

"It would certainly seem that way. Furthermore, if we once again reflect on your schools, and this rather fashionable expression…for as long as anyone can remember…such and such, this is because none of you can remember anything beyond your personal lifetimes. For all the generations you must have had passing by these last few centuries, I guess none of you ever wrote anything down about your experiences, despite your schools teaching, or not teaching you anything."

"Oh, well, that's just lovely!"

"Therefore, it seems you are completely unaware that you never took a direct hit on your walls during this time from all those enemies you are so afraid of. They are all under orders not to attack you."

"And another one!" she screeches.

"But wait," a man interjects. "How would you know this? Are you able to just go up to one and simply ask?"

"Technically, yes. We captured a ranking Flame Elf official and did just this," the priest shrugs. "We found out from their side what happened and redeemed her back to ours. So, Sargeras no longer has control of her. But she also told us you have someone on the inside managing you, and this now points to the Governor. He apparently works for them."

"Gods' pity!" the man retorts. "So, what is it you're saying here? If we go up to him and start complaining, he just calls in his blokes out there to clean up?"

"This is what we are concerned about now. His friends are the Suuden-Aryku, the ones producing this device and these implants, and he seems to be in league with your enemies. So, we must first take care of those outside before we can take care of those inside. Right now, we are making a number of secret movements, like us here in this temple, and the Guard is taking charge of your schools. But neither the Governor nor the Dean can know of it, or else…you know what happens. The Suuden-Aryku do not need to march on your city, as they have ships that can travel between the stars, and they can park one right over your heads and blast you from the sky above. The Daanen-Aryku tell us they did this on many occasions as they were being chased from one world to another."

"Whoa, hold on there," another man calls out. "I don't think any of that was on my school roster, not that it surprises me by now. Where do these Daanen-Aryku actually come from if they're being chased so far?"

"This is a good question, so let's touch on it briefly. The Daanen-Aryku and the Suuden-Aryku are one and the same society of people, with the only real difference being Sargeras. He arrived on their ancestral home world, called Azgarén, once long ago. He then offered them, it would seem, some sort of great gift if they would give themselves into his service. This was clearly an attempt to corrupt them. A portion of their people chose not to take this and tried to run away. They began calling themselves Daanen-Aryku, while the rest maintain the original name. The Suuden-Aryku gave chase, probably out of spite for not joining the corruption…and well, here we are."

"In all the bleedin' hells," the man groans. "Don't these people hold anything sacred?"

"I think we should point our fingers mostly at Sargeras, and we know he most certainly does not. His history, just those portions we are seeing here, to say nothing of what might have come before, is simply inexcusable. For instance, if we go back to those Flame Elves a moment, they are also down to their last city, as it seems. He used their entire population for one thing or another, then to stop with the last of them, probably because he wants to preserve them for something special."

"Oh grand, now I'm actually feeling sorry for the blighters."

"We are currently working on that, but it is one more covert operation we need to take, so Sargeras and his agents do not know of it before we are finished. We need to take a number of these actions, as we have come to understand who Sargeras actually is, and we are surprised to see he still exists at all."

"Uh oh, I'm not so sure if I want to ask about that one."

"Maybe so, but a brief mention might help. We hold knowledge of a special history shared with us by the Estelar. It is passed down to us by our Lord and King, who is privileged to know of it. There was once a race of beings they called Primordials, a rival godlike society that was discovered committing a number of atrocities on younger lifeforms, which is to say, beings more like us. They used them as toys for their amusement. They were punished for this, but it seems Sargeras is still out there, and even worse, he is leading his armies in our direction at present, and ours is the direction the last of them fell. This cannot be a good thing."

"Aye, you got that much right!"

"We think he ran away from that last battle and went into hiding, but now he is coming out. We have informed the Estelar of this, but we all generally agree, if he has been hiding for so long, he might be watching for them. Therefore, we must make the initial advance, not them, or else he might run again, and we could lose him."

"Grand…"

"Aren't these gods supposed to be all-seeing, and whatnot?" asks one woman.

"Such terms are often used to describe gods," the priest replies. "But the truth is they are not…not in such a sense as to imply an infinite quantity. They are beings who exist on a scale much higher than ours. But just like with us, where we might find our attention focused on one or another point of interest, so they might as well. Their capacity might be much greater, and perhaps now they might be watching him, now that they know of him, whereas at first, they thought the Primordials were all dead...end of story," he shrugs.

"Wow, now that pinches the idea a bit."

"Aye," reflects a male member. "They stopped looking after a while."

"Indeed," the priest affirms. "So, we have the Daanen-Aryku, which we think were playthings for his amusement along the way, even up until their last home, the world they call Ruuki uy'Daan, which was also home to these orcs. They tell us they found Flame Elves inside their ship, causing it to crash here intentionally. This is surely the work of the Suuden-Aryku, and further reason to think this world holds special purpose for him. Then he sends orcs at us for whatever reason, and this brings us back here. And his agents are not at all pleased with it."

"I'm sure of that!" another man chuckles. "How is it actually going for you out there?"

"The orcs are on the run, now pushed back by several hundred miles from their closest approach."

The crowds gush forward with another round of oohs.

"The Suuden-Aryku are learning not to toy with us out by the Naarg uy'Sodrad, and the Flame Elves were apparently told not to spend themselves on us at all. So, we are going to them instead with our covert interactions to bring them home. And then we have ourselves here with you. But this city seems to be a focal point for these conspiracies, and we need to step around it gently. We will take care of it, not you. You just go about your business and listen to our instructions, should we have anything important to pass along. In the meantime, we are here to help you learn the ways of the true gods out there, and to assist in the removal of these devices from your bodies."

"You can do that?" asks one member.

"Yes, we can. Our medicine is much more advanced than what you apparently have here. The Daanen-Aryku can also do this, but we do not necessarily want to see a lot of people wandering around out there in open view of our enemies. We need to be discreet in our actions."

The assembly collectively agrees.

"Now, good citizens," the priest prepares to wrap up. "If you wish to find true solace in the worship of the gods, I will present to you one to begin you on your journey."

He directs the other priests standing around the dais to remove a cloth shroud that was covering a tall marble statue placed on the platform. It reveals a male figure ornately clad in a magistrate toga. His right hand was held up wearing a gauntlet and revealing an open palm. His other hand was holding an inverted sword standing on the pedestal base.

"Remember what I said of our...faith," the priest proclaims. "This is where it comes from. This is Lord Torm. He is a member of the Estelar, the true gods of the realms. They preside over all of Creation, which is to say all places and all things. We exist inside a universe here. If you look up at the nighttime sky, you can see a portion of it. This is just one of many. Tae'Eladar is in another, and the Suuden-Aryku come from yet another. These concepts might seem difficult to learn at first, but with a bit of time and education, I think we can overcome this."

He pauses to observe their faces before continuing.

"Each member of these gods has their specialty, and Lord Torm presides over the domain of Justice and Law. They hold dear a philosophical doctrine called the Measure of Balance. We will teach you what this means. But unlike the alleged gods your old priests were described to you, these do not simply demand you to accept their words without question. They are scholars and advisers, who choose to inspire their Children to grow and learn."

+ +✦+ +

"This provides us with confirmation on another aspect of the Governor's involvement with the dwarves," the General relates.

"Leesa reported that the Dean was taking a couple of smallish barrels up there, along with a few other common goods, to resupply the dwarves in their enclave. The barrels she described sound exactly like these fertilizer containers we found inside their farming chamber."

"She is proving herself to be quite a clever young agent," Thaelyn admits. "I think Marelle would be proud," he looks across the table at her.

Marelle smiles as she listened to the late afternoon review.

"She also took photographs of the other contents of the basement," the General continues. "There was not much of extraordinary importance, several boxes containing a number of odd supplies, another couple of those barrels, and such like. But she did take note of one very unusual feature. Here, look at this."

The General slides a photograph from a recent stack into view. The image showed what was clearly an alien device nestled in a corner of the room and partially hidden behind a rack of shelves. It included a circular plate on the floor inside a partial tube-like chute standing upright. It was large enough to fit a Suuden'kai male, and then some.

Thaelyn studied the image and turned to Lieutenant Lapäli for his opinion.

"Yes, Your Lordship," Padriyl affirms. "I can already tell you this looks like a type of personal conveyor. I can't say I've ever seen a design like this, but the arrangement of components gives me the impression the Suuden-Aryku have managed to improve the technology to provide one small enough to fit into tight spaces and carry individual people. My only question is the power source, as these things would require a substantial amount to provide for their operation."

"Well then, Lieutenant," the General offers. "Perhaps this might provide an answer."

He pulls out another photo and places it into view. This one showed a hatch-like door set into the basement wall. Next to it was a control panel with a numeric keypad.

"Yes, this could easily give us an answer," Padriyl accedes. "If this is secured by a keypad lock, then it must be a sensitive area, and this might suggest the control center for a power source, possibly a fusion reactor, although it would have to be a very compact one, and I must also wonder if it is staffed, or monitored remotely."

"If the Governor has such a close relationship with them that he owns one of these," Thaelyn reflects. "Then he is no simple agent working to manage the city. And this further causes me to wonder who, and for that matter, what he actually is, if we consider our other suppositions about him."

"Just for reference, what do you mean?"

"He is said to be managing the city, as it was stated by Priestess Sehnisavain during our initial interview. He is suggested to hold some form of authority over the Suuden-Aryku, at least insofar as their patrols out by the Naarg uy'Sodrad are concerned. Recall our patrol dressed as the Allegiance Guard. Marelle tells us that her recollection of other officially sanctioned Guard patrols, those sent by the Governor as part of his diplomatic plays in the eyes of his neighbors, all came home safe without any signs of trouble. But ours came under immediate attack, and by no less than a most unusual raiding party using adamantium armor and swords."

"Yes, I recall this, and you suggested this was to make a visual display for the supposed disobedience of the Guard going out against orders."

"Yes, as this was not sent by the Governor. And so, this one patrol would be made an example. But how and why would the Suuden-Aryku choose, if by their own accord, this one occasion to make this rather prolific example. It seems far more likely they were instructed to do so, and for this precise reason."

"Meaning to say," Marelle interjects. "By someone who would know the difference of whether or not he actually sent it...the Governor."

"Correct, and this infers he holds a substantial amount of leverage over the Suuden-Aryku High Commander, who by definition is the highest-ranking officer in their military, and should not normally submit himself to anyone else."

"And this is where we have our argument," Padriyl continues. "Regardless of the whole society giving themselves to Sargeras, and whatever orders he issues for a chain of command, the Suuden'kai HC is apparently offering himself to serve under another authority, and not a native one. I think I would wish to point out one other aspect of this, and that being a human, with respect to those present, would be a poor choice as a CO over a Suuden'kai HC, at least as much for the required technical expertise."

"Very well," Thaelyn nods. "This does offer a valid argument."

"So, we must be missing something important here."

"What about the big guy himself?" Relissa muses. "Can he be putting on some kind of show for us out here?"

"This is a fine suggestion, Relissa," Thaelyn considers. "And I suppose he could manifest his image in one form or another. But the question here must be, would he actually come out this far, possibly to expose himself to his enemies, and especially if he is launching assaults on Tae'Eladar with those orcs?"

"Aye, that's a good one."

"Therefore, we have a missing piece, and this one piece could be a most important one, especially when compounded by these other factors, including the Governor's apparent management of the dwarves."

"Could it simply be the Suuden-Aryku are playing with us?" Marelle wonders. "It's obvious they like playing with the Daanen-Aryku. Maybe this is some kind of game to them...or maybe I should say Sargeras."

"I will admit, by the stories we carry down of the Primordials, they did enjoy playing such games, and this would be a rather elaborate one. But we still need to ask the question about the adamantium."

"Yes, and then there is that..." the General adds. "According to our young agent, she overheard the Governor in conversation with the Dean on his return that they would schedule a pick-up in two days' time."

"Very good, General," Thaelyn considers. "But on this occasion, we are not going to allow him his prize. Whatever the Suuden-Aryku are using this for, we are going to deny them this particular shipment."

"Of course, but how would you suggest going about this?"

"General, I must now apply myself in ways that are not to my greatest pleasure. But in times of war, this is precisely as I would teach our people. We must make use of falsehood and deception in the eyes of our opponents. I do not wish them to know it was us performing this deed, in order to distract their attention, and perhaps to buy us some more time."

"Your Lordship," Marelle offers. "It's my understanding you would normally teach this to your military recruits. To know everything about your enemy, but not to allow him to know you the same. I certainly wouldn't hold it against you to follow your own teachings, regardless of the fact you're a Celestial that doesn't like lying to people."

"Thank you, Marelle. In this case, we must create a scene of misdirection. Since we are already at war with the orcs, and since we are already using them as a distraction with the Flame Elves taking hits, just in case the Suuden-Aryku should call in for an update, then we are going to expand on this for the mines. However, here we have a complication, and that is the distance for them to travel to reach those mines."

"Yeah, that would be a big complication. You've pushed them pretty far to the south by now. Well out of walking distance to those mines, assuming they were ever within walking distance to begin with."

"And so will be our new deception, and we will have Sehnisavain corroborate with us to build on this deception. Although she tells us the High Commander has not yet called in for a status update, she is going to reveal to him that her people are coming under random attacks by orcs using portals. Whoever it was, whether Sargeras or some agent, who taught them this practice, we are going to take this heresy of teaching a lesser society such superior workings as portals, and turn it against them, claiming the orcs have evolved this by now in their time of need to use it as a weapon."

"Jiggers!" Relissa moans. "That's simply rotten," she chuckles.

"The Priestess will make claims of sightings of orcs appearing out of portals to make surprise hits, since they are also outside your common walking distance. So far, her people are attending to it, so she will not require reinforcement. In our case, we are going to suggest a surprise hit by a band of orcs that somehow managed to direct a portal at the space up there and hit the Suuden'kai transport crew. But our people must hit them hard and fast to take them down before they can call in any sort of distress message."

"All right, so we hit them hard and fast," Marelle muses. "But when, where, and how do we confiscate the goods?"

"This must be carefully timed. We cannot know precisely how quickly the Suuden-Aryku can respond to the situation, but we want them to respond to find their comrades fallen and due to an obvious orcish attack."

"So, we need to hit and run, and leave behind things like orcish weapons at the scene."

"My Lord," Relissa interjects. "If we're going to make such a quick hit, I'm wondering how we're going to make the rest of them think it was by orcs using portals, rather than just a bunch that happened to run by."

"This is a good point," he continues. "We are going to falsify a distress message by what will sound like the Suuden'kai crew members. Since we are speaking of the same basic race as the Lieutenant here," he looks up at Padriyl. "He will be the voice on their communications channels. Do you think you can do this, Lieutenant?"

"As far as I can tell," he admits. "The language hasn't really changed in our absence, although the manners are going to be a little shaky because we have not actually carried a conversation with any of them since we left Azgarén. However, the description by Priestess Sehnisavain tells us they tend to speak in flat monotones, which should be easy enough to replicate."

"Good, you will be our Suuden'kai survivor that just barely manages to call it in before being the last to fall."

"And jiggers again!" Relissa yips. "So, now he has to play a role of being under attack, and then dying on their trans-com."

"Indeed, and Marelle, you seem to hold some experience at roleplay, so perhaps you could practice a little with him to get his performance just right."

"Wow, I'm getting a lot of new students lately," she smirks.

"We also need to remove the adamantium, and this will take time, as the stockpiles are growing rather large by now. We should do this before we make our distress call, then have our people leave just afterwards."

"This will sure add to your wealth, I'll bet," she accedes thoughtfully.

"Technically speaking, Marelle, this is not our mine, and for that matter we cannot accurately claim it to be yours. But for all that your people have suffered, you probably deserve it more than we."

"Your Lordship, I'm sure our people would thank you greatly for this, but let's also remember we don't know how to use it."

"This is true, and neither do any of the elven societies here. For now, I will order it to be removed and stockpiled in storage somewhere until we can decide later. We are building a new military research center back home as part of our agreement with the Daanen-Aryku to develop our conjoined studies for use in the latter parts of this war. Perhaps we can store it there, and make use of it for some future application to benefit us all."

"That sounds fine by me. What about the iron? If orcs are stealing stuff, they might want that as well," she smiles timidly.

Thaelyn eyes her suspiciously.

"Yes," he sighs. "I suppose you do have a point, and orcs are known to be scavengers. Very well, if we have the time for it, do so. We might need to use portals, and just toss everything through to remove it quickly. We can allow our people on the other side to clean up at their leisure."

"That makes sense. One for the iron, another for the adamantium."

"Good, then we shall prepare ourselves for this occasion to

coincide with their arrival. Our scouts will call it in once they have a sighting."

"How do we feel on those dwarves and their reaction to us for this visit?"

"The scouts tell us they seem completely oblivious to intruders. Even the Dean's visit resulted in virtually no response. So, I will not concern myself with that unless something unusual occurs. In the meantime, we should prime ourselves with Priestess Sehnisavain and her status update…since the High Commander does not seem to have in mind to make so many of his own."

"All right, Priestess, do you have your lines ready?"

"I believe so, it seems fairly straightforward," she smiles demurely. "This may actually be the most entertaining moment of interaction I have yet to enjoy with that man."

"Well, just try not to break out laughing until after you finish."

"Of course, Master Cydulean," she grins.

Sehnisavain and Cydulean, along with Sumisal and Ilothonna, were in the High Priestess's office at the temple in Kynesoth preparing to make a call to High Commander Geilv to report on the condition of the Flame Elves and their sudden situation of war with the orcs. Sehnisavain was most often the one to communicate with the High Commander since she was the lead authority in the city. She picked up a trans-com from a side table and began dialing in a familiar number.

"Commander Geilv, speaking…" ushers the emotionless voice on the other end.

"Commander, this is High Priestess Sehnisavain in Kynesoth."

"Yes, do you have a report?"

"In fact, I do. It might interest you to know that we have come under attack."

"An attack? The invaders are attacking you?"

"No, not the invaders…they do not seem to show any interest in us so far. I'm actually referring to the orcs in this case."

"Orcs! Why would the orcs attack you?"

"We believe they have taken offence to their recent exclusion from our alliance. As I'm sure you must be aware by now, the invaders are apparently making quick work of them on the western frontier. We believe the orcs are now holding a grudge against the rest of us for not offering support, and are taking it out on my people since we are likely the most convenient."

"Do you require assistance?"

"No, that will not be necessary, Commander. I'm sure we can handle a few orcs. It is giving my people some much needed exercise for the lack of activity in other areas. Our only real concern is to be ready for them once they emerge out of their portals."

"What? Portals? They are using abnormal conveyance to reach your position?"

"Well, yes," she responds casually. "Their lines are much too far by now to walk the distance, and they have apparently improved on those teachings you once gave on how to use portals. Now they are using them to launch offensive strikes in our direction. But as I said, our people are managing well enough for now."

"Understood. You will advise if the situation changes. Is there anything else to report?"

"That is all for the moment."

"Acknowledged. Base Prime out…"

They end the link and Sehnisavain turns to the others in the room with a naughty smile.

Tristeen was once again in her morning alchemy study in the basement of the academy. Jared was also at his usual table across the room. As before, they pretended to be focused on their work, while at the same time peeking over their shoulders at the instructors who were still hovering intently around the elaborate conjuring circle they were laying down.

Tristeen took up the same table along the rear wall as she had once before, just opposite the circle, and as such, she could overhear some of the heated debate the instructors were having over the final details of the markings in the circle. Due to the clearly determined nature of the instructors, and the meticulous review of their work, she decided to make another of her little displays, just to shake things up.

"Wow, that's quite a circle you have down there!" she remarks innocently, but also boldly, to draw the attention of the room.

The sudden announcement shook the instructors who were so intensely focused on their efforts. They turned once again to find the smiling face of the young mid-classman peeking over their shoulders.

"You know," she continues unabatedly. "Something that fancy could win first prize at the bazaar over in the Upper Ward."

"Acolyte Macaid, if you please," the first instructor moans. "We are very busy and cannot be disturbed in our work."

"Oh, naturally, I'm sure you have to be very careful in…whatever it is you are supposed to be doing. After all, I remember very precisely you said this was not something for a casual demonstration. In fact, by the appearance of those glyphs, good gracious! I may not know as much about conjuring, but the few things I've been able to put together, something that tightly packed would represent a very strong warding circle, am I right?"

"Well, yes, but…"

"And if it's such a tightly packed warding circle, whatever it is you might want to conjure inside of it would have to be very dangerous, right?"

"Well…"

"And if it's so dangerous… Ye Gods! We certainly wouldn't want it getting loose in the city, right?"

"Acolyte Macaid…"

"And yet, you told me this might end up as a lesson for the upperclassmen. Wow! It makes me wonder what those upperclassmen are going to do with something that could possibly tear this city right down to its foundation!"

"Acolyte!" he shouts. "If you don't mind…"

"Instructor, I do mind!" she returns in kind. "You people don't even teach the mid-classmen anything more potent than how to make a few holiday sparkles, and yet you're hoping to teach the upperclassmen how to conjure up something that could rip this building apart? If I should see this thing roaming around on the streets tomorrow, I'm bringing the Guard over here and hauling you out by the heels. Do you understand, instructor? We do still have laws in this city, and you are not the ones making them. I am quite sure the safety of this city is more important than your wild aspirations to study things that shouldn't even be demonstrated!"

She turns abruptly and resumes her work without another word.

Her outburst had everyone in the room watching, and the instructors felt their eyes on them. They glanced around cautiously, and then returned to continue their review of the circle, although much more guarded.

Later in the day, Tristeen and Jared met in the main hall for a private conference, along with some others who were now participating.

"Tristeen," Jared begins. "That was a little brazen, don't you think?"

"Jared, I don't see anything wrong with what I did down there. First, they're putting together something I don't think any of us has ever seen put together before, regardless of the fact of what we think they hope to use it for. The simple fact that they're drawing up a circle like that is cause enough for concern."

"Aye," Sara admits. "I have to agree with her on that one. That bloody thing isn't for any casual mumbling."

"Second, they told me last time it was for a possible future study for the upperclassmen. They also said it was not for casual demonstration. What in all the hells is it for if they're not going to demonstrate their work? That's a lot of effort to draw up a circle like that just for the artistic presentation."

"Right to that, Tris," Jon affirms. "That sure isn't for any first prize, like you said."

"And finally, I think it is entirely appropriate to mention the safety of the city. If this really is for something big and nasty, their recklessness needs to be addressed in the eyes of whatever law we might actually have in force around here."

"All right, Tristeen," Jared relents. "Ease off a bit. I can't argue with you on any of this. And I suppose I have to admit, someone needs to put down a foot or two with these people that they don't own the city and its people, even though they behave like they do."

"Right," Sara agrees. "To let something like that out in the streets, accidentally or not, is a clear danger that needs to be addressed! You can't expect somebody to simply sit back and take it after a show like that parading around!"

"And to make a statement ahead of time is surely to be expected," Tristeen asserts. "Regardless of their preference that we keep our mouths shut, you simply cannot do that! Not if a demon is sent running through the plaza. You need to take action, and they ought to know it."

"Granted that," Jon considers. "But do you think it'll actually stop them?"

"Probably not, but the words needed to be delivered as a prelude that they know there will be repercussions following."

✦✦✦✦✦

"And this was that young noble girl, Acolyte Macaid?"

"Yes, Dean," the first instructor informs. "She even went so far as to threaten us by calling the Guard if something should be seen on the streets outside."

"Indeed, such insolence. Very well, we shall watch her closely, and if the dear young do-gooder believes we did something inappropriate, we shall make our proper appeals with the Governor and his authority in this matter. The Guard, for as much as they also seem to be neglecting their loyalties, must still follow the Governor's will, as he is the final authority in the city."

"Dean," the second instructor relates. "Some of us have been noticing a subtle rise in the level of curiosity of the students in this matter, and I think Acolyte Macaid's outbursts have been invoking a level of suspicion and mistrust amongst our student body of late. If this conjuration should go about as planned, it is likely they will turn on us, especially after this episode in the basement today."

"You think so?" he mulls deeply. "Then we might have to make special provisions to bring things back under control. I will report this to the Governor, as I'm sure he will want to know."

The two instructors bow and leave the office. The Dean sits quietly for a few moments longer, and then gets up and makes his way downstairs and out a back door. He often used this mode to sneak away across the plaza behind several other buildings and through the back door of the Governor's Manor, in case he needed to make private visits to deliver special reports. Once inside, he enters the main foyer and makes his way upstairs.

The noise of his commotion on entering the building and stomping up the stairs caught Leesa's attention. She peeked through the doorway of the office and followed him with her eyes.

The secretary had taken notice of her attentiveness, and was becoming curious as to her manners by now.

"Is there something occurring out there, Leesa?" he inquires casually.

She turns to his address and smiles.

"I need to make a quick run, if you please," she points delicately out the door.

She steps out of the office and discreetly removes her shoes, then quickly sprints up the stairs on tiptoe to listen at the Governor's door again.

"My Lord," the Dean announces. "We are developing a little problem over at the academy, I think."

"Oh wonderful, now what?" the Governor moans.

"Well, I suppose this is to be expected, at least somewhat. Some of the students, a few in particular, are taking notice of our work in the basement and becoming curious, perhaps even nervous. And one in particular made a statement of going to the Guard, if whatever it is we hope to be conjuring should get loose on the street."

"Really! They would do that now? Fabulous, and who is this over-righteous civil watch wannabe?"

"Acolyte Tristeen Macaid, a noble heiress to the Macaid family. She has traditionally behaved as a mild and very dedicated individual, but lately has become rather outspoken on our responsibilities to the city."

"Indeed, one of the nobles, is it?" he muses pensively. "They were trouble for us once before," he mutters privately. "I had thought they were reduced to just bystanders, but it seems they still hold a few old grudges. All right, Dean, I will need to consider this carefully. Those nobles tend to stick together, and if something…unfortunate… were to happen to one, it might stand out too much. Their names carry weight, and I wish to keep this situation within some measure of control. The rest of these people might still hold value. We do not want any of them turning on us. By the way, what about those rumors of unrest you heard once?"

"Well…" he pauses in consideration. "I might say they are quieting, but at the same time, I cannot be sure if it is a simple thing like a passing fancy, for instance relating to the recent events outside, or if the voices are quieting only when I enter the room."

"Oh? Is this to say they are suspecting you of something that now they are hushing up on you?"

"All I can say for sure is when I visit a local tavern, the room goes eerily quiet of the usual chatter. Then, it starts up again on so much general nonsense as to seem like they are diverting themselves."

"I see. This is not pleasing to hear, and it suggests that Thaelyn fellow is influencing our people in some way, possibly through his involvement with those farmers and such you said were going outside again to reestablish themselves."

"Maybe, and so it might be filtering down by now."

The Governor pauses to look out the window onto the plaza, quietly pondering his thoughts.

"Dean, as much as it might pain me to say this, we should delay our activity for a few days. We'll put a bit of distance in our actions in order to dilute the youthful ambitions of this young lady and her presumed responsibilities to the city. Your instructors have been attempting to play this out as a study of some sort, correct?"

"Yes, my Lord, this is the story they're giving...a study for a potential lesson, but only on condition of its viability."

"All right, good. We'll play on this for now. Have them finish with the circle, but do not conjure anything just yet. Do you still have that message I gave you?"

"Yes, it's sitting on my desk."

"Hold on to it until I give my word. Tell your instructors to appear as though they are indeed studying the finer points of this circle design, at least in the eyes of those unsettled students of yours. I need to think of what manner of procedure we can use here to maintain containment of the larger situation, while at the same time affording us our solution to this little problem."

"Very good, my Lord, then I will be on my way."

The Dean bows and begins to leave.

Leesa once again had been listening at the door until she heard the conversation wrapping up. She then quickly darted off to her favorite closet to hide.

The Governor waited for the Dean to depart. He turned again to look out the window and continued mulling the situation in his thoughts.

"Yes, those students would dare think they hold any such responsibility to anything. Their only purpose is to follow orders. It would seem this whole city needs a refresher to inspire them back into their proper place. And it will need to begin with those students."

He sits quietly for many long moments trying to think of an appropriate solution, mumbling to himself of odd mechanisms and peculiar artifacts, then to anomalous agents and obscure concoctions.

"Hmm, something that could appear on the surface as harmless, yes. After all, they play with their alchemy enough, so we will simply give them something new to play with. But it needs to be effective, and at the same time..." he chuckles wickedly. "Yes, I think I have an idea. How marvelous..."

He reaches into his drawer and pulls out his trans-com to dial a familiar number. He then waits for it to answer.

"Commander Geilv, speaking..."

"Commander, I have a special order I need to make back home. Take this down and forward it for me. Have it marked as a rush order."

"Acknowledged. Also, I have a report."

"Wonderful, not you too," he sighs. "Very well, what is it?"

"The elves have come under attack."

"What?!" he roars. "He's attacking our little Flame Elves now?"

"Negative, Thaelyn is not responsible. The elves are reporting orcs attacking at random on their outer lines."

"Orcs! Those beastly curs would dare offend us now?"

"The High Priestess of Kynesoth reports she believes this to be in retaliation to our absence of support while the orcs are under attack by the invading armies."

"Oh, well, I am so sorry for their sour attitudes, even though they are the ones who brought him here in the first place. What is the situation down there? Are they requesting support?"

"Negative, she reports they are holding the lines against the orcs as they launch their attacks through their abnormal conveyance."

"Excuse me?!" he shouts again. "Portals, Commander, they're called portals!" he pants. "Those brutes are now using portals against our people?"

"Affirmative, the High Priestess believes they have improved their knowledge and now employ these...portals...in new designs, striking at random and pulling back."

"This is intolerable, Commander! All right, fine, keep on top of it. I want to know if the situation gets any worse. Now, as to my special order…"

A new day was dawning and the scouts surveying the dwarven enclave to the north had staked out several locations to hide in preparation of the arrival of the Suuden-Aryku transport believed to be on route to pick up the stockpiles of metal. The front of the enclave was a large neatly quarried boxlike shape carved into the side of the mountain. It would make an excellent landing pad, although a tight squeeze, for an aircraft to settle into place. And since the Suuden-Aryku technology, same as with the Daanen-Aryku, was largely hover-enabled, a VTOL craft was expected to be arriving.

Thaelyn and the General gathered in the tactical office for a morning review.

"If we were to make a few assumptions," Thaelyn begins. "And say they might send it as the first order of business in the morning, then it comes down to how quickly it travels and how far their home base is."

"And this would allow us some idea of when to expect it," the General accedes.

"Correct, although there are still many variables, not the least of which is their course heading for the flight path."

"Yes, it could be almost anywhere. Our scouts have taken positions on the ridgeline to the east and will watch for anything passing along within view. This might at least give us an impression of their direction of travel."

"Good, but keep in mind not to be seen at the same time they are out there watching for this transport."

"Indeed. Fortunately, the Suuden-Aryku seem to have pulled back most of their forces and fortified themselves within their outposts by now. I think they have finally taken the lesson in front of the Naarg uy'Sodrad."

"Perhaps, but this only confounds our interpretation even more.

They hold superior firepower, especially if you consider their bombardment potential, and now they hide inside their fortifications."

"This must be related to the discussions we had of our own potential, for our use of magic, our mage shields providing us cover from their weapons, and our use of portals. If their main focus is on trying to remove you personally, I would say they are simply in a standby condition awaiting further orders."

"I would agree, but it also defies logic of who is actually in charge here. Leesa reported last night that the Governor consulted with the Dean on placing their action on standby as well, and largely due to an issue of the students in the academy becoming nervous over the implications of conjuring something that could pose a danger to the city. This does not bode well for at least a few reasons, and it also demands us to ask where is that next attempt they are preparing."

"Just out of curiosity, how would you interpret this?"

"In the academy? This is clearly a stall tactic, maybe to soften these attitudes of the students. But if the Dean and the Governor are such that they tend to play God with other people's lives, as would be demonstrated by these fabrications and enforced by this plague of theirs, I am tempted to say these students, who are expected to be as subservient as all the rest, might become expendable if they should present themselves as anything else."

"Gracious! Then we should offer some manner of warning to them."

"Yes, pass these thoughts to Acolyte Sarens and see if he has anything to offer. I might even go so far as to suggest we should evacuate them if this becomes serious."

It was late morning, and the scouts in front of the dwarven enclave were nestled neatly into their nooks. They had concealed themselves with natural cover, hiding within shrubbery and between rocks. They scanned the skies for anything arriving from above. Then one of them takes notice of an object coming into view.

"Oi…" he emits softly. "Look there, what do you make that out to be?"

"Well, mate, I'll tell you what it doesn't look like, and that being any kind of bird I ever did see."

"Right! Looks like those bloody Suuden-Aryku have got themselves a right dandy flying ship fluttering about."

"Aye, and a big one, to be sure… Look at the flippin' size of that thing!"

The large transport vessel came in smoothly across the ridgeline and began to line up with the landing zone slot in the boxlike space across the way from the scouts. It hovered above the ground and lowered its landing gear, then slowly began its descent into the space in front of the enclave's front door. The scouts watched and waited as they studied the large vessel for its graceful control under the expert management of its pilots.

"I'll say one thing, it would take a bit of talent to fly one of those, I'll bet."

"Aye, to be sure… But now we need to call this in."

"Right, and we need to check on how many of them are inside there. For as much material they need to move down inside those mines, it might be a while for them to finish up."

"Good enough. This will give our people some time to make our move."

One of the scouts casts an invisibility cloak on himself to go investigate the transport and its crew, while the other one pulls out a trans-com to make a call.

As the day progresses, Thaelyn and the General are assembling an assault team to launch against the Suuden-Aryku transport. Marelle, Relissa, and Lieutenant Lapäli were just arriving back through the gateway to join in the affairs.

"Ah, you are just in time, we have work for you up north," Thaelyn announces.

"Have they arrived?" Marelle responds enthusiastically.

"Indeed, they have, and they are well underway in loading up their supply. But fortunately for us, the stockpiles are large enough that it will take some time, and this allows us ample opportunity to make our move."

He directs them around the table for a briefing.

"Here is our plan," he begins. "Marelle, you and Lieutenant Lapäli will be teaming up on this occasion. With respect to the Lieutenant, you already have some experience with our people, and we need to be sure this follows smoothly. Therefore, I am making you the team leader. Your first objective is to neutralize the crewmembers, and prevent them from reporting back to their home base. My suggestion is to use our scouts as a stealth strike force. They can hit from the shadows and take down their opponents quietly and efficiently."

"Is this anything like the assassin that tried it with you?" she grins delicately.

"Indeed, but ours are much more talented," he chuckles. "Once we have secured the area, you must package up and remove the materials as quickly as possible. We will provide bags to carry it, and several mages to send it away using portals. We will also provide a number of orcish weapons collected from our refuse dump to distribute around the scene, and make it appear these were used to dispatch the crewmembers. Once the materials are fully removed, you will have Lieutenant Lapäli play his role on their communications channels to send off a fake distress message revealing foul play on behalf of the orcs using portals to launch a sneak attack. When this is done, you must depart the area."

"All right, sounds easy enough. Hit hard, leave a few clues, pick up and go."

"Excellent. We have a mage outside with a rune to the area. Join your team and be on your way."

"Um, my Lord," Relissa raises a hand for attention. "Do you think you could let me out of the cage long enough to give a hand?"

"Would you like to participate in this venture?"

"Well, Marelle's been getting all the fun lately, and I figure someone needs to keep an eye on this round-ear," she thumbs playfully at her, "just to make sure she doesn't trip over anyone's feet."

"Indeed!" he grins. "Well, this should be a fairly straightforward operation. I do not see why you could not be a part of it, and it might give you some valuable experience and a little fresh air to spend your energy."

"Aye!"

The meeting breaks up with Marelle and the others joining a squad of troops waiting outside. A mage opens a portal, and she leads them through.

Once again, they arrived inside a gully. It was closed on one end and leading out to the west. The terrain was rugged, with the only unnatural feature being the road cut into the slope and winding away on the opposite side of the gully in the direction of Rolsklinde. She observed the bridge that crossed the gully up to the wide area that seemed specially carved as a clearing in front of the entrance. From her viewpoint, she could not accurately see the vessel.

"All right," she orders. "We need a scout to go under his cloak. I want a quick survey of the front to tally up numbers and what they're doing."

A scout steps forward and nods, then quickly casts an enchantment on himself to go invisible. Marelle and her team waited several long moments for him to return. Eventually, he arrived back and dispelled the cloak so he could interact with the team. Marelle was startled by the sudden appearance, but quickly composed herself.

"What do you see up there?" she asks.

"I see three workers currently inside the vessel, but I recall from our report there were more moving to-and-fro, a total of seven, by the earlier count."

"All right, good, bring some help and deal with them. Make it quiet, and then set up ambushes for the rest. I want them mostly found outside for the others to discover."

"Aye!"

The scout selects several others, and together they cast cloaks on themselves to attend to their tasks. Marelle and the remainder of her team keep to the gully for now until the initial job was complete. In the distance, she heard the moans of the victims falling, and secretly mourned to herself about the unfortunate demise of they who were probably just as much subjugated minions as the Flame Elves and the dwarves were stated to be. But she couldn't allow herself to feel remorse at this moment. It was necessary to create this image in order to preserve even more lives elsewhere.

Time passed and the sun beat down on them in the rocky hillside. Marelle and her team waited patiently until finally the lead scout returned with his report.

"Lieutenant, it's done. The last of them is laid out, and we don't see any more walking about."

"Good work, let's go."

She waves her team into action, and they rush around into the clearing towards the mine entrance. As the others move forward, Marelle pauses to study the huge vessel, and whistles in awe of its size. Relissa and Lieutenant Lapäli follow at her side.

"Jiggers," Relissa moans. "That's a big one!"

"That would account as a heavy transport," Padriyl accedes. "They must be expecting to carry a large load."

"Well," Marelle admits. "They did say the stockpiles were huge down there."

The transport was indeed a large vessel, and just barely able to squeeze into the clearing. The bottom stood nearly even to Marelle's head, and the body was even greater in proportion, to accommodate the tall Suuden'kai occupants. It was not perfectly cylindrical, but instead somewhat oblate side-to-side.

Marelle studied the alien transport for its size and apparent utility. She reflected on her experience with the gryphons she was riding earlier when she was conducting her investigation of the plague and the implants. And although this was clearly an artifact of very elaborate technology, she could already see familiar features.

There were no true wings as would be present on a traditional aircraft, or even a winged creature like the gryphons. Instead, it had a set of elongated pods representing the propulsion nacelles mounted on short brackets on either side along the rear quarter, and a smaller set up near the front for maneuvering. The length of the vessel was impressive, and she guessed it had to be a good ninety feet long, and it stood on a tripod of sturdy legs.

The group moved around to the rear where they saw a loading ramp leading into the cargo compartment. They peered inside the cavernous interior, which had to be at least fifteen feet across, and lined with racks of shelving. Arranged on the shelves were large numbers of storage boxes that the Suuden'kai crewmen were apparently using to contain the adamantium ingots.

Several scouts appeared on the road leading up to the mine. This was the local team surveying the area. They made their approach to report in.

"Lieutenant Carronel?"

"Yes," she turns to their attention. "Are you the local boys?"

"Right to that! We figure you could probably use a few extra hands, and we know these tunnels well enough by now to help you find your way through."

"Excellent. Relissa, would you give us a hand by acting as a traffic guide?"

"Sure! That sounds easy enough."

The scouts lead Relissa into the enclave up to the main feasting hall they found earlier.

"All right, through that tunnel over yon," the first scout relates. "We have a passage leading down to the adamantium forge. If you can stay here and direct the flow from this point, we'll continue further on to assist."

"Aye, right and dandy…"

Marelle and Lieutenant Lapäli continued to supervise the work outside.

"Padriyl," she asserts. "Would you like to make yourself useful and coordinate our people to begin loading up?"

"Absolutely!" he affirms. "Do you want us to return it outside, or use those portal runes down below as we bag everything?"

"Hmm," she glances around the neatly arranged racks of shelving. "This is such a nice arrangement here."

The Lieutenant took notice of her extended lull as she studied the transport.

"You know, we don't actually have any orders for interacting with the vessel itself."

"True, but it sure would be a nice prize to take home."

"I'm sure it would be, but…"

"You really think so?!" she yips eagerly. "So then, what you're saying is, we need an excuse."

"Um, wait, Marelle, I didn't actually say that."

"No, you didn't, but if we did have one, we would need to make it a good one, right?"

"Marelle, you're not seriously thinking of…"

"Actually, the more I think of it, the more serious I get. Padriyl, humor me a moment with an idea. First, let's consider if we could use this somehow. How would we use it, and what excuse could we make for it? We have orcs making a surprise hit. They apparently want to steal everything, even though they're not especially talented at using metal. But they certainly are known for scavenging stuff."

"Well, yes, I suppose you have a point."

"And naturally, this transport would make a great carrier for the metal. But it could also be used to carry people, couldn't it?"

"Um…well, actually," he muses. "As a troop carrier, with all these racks in the way, it might not be ideal, but it would certainly prove useful. And I suppose you could always remove the racks. So, are you now suggesting these orcs are learning to fly?"

"The Suuden-Aryku made the mistake of teaching a lesser society superior knowledge. This could open the door for all sorts of stuff. Surely, somewhere along the way, these orcs probably saw something, and once you get it inside your head…"

"Oh dear cu'Nar. And you're going to make me an accomplice to this little game?"

"You're already an accomplice to a game. We're just adding another crinkle to it. And I think I know of a way to use it."

She glances back inside the cargo compartment.

"This is apparently only for the adamantium, not the iron."

"Then what do we do with the iron?"

"Bag it and portal it. We'll send it home separately. Then have our people pack the adamantium in these boxes and load this beauty up. We're taking her home."

"Um, should I mention I'm not qualified as a pilot?"

"Ooh, too bad about that, but then neither am I," she grins brightly.

◆◆◆

"I don't trust them," Tristeen huffs. "Yesterday, they're fidgeting over that circle like it's a newborn baby, and today they're virtually patting themselves on the back for a masterpiece of artistic design."

"This must have something to do with that presentation you made yesterday," Jared relents. "It has to be."

"Exactly, and therefore, the reason I don't trust them."

"You mean, above and beyond the usual reasons you don't trust them?" he grins gently.

"Well, yes, that too," she smiles briefly. "This is obviously a tactic to waylay our suspicions. They're trying to make us think they don't really have any untoward ambitions with that circle, just playing with pretty designs and fancy drawings."

"All right, so what do you think is next?"

"What I think is I want to talk to Willit again."

"All right, do we go together, or do you prefer I stay here and keep watch on the place?"

"Jared, I think it would be a bad idea to leave these people unsupervised. The trouble is, if they're in league with the Suuden-Aryku, none of us is truly safe. Leesa told me they replaced the priests in the temple with more agents, so we can trust them if nothing else around here. My advice, for lack of anything better, is if you see trouble coming, run over there for help."

"All right, should I pass this around to the other students? Seems like good advice."

"Yeah, do that, just in case. I'm going to the Ten Eagles to see what Willit has to say."

Tristeen and Jared were again sitting at a table in the main hall of the academy. As their meeting concludes, she gets up and strolls outside, then makes her way to the lower district. She keeps to a brisk pace to hurry herself along, feeling a sense of pressure building for the tension levels revolving around the academy, the instructors, and the Dean.

She arrives in front of the Ten Eagles tavern, which was becoming a very familiar setting for her and the others to carry on their private meetings. Unfortunately, as was the case with Leesa the time before, that same half-drunk man saunters over as soon as she makes her appearance inside.

"Ooh, lookie here!" he croons. "Now here's a pretty little one, with such long golden hair! Is that a bath robe you're wearing? Aw, why do you need that in here when we can all share a great time together?"

Tristeen turns to see the man approaching determinedly. But before he could get within reach, she turns and waves her hand in an elaborate circle, then thrusts it up in front of his face as a ball of flame rises up from her palm.

"Carefully, good sir," she announces coolly. "My friends often describe me as a little too hot to handle."

The man instantly halts and jerks back at the obvious display of magic.

"Whoa! Easy does it there…" he slurs. "You're one of those, aren't you! Yeah…I don't want to mess with no…(*hic*)…wizard!"

He stumbles back a couple of steps and then turns to hurry away.

Tristeen continues to the table where Willit made his consultations. Once again, like with so many others in the room, his attention had been called to the disturbance.

"That poor man," he mourns. "He's not having very good luck with women lately," he grins.

"Well, if he could get his nose out of his cups long enough, he might do better for the smell at least."

"Tristeen, you look a little upset. What's going on up your way?"

"It's those instructors, Willit. I don't trust them one bit."

"This much I knew already. What else?"

"They're taking a new strategy with that circle today, lauding over it like it's some great artistic achievement. Jared and I both feel this is just a tactic to stall for time, hoping to make us settle down before they do anything. The question is, when are they going to do it, and what are they going to do in the meantime?"

"Right, I get it. Well, I have a few words for you as well."

"Oh, anything good?"

"Nope, bad...very bad... The Dean reported to the Governor, and neither is happy the students are showing up anything other than their absolute obsequious dedication."

"Oh, wonderful! Don't we have anything like law and order in this city?"

"Not by their estimation. The Guard may be on our side, but I guess neither the Dean nor the Governor cares much about it."

"Grand..." she sighs. "All right, I suppose if you've got friends like the Suuden-Aryku on your side, who cares about law and order? What are we supposed to do about this?"

"The word from down south is to be really careful if the Dean or the Governor should give any instructions you don't personally agree with. The students may be made expendable just to clean house."

Tristeen stops and gapes at him in shock. She slowly hauls her mouth back into position as she turns to glance around the room; just in case anyone was watching.

"Willit!" she whispers urgently. "You think they would dare do something against us?"

"In a city that kills its population with a fake curse by presumed enemies and their alleged blood rituals...almost anything is possible."

"Dammit!" she scorns. "Fine, so how do we protect ourselves now?"

"Be aware of what the Dean is doing and band the students together. The General down there tells me we may need to evacuate you to safety if it gets really bad."

"Gods above, my mom is going to flip if she gets wind of this," she slumps to the table.

"Scout Moonshimmer, this is the last of it," informs a guard on his way into the room.

"Aye, and a right grand job of it, too."

"We're moving outside now. Our instructions are to pack it up and head out."

"Right behind you…"

Relissa and the other troops inside the dwarven mine had finished packing up the adamantium in their boxes, as well as supplementing it with a couple dozen bags to take up the overflow. The iron had already been packed up and removed using portal runes, and now they were on their way out.

Marelle and Padriyl were inside the transport, studying the controls and trying to figure out how they might fly the thing.

"My best qualifications would be at the navigator's console," he admits. "I can track our position from there based on the transponder signals from their locator beacons."

"And since neither of us really knows anything about flying, it probably doesn't matter who sits up here. So I'll take that seat."

"Maybe we could have Relissa sit in the copilot's chair to assist you."

"Great! I'm sure she'll be thrilled," she giggles.

The last of the boxes were being loaded, and the bags tied down to the shelving supports. Relissa makes her way outside the enclave with the final delivery from the troops and joins the others inside the vessel.

"Marelle?" she calls into the compartment.

"Up here in front."

She makes her way forward to find both Marelle and Padriyl taking up seats in the cockpit. She halts abruptly.

"Um, Marelle," she inquires timidly. "What are you doing?"

"Oh, hey! You're just in time. Take a seat over there."

"That's not what I bleedin' asked, you round-eared bugaboo!"

"Oh, well, we're just getting ready to deliver all these luscious goods back to camp, like we were told to do."

"Buggers to you!" she shouts. "I don't remember any words talking about flying the bloody ship all about."

"Calm down, Relissa, we have it all under control, and a great little idea to make an excuse for it," she smiles disarmingly.

"Jiggers, maybe I should've stayed back home in my cage."

Relissa reluctantly takes up the copilot's seat and nervously watches Marelle and Padriyl making their final checks.

"How are we doing back there?" Marelle shouts to the rear of the vessel.

"That's the last of it," replies a guard. "Are you sure you know what you're doing?"

"If I could answer that, I probably wouldn't be sitting here."

"Aye, that's what I thought. Right, so we've got the orcish weapons in place, and the scene looks like it got hit by surprise out here. We're just waiting for the word to jump out."

"All right, hold on. Padriyl, how do you feel about all this?"

"I feel like my horns are sagging," he responds nervously. "But I guess we're as good as we can be. Just take it slow and easy until we can get a feel for it."

"Good, then we need to make our report. I'll call in that we're ready, then you call in the fake distress message."

"Understood."

Marelle takes out her trans-com and dials in the number for the General.

"General Gabarleine here…" he answers.

"General, this is Marelle. We are ready to send off. The scene is set, and we're getting ready to make our fake distress call."

"Most excellent, Lieutenant. Did you encounter any difficulties with the dwarves along the way?"

"Nothing. They completely ignored us."

"All right, at some moment I would imagine we will need to

contend with them. As I recall from the study made by the Daanen-Aryku, those mushrooms they're eating are not only very potent with this drug effect, but apparently lightly tainted with heavy metals. We cannot allow them to continue this way for much longer without them falling deathly ill."

"Got it, but we'll need to liberate them from the Suuden-Aryku first, and I'm not sure how we plan on doing that just yet."

"Agreed. Very well, as you were, Lieutenant, and I hope to see your return soon."

They end the link and Marelle turns to Padriyl.

"Your game now, Padriyl," she smiles.

He gets up from his seat and waves to a group of guards who were standing by and holding large wooden clubs, along with shields to bash them against. This would serve as background noise. He pulls out his trans-com and brings up a photo he made earlier of one of the Suuden'kai crewmen and a name badge. He takes a deep breath and then engages the com-link on his station. As the connection is made, he points to the background performers, which then begin making a series of war cries outside the vessel, along with sounds of crashing and other warfare.

"Base!" he shouts urgently in a flat monotone. "Emergency! This is Ensign Sadraan of the resource collection mission. We have come under attack."

"Ensign Sadraan," issues the response. "Who is attacking you?"

"We have been ambushed by a raiding party of orcs. They arrived through their portal conveyance in a surprise attack. They have killed the other members of the crew and are attempting to get inside the transport."

"Ensign, you must try to evade. Can you escape with the transport?"

"They are attempting to steal the shipment!" he hollers. "They are coming inside!"

He waves for the background performers to advance, and thus their sounds grow louder in the cabin. The group shouts orders and harsh language in orcish, and bangs their clubs against their shields to make sounds of things being smashed.

Padriyl continues his act, "I am unable to escape, they… Aarghhh…"

He fakes a death cry on the com-link and the guards make a rush of loud victory shouts, followed by another series of crashes until they turn off the com-link a moment later.

Marelle and Relissa both watched the scene behind them from their seats.

"Jiggers," Relissa relents. "If I was on the other side of that, I'd have a whole swarm of wiggles crawling up my back."

"Nicely done, people," Marelle applauds. "All right, everyone back to base. Mages! Bring our people home. Those of us here are taking the scenic route."

"Marelle, are you really sure you know what in all the bleedin' hells you're doing?"

"Well, in theory, yeah."

"In theory?!" she screeches. "You know, between you and that oversized door-knocker, I don't know which of you is worse."

"Um, which one are you talking about, in this case," she glances at Padriyl.

Relissa follows her glance, and then back again.

"Aw, buggers, it must run in their blood. So, what are you… um, we…doing here?"

Marelle gestures to Padriyl to close the rear door. He gets up and walks over to a control panel on the side, where he presses a button to bring up the ramp and seal off the opening.

"Now Relissa," Marelle asserts. "Follow along with me and pay attention. We'll start with this console here in the middle between us."

Marelle directs Relissa's attention to the center console and a series of levers in two groupings.

"You see these levers here?" she continues. "The set on your side is power for lift, something called a flux cushion. It's what takes us up off the ground. We're in a really tight space here, so we need to go straight up to get out without hitting anything. I'll leave that to you."

"Oh, thanks!"

"We need to handle everything real gentle, since we don't know much about how this thing performs. There are two levers, and we think you do both of them together. It's important."

"You only think?" Relissa gasps.

"Next is this other set. This is another kind of power for moving forward, called a throttle. Or maybe it's the other way, and that set is for forward and this one is up... Either way, once we get off the ground, we'll know for sure."

"Marelle," she whimpers. "I really wish you'd make up your bloody mind on that before we get off the ground!"

Marelle grins mischievously.

"This small lever back here, he says, is probably for the landing gear."

"Probably. Right then, and what's this landing gear?"

"The leg things under us."

"Uh huh..." Relissa turns to glare at Padriyl, who seemed to be enjoying the show.

"Now, to this big part up front here..."

Marelle brings her attention back to the front console. Padriyl moves forward to peer over her shoulder and help with translating the language. Together, they begin powering on the various flight systems. Section by section, the console begins to light up with readouts and status indicators. As she continues activating the panels, a soft whirring sound rises up.

"Um, what's that noise?" Relissa asks tentatively.

"That's simply the vessel coming to life," Padriyl affirms.

"You sure it's not going to go boom on us?"

"Oh, come on now," Marelle soothes. "Relax and pay attention, I need your help on this."

Relissa forces herself to focus her attention on the panels of lights. Several indicators start flashing yellow and then turn to a steady blue.

"Should we be worrying over what any of these are about?" she asks.

"As far as I can tell," Padriyl observes. "Most of these are status indicators. Blue is usually an indicator of a good condition while red is not, and yellow is most often used as a warning or an interim until it stabilizes."

"Aye, fine then."

They wait a moment longer until the lights settle, and the video monitors show a final result.

"All right, I think we should be ready," he affirms. "The pre-flight diagnostics are done, and it all looks good. Now remember, until we get a feel for it, go slow and easy to see what happens, and be ready to pull back if we have the wrong ones."

Marelle looks over at Relissa to judge her readiness. If a dark elf could ever appear pale, Relissa was a few shades lighter by now. Marelle reaches her hand across to comfort the poor girl.

"Relissa, make yourself comfortable. If we're going to do this, we're doing it in style. I don't know what sort of style, but it'll be one for the books. Reach down to those power levers and remember to move them both together. Take us up slow and steady."

Relissa braces herself and reaches for the pair of levers on her side of the floor console. She wraps her fingers around the T-handles and begins pushing forward gradually.

She delicately pushed the levers in tandem. A humming sound was emanating from somewhere behind them. Marelle looked out her window and saw the pod on her side beginning to glow slightly. Padriyl sat in his chair at the navigator's station monitoring the power readouts and positioning sensors.

Relissa's hands were sweating, but she pressed on, moving the levers in tiny increments. From out her window, Marelle saw movement. The ground was pulling away under them ever so slightly.

"Good, we're doing it!" she proclaims. "Go a little faster on that, let's bring ourselves out of here, but keep your wits about you."

"Wits? I think I left those back in the camp!"

Relissa pushes just a touch harder on the levers, bringing them forward a tiny bit faster. The craft is pulling upward more readily now. Marelle looks out into the gully to see the last few soldiers cheering her on as they were still departing the area.

"Keep it going, you're doing fine. We have room, but we still have a way to go before we clear these walls."

Relissa feels slightly more confident and brings more of her attention to the control, briskly glancing outside her window to see how it appears on her side. She pushes a little harder, and the vessel makes a slow but steady climb up.

"For as much as I'm pushing this thing, it doesn't seem to be going very fast."

"With all that cargo back there," Padriyl offers. "We're likely to be overloaded, so it might seem sluggish."

"Take us up more," Marelle encourages. "We're almost there, but then we'll need a lot more to get over the mountains around us."

"How high are we going?" Relissa asks.

"There are certain standards we follow for a cruising altitude," Padriyl informs. "But since none of us actually knows how to fly, I'm just going to say, get us over those mountains, and pray to your gods we don't crash."

"Jiggers, and thank you, Officer of the Daanen-Aryku Sentinels!"

"We aim to serve," he chuckles. "But it might help you to know, from what I recall of our design standards, the flux cushion offers what we call an operating floor, which is a minimum operating distance from the ground, or more accurately, sea level. Therefore, since we're up here in a mountainous region, we need to set our floor to be well above the ridgelines here. That might also be the reason you need to apply so much power, is because we're already at altitude."

"And what about that bit you were talking about of standards for flying?"

"The flight control wheel will take us up and down after that, but never below the floor setting on those levers."

"Hey, that's not a half bad idea you people had there."

The large vessel slowly wends its way up past the edges of the carved area in front of the enclave. The nacelle pods were now just above the tops of the rocky walls.

"Congratulations, Relissa," Marelle offers. "You got us out of that hole. That was probably the trickiest part right there. Now, push it a little harder and take us up till we're roughly above these mountains. I think by now we should have some freedom to play with it."

Relissa pulls her hand off briefly to wipe the sweat away, then repositions herself on the seat to make ready for a more serious performance.

She reaches back down and pushes the levers again, still cautiously, but a bit faster than before. The humming becomes more prominent as the vessel makes a distinct rise into the air. They watch from the window to gauge their altitude by the surrounding terrain. When the landscape is a comfortable distance below them, Marelle gives the order to stop.

"Don't forget the landing gear," Padriyl advises.

"Aye," Relissa responds.

She reaches over to the small lever at the rear of the floor console and pushes it gently until it softly snaps into a forward position. From somewhere underneath comes the mechanical sound of movement…a clunking, followed by a long whine. Relissa and Marelle each instinctively become rigid and hold their breath.

"Is that normal?" Relissa mutters.

"Yes, it is, don't worry," he calms.

The sounds continue with another clunking and two short beeps from the console itself. A light on the console changes from the lowered point to the raised point. The two women turn to look at each other and breathe sighs of relief.

"Right…" Relissa begins in a faint attempt at humor. "Now, if we fall and die, I'm making sure I haunt both of you."

Marelle lets out a smile, hoping to hide her own trepidation.

"Now, we take a little ride together."

She carefully takes hold of a control wheel situated in front of her and angles her view forward through the window.

"What does that thing do?" Relissa asks, looking over at hers in a similar position.

"This is the flight control wheel he was talking about. It controls which way we go. If you turn it, the vessel turns along with it. Also, pull back and we go up, push forward and we go down."

"Aye, but not below that floor thingy, got it."

"All right, you're handling the throttle. I'll take the steering. Keep a watch out the window and let's take it slow and easy until we can get a good feel for it."

"I would also advise we make a steady climb," Padriyl suggests. "At least until we hit a comfortable cruising altitude and speed. Then come back down as we approach our destination."

"So, does that mean I work this flux lever?" Relissa wonders. "Or just the throttle bit?"

"For now, I think only the throttle. We won't worry about the flux until we come in for a landing, and we need to lower ourselves back down."

"Fine and good..."

Relissa reaches down and takes the throttle levers. She pushes them forward gently while watching the terrain. The humming sound gets bolder, and the landscape under them shows signs of movement. She continues advancing the levers until the movement shows a significant increase.

"Do we know how fast this thing can go?" she asks.

"I could give a few suggestions," Padriyl admits. "But these would be in measurements native to my people, so they might not mean much here."

"Aye, fine to that, but how about a rough guess?"

"Fast, I would expect. If they follow our usual specifications, at least as far as my old studies taught me in school, this thing is probably subsonic, but still able to go...oh, let me think of the measurements you people use...maybe around five hundred miles per hour or so."

"Jiggers, that's right quick! Are you thinking of taking us up that much?"

"Well, personally, I don't know…" he hesitates as he glances at Marelle.

"I'd like to give it at least a little exercise," Marelle admits. "After all, this might be the last run for this thing for who knows how long."

"Marelle," Relissa whines. "When you use words like 'last run', I really wish you wouldn't talk like that."

"Oh, Relissa, you know what I mean. Once we get this back home, they'll probably move it to storage, and it'll just sit there collecting dust."

"Aye, I know. But, um, do we really want to go romping out in the fields today?"

The vessel creeps ahead, passing across the gully and over the rocky slopes on the other side. On the ground below, the road winds its way through the pass to the south.

"Give us some more power," Marelle issues. "I'm sure we can do better than this."

Marelle holds the wheel firm and steady in her hand while Relissa takes up the power another notch. The vessel moves along, increasing speed slowly and steadily. The terrain below is now passing by effortlessly, but ahead of them they see another row of mountains.

"We have a ridgeline," Marelle observes. "I'm pulling up gently."

She pulls back on the wheel and observes out the window. She carefully gauges how much she needs to pull in order to gain additional lift until the ridge passes comfortably underneath. Ahead of her, the mountains descend into foothills, and in the distance, she can see the land smoothing out into a valley. On the horizon, she can just make out the city features of Rolsklinde.

"I remember when I was riding that gryphon," she reflects. "The absolute freedom to move around out there, without anything in your way."

"From what I recall," Padriyl admits. "A lot of pilots say that. I never trained for it myself. My position was mostly in ground forces and local security. But I'm aware pilots often feel a deep sense of freedom when travelling up there. I don't mind flying as a passenger, but as a pilot, this requires some serious training."

"Do you think your people could teach someone like me?"

"Do you actually want to learn to fly, Marelle? With respect, your society is still rather far from that level of technological proficiency."

"Granted, but I think we'll be seeing a lot of changes in the coming years as we're chasing the Suuden-Aryku. And this feels so good."

They move past the remainder of the hilly terrain and into the prairies beyond.

"Relissa," Marelle suggests. "I think we're clear enough from the nasty stuff, so let's see what this thing can do. We'll take it carefully, but I want more speed, and I'm going to practice a few turns."

"If you say so," she responds timidly. "I guess we only live once. I was just hoping for a little more time on my side of it," she quips.

Relissa gently pushes the throttle levers forward. The craft increases speed, now moving along at a rapid rate, and the land under them rushes by. Marelle compensates by pulling back on the wheel to gain more altitude. Padriyl monitors the readings on his station and advises as necessary to achieve a comfortable operating condition.

"When I was on that gryphon," Marelle recalls. "The driver put us inside that bubble thing. Relissa, you took a ride once. Do you remember that?"

"Aye, and it tussled me a good one when he took us faster than what sound travels."

"He had you travelling supersonic?" Padriyl asks incredulously. "On a gryphon?"

"Aye, by three times yet. Those bubbles of theirs are a fine bit of sparkling."

"Incredible, and using magic. I wish I could find time to study that."

"Just take a few lessons in his academy. You'll have your horns twisted up tight real quick, I'll bet!"

"Well, Relissa," Marelle concludes. "If this thing can apparently go faster, let's see what it can do."

Both Relissa and Padriyl glared at her for her daring to tempt the fates.

"You heard me people. If we can do it…let's do it! Take us higher on those levers. We'll go a couple more of those notches. Take it slow, so I have time to bring us higher along the way. We'll light the fire and see what we've got."

"Jiggers…Marelle," Relissa moans.

"Come on," Marelle smirks. "How many times have you ever played in one of these before?"

"Aye, you got me on that one. And I think a wee bit of my own mischief is coming back at me now."

Relissa reluctantly reaches down for the controls again and gradually increases their thrust. Along the way, Marelle pulls back, and they make a steady climb. Trees and shrubbery shrink to little more than dots and blurs on the land below.

Marelle begins a slow turn to the right, angling off to the southwest, passing around the west side of the city.

"One thing I think we do not want is to be seen in the skies over the city."

"Right, we don't want any of those city folks looking up and getting any shivers from it."

"And if we're trying to be discreet, the last person we want to see us is the Governor."

"Aye! You got that one right."

They start moving away from the city into the open terrain beyond.

"Good, let's try it. Give us some more speed, slow and steady."

Relissa grips the throttle and presses it forward. They hear the humming sounds of the engines pick up speed, and the wind outside begins gusting past, while the land underneath advances rapidly.

Marelle continues pulling up to gain more altitude, providing greater comfort for their maneuvers. She tries a gradual turn to the left, then to the right. As she gains confidence in her management of the controls, she makes another set.

"Do you feel that, Relissa?"

"Ugh…Marelle… Aye, I feel something, and if you do any more

of it, I'll be turning right at you for the favor!" she balks, holding her hand up to her mouth.

A wide grin spreads across Marelle's face as she feels the power of control under her.

"Imagine," she marvels. "Padriyl, your people would fly things like this all the time on your world. And the Naarg uy'Sodrad itself, what do you think, maybe a hundred times this size?"

"Oh, much more than that, easily," he admits. "That thing is truly massive. Half of it is buried, so it doesn't show up as well."

"And able to move from one world to another as easily as we might walk across a room. Relissa, do you realize we're the first of our kind ever to do this here?"

"I envy you two a little," Padriyl accedes. "Maybe myself too, for this small role. But this is a special moment for you…so long as you don't foul it up," he chuckles.

Relissa looks out the window at the rapidly scrolling scenery. Hills and valleys passed by fluidly. The flight mechanics of the vessel almost seemed soothing after a while. The notion of achievement was not entirely lost on her. They were operating a vessel completely outside their ability to grasp, scientifically or technologically, and it felt good. But in the end, as she continued to look outside, she remembered their intended task.

"Aye then, I'll give you that much, but now I think we should be turning back. Neither of us has really been out this far on our own. We wouldn't want to get lost."

"Yeah," Marelle sighs. "I guess you're right, but it sure was fun. I'll bring us back around. Padriyl, you said that station monitors our location?"

"Affirmative, you should bring us around to, um…well, you can't read our language."

He gets up and peers over her shoulder again and locates the digital readout of their compass heading.

"You need to bring us around to zero-seven-three on this gauge. Turn left till I say stop."

She obliges, and the vessel makes a gradual left turn back in an easterly heading. When they meet with their new course, she levels out and Padriyl returns to his seat.

"It shouldn't be far from here," he affirms. "But we'll have to play it by touch since we really don't have any proper ground control to guide us."

They continued briefly until they saw the western ridgeline of the valley coming into view on the horizon.

"Bring us down a bit, Relissa," Marelle directs. "We don't want to overshoot it. And Padriyl, you should probably call in and tell them we'll be arriving soon."

"Right, this should be fun."

"What do you mean?" Relissa asks.

"She didn't bother telling them what we're doing out here."

"Oh, Buggers!" she shouts. "That ties it!"

Marelle begins a careful descent as Relissa pulls back on the throttle. And as they make their approach, Padriyl takes out his trans-com to dial in a call.

Thaelyn was inside the tactical office, as usual, sitting at the table with the General, when his trans-com rang out. He picks it up to answer it.

"This is Thaelyn."

"Your Lordship, this is Lieutenant Lapäli. We are on our way in now."

"Lieutenant, I was wondering what was taking so long. Were you delayed for some reason?"

"Um, well, you might say that...sort of."

"I might say that...sort of," he raises his brow. "And how do we define the sort of component of that statement?"

"Well, this was actually Marelle's idea, so I want to emphasize her, um, inspiration for the cleverness of the notion, but we're flying the transport down into the camp."

"You are flying it?" he intones warily. "Excuse me, but I do not specifically recall that portion of our meeting."

"Yes, but she had a revised thought come to her up there, and she wanted to present this to you personally."

"Oh, naturally, to present this personally… Very well, so you are flying it down here for her?"

"Um, well, not exactly. I'm actually sitting in the navigator's seat."

"The navigator's seat," he ushers cautiously. "Why are you in the navigator's seat?"

"Well, this station is a little better suited for my training than, say, the copilot's seat."

"The copilot's seat?" he mentions worriedly. "Why? Who is sitting in the copilot's seat?"

"Relissa is taking that seat."

"Relissa?" he surges. "What is Relissa doing in the copilot's seat?"

"Well, because Marelle is in the pilot's seat."

"Marelle!" he shouts. "What is Marelle doing in the pilot's seat?"

"She's flying the transport."

"Oh, Dear Blessed Powers Above!" he shrieks.

Thaelyn jumps out of his chair and dashes out of the building, followed by the General.

"Where are you presently?" he asks urgently.

"We're coming in across the western ridges of the valley."

Thaelyn strains to catch a glimpse of the transport through the trees, then to see it slowly making its approach from the west.

"Powers pay witness…" he mumbles. "I have a sighting. And you say Marelle is piloting it? Our little Marelle…"

"Yes, Your Lordship, and doing quite well at it."

"Incredible. And you say Relissa is her copilot?"

"Yes, and the two of them are working together at this."

"Is that so! But with all due respect to those two ambitious young ladies, neither of them comes from a society with the first concept of flight, powered or otherwise."

"Yes, well, I tried telling her that before."

"Oh, did you now!" he retorts. "She barely understands how to use a trans-com, and yet she directed herself to fly that technological behemoth with a Night Elf who talks to squirrels!"

"Um, well…"

Relissa was listening to the passionate exchange and began snickering at the implications.

"Anyway," Padriyl continues. "We have the settlement in view, but I'm at a loss of where we might set it down."

"At a loss?!" Thaelyn gasps. "You? At a loss?"

He turns to look toward both the north and south gates, trying to gauge which would hold the largest space for a landing. He then runs off to the south side and the large clearing just outside the gate.

"Lieutenant, I believe the space outside the south gate would be sufficient. Bring it in carefully."

Marelle and Relissa cautiously guide it in, with Padriyl's help for speed and altitude. Relissa hits the lever for the landing gear as Marelle eyeballs her positioning relative to the ground. Thaelyn offers a few notes from his perspective, including hand signals to direct them into place, and together they bring it gently down for a landing. Padriyl then assists Marelle in powering down the systems while Relissa strolls to the back door and opens it to the fresh air outside.

Thaelyn glares at the young dark elf as she comes into view. He then turns to examine the General for his impression. The General was beaming at their obvious level of accomplishment.

"My dear young Relissa," Thaelyn begins.

"My Lord, before you go and say it, I was hoodwinked into it, blindsided."

"Really! So we might suggest you only played a minor support role on this occasion, for the apparent outcome?" he raises his brow suspiciously.

"Well, I guess, when you consider the wee bit of fun we had, um, aye."

"Fun...should I ask this question. What manner of fun?"

"Well, we figured this is the last time this little bugger will be seeing any real business, so we had to give it a good run."

Thaelyn turned and covered his eyes at the suggestion. He opened them again to look at the General.

"General, do you recall that private list I sometimes bring out?"

"Yes, my Lord, although it's been a good long while for it. Are we to bring it back into service?"

"Indeed, and you will put this young lady's name on it. But place her as the second one on the list, as it would seem the other one deserves the honor of being Number One."

"Good gracious, such an honor as that!" he smiles.

"Um, my Lord," Relissa hesitates. "What list is this?"

Thaelyn sighs as he tries to pull himself together.

"Since my early days, I began a special list to record those people who make themselves known with such unique and noteworthy qualities that I must watch them very closely," he eyes her carefully.

"Oh, one of those," she chuckles weakly. "Well, it wouldn't be the first time."

Soon, Marelle and Padriyl come outside, after the vessel had been powered down.

"And here is the mastermind of this conspiracy," Thaelyn continues. "Oh, and let us not forget her other accomplice, the dear Lieutenant Lapäli, of the prestigious Daanen-Aryku Sentinels. General, we should not neglect him, so place him down with an honorable mention, will you?"

"Absolutely, my Lord," he affirms buoyantly.

"All right, so what is this miraculous revelation you had up there that would drive you to perform the otherwise implausible act of flying this cantankerous monstrosity all the way from the mountains in the north to wherever it was you took your little joyride, and then back here, hmm?"

"Yeah, right, so here it is," Marelle begins her sales pitch. "First, we have this wonderful cargo transport that was all nicely arranged to carry what might be hundreds of boxes, all neatly stacked on shelving. Here, look, I'll show you."

She leads them around to the ramp and up into the cargo compartment to demonstrate the racks of shelving and the large assortment of boxes, plus many bags tied to struts.

"Very well," Thaelyn admits. "I suppose this is indeed a very nice arrangement, and it further goes to show how this is apparently a routine procedure for them, if they are configuring such vessels as this so professionally. I must now wonder how many of these shipments they have been transporting during their time here."

"If they're configuring this with such precision," Padriyl offers. "And also going so far as to make custom boxes to pack the ingots, this must be a very routine procedure with a long history."

"Indeed, and this further complicates our interpretation of their ultimate goal for it."

"Anyway," Marelle continues. "It just seemed like it would be so much easier if we pack everything inside here and bring the whole thing back, rather than piecemeal as individual bags, which would take a lot of manpower to move around. Then I had another idea, and with Padriyl's help to work out a solution…"

"Oh! So, he actually did play a more prominent role in this?"

"Hey, I believe in giving credit where credit is due. After all, I needed his help to decipher all these controls."

"Oh dear cu'Nar," Padriyl mumbles privately. "Here we go."

Thaelyn nods as he examines the two of them.

"General," he calls out. "Perhaps you should elevate his mark to one of higher stature than a simple honorable mention."

"Naturally, my Lord!" he replies cheerily.

"So, he helped with the translations," Marelle resumes. "And together with Relissa to work the throttle and flux field controls for me…"

Thaelyn eyes the young dark elf again for her collusion in this affair. She simply smiles innocently, even though she knows it won't pass.

"I will admit your performance at bringing it in, and setting it down here, was very neatly executed. So, I will congratulate you on this."

"Thanks, my Lord," Relissa admits.

"A throttle and, what is it…flux controls?"

"Yeah," Marelle responds excitedly. "Apparently, as Padriyl explains it, their technology uses a flux field to elevate the vessel off the ground as a kind of cushion, giving it a minimum operating floor altitude, and from there you have the control wheel to guide the thing in all directions, including up and down, but the flux settings keep you at a certain minimum elevation above sea level."

Thaelyn found himself entranced by her remarkably technical description of what ought to be well outside her level of scientific understanding. As she explained her lessons, he began to realize she held a better understanding of flight than might otherwise be expected.

"Then," she rambles. "As we increased thrust, it became necessary to also increase altitude, to maintain certain principles of flight as what the Daanen-Aryku normally use. And after doing this for a little bit, taking it for a little drive out west and back, I got a real good feel for it."

"So, is this to say," he considers. "Now you want more?"

"Yes, actually, I'd love to have them teach me more."

"Most interesting. Well, I suppose if you hold such a gift, we should not overlook it. But let us come to that when we have more time. What about the aspect of it sitting here in our camp? This is the part I am particularly curious about."

"Right, about that," she submits. "The way I figure it, we have a couple of things occurring here. For one, we have orcs stealing adamantium, which seems a little bit odd if they don't even know how to use iron properly, right?"

"Yes, this does actually follow in an odd manner, unless we are to say they are stealing it in the hopes of finding a use for it, or simply to deny it to the Suuden-Aryku."

"But what about the rest of it?" she waves at the transport. "If these orcs have been exposed to the Suuden-Aryku and their technology, including being taught how to use portals, what else might they have learned, or could learn if they apply themselves. I learned how to fly this thing, with a little help of course, in minutes! Could they learn this, and further to realize they could load up an army inside here and deliver it into battle somewhere?"

Thaelyn drew back in deep thought, instantly realizing the obvious implications.

"A troop transport..." he muses thoughtfully. "Indeed. If the controls are in fact so easy to understand...pull this, push that...that a band of orcs so determined to survive in the face of such powerful foes, and so disgruntled by the lack of support from their alleged allies, they might be driven to do almost anything."

"And then, we use this to exaggerate our orcish attacks on Kynesoth by claiming they're setting down hordes outside their walls. We could have Priestess Sehnisavain call in a report, accusing the Suuden-Aryku of turning coat on them, thinking they are the ones piloting the thing, when in fact it's orcs. This could also give us an opportunity to play a trick on the Suuden-Aryku themselves once or twice, if we can hit an outpost fast enough and make it look like orcs, just like up north. What do you think?"

"What I think is I am beginning to understand why your Captain said you were trouble. I also think we need to remove this from sight quickly before the Suuden-Aryku see who truly owns it. General, we need a mage with a rune," he emits urgently. "Let me see… Yes! Have him go out to that new military research base we are building. We have more than enough space out there for storage. Mark a rune and return back promptly to move this."

"Right away, my Lord!" he replies.

"And as for you, young lady, along with your accomplices," he eyes Marelle and her team.

He smiles and reaches out to squeeze them each on the shoulder.

"Very nicely done," he nods. "This gives us a few curious new twists to play with. You should now find some rest. We will review these ideas later."

Chapter 8

ANTICIPATION

A tonal announcement arose from the Governor's drawer. It was late in the day from Marelle's expedition to the dwarven enclave. The Governor reaches over to take out the trans-com and answers the call.

"Yes, Commander?"

"I have a report."

"It would seem you are especially active with your reports lately. What do we have this time?"

"Another attack…"

"Oh grand, so those infernal orcs are still bothering our little Flame Elves. What have they done this time? I hope the elves are still holding their own. I would wish to keep them around a while longer."

"Negative, this is not the elves. This is our supply transport for the metal."

The Governor's face suddenly drops, and he comes to attention in his chair.

"Commander!" he ushers sternly. "What about our transport! Are you saying that man has found our operations up there and is attacking the dwarves now?"

"Negative, it was another ambush assault by the orcs."

"What?!" he screams. "In all the blazes of Creation! How could those bestial creatures find their way to the mines?"

"They used more of their abnormal…uh, portals. We received a distress broadcast of a surprise attack. The message stated the orcs were attempting to steal the metal. Then the message broke off. We sent a team to investigate. They found the crew dead and the metal and transport missing."

"Excuse me!" he shouts. "How is it possible the transport was missing?"

"Unknown. We can only surmise the orcs have pirated the transport along with the metal."

"And the dwarves? What about them?"

"Unchanged. They still perform their work."

"Something is wrong here…but unless…wait, of course! Blast! Those orcs must've realized the importance of keeping the dwarves to perform their work, and will use this to take their supplies directly; now that they have an index to that location. Commander, you need to find that transport, and then punish whatever group it was that took it."

"Affirmative."

"What about the elves, anything new on that side?"

"Negative, there is no new information."

"Good, then hopefully they are keeping the upper hand. And Thaelyn, what is he doing down there?"

"The situation is unchanged. He continues his assault on the orcs and no one else."

"There is something wrong with that as well. He was defending the Daanen-Aryku's position, but he doesn't make any outward assaults to take their fight to the enemy. I think we are in a stalemate game there. He doesn't want to make a charge against us the same as we do not make one at him. Very well, so much the better…it gives us time to prepare. Maintain your condition, Commander, and look for that transport. If these infernal orcs are actually learning to fly now…"

He grumbled something unintelligible and ends the link, then tosses the unit back into the drawer.

"Four hundred years…" he moans. "And even more before that, if you count all those early survey expeditions."

He leans back in his chair to continue his thoughts.

"Patience, good fellow," he soothes to himself. "We have all the time we need. It's only one shipment. It won't make that much of a difference in the grander picture. And I doubt those orcs will find any proper use for it, not unless they try tying them to sticks and using them as clubs."

"High Priestess," Cydulean announces. "Our people outside tell us the circle is ready for the planting. I presume you would like to participate?"

"Indeed," Sehnisavain responds. "This would be both a fascinating process to watch, and if I could be permitted even a small role in it, it would make up for so much of my own torment for all those years spent under that creature's control."

"Absolutely, as I thought. Priestess Rumoren will need to perform the actual planting, since she is the one specially blessed to make use of Shescellaie's staff, but you could surely contribute by bringing the life-seed into the circle and handing it off."

"Very good. This will do nicely for me."

Sehnisavain and her attendants in the temple in Kynesoth had been overseeing the hasty refurbishing of the shrine outside their temple. Since the time of her return and the delivery of her speech, they have been digging out the area of the old circle once used by the previous Tree of Life, and hauling away cart after cart of waste material to a dump site outside the walls. The result was a huge hole excavated in front of the temple, reaching a full man's height into the ground.

Master Cydulean and Priest Sumisal, both of whom were still impersonating local priests, then coordinated the delivery of many truckloads of bags of fresh soil from Tae'Eladar, including bags of mulch to mix into it. This was used to fill the hole and to provide a rich bed for the new tree. The soil was packed down as each layer was added until the hole was returned to the surface.

The druids that were coordinating the affair made routine checks of the soil conditions and firmness along the way. The local citizens often worked in rotating shifts, beginning in the early morning, and continuing until the late evening. The process was laborious due to the continued influence of Sargeras and his songs attempting to govern them to his cause. But the inspired motivation brought by realizing his involvement in the horrors of their world, and what he made them do, drove the people to force themselves against his songs to seek their freedom.

Sehnisavain's two daughters, Tyshalis and Rhyvanith, had returned to the city for the occasion to observe the ceremony. Now the three of them were joined by Ilothonna and Kerali as they stepped outside to see a circle of druids lining up around the fresh shrine. A large body of local citizens also stood around to watch the ceremony, each of them hoping to find their freedom at last.

The druidic High Priestess waited on the north side of the circle for Sehnisavain to join at her side. Sehnisavain made her approach while the rest of her group remained on the temple steps, but then she halted abruptly as she remembered her shoes.

"It's been so long," she admits bashfully. "I almost don't recall the proper manners for it by now."

"It's quite alright, High Priestess," Rumoren offers. "We will remind you, and help teach the rest."

Sehnisavain pauses while she removes her shoes, and then steps up to Priestess Rumoren. The druidic priestess pulls out a large nutlike seed from a pouch on her belt. She cups it gently in her hands and holds it out for Sehnisavain to take into hers. The elder woman gazes at it dreamily as she forms her hands into a cup to receive it.

"I've never actually seen a life-seed before," she relents. "I recall stories, but these are ancient from the times when we first arrived and began to settle."

"And today, you will become a part of a new life for your people here," Rumoren affirms.

Sehnisavain takes the seed gently into her hands, while Rumoren steps around her to enter the circle proper. She takes up the staff of twisted vines, the same one used by Thaelyn in times past for the service he provided in Solinaia, and that first day in the Badlands, and signals to the druid circle. They begin a low chant.

Rumoren waited a few moments for the chanting to build up enough energy to make a single tap of the staff on the ground at her feet. As with Thaelyn's example before, the tapping emitted a soft echoing effect through the soil and a spray of energy radiating out from the base of the staff.

She then stretched the staff out at length and made a slow clockwise spin while she invokes the magic of the staff to rain down sparkles of energy to enrich the soil around her. She completes the circle and sets the staff off to her side, where it stood upright on its own. Now she waves to Sehnisavain.

Sehnisavain took a deep breath to try to relax, but it didn't seem to work. So she carefully stepped forward into the circle and slowly up to Rumoren.

"I'm simply too old for this," she moans as she feels herself becoming shaky.

"You are doing fine, High Priestess. Just a little more..."

Sehnisavain arrives in front of Rumoren, and they make the exchange. Sehnisavain relaxes and breathes a sigh of relief as she backs away and kneels in prayer.

The druid circle continues its chanting while Rumoren holds the seed up briefly to the sky. She then kneels down to scoop out some dirt to make a hole for it.

Tyshalis and Rhyvanith both studied the process intently until Tyshalis turns to her sister to whisper in her ear.

"Remember this, Rhyvanith," she instructs. "One day, we might be doing this for our people, if we should ever build any new cities."

The younger girl nodded as they continued to watch.

Rumoren set the seed into the hole and covered it up gently, packing the soil around it, and then stepping away. She takes the staff again and waves it over the seed, sprinkling more particles of sparkly energy onto it, then steps back and waits.

In a few short moments, the soil on the little mound began to stir. Several small bits dislodged, and a small sprout pops up. The sprout then began to grow at a phenomenal rate.

Sehnisavain watched in amazement at how fast the young tree was rising above the ground.

"Dear Protector, is that normal?"

Rumoren simply smiled as they continued to watch the sprout grow into a sturdy young sapling, reaching well over the druid's head until it finally came to a stable rest. Rumoren then joined at Sehnisavain's side to kneel in reverence of the new tree.

"We should give it a short while to fully awaken," Rumoren advises. "Then we can begin to redeem your people."

<hr>

"Dean," the Governor informs. "I have a remedial task to be performed that I believe will attend to our little disobedience with the students over there."

"Oh? What sort of task?"

"I am expecting a delivery very soon that we will employ for a new class project. We should send word that all the students are required to participate, just to be sure they all receive the full… benefits…of this lesson, and in so doing we should no longer need to concern ourselves with that aspect of our troubles. Then we can move forward with the rest."

"Excellent, my Lord," he affirms. "What sort of delivery is this?"

"The delivery will be a special elixir to tame their ambitions somewhat. I will have you schedule this as a morning activity once the delivery arrives. But it is important they be secluded for privacy, and for this, I suppose we will need to make use of the basement, since it will afford us to isolate them during this time."

"The basement," he muses. "Indeed. Well, if you say so, my

Lord. I just hope they don't get any improper motives about our circle while they're down there."

"Oh, let us not worry about that, Dean. I will consider this a worthy expenditure if we should find ourselves in need of tidying up. I will let you know when the package arrives. In the meantime, simply keep up the image of harmlessness down there so we do not have any more incidents with those rabble-rousers."

"Very good, my Lord, then I'll be on my way."

The Dean had been visiting with the Governor for another meeting. He turned to leave the office, then to descend the stairs and exit out the rear door, returning to the academy via his private route.

Just down the hall from the Governor's office, Leesa was peeking out through a crack in the door of the closet she used to hide herself. She quietly emerged and closed the door behind her, then tiptoed downstairs to the foyer. As she arrived on the ground floor, she began to place her shoes back on her feet.

"Ahem…" ushers a voice from the door of the secretary's office.

Leesa looked up to see the secretary staring out the door at her. She felt a sudden cold snap, but it was not entirely unexpected, as she was taking notice of him taking notice of her recently. She knew this was likely to occur, eventually.

"Uh huh…" she retorts quietly. "I was wondering how long it might take for you to get enough gumption to get out of that chair of yours and check out the world around you. You seem to spend all day with your nose in that book."

"And you? Why would you apparently want to go listening at the Governor's door?"

"I'm an agent working on behalf of the Guard, that's why. That man up there, along with the Dean, are both labeled as crooks."

"An agent?" he asks curiously. "What do you mean, crooks?"

"My impression is you don't have a clue what he's doing up there, just like the rest of the people in the city. Have you heard any of the talk going around?"

"What talk?"

"Well, for one thing, the new priests over there, and what they're passing around quietly. And if not that, any general chatter in the alleys and taverns."

"Um, well…no. I'm not much of a temple-goer, and I don't usually make it a habit to visit taverns that often."

"Wow, you suddenly sound like a really dull guy," she giggles. "All right, listen close and try to understand. I don't have a problem with you personally, but this city is in deep trouble, and the people at the top are the ones causing it. I'm a spy sent to watch these two," she glances upstairs. "Your previous assistant didn't just take ill; he was taken away. The same as with those original priests. Lives are at stake here, and anyone who gets in the way of saving what's left of it is removed to make room for those who will help save what's left of it. Get it?"

"I get your meaning, but it doesn't answer anything else. Who is doing all this and why? You say you work for the Guard, but isn't the Guard supposed to be working for the Governor?"

"Not anymore. The Governor likes lapdogs, people who only do as he tells them and nothing more, and certainly not any real work to actually solve problems. We have information that says he doesn't hold a proper right to be there in the first place, and worse is he's responsible for a lot of foul deeds in the city. Case in point; the curse and the Plague. He is the one doing it, with his false priests and their so-called blessing at the Festival. He's part of a conspiracy that took over four centuries ago by forcing the original governing council we once had to step down so someone new could take over… or else everyone dies of a new plague."

"What?" he winces.

"It was a ruse. There is no such thing as a plague. He faked it to become governor and took over. Now he owns the academy and the temple, and uses them to feed the rest of us a bucket load of hullabaloo to turn us away from people we're supposed to be friends with. He's in league with the real enemies out there, and giving them half the iron we're supposed to be getting in here. And as for the Guard, they're expected to sit and stay, not do any real work to correct any of this. Well, Captain Kholgard is tired of it."

"So, he put you in here?"

"I'm actually working for my cousin, who is working for those people in the valley. But, if you want any more than that," she asserts with a finger, "go visit the priests in the temple. They serve Lord Thaelyn down there, and they work for the law. And that law is doing more to solve our problems than any of us ever did, all thanks to such lovely expressions as, 'if you can't trust our authority, who can you trust', and made worse by, 'for as long as I can remember…' such and such, where people like the Dean, and that guy upstairs, keep us blind and ignorant of what's going around our heads in plain sight."

"You must be kidding! So that's where it all comes from."

"Talk to the priests, and tell them I sent you. But for now, I have work to do, and it doesn't involve running errands for that guy upstairs. Those students over there are in danger."

She heads out the door and across to the academy.

The secretary watches her through the window, asking himself what she was raving about with that last statement.

Leesa rushed through the doors of the academy. It was still early in the day, and Tristeen was in her alchemy study in the basement. Leesa strolled casually through the main hall and down the corridor to the basement to check on her. She saw Tristeen at the far table performing her work. On this day, however, the instructors were absent from their studies of the circle, instead cordoning it off to prevent anyone from tampering with it. So Leesa tenderly stepped inside to speak to the girl.

"Tristeen," she whispers.

Tristeen turned when she saw Leesa approaching.

"It's probably not smart to come down here."

"Yeah, well, besides that, I have a few words for you."

"All right, what?"

"Be careful the next time the Dean gives you a special lesson. He and the Governor have something cooking up, and it's not good."

Leesa then turns and discreetly leaves the room.

Tristeen watches her as she makes her abrupt exit, suddenly feeling a shot of anxiety rushing through her. With nothing else to do, she simply returns to her work, briskly peeking over her shoulder at Jared working his table across the way.

✦ ✦ ✦ ✦ ✦ ✦

"This is going to take a long time," Cydulean observes.

"What's the full population of this city, High Priestess?" Sumisal wonders.

Sehnisavain and the others were overseeing a systematic process of bringing people up to the tree for their redemption. The process involved bringing them up in small groups and placing them in physical contact with the tree, in order for the tree to remove the effects of Sargeras's songs.

"I don't know if I could give a proper answer to that," she relents. "I haven't taken a full count, not since the days when all this began."

"Given the size of this city," Cydulean considers. "If it's fully populated, I might suggest upwards of forty thousand."

"Many of our people live in family groups, so you might see a denser clustering effect than what I was noticing in your home city."

"Then perhaps more like fifty?" Sumisal suggests. "And if we only have room for a dozen or so under the tree at any given moment, even if we try pushing ourselves, and then waiting for them to recover, which requires at least two or three hours of rest…gracious, this could take…um…" he waves a finger in the air as he tries to calculate the number.

"Longer than I think any of us would actually care to wait," Cydulean accedes. "Sumisal, I think we should not depend on this one tree for our support. We need to think on a larger scale, especially if we hope to remove these songs from their minds and free them more efficiently so we can be on with our other needs."

"All right, so what do we do?" he inquires. "Do we recruit other groves? We would need to remove these people to Tae'Eladar for that, and somehow herd them through the gateway network to each of our cities back home. That's a lot of people to move, virtually none of whom would know their way around or speak the local language to ask directions."

"We'll need assistance, to be sure."

"What about us?" Tyshalis asks. "My sister and I have been learning a little bit. We can help in B.T. at least."

"That's good for a start," Cydulean admits. "But we'll need a lot more than that."

"Amariyn," Sehnisavain offers. "She and her people. Could they help us? How many of them know their way around your world by now?"

"Probably not nearly enough to suffice our needs..."

"Wait a minute," Sumisal interjects. "They might not know their way around, but they can certainly help with the language. They maintained their knowledge of Elvish, and this is a common study in our schools. So, all they need to do is set themselves up at certain waypoints, and act as traffic guides to conduct the flow."

"Ah, perfect! Then, the only thing we need is to allow passage to Tae'Eladar and guide them along."

"Like the portal thing you have up in Firstfall?" Rhyvanith asks.

"While that would certainly be a good example," Sumisal agrees. "We need to do this without the Suuden-Aryku getting curious if they should notice any mass migrations moving in and out."

"Oh, you mean if we send people walking up there...right."

"Then we need to use portals here," Tyshalis asserts. "Lots of them, by the sound of it. And for this, we'll need to bring more of your mages in, I suppose. And here is where things start getting complicated."

"Um, how do you mean that?" Rhyvanith wonders.

"First, we need to be sure we contain these people with their motivations to actually behave themselves and do as they're told while they're essentially wandering around an alien world with alien people. Next, if the Suuden-Aryku are watching us, we don't want to move everyone at once, like Priest Sumisal said, and have mass migrations coming and going, even if through portals."

"All right, what about this idea," Cydulean offers. "We call people inside the temple, which is generally out of view of any observers outside. We can make it appear as if the people are attending a service of some kind. If we can move them in large enough numbers, perhaps a few or several hundred at a time…" he pauses to examine the structure. "This building is rather large. How many can we seat inside here?"

"A lot, actually," Sehnisavain responds. "In the old days, our city was once a primary haven for our people. We had our own citizens, and occasionally visitors from the outlying farms and villages. As such, we built this magnificent temple to house a large number of worshippers. We can comfortably seat eight hundred at a time in here."

"Eight hundred…" he muses and pulls out a small journal book from a pocket, along with a pen. "If we suggest around fifty thousand, and the timing seems to be maybe three hours per redemption, by the time they wake up. Then eight hundred at a time…" he scribbles his notes in the book. "And if we make these runs…well, what do you think, from first light until late eve?"

"Maybe," Sumisal considers. "Unless you think we should run this through the night."

"That means somebody will be working really long hours," Rhyvanith moans.

"Well, no," Cydulean infers. "We would simply need to arrange some scheduling. All right, if we rush this, and go the full day and night, simply to get it done…since we don't know what the Suuden-Aryku will throw at us next, and we want these people redeemed from those songs as quickly as possible…"

"That last note we got from up north," Sumisal recalls, "is suggesting those awful orcs are learning to fly a Suuden-Aryku transport. This will surely make trouble for us," he chuckles.

"How clever of them," he smiles. "So the Suuden-Aryku may be getting anxious by that time."

He continues with his figures until he comes to an approximate conclusion.

"This looks like just over a week of constant work."

"But eight hundred at a time?" Sumisal wonders. "Surely, we can manage more people than that at our trees, especially since all of ours are fully mature groves with the mother and six daughters."

"Right, that alone multiplies the capacity greatly."

"What if we double up on that number? Maybe even triple or so. I think we can push a thousand and a half, or even two thousand, and not make such a grand scene by anyone watching. It's only for a few hours at a time, and then they come back out."

"So we cut the time in half or better," he considers. "We'll need mages with way-lines, enough to cover this plus relief crews to replace them on occasion. Even we mages can get tired once in a while," he laughs heartily.

"So, what you're saying is," the Governor's secretary states. "I'm working for someone who is apparently working for the Suuden-Aryku, and who is responsible for this plague," he points at his shoulder for reference. "And that he took control, or at least his predecessor took control of our city away from the old government, and also took authority of the mage academy, which means the Dean…no wonder he makes so many visits…and the temple, which is where you people came in, and well, basically keeps us under his thumb?"

"In a nutshell, yes," Priest Garrain affirms. "And right now, we're trying to inform the people of it, but quietly, so we don't let him know what we know, and cause him to call on his friends out there to make even more trouble until we can make a move of some kind."

"What kind of move? I should think that simply going in and nabbing the guy would be enough. I always knew he was a hard fellow to get along with, but this…" he shakes his head.

"This might be true, but we still have a few questions to answer about his true identity and how he might hold such authority that he can actually give orders to the Suuden-Aryku military."

"Meaning to say what…he might hold military authority? But if that's the case, he couldn't be a simple spy or some kind of criminal who took illegal control."

"Right, and this is where Leesa comes in. She's in there trying to learn more about him. She recently discovered some Suuden-Aryku equipment in the basement, which clearly ties him in with them, and rather intimately, to be sure. Whoever and whatever he actually is, we're trying not to take anything for granted so far."

"All right, I understand, and I'll keep your secret as best I can. I just hope you'll give me fair warning if his friends should decide to drop by for a visit," he chuckles.

The secretary bows his head and leaves the temple to return to his desk. On entering his office, he finds Leesa again attending to her assistant duties. She looks up at him and smiles pleasantly.

"Did you enjoy your little walk outside?" she asks innocently.

"I, uh…yes, actually. You know, you were right, going out and stretching the legs can be very refreshing."

He pauses to look out the door before turning to her, and leans in discreetly.

"Just who are you?" he whispers. "You look like a noble in those clothes, but I wouldn't expect one of them to come outside and get their hands dirty."

"Maybe not in all cases, but we do have one over in the academy. As for me, I'm from the lower district. My cousin is in the Guard, and she recruited me to help."

"You look a bit young to be doing this sort of work."

"Young or old, it still needs to be done. And in my case, I can use this to my advantage."

"Great gods," he shakes his head. "So you're actually playing into it? Aye…" he chuckles. "And she must've taught you well. And by the way, you really do look good in that dress," he smiles and returns to his desk.

Leesa repays the smile and then continues with her work.

Amariyn was making a visit to the tactical office in Firstfall. It was morning and Thaelyn was in conference with the General again.

"Your Grace," she announces. "A pleasant greeting to you, I hope all is well today?"

"Ah, Lady Amariyn, indeed… Come in."

"In accordance with your request for aid, I'm arranging a large number of our people to arrive here shortly to assist with the, um… Well, I suppose we might still call them Flame Elves, at least so far, until they make their conversion. How do you wish to proceed?"

"We will begin by arranging them along certain thoroughfares back home to act as guides, where they will direct the flow of the, eh, yes, I suppose you are right. We will call them Flame Elves for now. At least until after they reach the trees, and then we will grant them back their proper titles."

"Of course, and I will be especially happy to see things return to a familiar portrayal, at least as far as this awful war is concerned."

"Absolutely. Then we must return them home again and prepare for the next volley. We are trying not to make a large showing of people moving around, just in case the Suuden-Aryku may be monitoring them after our little plays with the orcs. By the way, General, we need to lay down at least one new play in the eyes, or perhaps I should say the ears, of the Suuden-Aryku where that transport is concerned."

"Right," he nods. "And I have been contemplating this for a while. Among other things, we should have Priestess Sehnisavain declare the need to call in her outer guard posts to consolidate their numbers for better defense inside the city walls. After all, if the orcs are landing an assault vessel, those outposts would be in a vulnerable position."

"Indeed, they would be."

"This further gives us an excuse for pulling them in for our needs to redeem them."

"Very good, and so the orcs crash against their walls, but elves are well-known to be master bowmen, and if to place a few lines of these on their walls, I think those orcs would not last long."

"Naturally. And here is where we have the Priestess make a daring accusation that the Suuden-Aryku are the ones delivering the orcs."

"Um, excuse me, General," Amariyn wonders. "Is it actually wise, at this moment, to have her making such a statement?"

"In this case, the Suuden-Aryku High Commander will know he is not responsible for sending any attacks against the Flame Elves, so he will refute this. But in her eyes, we must reference the Suuden-Aryku delivery vessel, and therefore it must be Suuden-Aryku flying it. The issue of it being stolen will then come out in conversation as the High Commander will likely explain the loss of one such transport to the orcs."

Amariyn shakes her head and chuckles.

"I am so very glad I'm not in the military. This level of intrigue would be the end of me. So, she makes it appear she believes it to be the Suuden-Aryku sending this transport when, in fact, it's orcs, and for what purpose?"

"We are building an image here," Thaelyn relates. "We are suggesting the orcs are evolving their capacity to become a threat to more than just the elves. We hope to use this for a later assault on a Suuden-Aryku outpost, but we have yet to plan this."

"How interesting. Well, I certainly wish you luck in this. But how do you hope to finally rid this world of these heathens?"

"There are still a number of variables in that equation, so we will move forward step by step until we can satisfy a few. One thing that does come to mind, however, is we will need to remove the Flame Elves from their perspective of interest."

"And how do you propose you would do that?"

"Somehow, they must come under attack. It must be sudden and unexpected, and perhaps also very mysterious. We want the Suuden-Aryku to become afraid of us."

The activity levels in Bya'an Tamoranth were becoming vigorous today, as a large gathering of Night Elves was assembling in the city's main terminal hub for their gateway network. The scene was drawing the attention of the locals, as the sight of any dark elf on the streets was an anomaly, due to their hostile relationship to the infamous Drow. The Night Elves were still a new sensation for some, and this occasion was especially noteworthy.

Slowly, they began dispersing through the gateways to other cities around the continent, taking up positions along established routes between the local terminal stations and the city grove districts.

Once the traffic guides were in place, a group of mages in the temple of Kynesoth were given instructions to begin opening way-lines while Sehnisavain and her people called in their citizens by the hundreds. One by one they filed through the portals directly to Tae'Eladar, arriving in the gateway hub station at a designated gathering point, then to be directed by the first of the Night Elf tour guides. Some were sent to the grove district in the capital city, while others were redirected through the network to other cities.

As each one found their way along the route, they arrived at a grove of the mother tree and her daughters. All seven of the dryads had emerged from their trees for the occasion to give a healing touch to the arriving elves, sending each one into a restful sleep within the circle.

The elves slumbered for only a few hours before waking up free of the horrid songs of Sargeras, instead now feeling the refreshing sensation of harmony and nature's bliss, a feeling of oneness of spirit with each other and the world around them. But they knew they could not remain long, as they needed to return home to allow the next group to follow. And so it would continue for the next several days.

In the tactical office in Firstfall, Thaelyn and the General monitored a series of reports and tallies coming in on the activity of the Flame Elves.

"Our auditors will continue with a census until the last of them is processed," the General reports. "This will give us a much better estimation of their population count, and it could possibly serve us later if we carry any further interactions with them."

"Excellent," Thaelyn affirms. "And we must be sure we maintain a close relationship and discussion of our affairs where this war is concerned, in case we need to make any hasty evacuation procedures."

"Absolutely, and for this, I might recommend we keep a band of mages on-hand in case we need to send them down there to bring those people out quickly. We should bring them directly to Tae'Eladar for this point, not up here."

"Good, see to it."

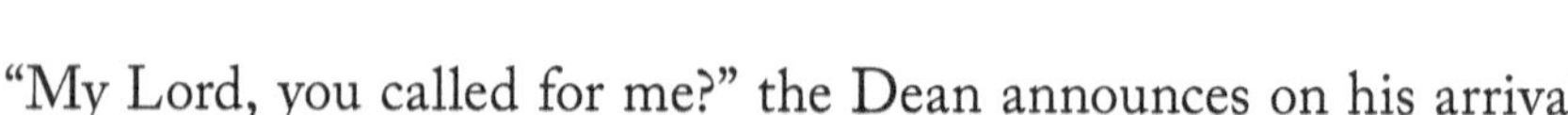

"My Lord, you called for me?" the Dean announces on his arrival in the Governor's office.

"Yes, we have that delivery I mentioned," the Governor asserts. "It's been stored in the basement, as usual, so I will have you carry it back and put it somewhere convenient until your lesson is ready."

"And just for the proper understanding, how do we apply it?"

"It's a very simple application. You have two boxes, each filled with vials of an elixir. Hand them out to each of your students. One per person should be adequate, and have them drink it down. Then send them to their study in the basement. I should think you can simply give them a few tasks and leave them be for a while, and all will be fine by the time we are ready for our next objective."

"And this is when we call that man up here for his little surprise party?" he grins.

"Yes, and I hope to have a front row seat to enjoy the performance."

"Very good, my Lord, I'll be on my way then."

The Dean turns to leave the office. As he exits into the hallway, he takes note of Leesa, apparently searching for something in the closet at the end of the hall. He studies her for a moment and notices she is missing her shoes, so he approaches to inquire about this.

"Eh, Leesa, where are your shoes?"

"Oh, I'm trying to give my feet a little rest," she replies chirpily. "All this walking around, and those shoes pinch a little."

"Ah, I see. Eh, perhaps you could give me a hand for a moment?"

"Oh, do you need something?"

"Yes, I need to carry a couple of items from the basement over to my office. Do you mind?"

"Not at all!" she affirms eagerly.

She grabs her shoes from the floor next to her and quickly slaps them back on her feet, then follows him down into the basement again. He locates a set of blue boxes with lids tightly sealed on top. There were labels affixed to the lids with lines of writing and other strange symbols and graphics.

Leesa tried not to make it seem as though she was paying attention to the design work on the labels, instead simply to lift one box and wait for him to lead the way out of the basement. He closed and locked the door, then brought the two of them outside. As they progressed across to the academy, she followed behind by a step or two, where she discreetly pulled out her trans-com from the hidden pocket under her beltline and quickly took a snapshot of the label on the box, then stashed the unit back into hiding. When they arrived at the academy, they travelled up the stairs and finally into his office.

"We'll set these down right over here," he points off to a corner.

The two of them place their loads side-by-side on the floor.

"Is there anything else?" she asks.

"I believe that is all for now. And thank you, you certainly seem like the sort of person we could use more of around here."

"Aw, I bet you say that to all the pretty girls," she coos sweetly.

She smiles brightly and then turns to leave.

The Dean watches her as she departs, then takes up his chair in contemplation.

"I wonder how old that girl is," he mumbles quietly. "She certainly seems like the obedient sort, and doesn't ask any unbecoming questions, unlike some of those we have downstairs."

He ponders the notion a moment longer.

"One of the noble families…hmm, perhaps, yes, I seem to recall some tales of those women and their tea parties. All gossip, and no determined thought on city affairs."

Leesa returned briskly back to her desk in the secretary's office, where she again pulls out her trans-com, this time to make a call. The secretary observed her using the odd device and directed his attention at her. She turned to catch his gaze, but then placed a finger to her lips to offer silence.

"Lieutenant Lapäli here," answers the voice.

"Lieutenant, good," she offers. "This is Leesa. You're in the settlement again?"

"Yes, I just returned a short while ago after today's class. What do you have?"

"I need to send another picture to you. Are you ready?"

"Absolutely. What is it this time?"

"The Dean had me help drag a couple of boxes out of the basement over to his office. It has something to do with that lesson he's supposed to give to the students over there."

"This doesn't sound good."

Leesa now follows a familiar procedure, which she has learned and practiced several times by now. She pulls up the main menu on the trans-com and selects an icon for the photo library.

The secretary was becoming curious as to the strange device and its operation. He steps around his desk to observe.

She brings up an index of her recent photos and touches the thumbnail icon for the newest one. This brings the image onto the display. She follows this by pulling up a local options menu and selecting a feature to send the image along the current com-link. The secretary gazed at her for the obvious professionalism of her work.

Leesa then returned to the link to talk again.

"Are you getting it?"

"Yes, I am. Very good. Is there anything else?"

"That's all for the moment."

"All right, I'll take a look and pass it along."

They end the link, and she stows her unit back into her pocket.

"Young lady," the secretary mutters. "If I didn't know you were working to save so many people, I might say you were a danger to society."

"It certainly is interesting work," she smiles amusingly. "I wonder if I could take up a job of some kind doing this."

The two of them return to their desks and continue their work.

"What do we have there, Lieutenant?" Thaelyn asks after the call finishes.

Padriyl paused a moment to study the image he received from the link.

"Interesting, this looks like it came out of some kind of industry, like a medical research facility, I think."

"Can you make out what it is?"

"I would need to run this past Med-tech Tad'vaal to get any kind of answer, but this label says it comes from someplace with a company logo of ARC, and it looks very professional, like it came out of an automated production line."

"How quaint... But does it give a description of the contents?"

"All I can say is it's something called a Kajik'tav Serum. I don't know what that is, but I find it very interesting that it has a name of any kind, and why it might be here if this is from some kind of medical industry."

"Indeed, so we might suggest a medicinal agent, but likely one designed for your species, not necessarily that of humans, and therefore we must ask what effect it would have if given to someone here."

"That's simply scary. And worse is that someone actually thought of using it. And even worse is if that someone is so familiar with our medical agents to call for one here."

"If this is the case, he cannot be local."

"Are you ready for this one, Priestess?"

"This should be a rather interesting conversation, Master Cydulean. He has never demonstrated even the tiniest amount of emotional content, so I wonder how he might react to this."

"Indeed, then this might prove to be a rather interesting study."

Sehnisavain and her cohorts were again in her office at the temple in Kynesoth. As before, she was preparing to make a call on her trans-com. She settles herself into her role and takes a deep breath, then dials the number.

"Commander Geilv, speaking…"

"Commander!" she announces harshly. "How dare you assault us! Are you now turning on us the same as you once claimed to be with the orcs?"

"What? I do not understand your meaning. We have made no aggressive movements in your direction. Why do you accuse us of this?"

"Do not play coy with me, Dear Sir!" she shouts angrily. "We just now fended off a large assault wave of orcs crashing against our walls. Our outer watch posts had to rush back inside the city for safety, just as we closed the gates. Fortunately, our archers were able to repel the invasion, but the fact that it was launched from one of your transport vessels is an outrage!"

"Wait, settle yourself. We did not launch any attacks on your position. You say this was orcs attacking you?"

"Yes, orcs, of all the creatures that would dare tarnish our lands. But, if you're trying to claim it wasn't you who sent them, then how do you explain the fact that our people witnessed one of your transports dropping them outside our walls?"

"A transport…" he pauses briefly. "I will ask you to clarify. The transport, was it a large cargo supply vessel?"

"I wouldn't know one from the other, but the reports did say it was huge, and with a large number of orcs pouring out the back end of it. Then it picked up and flew away."

"High Priestess, be advised we suffered an attack on a supply collection mission to the north. We received an emergency broadcast describing an ambush attack by orcs arriving through portals. We sent a team to investigate and found the transport missing, along with the materials it was collecting."

"Oh, wonderful! So, you're trying to tell me these beasts are learning to fly now? Commander, this is an outrage, and even more so for the apparent influence your people gave to inspire them in the first place," she pauses to catch her breath. "Very well, Commander,

I will share this with our people, and further to give orders for all our remaining outposts to return home for safety."

"Understood. Did your people observe the direction of the transport as it departed the area?"

"All they were able to tell was it headed off generally to the south and west. Our last reports said the orcish lines were simply too far away for us to see them from our home territory."

"Acknowledged, we have scout ships attempting to locate it, but so far, they have been unsuccessful. You will advise if you receive any more sightings."

"Of course, and do try to resolve this quickly."

They end the link, and she turns to the others in the room with another naughty smile.

The Dean was in his office holding a meeting with several of his instructors. Together, they had been preparing a stack of notes to be delivered to the student body.

"We must be certain to have full attendance for this special lesson," he advises. "Therefore, we will deliver these to each of their respective homes as a reminder to be punctual for the opening bell."

"Of course, Dean," replies one of the instructors. "But what do we do with the circle downstairs? If we're putting them in the basement for this lesson, should we be concerned about our earlier work?"

"At this moment, we'll take things incrementally. The Governor informs me that we can make an allowance for time in this case if we can solve this other concern of the students and their nervous anxiety. If anything should happen to the circle, we will simply make the necessary adjustments and proceed from there."

"All right, then we'll start sending these out right away. How long do we expect this lesson to continue?"

"According to my instructions, we will give them a series of tasks to perform down there and just leave them be for a time. I will check on them later to ensure they have become more compliant."

"Um, just for the sake of asking," offers another instructor. "Do we know what this new elixir is about?"

"The Governor simply tells me it should soften them up a bit, so they are not quite as edgy. Afterwards, we will proceed with the circle again."

As the meeting in the Dean's office was wrapping up, another event was occurring in the Governor's office. Leesa and the secretary had both halted their work efforts to listen to a tirade of stomping and pounding from the floor upstairs, accompanied by a series of loud screeches.

"Um," Leesa dithers. "Is this normal for him?"

"In all my time working in this office," the secretary relents. "I've never heard quite as much shouting up there as I have been recently."

"Recently..." she muses. "Can you make out the words?"

"Not at all. And furthermore, who is it he's supposed to be talking to, if we didn't see anyone go up there?"

"Yeah, and then there's that. My best guess is if he's got Suuden-Aryku devices in the basement, he's probably got a trans-com up there."

"That doesn't sound good. So, he's in contact with them somehow?"

"Must be, if he's able to give them orders," she considers. "But if something out there is getting him so riled up, I'll bet we're playing a few good rounds on him."

Upstairs in the Governor's office, he was once again cursing into his trans-com.

"How, Commander?! How can these pestilent animals learn to fly a transport, and then use it as a troop carrier! You must find it and destroy it. What is the condition of the city down there?"

"Stable, the High Priestess reports they were able to repel the invasion effectively using their city defenses."

"Good, at least they can accomplish that much. Keep me advised if you should hear anything else."

They end the link, and he settles back into his chair to take a few deep breaths.

"This operation is starting to fall apart," he mumbles to himself.

It was late in the day when Thaelyn was making some new plans with his officers in Firstfall.

"Lieutenant," he instructs. "Can your people put together another countermeasures device to interfere with the Suuden'kai communications network?"

"I'm sure we could piece something together," Padriyl replies. "We could simply copy the design we're using around the ship from your earlier instructions. What do you plan on using this one for?"

"Priestess Sehnisavain tells us she is aware of a Suuden'kai outpost that serves as a small waystation for transporting goods into the region. This is what they were using once to deliver supplies to the Flame Elves, and sometimes the orcs. It is a fairly small outpost, presumably manned by only a few score of troops. If we can block their communications to prevent them from calling for help, then hit fast and make it look like another orcish raid, I think we will invoke a reaction by the Suuden-Aryku that they are coming under attack from an otherwise unknown vector."

"You know, they probably have ships up there right now looking for that transport."

"Likely so, but if we then transmit another of our distress messages, I think this would override any truth or fiction they might be entertaining about the presence of a phantom transport making trouble."

"Oh dear cu'Nar, so it's a phantom ship now," he laughs.

"General, this outpost is said to be due east of Kynesoth. Send a few scouts down there and have them survey the area. We will strike once we have the jamming device ready, and a fair understanding of their movements. We should also make a study of those staging posts they were using against the Naarg uy'Sodrad."

"Of course, my Lord," he responds. "I must wonder what sort of reaction they might have to this one," he smiles.

Chapter 9

AMBITIOUS INSPIRATION

"Tristeen, you have a note down here from the academy."

"A note?"

Tristeen was just pulling herself together after an early breakfast when her mother called about the delivery of a missive from the Dean. She rushed downstairs, still in her nightgown to take a look. She picks at her long blonde hair, pulling it out of her face and running her fingers through it as a crude effort to comb it while she reads the note.

> *"The academy will be conducting a special exercise in the morning that will involve a test of a new elixir designed to improve student performance in future projects. Precision is important in this experiment. Therefore, the exercise will be conducted in the basement to prevent any disruption that may come about due to outside disturbances. Participation is required for all classmen. Attendance begins promptly by the first bell."*

"And here we go…" she muses quietly.

"Tristeen?" her mother asks. "Is there something wrong?"

"Mom, you remember what I've been telling you about him, right?"

"Yes, although it seems so sinister."

"Well, here it is…the beginning of the end. He's doing it."

"Doing what?"

"Cleaning house…"

She now turns and dashes upstairs to finish dressing. Several moments later, she runs out of the house and down to the academy. She bursts through the doors into the main hall where she found several other students assembling, including her friends Jared, Jon, and Sara. They all gathered together in a huddle.

"Tris," Sara begins. "I'm a right bit scared now. What do you think he's got up his sleeve for this one?"

"Leesa told me to beware of any new projects he brings out, so I'm going to the head of the line to see what he's got up there. New elixir? Pshaw! Has anyone here seen those instructors working the alchemy tables, or were they too busy gloating over that circle?"

"Aye," Jon admits. "She's got one there. He said in that note they've got themselves a new elixir to make some fancy work on us. Bully to that, I say! Fancy work to make us all soft and cuddly, mayhap."

"All right, everyone," Jared asserts. "We need to stand together on this. He can't make any moves if we're all holding firm at once. Even if he calls all of his instructors to his side, we still outnumber them. Let's see what this is about and move ahead wisely."

"This is likely where we'll just have to walk," Tristeen relents. "Fine, so much the better. I'm sick of this place by now. We're not learning anything useful anyway, as much as it pains me to say that. I had my hopes to learn what magic was about, but this place barely even teaches what it could be about."

"Aye," Sara affirms dejectedly. "I have to admit, you're right. It was a fine tingle in my bosom dreaming of what I could learn. But if the only thing they wanted from us was to play like mice in a cage, I'd be better off working upstairs at the Ten Eagles."

"Sara! Don't even say that. We'll stick together and find a way. I won't have any of my friends working at the Ten Eagles."

The student body continued to gather in the main hall. The room was becoming crowded by now for all the people clustering around. Finally, the Dean makes his appearance in the rear door, ringing his bell to gain their attention. He begins making his announcement, calling out in a well-pronounced voice for everyone to hear.

"We have a special assignment scheduled for today," he declares. "Everyone is required to participate in this session, regardless of class duties or associate grade. The session will take place in the basement, for reasons of the delicate nature of the study material. It is imperative we provide this isolation to ensure we achieve the purest results from this study."

The Dean makes a quick survey of the room to gauge the reactions of the students before continuing.

"Along the way, we will be testing a new elixir that was only recently developed by our top alchemists. This is stated to improve our study efficiency and our attentiveness to the most critical aspects of those lessons we offer. Naturally, as you know, the study of mage craft involves a considerable amount of intensive review. Therefore, it becomes apparent, from time to time, that we must rise to meet the occasion of serving our city's needs."

He again pauses to check their expressions.

"In addition, it has come to my recent attention that some of you are concerned over our recent studies in the basement. I will assure you that this effort has been very carefully considered, and as part of our obligation to serving our people and our city, you should know that today's assignment has been devised to lead us in a positive direction to see these obligations fulfilled. Now, without further delay, we should begin with the lesson. Please follow me..."

The Dean leads the group through the doorway at the rear of the hall. They turn right and proceed down the corridor, eventually rounding a corner to the left and continuing until they reach the basement door.

Tristeen rushed into position, excusing herself in front of the other students to take the lead. As they arrived at the basement door, the first thing she noticed was a small table with a blue box sitting on top. The lid to the box had been removed and was lying next to it on the table. Nearby, she saw a second box sitting on the floor, and a waste barrel just in front.

The Dean turned to face the assembly, making himself ready to start handing out the vials from their packaging, when he noticed Tristeen at the head of the line. She smiled innocently at him. He felt a soft loathing for the girl for her interference in his activities, but he held himself steady as he prepared his next announcement.

"As you can see here, we have enough supply for everyone, so we will begin handing them out, one to each of you, and you will imbibe them and toss the empty vials in this barrel here."

"What's inside?" Tristeen inquires innocuously.

"Huh?" he retorts. "Oh. Well, so far, this is a secret formula that needs testing for its accuracy."

"Ooh," she croons. "A secret formula, and you want all of us to test it for you? Why, wasn't it tested in the lab already?"

"Well, yes, of course it was, but now we need a working example in the field to demonstrate the efficacy of the formula."

"Oh, yes, but of course!" she yips excitedly. "And so you need this working example on all of us students, since we're the ones who will ultimately be using it, right?"

"Exactly, now if you will just…"

Tristeen spontaneously directs her attention at the neatly packed array of bottles in the strange box. She pulls one out to examine it closely. It fit easily in her palm and resembled a slim, hexagonal shape.

"Wow!" she holds it up for display. "Hey look, everybody, we must've got some new bottles in the lab! They're hexagons now!"

She continues to examine the vial as the Dean tried to regain control of the situation.

"Acolyte Macaid," he asserts. "If you don't mind, we need to focus on our assignment here."

"This is pink!" she shouts, ignoring his statement. "Has anyone ever seen a pink elixir before?"

"Acolyte Macaid!" the Dean urges sternly.

Tristeen now examines the box more closely.

"This is a very strange box. Hey Jon, Sara, Jared, come over here and look. Have you ever seen anything like this?"

The three friends join alongside Tristeen, and the Dean felt himself losing containment of the situation as the four of them are now inspecting the foreign container.

"Will you all please…!" he shouts.

Tristeen now picks up the lid sitting behind the box. She begins examining the label on top. The Dean reaches for it to take it back, but she simply slaps his hand away.

"Excuse me, young lady!" he protests.

"Sara, look at this here," she interrupts. "Have you ever seen anything like this before?"

Sara takes the lid and studies it closely.

"Nope, not anything like I ever saw before. It's not wood or metal. Jon?"

She passes it across for him to examine next. The Dean tries again to take the item away, but this time Jared catches his arm and pulls it back firmly while solemnly shaking his head at the action.

"It's solid, a bit stiff, but you can still bend it," Jon considers. "But it doesn't look like any kind of fabric or leather that I can see. Blue… I can't think of anything we might make around here that's blue like this and not otherwise made of a dyable material like cloth."

"Aye, and this color looks like it's inside here, not something on top of it, like paint."

"Right, and even though it's stiff and I can bend it, it just flattens out again. Metal doesn't do that."

"Will you people stop talking so much nonsense!" the Dean barks.

Tristeen holds her hand out and Jon passes the lid back to her. She returns to studying the label.

"This here looks interesting," she observes. "It looks a bit like writing. Does anyone know what it says? Because it's not anything I ever learned in my language classes."

"What language classes were those, Tris?" Jon asks.

"Hey! You're right. We don't get any language classes around here, except maybe to learn our own, and this isn't ours."

The Dean was starting to feel a cold shiver run through him as it was becoming clear this box had foreign origins. He now had to make up an excuse for it.

"I will have your attention, people!" he roars. "This is an important project we have here, and this nonsense of the box and that ridiculous bit of paper is not why we have assembled here."

"This doesn't look like paper to me, Dean," Tristeen asserts. "I don't know what it is, but paper it is not."

"That is entirely beside the point! We are here to conduct our studies, and you will oblige as part of this student body."

"Or what, Dean?" she retorts firmly. "You'll expel me like you did Haran, all because he disagreed with your principles about what service we owe to our city and its people? This box isn't made of any recognizable material, yet it looks very neat and professional. And this label is written in a foreign language. All right, let's say you just happened to find some odd box somewhere and are reusing it, for all the shortages we have in the city. Can you at least tell me what sort of ingredients it has? As a noble, to say nothing of my friends or anyone else in the city, I'm rather particular as to what I put inside my body. I'm not drinking anything unless I know what it's made of."

"Blast it, young lady..." he curses. "It's a very complex formula, and quite more advanced than anything I'm sure you've ever studied in the labs. Even I wouldn't know every little detail of it, as the alchemists who made it are keeping it as, eh...a trade secret, you know."

"Oh, a trade secret? Master alchemists, is it?"

"Yes, the best in the trade. Now if you will simply..."

"So, the Dean of the academy," she interrupts again. "One of the most powerful men in the city, is submitting his authority to a third party, and on the presumed expertise of that third party he is also submitting the health and welfare of his students to whatever that third party has created, without even knowing what is involved in the creation of it. Do we at least have some sort of test results from their original lab studies?"

"Damn you nobles!" he spits. "Can't you just do as you're told for once and be done with it?"

Tristeen felt a sudden surge of rage flush through her for that statement. She steps in and swings an arm around for a solid slap across his face.

"You just remember, Dean," she scorns. "I'm the noble, not you. And I hold considerably more responsibility for the safety of this city than what you seem to care for. You want us to drink this and then lock us in the basement…for how long, Dean? Until whatever this is drives us back into our cages for you and your instructors to poke sticks at? Not today, Dean, because I suspect once we're put back in our cages, you and your goons will go back to your circle over there and finish whatever it was you were planning before all this got started."

"You have no idea what you're playing with, young lady."

"Dean, I think I have a few ideas of what YOU are playing with, and I think you don't know half of what's on the other side of it."

Now she turns to the assembly and announces boldly.

"We are done here, people. This place has been taken over by hoodlums and maniacs. If they want to play God with people's lives, let them do so with their own, not ours. Everybody outside…"

She returns to look at the Dean again. He was clearly fuming. She again examines the box, and then has an idea flash into her. She grabs the lid and places it back on top, then picks up the box to carry it away. The Dean tries to stop her by reaching out to take it back.

"And just where do you think you're going with that?" he spurns.

Sara takes the initiative to step in and assist, delivering a firm knee to the groin, which causes him to let out a loud moan as he doubles over to the ground.

"I've been waiting a long time for that one," she affirms.

"Grab the other one," Tristeen orders. "Whatever this is, don't let him feed it to anyone else."

Sara takes the second box, and the four of them follow the rest of the assembly out of the building.

"Everyone, over there to the temple," Tristeen issues.

"Why the temple?" Sara wonders.

"We've got friends in there."

The two young women, along with their male counterparts, lead the procession across the plaza and into the temple.

"Everyone inside, quickly," Tristeen emits. "I don't want a lot of people to see us duck inside here."

The students all hurriedly file inside the temple, and Jared closes the door behind them.

"Right, then," Sara relents. "What are we supposed to do in here, pray to our false gods to help us?"

"Easy does it, Sara."

The sudden arrival of the large assembly of young people in mage robes drew the attention of several men from the head of the room. Most of them were priests, along with one who was in professional attire.

"What happened here?" Priest Garrain asks urgently.

"We made a stand against the Dean over there," Tristeen relates. "Right now, he's hotter than an overstuffed teakettle, and we need help. I'm told you can get us out of here, is this true?"

"Indeed, it is. But tell me first, what actually happened to cause this?"

"Look here," she opens her box to show the contents. "He claims this is for some grand new alchemy experiment we're all supposed to drink, and then sit in the basement and wait for something. Leesa told me this is likely from the Governor, and probably to make us quiet down for all our grousing of that circle he's drawing in the basement."

The professional man came in for a closer look, pulling out a bottle for review.

"Um, my pardons," Sara wonders. "But you don't look much like a priest. Who are you?"

"My name is Master Dastien. I'm a mage in the service of our Lord Thaelyn and his most noble Order of Tyr."

"Oh, wow…a mage, is it? I hope you're a mite better than the ones we have over in the academy," she smiles sheepishly.

"Not to worry, young lady, we are a much different folk than your own example. This here…" he directs to the vial. "This looks like formed glass from an industrial process."

"What about the box?" Tristeen asks. "Can you tell what it's made of, and this label here?" she points at the lid.

One of the priests takes the lid to examine it.

"This looks a bit like the Suuden-Aryku language to me."

"Suuden-Aryku!" Sara yips. "Buggers to that, I say!"

"This box looks like a synthetic material," Master Dastien admits. "Our industry is only just recently entering that stage of development where we're experimenting with synthetics."

"So, this box is of Suuden-Aryku origin," Tristeen sighs. "And what's inside here, do we know?"

"This is likely that shipment the Governor ordered recently," Priest Garrain offers. "The one Leesa photographed for us. I recall mention of a name, but it doesn't mean anything to me."

"All right, well anyway," Tristeen asserts. "We need help. I want all these people removed from here. I was told you could somehow evacuate us, right?"

"Yes Ma'am," the Master affirms.

He reaches into an inner vest pocket and pulls out a rune stone. Sara studies it carefully.

"What's that?" she asks tenderly.

"This is what we use to create portals. From here, you will go straight to our settlement in the valley to the south."

"Bloody hell!" she yips. "Now that'd be a fine bit of sparkling, if ever I did see. Could you teach this sort of thing to someone like me?"

"Absolutely, although you would first need to study our language before you could enroll in our classes. Would you be interested in trying out for one of our academies?"

"Um, well, how do they treat people over there?"

"From what I've been hearing of your own academy, you should know that we'll expect nothing less than superior results from your studies if you should wish to become productive in any sort of career," he grins.

"And you even give jobs for this? Aye, I think I might want to take a wee look at that. It beats all the hells out of working the Ten Eagles!"

Master Dastien holds out the rune and enchants it, causing it to glow with the ring of energy circling in his palm. Sara gazes at it longingly.

"I'm feeling those tingles again, Tris," she coos.

"Well, hold the thought for now and just get out of here. Jon, take this box," she hands it over to him. "Deliver these to that Lord Thaelyn and tell him I sent you."

"Wait now, Tris!" Sara protests. "What about you? You're not coming along?"

"I need to stay here and watch that maniac. But I want all of you out of here. Go now, and find a good life for yourself. Don't worry about me, I'll be along eventually."

Sara gazes at her friend pensively, and reaches an arm around for a hug.

"Right, you do that, and I'm holding you to it. Now, how do I use this rune thing?"

"Simply touch your hand to the stone," Master Dastien replies. "Watch your step as you come out, and then move away for the next person. We tend to use a timing practice to move groups of people quickly."

"Aye!"

She steps forward and gingerly reaches out her hand to touch the stone. An instant later, she is enveloped in a flash and sent away.

"Gods above!" Jon mutters. "And to think, they barely taught us how to make fire."

He then follows behind, and the rest begin to follow after that.

"I'm staying with you, Tristeen," Jared proclaims. "You're not taking this alone."

"Thanks, Jared," she submits. "But from this moment on, we need to be extra careful."

Sometime later, a feeble knocking comes at the Governor's office door.

"Yes?" he calls. "Come in."

The door opens to reveal the Dean limping and hunched over. The Governor stares at him as he enters the room.

"What happened to you?" he yelps.

"I had a little problem with one of the students."

"Just what did you involve yourself with that it would bring this sort of condition?"

"I, uh…well, we had something like a rebellion."

"A rebellion?!" he shouts. "What happened over there?"

"It was that same young lady, Tristeen Macaid. She took the lead and began interrogating what the elixir was, where it came from, what was inside, and so on. I tried to put it to rest that it was a special recipe we were demonstrating, but she came back with all sorts of arguments that I wasn't disclosing the ingredient list, or the test results from the original alchemist labs, and well, it just went around with her finally leading a revolt, and they all walked out."

"And how does this relate to your unfortunate posture?"

"She took the boxes, and when I tried to recover them, one of her cohorts kicked me…down there," he glances at himself.

The Governor almost felt a note of amusement come into him, but he quickly checked himself for the clear change in circumstances.

"Where did they go, do you know?"

"They left the building, this much I know, but I was on the ground and couldn't move for several moments, so I couldn't follow them."

"All right, if they're gone from the building, they could be anywhere in the city by now. And I think I will not waste any more time on them. If they simply walked away, either they won't bother with anything else, or we'll deal with it in other ways. What about the circle, did they do anything to it?"

"No, this was outside in the hallway."

"Good, then we should move forward quickly before anything else happens. I want you to send out that note immediately. We'll take care of that man and then move to the rest in a more fashionable order."

"Um, my Lord, I would love to oblige, but I have a small issue."

"Oh grand, now what?"

"I don't have any runners. Those were my students, if you recall, and they're all gone now."

"Oh, but of course. Then perhaps we could use mine on this occasion. That young lady downstairs seems eager enough to please. Call on her to deliver this and make it quick."

"Right away."

He turns and hobbles out of the room, then proceeds downstairs to the secretary's office.

"Leesa?"

The girl turns to the address from her desk.

"Yes? Oh, Dean, look at you. What happened, are you injured?"

"Oh, it's alright, I'll be fine in a moment. It's only a minor discomfort. I have a need of your service to deliver a very important note. I would send one of my own runners, but unfortunately, um, they're all out at the moment."

"Oh, well sure! What kind of note, and where is it going?"

"It's um, a note that needs to be delivered to the valley to the south. Are you aware of those new people down there?"

"I've heard a few stories."

"Right, good, well, um, the Governor has been making a few new trade proposals with them…you know, to expand on our trade relations."

"Oh wow, so we're setting up a new trade partner, like with the dwarves up north?"

"Yes! But the negotiations are delicate to make sure we can

establish a profitable exchange. And this note is a necessary response to a recent offer they made. So, it's very important to deliver it promptly."

"Oh, of course... Um, that's a long walk though."

"Oh no, silly young lady," he chuckles. "I would have you take a horse on this occasion. Can you ride a horse?"

"Hmm, riding a horse, I suppose I could do that. Is it hard?"

"Oh, not at all!" he retorts supportively. "It is actually quite easy, as the horse does most of the work."

"Oh, goodie... But, um," she glances at her dress. "Maybe I should change into something more appropriate. I recall something once about how young ladies shouldn't be romping around on horses in a long dress."

"Oh, well, I suppose if you must, but be quick about it. Now, follow me to my office, that's where I have the note."

The two of them leave the Manor and return to the Dean's office, where he finds the note on his desk.

"Here it is, now be sure to give it to the one they call Lord Thaelyn. He's the one we're making these negotiations with."

"Do I need to say anything to him?"

"Oh, I think not. The note should be all there is. Just drop it off, and return back promptly."

"Good, I'll be back before anyone knows it."

She smiles and briskly leaves the room, while the Dean sits down in his chair and tries to recover from his earlier ordeal.

Leesa steps outside and casually glances up in the direction of the Governor's window to see if he is looking outside. She doesn't see anything, so she begins stepping out into the plaza until she gains a perspective of the Dean's window. He could not be seen either. So now she makes a mad dash across to the temple.

"Master Dastien!" she shouts. "He's doing it!"

"Doing what, Leesa?" he replies back.

The two met near the head of the room. She shows him the note the Dean gave her.

"This is supposed to be delivered promptly to Lord Thaelyn down there. I think it's that note to call him up for the little surprise party, as the Governor calls it."

"Grand. And the timing seems convenient enough. All the academy students just walked out on the Dean."

"They did? Oops, that might make trouble for someone."

"It would appear that way, and the first example would be His Lordship. All right, I will send this off immediately. I would suggest you remain here for now, and occupy yourself with something until such time as you might normally have made the journey down and back."

"All right…"

"Eh, knock, knock?" Sara utters timidly through the door of the tactical office in Firstfall.

The disturbance draws the attention of Thaelyn and the General, both of whom turn to see the young mage student standing in the doorway.

"Yes, young lady, come in," Thaelyn issues. "Can we help you somehow? You appear as one of the students from the academy up north, correct?"

"Aye, and begging your pardons, but the man outside here pointed me at the door when I mentioned your name."

"Indeed, we have this trouble with the difference in languages."

"Aye, um, I was sent here by your people up in the temple…well, we all were," she waves at the large assembly outside. "Jon and I need to deliver these boxes to you, compliments of Tristeen Macaid, who led all of us on a revolt away from the Dean."

"Indeed!" he chuckles. "And what sort of reaction did he have to that?"

"Not a good one, you can be sure of it," she smiles. "We're told these are probably from the Suuden-Aryku, and the Dean wanted us to drink this and sit in the basement for some odd reason none of us was pleased about."

Thaelyn waves the girl in, followed by Jon with the second box. They set them on the table for Thaelyn and the General to examine. Thaelyn studied the label.

"Yes, this would be that item Leesa photographed for us. I should thank you for bringing this to us. This will prevent the Dean or the Governor from trying to use it elsewhere."

"That's what Tris said," Sara affirms. "She's a right smart one, she is!"

"I would wish to meet with that young lady at some moment. She is becoming quite instrumental in our affairs up there. I think it is quite likely she saved a good many lives today."

Sara and Jon glanced at each other and smiled at the appreciative thought.

"Um," she continues. "So, now that we're here, I think we'll need to know what to do with ourselves after this."

"If you are here to be evacuated, I would offer you to stay with us for a while. I can make temporary arrangements if you like, or if perhaps, you have another direction you wish to take, we can discuss the possibilities."

"Your Master Dastien up there said something about an academy. I've always wished to study as a mage, but ours was a bloody flop. Can you suggest something about that?"

"Indeed, we have a number of courses available for study, depending on your field of interest. For this point, I might have you confer with Haran Carronel over in the guildhall."

"Haran!" she yips. "Bloody hell, so this is where he's been hiding? Most of us thought he'd completely flown the coop. What's he doing down here?"

"He took sanctuary after his encounter with your Dean and later chose to take up residence on our world as a new citizen. Ultimately, he plans to attend our academy, so he would make a fine tour guide for you and yours if you like."

"Well now, I could use a wee bit of that."

"I might also recommend, if you have not already done so, to have your implant devices removed."

Sara stared at him a moment, then recalled her shoulder. She impulsively brings her hand up to it.

"Right, um, does it hurt? Where do we go for that?"

"For this, I would direct you to my wife at our temple in our home city. She will help you further. Bring all your friends with you, as well. We will take care of each of you."

"Um, I don't have a lot of coin on me…my family isn't one of the wealthiest, you know."

"Young lady, this is far more important than what coin would account for. We will not charge you for this particular service," he smiles.

"Wow, that's a right noble offer. I can't pass that one up!" she smiles tenderly. "If only our own priests were as prim and proper. But all they could do was fill our heads with their guff about these false gods, and this promise of saving us from the plague, when in fact they were the ones doing it."

"Yes, and this is one of those things that aggravates me the most, is their sacrilege of the true gods out there. This is especially true for the elves and what happened to them. This creature, Sargeras, is an abomination that should not exist, and if he were to know just how close we were to him…" his voice cuts off suddenly, and he pulls back from the table in reflective consideration.

The General took immediate notice of this and came to attention.

"My Lord, is there something amiss?"

"General," he grins brightly. "I just had a rather delightful idea to solve one or more of our variables. Send word to Aerlie to meet us here. And have her bring several of our ranking priests with her."

"Your Lordship," Marelle considers. "Don't you think this might be a bit risky for your methods to date?"

"The risk, in this case, is a measurable one. I believe we can accomplish this without compromising any of our other efforts."

Marelle and the others have returned from their classes and

joined with Thaelyn and his officers, now including Aerlie, who was visiting from the city.

"But jiggers," Relissa moans. "You'll be stirring up a pot of nasty ones with it."

"Maybe so," Aerlie affirms. "But we think the risk is still manageable. And it would make perfect sense to the casual mind."

"Oh, I need to hear this one," Marelle smirks. "The casual mind… And just for the fun of it, how do you figure this one?"

"Like all things in this war, it would go in steps, beginning with a missionary. We've done this before, or at least Thaelyn did in those early days when he was taking control of Tae'Eladar. There were a number of nations that were ruled by some very corrupt influences, so he sent missionaries to soften them up before hitting them with anything harder. We are an official sovereign member of this world now, by merit of the inclusion of Solinaia. This means our kingdom holds political influence, as well as perhaps cultural and religious guidance."

"Jiggers!" Relissa yips. "That's a new one! So, now you're going to go out and start spreading your gospel around to all the neighbors."

"And since we have a human society which is apparently just as lost as the rest of you, it seems only right to share our great gift of wisdom of the true gods out there," she smiles harmlessly.

"Aye, and what do you think the Governor would say about that?"

"Technically, there is nothing he can do about it, except to file a political complaint, which in our case will fall on deaf ears, much the same as our call to arms did with him against our mutual enemies. Any other society might consider this tantamount to war, if to interfere with their internal affairs, but in the absence of a true army, and certainly one to match our own…"

"And now Buggers! You're going to hogtie him with his own hullabaloo."

"Um…" Marelle interjects. "Should I remind everyone here of the Suuden-Aryku? Not that they've been matching you, but, um…"

"Indeed, Marelle," Thaelyn responds. "But we have a few interesting stipulations here. One is our previous statement of attacking us directly for reasons of our portals and other things that would make us very difficult to remove."

"Right, and so the reason they haven't done so already."

"Next, he is essentially ruling that city as a covert operation for all his lies and deception. To call in the Suuden-Aryku to that location is to expose him. And he would not likely wish this if he can find another…covert…solution to it."

"Great! So, you're basically backing him into a corner."

"But the most important point here is to give us an excuse for the people of Rolsklinde to turn away from the rhetoric of the Dean and those priests. It would relieve us of some of our own covert operations, and relax our posture on that side. If the people are allowed to openly realize the crimes of the priests, this takes away one of the Governor's tools, without necessarily pointing a finger directly at him."

"Unbelievable."

"Then, by sending our missionaries to teach them about the true gods, we can bolster them against any further attempts by him to corrupt them back to his side. They will be wise to it now."

"Wow."

"This also reflects well on teaching them about the world around them, as they will have people from outside coming in and sharing their stories. The Governor held so much authority because he was isolating them with no interchange of information. We are going to break that. Even with the Suuden-Aryku behind him, he cannot stop the free flow of knowledge."

"All right, I suppose so, but he can still burn the place to the ground."

"Perhaps, but as Aerlie said, we will take it in steps. We are still playing on our assumptions of them holding back from us. And furthermore, by opening our cultural borders, and sending such enlightened people as Relissa here to spread our gospel…"

"Ay!" she protests. "Don't you go pointing your fingers at me!"

"Oh, come now, Relissa," Aerlie soothes. "You'd be perfect for the job. You made first contact, you were touched by the spirit, you learned about your heritage…what better representative of the Night Elves could we ask for to share the story of your people with all those unfortunate souls who seem to think you conduct unholy rituals at blood altars.”

“Jiggers, hoodwinked again…and just like Haran that one time.”

“And…” Thaelyn continues. “This could open up a few other opportunities for us, like with the Daanen-Aryku and their story. This would sap away at the Governor’s position of control. It is also non-military, so if we avoid a direct fight, the High Commander has no immediate cause to attack us, unless the Governor somehow orders it, assuming he holds that level of authority. But if his true interest is to see me removed, we can keep his focus on me rather than anyone else.”

“This actually brings us to his note,” the General mentions.

“We got one finally?” Marelle asks.

“Yes, it came in earlier today. Apparently, according to Master Dastien, the student walkout at the academy prompted them to push ahead with this other action of theirs. This suggests they are becoming impatient with our dear Lord and King,” he smiles.

“What does it say?”

“It’s written as a personal request from Captain Kholgard for an urgent meeting on some issue of city defense.”

“And how do we respond to this?”

“Personally,” he suggests. “I am of the opinion that this could represent a turning point. Conjuring up whatever these people have in mind, just like we mentioned earlier, seems like an act of desperation, or at least a simple lust for power. However, whatever it is they bring out would likely require a sizable opposing force to put down. If he expects this creature to dispose of his problem for him, we must then ask ourselves how he would dispose of the obvious problem left behind from it.”

“Meaning the creature, I presume, rather than him,” she points gingerly at Thaelyn.

“Correct. Now we have a paradox with only one viable pathway, and that would involve the Suuden-Aryku military, but this also means exposing his connection to the population. If his purpose is to conceal himself from them in order to one day make use of them somehow, he would not as likely wish to reveal himself or his connections out in the open. He has essentially four centuries of fabrications behind him to conceal his actions. Would he wish to sacrifice all that in one movement?"

"And so, the only real alternatives are to go ahead and reveal himself, or let it go entirely, where either of these would likely mean the end of our city and its people. Then how do we proceed with this? Ignore the message and take more subversive actions to undermine his position?"

"At the very least, I would say we should stall for time. We can send Captain Hagmaert up there as a representative. He will claim our Lord is currently very busy with his tedious affairs of the war with the orcs, and cannot get away immediately, but he promises to make the effort once he can find a proper moment. This releases us, at least for now, but with the promise of finding our way in the foreseeable future, in order to keep the Governor's focus on his target."

"But just a moment..." she asserts with a finger. "You'll send Captain Hagmaert, but who is he going to talk to, if the message actually came from the Governor?"

"Oh, well, if the Governor and the Dean are so interested in our Lord's visitation, they will probably be keeping a close watch for him to arrive, do you think?"

"Yeah, probably."

"And if they should see a splendid carriage arriving in that plaza of theirs, one or the other should take notice, do you think?"

"Yes," she grins. "But if they see the Captain stepping out, they might not want to call on their pet just yet, and instead try to understand why he is arriving rather than His Lordship, right?"

"Yes, and then we will offer our explanation to buy time."

"And hopefully they will accept it."

"We will intensify their focus," Thaelyn affirms. "These new plans will serve to inspire them to want me even more. I am going to make personal trouble for that man."

"Um, my Lord," Relissa wonders. "Does the Captain speak our language yet?"

Thaelyn sits back in his chair and sighs heavily.

"Not yet…"

The next morning, an ornate carriage arrives in Firstfall from Tae'Eladar, along with the horses to draw it. They arrived separately via portals, as a matter of convenience, and the horses were now being harnessed up. Captain Hagmaert, along with a mage to serve as a riding companion and support, were preparing to leave.

Thaelyn had once again found himself in need to conduct a meld to share the language. By this time, he was feeling almost giddy due to the number of times this process had to be performed.

"My Lord," the Captain offers. "Perhaps once a few of these operations are complete, you can send our agents elsewhere, rather than having to apply this so many times."

"Captain," he responds. "While I would be very pleased with this, I am not holding my breath for it so far. Now, you understand our objectives, and do be careful, just in case they become irate with my lack of attendance."

"Aye! I'll make a good show of it, and if this mage over here can keep his eyes open long enough, maybe we'll be back by suppertime."

Thaelyn smiles and sends the two men on their way. They load up in the carriage and head out the north gate.

The carriage was pulled by two white horses dotted with light gray spots, and the carriage itself was a nobleman's ride, skillfully crafted with white and blue enamel trim and gilded borders.

They sped along across the countryside, crossing the grassy fields until they eventually came to the pass leading up along the mountainside. They navigated their way to the crest and carefully down the other side, then continued north to the city, passing the southern watch tower and several new outlying farmlands until they arrived at the city gates.

The guards at the gate passed them through and they found their way along the streets, moving towards the upper district and the large plaza with the Governor's Manor, the academy, the temple, and the city barracks.

Tristeen had taken up sitting in the park area on the far side of the plaza, between the barracks and the Upper Ward. She didn't dare return to the academy after the walkout, but she also didn't want to let the academy out of her sight. The trouble now was that she couldn't actually see what was inside the academy to monitor their actions. Needless to say, she took notice of the unusually opulent carriage as it entered the plaza and came to a rest right in the middle.

"Who is that now?" she mutters silently.

The Dean was first to take notice, as the Governor had his attention on his desk. He looked out the window of his office above the academy to see the lavish vehicle and instantly jumped out of his chair to see who it was. But the man he saw getting out didn't look the same as the one he saw that first day. This one had a unique set of military attire, and an ornate helmet with a crest on top.

"What... Who the bloody hell is that?"

He turned to leave the office and rushed downstairs to investigate.

Captain Hagmaert had stepped out of the carriage and now stood there perusing the scenery, as if a tourist on vacation. The mage he was travelling with stayed in the carriage waiting to offer support if the situation got ugly.

Tristeen gazed in wonder at the neatly accoutered military man, also asking herself who this was, as nothing about him resembled anything recognizable.

The Dean rushed outside to meet with the visitor.

"Eh, hello?" he emits tenuously. "Are you looking for something?"

Captain Hagmaert turned to the man in the elegant wizard's robe and began his play.

"Ah, good man, indeed!" he replies exuberantly. "Yes, as a matter of fact, I was searching for someone, but perhaps you could assist instead. Might you be someone of authority here?"

"Me? Oh, but yes, of course. Where are my manners? I'm Dean Malorn of the academy here. And who might you be?"

"Ah, good Dean, yes… I am Captain Julian Hagmaert, in the service of our dearest Lord and King Thaelyn of Tae'Eladar. Good greetings to you," he bows politely.

Tristeen could just barely make out the words at this distance, and she studied their interactions carefully, trying to understand what was occurring.

"Captain Hagmaert, is it?" the Dean muses. "And what is it that brings you here?"

"Indeed, I am responding to a missive received only just recently at our station concerning a small matter relating to the city. It would seem my Lord was requested to make a visit to discuss one thing or another. Unfortunately, since this is my first time here, I am uncertain of where to direct myself on this occasion."

"Oh! That, yes, I actually know about this. As a member of the city authority, I'm aware of this message. But why are you here and not him?"

"Ah, much to his regret, he is unable to attend immediately, and sent me instead to deliver his kindest apologies for the delay. He has been especially busy of late in his affairs of war against the orcs; don't you know. A nasty bit, that. As a matter of fact, I do seem to recall your face during one of his early meetings. You and another man, who was that…" he ponders a moment.

"You mean the Governor?"

"The Governor, yes!" he rejoices. "I recall the two of you came to meet with us once, but unfortunately, it seems we were unable to arrange a proper accord at the time. Such a pity. But, he does have his obligations to his people, and he must continue with this as a high priority. You know, as any good king would do," he grins brightly. "Therefore, he sent me in his stead to see if perhaps I could represent him in this affair, or to see if this could wait some modest amount of time until he is better available."

The Dean was disturbed by the assertion, but he didn't dare allow himself to show it. Instead he knew that any arguments at the delay would seem impolite and could alter the final outcome of him arriving at all.

Tristeen listened attentively. The Captain's manner of speech was eloquent and flamboyantly chivalrous.

"Is this how you people behave down there?" she mutters privately. "Gracious! Don't go anywhere near my house, or my dad will haul you in for one of his more elaborate political debates, as well as tea, biscuits, and maybe a meal or two!"

"A postponement, you say?" the Dean considers. "Eh, this is most unfortunate. How long do you suppose this delay might be?"

"Oh, my dear Dean," the Captain responds optimistically. "I truly wish I could answer that. But war is a very dirty business, and fraught with so many unexpected inconveniences. However, he does promise to make every effort to see a proper moment to attend to this, and hopes this does not diminish our relations at all. Can I trust you and yours can permit this unfortunate interruption?"

"Oh, well, I suppose we can't make any arguments about this. After all, as you say, if his business keeps him so busy," he titters. "But I would wish to emphasize the importance of this meeting, and I do believe our authority figures would desire for him to make every effort. After all, we regard our city very highly, and would wish to see to its every need. We feel that his participation would be of great benefit to us all."

"Jolly good!" he exalts. "Then I shall return to him with this most positive reply and impress upon him the great importance of this occasion to see to our full and proper political relations. And now, without further ado, I should kindly take my leave," he bows again. "Good day to you, Dean."

The Captain returns to the carriage and they take off again down the road. The Dean watches them a few moments longer, and then proceeds to the Governor's Manor.

Tristeen continued to watch from her seat in the park.

"Regard the city highly, my noble backside, Dean," she scorns quietly. "As for you, Captain, that was a stall tactic, and a good one too," she smiles softly.

In the Governor's office, the Dean was reporting in.

"Blast!" the Governor curses. "Can't that man at least be punctual to his own death?!"

"There wasn't much I could do about it," the Dean relents. "If I were to argue, it might spoil everything."

"Agreed, Dean. Then we shall bide our time and show a little patience for him to find time away from his reckless rampage across our world, fighting those beastly mongrels. Maybe along the way, he might solve a few of our own problems with those creatures."

"Very well, my Lord, then what should I do in the meantime? I find myself with very little occupation now that the student body is gone."

"I don't know, Dean. Maybe you can rearrange your bookshelves, or lead your instructors in a singalong. One thing I would advise is to see about the schools and their teachers. It came to mind recently that if your students are now so opposed to your manners, they might try spreading this to others of a similar influence."

"Oh, yes, very good. This will give me some occupation."

The Dean bows and leaves the office.

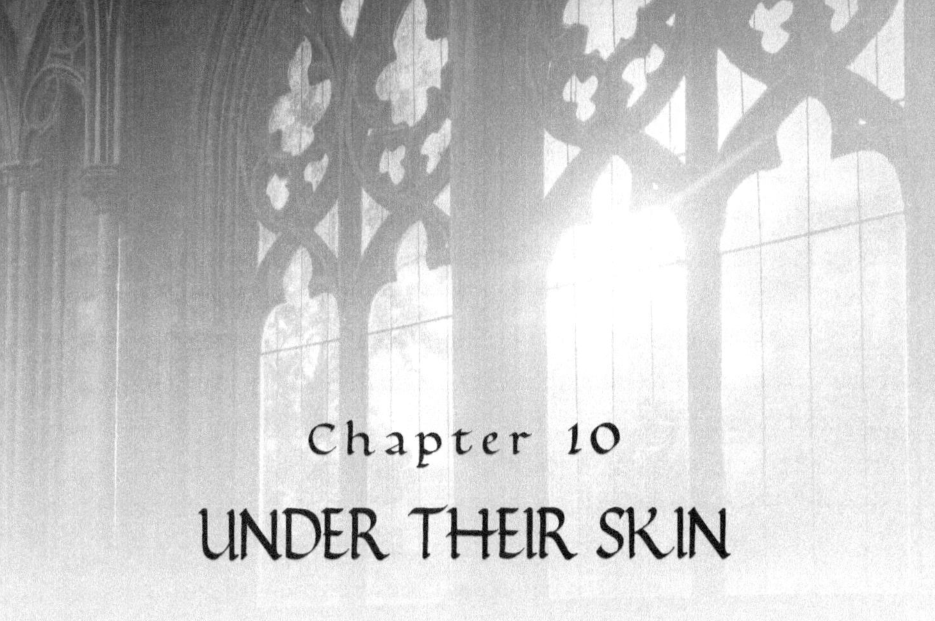

Chapter 10
UNDER THEIR SKIN

"**I**s that the last of them?" Cydulean asks of Sehnisavain and her attendants.

"Yes, finally," she sighs. "It took just over four full days of constant effort, but I had my people going door to door to make sure every citizen was accounted for."

"Good, my last word from our auditors said we were up around fifty-two thousand population, in case you were interested. That's a good healthy number for this city."

"But a paltry one for what was once our full population in this world, I'm sure."

"Indeed, but yours isn't the only one."

"I know, Master Cydulean, but now we need to prepare ourselves for whatever is coming next. Do they have any new plans for us?"

"My latest understanding is the orcs are lessening their interest in you, and will soon discover the first of their new targets. Naturally, we will keep you informed when this first target has been found, and so unfortunately destroyed, but this is a time of war, and these are the manners of orcs, as it seems," he smiles.

"Of course, but what do you suppose the owners of that next target will think of this?"

"That remains to be seen so far. Ultimately, we hope to see a pullback as a defensive move."

Sehnisavain and her people had been making their migrations to and from Tae'Eladar for the last several days, with the help of a series of mages and their portal way-lines inside the temple. The elder Priestess and her younger counterparts, along with a host of others, struggled to take up the work shifts and see every citizen of Kynesoth redeemed at the trees on Tae'Eladar, as well as the local one. At this moment, the full population of the city had finally found their peace, with the only thing to look forward to being the Suuden-Aryku and the continued uncertainties of the war.

In Firstfall, a missionary expedition was preparing to head out to Rolsklinde. A number of coaches had been imported to transport the assembly, along with teams of horses. This was the first part of Thaelyn's new exchange program to introduce the local people to his kingdom and its culture, along with its history, social customs, and other important aspects of what was essentially an international political exchange, even though the exchange was occurring across worlds.

The arrival of these larger coaches quickly gave rise to the obvious question of the local roadways, or lack thereof. Therefore, Thaelyn started putting out the word for laborers to arrive and make improvements to their local infrastructure, such as laying down a proper road from Firstfall to the north, travelling past the farming settlements up there, and further to the mountainside pass. They would also make improvements to the pass itself to accommodate more efficient travel over the mountain on the way to Rolsklinde. He further gave instructions to lay down an improved roadway leading out from Solinaia.

For now, however, the coaches would make their way, albeit slowly, across the open terrain to the city. They carefully traced their way along the narrow mountainside pass, over the crest and down the other side, then along to the city itself, arriving at the gates and passing through. They made their way along the avenues to the upper district until they arrived in the plaza and parked alongside the temple.

Once again, Thaelyn and Aerlie had to apply themselves, at least one time each, to yet another melding to give a couple of these people the language skills. This one aspect alone was the most burdensome. But the demands of the war, and the rescue of the city and its citizens, played its role in seeing this necessity through.

The missionaries disembarked from their transport and gathered in front of the temple. The local priests, who were Thaelyn's hidden agents, played their part by sending out criers to draw the people into attendance for a community service. Then they openly welcomed the visitors in the eyes of all those who might be watching, such as the Dean from his window.

The Dean, with so little else to do, found himself staring out the window much of the time. When he saw the arrival of the train of coaches, he lurched forward in his chair to gawk at the abnormal display.

"What in all the hells is that now?" he shouts.

He jumps out of his chair and again rushes downstairs to investigate. Once out in the plaza, he gazes at a cluster of people in ornate robes, all of which appeared priestly in design, but of foreign origin.

Tristeen was again outside in her usual spot in the park, which secluded her from view by the academy. She also took notice of the clearly unusual arrival of a series of coaches. She further observed as the Dean rushed outside for his own inspection. Although she had no idea what was going on, if it had the Dean in a fluster, it was a good thing. She smiled mischievously.

"What are you people doing this time?" she muses quietly.

The local priests led the foreign congregation inside while the Dean hurried across to inquire what was happening.

"Eh, excuse me, but who are you?" he asks one of the priests.

Priest Garrain of the temple turned to his address, as he was hoping the Dean would come out, and was expectantly waiting for him.

"Ah, Dean!" he announces comfortingly. "How nice of you to join us. We are entertaining a group of foreign missionaries who have travelled all the way from the Kingdom of Tae'Eladar to visit our fair city. Would you care to come inside and meet them?"

"A what? From where?" he blurts nervously. "Missionaries! Here? From there...I mean him?"

"Oh, yes, it is a most extraordinary occasion. It seems he recently got the impression that our city desired to make a deeper bond of relationship, so he is sending these people to share some of their cultural and social beliefs with us."

"No! I mean, yes... I mean...what? How could he possibly get the idea we want anything to do with him? I mean, um...what I mean to say is where did he get this idea?"

"Ah, well, I suppose it might be related to the visitation I happened to take notice of two days ago by that officer of his."

"Gah!" he screams and slaps his hands to his temples. "And you're actually letting them inside here? By the way, who are you? I don't recognize you from the last time I checked in here."

"Oh, that! Yes, but of course, how silly of me. You probably missed that. My name is Priest Hernan Garrain. We were recently inducted into service as the previous ones were retiring."

"Both of them?" he tries looking around the man to see the other priests.

"Yes, and we have found ourselves already involved with so much work trying to improve the services that the people were in such need of in this city."

"Services!" he yelps. "What services! Eh, that is, what services are you trying to improve on?"

"Well, Dean, surely you know there are many in this city that look to the gods for their support, right?"

"Oh, well, yeah, there's that, of course."

"And surely, as you must be aware, there is this horrible plague that is always in the back of their minds."

"Well, yes, there's that too."

"And so, they are always in need of comfort in these hard times to reassure them that our gods will watch over them."

"Oh, right! Yes, of course! And you're doing this?"

"Oh, what a silly question, Dean…" he smiles harmlessly. "Of course we are! But this new arrival of missionaries is a rather fascinating one. We are curious to learn of our new neighbors and their ways."

"Neighbors?!" he shrieks. "He's calling us neighbors now?"

"Well, in a manner of speaking, I suppose so. After all, he does seem to have occupied that valley down there rather sufficiently by now."

The Dean screams as he runs in a circle, then takes off in the direction of the Governor's Manor.

Tristeen was doubled over on her bench with both hands covering her mouth, trying to hold back her laughter at the clearly evident display. Witnessing the Dean's torment by this otherwise innocuous demonstration of the Governor's own tricks being played back at him was enough to make all her experiences in the academy worth the suffering.

✦ ✦ ✦ ◆ ✦ ✦ ✦

"Your Lordship," Padriyl announces as he arrives in the tactical office. "I just received word that we have a simple jamming device ready. It's not pretty, but it's functional, and should serve to interfere with the Suuden'kai communications network well enough to disrupt any outbound calls, at least for a short period."

"Excellent, Lieutenant," Thaelyn responds. "Our scouts tell us that outpost is only lightly guarded, so I guess they do not consider themselves under any immediate threat in that location."

"Jiggers," Relissa moans. "That's already a bad thing," she grins. "Especially with you around…"

"Indeed, and now they are going to realize their latest problem with the orcs. There are no other installations in the near vicinity, and therefore their relative isolation will be their undoing. We have already marked several runes in the local region to create a small way-line, and now we are just waiting for the jamming device to finish the equation."

"All right," Padriyl offers. "I'll call to have it brought here right away. When do you plan on launching this round?"

"Assuming there are no unexpected movements, we will send this one out just after your class tomorrow. This should allow adequate travel time for a transport to reach that location from wherever these devious little orcs are hiding it. We will cover our full team with stealth cloaks. The plan will be to send them directly into the middle of the camp and hit from all sides. Then, we want to raid that camp for all it is worth, as orcs are known to be scavengers. Whatever we cannot carry away, we will burn to the ground, as orcs are also known to raze what they do not want."

"Buggers!" Relissa shouts. "Now that's a scene! Those bloody Suuden-Aryku will be peeved for sure after this one."

"We will have the Lieutenant use their local communications relay just before taking it for ourselves. This will be to send another distress message, just to let them know who did it. I want everything we acquire to be taken directly to Tae'Eladar and delivered to the new research base for storage."

"Removing it fully from their sight," Marelle muses. "And giving us a few new toys to play with," she snickers.

"Lieutenant," Thaelyn asks. "Do you think your Commander would mind placing you temporarily under my command for this mission? I would like to place you in charge on this occasion. I think it is time for you to earn another mark on that rank of yours."

"I'd need to call this in," he considers. "But I think he should be agreeable. I'll admit, however, I've never led an assault mission before, although my experience working with you has certainly taught me a few things."

"Excellent. I will share with you a few important pointers before I send you out. Next is Relissa. I would like to prepare another envoy mission to Rolsklinde, this time with a delegation of Night Elves."

"Um," she relents. "Is this where you have me giving out a history lesson?"

"Well, I would surely wish to see you share a little of your personal style," he smiles. "I was thinking of involving your mother for her priestly experience, as well as your father for his historical perspectives. As for you, I am quite sure you would do well to represent us as my assign in case the Dean should come around asking questions about this special moment," he grins.

"Oh buggers!" she chuckles. "Right, this'll be a good one. But give me a wee bit of time with Marelle, just to be sure."

"You have until tomorrow afternoon. I will send you out after you finish your class."

"Aye!"

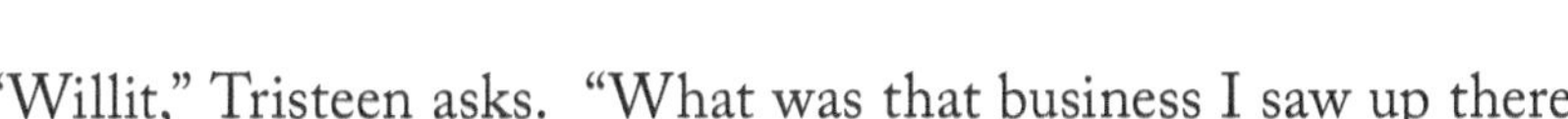

"Willit," Tristeen asks. "What was that business I saw up there at the temple today?"

"Word on my side is they're working to solve a few things. For one is to build up the people with the justifiable potential to learn a few things about the world."

"And the Dean and the Governor, what do you think they'll say to it?"

"Other than to grouse at the top of their lungs for all their hard work going down the pipes? They want him to come in for his final show. He's just making a little noise along the way."

"And where will this ultimately lead?"

"These newfound relations will lead to a chain of events to discover a few things, like the lies made by the old priests and the Dean. Once the people know, which is to say it's out in the open, the guys at the top lose their edge. What we need to be careful of is how eager the Governor is to remove him, or if he has in mind to do away with all of it. Conjuring something big will require something big to dispose of it, as well. Who will do that if the Governor is trying to keep his secret relations?"

"You're talking of the Suuden-Aryku in this case. So, what happens? He calls up something big, it romps around destroying things, and either he calls the Suuden-Aryku to kill it, if they can actually do that, or it continues romping around destroying things."

"If he's managing us for a reason, that reason must be to use us for something. So, the real question is what he will do if we're no longer useful, like if we discover all his secrets. Conjuration or no, this is a turning point. Because even if to call in the Suuden-Aryku to take care of it, this still reveals his biggest secret. He's losing control here...he has to if we want to win."

"Great!" she relents harshly. "So, he's cutting his throat along with all of ours."

"He's lost the Night Elves and their potential. He's also lost the Flame Elves, although he doesn't actually know it yet. But he also has to lose us if we're ever to get rid of him. And his pet orcs are out there about to make their own trouble."

"The orcs? They're making trouble for him, as well?"

"As far as he knows..." he grins broadly.

"All right, Lieutenant, make us proud," Thaelyn asserts.

"Affirmative, Your Lordship," he replies. "This should be a very interesting experience. In a way, I wish my father could see it."

"Your father?"

"Yes," he lowers his head. "He was lost on Ruuki uy'Daan."

"I feel for you, Lieutenant. Then make this one in his name."

Lieutenant Lapäli was preparing his team in Firstfall. It was the day after their meeting, and he had just returned from his daily language course. A full platoon of troops had assembled and were waiting for their raid on the Suuden-Aryku camp.

A collection of mages began opening up their portals, and Padriyl led his team through to a secluded gully not far from the Suuden'kai outpost east of Kynesoth. There, they crouched low until they had fully assembled.

"All right, people," he states. "The plan is to advance using stealth, open up within their camp, and hit by surprise. We can't allow them to get their weapons or any other equipment, especially their com-systems. Also, we don't want to make any excessive noise or dust that might draw attention at range. Once the enemy is down, we start carrying off everything that isn't nailed down, except the com-system. We save that for last. We have bags for the small stuff, and I'm told the mages will use their rune stones to transport the larger items independently. Then I'll make the fake call for help. After that, we take the last few pieces, and burn the rest. Got it?"

The rest of the team responds with a muted 'Aye' and Padriyl glances around to survey the region. The area was quiet and seemingly empty, giving a slight sense of vulnerability due to being so exposed. Not far away, he could just catch sight of the camp popping up above the terrain. He returns to his team.

"Who has the jammer?"

"Here," replies one of the scouts.

"Good, we'll engage it and carry it with us. We'll use it like a portable model on your back."

The scout steps around to allow Padriyl to examine and activate the jammer before continuing.

"One thing before we go," he submits. "I've never had one of these cloak things before. How does it work?"

"I'll cast a cloak on you," responds a mage. "And you'll then move carefully and quietly along the ground. If you make any noteworthy sounds, you'll break the enchantment. So, you cannot speak or interact with anything until you're ready for that. Also, you won't be able to see the rest of us, but we can see you and each other by a special glyph we receive as part of our training and augmentation at the guild runemancer's parlor."

"An augmentation? Are we speaking of something installed into your bodies?"

"Onto, would be a better word. If you're familiar with the concept of a tattoo, this is a magical form that becomes a part of our bodies as we pass through our training. This is what allows us to see and interact with each other, even while cloaked."

"Aye," offers a scout. "We can use a silent hand language while dark, and this lets us communicate without the need to speak."

"Great cu'Nar, that's simply dangerous," Padriyl chuckles and shakes his head. "I noticed you used a term there, I think. Dark?"

"Aye, we use a whole basketful of words for this. Would you like to learn a few?"

"Sure, what can we use here?"

"Right then… When we go into a cloak, we say we go dark. To sneak along and keeping away from any others around us, we might say to move short and sly to the shadows."

"And for those times when we need to hit somebody," a soldier adds. "If to take them as captives, we don't want to kill, right? So we say to hit them soft, or if to kill, hit them hard."

"Interesting," Padriyl admits. "You people have developed this almost as an art form. Ours is not a militaristic society, so this is new to me."

"Fine to that. We can't all be soldiers. We respect each other for our best gifts, not how we fight wars."

"All right, so we'll all go dark, then move short and sly into their camp, and hit them hard. Right?"

"Right to that, Lieutenant, you'll be one of us before you know it."

The mages start casting their cloaks on the group, covering each one with an invisibility layer.

"Lieutenant," the mage offers before he finishes. "We'll follow behind you and wait for your signal. A simple wave of the arm will do. We'll take care of the rest."

He nods, and the mage finishes with a cloak on the two of them.

Padriyl found himself covered in a strange cloaking aura where he could see out, but couldn't see himself or anyone else around him. He had to focus himself on his presence of mind, knowing where his body parts ought to be, rather than actually seeing them, so he could move effectively.

He began slowly moving forward towards the camp. He was

nervous, not only about leading a military advance on an enemy outpost, but the strange manner in which he was doing it. He forced his breathing to a slow and steady rate, trying to reduce any sudden or outward reactions that might break his enchantment.

They moved along carefully, keeping a close eye on the activity within the camp. The Suuden-Aryku troops were mostly attending to their duties or sitting around in conversation. A few were walking between the outpost structures.

As they moved in closer, Padriyl felt a tang from his conscience that they were about to attack an unsuspecting outpost of simple workers by the appearance of it. But he had to remind himself of how many of his own people, most of whom were workers, scientists, medical professionals, schoolteachers, and others, had been indiscriminately slaughtered by these same people. The thought brought his temper up as he reflected on so many innocent people killed. This here was repayment for the favor.

He mulled this thought in his mind, but even though he was a soldier in the Sentinels, he was not a murderer. Payback? No, he didn't dare suggest such a thing, because this would make him no better than the others. The murder of one unassociated body for the murder of another is not a justifiable solution. His society was more sophisticated than that. They had to hold onto their values. This was war, a business of killing to fight for a cause. People die, innocent or not. It's an ugly thing, but business is still business, and it relates to a larger demand.

He brought them within range, just on the outer edge of the camp, and hunched low to study them a moment longer, looking for a good opening. He then raised his hand and swung it forward.

He sat there silently and waited for the action, feeling a sense of power now coming into him for the authority of control. But he kept silent as he allowed the soldiers to do the work.

In a moment, he saw the result, as a full platoon of troops popped into existence in the middle of the camp, striking at any Suuden-Aryku trooper within range. The enemy soldiers fell in cascading fashion, with none of them expecting the assault, nor with any time at all to respond. It was over almost as quickly as it began.

Padriyl stood up and strolled forward, examining the work made by his command. The scene was a scattered array of bodies on the ground, with the remainder of the team searching the structures for any stragglers. With nothing else to do, he decided to bring up a hand and snap his fingers as a way of breaking the enchantment and becoming visible again.

"Nice work people," he admits. "Maybe, one of these days, I might have a chance to learn more about this magic of yours."

"Aye!" a guard responds. "We've got some fine courses for study back home."

"All right, let's pack everything up and move it out. We'll leave the com-system for last."

"We've got some vehicles over here," calls a guard from around one of the structures.

Padriyl steps around to examine the find and sees three large hover coaches parked behind the building.

"This looks nice. We'll take them. We can use them to load up some of this loot along the way. That'll save us a little work to transport things."

"Are the orcs learning to drive now?"

"Hey, if they can learn to fly, anything is possible!"

The soldiers pulled out a collection of bags they were carrying in their slimline backpacks. They picked up every small item that was lying around, and any gear that might look interesting from the bodies.

Padriyl waited for the scavenging team to conduct their work. He occupied himself by studying a series of terminal displays left behind by the ranking officer who filed the local reports for the outpost.

"This outpost is designated as Therinë-012," he states.

"Is that so!" responds a soldier. "Well, that's a fine one. Um, what of it?"

"It would make sense to know of it so we can ID ourselves in my report. That way, they know who we are."

"Ah, right to that!"

"And don't forget, we need those orcish weapons."

A mage pulled out a blank rune to mark it in a convenient location, then another one leading back to camp, and used that to send the first one away, giving the people in Firstfall a means to deliver several bags of collected orcish weapons from their landfill. A moment later, they arrive at the marked location.

The soldiers took the orcish weapons and distributed them around the bodies, placing them in such a way as to make it appear those were the weapons used to make the attack.

The larger pieces of equipment were sent away by rune transport to a receiving area at the new military research center on Tae'Eladar. There, a set of workers were hauling the items away to the local storage areas. The bags of smaller items were stored inside the vehicles for efficiency of transport.

"Now, how are we going to move these vehicles?" asks one mage. "They're too bloody big to move by hand, and I'm not one to know how to drive them. They'll never get them out of the way to make room for the next."

"Aye, I think what we'll do is one of us will go back, take a few extra runes, and mark a line of them, one for each, and bring them back smartly."

"Aye, a good one, that."

A mage steps forward and pulls out a rune for Firstfall, then departs. He arrives at the local receiving area to retrieve the marked rune he made earlier to the outpost, plus three blank runes. He then recruits another mage to open a portal using a rune they held in the tactical office leading directly to the research base. On arrival, and finding a suitable location, he marks the three blank runes, and finally uses his outpost rune to return.

"Here we go, lads!" he announces, and begins handing out the new runes.

Two additional mages came forward to take their runes, and between the three of them, they lined up and sent the vehicles on a far journey.

"Lieutenant, we're all set here," announces one of the soldiers. "Just this com-system left to go."

Padriyl examined the unit, which was a large self-contained transmitter station and network link. It was a portable unit that could be quickly deployed in the field and relocated, as necessary. It included a small fold-out chair and a terminal console. He sat down to study the interface, locating the frequency selector and microphone.

"All right, I need a name from someone known to work here," he states.

He examines several of the bodies, choosing a ranking officer. He returns to the com-system and sits down, then engages the relay and begins his play.

"Base Prime! Urgent!" he shouts. "This is Lieutenant Hak'lanal of outpost Therinë-012. We have come under attack. Respond!"

"Therinë-012, we are receiving you," the voice responds. "What is your situation?"

"We are taking heavy losses. It was a surprise attack by orcs. They set down in a heavy transport. We had no opportunity to prepare."

He then turns to the team and waves for them to make an advance from a distance, calling out shouts and banging their weapons against their shields to simulate the sounds of battle.

"They are entering the camp!" he shouts. "We cannot... Aaagghhh..."

He waves for them to continue advancing near the unit, still shouting and banging their weapons until he turns off the transmitter.

"All right, people, let's finish up fast," he orders.

The mages send off the last of the equipment and set fire to the buildings. Then they open their portals and leave the area.

Relissa's mother and father had been preparing a delegation to make a journey to Rolsklinde as part of the next cultural exchange effort from Thaelyn's kingdom. As before, they gathered up in a carriage, in this case leaving Solinaia. One other priest joined the two elder Night Elves from their local temple, and together they departed from the city to arrive at the south gates of Rolsklinde.

Relissa had only recently returned from her classes and was sent directly to the city by rune transport, which arrived at generally the same location outside the gates. There, she met with the carriage, and together they proceeded to the upper district and the temple.

The prim elven buggy travelled along the streets to the upper district, and like before with the Tae'Eladaran carriages, they arrived in the plaza and pulled along the curbside near the temple.

Tristeen had made it a habit by now to take her favorite seat in the park across the way. When the buggy came into view, she began to study it. She had never seen a carriage of this design before, but then she had never seen Night Elves before either. Even though she knew the Dean was likely to come out again, this time she wanted a closer look, so she got up from her perch and cautiously circled around the outer edge of the plaza to the corner of the temple.

The priests came outside to greet their newest guests, while a group of criers rushed into the streets to call on the people to attend the special service. Soon, a gathering of citizens began to form near the temple entrance.

The Dean once again took notice of the arrival in the plaza, and more so of the criers shouting in the streets. He glared out his office window in shock at what he thought he saw, and once again leapt out of his chair to rush outside to investigate.

Relissa and her entourage were making their greetings with the priests of the temple. It was at least as much the formality of the greeting as it was a delay tactic to make sure at least the Dean, and maybe also the Governor, could witness their arrival. When the Dean made his appearance, he gawked at the assembly.

"What is this?" he blurts abruptly. "Who are you people?"

Relissa, along with both her parents, and the Night Elf priest, all turned to face him, each of them offering unnervingly pleasant smiles. Relissa steps forward to introduce her group.

"A pleasant greeting to you!" she begins in an unusually, for her, polite form of speech. "We're representatives from Solinaia stopping by for a little visit and a bit of cultural exchange."

"Why?!" he charges.

"Oh, well, we figure it's been so long since any of us had the chance to make it out this far…you know, because of this awful war and such. But now that we have a bit of breathing space, we feel it's important to reestablish our old relations."

"Old relations?" he howls. "We had old relations? Um, what I mean is, of course, we had old relations. But why would we want… um, I mean, what makes you think…er, that is to say, why would you choose this moment to come back?"

"Oh, right!" she smiles warmly. "Well, it seems like as good a time as any, and we heard recently you were opening your doors to visitors from outside for the first time since all this recent hullabaloo got started. So, we thought we might make a quick visit to make up for old times."

"To make up…!" he shouts nervously. "But this…with you being here…and then talking…"

"Speaking of talking, we should be getting inside. We have so much to talk about from these past four hundred years."

Relissa smiles politely and directs her group inside the temple.

Priest Garrain was still standing outside as the latest visitors passed through the door, along with a host of parishioners.

"You!" the Dean barks. "Why are you inviting them in here? We're not supposed to have these people here. They're supposed to stay at home!"

"Stay at home?" he mulls placidly. "Oh, but Dean, it is not my place to tell people to stay at home. After all, I am sure they have their own free will to travel if they should desire it."

"Free will!" he shrieks.

"After all,'" he continues. "The world is a big place, and people seem to like to get out on occasion. And more than that, they like to visit their neighbors."

"Neighbors?!" he screeches. "They're not neighbors! They're elves!"

"Yes, I did take notice of this, and also that they live in this world right alongside us."

"Alongside?"

"Indeed. I'm sure you must recall their city is but a short distance away to the west, and that most surely makes them neighbors. And besides, we have learned something recently."

"Learned something! What are you supposed to be learning? You're priests!"

"Why, Dean," he smiles irritatingly peacefully. "You are so remarkably attentive to detail. And so, as priests who are trying to give comfort to our people, we have learned that our predecessors have been spreading a lot of old folklore about the elves that may not be completely accurate. Why, in my interview with these people, they informed me that they do not apparently perform any unholy rites as we once thought. Can you imagine that? Who would be so unkind as to suggest such a thing? I tell you, Dean, these old rumors need to be corrected!"

"Corrected?!" he screams. "They're not supposed to be corrected! This is what they were made for!"

The crowds of people who had been gathering around the temple all suddenly halted and turned in his direction at his boisterous statement. He instantly realized they were all staring at him for his accusation.

Tristeen decided to step into view at this moment and get involved.

"This is what they were made for, Dean?" she announces boldly. "By whom? He said these are old folktales. Folktales are supposed to be gossip and hearsay handed down by our ancestors, usually based on rumor and superstition. But made for? You're an educator, Dean, or at least you're supposed to be. It should be your job to correct these old unfounded stories. But I guess you don't really care to do that. Not if you seem to believe they're made for something."

"And just what are you doing here!" he spits.

"Why, I live here, in case you forgot," she retorts demurely. "Much like everyone else in this city, and like the elves in theirs. And like some people, I hold an interest in going outside to see things, rather than staying at home, as certain other people would prefer me to do, and listening to all their fabricated nonsense. So, if I've been listening to folktales that aren't correct, and even worse, were made for some reason, my goodness! I think I might want to hear the real story from those people who should know it best. Because it would seem ours do not. Especially if they who claim these stories are intentional are in fact the ones creating them."

As she finishes, she curtly turns around and follows the rest of the people into the temple.

The Dean glares at the girl, then at the priests and the others around him as they all proceed inside the temple. But he knows by now his argument has already been exposed, and this little secret is no longer a secret. Worse, his own arrogance has been revealed publicly. He forces his body, which was rigid with anger, to rotate in the direction of the Governor's Manor.

Leesa was peeking through the window when she first heard the ruckus outside. When she saw the Dean heading in her direction, she quickly returned to her seat and pretended to be working.

He came inside and shambled up the stairs, then to the Governor's door. He rapped on it just two times, slowly, and then opened it to proceed inside.

"My Lord..." he moans.

"Save it, Dean!" the Governor growls. "I could hear it out the window. You succeeded in making a scene for virtually half the city."

"I'm sorry, my Lord, my surprise got the better of me. But what could make those people suddenly show up here?"

"I think it becomes clear, Dean. It's all him! Clearly, if he's been interacting with our people in any way, like the captain over there, and who knows how many more, he's likely heard a few things by now. And since he's not bound to those same restrictive measures we have so carefully crafted around us, he's free to move about and share it with the rest of the world. He needs to be destroyed; do you hear me?!"

"Yes, my Lord. But unless you are to suggest we try conjuring that thing and hope it simply meanders its way down to the valley, I don't see how we can use it without him actually being present."

The Governor sits back and contemplates the suggestion, then forces his own temper down by taking several deep breaths.

"Patience...yes, patience. Time, this is what we need. We have plenty of it. We will take care of him, and then the rest. And I will desire to see something special for the rest at this point, simply to repay them for this most insolent manner of daring to disobey their confinement. We had them right where we wanted them, but then he comes along and lets them all out."

"Technically, he came here to destroy the orcs. By doing that, he let the others out incidentally."

"I don't care what he came here for! Those infernal orcs drew his attention, and now he's spoiling everything we built. Once this is resolved, I'll be paying him back a special favor for this little inconvenience."

The Dean simply bowed and turned to leave.

Leesa was still downstairs, this time choosing not to go up to listen. She knew this was only relating to what happened outside, and not likely anything important. She was peeking out the office door when she saw him work his way downstairs, apparently beleaguered from the day's events. She ducked back into the room as he passed through the foyer and out the door on his way to his own office.

Sometime later, after things had settled down a bit, a tonal ring ushered out from the Governor's drawer. Reluctantly, he picked it up to answer it.

"Yes, Commander, what is it this time?" he inquires sourly.

"I have a report of another attack."

"Spare me the intimate details, Commander. What and where?"

"Outpost Therinë-012 by orcs arriving in the stolen transport..."

The Governor sat there a moment as if in a daze as the message sank in. Then his eyes began to open wide, and he jumped out of his chair. He erupted in a bellowing wail that shook the walls, followed by slamming his fist on his desk, cracking it down the middle. The reverberating force rattled the flooring and by association the ceiling downstairs. This caused both Leesa and the secretary to jerk around at the disturbance.

"What in all Creation!" the Governor screams. "How can a band of renegade orcs be so resourceful? What happened, Commander? How can they possibly attack one of our outposts?"

"It was a surprise hit. A transmission was made by the outpost commander of a sighting of a heavy transport. It set down and unloaded its complement before they could respond."

"Insufferable! At the very least! And even more so that you can't find that elusive little wreck."

"A support vessel was sent to investigate and found the outpost ransacked and destroyed."

"Ransacked... Oh, but of course! They're orcs, don't you know? They love little shiny things. Should I ask what sort of loot they managed to pick up on this occasion?"

"Our team found all the base equipment missing, including many personal items and three ground vehicles."

"Ground vehicles!" he screeches. "Oh joy! Now they'll be chauffeuring themselves around as a fully outfitted task force. Commander, you will do whatever is necessary to find and destroy those orcs. Have we heard anything else from the elves?"

"They report no recent activity."

"No recent activity..." he halts a moment to think. "What does that mean? The orcs are refocusing themselves on us now?! Blast! They're going straight for the heart! Commander, you will pull back all nonessential outposts from the frontier edge. Let's see how eager these little creeps are to find us."

He ends the link and tosses the unit back in the drawer, then sits down in another vain attempt to calm himself.

✦ ✦ ✦ ✦ ✦

"Um, Your Lordship," Marelle hesitates. "I don't want to argue this process, but the risk factor is getting a little bit bigger, don't you think?"

"It is all part of a progression, Marelle," Thaelyn comforts. "Recall what we said before. We are not…yet…pointing any fingers, instead taking this as an indirect approach to a series of discoveries that will ultimately reveal the truths of the world."

"With the final one being those implants…"

"So far. But until then, we have one more promise to keep. Lieutenant, how do your Elders feel about making a visit?"

"While they understand the need to play a role," Padriyl affirms. "They're no less nervous for making the appearance up there. We also have the issue of language, as neither Elder Girhani nor Elder Vankkar ever learned the local tongue, to my knowledge."

"Do we have an interpreter to follow along?"

"Yes, we're assigning one of our interns, Likha Vuurti. She's Med-tech Tad'vaal's assistant, and while I don't like using this depiction, she's not as critical to keep hidden away as the Med-tech herself, or such like my mother."

"I believe I understand, but I think we can be fairly certain of our outcome here. Just remind them we have people inside the temple to help if they need it. But to have Daanen-Aryku representatives is important to complete the image. At this point, I think it makes no less difference for the risk factor than it did for the Night Elves."

"Yes!" Marelle interjects. "It's all imminent disaster waiting to happen," she chuckles ironically.

"Oh, come now, Marelle. If they have struggled to tolerate it for this long, it is very clear by now that they want me more than anything. I am the wildcard here, the loose cannon unraveling all of their intrigues. Therefore, I must be their first target to remove before they can hope to play whatever new tricks they have in mind to restore their sense of order."

"Right, and this means trouble on a grand scale for the rest of us!"

"Likely so, at this point," he relents. "This may bring us back to the General's idea of a turning point, which is likely unavoidable, no matter what we do. And here is where we should make ourselves ready. We must win this battle. But to do so, he must lose, and this must include losing whatever authority he might hold on anything."

"And how do you plan on doing that?"

"First, I will need to reinforce the idea that I have not forgotten my political obligations to my dearest neighbors," he smiles. "And for this, we will send our dear Captain up there again to explain that I am just now returning from my most recent campaign to crush our most hated foes, the orcs."

"Um, wait, I think I missed a small detail here. You've been away on a campaign?" she asks, intriguingly.

"Why yes! It is actually not uncommon, at least in our world, for a noble Lord, or even a King, if they are ambitious enough, to lead their own crusades. It is a sign of dedication and leadership, to symbolize their strength and authority in the eyes of the people. And I have a long history of this sort, though I will admit I have not engaged in this here because our armies are so widely dispersed."

"Just being here in this office would be good enough in my eyes," she smiles. "You're right smack in the middle of it."

"Perhaps so," he agrees. "But without the Dean and his spies watching my every step, we can claim I have been away somewhere. This would further work to confound the Governor and his designs to rid this world of my menace if he were to learn that I do not stay in one place."

"Gods' pity!" she wheezes. "He'll be fuming for sure after that one."

"And it also lends a bit of credence as to why it took so long for me to respond to his summons."

"Right, good…"

"But naturally, before I go up there, I need to refresh myself," he grins.

"Uh oh…refresh yourself?" she mumbles tenuously. "And what will be happening up there while you're refreshing yourself?"

"Your people will rediscover the true gods," he reveres with raised open hands.

"Oh dear gods…and literally…"

"This is where we hit home the idea of the implants. Your

delightful priests up there, after four long centuries of trying, are finally going to realize the cure to your dreaded plague."

"Bloody hell!" she gapes. "This will send both the Dean and the Governor flying straight through the roof!"

"Indeed, and then I will make my grand appearance on their doorsteps to attend my fated encounter."

"Can I watch? This should be good."

"It might also be dangerous, especially if you consider that conjuring of theirs."

"Right, but if you're planning something, you'll, um, hopefully, be dealing with it. At least, you'd better bloody well be dealing with it, or it'll deal with everything else," she chuckles ironically. "So, if I just take up behind a wall or something to the rear…"

"Perhaps inside the barracks building, which is at the far end of the plaza, correct?"

"Yeah…"

"All right, we will see about forming a line of defense in that direction, and draw the creature's attention to us, rather than anything else out there."

"Who is 'we', in this case?"

"Well, I suppose I might involve Aerlie at my side, if only for appearances. After all, I want to them realize how…simple…we are."

"Oh, bloody hell!" she yips. "If even for a tiny bit of that!"

"But I will also have my elite guard present," he grins.

"Eh, you have an elite guard?"

"But of course, Marelle!" he responds jovially. "After all, what proper King would travel abroad in hostile lands without his finest bodyguards?"

"Gods above, this I have to see."

The next morning, a Daanen-Aryku hover-shuttle arrives in Rolsklinde. This, among all the recent visitors, was the most bizarre sight to be seen driving along the streets of the city. People stopped and stared at the alien vehicle as it glided along above the ground, with no wheels or anything else apparently supporting it. Like all the others, it made its way to the upper plaza and parked in front of the temple. And once again, Tristeen was sitting at her favorite spot, watching the academy as part of her own spy campaign to keep up with the local events, when it came into view.

"What is that thing?" she mutters quietly. "That simply has to be the Daanen-Aryku, for all I've heard of them, but a flying coach?"

As usual, the priests sent out their criers and welcomed their visitors with open arms. And also, as usual, this drew the Dean's attention.

The Dean had been sitting at his desk, shuffling through a set of papers, the same set he had been shuffling through for several days, since he had nothing else to do, until he heard the telltale voices of the criers shouting in the streets. He stiffly came to attention and stared into the distance ahead of him, then slowly turned to the window and cautiously peered down into the plaza. There he saw the Daanen-Aryku delegation of three people arriving.

"Oh, how lovely…" he muses coldly. "Now we have them making a visit."

He stoically rises from his desk and begins moving mechanically out the door and down the stairs, then exiting the building. As he emerges outside, he sees the excessively tall Daanen-Aryku delegates meeting with the priests across the way.

"Gods above…look at them," he wheezes.

He creeps forward uncertainly, keeping a careful distance from the imposing figures until he comes within speaking range.

"Eh…" he beckons timidly with a finger. "Excuse me? Um, you're new here. Might you be those Daanen-Aryku I've heard about?"

"Indeed, we are!" announces a young female in a professional dress. "My name is Likha Vuurti, and I'm acting as an interpreter for these two, who are members of our Elder Council. Here we have Elder Santari Vankkar," she directs to a male as he bows his head politely. "And then we have Elder Opadna Girhani," she directs to the other one, who also bows.

"Of course, naturally," he emits satirically. "You would have to be those in particular. And to what do we owe this fabulous occasion of your visit?"

"We've been hearing from the other races lately that you are accepting visitors for enhanced political relations. Since we first arrived here, we've had a lot of problems with the Suuden-Aryku assaulting our borders. Fortunately for us, that new arrival in the valley to the south, Lord Thaelyn, made some arrangements with us to assist in our defense, and now the Suuden-Aryku seem to have halted their attacks. This gives us a bit of freedom to finally send out delegations to meet with our neighbors in this world."

"Neighbors... Yes! But of course," he titters. "Neighbors... because you live so nearby," his tittering becomes more of a giggling. "And now you want to make a better acquaintance. Why not! And, OH! I suppose you have a few exciting tales to tell, am I right?" he begins laughing senselessly.

"Oh, absolutely!" she affirms joyously. "We have a few thousand years of stories to tell. Although, I doubt we have the time for all of it at once," she grins brightly. "But most important is to help these people understand who we are as a society, since ours is probably very different from yours, and you might feel a little, um, well, uneasy for it."

"Oh, but yes!" the Dean chortles loudly. "Indeed, why didn't I think of that? Well then, I shouldn't keep you. Ta-ta!" he waves gaily.

He turns and begins ambling back towards the academy, cackling insanely and uncontrollably.

Tristeen watched the show with a wide grin forming across her face.

"Congratulations, people. You broke the bastard."

Midday was passing, and Relissa, Marelle, and Lieutenant Lapäli were returning from their classes again, this time to find Aerlie in the tactical office in a meeting with the rest.

"My Lady," Relissa calls. "What brings you here today?"

"I'm simply delivering a few boxes," she replies. "We've been preparing a number of pamphlets with some of our hymns translated into the local language. This is in preparation for tomorrow when we hope to call the people into attendance for their first official service in the eyes of the true gods," she smiles pleasantly.

"And this is where all the native hells are going to break loose for us," Marelle chuckles sarcastically.

"This is actually in preparation for our next movement," Thaelyn asserts. "Part of which involves the removal of the Flame Elves from the equation."

"Right, and this part should be good. How are we planning this? We have them on our side by now, so all we really need is to simply give the word and have them walk through a portal to Tae'Eladar, as I understand it. And we'll keep them there until things blow over… or blow up, whichever comes first."

"Your confidence is most inspiring, Marelle," he grins. "And indeed, I feel timing is becoming an increasing concern here. We decided once to reintroduce the people of this world to the true gods. The Night Elves have their dedication already. The High Elves are in rehabilitation, so it should follow nicely enough for them. But the human population is still several steps away, and this is where I feel our soft underbelly may lie."

"Oops!"

"Among other things, we need the Captain to go back up there with our reassurance of my visitation. We want to keep their focus on me, rather than anyone else. But at this moment, we will need to make a few statements about who these people are dealing with. It is unavoidable at this point, as they still seem to be working on the assumption that I am just a simple man. One of these will relate to me actually going out there and conducting some of my own work."

"All right, sounds good so far. This actually reminds me of our trip out to see that portal."

"Indeed, this is a good example. If the Governor and the Dean are so complacent to sit at their desks all day, they will need a subtle awakening that some of us actually do go outside, rather than stay at home, as Relissa's report of her meeting suggested."

"Aye!" she asserts. "He didn't like the idea of us coming out of our holes to talk about anything."

"And more so to say this is how I built my kingdom back home. I went out there and did it myself. This is where we make the statement that I am not some…simple man…who just happened to be born into such a lovely place as Tae'Eladar with a silver spoon in my mouth."

"Nice," Marelle admits. "But this sounds like it could open something up."

"Yes, and this will naturally follow with a few words of HOW I built it, including a reminder of our full military using such fine equipment as what those two were drooling over on that first day, as well as magical enchantments to enable us to overcome virtually any foe."

"Uh oh…and I'm guessing right now this will relate to that conjuring…your demonstration using this elite guard of yours."

"Very good. This is to make us known in the eyes of those who have so far been holding back, thinking they can simply take me out, and perhaps later try more of their devious manners on the rest."

"Yeah, and if we go back to your use of portals and such, suddenly this makes you look even more dangerous."

"But we also need to make a new suggestion, and this is to further emphasize that I am no simple man, as I am not even native to Tae'Eladar."

"Oops! So, you're opening up a little?"

"Now there's a fine one!" Relissa asserts. "So, you're basically saying you come from somewhere else, and essentially built your own kingdom over there."

"And a full world of it, no less," Marelle adds.

"This should change a few perceptions in their minds," Thaelyn resumes. "Assuming they even pay attention to it, as their arrogance might simply override the suggestion. But my demonstration with their conjuration might further prove these words."

"Aye, I'll bet that much," Relissa grins.

"Now, we can make a number of other statements along the way, possibly relating to these new gods we are teaching them about, and maybe also my divine mandate to perform this task. But the real question becomes how effective this would be in their minds, especially if they do not know who these gods are, and perhaps hold no such dedication, if you consider the priests you had in there previously."

"Right, your gods might mean nothing to them if they don't even believe in anything to begin with."

"Indeed. Here is where we had an idea where the Flame Elves are concerned, if we suggest those same gods physically arriving to carry them away to their salvation."

"Holy Buggers, and literally so!" she chuckles. "That'll make a grand showing, to be sure!"

"But at the same time, we also find ourselves with a paradox, thanks largely to Marelle's delightful young niece," he grins playfully as he leans back.

Relissa and Marelle both eye him carefully, glancing at each other along the way.

"Oh dear..." Marelle mumbles. "I'm starting to feel a few of Relissa's wiggles now."

"Ay! Save some for me," Relissa gripes. "I'm still using them!"

"So, um, what did my delightful young niece do this time?"

"She is proving herself to be quite observant. In fact, I would wish to see her enroll in some manner of formal training to see if we can bring this out more," he smiles. "She has been reporting on a number of occasions in recent times of the Governor shouting in his office, even having tantrums with his furniture, and apparently to no one in particular, as she did not see anyone go up there for a visit. Therefore, she is surmising this must be to the Suuden'kai High Commander using a trans-com."

"Reporting something in?"

"Possibly, or perhaps hearing a report from out there. But this is where the paradox comes in. She reports he is not using the local tongue. So, if we suggest, much like with Sehnisavain, he at one time learned the Suuden-Aryku language, he might be able to speak to them as an attendant reporting in. But shouting? No, this is not the manner of an attendant reporting something, even if to speak of such unpleasant visitors whom he would much rather have stay at home."

"Oh great..."

"Therefore, I must once again suggest he holds a higher representation. Let us examine the pieces again. He was apparently instrumental in directing an assassin at me here, and likely that rogue Suuden-Aryku patrol using adamantium. I cannot accept that a Suuden'kai High Commander would choose methods such as these if I were so undesirable to have in this world."

"And surely not with adamantium."

"Correct. These tantrums Leesa has been reporting in the Governor's office must be related to our actions in the field, most notably the recent ones. We are unraveling some very delicate plans that someone must have gone to a lot of trouble to create and over a long period of time."

"Oh, I'm so terribly sorry to hear that," she jests.

"Then we have that Suuden-Aryku technology in his basement, including a conveyor device, which ties him in rather intimately with them. And if he holds such intimacy that he can literally scream at the High Commander for his losses out there, this is not an attendant we are speaking of here. This is someone in a control position."

"Uh oh..." she moans tensely.

"Buggers!" Relissa whines.

"Previously," Thaelyn continues. "We suggested he could be part of a criminal organization, but I think not at this point. For this, we must recall his apparent knowledge of Suuden-Aryku medical technology for that special order of his. Therefore, he must be very familiar with their ways. And this means, he is not likely a local resident."

"And another bugger."

"Then, if Sehnisavain tells of someone managing the affair up there, and that same someone holds such authority that the High Commander would take this level of abuse out of him, this leads us in a new direction for our suspicions, and it is not a pleasant one."

"I'm not sure I'm going to like this," Marelle murmurs. "But go ahead. Where do we start?"

"As for myself," the General offers. "I would first mention that he has a temper. The timing of these outbursts seems appropriate to our most recent orcish plays. What this tells me is not only is he very upset about the orcs bringing us here, but now he's upset that they would dare turn on his associated forces. If we say he holds a control position, the Suuden-Aryku must work for him, not the other way around. And for this, there are very few choices but to say he is an agent of Sargeras, one of high enough rank that he is the one in control, not the High Commander."

"Cu'Nar's grace, General," Padriyl winces. "I really didn't need to hear that one."

"My apologies, but this only exacerbates the suggestion of a control figure. I have to reflect on Relissa's statement once. Your entire society gave themselves to Sargeras. At this point, I might have to suggest that none of your native people are in control of anything. Instead, he is."

"Yes, I suppose I would have to agree. Further, that we do not normally maintain a true military, and yet here they have one."

"Next, if the High Commander is allowing himself to take this level of abuse, he must be very subservient to this man. This brings us back to the control devices the Med-tech once described in those Suuden-Aryku bodies she recovered. He must also have one, and if this is the case, the Governor, or whoever he is, must be related to Sargeras as the one who put them there."

"And so, he is the one chasing us halfway across Creation, not Sargeras?"

"If we reflect a moment on this," Thaelyn muses. "Sargeras was supposedly the one delivering those songs into the minds of the Flame Elves. But if our comparatively simple play out there was enough to turn them around, his strength must be severely lacking. Could it be the distance from Azgarén? Could it be his long slumber after an eternity of hiding?"

"Or…" Aerlie interjects. "Could it be he is in a barren fold?" she smirks. "If he is described as a divine entity, he might need this no different than the Estelar."

"Precisely! We must remember that detail. I must admit, it is so familiar to see the Estelar existing virtually everywhere, to not see them in any particular place is unusual, perhaps even abnormal, and perhaps to the point where we might forget their habitation demands…the dynamistic flows…which would be the same for him."

"And therefore, he would probably need help to survive there."

"Indeed. This agent might therefore not be as dependent on the flows, whereas Sargeras could be mostly resting at this time, perhaps trying to conserve his strength. As such, he would need someone else to do his work, and with such means as propaganda and misinformation to provide his control measures. This agent may not be as potent, for this point."

"In all the nether-space," Padriyl relents. "And that really does make sense."

"And here goes another Jiggers!" Relissa groans. "So, my idea of the big guy could be right, at least by a wee bit?"

"Possibly," Thaelyn offers. "And this would naturally lead us to a few other discrepancies, such as the adamantium. If the Suuden-Aryku are not personally capable of using it, and no one else on this world knows how, and further if to say the dwarves are simply slaves to mine it for them, then it must be someone else with higher knowledge, or certainly that sort of knowledge to allow them to understand this. This might also offer us a clue as to who wants it, as it cannot be any of the local players. But now we must ask why, what is his purpose?"

"Nothing good, I'll bet," Marelle moans.

"I would agree, especially if this path is leading him right back to where it all started."

"I might suggest it can't be for armor, or else we'd see a lot more of it, especially after that run you had out there. They must know who those people are by now, but they didn't augment their troops to counter it."

"No, they did not. I might therefore suggest it reaches beyond our current knowledge base as something very unique and specific. We can also say if he holds such dedication of purpose as to want me personally out of the way, rather than to use his superior firepower of the Suuden-Aryku military, and instead to conjure up something from beyond this world, he does indeed seem to enjoy playing games."

"And so, we suggest this to be an agent. But is this simply an agent, or could it be the agent?"

"And how is it that he appears human?" Padriyl wonders. "I've met the man on several occasions as part of our early diplomatic relations."

"Early? How early?" Thaelyn wonders.

"Um…oops," he slaps his temple. "Yeah, that's a good question. This was when we first arrived."

"And did you know back then how long human lifespans were?"

"Not specifically at that time. And I suppose I didn't pay as close attention to it on the subsequent meetings. Although granted, there weren't very many to follow after."

"Very well, but if he relates to Sargeras in any way, he may carry an exceptionally long lifespan. And if he appears so perfectly human, I might have to suggest he is able to alter his form…a shapeshifter."

"Oh, wonderful!" Marelle blasts. "That makes my day. It could also answer the part of how he became our Governor, maybe also how he stayed there during all this time."

"Aye!" Relissa interjects. "And our trees, who killed them, and how?"

"And if he holds a sufficient lifespan," Thaelyn suggests. "He could also be the one directing the orcs during that ancient migration, and maybe all of you with that strange portal that should not otherwise be on Tae'Eladar. That would require some very privileged knowledge to build."

"And us with that wild jump?" Padriyl offers.

"If he had a way to infiltrate your crew, then to sit at your navigation console," Thaelyn nods. "He likely knew the way to that world already. This might also account for your stories of how they always found you, if he was riding along and sending out reports."

"Argh!" he grabs his horns and slumps to the table.

"You know, Thaelyn," Aerlie asserts. "For this point, I might suggest he is not a simple agent at all, but rather a servant creature of some kind. After all, the Estelar have theirs, so why not a Primordial?"

"You are absolutely correct. I might also have to admit to an occasion where Sehnisavain mentioned such words as 'that creature who leads the rest'. I originally misinterpreted the statement, thinking she was referring to the High Commander, but it also seemed disjointed from her other references to him."

"Maybe so, but this would be a surprise, no matter how you look at it," she smiles. "Then, if this is the case, his kind might hold just the sort of knowledge, as well as the capacity to perform all of this. He could fold space directly, alter his form as necessary, and depart the area before anyone takes notice…the perfect spy to make trouble for you. And he might also hold the motivation to make this journey back home, if only to make trouble for those who once made trouble for the others."

"Well, that's just flippin' grand!" Relissa grumbles.

"Yeah," Padriyl rests his head in his hand. "And there go my horns for the week."

"Only for the week?" Marelle chides tenderly.

Thaelyn turns to glare at Aerlie as she stood behind him. He frowned deeply at the implications.

"This does not bode well, my dear."

"No, it does not," she relents. "He's going home, but it's not his home anymore. And even worse, he may be alone, and yet he is still trying."

"Buggers!" Relissa scorns. "My Lady, that's not a nice thing to think about. He must have one bugaboo of a plan if he's hoping to spring this on anyone by himself."

"This might now suggest the reason for the huge volume of metal, all of it being ingots, which might need to be processed further to make anything useful out of it."

"But not by anyone local that we are aware of," Thaelyn muses.

"Maybe more of that higher knowledge, and elsewhere, so he can monitor it better. This world seems more like a playpen than an industrial center."

"Very well," he sighs. "We need to see if we can confirm any part of this and learn who our true foe is out there. This might also demand us to modify some part of our plans up in the city. Lieutenant," he directs to Padriyl. "Do you recall if Sargeras was accompanied by anyone on his arrival to your world?"

"I don't personally know of anything, and whenever we spoke of it, it's always Sargeras this, Sargeras that. So, if anyone else was travelling with him, he didn't stand out much."

"Or maybe this is more propaganda to delude you. If he was travelling with you during this time, watching you, reporting on your location, even directing your ship on occasion, then I doubt he would want to hear his name mentioned so often. If Sargeras was still on Azgarén, this other one may have been pointing a finger in that direction to distract you."

"Like he did so many of us," Marelle accedes. "This is his pattern. But then, who can we ask that might know anything…Commander Nazég, maybe?"

"I can't be sure if he would know of it either," Padriyl considers. "But wait. Oh! Yes! Velen! He was present at the time! If anyone would know, he should be the one."

"Ah!" Thaelyn croons. "Then, is it possible to ask him?"

"I might also wish to clarify with Sehnisavain," Aerlie notes. "You know, to cross-reference the names. It's one thing to say so-and-so arrived on Azgarén, but it's another thing to say he's here with us now."

"Good point. Perhaps you can attend to that while the Lieutenant makes his call."

Aerlie calls in one of the pages waiting outside the building to run her errand. The young man dashes off through the gateway back to the city while Padriyl brings out his trans-com.

"This...creature..." Thaelyn muses. "He could be dangerous for a number of reasons. If he can change shape, this means he could impersonate almost anyone. I wonder if this could be part of his plan to take me out. Isolating me, and then removing me, perhaps along with any witnesses... He could then try impersonating me, and corrupt our people back home."

"Oh please," Relissa groans. "We don't need another of those."

"That would be extremely problematic, I think," Marelle admits. "He has no idea just how goody-goody you really are. Furthermore, your relationship to those same gods he is supposed to be hiding from," she giggles.

"Indeed!" Thaelyn smiles. "This would likely backfire on him rather quickly. But then, if he is indeed a servant being to one such as Sargeras, could he also be a leftover from the old Celestial War?"

"This might make sense, Thaelyn," Aerlie responds. "We are speaking of running away, and hiding in a barren fold...not the sort of place I would go if I needed the flows to survive."

"Granted, so it could date back to the beginning, and possibly offer a clue as to how he evaded them in the first place."

"And the Estelar might not normally look there if it doesn't represent a likely place to find one such as he."

"Indeed!" he nods. "And this other one, not being as dependent on the flows, could serve as a caregiver during this time."

"Yes, if Sargeras is in a dormant or low energy condition. But I would imagine his servant would need to pay special attention to him to maintain him in that place. He must be supplying him somehow."

"Ugh... I cringe at the thought of how he is doing that. There is not much you can offer as a substitute to the flows."

"Holy bum-creeping jiggers," Relissa murmurs. "By the words going around today..."

Padriyl had his trans-com out and anxiously dials in the number for Commander Nazég. He puts it up to his ear and waits.

"This is Commander Nazég speaking."

"Commander," he urges. "We have a problem here that needs an expert opinion. I need to speak with Master Velen."

"Oh? What is this about?"

"Sargeras…and Velen is likely the only one who might be able to answer this by now, being the last survivor from Azgarén."

"The last survivor?" he muses. "Wait, Lieutenant, what are we speaking of here?"

"We're having a long and difficult debate over here, and I've pulled out at least a week's worth of horns, although Marelle suggests it might be more than that by now…"

"Oh, really! She said that?"

"Yeah…" he chuckles feebly. "We're trying to understand that Governor up there and his apparent level of control authority over the Suuden'kai military. It's more than just giving advice, because he's apparently in that office of his, likely using a trans-com, and screaming at the HC for all our recent plays and their losses. This now suggests he owns them, not works for them."

"Uh oh…"

"Combine that with those implant devices in the Suuden'kai military, and who put them there, then his special order for that medical package, and everything else we've seen so far, and he can't be local to this world. Instead, he must hold intimate knowledge of our people and our world, and therefore, he might work for Sargeras directly."

"Cu'Nar's eyes, this doesn't sound good for us."

"Yeah, he could be the one to give away our position if he was a spy riding along with us, and even to program that wild jump."

"In all the nether-space, now that would make perfect sense!"

"Therefore, Velen… We're asking if Sargeras was alone when he arrived, or if there was someone else with him, and could this guy be the same one?"

"Got it…" he moans. "Yeah, I see your point, and I don't like it at all. All right, hold a moment. I think he's in his library again, but he doesn't carry a trans-com, and there's no terminal in there. I'll have to walk us over."

Padriyl waits while the Commander makes his way through the Naarg uy'Sodrad to Velen's favorite room. He drums his fingers on the table, and the rest of the group waits along with him. Eventually, a new voice comes on the line.

"Master Velen?" he utters respectfully. "This is Lieutenant Lapäli… Yes, Tudorin's son… Uh, well, I'm fine, thank you. The Commander keeps me busy, and my work here with His Lordship has been vigorous to say the least…"

Relissa and Marelle exchanged a cute smirk at the conversation, then look at Thaelyn as he also smiles and nods. He glances at Aerlie, who was similarly grinning.

"Right," Padriyl continues. "I'm calling about something very important, and you might be the only one to remember at this point. Can you recall back to the day when Sargeras first arrived on Azgarén…? Right, and yes…the Council of Elders, I've heard of that one…" he rolls his eyes and glances tediously around the room. "Of course, and this is when the cu'Nar came in…uh huh…"

Marelle and Relissa were now struggling to hold back their giggles for the obvious history lesson occurring right now on the line.

"Yeah, that part about the ship arriving in orbit. I'm sure that got a lot of people talking…"

He lays an elbow on the table and rests his head in his hand while he continues to listen.

"Jumping from world to world… Right… Uh huh, so many, I certainly wouldn't want to be in that position… Oh, yes! Of course, I'm sure that wild jump was a fun one. I can just imagine everybody screaming at the top of their lungs as we're falling through a hole so big, it took us completely out of our home universe!"

Aerlie steps over to wrap an arm around Thaelyn, as the group continued to listen.

"Yeah," Padriyl continues. "And then we have that, so conveniently to arrive right next to a star system with a habitable planet. You know, I've heard the Commander make a few comments about that from time to time, and we also just mentioned it here. It's enough to pull your horns out at how…coincidental…it was. But anyway,

Master Velen, I'm currently in conference with His Lordship and the Lady Aerlie… Uh, yes, of course, I'll pass your well wishes along, and I'm sure they'll be happy to hear it, but we have an important question for you. It dates back to Azgarén and the time Sargeras first arrived. This is something that's important to understand in our discussion right now. Can you recall if he was alone, or travelling with someone?"

He waits several moments while Velen struggles to recall that precise moment. The rest of the room holds silent while he apparently gives his reply. Padriyl closes his eyes and sighs deeply.

"Oh dear cu'Nar," he relents breathlessly. "All right, this is what we were afraid of. Why is it no one recalls the name…? Really! So, he seemed more like a spokesperson to you…? Of course, then the cu'Nar showed up, and boom, there we go. So, in the relatively short time you had, Sargeras was played out as the primary figure for these offers? Well, I suppose that makes sense. But it would seem this other one is the one we should be paying closer attention to. We think he could be the one making all this trouble, not Sargeras proper."

"Lieutenant," Aerlie interjects softly. "Ask him if he recalls Sargeras's physical condition at all."

Padriyl nods silently and refers into the trans-com.

"Master Velen, Lady Aerlie is also asking if you can recall Sargeras himself, what sort of condition was he in when he arrived, do you know?"

Again, he waits as Velen struggled to recollect the old memories. He listened several moments longer, and then nodded.

"I see. This is interesting. All right, Master Velen, allow me to report back on this later. I need to bring this to our meeting here. Thank you."

They end the link, and Padriyl pauses a moment to compose himself. Thaelyn gazes at the junior officer as he holds his posture and takes another deep breath.

"So here we have it," Padriyl begins. "You were right in your suppositions. He wasn't alone. Master Velen tells me it was a very long time ago, and his memories are weak by now, but he did recall two of them arriving, and Sargeras was also said to be in a poor state of health, or so it seemed."

Aerlie nods contentedly.

"This is how I might expect someone to be who is dependent on the flows and in a barren fold. He would be weak, perhaps struggling. It would be like a fish out of water, or one of us trying to survive without air to breathe for an extended period."

"Interesting. But anyway, the other one was representing himself as something like an attendant of some kind. His impression is that of a bodyguard or personal advisor who was assisting Sargeras during this time, although we left very soon after, so we didn't see where this went. But they arrived together and requested some sort of aid and then offered this exchange of superior knowledge as payment."

"I recall some of this from Kaliya, I believe," Thaelyn admits. "And then your people escaped on your ship, provided to you by these cu'Nar, followed by the chase, leading ultimately to Ruuki uy'Daan, and finally here."

"Right, and with him possibly travelling along and giving away our position each time, then to program that wild jump. The Commander didn't like that one at all."

"I doubt he would, but at least we have a potential suspect to give reason for these events. What about this individual, did Velen give a name?"

"All he was able to recall was the name Darumon. I hope that's enough."

Sehnisavain was just arriving through the gateway at this time, and making her way across to the tactical office. She peeked inside to announce herself.

"Your Grace, you called for me?"

"Sehnisavain, yes!" Aerlie smiles pleasantly. "I hope we didn't disturb you in your work."

"Oh no, I was just reviewing several details with the girls on how to organize some of our people for their rehabilitation lessons. What is it you needed from me?"

"We are in an important discussion here trying to understand a few details that seem to have been eluding us."

"I see, and is there something I can do to help?"

"Yes, you once mentioned this reference to someone or something that is in the position of control over the Suuden-Aryku military, and our recent interpretation is you are not speaking of the High Commander. Is this correct?"

"Yes! Oh, my apologies, if I neglected to be more precise. He is a rather unpleasant individual. I do not know what race he belongs to, but he is uniquely different in his appearance."

"Interesting, how does he appear?"

"Whenever I saw him, he appeared not much taller than an average man, but his skin was dense and a bit like rough leather, dark reddish in color, and with a number of bony ridges and small spikes. He also had two thick horns coming out and angling forward. He wore some sort of black plate armor and…oh, his eyes tended to glow a bit with a soft yellow."

"Well now, this certainly does represent a new one. But now, do we have a name for him?"

"Yes, he addresses himself as Marshal Darumon."

"Interesting…" Thaelyn considers. "A military marshal, is it? How quaint… And also, how very disturbing to see him here."

"Do you know of him?"

"We are sitting here trying to rationalize a few things, and Lieutenant Lapäli just got word from Master Velen of an attendant of some sort arriving alongside Sargeras in their old home world. This must be him. This could answer a number of questions on who is responsible for all your woes on this world, including your trees, your holy relics, and also the Governor up in that city, as we are suspecting he must be the one in charge, and perhaps a shapeshifter impersonating a human."

"Dear Protector! A shapeshifter? That would indeed pose a problem."

"Yes, but now we need to discuss how to deal with it. I will allow you to return back to your work and brief you on our results later."

"Of course, Your Grace, and I do hope you are able to find a solution to this one."

She bows and leaves the building.

Thaelyn went silent for a long moment and slowly rose from his chair to pace around the room briefly.

"A military marshal… This is certainly a prestigious rank if it is in fact true. And with so many other falsehoods going around, how can we be sure of this one. However, it would certainly offer a few possibilities."

He begins pacing back in the other direction as he continues his thoughts.

"The rank of marshal most often reflects upon a land-based military, not as much a naval force. However, if your people on Azgarén submitted themselves to Sargeras, and it would certainly seem their military has submitted itself to someone, and further, if that someone represents himself with such a prestigious title, they might follow it anyway. Then, if to say they are asking for aid, and further, as you and yours have said before, you are not a militaristic society to begin with, then he must have changed that as he brought them under his control."

"Jiggers," Relissa moans. "So he comes in, makes a deal they can't refuse, and takes over the place."

"Control…" Padriyl muses. "Those chips the Med-tech was talking about once, and therefore the HC submitting himself to a higher authority that is not part of the normal chain of command."

"Correct," Thaelyn submits. "And doing so with such obedience that he takes all these tantrums from the Governor. This can be problematic already, because if we take out the Governor, the High Commander may become a wildcard on us for whatever he might perceive as a threat, and with no more control effect keeping him in line."

"And that's an even bigger jigger!" Relissa groans. "So, how do we get the bugger to bug out?"

The room all turns to glare at her for the odd statement. Relissa instinctively winces as she ducks her head and covers her mouth when she becomes the center of attention. Marelle reaches over to pat the girl on the shoulder.

"Aye," Relissa relents timidly. "That one just sort of happened."

"Thaelyn," Aerlie muses humorously. "Do you have any lists for such a thing as bloopers?"

"Not specifically, but if you would wish to indulge…"

They share a quick laugh before continuing.

"Let us now apply this to a few of our key points here," Thaelyn offers. "He must have been planning something for a long period, if we involve the orcs, including that first invasion and then the second, and also the migration of your people. Later, we have the apparent centering on this world and the events occurring here, which now includes the arrival of the Daanen-Aryku. If he is a leftover from that same period, it is likely he is taking at least some small amount of pleasure along the way."

"This would also explain his actions up north," Aerlie mentions. "He is actually playing with you."

"It's just so unbelievable," Marelle gasps. "That someone could find so much joy in something like this."

"Yes, I must agree, Marelle," Thaelyn nods. "And no doubt, this was also the issue with the Estelar in those early days. So, he arrives on Azgarén, persuades them to follow, and creates a true military out of them, augmented with all these enhancements to ensure they perform according to his desires. Here we can now describe his pursuit of the Daanen-Aryku, as no doubt he is most likely displeased that your faction tried to escape. And in the traditions of the Primordials, he gives chase, but with the purpose not to destroy you outright, instead to take pleasure from it for as long as possible until we arrive here."

"Cu'Nar help us," Padriyl moans. "I'm trying to imagine the Council right now listening to this."

"I hear the sounds of many horns dropping," Marelle grins.

Padriyl glares at her lightheartedly and bumps his elbow into her shoulder. Thaelyn and the others simply smile as he continues.

"But along the way, we may need to consider what capabilities he might have to enable all this. If he is a servant creature, he might not be quite as potent as Sargeras himself, but certainly he would have some fascinating skills. For instance, if we consider the elven trees and their holy symbols. According to our best estimates with the elves, those trees were all killed at very close timing together, perhaps all within a single night or thereabouts. If to simply impersonate a local, he could just walk right in and do it without hardly any question, but the entry and exit would still be an issue here."

"He'd have to be in all places at once," Marelle considers. "That might be a little hard to do."

"It would certainly be problematic if you consider how many cities there might have been. But let us consider. The Estelar have their servants, such as the seraphim, and such beings as these are able to fold space."

"Um, just for the sake of..." she innocently redirects to Padriyl and lays a hand on his shoulder. "Yeah, just for the sake of this guy not losing next month's horns," she grins. "And for those of us who are not quite up on the abilities of demigods, what is that?"

Thaelyn smiles as he passes his gaze at Aerlie. He then tries to simplify things.

"Folding space, in this case, is to use the power of one's mind to bring two points together within space and create a brief link, in some ways like with our portals, and simply step across the boundary."

"Great cu'Nar," Padriyl groans. "With the simple power of one's mind?"

"Indeed, there are those who are so advanced that they can do this, including many of the Celestial races. Within the Outer Planar region, which tends to be more malleable to the authority of the mind, I can also use this to some extent. And so, in this way, he could move between virtually any two points in space...and we are literally speaking of any two points, not necessarily on the same world or even the same universe."

"Well, Marelle, I thank you for trying, but I think my horns are gone for the rest of this month, and maybe the next one."

"Aw, poor guy," she mourns. "But this would sure be a good

example of a godlike power. It would allow him to zap from city to city and do his dirty deeds, then leave without anyone seeing him."

"It could also allow him to come and go with the Daanen-Aryku," Thaelyn affirms. "This long pursuit of theirs, where he could follow them during their jumps to identify their next landing zone, then return home to pinpoint their next military target."

"And if he already owned Ruuki uy'Daan," Padriyl suggests. "He could just sit down at our nav station and program the coordinates while the Elders were arguing over the details."

"Quite possibly. And if he had in mind to chase you into a new universe, it must also be premeditated, as this is where he would find his adamantium."

"Great."

"He must've been preparing for something during this time," Aerlie offers. "They were running for thousands of years before arriving here. What took him so long if he already knew the way?"

"This is a good question," Thaelyn nods. "But one we might not have an answer to at this time, unless it is simply to develop the resources on his side."

"What about the Flame Elves and these songs?" Marelle wonders.

"If we consider Darumon is maintaining his Master somehow, perhaps to give him enough power for it, Sargeras might be just strong enough that he could exert himself for this much. But as we saw, it was not so strong that we could break it. So, our earlier discussions on this might still hold."

"And the orcs?"

"This could go multiple ways, but at this point, Darumon, or maybe Sargeras, could simply pose as a god image and cause them to follow regardless. And in fact, we are aware, from our old history, the orcs of Tae'Eladar did worship a god of war. This recent incursion simply made matters worse."

"All right, and I think the rest simply falls into place as a work effort with him impersonating a human governor in our city."

"And using a lot of falsehood to augment his plans. As for the Governor, if it were me managing such a complex affair as what we see here, I would certainly wish to place myself in a central location. If this world is a type of jumping off point, he might wish to gather his belongings here. He finds the dwarven world, takes it, maybe brings a few here to supplement his efforts, but I think if he is using a heavy transport to retrieve such a large supply of material, he must be delivering it somewhere special for processing, and I doubt it could be this world."

"Maybe the world with the dwarves?" Marelle suggests. "It's the only other choice, unless he found another one."

"I would likely suggest, if he has such as the Suuden-Aryku working for him, worlds are aplenty out there," he chuckles.

"Right, I get it," she smiles.

"But we still need to know what he is doing with it. And for this, I might need to consult with someone higher up."

"Ouch!"

"So, here we are…" Relissa reflects. "At first, we were thinking we've been bamboozled by some wonky nit, then maybe the big guy himself, but all the way over on Azgarén, when it's actually his flaming crony right here in our backyard."

"Maybe so," Marelle admits. "But, if he isn't as potent as a true god, and needs to play a lot of tricks to get things done…well, we need to play a few more of our own, right? If we can't take him out directly, how do we get him to leave?"

"Indeed," Thaelyn wonders. "If his military out there is regarded as a wildcard, then we need him to depart the area voluntarily. But how do you convince one such as he to, um… Who might… Ooh…" he coos with a broad grin stretching out.

"Thaelyn!" Aerlie gazes at him and smiles. "That's simply mean," she giggles.

"But my dear," he shrugs casually. "This is war!" he smiles some more. "And we find ourselves having to invent a few new tricks."

"Are you two playing inside each other's heads again?" Marelle teases. "Want to share it?"

"We want him to depart from this world, along with his blessed military. And he thinks he owns the place. But what if he should discover he does not…suddenly."

"Um, right. I'm actually afraid to ask this now, but how do we do that?"

"By presenting before him exactly that which he and his Master have been hiding from all this time."

"And this follows nicely with our existing direction," Aerlie adds. "We will simply exaggerate the effect. We were thinking of using the Estelar as our excuse for the disappearance of the Flame Elves… physical evidence of 'gods' who actually do get involved in things. But he should know of them personally. And if we call unto them to make them realize we have some lost Children on this world, and further to realize where they came from and how they were abused along the way…"

"Oh buggers!" Relissa moans. "Aye, that'll do it!"

"And so, we will make it seem they're coming to reclaim everything, and also to investigate who was responsible."

"And surely," Thaelyn concludes. "This Darumon would not wish to be present for it."

◆◆◆

"All right, Captain, are you ready for this one? It is a complex script to follow."

"I believe so, my Lord. It's a tidy little game, but I feel I understand the direction of it. We'll take it a few steps and let them fish for more."

"Good, then be on your way and give them something new to think about."

Captain Hagmaert was just finishing his last-minute briefing before loading up in his carriage and departing for Rolsklinde. As before, the vehicle sped along the open terrain to the mountain pass, travelling up and over, and further north to the city. It made its way along the streets and into the plaza in the upper district. And just like the previous time, they pulled to a stop in the middle of the plaza to present themselves to anyone of interest.

Tristeen was still sitting in the park; watching and waiting for anything new to happen after the morning arrival of the Daanen-Aryku delegation. Now she sees the return of the elegant carriage.

"That's him again," she mutters. "Now what's he doing? I'll bet it's a follow-up report."

The Dean had been gazing dreamily out the window when he also took notice of the return of the carriage. He jerked forward in his chair and stared at it, watching to see who stepped out this time.

"Is it him now, finally?" he pleads anxiously. "Oh please, let it be him."

Captain Hagmaert steps out of the carriage, proudly displaying himself to the local scene, and again casually glancing around the area as if looking for someone to talk to.

"Blast! Not that one again. All right, fine…let's see what he has to say for himself. Maybe he has further word for us."

The Dean dashes out of his office and down the stairs again, and then hurriedly strolls outside to make another meeting. The captain quickly notices the man's approach and calls out to him.

"Ah, my good fellow again!" he announces joyously. "You are Dean Malorn, if memory serves, am I right?"

"Yes, and I see you've returned to us…eh, Captain. Do we have any new word for His Lordship's arrival?"

"Indeed, I do have a most promising word or two for you. I have just received news that my most noble Lord and King has returned from his latest campaign on the far frontier against those most despicable fiends, the orcs, don't you know?"

"Huh? He's returned from somewhere? What do you mean? He wasn't in that camp of his down there?"

"Oh, no!" he refutes exuberantly. "He often carries his campaigns personally. We have something of a history of this, you see. It's so marvelously inspiring for the troops when your noble Lord leads you on these crusades."

"Really! How nice…" he titters.

"And indeed, His Lordship has such a history during his long tenure of service. Even as far back as before he became King."

"Before he became King? So, he was doing this as a prince, I suppose."

"A prince?" the Captain muses. "No, he was never a prince…a duke at one time, but never a prince. He was not actually born into royalty."

"Not born into…" the Dean flusters and shakes his head. "Not born into royalty? But how…well, wait, I think I get it. He was a duke…that's a noble title, right?"

"Indeed, it is, my fine fellow, and he most surely earned that one after being knighted twice by two different royal authorities."

"What?!" he shrieks.

Tristeen found herself fascinated by this display as she watched from her park setting.

"Are you actually telling the truth?" she mumbles. "Or simply making up a story?"

"Knighted twice?" the Dean yelps. "How do you get knighted even once, let alone twice? Is this to say he wasn't even a noble before this?"

"Absolutely!" the Captain declares. "He started out a humble man, but with high ambitions. Then, over the course of his early years, and after so many fine and extraordinary deeds during his time travelling from one side of our world to the other, he first earned his fame, and then his title. And in fact, this is generally how he forged his kingdom, bringing all the nations together as one glorious body the world over."

The Dean felt himself stumbling, and nearly falling over backwards, gaping at the man for the outrageous suggestion.

"You must be joking! How can one man do all that?"

"Well, naturally, I shouldn't say it was simply one man. He was surely instrumental in directing these affairs, but in fact it was his most holy Order of Knighthood that did much of the work…again, with him leading on many occasions."

"A holy Order of Knighthood… You mean his military, I suppose."

"Yes, technically, this is a military body, but unlike your simple city guard over yon, this is a body dedicated of holy purpose in the eyes of our gods, and driven to succeed in the face of even the most horrific of foes…and we have seen a fair few of those in our time," he finishes nonchalantly as he preens his fingernails.

"You…they…his…" he stammers. "Um, and how long did all this actually take? I mean, we're talking about an entire world here, right?"

"Oh, most certainly, and you can be sure it was a grand effort. He worked his talents on all sides of it. Indeed, I could tell you some stories, but then, I would not wish to bore you with such trivialities as the elaborate political agreements and unions he made, to say nothing of those few miscreant nations that felt they might hold better opinions of things."

"Miscreant nations?" he shouts. "What kind of miscreant nations?"

"Ah, would you actually like to hear of one such? Jolly good! Naturally, you cannot expect everyone to see the wisdom of his guidance immediately, especially if they love their own positions of authority so much. But let me see… Oh! Yes, this is a good one. Within our main continent, there was once a nation to the south called Menenbahd. A nasty one, that. It was once ruled by a crime lord who dominated over everything around him. Crime was rampant in the streets, and in fact one could say the term lawless was entirely moot, as the law, if you could call it such, was that of the criminals themselves. They had such things as theft, drugs, slavery, and other vile deeds virtually everywhere!"

"Incredible! What happened to it?"

"My Lord happened to it, to be quite honest. One day, he decided it was simply pointless to make any sort of negotiations with it, or even to try outlasting the ruling power, as it was clearly obvious that another of a similar sort would simply replace the previous one. So, he sent our armies down there to conquer it," he finishes curtly.

"Conquer?!" he shouts again.

"Yes, but not to worry, Dean," he soothes. "As they are much happier now!" he smiles buoyantly.

The overly exuberant expression on the Captain's face sent chills down the Dean's spine for the ramifications. He started having visions of a nation pushed together so fiercely that the people were made to quit all their earlier practices and take these instead.

"And besides," the Captain resumes casually. "It was Fated to occur this way. After all, it was his divine purpose in our world… to bring it all together under one rule…whether they liked it or not."

"What?!" he screeches.

The Dean slaps his hands to his cheeks and wails as he scans the area hoping to find an escape. His voice bellowed across the plaza, drawing the attention of many people around the area. Tristeen continued to watch, with another grin forming on her face, but also intrigued by the story.

"Divine purpose?" he gasps. "How can he have a divine purpose?"

"Ah, this is such a fine one to ask!" the Captain asserts enthusiastically. "This is where we need to delve into a bit of our history. You see, ever since that day he first came to our world…"

The Dean wheezed and stared at the Captain with his mouth agape. He tried screaming, but on this occasion, nothing was coming out. He stumbled back a few steps, pounding on his chest to force his lungs to start breathing again before he could emit any new words.

The Captain had to force himself to maintain his composure for his acting role, but deep down he was enjoying his little play.

"First…came…to your…world?" the Dean gasps breathlessly.

"Oh, but of course, did I forget to mention that? How silly of me. Yes, indeed, he is not a native resident of Tae'Eladar."

"But…but…where does he come from?"

"Oh, he has a tendency to keep such things to himself…you know, as personal detail. But his story tells of how he once served his Father in his grand court as an inquisitor and adjudicator, galloping across the realms putting down so many rampant deeds, and finally coming to the end of his contract, now with the freedom to choose his own way, so he came to us."

"Gah!" the Dean screeches and backs away.

"At first," the Captain continues. "He arrived as nothing more than a man seeking his fortune…or so he thought. But as he began to draw so much attention to himself, due in large part to his native manners and qualities and how he first arrived, our people began to see him as something of a messiah!"

The Dean shrieked again, slapping his hands on his head, and backing away another few steps.

The Captain observed the Dean's continued outbursts and knew he was making an impact. He casually glanced around the area as the Dean recovered from his most recent shock and discreetly took notice of a face peeking out the window of the Governor's Manor. Silently, he wondered if this might hold a similar effect on him, or if he would simply shrug it off.

"This naturally brought disciples to his side," he continues. "And as a soldier, these disciples became his Order of Knights, by the way following the same gods he held so high. It wasn't until sometime later when we learned that he was in fact directed to come to Tae'Eladar by a being of some unique faculty that apparently engineered our entire world just for this purpose!"

"Huh?" he blurts. "Engineered…an entire world?"

"And further to install our Lord and King to bring all those miscreant nations under one rule, since they weren't apparently doing this on their own, and as such, creating a virtual utopian paradise!" he boasts.

The Dean was turning pale by now, and questioning whether or not such a man could be killed at all, to say nothing of by his conjuration.

Tristeen leaned forward in her seat, listening intently to the story. Even though it sounded absolutely amazing, it also sounded equally unbelievable. But she couldn't help herself but to imagine if such a thing might actually be true.

"This sounds like a lot for one man, don't you think?" the Dean submits timidly.

"Oh, I suppose it might, if we were speaking of your more conventional example. And I should once again remind you of his army of knights. So, we cannot say he was truly alone in all this."

"But of course."

"Further, as he expanded his holdings, that army also expanded in numbers."

"Oh, well, yes, I suppose that might follow."

"I might also say that with these new acquisitions, came additional wealth and power. And from this, that army was further augmented with all manner of extravagant equipment. So, they are not your average example!" he emphasizes with a finger. "Indeed, due to his point of origin, his native knowledge, and his abilities, and what he brought to our cause, he is hardly what some might call…a simple man!"

The Captain eyes the Dean demurely, trying not to imply any determined meaning other than the obvious suggestion. The Dean watches him, and quickly reflects on Haran's report regarding Thaelyn's initial arrival, and the words spoken at that time.

"In fact," the Captain accedes thoughtfully. "There were many people in our world who once thought him to be as much, and you can be sure they sent such as assassins, and even worse, at him. This simply made him angry at their belligerence, and subsequently he went to war with them."

"Oh, dear…"

"I recall one time when we found ourselves at war with this one guild of exceptionally powerful mages. Oh my goodness, what a mess that was…"

"Really? What happened?"

"They were a foul bunch, very corrupt with their gluttony for power. They held a tyrannical rule over the local lands, you see. They lived inside this large and very well-built fortress in this one city. And they tried at least a few times to do away with our Lord, but to no avail."

"Uh oh…"

"This simply marked them for extermination."

The Dean's face went blank, and he could feel the blood rushing out of it.

The Captain continues, "By the time that battle was won, half or more of the city lay in ruins, as they were so intent on preventing him from taking over any part of it. Those poor people were scattered all over the countryside trying to escape from the fires and chaos those mages brought down."

"Wow! And your armies?"

"I will admit we did take a few casualties here and there…it was a vigorous battle, you know. But for the level of devastation left behind, I might say we did quite well on that one."

"Yeah…" he sighs feebly.

"And this is clearly a testament to the training, as well as the diversity of troops we put on the field, including the mages and priests who travel along with them."

"Huh? You put mages and priests in there too?"

"Oh, but yes! A well-organized army is not simply about the frontline soldiers. They need backup troops, in the form of archers, as well as mages for additional firepower, and priests for field augmentations and occasional healing."

"On the field?!" he yips.

"Well, better this than to haul their limp bodies all the way back to a city and a temple healer's ward. This way, we can put them back on their feet to face down whatever it was that sent them to the ground in the first place."

"Great gods!" he shouts. "What does it take to kill you people? I mean…um…"

"Indeed!" he chortles. "And I'm sure you are not the first to ask that one! And our full army is like that. Why, if it were not for his most inspired teachings, and his determination to see us succeed by any means, I doubt we would have accomplished even a fraction of what we did. For instance, take the magical studies."

"Why, what about them?"

"Once upon a time, it was such that the Art was limited to only a privileged few. But the extraordinary utility was so enticing that he simply had to create a properly structured education program for all our people, beginning with the middle childhood years…"

"Children?!"

"…And continuing into early adulthood, both for a civilian course as well as a military one. Since then, much of our civilization, for virtually all walks of life…whether trade crafts, industry, arts and entertainment, even sporting activities, might use it to some degree or another."

The Dean was panting as he delicately glanced over his shoulder at his academy.

Tristeen also listened, and even though it seemed surreal, she tried to imagine a world where everyone studied magic and used it in their daily lives.

"Really?" the Dean relents gingerly. "Um, but how much do you actually teach? You know, just for reference. I'm something of a mage also, and so from one to another, you know," he titters.

"Truly now? Well, ours are full academies with a robust student body and a well-structured curriculum of studies. We have nine full Circles of study courses, and if one were to take it up that high… well, we will just say you would not recognize the place after they are finished with it," he chuckles. "Just take that valley to the south as an example."

The Dean gasped as he quickly reflected on the Badlands valley during his visit. Whatever forces were involved in turning a desert wasteland into that fertile oasis was no simple wave of a hand as he taught in his academy.

Tristeen continued to watch and listen. She found herself wondering how these academies might appear as compared to her own. She quickly reflected on Master Dastien in the temple when he so casually opened that portal to evacuate the students. It seemed so effortless, such a common practice, like he had done it all his life.

The Captain continues, "And we give this not simply to those who would specialize in the Art, for instance as a professional demand, but also they who might wish to take up supplemental studies to complement their other skills. In fact, the schools back home mandate at least the first few grades as required study for everyone."

"Mandate… And we are speaking of common citizens here?"

"Indeed, and it has truly changed our world."

"Good gracious. And so if we reflect on those orcs out there…"

"Oh, pshaw," he waves it off. "They are not even a challenge for our most basic frontline fighters. And our mages could wipe them out with just a few salvos of elemental bombardment. But one of our finest applications is not simply the conjuration of magic, but the enchantments we use. Oh, yes!" he heralds. "This is where our military finds its most noteworthy reputation for being such an unstoppable force."

"I'm almost afraid to ask. How come? What do you do with enchantments? Are we speaking of your armor, perchance?"

"Absolutely! You cannot go out and conquer a world without at least a few sturdy enchantments on you somewhere."

"Well, yes, I suppose."

"And ours very often involve more than one, to provide multiple forms of protections for the armor, and multiple forms of additional damage potential for the weapons."

"Multiple? Isn't that a little like overkill?"

"That would largely depend on who, or what, you are fighting, as everything has its strengths and weaknesses."

"I see…" he whimpers, once again reflecting on his proposed conjuration and what hope it might have to fight something like this.

"But it is not simply the equipment," the Captain asserts. "As even the soldiers themselves need a little. They carry a myriad of enchantments on their bodies, both arcane and divine, which make them nearly impossible to kill."

The Dean's eyes bulge, and he began to feel faint. He unconsciously falls back another step, catching himself as he glares at the Captain's smug expression.

"This is one of the gifts our Lord gave to us as he was building our military," he admits. "And why we were so successful at uniting our world. We spend a lot of resources in training our people, so we don't want them so quickly falling to the side in battle. We want them to stay on their feet!" he asserts firmly.

"Great gods," the Dean wheezes.

"Prior to this, well, our world was just one nation bickering with another with little or no final result."

"Yeah, I'll bet."

"Then, one day, he found his true love. Oh, what a day that one was! Even his Father showed up at the wedding, much to our surprise, and revealed to us that she was also Fated to arrive, unknown even to our Lord!"

"Huh? Wait a minute, I'm not sure if I follow. Where did she come from?"

"Well, technically speaking, she was born on Tae'Eladar, so we can say, in her case, she is a native, at least by merit of her birthplace. But she is actually another of the same, simply hidden away by that same fascinating individual who was engineering everything, and this was simply another piece of it. Then they joined in marriage and finished uniting the remainder of the world together."

"Uh huh… But, um, this is all a lot of work to unite a full world, isn't it? I mean, even with a super army, this should take some time, wouldn't it?"

"Yes, we can most certainly say it did. You see, our Lord would prefer to use political means as much as possible, rather than resort to war. It's so much tidier, you know," he smiles cutely. "But one way or another, it had to be done. This falls back on that divine mandate, and time was certainly on his side."

"Why is that?"

"It has to do with his point of origin, you see. Where he comes from, well…" he seems to pause in contemplation. "Perhaps we can simply say, they have a tad longer lifespans out there."

"A tad longer?" the Dean winces. "How much is a tad? Can you give me a hint?"

"Well, I suppose it's really no secret…after all, our full population knows about it by now. When he first came to us, and up until he finally united those last few nations into his kingdom, I believe we are speaking of a good half a millennium, to be sure."

"Half a… Half a…" he pants.

"But I feel we should also include the additional two and a half centuries we were made to tolerate those orcs until we finally declared genocide on them."

"Genocide!" the Dean screams and jumps back a couple more paces.

"Yes, they had been with us for a good many millennia by that time, and never once cooperated with any of our efforts. So, one day, we finally had our fill of it, and decided to remove them. This also coincided with the unfortunate conflict of your world spilling into our lovely home."

"Oh grand…now I'm really sorry those orcs ever went over there. So, we're saying, um…half a millennium, which is five, and then two and a half more… This comes up to seven hundred fifty years!" he grimaces.

"Yes, I suppose this would account for his time in our world so far. My, how it seems to fly by," he grins.

"Fly by!" he yelps. "Egads, man, how old was he before this?"

"Oh, he was a full millennium before this ever happened."

"Gah!" he screams again and hops back another step. "How can a man live so long?"

"Indeed, this is a truly fascinating question. There can be many ways in which to answer this, but we simple people are often not ready for such elaborate wisdom. He and his, however…well, they are indeed privileged, and very likely to prove themselves to be all this and more for a good long period to come. We on Tae'Eladar are blessed for this point."

Now the Dean collapses to the ground, panting.

Tristeen was fully entranced by the story, dreamily imagining a world filled with such people that could look up to those of such high esteem that they might stand amongst the clouds. It still seemed entirely fantastic, but if it was reducing the Dean into a pool of his own sweat, it was certainly worth the admission price.

"But anyway," the Captain concludes formally. "Returning to our business of my Lord and his meeting, he wants you to know that he will be arriving on the day after tomorrow, just after he refreshes himself from his latest crusade. I do hope this is to your liking. And with this message delivered, I must be on my way. I do have so many other chores to attend. Cheerio, good chap!"

The Captain bows and pertly turns around as he climbs into the carriage again, then takes off down the avenue.

Tristeen gazed in awe at the presentation.

"You people must be a theatrical group," she mutters to herself. "At least in part. But if any part of that is true, the Dean and the Governor don't stand a chance against you, with or without a conjuring."

The Dean pulls himself off the ground and slogs his way towards the Governor's Manor. He trudges up the stairs and knocks once as a glancing blow on the door before opening it, then nearly falls inside.

"Um…"

"Dean!" the Governor screeches. "How can you be so inane?! Can't you see that man was toying with you? I was watching from up here, and could hear most of it, and it was quite clear to me he was filling you with as much rubbish as you could tolerate without exploding from it."

"Of course, my Lord, it's just that it was so well-played. I guess I got caught in the moment. But I suppose I did put on a good show for him, if his ploy was to try fooling me with his rhetoric."

"This much I will certainly agree with. But now, did I hear him say that man was scheduled to arrive in two days' time?"

"Yes, my Lord, this is the final word."

"Good! It's about time. Be ready for him, and when you see him, send that creature out there to finish him!"

"Right, my Lord. But, just for the sake of mention, what if any of that might be true. We know his men use adamantium and mithril, and from some of those reports, they did seem to be quite proficient at magic."

"Yes, I will agree on this much. Enchanted weapons, and even a form of physical technology from it…they've must've progressed far on that world of theirs. I can perhaps accept this much, if only for our observations. But the rest of it is clearly rubbish, and simply to brag him up in our eyes."

"What about the part saying he came from somewhere outside their world?"

"Again rubbish. They don't have anything…ehm…well," he coughs to clear his wording. "I find it highly unlikely someone would settle down on a world just for the sake of…well, anything that man was suggesting. It seems so…implausible, yes. After all, why would someone with such extraordinary qualities as what he was claiming trouble themselves with so much trifle as uniting a bunch of squabbling little peasants into anything at all?"

"Yes, I suppose," he chuckles feebly. "Anyway, I should get back to my office. I'll put my people back to work on that circle to ensure all is ready."

He bows and leaves the room.

The Governor glances out the window again, peering down into the plaza.

"If even a small amount of that is true…" he grumbles. "It would mean something dire has occurred over there since my last visit. But where could he have come from? That entire fold is still shredded from that old battle."

Chapter 11
SUBVERSIVE INTERPLAY

"Commander Geilv, speaking..."

"Commander?" ushers a soft, indistinct voice.

"High Priestess Sehnisavain, do you have something to report?"

"I'm not sure," she wavers distantly. "Do you hear that?"

"Hear what? I do not hear anything from my station."

"His songs..."

"Songs? I do not understand your meaning."

"Him, his songs, they seem to be fading. Something...I think... is happening."

"You are not making sense. Who is it you are referring to?"

"Our Lord...the one who lifted us up... But his voice, it's as though something is interrupting it. I cannot be sure. Perhaps I am simply weary. Forgive me, Commander, maybe I simply need some rest."

"Agreed. Do you desire assistance?"

"No, I'm sure that won't be necessary. But...well, yes, perhaps if you could simply check in tomorrow, just to make sure all is well, I would appreciate it."

"Understood. I will contact you tomorrow."

They end the link.

Sehnisavain puts down her trans-com and grins at Cydulean and the others in her office.

"It's really a shame he doesn't seem to have any emotional display. I'm sure this would make for a very interesting reaction once it's fully played out."

"Indeed, Priestess," Cydulean admits. "I would love to see the look on his face, or at least that of the Marshal, once he learns of it."

"The Marshal would be the most enjoyable of all, I'm sure."

It was late afternoon and Thaelyn's most recent plans were in progress. Sehnisavain was beginning a new play which would carry over time until the eventual liberation of her people.

In the meantime, Aerlie had been sending secret deliveries to the temple in Rolsklinde, using rune transport rather than overland methods. This included boxes of translated hymns and other materials to teach the local people of the true gods. Another iconic statue had been ordered from a sculptor's supply warehouse on Tae'Eladar to add into the mix. This would offer another divine image for the people of Rolsklinde to become familiar with. She was also assembling a large choir to be delivered secretly the next day for their latest presentation.

"We have delivered our briefings to our priests up there," Thaelyn reports to his latest meeting. "This will give them something new to offer our dear Dean when he no doubt comes to investigate our latest performance."

"This should be good," Marelle grins. "I wish I could see his face."

"In addition, it is also where we will need to open ourselves up a bit with our indirect references to his and the Governor's maneuverings. And since my arrival is scheduled to occur soon, I feel confident they will wait until that moment before they take any other actions to correct for all my continued intrusions of their delicate affairs."

"You know, when you put it that way, it sounds scary."

"Oh, we are only just beginning, Marelle," he smiles. "Once we are finished with our little play up there, I think I will also choose this moment to investigate the academy for its involvement in an unfortunate instance of theft, and see if I can arrange a proper resolution to it. And if the Dean should behave in his traditional manner, I will ensure he fully and completely understands who his opponent is in this matter. We need to reinforce the Captain's play, and naturally, this will once again filter back to the Governor."

"Jiggers," Relissa moans. "Marelle, you said this sounds dangerous, but maybe we should ask for whom?"

✦✦✦✦✦

The next day, a midmorning service was commencing at the temple in Rolsklinde. The temple bells were ringing, and people were being called to attention in the plaza in the upper district. Citizens were arriving from all across the city, even though seating was limited inside the temple proper. The commotion represented a familiar occasion except for one thing…it was the wrong time of year.

The Dean was in his office, once again trying to find an occupation for himself by reviewing a series of accounting papers for the academy supply stores. When the bells began to chime, his attention was instantly diverted away from his work. He lifted his view to stare into the distance, furrowing his brow and darting his eyes to-and-fro as he tried to fathom the meaning of the bell ringing. He slowly turned his gaze over his shoulder to peer outside into the plaza, and there he took notice of the people coming into attendance in front of the temple.

"What in all the hells are they doing this time?" he mutters. "Are we receiving more neighbors? Who's left in this world, except…well, no, they wouldn't be coming here…or would they?"

He glared at the activity outside, trying to isolate any new arrivals, but there were no carriages, nor anything else that would indicate a visiting delegation of any kind.

"They only ring those bells for the Festival. But that's in the springtime, and this is autumn now. What are they doing down there?"

He sighs tenuously and gets out of his chair to once again trudge downstairs to investigate.

The priests of the temple were welcoming their parishioners

inside and directing them into the seats. A large choir had arranged themselves on the platform in front and was raising their voices in harmonious song to welcome their guests. The melody was bold and enlightening, and it echoed through the temple and out into the plaza.

The Dean exited the academy only to be presented with the abnormal merriment of song ushering out from the building across the way. He halted briefly to survey the area before continuing across the plaza. In front of the temple doors, he found the lead priest directing the flow of people inside.

"Eh, excuse me," he announces calmly. "But what is going on here today?"

"Ah, Dean!" Priest Garrain replies jubilantly. "Such a joyous day it is! We are in celebration, and calling on the people to join us for this grand occasion. Perhaps you would like to participate?"

"Uh, I've never been much of a temple-goer. Traditionally, there was never that much to be gained in it for me. But what I'm most interested in is why you have these bells ringing. Isn't it the wrong time of year for that?"

"Oh, Dean, we simply decided to make use of them because they were so convenient. After all, why have bells if you only allow them to sit and collect dust most of the year. But if to use them to bring the people into attendance, it would surely promote our efforts at providing for their greater comfort, would it not?"

"I, um, well, all right, if you say so. But what is going on inside there? You people never did anything like this before."

"But of course, you are right. It has recently come to our attention…you know, due to the people being in such need for their comfort in these hard times… Eh, you do recall our discussion from a few days ago, correct?"

"Yes, you mentioned improving your, um…services."

"Right," he affirms fervently. "And the people do need these services from time to time to give them a sense of calm that the gods are indeed watching over them and will one day deliver them from all this terrible hardship we face in this world."

"Uh huh…and so you're improving your services with this new

bell ringing and some kind of singing inside there," he peers over the priest's shoulder to see inside.

"Ah yes, indeed. Here, come with me and I'll show you. You might find this rather interesting."

The priest waves at the Dean to follow, and together they go inside.

On entering the temple proper, the priest demonstrates to the Dean the activity of the people and the choir in front. The worshippers all had pamphlets in their hands and were trying to follow along with the songs being sung by the choir. Since the songs were essentially new to them, the people simply listened as they tried to become familiar with the melody.

The Dean looked around the room, feeling partially stunned by the volume of people in attendance and how attentive they seemed to be to the presentation up on the platform. The choir was dressed in neat uniforms involving white and pale blue gowns for the women and suits for the men. The professionalism of the display was shocking to the Dean's eyes, as they never before had a choir. He stood there gawking at it as he glanced at the people who were so focused on the performance.

"Where did those people come from?" he mumbles to himself.

"My pardons, Dean?" Priest Garrain feigns an attention lapse. "Oh, you mean those up there. Yes, of course. We have realized that people have a tendency to respond to songs. I must admit, we learned this from our recent interactions with some of those delegations who visited recently. For instance, the Night Elves told us that they often used song to recall the worship of their gods and to offer up their devotion. This would then lift their spirits and grant them a sense of belonging to their local community and the spiritual union they share with their gods."

"Really!" the Dean retorts disdainfully. "They said this?"

"Absolutely, and in fact we found ourselves curious as to this process. After all, as I'm sure you already know, we never held such a service like this before, and it caused us to wonder if it could be useful to aid our own people, especially in the face of this awful plague."

"Oh!" he reconsiders. "So, you're thinking you could give our people a better sense of, um…containment, I suppose would be a good word for it, that they shouldn't worry as much about this plague being pressed down upon us by those horrid Flame Elves. And so, by using song, you can keep them under better control, saying that one day…" he coughs for emphasis, "…we'll see our salvation from it…right?" he raises his brow expectantly.

"Indeed, Dean," Priest Garrain admits reassuringly. "You should know that we have everything under control here. And in fact, we feel confident that we can give these poor lost Children even greater hope than they ever might have known before. For we have rediscovered the True Gods!" he rejoices with open hands.

"Huh?" the Dean blurts spontaneously. "What do you mean, true gods?"

"Ah yes! This is a very interesting one to tell. Firstly, the elves apparently have a full pantheon of true gods they call the Seldarine. By the stories I heard, this body has been their dedicated pantheon since the beginning of their kind, and this accounts for all the elven races, not just the Night Elves."

"All of them? Wait, you can't be talking about the Flame Elves in this, can you?"

"Well, technically speaking, it was, at least until this awful war came to us. The Night Elves tell us that the others were once called High Elves, and yes, they did share in this same worship, at least until this creature called Sargeras showed up," the priest leans in and hushes his voice, discreetly darting his eyes around the gathering. "You know… Him."

The Dean catches his direction and follows along with the insinuation.

"Ah, yes, right, I understand your meaning. And this is when they ultimately turned to join the Suuden-Aryku and the orcs, or some such, right?"

"Right, but before this, they also worshipped the Seldarine, and in partnership with the Night Elves. But now, here is the clincher. Apparently, none of us is native to this world."

"What?!" the Dean shouts. "Not native? How... What in all the hells are you talking about?"

"This came out of those missionaries; do you recall them? They came from Tae'Eladar, where we have humans and the remainder of the elven nations. Apparently, this is where we originally came from...all of us."

"Gah!" the Dean shrieks and once again slaps his hands to his temples.

Priest Garrain continues, "Once upon a time, apparently thousands of years ago, the elves were in a process of migration. They originally came from another world entirely and arrived on Tae'Eladar, where they found the early human population. Then, some of these elves, in this case a clan once known as the Ssri, and another that was now calling itself the Cala clan, moved forward, along with some of those humans, and apparently found this world."

"How?"

"Oh, but indeed, this is a curious one. Apparently, as the story goes, someone inspired them with the discovery of a most mysterious portal device that was activated by a strange artifact. This led them to our world here. Even more curiously, this also seems to have occurred at approximately the same time as the discovery of a new arrival on Tae'Eladar, which they apparently described as man-beasts. How strange..."

"Man-beasts?" he muses.

"Yes, according to that Tae'Eladaran delegation, this might represent the first orcish invasion."

"Orcs! Wait a minute! The first one? How long ago was this? I remember something from that captain out there recently."

"Yes, indeed. This most recent invasion simply stirred up a preexisting migration and settlement effort they had way back in those early days. But we are speaking again of thousands of years ago."

"Thousands of years ago, yes, this is what he said. Then, how many orcs are we speaking of by this time?"

"Oh, wow. As I recall their statements, they occupied a large nation on the southern side of their main continent. Probably in the millions, to say the least. No small matter, that."

The Dean wheezed at the clear magnitude of the suggestion and reflected on the previous discussion with Captain Hagmaert about them.

"A nation of them…millions…and then genocide…"

"Yes, according to their stories, those orcs simply would not behave peacefully. So, out they went," the priest waves a hand casually. "But anyway, back to the migration of our people to this world. The elves brought with them a number of things that were important to them, some of which apparently belonged to their worship of the Seldarine, and established themselves on this world, then to expand their population to cover the greater portion of it."

"Uh huh…" the Dean gushes. "And why should I care about any part of this? Or anyone else, for that matter."

"Well, clearly this is a part of our history, and the people do need to understand the relationship. I've heard some say those people in the valley are invaders, when in fact they're our distant cousins who finally found us."

The Dean screamed again at the implications of anyone related to the local populations now discovering them, and by merit of this relationship, trying to interact with them.

The priest continues, "Some might even suggest they are no more invaders than they are simply reacting to the war here going over there. Such a pity, that."

"Yeah…" the Dean wheezes. "A pity…"

"But now we come to another important aspect of this new knowledge," the priest offers. "On Tae'Eladar, the humans also hold their worship of the True Gods, and in their case a different set."

"A different set?" the Dean screeches. "Just how many are there?"

"Ah, this is actually a very good question. It would seem these gods, all of them, are part of a large society called the Estelar, and they rule all of Creation. There are simply no other gods out there. Either they at one time merged with the Estelar, or they were destroyed by them."

"Gah!!" he screams again. "What do you mean? These Estelar kill other gods?"

"It is better to say they follow a certain philosophy called the Measure of Balance. They believe all things in Creation must balance. And for those who do not follow, or simply cannot tolerate such a concept, either they must conform, or be removed."

The Dean's face went blank at this statement. He simply stood there as the priest continued his explanation.

"I suppose we could associate this as a form of law enforcement, if only on a godlike scale. They own Creation. They set the rules. And if we continue on this same scale, any creature so potent that it can afflict itself on anything else out there, such as to bring devastation upon whole societies, even whole worlds, the 'rule' of the Measure of Balance must be enforced absolutely. And by saying absolutely, we cannot be speaking of something as simple as placing someone inside a prison cell. These are gods, after all. So, it's much more of an all-or-nothing circumstance. Do you see?"

"Uh, yeah, I suppose I can. But gracious, that sounds harsh."

"Here, let me demonstrate," the priest directs. "Do you see those up there," he points at the two statues on the platform. "They were donated to us by the priesthood of Tae'Eladar to help us better understand the Estelar, at least as it relates to the human population. The first one is called Lord Torm, who presides over Justice and Law. By worshiping him, you accept and agree to the principles of Justice, and simply will not tolerate any criminal actions or other such malpractice of Law. This means, technically speaking, that you become a law enforcer in his name."

"Gah!" the Dean screams yet again, and glares at the priest for even stating such a thing.

"The next one is called Lathander, sometimes known as the Morninglord. He presides over birth, youth, and renewal, among other things. I'm told the priests of Tae'Eladar often give worship to him in order to receive blessings to use amongst their population to heal injury and correct for illness. Through his teachings, the people have learned ways to live longer and healthier lives."

The Dean wheezes at the mention.

"Of course, they say there are more out there," the priest implies. "So these here are simply a starting point."

"A starting point?" he gasps. "You're kidding me!"

"Ah, but Dean... Think about it for just a moment and how it relates to our situation here. The people of this city have been suffering from this plague for how long now? And in all that time, they have sought the comfort of the gods to guide and protect them from this awful curse, is this not true?"

"Well, uh..." he vacillates. "Yes, that was the purpose of it, but..."

"But four centuries, Dean, and I would think at least a few of them are growing tired of waiting for this alleged salvation these gods were supposed to bring. But..." he emphasizes with a finger. "If we were to bring the image of the True Gods back to our people, it would give them a renewed sense of hope, maybe even a greater sense of comfort and relief that those gods are indeed watching over them and offering their support, is that not right?"

"I, uh...well, yes, I suppose I can see your meaning. But, true gods, as opposed to, um, the ones we had in here before?"

"Ah, but of course, you are right. Look at it this way, as I think it would tend to stand out after a while. Four centuries, if anyone is actually paying attention to it, is a long time to wait for salvation, and those old gods simply were not living up to their names."

"Ah! I see it. Therefore, these others, and calling them the True Gods. Oh, yes," he nods confidently. "That's rather ingenious, actually. And so, you're trying to improve your services, and with new god images, so the people aren't, um, so anxious about this awful war and the curse we suffer so often!"

"Very good, Dean, I am so glad you can see the greater wisdom of it. Personally, I thought it was a splendid idea to bring this into our temple, along with these songs to help encourage the participation of our citizens to this new worship."

"Of course! Yes, this is actually very clever," he agrees haughtily as he glances around the congregation. "And just look at how many you have in here. Gracious, I haven't seen it this busy in all my years."

"Oh, indeed! And see how attentive they are. They truly do appreciate this new service."

"And so, you're using those bells now to bring them inside for all this."

"Absolutely! They certainly do come in handy. And especially on this most glorious day, because along the way, we have discovered a fabulous revelation!" the priest rejoices with his hands raised in praise.

"A what?" the Dean blurts in surprise at the sudden shift in tones. "A revelation? What revelation?"

"Oh yes, Dean, this is the reason we are calling all the people of the city to our attention today. We found the cure!" he shouts.

The Dean gapes at the man for his audacity to make such a claim.

"A cure?" he wheezes. "What are you talking about, a cure?!" he yelps. "There is no cure, that's the whole point! It's a curse by the Flame Elves, not something you can cure with a simple remedy or a wave of the hand!"

"Indeed, Dean, a simple remedy, like an elixir or some such, this would not do at all. And a waving of the hand…well, I suppose that might depend on the hand, of course. But for little people like us, oh come now, that is just silly, don't you think?"

"Yes! Silly, that's exactly right. So, this idea of a cure is also silly. Because it's a curse! And you can't stop a curse, right?"

"Oh, but my goodness, how true it is. I mean, first you need to know who is casting the curse. Although it is so often said to be the Flame Elves. But then, you need to know where to go look for it, what with all their alleged blood altars and such. Coincidentally, this was one of the long-standing complaints by some people, that those old gods, after four hundred years of people praying to them, did not point the way to it. You do know how they were described as all-powerful creations, right? Well, Dean, the definition of an all-powerful creation is one where nothing stands in its way of solving a problem. Unfortunately, those examples apparently failed."

"Uh oh…"

"And of course, the next thing you need is a city authority, like the Allegiance Guard over here, to actually go outside and do it.

But I once heard how they were only told to stay at home and pick up drunks off the streets. I cannot imagine who would say such a thing as that. But for the clear lack of them being given orders to go out there and find those blood altars, which were casting those curses, which were killing our people, well, it stands to reason there is a clear problem occurring somewhere in our local law enforcement. What do you think?"

"Um…"

The Dean suddenly felt a cold spike arriving as he paused to consider the implications of that statement. The obvious direction was now orienting along those same lines as these new gods and their teachings. And since he personally knew where the curse actually came from, this was now suggesting something had happened. But the question was how this man could be behind it if he's supposed to be following the traditional methods of his predecessors.

"You know, Dean," Priest Garrain begins a bit more seriously this time. "I recall a conversation I was having a while back with one of the citizens here. Four hundred years…this is how long those awful Flame Elves have been pressing this curse. And also, four hundred years is how long the people of this city have been praying to their gods for deliverance. And curiously, for some odd reason, none of them have ever truly paid attention to the great passage of time, and the lack of results. And yet, people were dying left and right. This is very curious."

"It is? I mean, um…yes, I suppose."

"But then I am reminded of that famous saying, 'for as long as I can remember…' Well, you know the rest. After all, this is pounded into their heads so heavily in the schools, how can one miss it. Which simply means they can't remember anything beyond what they personally experienced in life, as the schools aren't teaching them anything else."

"Oh, dear…" he mumbles.

"And this is made worse, as people are dying, Dean! If you have people dying of something, you might think a proper form of law and justice…" he glances briefly at Torm's statue, "…might do something about it. At the very least, this would be murder. And we say we are at war, so why isn't anyone fighting it?"

"But...but..."

"But I am sure the city's authority knows what it is doing. After all, if you can't trust them...even if they do order the Guard to stay at home and pick up drunks off the streets, then who can you trust?" he laughs satirically.

"Uh, yeah..." the Dean titters faintly.

"But not to worry, Dean," he comforts. "In the absence of all this, we simply have to resort to our own means. The Guard isn't doing it. The city authority isn't doing it. So, it must be the priesthood to do it...with our new gods directing us. And as such, I am pleased to say we have finally realized a solution to it, and it is so very simple."

Now, the priest reaches out and abruptly hooks a thumb under the Dean's collar, pulling it away to reveal his shoulder, where the priest could see a clear scarring from a crude surgical procedure. The Dean instantly reacted by cocking his head to follow the action.

"Ah," the priest croons. "But I see you must already know of it, Dean. By this scar on your shoulder, it would seem someone must've told you of the little implant device placed there at age twelve during the Festival of Passage. So, I guess you no longer have to worry about that awful curse by those awful Flame Elves and all their unholy this and that. I just wish you and your beloved priests would've told the rest of the citizens about it. Such a pity," he glares at him sternly. "Fortunately, Dean, we are here now, and we do follow law and justice."

The Dean turned to look into the eyes of the priest, who was now staring down at him.

"Who are you people?" he asks timidly.

"Priests, Dean. Actual real priests who worship actual real gods, and none of whom would conduct such blasphemy as what you people are performing in this city. His Lordship learned of your little curse out there and sent us to investigate. After just one day, we learned the truth. We then arrested those heathens you had working in here and installed ourselves."

"Arrested? But you shouldn't even hold any jurisdiction here!"

"What about your Captain Kholgard, or do you think you can keep him so tightly caged up in his office. He is your law, and he isn't too happy with how your city authority is running the place. Especially with people like you telling him to pick up all those drunks off the streets. And so, this is your answer."

"Oh no..." he whines.

"As for us, we follow a divine law, one that isn't limited to just our own world. The Estelar govern everything, including this place. Four centuries, Dean, and none of you spent even half an effort to correct this. These are your children, Dean! But if your city authority would prefer your law enforcers to play street sweepers, this might explain the source of it."

The cold spike running down the Dean's back was intensifying. He started backing away, glancing around the room, and feeling the eyes of everyone on him.

"I don't believe in anything like gods," he snarls. "And you shouldn't even be here!"

"Dean," the priest retorts. "As for your belief, I suppose I cannot blame you for the nonsense circulating in this temple of yours. But as for us being here... You might not want us here, and your Governor might not want us here, but you do not control the minds of these people who are suffering under you...they who have finally found the freedom to realize who is killing them and why they can't remember anything outside their personal lifetimes! Your Captain over there does not want to simply pick up drunks from the street, and by his authority, which is far more compassionate to the health and welfare of the people, he became our authority to go anywhere and do anything, in spite of you. We are law givers, Dean, and you and your Governor are on our list."

The Dean found himself backing away further as the priest continued his rant.

"First, you lie to us about squatting on that land when no one recognizes any such claim. You say your armies are busy elsewhere when your own Captain Kholgard tells us he is locked behind a desk.

Your supposed allies in this world believe you to be their friends, when in fact you feed your own citizens so much falsehood about them that you refuse even to recognize them as living alongside of you as neighbors. They are told you suffer frequent attacks when your own citizens do not recall any such thing within their lifetimes. These are called lies, Dean, and some of us take exception to them, including those who are trapped inside these walls because of them. You claim you are at war, when in fact this is much more like oppression. As for us being here, you invoked that by sending your orcs at us, and not just once."

"Me?"

"Whoever owns them, and the name Sargeras is plastered all over this world. And we are quite sure you are associated, as you seem very close to the Governor, who seems very close to your enemies out there. So, keep your complaints to yourself. We are guardians and protectors, and we do not take no for an answer, especially by people like you. Your priests were like this before we hauled them away by force."

"Fine, and so what? So what if we don't like someone? So what if we made up a few stories?"

"Indeed, I suppose what you like or do not like, and the stories you generate, are not my personal concern. Although you might want to consider the Captain's lecture yesterday. We do not tolerate prejudice. Instead, we destroy it. But I will leave it to these people and their suffering for this curse, and the offence to their children, to decide your fate. And I would imagine four centuries of lost family members will speak for itself."

The priest glances around the room at all the faces turned up to watch the exchange. The Dean followed along and felt a new spike of fear rushing through him for the public reaction that was welling up.

"Dean," the priest continues. "You do not tell us what to do or not do, including asking questions. We investigate things, as I believe my Lord once mentioned. And one of the things we discovered is the true history of this city."

"A true history? Grand. And what sort of true history do you think we have here?"

"It would seem, despite your effort at stunting the people's wisdom, a few did hold the presence of mind to record a few things, most notably the noble families, who seem to hold a higher level of responsibility than what I would imagine you might care for. They kept a number of old journals, where they describe the beginning of this curse, and a man who arrived with claims to correct it. He demanded to be made governor, with control of the academy and the temple, meaning people like you and the priests. This is often described as ransom and blackmail. And so, here we are, with your history so badly smeared, you do not even remember who you are, and your people suffering from something put there by your own authority figures. Here is where we come back to the statement of murder. And this makes all of you criminals. And in case I did not make it clear before...we are law enforcers. With or without your Captain providing his authority, your war came to our world, and you claim to be so unhappy over our intrusion in your lovely little garden. This gives us authority to put things right...our way! Because it labels you as a participant! And as such, any...authority... you might claim for yourself becomes moot."

The Dean was feeling very anxious by this time and considering a hasty retreat. He started backing away again, but the priest wasn't finished yet.

"My Lord told us of your claim of so many villains in this world. Well, my understanding is he will be arriving on the morrow. Maybe you can explain to him why your priests were infecting the people with this awful curse by those awful Flame Elves and slandering everything else out there. Maybe you can also explain that delightful new elixir you were going to feed your students recently."

"But what business is it of yours what we do in our city!" he screams. "Regardless of the rest of this world and any war out there?"

"The business of your citizens asking us for help after you offend them so often. Despite your lack of belief in the gods, Estelar or otherwise, you should take note of these, as we have met some of them personally on Tae'Eladar. We are not simple priests who wail at statues, Dean. We are employed by a society of beings of supremely advanced designs, such that they can be called gods. And they do not take kindly to their Children being so offended by people like you! And walls do not stop gods and their mandates! The Measure of Balance is the rule to apply here, and crime, no matter who commits it, or where they are found, still falls under their jurisdiction. And we are their enforcers."

The Dean now felt a heavy shudder rush through him. He glanced around nervously at the congregation, where all eyes were intensely focused on him. He began wailing and stumbled backwards. His wails soon turned to screams as he ran out of the building.

He crashed through the doors and stumbled into the plaza, zigzagging as he continued his screeching, crouching and jerking in all directions, as if expecting fire and brimstone to come down around him at any moment. He then turned an outstretched finger towards the Governor's Manor in a vague moment of impulse to report this in and dashed off towards the door.

Leesa was watching and waiting at the window. When she saw him coming in, she rushed back to her desk and pretended nothing was happening.

He barreled through the door and towards the stairs, then tripped and clawed his way to the top. He staggered up to the Governor's office door, burst into the office, and slammed the door behind him.

The Governor had been sitting near the window watching the events outside. He casually glanced over his shoulder at the Dean as the man leaned against the door in a cold sweat and panting. He then turned to look out the window again.

"You know, Dean, these last few days have provided me with a small amount of amusement at your antics out there. So, what do we have on this occasion that might cause you to behave as if the world was coming to an end?"

"Um, my Lord, we have a little problem inside the temple."

"Ah! Only a little problem, I'm so pleased," he retorts

condescendingly. "Might it have anything to do with those bells and that singing I've been listening to all morning?"

"Well, yes, partially."

"And should I assume it does not involve a second yearly occurrence of the Festival?"

"Yes, my Lord."

"How extraordinary. Very well, Dean, what is going on out there? And why did it take you so long to finally come back out?"

"Oh, well, the priest was explaining everything to me, and it took a bit of time."

"How pleasant of him. Priests are always so helpful."

"Right. First, it seems these aren't the original priests we had in there."

"Yes, I believe you mentioned a change of labor due to the old ones retiring, or some such nonsense. Although, this in itself is unusual, because they should've reported to me if they had anyone new coming in."

"Yes, of course, although I also have an answer to that bit now," he titters. "But anyway, as for the bells and such, they're changing their manner of worship, and are now using a choir, as you can surely hear, and he showed me a couple of new statues up on the platform for some new gods they're supposed to be following."

The Governor jerked around to glare at the Dean.

"What new gods?" he intones cautiously.

"They were talking about those delegations that came in recently. The Night Elves were apparently teaching the people about their worship of something called, um, the Sel-something."

"Seldarine, Dean. Yes, I know this name. The Night Elves are a stubborn group, holding onto this outdated belief. But the others proved to be a little more susceptible...well, never mind. What of it? This is a human city, not elven."

"Right, and those missionaries that came in told the history of the people of this world."

"History?" the Governor leans forward to his desk and raises his brow concernedly. "What about this history?"

"They say we're all apparently immigrants from Tae'Eladar, from something like thousands of years ago when the elves were inspired by someone to pass through a weird portal thing and carried some humans along for the ride."

"A weird portal thing..." he mumbles. "Someone actually remembers that?" he refocuses himself. "Right, so they're refreshing a bit of ancestral association. Well, I won't consider this to be too disastrous. Once we rid ourselves of that man and his unwelcome intrusion, we can work on breaking this again. What else?"

"He also mentioned something curious, and I recall this from that Captain, as well. It was an earlier invasion of orcs at about the same time."

The Governor frowned at the suggestion.

"Really! An earlier one, is it?"

"Yes, and so that Captain, with his statement of genocide against them...this is apparently to say a large nation of them being wiped out...on the scale of millions, so he says."

"Is that so?" he leans back in contemplation. "That would take a bit of effort, to be sure."

"And now these people brought some of their religion with them. Those two statues represent a couple of the gods they worship over there."

The Governor became noticeably tense at the mention. He came to attention and stared at the Dean intently.

"Which ones?" he emits worriedly.

"One is called Lord Torm, the other is called Lath...um..."

"Lathander," the Governor finishes. "He can be a problem, but the other one... Torm, is it? He isn't much to speak of. Last time I heard that name, he was a lesser deity."

"They say he rules over Justice and Law."

"What?" he blurts. "But that's not right. That was, um..." he pauses a moment to think. "Did something happen to the other one?" he mumbles to himself. "Hmm...well, these are just statues, so unless..." he halts unexpectedly as his thoughts begin to consolidate.

"Dean, what was it exactly that caused you to spill out onto the plaza screaming like a frightened animal?"

"They're not our priests, they're his. Ours were arrested and taken away. He's discovered all the lies we've been giving so far. For instance, our early meeting and your statements about land ownership, the false statements of the attacks, and our statements of being at war, but the Captain never being allowed to go outside the walls."

"Blast it!" he rages and pounds his fist on the desk. "All right then, so he's one to ask questions. And apparently, he desires to seek answers, not simply sit back so complacently, like everything else around here."

"Right. This was a large part of the debate. They're law enforcers, all of them, by the sound of it. They don't take no for an answer, they don't stop at walls, and our war spilling into their world, and us complaining over their arrival here to spoil our little garden, as he called it, makes us accomplices to the original cause. Therefore, boom, we're in it."

"Really! Well, now, they certainly do seem determined."

"And therefore, we are being described as criminals. This comes from a number of things, not the least of which are those lies."

"I see. What else do they have?"

"We can include the stories the old priests gave of the other races, which he's apparently working to correct, like with those delegations sent recently to meet the people."

"Yes, this could complicate things. If the people realize all the images we've been trying to create are false, this lets them out of their cages even more. I see a lot of people passing in and out of those doors, Dean. What does it look like inside?"

"Full to capacity, with people trying to study these new songs and learn the worship of these new gods. By the appearance of it, they're looking to tell everyone in the city. Like I said, he replaced our priests, and now it seems they're giving out new stories about these new gods they call the Estelar."

The Governor's eyes suddenly bulge. He yelps and jumps out

of his chair. He stumbles as he falls back a step, knocking the chair over in the process.

"They actually know their names?!" he shrieks.

"Well, yes, it would seem that way. I recall him saying he's an actual priest in worship of actual gods they meet on occasion in their world…and working for them in some form of employment."

The Governor shrieks again and falls back against the wall, then slides away past the window, nervously peeking outside to see if anything was coming down on the city.

The Dean couldn't help but notice the clearly evident reaction as a form of recognition. He raises his brow at the display.

"My Lord, what's wrong?" he wonders. "I mean, this is just a lot of bunk, isn't it…gods and religion and such? Just like you were saying about the Captain out there."

"Dammit, Dean!" the Governor gushes. "If these people have such a close relationship to those beings, that means something must've changed on that world since the last time…eh, I mean because that name isn't normally known to such common peasants."

"Uh huh…" he muses privately. "So, you mean the name is real? Which probably means we're in trouble here if our people are now learning who they are."

"Eh…well… What I mean is, it's an old name, Dean. To know of it means you would need to have access to some very old knowledge. Very exclusive knowledge, too. A bit like that book I loaned you once. You need to travel in the right circles for it."

"Yes, of course…and circles you are no doubt familiar with, unlike the rest of us. Interesting. Could this be related to what that captain said of him being from somewhere outside that world?"

"Eh…" the Governor hesitates. "Well, I suppose it does raise a curious possibility, and not a pleasant one, at that."

"All right. This might complicate things, because it now suggests the rest of his storytelling might not be so much storytelling. Anyway, if these people claim to have any kind of relationship, what does that mean for us here?"

"It means trouble, especially if they're starting to worship them here, and this simply draws even more unwanted attention to us."

"Oh, no doubt!" he mulls to himself. "And this brings me to the next point. The plague, he's found what it is."

"And blast it again! That man is insidious!"

"I suppose, if you consider what was said before, it should be expected, especially if they arrested those priests. Apparently, he conducted an investigation of the city and the plague. I can only imagine someone told him about it somewhere."

"Yes, naturally, why not?"

"They apparently discovered the part about the old priests and the Festival, and the devices in the shoulders."

"Wonderful," the Governor groans. "They must hold much greater knowledge than expected, which only further complicates things."

"I could possibly point at that captain and his statements of things he brought with him, which might include knowledge."

"Yes, it might. Although, to be honest, I thought some of those people had rules on this. Then again, in this long duration of time... who knows what he did?"

"But I'm sure this also contradicts the notion of the Flame Elves doing anything."

"Oh, but of course it does! Next thing you know, he'll be investigating them."

"And then, he learned something from the noble families."

"Oh grand, them again! Those nobles are becoming a serious annoyance. What is their role in all this?"

"They apparently kept notes of some kind dating back to those early days. It talks about the first governor, his promise of a cure, and his need to control the academy and the temple. But they're describing this as ransoming the city to take power. They're pointing their fingers at you now, and me as well, for my close relationship. We're next on the list, I think."

"Is that so!" he fumes. "So, they think they can bring some sort of legal action against us here in our own city? Pah! They hold no authority here! What are they suggesting in this case?"

"As for the authority, I doubt it matters. Captain Kholgard is apparently on their side, not ours. That represents authority. And you, and I as well, are being described as criminals, which seems to negate whatever authority we might claim. You refused to play nice, at least as much for refusing to cooperate in the war outside, which implies you want the war outside, and that means you are a participant in it...on the wrong side."

"Oh really! And what about our shortages?"

"I suppose one could say, if he's giving us all the spoils of that orcish rubbish, there go the shortages."

"Oh, grand, but you do hold a point."

"Therefore, it goes without saying that if any of his investigations should lead him to suspect you of doing anything other than sitting at that desk pushing papers, their war is breaking through our walls, like it or not."

"Yes, that determination of theirs. All right, I will need to consider this a moment."

"In addition, he said they're all law enforcers, I guess founded on the principles of this Lord Torm, and they don't stop at walls regardless, as their gods apparently own everything. Further, whoever owns the orcs is responsible for calling them here, and not simply due to this most recent invasion, but that first one as well, as the name Sargeras is written all over this world, it would seem, and that likely associates a few things. And they're not at all happy over being rejected as potential saviors by those who do not otherwise want them here...meaning to say those same people, and their assigns, who own the orcs."

The Governor glares at the Dean a moment as he ponders this suggestion.

"So, this is to say, it doesn't matter what we think. They, as law enforcers, are going to apply themselves to us regardless?"

"Yes, and by this divine mandate of theirs to step across any wall for it. And especially for the offence of the priests and those devices. They describe this as murder. And I suppose, despite either of us trying to keep them inside cages, particularly if you count four centuries of praying to gods who didn't do anything useful to solve our problems, as so many desired, the people started asking for help, and they simply responded. So, it sounds like it's outside our hands now."

"I see, and how typical. And further is I suppose you do have a point, assuming anyone was paying attention to the calendar date. And their entire society is like this? In all Creation, what have those orcs brought back to us."

"He also repeated that statement you once made of the villains of the world. So, whatever your original direction, it's been turned around now. And the priests are already taken care of."

"Oh, really!" he pauses to think. "Let me see. First, do they actually think they can pin any of this on either of us for any reason? You're an educator following in the footsteps of the man who preceded you. Surely, you can't be held responsible for anything your predecessors did."

"Um, about that, they must have some sort of word on the elixir you gave me for those students. They didn't seem happy about it."

"Uh oh...did they say anything about what it was?"

"Only that they didn't appreciate something unknown, and I'm going to suggest unpleasant for the students, which likely involves your statement earlier of calming them down somehow. I guess they don't like the idea of using this to quiet their grousing."

"And again, so typical. This also tells us where they went after walking out on you," he pauses in contemplation a moment. "Yes, law enforcers...pushing their values into places we don't otherwise desire them. But I wonder, if they went to them to report this, how does it relate to the original reason for the grousing?"

"I don't know. He didn't mention anything specific. In fact," he considers briefly. "His mention was offhanded, as a passing remark, only the elixir, and nothing else. He suggested that on his arrival tomorrow, I should explain why I was ready to give it to them for any reason. That, along with the priests and the device."

"All right, perhaps this holds some meaning, a form of imprecise knowing, and this unknowing can serve as cover for us until we finish with that man. Anyway, as for me, I'm just a governor, again following a process. Whoever that first one was, and whatever his motives, we're all human here, and this was four hundred years ago."

"Yes, I suppose, but in the modern day…"

"In the modern day, all manner of things could be possible, if you have the right, or perhaps the wrong people in certain positions, like those priests and whatever it was they were doing. After all, can anyone around here actually prove it was me instructing them to do this?"

"I, well…"

"If those priests did anything unpleasant, it was clearly a clandestine effort, maybe established by that first man and kept hidden during all this time."

"Yes, I suppose we could say that. But I should also inform you they looked at my shoulder and saw the mark from mine."

"They did? Well, I suppose this might be expected, if they are checking so many things. But let's say, oh…one day you felt a lump and went to a local surgeon to investigate, and he pulled out a strange foreign object from you, which he thought might have been lodged in there due to some accident or injury you received in your youth. That should be a handy one!"

"Yes! I like that one."

"As for the orcs, unless he has something that explicitly points at me owning them…" he chuckles coarsely. "He is simply grabbing at straws. And the simple fact that I might not want to fight is merely due to our unfortunate supply shortages, with or without his offerings of orcish rubbish, as our military might require something special to go up against all that. And how much of that rubbish was going to our military out there, hmm?"

"I, uh, don't know precisely, but I can certainly see your point."

"Right. And four hundred years can also cloud one's opinion of a success factor in the face of an unknown quantity."

"Oh, absolutely!"

"And if he doesn't like all the stories going around, I heard words outside they were being described as folktales, and I can't be held responsible for folktales."

"Of course, my Lord. Um, what about that mention of the name Sargeras everywhere?"

"I suppose that largely depends on how you define everywhere. If we say those orcs are following him, clearly, he will represent a potent image, and those orcs, being who they are, might see this as a god figure. Do you think?"

"Oh, from what I've heard, that does sound reasonable."

"And if he heard it anywhere else...well, those Daanen-Aryku might be a problem. They would also know the name. If memory serves, they were on that same world with the orcs for a while. Then again, knowing him, he might also learn of the name in relation to the Suuden-Aryku, maybe even those Flame Elves, since they all joined together at one time. This might be that everywhere, the union they share."

"Possibly."

"But you said he was mostly focused on the orcs? Well, my contacts say he hasn't moved in any other direction, so perhaps..." he pauses in consideration. "Anyway, if those priests are gone now, it would seem that part of it should be resolved, as they are the only ones to be found guilty of anything."

"Very good, my Lord. Let's hope we don't have any more surprises before the morrow, and he makes his personal appearance."

"Agreed. But you know, Dean, this is getting out of hand by now. We lost control of the Night Elves, and now we're losing control of the people here. This is going to take some serious action to correct."

"Yes, and especially with those priests over there describing all the lies and stories we've been telling. They're also emphasizing the four-century lack of anyone standing up to ask questions and demand corrective action for these...clearly evident...erroneous deeds. Like the plague, and those 'gods' our priests were praying to, and their clear lack of progress to solve the issue. This, in relation to that saying that goes around outside... For as long as anyone can remember..." he shrugs.

"Yes, perhaps this one has run its course by now. It would surely show up as a failing of some sort. This is just another example of the people coming out of their cages. So, whatever action we need to take, it must be carefully planned to correct these ambitions. I'll need to think about this. For now, go back to your office and try to find something for yourself until tomorrow. We'll work on the rest after that man is disposed of."

The Dean bows and leaves the office, then exits the building and returns to his own.

Leesa was again hiding in the closet as he made his exit. She picked up her shoes and tiptoed downstairs, glancing at her trans-com as she turned off the record mode. The video might only be that of a door, but the audio caught every word spoken on the other side of it.

The Governor sat down, trying to settle his own nerves from the conversation. He looked out the window again, but this time didn't care much for the view, so he reached up to close the curtains for a little privacy.

"Those accursed Estelar again," he mutters under his breath. "If those people over there have become so close, there is no point in trying anything else. Not without drawing them into play, and I can't afford that. I may need to pull back from this operation. Those insufferable orcs have brought back something I'm not prepared to deal with just yet. Not until the Agent is ready."

He reaches into the drawer for his trans-com and dials a number, then waits a moment.

"Commander Geilv, speaking…"

"Commander, we have a small problem developing here. Listen carefully. These invaders have apparently been divulging some critical details to the locals that might cause them to turn against us. We are essentially losing containment here, and the results may be irreversible, if only due to the relationship they have on that world of theirs with our larger opponents."

"Larger opponents? Are we speaking of Thaelyn?"

"No, Commander. In this case, I'm speaking about THE larger opponents. I have just received word about this. Apparently, they hold a closer relationship than previously expected. And this is an engagement we are not ready for. Therefore, we may need to conduct a tactical retreat to preserve our resources until we are fully prepared."

"What form of retreat do you suggest?"

"At the present time, let us first see about our precious little elves. They're not serving any immediate purpose for us, and I don't want that man down there getting any wild ideas about them. I'll have you call in a couple of heavy troop carriers. Then arrange for personnel transports to ferry them up to the carriers. Contact the High Priestess and have her prepare her people for evacuation in the morning."

"Acknowledged. Do you require anything else?"

"For the moment, Commander, that should be all."

"Understood, Base Prime out..."

Priestess Sehnisavain was in her office in casual conversation with her daughters, her two deacons, and the two agents, Master Cydulean and Priest Sumisal.

"Our people have so much to recall after this horrid domination," she reflects. "Virtually none of them even recall our native tongue anymore."

"Priestess," Cydulean soothes. "I understand the suffering you must be feeling right now, and although I cannot suggest anything where your local history is concerned, I'll ask you to rest assured we will help you with as much as we can. We have education courses back home that we can offer, and in your case, I think our Lord would be more than happy to offer at least the language classes free of charge, simply to give back that one very intimate component of your heritage that was taken from you."

"I would be very grateful for that. And with the help Lady Aerlie has already offered to reacquaint our people with our old gods, this will go a long way as well."

"What sort of association would you offer us," Ilothonna asks. "Once all this is said and done."

"There are many possibilities in front of us," Sumisal suggests. "As you already know, the Night Elves rejoined our society to participate once again in the body of the Tel'Quessir. You would be welcome to do the same. It might seem a bit alien to you by this time, whether for the domination effect or simply your long absence. But to become a part of your ancestral heritage would be to return to your roots. And as elves, we all know the value this holds."

"Yes, I would agree, but before we could come to that, I think we would need to further educate our people of our heritage so they would understand this relationship."

A tonal ring emits from the trans-com on the desk. Sehnisavain had been expecting this call, but the sudden announcement still jolted her after the pleasant interlude.

"Here we go," Kerali submits warily. "This is Number Two."

Sehnisavain nods and picks up the unit. She takes a deep breath to compose herself and places herself into the mindset of her new role. She answers the call.

"Hello?" she replies dreamily. "Who is this?"

"This is Commander Geilv. I am calling to follow up on yesterday and your apparent lapse. Also, I have instructions for you."

"Commander…ah, so wonderful for you to call…"

Sehnisavain harmonizes her voice in a fluid rolling, as though she was experiencing a euphoric hallucination.

"Yes, all is certainly well for us here. The songs are so soothing."

"Songs… High Priestess, are you well?"

"Oh, Commander, I feel so alive, more than I can recall since… Oh, for as long since…before it was taken from us. Such a sad day that was."

"Taken? What was taken?"

"The source, Commander," she sings. "That which fills us with the spiritual harmony of the world. We became lost, but now we are found again. The songs are revealing to us our true nature as a people."

"You are behaving strangely. Do you require assistance?"

"No, Commander, we could not be happier. We feel so free again."

"Your statements are strange, but if you are content that you are not in danger, then I have instructions for you."

"Ah, Commander, do you have something pleasant to share with us?"

"Affirmative. The Marshal requires you to assemble your people for evacuation. We will be sending transports beginning tomorrow morning to relocate you to a secure facility."

"How wonderful!" she elates. "And maybe we can also share our delightful spiritual revelry with you and your people, where we can join hand-in-hand with song and dance, in the traditions of our ancestors."

"Eh, I do not sing or dance. But I will certainly require a medical examination of you when you arrive."

"Fabulous, Commander, and do make sure you call in the morning to inform us when the transports are on their way. We wouldn't want to leave anyone behind!"

"Acknowledged, Base Prime out…"

The link terminates and Sehnisavain grins broadly for her performance. Both Tyshalis and Rhyvanith break out giggling at the preposterous conversation just played out, and the rest smile in agreement of a job well done.

"Does he have anything special to say?" Sumisal asks.

"Other than he thinks I'm going crazy and need medical help?" she smiles. "Yes, they're sending transports in the morning to evacuate us."

"So, they're evacuating you, are they?" Cydulean wonders.

"I'll bet this is in response to our people up in Rolsklinde," Sumisal adds.

"He's losing containment of the others and wants to preserve whatever he's got left. He's withdrawing."

"Did you see him this morning?" Tristeen whispers. "I think that was the best one yet."

"I was across the way from you, on the other side of the pews," Jared affirms. "I'll admit, I was never much of a temple-goer, but this new religion sounds right dandy. It doesn't make you grovel on your knees, like the old one did, but instead it encourages you to stand up and be recognized."

"These people seem to know their gods in ways most of us couldn't dream of," Willit offers. "When I was studying with them on Tae'Eladar, I paid a small visit to Lady Aerlie in the temple for a few pointers, and that place is a masterful work, just for the architecture, to say nothing of how many gods they support in it. Every race is represented for their own pantheon."

Tristeen was in a meeting with her two cohorts at their favorite table in the Ten Eagles. They had just recently returned there after spending time up in the temple to review the new service by the priests.

"Willit," Tristeen wonders. "What do you know of these Estelar? Did you learn anything while you were there?"

"They're an ancient society, or rather a collection of societies gathered up from all across Creation. It's said they've made it to the highest point of development, above all others, and the rest of us are described as Children under them. Now they spend much of their time governing the realms and watching over us, and occasionally giving advice to a few here and there. The people of Tae'Eladar are something of an exception to the rule for their closeness."

"Why is that?"

"I was wondering about this as well since it almost demanded me to ask about it. Tae'Eladar is in another universe, it seems. It's a bit like to say these Suuden-Aryku also come from another universe."

"Um, wait, what do you mean by universe? This isn't something they teach us in school around here," she smiles.

"Right..." he chuckles. "Look up in the nighttime sky and what do you see? You see a lot of stars. Well, apparently each of those stars is a sun, maybe a bit like ours, but at great distance. And there are more than you could ever possibly count out there, most of which are simply too far to see. All that space is a universe. Think of a big bubble, with all of this inside. We live in this one, the Suuden-Aryku come from a completely different one, and Tae'Eladar is in yet another. However, here's the difference."

He clears his throat for emphasis to break his statements.

"They don't have any stars in their sky. So, naturally, I asked about this. In their nighttime sky, it's a huge cloudlike thing in a myriad of colors, like those of a rainbow, but all twisted up. They call this the Ethereal Maelstrom. This is their universe…or what's left of it. They presumably had stars once upon a time, but then there was a war, known to them as the Celestial War. This is where these Estelar came in and found a local group of gods that weren't behaving nice with the little folk. They demanded them to conform to their principles of rule, but these others refused, and instead a battle broke out. These others are sore losers, so it seems, and they used some kind of weapon that literally destroyed the entire flippin' universe."

"Gracious!" she gasps.

"These Estelar apparently tried to save what they could out of it, and this means Tae'Eladar. It's a survivor, but it's likely one of the very few that still exists over there."

"And so, by merit of this condition of it being a survivor, they hold a closer relationship?"

"It would seem they do, and for a few reasons, with isolation being one of them. These Estelar believe the younger races need to grow and develop on their own, each with their unique qualities, rather than have someone come in and direct them to one thing or another. But in this case, being isolated as they are, the people of Tae'Eladar made a special pact to bring them a bit closer to their gods. Ordinarily, the Estelar wouldn't do this with such a young race, because it could affect how they might develop, as well as others this young society might deal with later, like those in near proximity in that universe. But being so isolated, this can contain the effect somewhat. So, the people of Tae'Eladar took special lessons, and now they can go out and help others while still following these same rules."

"So, they're working as a kind of extension of the arm for the Estelar. That must be a fascinating role to play."

"Aye! And being so close, with such big friends behind them, and a few in particular in the right places, you can learn a lot. Lord Thaelyn brought the whole world together under his rule, and he taught them about these Estelar, whereas before they were probably a lot like us, and how we might see the gods. Now, they move forward together with new ideas and new inspiration."

"But how does this relate to that captain and what he was saying?"

"I wasn't here when he was visiting, but if I were you, I'd probably listen up close. He was out there dropping clues they'll bring together later."

"Uh oh…and some of those were big clues…a little crazy, if to think about it, but still…"

"Maybe so, but they're getting some new ideas down there of how to finish this up. Also about who the Governor really is, but I think I should keep that part quiet so far. It's simply nasty. And now, they need to lay down the groundwork."

"All right. But you know," she muses dreamily. "I wonder what it might be like to live in a world like that."

"From what I've seen, they have a lot of fine qualities to their credit. Many different races all behaving like one big family, with virtually no crime, and everybody is very highly educated…and I'm talking bloody high head-splitting education!" he chuckles.

"How do they manage that, a lot of schools?"

"It's not just the schools, Tristeen. It's how they teach. I visited their academy once to check the mage studies. They can teach you how to turn the world inside-out, depending on how much you need for the job you have in mind, as well as everything else you can possibly think of to study in any school, multiplied several times over, and do it in less time than I'll bet you've spent in the academy here learning no more than how to stir a fresh brew in a beaker."

Tristeen gaped at the suggestion. She turned her gaze at Jared, who was similarly amazed.

"Willit," Jared submits. "How can you possibly learn all that even in a lifetime, to say nothing of the time we spent licking the Dean's shoes?"

"It's all in a special elixir, my friend," he admits. "I had to spend a few moments on this, simply to catch the full meaning of it. Apparently, some number of centuries ago, they found this formula for something called the Elixir of Visions. And bloody hell, if you ever, in all your flippin' life, wanted to learn anything about anything, this will dump it inside your head so bleedin' fast, you won't know what hit you until after you wake up with more academics to your name than the full spelling of it."

"But how does it actually work?" Tristeen whispers.

"All I can say is it speeds up your ability to learn, so they can throw a whole library of books at you, and you simply absorb each one."

"Incredible. I'd certainly like to take a look at that."

"Well, this will have to wait for now," Jared accedes. "So far, we need to figure what comes next with our own troubles. That Lord Thaelyn is supposed to be arriving tomorrow sometime, but do we know when?"

"My word is mid to late morning," Willit responds. "He's trying to time it with a little surprise he's playing with the Flame Elves down south. The two are supposed to throw a hard hit at the Governor for all his hidden dealings."

"What about that conjuring? Does he have any plans for that? The Dean was drawing up a really tight circle if you recall."

"Aye, he knows this, and I'm sure he'll play into it for a good show. He wants to make his own special appearance to let these people know he's not your average man who simply dresses up nice."

"I want to see this," Tristeen admits.

"It might not be smart to get too close, Tristeen," Jared suggests. "If the Dean calls up something really big, and it gets loose and starts wrecking the place..."

"I know, but I think I still need to be there to see it. And, if you're really so concerned about my safety, I know you'll be right there at my side," she smiles cutely.

"Oh bloody hell, Jared," Willit moans. "You stepped right in the middle of that one."

"Yeah," he relents. "And she's not one to let something like that slip by. I should've known better."

"All right, the three of us will go watch, but we need to keep back, just in case."

"We can camp out in the park across the way," Tristeen offers. "That's where I've been hiding these past several days. It gives a good view, and if things go bad, we can duck behind the barracks and run."

✦✦✦✦✦

"According to the report from Master Dastien," the General recounts. "The Dean's visitation this morning went forward generally as expected. Our people revealed their message in a well-played sequence that led him through a series of steps until he finally realized who they were and ran out of the building screaming," he chuckles.

"Sounds like fun," Marelle grins.

"Naturally, he went to the Governor, and according to the recording Leesa made of their conversation inside his office, the Governor seemed disturbed at the mention of the Estelar, but otherwise undaunted by our various investigations. They are now inventing a series of excuses to cover for themselves in case anyone comes asking questions."

"So…" Thaelyn surmises. "We will need to combat this to the point of refuting their validity. Either that, or as they did up there, simply exert our demands that their war spilled into our holdings, and therefore, we are taking whatever initiative is necessary to oppose whatever villains cross our paths in the service of those people who are made victims."

"Jiggers," Relissa winces. "Aye, but that's a hard line to take with peeps who don't otherwise cooperate."

"Perhaps, but the rules of war must apply here, and this will rise above any of their local laws. However, along the way, we will likely need to pull a few more of our own secrets out of the bag. Very well, this much is doable."

"What about the, ahem…Flame Elves," Marelle asks.

"The Priestess has made her second play. The Governor apparently made a call to the High Commander to have them evacuated. They are planning on pulling them out tomorrow morning, which works nicely with our own plans. The Priestess played her role as someone who is experiencing a type of delirium based on what we will describe as her true god rediscovering her people. My role will need to play into this, and timing may be an important factor to have our side ready before the High Commander reports the apparent disappearance of the people of Kynesoth. I need to plant a seed of our own conspiracy in the Governor's mind, and that seed must motivate him to seek an escape."

"We should organize our own evacuation of the elves for this eve," the General suggests. "We can send a number of mages to create a way-line directly back to B.T., maybe in the training fields just outside the guildhall. Then call the people to attention and pull them out."

"Good, make it so, General, and make sure you have them go door-to-door, if necessary, to collect all of them. We will have Priestess Sehnisavain and her people oversee the operation on both sides."

"But now, as to this movement he is ordering," he considers. "This already suggests a motivation to withdraw. Leesa's recording hinted that he regards the Night Elves as lost already, and with the local people becoming aware of all the fabrications he worked so hard on, he is taking the same position with them as well. I even heard words of how this will require a serious effort on his part to reverse."

"And no doubt, this reflects on that turning point we spoke of once."

"Uh oh…" Marelle groans. "But how do we interpret this?"

"Initially," Thaelyn muses. "This represents the typical mind of a Primordial and his ilk. Simply look at the rest of this world. If he actually cared for anything, he would not have devastated it. The stories tell us they held no true respect for life unless it served a purpose, like entertainment, or in his case, utility. And so, we might have ourselves a potential dilemma that we need to consider carefully. What might he do to these people if he feels himself losing control and therefore must pull back? In the tradition of someone who seems to enjoy destroying whole worlds in order to simplify his management practice, I hesitate to think of what he might have in mind for those who are so close to disobeying him. Just look at those students and his solution to that."

"Oh bloody hell, Your Lordship," Marelle groans. "And there's nothing we can do about it?"

"I will not permit him any more of his wanton destruction if it is within my power to do so. But at the same time, we might need to make a sacrifice, if only to preserve lives and cause him to leave without resulting in even greater loss. We need to remember that military body out there. I want all of them to depart as cleanly as possible. But 'clean' in this case must first consider lives, as property can be replaced."

"Like the city? Are we speaking only of Rolsklinde, or everything?"

"Buggers to that!" Relissa yelps. "My Lord, we need to safeguard ourselves a wee bit, don't you think?"

"If he were a common man," he considers. "We might hold an advantage. But as a servant being to Sargeras, this carries its own burden. If he regards the younger races so trivially, he will not simply allow them to better him. But we do have one special card to play, and this again revolves around the Estelar."

He leans back as he ponders his thoughts.

"First, we need to prepare ourselves to counter his actions in some fashion. The difficulty here is to understand what actions he might use on this occasion. Would he use his Suuden-Aryku military to attack from the land or air, or instead use bombardment tactics? Would he limit himself only to Rolsklinde, or include Solinaia as well? I already have in mind something for the Night Elves, as part of our play for Kynesoth, so this may offer us a solution on that side. But there is a distinct difference between your people and hers," he gestures mildly at Marelle while glancing at Relissa. "And this is that soft underbelly again."

"We're not as closely associated to the Estelar as yet," Marelle moans. "Right, I get it."

"The Night Elves kept their religion during this time, so we can use this, perhaps even to exaggerate it by saying with my help, they have grown even closer. This would allow us to suggest they hold such a deep devotion by now, especially after their reunion with Tae'Eladar, that those same gods are now watching them rather closely. We can even place emphasis on this after our recent events, suggesting Sargeras has essentially violated their sanctity here."

"Wow," Relissa muses. "If I said buggers before, that's an even bigger bugger," she snickers.

"Indeed, and if this holds any meaning to him, he will likely consider any direct action on your home will result in repercussions of the divine sort. However, Rolsklinde is another matter. Those people are only now reconnecting with their gods. The link may not be as profound for them to call the eyes of their gods upon the city to watch over it, and so he might consider it a risk worthy of taking if he is already on his way out."

"Oh, great..." Marelle moans and slumps to the table.

"Marelle, I fully understand and sympathize, and I will offer my help to restore what is lost. Cities can be rebuilt, so our greatest concern must be the people. We have a couple of potential options, but I must think ahead on these matters beyond what is immediately within our sight."

"Yeah, you tend to do that a lot. So, what do you see this time?"

"Do you recall once when I was teaching Kaliya about the butterfly effect? Well, here is one occasion to use it. These are lessons we learn from our Celestial origins. They teach us to see the future permutations based on what might be a series of progressive actions and their potential consequences, and often on a higher scale than what many mortal societies tend to consider."

"Right, I get it."

"Let us say I call in a little of my own divine might. I could surely call on Lord Torm, or any of the other Estelar, perhaps even a few seraphim to aid me in destroying Marshal Darumon immediately. This would remove his threat potential for this world and anything else he has in mind out there. However, here we have one immediate complication, and that is the Suuden-Aryku High Commander. So far, Darumon is controlling him, but without that control, he becomes a loose cannon."

"Right, and I recall our mention of that a while back."

"If we listen to Med-tech Tad'vaal, she suggested they have these neural implants that might control their behavior. Given that the Suuden-Aryku are not normally a militaristic society, I must therefore assume this effectively alters them to perform as the Marshal desires, meaning to say they do as he tells them…much like everyone else around here is expected to behave."

"Exactly, and if the Marshal is the one giving the orders, without those orders, the High Commander takes on his own initiative, and who knows what that means."

"I can tell you what it could mean," Padriyl offers. "As a society that doesn't hold any religious beliefs, they wouldn't have a clue about the power of a true god. Even I, who's been sitting here and learning so much, can barely answer that one," he chuckles.

"Aye!" Relissa grins. "Just look at that pile of horns sitting next to you!"

"Right! And even worse, if you were to bring one down in front of him, he probably wouldn't know what he's looking at until after he's sent up to meet one in person."

"That sounds really dangerous," Marelle relents. "For him, at least…"

"Indeed!" Thaelyn asserts. "And so we might have the High Commander destroying everything that remains in this world, at least until I call on the Estelar to help, and then he and his would be smitten to ashes. But this is a high price to pay for the simple interpretation, assuming the High Commander does actually come to the interpretation. Further, if he is under some form of artificial control, he might simply call in the remainder of their military, sacrificing everything he owns indiscriminately until his entire society is spent."

"Ouch! That's really bad!"

"I might also suggest Sargeras himself could get involved. If he were to lose his most faithful servant, who may be his only lifeline in that barren fold, he could take his own action, if only for his simple survival, and this could result in any number of repercussions, most of which are unfavorable. For instance, in a barren fold, he would need some manner of support, even empowerment, and a being of this sort could very literally yank it out of any lifeform within reach, including the full Suuden'kai population, leaving a dead world behind him."

"Oh, no!" Padriyl winces. "I may not hold any special love for them, not after all they did to us, but I think I wouldn't want anything like that."

"Indeed. Therefore, our only reasonable choice is to permit the Marshal to live, at least for now, until we can bring this under our control and find a better solution to it. If we can chase him away, we can pursue him on our own terms, and then see about resolving some of these other issues as the opportunities present themselves."

"But how do you suggest pursuing him?" he wonders. "Especially if we don't have any space capability."

"This is one question I cannot answer at this time. But if my expectations of Kaliya hold any value, this might offer us a step forward with some as yet unknown potential. It is all we have that I can be sure of, as I find it highly unlikely the Marshal will permit us to simply follow him in a more conventional manner."

"All right," Marelle continues. "So, we may have to sacrifice our city in the process, but we might ultimately save the lives of a lot of people, including the Suuden-Aryku."

"And this brings us back to how the Marshal might proceed once he makes his decision to depart. If he takes such offence over the people demonstrating their free will, he might wish to appease his sense of pleasure at seeing their lives made forfeit. This actually follows in the same trend as that elixir he was hoping to feed the academy students."

"My Lord," Relissa wonders. "What was that about, by the way?"

Thaelyn defers to Padriyl for the explanation.

"According to Med-tech Tad'vaal," Padriyl recalls. "The medical archives recognized it as a medical treatment for a rare lung disorder. This might seem strange on the surface, until you consider this is for our people, not humans. If given to them, and especially in the dosage those vials contained, it would cause a catastrophic collapse of the lungs, suffocating them in what she describes as a rather arduous and painful death."

"Jiggers, and to think he would actually come up with such a thing."

"Likely, he chose this for the effect, if we look back on that rogue attack out by the Naarg uy'Sodrad and his reasons for that."

"So, what are your thoughts on all this?" Marelle asks. "He might want to destroy the city, but how do we know what to look for?"

Thaelyn sighs as he considers the situation.

"My first concern," he muses, "and perhaps the most immediate, is in his basement."

"His basement?"

"Yes, that odd door down there that may lead to a fusion reactor."

"All right, wait a minute. Explain to me how this is important. Because this is Suuden'kai technology, right?"

"Lieutenant?" he again redirects to the Daanen'kai officer. "Perhaps you would care to indulge the young lady?"

"Right," Padriyl responds with a sigh. "Marelle, and everyone else, this could pose a very real and imminent danger to the city, or at least some portion of it, depending on the size and how it's configured. If he can set it to go critical, which means to become unstable, it could blow up."

"And what will that do to the city?" Marelle asks tenuously.

"Blow it up."

"Blow up the whole flippin' city?!" she yelps.

"Keeping in mind, this depends on a few factors. First, how big the reactor is. If it's a compact form, for instance, something only large enough to power the conveyor, it might not be very powerful. The explosion, in this case, could be limited to only half the city."

"Oh grand! Only half the city," she elates sarcastically. "That makes me feel so much better!"

"Right, I understand. This also depends on the fail-safes built into it, and if any of those can be disabled at all."

"Fail-safes…"

"Devices that are built into such things as these to prevent them from blowing up. If he can disable them, or somehow cause them to fail, he could do this. But here we have an unknown factor. Can he do this locally, or would he need to apply an override from another location?"

"Another location, like with the Suuden-Aryku?"

"Right. At one time, we were wondering if they could be managing this thing remotely. If so, the local consoles may be largely automated with comparatively little override authority. If this is the case, he might just ignore it altogether, go back to his base and give the order from there. Otherwise, if they can disable those fail-safes for him, he might set something to overload and then leave."

"And this might afford us a small amount of time," Thaelyn offers. "We would need to get inside there and somehow disable their command linkage. But for this, we need the access code to that lock, or else a means to break through it."

"A pulse rifle might do the trick if we're careful. The Suuden'kai design has a tendency to blow holes in things."

"All right, have one brought to us, maybe also a cutting torch, if we need to be more precise. And I will assign you to this task, as you would hold the best training for this regard. We also need someone who is trained in these reactors to quickly decipher the technical design and find a shutdown switch."

"Every reactor design we ever built has a scram switch on it. It's designed to be easy to locate and use in case of an emergency. I should be able to handle that, as well."

"Good, then this should cover us on that side. The only other concern would be any military action they might take, and for this, I think it would be prudent to call in a large number of shield mages. We may need to evacuate the city, so we will need those, along with mages and portal runes."

"I would suggest we send a few more scouts to observe the Suuden-Aryku," the General offers. "They have those forward staging posts near the Daanen-Aryku. They represent the most immediate threat potential."

"Agreed," Thaelyn nods. "We already have a line of observation posts along the eastern ridgeline, so let us involve a few more in sight of those staging posts. Equip everyone with trans-coms, so they can report back to us immediately if they see anything."

"What about those dwarves?" Relissa wonders. "Should we ask what he might do to them?"

"They should not be a concern at this time. He controls them with this drug effect, so they should not pose any sort of trouble for him. His primary concern would be those who are defying him. If he holds any designs on the dwarves, he might simply wish to relocate them to another area, or he might abandon them altogether. In either case, we will wait until he makes his next move, and see if we can acquire them for ourselves afterwards."

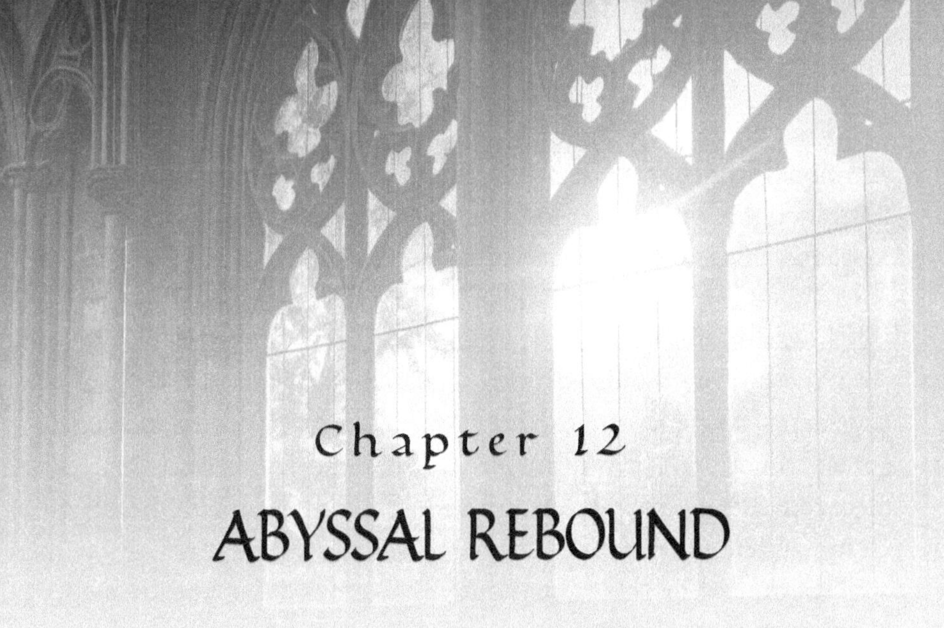

Chapter 12

ABYSSAL REBOUND

Throughout the evening and late into the night, the city of Kynesoth was busier than usual. Sehnisavain and her two deacons had been sending guard patrols into every neighborhood, calling out the citizens for a citywide evacuation.

Master Cydulean and Priest Sumisal oversaw the process with a group of mages opening portals in front of the temple. These led to a large practice field near the guildhall in Bya'an Tamoranth on Tae'Eladar. But this was simply the first waypoint. From there, Tyshalis and Rhyvanith coordinated with a group of Night Elves and local guardsmen to direct the flow further along to a tent city that had been erected just on the edge of town. This would serve as temporary accommodation for the High Elves until the situation stabilized back home.

Dawn was breaking on the horizon, and Sehnisavain, along with Ilothonna and Kerali, were the only remaining citizens still in their home city. Master Cydulean and Priest Sumisal accompanied them as they watched the sun coming up in the morning sky.

"All right, here is the deal," Cydulean begins. "Kerali will answer the trans-com this time, suggesting both Sehnisavain and Ilothonna have, and I quote, gone to meet their gods. She will also feel this delirium, and at this moment, it's becoming critical. After a few additional words, she'll run off, leaving the trans-com on the table for the High Commander to listen to her voice echoing behind her."

"And this is when the last of us leave," Kerali affirms.

"Right. But in our case, we will go directly to the camp up north. His Lordship might need our attendance later."

"And so, the Suuden-Aryku send their transports," Ilothonna considers. "Which brings them to our otherwise closed and locked gates. They find a way inside and conduct their own search, discovering the city to be abandoned. This goes back to the High Commander, which eventually goes back to the Marshal."

"Right, and by this time, hopefully our Lord has already made his play up north, leaving a nice little clue in the mind of the Dean and the Governor on what is happening out here."

"I wonder what sort of reaction he'll have to it," Sehnisavain muses. "Considering his obnoxious attitude, I'm sure it would be a remarkable one."

⁑⁂⁑

"My Lord," the General announces. "We have your, ahem, elite guard assembled and ready. It is surely a sight befitting of a King… if I may say so," he grins.

Thaelyn and the General were once again in the tactical office, this time awaiting word from Kynesoth on the events down there before taking their own action. Relissa and her group were given the day off from their classes in order to fulfill a promise to allow them to watch the events in Rolsklinde. Padriyl would accompany them, and he also requisitioned a small video camera to record the occasion. Aerlie would also attend, in part to offer her support, as well as her portion of the demonstration in the eyes of those who would be watching.

"I'm a mite nervous about this," Relissa admits. "Even with your elites out there…"

Thaelyn smiles as he steps around to the door to look outside at the gathering of soldiers.

A group of uniquely clad people had gathered into a huddle in the center of the settlement. They were unlike most of the other visitors that may pass through the little village, and represented a full squad of troops, consisting of a mix of elements.

Among them were four in full plate armor, glimmering as with the finest of materials. These were paladins, who accounted amongst the finest of knights and were dedicated as priests to their chosen god. These were not simple warriors, as they also carried divine power within their ranks. Then there was a pair of master archers equipped with enchanted bows. They didn't need traditional arrows, as the bows used elemental ammunition conjured on demand. Following this was a pair of mage Elders, the highest ranking within the Art. Lastly was a pair of prelates, whose divine association could call upon the seraphim themselves, if need be. Also among the group, in addition to those who would serve as the combatants, were a half dozen shield mages to create a defensive wall in front of the weaker elements.

A squadron of gryphons was also being prepared to carry them, where Thaelyn and Aerlie would ride the lead, the paladins would each ride behind gryphon drivers, and the shield mages would carry the rest, for a total of eleven gryphons.

Thaelyn returned inside the office to finish the meeting and wait for the call from Kynesoth. This would serve as their trigger to launch.

Tristeen, Jared, and Willit had assembled on a bench in the park, where they waited for the action. The plaza was just stirring to life as the morning brought the people out to conduct their daily chores and errands.

The Dean had his lead instructors review the conjuration procedures one last time in the basement of the academy in preparation for their act later in the day. Everything was waiting for the appearance of Thaelyn in the city center.

The Governor relaxed in his office, gazing out the window, hoping to catch first sight of Thaelyn as he came along the avenues in what he expected to be a fashionable carriage, as would be typical of such a man.

The morning was progressing when a tonal ring came out from the trans-com on Sehnisavain's desk. She directed Kerali to pick it up and answer it. The younger priestess now had to compose herself for her own performance, taking a deep breath, and touching the answer button on the display.

"Yes? I am here!" she exalts joyously.

"This is Commander Geilv. Who is this speaking?"

"Oh, how wonderful! Commander, we are so overjoyed. He's here at last!"

"Who is there? Are you under attack? Who are you?"

"Oh no, nothing like that. This is Kerali, Second Deacon to the High Priestess. He's here! Our Lord has come for us!"

"I do not understand. Where is the High Priestess?"

"Oh, she's already gone. He took her up, along with Ilothonna. They've joined with our Lord, the Protector! The gods of our ancestors have found us!"

"I… Wait, you say she has gone to meet with a god. Is this to say she is dead?"

"Dead?" she giggles. "Oh, don't be silly. We're all being taken up. Everyone! The Protector is calling on his Children and carrying us away from our sorrows."

"Who is this Protector?"

"He's the leader of the gods of our ancestors. We've been lost for so long, and finally he's come for us. Oh, wait. I see him!" she shouts. "I'm here!"

She drops the trans-com hard on the desk and starts moving away.

"Here I am! Take me, oh Lord. Bring me up!"

She starts out the door with her voice resounding through the halls. The Commander listened to the echoes on his side of the com-link until he resolved there would be no further communication, so he ended the link.

Within the Suuden-Aryku planetary command base, where Commander Geilv made his operations, he studied the communications station and its operator for a moment. The officer gazed at him curiously for the strange message they received.

"Contact our transport convoy," the Commander issues. "Have them make haste to their destination and investigate the situation. But tell them to approach with caution."

Master Cydulean and the others were content that they had done all they could for now, so he pulled out a rune and transported the group back to Firstfall. On their arrival, he reported in with Thaelyn.

"My Lord, it is done. The Commander has called in, Kerali gave her performance, and we believe he has his people on their way, likely by now in a hurried state to see what is occurring."

"Good, then we should not delay ourselves. General, send Relissa and the others up there to Master Dastien, and have him assist them in finding their places."

"Right away."

The General waves for Relissa, Marelle, and Padriyl to follow outside, where they met with a mage and a rune to an arrival location inside the temple. He sends them away to the city where Master Dastien greets them.

"Welcome, friends," he announces. "We are going to cast invisibility cloaks on you, and have you sneak over to the barracks where you will find shelter. This will keep you out of the eyes of anyone who might be observing the plaza. And I'm sure at least one or the other of the Governor and Dean will be watching today."

He begins casting the cloaks, and one by one the group moves outside and across the plaza, unseen by anyone watching.

Back in Firstfall, Thaelyn was assembling his troupe on their gryphons. He and Aerlie took the lead, and the team paraded out the north gate of the settlement. He takes the lancelike staff from its mounting on the side and raises it up to signal to the others, then calls to the animal to charge forward.

Each in turn now chases along in a fury of motion, like a stampede of determined predators, building up speed and flapping their wings to gain lift. They rise up in an arc above the local tree line and take up a V formation.

Thaelyn again raises his staff, and each of the drivers calls out their chants to link up with his lead control. Energy bolts spark between their staffs, forming virtual towlines with his. They collectively set their staffs into the mounting hooks on the gryphon collars and Thaelyn now calls a new chant to engage their transport spheres. The assembly becomes instantly shrouded in energy bubbles, and they all rocket away at supersonic speed.

The travel time to the city was negligible, but this was not the issue. It was the demonstration of their arrival that counted. They came into view of Rolsklinde rather quickly at altitude, and Thaelyn carefully timed his exit from the spheres to occur over the city proper, causing the sonic thunderclap to echo down from directly above.

Tristeen and her friends jumped at the unexpected announcement. Hearing thunder wasn't as much a concern, but on a clear sunny day, it was something of a surprise. They instantly jerked their view to see what was occurring up there, only to find the sudden arrival of a number of otherworldly beasts.

"Gods above!" she gasps. "What are those things?"

"I don't know," Jared relents. "But I doubt they're gods of any kind."

"Those are gryphons, my friends," Willit affirms calmly. "And it doesn't actually surprise me that he would use them on this occasion."

"Why is that?" Tristeen wonders.

"Just for show, I suppose. If you really want to make an impression, do something no one would expect."

"But, dear gods, they can fly on that world of theirs?"

"It's a very curious place, Tristeen."

The Governor also jolted slightly at the sudden shockwave. He had been expecting ground transport of some kind. But when he saw them arriving by air, he was somewhat amused.

"How clever of them," he accedes. "It would seem that man has taught these people a few interesting tricks. But now what, he has an escort? Well, of course, I suppose I should've expected as much."

The Dean reacted much the same as the rest. He was studying a new stack of accounting papers when the booming rattled the window and seemingly the walls. He pulled up abruptly to examine the room, and then slowly turned to look outside, focusing on the plaza pavement below.

"I swear," he mumbles. "If those people are playing another of their tricks on us..."

He glances at the plaza, carefully surveying the grounds for any strange events. He didn't see any carriages or other new arrivals, and no one appeared to be conducting any sort of activity that might invoke a loud noise. But he did see a lot of people halting in their tracks and looking skyward, many of whom were pointing at something. This naturally caused him to follow their direction.

In the sky above the plaza, he saw a flock of overly large creatures with powerful legs and claws, birdlike heads, and huge wings. They were gliding along in a graceful descent, circling downward and angling along the main avenue leading into the plaza.

"Dear gods!" he shouts and pulls back. "Is that what he uses to travel about? Even without his portals, he would still be dangerous, if to bring those into play."

The gryphons made a determined descent into the city, lining up with the northbound avenue, and then veering around into the plaza, where they slowed themselves to settle for a landing. The people all shrieked and ran off in different directions to vacate the area, leaving the plaza mostly empty of foot traffic.

Tristeen gazed in awe at the obvious splendor of the beasts, but she quickly felt a note of trepidation flash into her as they landed and began moving in her direction.

"Um, should we move?" she hesitates.

The three friends move away from their bench as the first of the creatures arrives at the near side of the plaza, with the rest following close behind.

Thaelyn brings his convoy to a halt and detaches his harnessing.

Aerlie follows suit and they begin to dismount. The animals laid down to allow them easier access to the ground, but Aerlie uses her wings, as a common tradition in her case, to flap her way off the animal, while Thaelyn uses the little stepladder on the side to climb down.

"Who, and what, is that?" Tristeen whispers urgently to her friends.

"That's Lady Aerlie," Willit responds.

"Wait, I heard that name before. Who was she again?"

"His wife and Queen…"

"Her?" she gushes. "But she's completely different. You mean they actually do this on that world?"

"As I understand it, humans and elves sometimes mix it up, and you may want to mind yourself a bit. It's said she has extremely sharp hearing, and they both speak the language."

"Oops! Um, I'm sorry, I didn't mean anything bad. It's just a little surprising."

Aerlie was joining with Thaelyn and the others in front of the barracks. Of course, she could hear the voices, so she simply turned in Tristeen's direction, nodded and smiled politely.

The Governor glared at the procession as they made their way toward the barracks. He expected them to travel in that direction. After all, the note calling Thaelyn up here was presumably from Captain Kholgard. He then turned towards the academy.

"Dean," he murmurs. "I hope you are as attentive to this as you have been to all the other nonsense that has been occurring lately. I will be expecting a fine show to come about soon. Then finally we can find a few of our own solutions to this menace he created."

The Dean had already jumped out of his chair and gone downstairs. He called on his people, and together they convened in the basement.

Thaelyn and Aerlie were preparing to meet with Captain Kholgard in front of the barrack gates. The rest of the entourage was lingering loosely in near proximity in the plaza. The gryphon drivers were leading the animals into the park area to find shelter and to move them out of the way.

Tristeen and her friends felt an even deeper sense of uncertainty as the gryphons were being guided into place and settled down close by.

"Um, do any of those people speak our language?" she asks.

"Probably not," Willit responds. "Why? Do you want to go up and pet one of those things?" he grins mischievously.

Tristeen gawks at his display, and then glances back at the animals, which clearly seemed to be well-mannered.

"I suppose this is turnabout for me making you come up here to watch," she chuckles softly. "But is it actually possible?"

"Well, they use them like we use horses, if you don't count the claws and beaks that could probably rip you in half," he smiles.

"Oh, wow, Willit, you're so comforting."

She edges closer to the animals, and tries waving to attract the attention of one of the drivers. The man looks up at her and nods, then waves the group over.

Tristeen and the others creep up slowly, and carefully lay a hand on one of the gryphon's shoulders. The creature seemed to respond favorably to the attention, cooing to the visitors as it surveyed the scene and the other people coming out of hiding around the plaza.

"Feel this," she mutters as she strokes the animal's shoulder. "That's solid muscle under there."

"Aye," Jared affirms. "That's a good solid piece of meat. I think ripping you in half would be the least of your worries."

"Jared, you're not helping. But all things considered, they seem very gentle."

Captain Kholgard was emerging from his office to meet with his visitors. Marelle and Relissa were lurking just behind the wall and came into view to wave hello, along with Padriyl who was keeping discreetly behind the others with his video camera.

"Your Lordship," the Captain announces. "I would like to say welcome to the city, but the Lieutenant tells me this isn't such a fine day for it."

"Indeed," he nods. "But we must still play our roles, Captain, so let us pose like we are having a pleasant conversation. Should I reacquaint you with my wife, Aerlie," he gestures politely at her. "And a number of what we shall describe as my elite guard."

"An elite guard?" he muses. "So, do we have any idea what that porker has up his sleeve today?"

"Based on the descriptions we have from our spies; he was drawing up a very elaborate conjuring circle in his basement. This suggests to me he is hoping to bring forth a rather potent creature, although the precise sort is uncertain so far. For all that he purports of himself, I must question his integrity, and not simply that of his mental stability, but also his prowess to actually work any significant amount of magic at all."

"Mental stability," he chuckles. "That much I'm certain he's falling short of. As for the rest, I don't claim to know anything about magic, and personally, based on our history with those wizards, I don't care much for it."

"The utility value is actually very evident, if only to use it responsibly. We teach our full citizenry these skills, and it has greatly improved our way of life back home."

"Really! Well, I'm just an old soldier, so don't pay much mind to my groaning. I'm happy enough to see all the help you've given us, and I hope one day we can get rid of those two so we can find something new for ourselves."

"Indeed, Captain, these are my thoughts as well. But unfortunately, I believe your governor is one who might not care to go so quietly into the night. Therefore, we must be ready to take some extreme measures to preserve the lives of these people."

"Why is that? You think he might call on his friends out there after all?"

"I am certainly of the opinion that he will not go down without a final word or two. So I will ask you to keep your wits…" his voice cuts off as he senses something.

Aerlie felt it as well, and the two of them appeared to drift off suddenly.

"Buggers, three times over!" Relissa whispers harshly. "It's coming."

Aerlie turns to her husband.

"Thaelyn, that's a strong one."

"Indeed, Negative Chaotic, a big one...a greater tanar'ri, how quaint. Perhaps he does know a thing or two about conjuring. But his ambition is no consolation for his ability to contain it."

"Well, if you recall, containment wasn't his priority."

"Oh, yes, of course, how could I forget that..." he shakes his head ironically. "Captain, get your people behind these walls and stay there."

The Captain orders his guard members to take up within the safety of the barracks while Thaelyn and Aerlie both turn to their troop contingent.

Tristeen and the others were watching intently, and when they saw the sudden shift in posturing, she had to wonder what was happening.

"Willit, you said she can hear really well. Does this mean she hears something? Because I don't hear a thing so far."

"I saw both of them reacting to something," Jared offers. "This must go a bit beyond simple hearing."

"How can you react to something if it's not even in the local area, not in sight or sound?"

"These two are special," Willit offers. "They have some special senses, but that's all I can say."

Padriyl was hiding behind the wall with his arm reaching around holding the video camera. Marelle and Relissa were cowering under him and peeking into the plaza.

"Aerlie," Thaelyn inquires. "What do you hear so far?"

"Crashing sounds, like something big is trying to free itself from the confines of that building over there."

"Yes, I suppose so. The Dean will have himself a fair amount of repair work ahead of him before this is done."

The Governor watched the scene from his window. He could see them turning away from the Captain, and apparently looking in the direction of the academy.

"What are you looking at?" he wonders quietly. "Do you hear something? I should think you are too far for your little ears to hear it yet, but you seem to be aware of it."

He continued to watch, and he opened the window slightly to listen in as well. He could just make out the sounds from within the academy building.

A quick knocking came at his door and the Dean nervously stepped inside, closing the door solidly behind him.

"Gracious, that thing is big!" he wheezes.

"It would seem you managed to escape from it, however," the Governor replies. "Very good. Now, let us sit and watch the show."

Tristeen and the others were huddling near the gryphons, feeling a gentle sense of comfort taking shelter by their side. By this time, they could also hear noises.

"Do you hear that?" she utters anxiously. "It sounds like something is tearing the place apart in there."

"Aye," Jared agrees. "Not that it matters to me by now. I don't go there anymore."

"Yeah, but that's not really my point. It's that…"

At this time, the front doors of the academy burst open, shattering into splinters, and spraying debris out into the plaza.

The people who had been gathering around to observe the strange visitors all turned abruptly to find a monstrous creature emerging from the building. Panic ensued as they screamed and ran off in all directions.

"Bloody hell!" Jared shouts urgently. "If I ever thought the Dean was mad before, I didn't know the half of it!"

The gryphons instantly took notice of the disturbance and sensed the great danger arriving in view. Those nearest to Tristeen and her group jerked to attention, and she could feel their muscles tensing up. One animal quickly responded to its training by taking a defensive posture in front of the group, calling out an alert to the others and bringing them into a cluster formation.

"What are these beasties doing?" Jared yelps.

Tristeen glanced around and made a hasty assessment.

"Keep your calm," she asserts sternly. "They're forming up around us, like a family group defending its young."

"Great gods! Now that's a defense I don't mind having around!"

Thaelyn and Aerlie both gazed at the creature coming into view. The guard troop also turned to see it, and instantly went to action, taking up a defensive stand.

"Shield mages forward!" Thaelyn commands. "Form up a wall. Support troops to the rear."

He quickly surveys the area and notices the trees in the park. They were old trees with several sturdy branches that appeared low enough to act as perches.

"Archers, take up in those trees and wait," he directs. "Mages and priests to the sides, warriors on the flanks…"

The troops quickly rushed into position. Tristeen and her group watched the activity and the professional direction of the soldiers. Then she saw the archers arriving in the park. She directed the others to watch.

The two archers pulled out something from slots on either side of their belts. These appeared to fit onto their hands, almost like gloves, but with spiked teeth in the palms. They used this to grip the nearby tree trunks and climbed nimbly to the first branches, where they perched themselves for a clear shot at the creature.

"I've never seen people do that before," she mutters. "Are those archers? They have bows on them."

"Aye," Jared admits. "Looks like it. They look a bit like elves too, but none I ever did see before."

"Those are called Wood Elves," Willit offers. "So, climbing trees is natural for them."

"Fine then," Tristeen accedes. "But now, look at that row of mages out in front."

The shield mages were busy conjuring up their projected defense, which resembled a tower shield by design, but was another example of their Infinity Shield being held in place as a portable wall. All six of them were lining up to create a defensive barrier. Tristeen and her friends gazed at it.

"Is that a magical shield of some kind?" she wonders.

"These people are a good bit more advanced than we are, Tristeen," Willit suggests. "That's the thing they've been using against the Suuden-Aryku, I think."

The paladins took up in pairs on either side of the barrier while the rest were stationed along the rear.

Relissa and Marelle peered around the barracks wall. Their eyes beheld a towering beast of gigantic proportions lumbering into the plaza. It held its bulk upright on two powerful legs that ended in claw-like feet. It had two pairs of arms, the lesser of which were muscular and terminated in hands, similar to humans, while the upper pair was huge and ended in large pinchers. Its head was shaped almost like that of an ape, but with a wolf-like muzzle, and sported two long black horns protruding out the top. It stood far above the height of a normal man, and more than twice that of Thaelyn. As it stepped across the plaza, the ground under it quaked.

"Did I say buggers?" Relissa barely squeaks out the words.

"Yes, you did," Marelle whispers painfully. "Times three..."

"Then I think I need a new word for this one."

Across the plaza, looking out the window of the Governor's Manor, the Governor and the Dean observed the sight outside.

"Anyway, my Lord," the Dean offers. "As you desired. My only real concern at this point is how we might dismiss it when it's done."

"Do not concern yourself with that for now. I have a few ideas."

The demon stood there in front of the academy a moment as it gained its bearings. It paused to gaze at all the little things scurrying around, then it took notice of the soldiers on the far side and turned to glare at them.

"Is this all they have for me?" it grumbles in a harsh and sinister language. "They promised me something special."

It begins to lumber forward.

"Wait... I smell goodness nearby."

Thaelyn stepped forward between the ranks of the shield mages, presenting himself in easy view of the creature. Tristeen watches him.

"Is he actually doing what I think he's doing?" she gasps.

Thaelyn gazes at the monster, and then suddenly a recollection stirs.

"Well, well… Who do we have here?" he mumbles to himself.

Aerlie notices his mention and steps up behind the mages.

"What do you mean?" she asks.

"I know him."

The demon focuses its attention along the direction of its senses, detecting the presence of something familiar.

"A Celestial!" it acknowledges in its native Abyssal tongue. "How nice. So, there is something worthy to fight after all."

He peers closer trying to identify his opponents.

"How curious. A hybrid pup? And what is this pet standing next to him? How delicious! Two for the price of one."

Thaelyn takes another step forward and calls out in a bold voice using the creature's native language.

"Navaatu! It has been a long while since our last meeting. How is that scar feeling today?"

The demon was curiously intrigued by the mention. It moves in closer for a better look. But as he gets within range and looks down into Thaelyn's face, he makes a shocking revelation.

"YOU!" it growls loudly. "I remember you! A thousand years have not dulled the memory of our last meeting…Thaelyn, Scion of Celestia!"

"Great gods!" Tristeen wheezes. "They can speak to each other?"

"Aye, and not just that," Willit responds tenderly. "But did I just hear it call his name?"

Tristeen stares at the man worriedly before returning to the scene in front.

The Dean and Governor both watched, and the Dean felt a soft shudder rush through him.

"Uh oh…" he whispers.

"Dean!" the Governor urges. "What am I hearing out there? Those two are communicating!"

"It would seem that way," he relents weakly. "And I also heard a word I would not normally expect to hear from him."

"Which one, that man's name? Even I can hear that much."

"Yes, then perhaps I should say two words, as Thaelyn also used the creature's name. This is the one we were researching for so long in order to call it up."

The Governor glared at him momentarily.

"Dean, I don't like the sound of that!"

"Neither do I. But maybe this is simply relating to his origins, for instance, if he is not native to Tae'Eladar. Maybe he simply brought some privileged knowledge with him."

"Knowledge is one thing; personal acquaintance is another completely."

The Dean could only gaze uneasily at the scene and shrug.

Navaatu glared at Thaelyn as the two stared down at each other.

"Indeed, you do recall me," Thaelyn affirms. "But in those thousand years, Navaatu, I have grown even more powerful. In addition, I have become King over the Prime domain of Tae'Eladar."

"And do you suggest this puny mortal flesh would be of any concern to me?"

"Come forward and test it, as I am sure they could use a bit of sport. And if it pleases you further, I will offer a lovely little prize. I still carry Amaunator's Flame!"

"You Positive Ordered infidel!" Navaatu roars violently. "That was once mine!"

He lets out a bellowing wail that sends waves across the plaza, rattling windows and shaking the walls of nearby buildings. He then charges forward.

"Dear gods!" Tristeen gasps. "Can he actually be more insane than the Dean?"

Thaelyn waves for the front line to rush forward, taking up a new position in front of him. They reestablish their wall as the huge demon advances.

Navaatu observes the mages taking up in front of Thaelyn and chooses to break through their line with a simple lunge. He leaps into the air to come down on them from above, hoping to crush them under his feet.

Tristeen and her group, Relissa and hers, and also the Governor and Dean, all watch as the demon's enormous bulk flings into the air and descends onto the line of shield mages.

The mages lifted their shields, angling them up to deflect his arrival. As his feet make contact, the impact of his inertia ripples through the projected apparition, being absorbed fully and ineffectually. His motion instantly comes to a halt, much to his surprise, and everyone else, except for Thaelyn and his people. Almost immediately, the demon feels he is losing control of his footing, and begins teetering backwards, sliding off the shields and falling flat on his back with a tremendous thud.

Tristeen gawks at the sight, completely at a loss to understand what she just saw.

Relissa and Marelle glanced at each other.

"That's one mighty bugaboo of a shield they have there," Relissa offers quietly.

The Governor glares at the scene trying to ascertain what just happened.

"In all Creation," he mutters. "And with no collateral effect underneath… Blast it!" he scorns. "Those mongrels have an inertial absorption shield!"

"A what?" the Dean wonders feebly.

"Inertial absorption… The creature's force of motion, inertia, was simply absorbed into the shield with no residual effect to the mage underneath. Those shields are even worse than I thought!"

Navaatu was stunned briefly by the impact. He slowly began to pull himself back upright.

Thaelyn waved at his men to begin their assault. The paladins came in from the flanks while the support troops took their own stances.

Tristeen again glanced up at the archers in the trees. They were beginning their attack, but she noticed something strange.

"Um, aren't they supposed to have quivers or something for their arrows?"

"Well, not being an archer, um," Jared relents. "I suppose they should."

Then she notices the archers pulling back their bowstrings, even without arrows loaded, and she saw the formation of an elemental shape appearing.

"Gods above, look!"

The three of them turned to study the archer with his bow firing off a series of elemental ice bolts.

"Those things are enchanted!" she gushes excitedly. "They don't even use normal arrows!"

"Beats all the hells out of anything we've got," Jared admits. "Shortages or no…"

The archers launched a volley at the demon, and each one made a solid hit, freezing a portion of the creature's body at the point of impact. Navaatu lets out a howling wail for each hit.

The mages cast their own attacks, again using ice magic as the preferred weapon against a demon, hitting him from different sides and wrapping his body in a brief casing of frost. Then the priests make a turn with divine smites, pummeling him to his knees.

Now the paladins arrive for their assault. They call on their holy chants to engage a divine aura of protection, and then lay into the creature with their dual-enchanted swords, inflicting both ice and electrical damage along with the slashing of the blades.

Navaatu found himself becoming overwhelmed, but his stubbornness forced him to retaliate. He swung one of his powerful claws at a nearby paladin, smashing into him and sending the warrior hurtling through the air into a building across the way. The knight slammed into the wall and tumbled to the ground.

"One down…" the Governor muses contentedly.

Tristeen and her friends all gasped at the devastating hit the man took, leaving a clearly evident fracture in the wall as he fell away.

But he wasn't dead.

The knight slowly pulled himself to his knees. He was obviously in pain from the force of the blow, and his armor appeared dented, if only slightly, due to the ribbing underneath reinforcing the structure.

Physically, he was stunned, and felt a tinge of pain in his chest, possibly from a cracked rib, as well as bruising. But his conditioning from his training, along with the augmentations from the Draconic bonding and magical glyphs applied to his body, made him far more durable than an average man.

He unlatched a portion of his armor to reach underneath and then removed one gauntlet. He then raised his hand to call on a divine healing chant. His hand began to glow, and he placed it under his armor to touch the affected area. He immediately felt relief from the pain. With this minor concern resolved, he reassembled himself, picked up his sword and shield again, rose to his feet, and let out a renewed battle roar before charging back into the fray.

Tristeen found herself stupefied at the sight.

"He's not dead?" she mumbles.

"Worse than that," Jared observes. "He looks a mite angry now."

"Angry!" she shouts. "The man should be dead, not simply angry for something."

"What is that?!" the Governor rages. "How can he still be alive?! That should've been a fatal blow. In all Creation, what does it take to kill these people?"

Navaatu turns to see the return of the man he thought he just put down, and he seemed somewhat amused at the sight.

"How delightful," he muses. "You have reinforced their bodies. All the better to make our sport."

"They carry draconic blood in them, Navaatu," Thaelyn affirms. "They are not as fragile as the common mortal."

"Draconic! How could you apply this to them?"

"I had help, and she stands at my side to build my Kingdom."

The demon roars again and takes on a new fury. He makes a broad sweep with an arm, knocking some of the knights off their feet, then reaches out to grab one as he returns. He catches the knight around his midsection in one of his pincher-like claws and lifts him up.

The paladin finds himself in a predicament, so he resorts to bringing up his sword and plunging it hard through the demon's arm, piercing the tendons to weaken its grip. This invoked Navaatu to emit another loud scream and to try flinging the knight away. But the knight held tight to his sword and hooked an arm over the claw for added support.

Navaatu swung his arm out and back, trying to dislodge the knight. As he made the return, the knight saw an opportunity to use his momentum to land a solid kick to the creature's muzzle, then levering himself to straddle the arm where he pulled out his sword and threw himself off to tumble away on the ground. Navaatu reeled back and shook his head to refocus himself after the impact.

Relissa and Marelle watched in wonder.

"Jiggers! Is this what they teach in that academy of theirs?" she shudders. "I'm going to have my work cut out for me."

Tristeen and her friends also gazed at the action.

"They're all insane!" she whines. "That guy just kicked that monster in the face."

Navaatu let out another roar of outrage for the assault, but before he could retaliate, he was getting hit by another series of elemental arrows and mage strikes.

"Dean!" the Governor shouts. "This is not going well! Those people are virtually indestructible out there! No wonder they're doing so well against the Suuden-Aryku."

"My Lord, I don't know what to say. How could I have known they are so well-practiced?"

"This is not simple practice. This must relate to all that nonsense the Captain spoke of. That one who took what should've been a fatal hit, and he barely felt it. That's not normal, Dean. They must have more enchantments than what's just on those weapons of theirs. In fact, it wouldn't surprise me if their bodies were somehow modified. In all Creation, if a man could actually create an army of this sort," he pants. "That world has become extremely dangerous. I'm not surprised the orcs are extinct. And now he's here!"

Navaatu was showing damage across most of his body by now. The paladins had cut through several critical tendons, leaving gashes across his arms and legs.

Thaelyn had been holding back so far, allowing his people their exercise to make a noteworthy show for the Governor that his military was not to be trifled with. But now he had to deliver the finishing blow.

"Navaatu, this has been a good game thus far," he asserts. "Now, do you recall my mention of your little prize at the end? Well here it is!"

He pulls out his sword from the sheath on his back and holds it up.

"Here we go, peeps," Relissa cautions.

Navaatu gazes at it greedily, but before he can make any movements, Thaelyn quickly glances at Aerlie and nods. She begins a complex spell cast, while the paladins laid the final blows on the demon's arms to occupy them. As her spell becomes ready, Thaelyn pulls the sword close to his lips and speaks softly into the weapon. Tristeen and the others watch as the sword erupts in a brilliant blue column of plasma.

"Oh dear gods," she mutters. "That thing's activated by a Word of Power!"

The Governor glared into the plaza at this new demonstration.

"That's no ordinary sword, Dean," he mumbles guardedly.

"Indeed, even I can see that."

"Yes, but my point is it should not be in the hands of an ordinary man, either."

The Dean turns to gaze at the Governor briefly before returning.

Aerlie sends her spell off, invoking a large ethereal fist to appear flying off at the demon and slamming into its chest. The force of the impact hurled the demon several paces backwards, lifting it up and causing it to fall to the ground again on its back.

"Gods be blessed," Tristeen wheezes. "What was that!"

"Don't ask me," Willit winces. "That one's not on the books back home."

Thaelyn charges forward as his guard pulls back, allowing him space for his own maneuver. The demon struggled to hoist itself back upright, just barely coming to its feet when Thaelyn leaps in with a downward slash across its torso.

Navaatu screeches from the pain and reactively tries swiping at him with his right claw, but Thaelyn ducks underneath, then spins on a heel and swings his sword in a wide arc, cutting neatly through the creature's right flank. The strike causes Navaatu to recoil back, letting out an even louder howl.

Aerlie moves forward and conjures up a double-handed lightning bolt, sending it out and striking the beast in its midsection. The heavy jolt stunned the creature, dropping it to its knees as it tried in vain to refocus itself.

The Governor and the Dean gawked at the ferocious display of just these two people.

"In all Creation," the Governor gasps. "These two don't even need an army! Just look at them!"

Thaelyn moved around to the side. He shouts an attention-getting roar at the demon, causing it to swivel around and swing its powerful upper arm at him. Thaelyn ducks and rolls under it, quick to find his feet again and orient for another slice. He brings his sword down hard on the demon's outstretched arm, severing it at midpoint. Navaatu's increased howling now rattles the surrounding buildings.

The Governor's breathing was quickening as he began to realize the sheer power of just these two people in combat, to say nothing of their military.

Aerlie prepares one more spell, a heavy ice blast aimed at the beast's upper torso. She sends it off, encasing it in a block of ice, and this allows Thaelyn to make another approach, flipping his sword around for a reverse jab in the demon's left flank.

Navaatu staggers in a daze with multiple critical hits, and further as he tries to break free of the icy prison.

"And here is where we part ways for the second time," Thaelyn asserts. "Say hello to Cyric on your way back. Tell him, I have not forgotten the Spellplague."

Thaelyn now orients his sword for an upward thrust and pierces through the demon's torso, under the ribcage and through the center.

The shock of this new hit invokes a reflex to break the remainder of the ice spell, and Navaatu screeches in agony. Aerlie rushes up to

Thaelyn's side and stretches out an arm, then recoils it back slowly as she forms an energy well within her palm. A sound like muted thunder coils up in her grip until she releases it in a forward thrust. The sonic impulse lashes out at Navaatu, rattling what remained of his body and knocking him once more onto his back.

Navaatu let out a final tumultuous roar as its body erupts into flames and is consumed down to nothing.

Leesa and the Governor's secretary had been watching through the window in the Manor. He turned away from the spectacle outside to gaze at her.

"And you work for him?" he whispers imperatively.

Tristeen and her friends were in shock over what they had just witnessed. She couldn't speak immediately, and neither could Jared. Willit was the only one to find his voice.

"Well, um," he ushers delicately. "I guess that takes care of the Dean's little surprise party."

Both Tristeen and Jared turned to gape at him for his remark.

"Do you think?" she blurts frantically.

"Dean!" the Governor shrieks. "This is intolerable! In fact, this is beyond intolerable! I don't even have words for it, it's so intolerable! You need to get back over there and cover this up. I don't care what you have to say or do, but get rid of him. Tell him it was some bumbling accident by one of your students."

"Um, but my Lord, I don't have any students anymore."

"Oh blast! Then make something up…one of your instructors if no one else. Grovel on your hands and knees begging for forgiveness, but something! I need time to think. Something must've happened over there that defies reason."

The Dean nods and takes off in a hurry. He rushes downstairs, barely taking notice of Leesa and the secretary staring out the window, and then dashes out the back door. He followed along the alleys out of view in the corner of the plaza, and around behind the academy.

From where they stood, Tristeen and her friends could see part of the alley behind the academy, and she caught a glimpse of hurried movement scurrying along.

"There!" she points. "He's going back in. I'll bet he's going to try inventing some new excuse now."

Tristeen gets up from the group and begins moving towards Thaelyn and his people.

"You stay here," she directs. "I'm the only known rabble-rouser around here, so let's not get you in trouble also."

Thaelyn was standing down his troops from the combat condition, and returning his sword to its sheath. Aerlie called on the prelates, and together they moved in to check the troops for any additional injuries.

Captain Kholgard came out of hiding behind the wall as Thaelyn returned to speak again.

"Your Lordship," the Captain offers. "I don't know where you people learned to fight, but that was some show you put on. If those two porkers weren't afraid of you before, they ought to be by now."

"Indeed, Captain, but this may not necessarily be a good thing. Now they may behave like frightened animals, and we cannot be sure what their next move will be. And yet, regardless of this, I must now finish it by planting a few carefully chosen words with the Dean. Naturally, we cannot allow such a thing as a demon running loose in the city to go without some casual mention."

Tristeen arrived near the group and approached the last few steps reverently.

"Um, Your Lordship, I presume," she calls softly.

Thaelyn turned to see the distraught young lady with the long blonde hair.

"Yes, young lady, do you wish for something?"

"I, uh…well, I'm actually one of the people helping you. My name is Tristeen Macaid, perhaps you've heard of me?"

"Ah, but of course," he smiles. "So, you are the young noblesse who has been making a few of her own statements up here. Please, come forward."

"I don't want to disturb you, but I guess I am, anyway. That was a very surprising show you and your people put on. My friends and

I are shocked by what that horrid little man conjured up. If I'm not mistaken, I think that was a tanar'ri, am I right?"

"Indeed it was, but it is also rather curious you would know that word."

"It is? Well, maybe so. I saw it referenced once in a strange book the Dean owns."

"A book…is this the one I heard once mentioned that he was using to call forth this creature?"

"Yes, the same. It talks about something called the Outer Planes, and things that live there. I have no idea where he got it, but it doesn't look like anything I've ever seen before."

"In what way," he asks concernedly.

"For one thing, the binding was thin and looked like it was some kind of silvery metal. The pages weren't paper, but something shiny and smooth. I have no idea what they were. And it was bound on a spiral metal coil."

"This does not sound like the sort of book I would expect to see in a society like yours, with respect. Ours is a bit more advanced, so these materials might be better known to us, but next is what was inside."

"Right, I recall a bunch of names, places like Baator, Gehenna, Carceri… And things like Tanar'ri and Baatezu…"

"And this is where you learned the name of that creature, or at least the general faction term."

"A faction?"

"Yes, Baator is home to one faction called Baatezu. The Tanar'ri are found in an opposing domain called the Abyss."

"Interesting, but they all look like demons to me."

"Yes, to the layman's eye, they might. But more appropriately, Baatezu are better described as devils, being from an ordered hierarchy of social structure, whereas the Tanar'ri are demons with a fully chaotic social climate."

"Order versus chaos, now there's an interesting concept. What about those names, and a few others like, um, Hades, Elysium, Mechanus…?"

"These are the names of the various locations that can be found out there, most of which you have mentioned thus far are located in the Lower Planes."

"Yeah, I recall this as a section heading. He had it open to that part at the time I saw it."

"I suppose this makes sense if he has any interest in conjuring a demon. At the same time, the name Hades is an older one, and no longer used. But still, it would seem someone did their homework on the topic. And in a society so far removed from the core of the realms, and where so much of your other knowledge seems to have been erased by this conspiracy of yours, I must ask myself where he found it."

"Based on how the thing appears, we're thinking it's not local, but maybe has something to do with the Suuden-Aryku."

"While I may admit the Suuden-Aryku could have contributed to its manufacture, I doubt they would hold this precise knowledge. I suspect they come from a place even farther removed than you, and likely with no true knowledge of the magical arts or anything they might otherwise describe as mysticism," he chuckles briskly. "In fact, this seems much more the sort of study resource we might have in one of our own libraries, rather than what I would expect in yours."

"Um, may I ask why?"

"My presence on Tae'Eladar gives my people the advantage to know certain things, but generally speaking, most mortals should not otherwise have access to this level of detail."

"Um…" she suddenly feels pale at the mention of those words. "Just how do you mean that? Most mortals…and your presence on your world? Because I'm recalling what your Captain said a couple of days ago."

"Ah, but of course," he smiles. "We can say for now that I am not your average man. Beyond that, I must be careful of my words in such places as this," he discreetly rolls his eyes towards the Governor's Manor.

"Gracious," she flusters. "Sure, right. And so, his words that you're not native to that world. I'm getting visions now, especially since you and that thing seemed to know each other."

Tristeen feels a cold sweat forming on her brow. She raises a hand to rub her face.

"Well, anyway," she continues. "A moment ago, I saw the Dean running around the alleys behind the academy as he was going back inside. He was probably over at the Governor's office before this. Are you thinking of going over for a little chat, perhaps?" she curls a tiny smile.

"I think it might be prudent at this time. And, in fact, I would not wish to delay this any longer, as I have another matter of timing working against us at present."

"Which one is that?"

"It has to do with the Flame Elves to the south. I need mine to occur before the Governor hears the rest of it on his end."

"All right, fine by me. Um, would you mind if I tag along? I'd love to see the Dean's face after all this."

"I would not wish to place you at any undue attention," he cautions.

"I'm sure I already have plenty of that. But don't worry, I can handle myself."

"Very well," he grins. "However, your Dean is not really the problem here. It is your Governor. We have recently come to a new understanding where he is concerned."

"And what is that?"

"He is not native to this world, and neither is he human."

"Really! Well, wait a moment, how would this relate to our questions of the transition from one to another over the years?"

"My belief is he must be the original one. He would represent a being of some rather profound capacity, and not one to be underestimated, especially if you look at what he has done to this world. And we believe his activities are not limited to this one."

"Oh wonderful, then how do we get rid of him?"

"These are the words I will share with the Dean, and from there to be passed along indirectly. Let us go now and attend to this."

Thaelyn peers inside the barracks to the others in hiding.

"Marelle, Relissa, would you care to join us?"

The two women come out and join by his side. Tristeen catches the names and turns to study them.

"Are you the famous Marelle Carronel I keep hearing about?" she asks.

"Famous?" Marelle responds curiously.

"Well, to the point where I keep hearing your name mentioned every time something is turned upside-down around here," Tristeen grins.

"Oh, that," she giggles. "He keeps me very busy, which is a good thing."

"Aye," Relissa adds. "Like that bit with the Suuden'kai transport. Let's not forget how you got your name on that special list of his for flying it around the countryside."

"A what?" Tristeen wonders. "A flying transport?"

"Right, she got this wild idea to bring it home with her, even though she hasn't a bloody clue how to fly the bleedin' thing."

"Oh dear gods, that must be a story."

"Come along, dear Children," Thaelyn coos. "We can carry the pleasantries later."

He leads the group across to the academy, which includes Tristeen, Relissa, Marelle, and Captain Kholgard, as they all enter the academy building.

The Governor was still watching from his window.

"I see a Night Elf in that group. How did she get here? She must've been hiding inside the barracks. No doubt, she is one of those working with him in that camp of his. And another one, who is that? She seems too neatly dressed for a soldier. I wonder if she is that troublemaker the Dean mentioned."

Thaelyn and the others passed through the main hall inside the academy. Where once the walls were lined with bookshelves, many were now broken and the books scattered across the floor, half of them still smoldering. Most of the tables were overturned, some of them smashed and others burning.

Thaelyn moves among them casting several small cantrips to douse the fires. Tristeen watches and decides to lend a hand.

"I don't know why you would trouble yourself with that," Marelle comments. "Not after all these people have done lately."

"This is supposed to be a place of learning," Thaelyn admits. "And despite who manages the affair, I would not wish to see these fires spread to the remainder of the building."

"He's right about that much," Tristeen offers. "If this place goes up, it could spread to the rest of the city. And considering everything else, I don't think we have enough people currently in their right minds to fight it."

They quench the smoldering embers and proceed through to the rear door, which was also torn apart. Beyond that is the corridor stretching in both directions. The walls bore deep grooves etched into them, left behind from the passing of an exceptionally large creature.

"Would someone happen to know which way the Dean's office is from here?" he solicits.

Tristeen steps forward and points off to the right.

"This way to the stairs, up, and then turn left."

The assembly turns down the hall, passing by classrooms and workshops. Other hallways turn to find more rooms deeper into the structure. They approached the stairwell leading up. Looking further down the corridor, they continue to see signs of the demon's passage coming out from another hall leading off to the left.

"I would guess that leads to the place where the creature was first summoned," Thaelyn muses.

"Down that way is the door to the basement," Tristeen offers. "That's where they were drawing that circle. That's also where the Dean tried to lock us up with his experimental elixir. By the way, do we know what that stuff was?"

"Actually, yes. The Daanen-Aryku tell us it is a medicinal agent to treat a rare lung disorder which can cause breathing difficulties."

"But this is for them, I suppose. What would it do to us?"

"Indeed, Med-tech Tad'vaal, their chief medical expert, suggests it could cause a constricting effect, especially in overdose form, and you being human would only complicate matters for the quantity in those vials. This would effectively cause your lungs to constrict violently and result in what she believes would be a painful, suffocating death."

"Grace of the Gods!" she groans bitterly. "That man would actually do such a thing?"

"I must ask myself if he actually knows of it, especially if this was ordered and delivered by the Governor with instructions to feed it to you. The Dean, like so many others, may not hold enough privilege to ask questions about it."

"Wonderful, so not even he knows everything, which is actually a little ironic, when you think of it."

"This brings an important thought to my mind while we are here. The reports I have been receiving during this time, such as from our priests and my Captain during their meetings with him, suggest our plays have been taking their toll on his mind, if only partially. I am forming an opinion that he became buried under a mountain of intrigue by the Governor during his career, to the point where he became as one with him. Our recent plays may have been slowly chipping away at this, and now I wish to test this to see what sort of result we have. I am wondering how this might affect our overall outcome after today's show."

They reached the top of the stairs and turned left, then proceeded down the hallway to the Dean's office door.

"All right, listen." Thaelyn turns to the assembly and speaks softly. "I have a need to carry this conversation with him in a certain manner, so if you have any words to share, try to keep it succinct. I must deliver a number of suggestions to him, and no doubt he will try to present a similar number of excuses for his actions."

Tristeen and the others nod as Thaelyn prepares to knock on the door.

"Y-yes? Who is it?" ushers a weak voice from within.

"Dean Malorn, I believe you should already know who this is. I am here with questions. And considering the state of this building, and the plaza outside, they demand answers."

"Uh, yes... Well, um, please come in."

Thaelyn opens the door and steps inside. He is followed by the others in the group. As instructed, they keep calm and silent, and hold back.

"Your Lordship," the Dean announces apprehensively. "It's such a surprise to see you here…uh, how nice."

The Dean stood behind his desk and glanced at the assembly, which included Tristeen in the mix. He glared at her for her persistent meddling presence.

"You again," he mutters scornfully.

She simply smirks at his reference.

"I once said if I should see any odd creatures prowling around the plaza, I would go to the Guard. Well, here we are. This is Captain Kholgard," she thumbs at the man behind her. "Say hello, as I somehow doubt you might be personally familiar. Especially, as you once said, he should be spending his time picking up drunks from the street."

"Really! And just where did you hear that statement?"

"I'm sure half the academy heard it when you and Haran had that little talk in here once. I was standing just outside listening."

"Oh…" he relents softly. "And what now? Are you going to arrest me for something? It was an accident."

"Oh, an accident," she muses derisively. "You know, your instructors once told me this was far too dangerous to demonstrate. I guess someone took a differing opinion to that somewhere."

"They were simply attempting to understand the mechanics of a conjuration, and since the circle was so carefully drawn, it was deemed to be safe within the constraints of the procedural outlines."

"Are these the same procedural outlines once defined as too dangerous to attempt? Or are we speaking of those that were described to be at your personal discretion? And then, where did those procedural outlines fail that they let out such a huge monster like that on the streets?"

"That is as much a mystery to me as it is to the rest. But I will be conducting a careful review to discover who was ultimately responsible for this failure."

"Well, let's hope you discover this before you attempt any more of these experiments. And especially if you should ever hope to teach this to the upperclassmen, as it was once suggested. If your finest instructors can't hold it back, I'd hate to see the results of your students with all the mistakes they tend to make. But, oh wait, I forgot, you don't have any more students. Sorry," she grins impishly.

Thaelyn observed the interchange and found it rather amusing for Tristeen's play of words.

"Dean," he begins. "You are a curious piece of work. My people have shared with me a number of fascinating accounts of their experiences up here. However, that being said, I think our first order of business revolves around a few key points of concern regarding our past interactions."

"What past interactions!" he blasts. "I haven't had any with you. Well, not other than those priests of yours in the temple, which you somehow managed to sneak in under our noses."

"I did not sneak in anything that was uncalled for after you began sneaking in yours. Those spies of yours we discovered observing us in a time of war. I am a soldier as much as I am a King and a protector of my people. Despite you and your Governor, neither of whom seemed as interested in fighting this war, I hold my obligations rather dear to me, and I take offence to people spying on me who are not otherwise friendly to my cause."

"Oh, those!" he recalls uneasily. "Um, they were just runners with, uh…instructions to keep us abreast of, eh…how well you were doing down there. This is our world, you know, and we do feel a need to know what is occurring out there."

"Dean," Tristeen interjects. "He's right about one thing; you're a piece of work, and not a fashionable one at that. Do you recall Haran? As I said, I was standing just outside this door when you screamed at him that his famous report was to be filed in the trash. Furthermore, some of those runners are my friends, and they told me precisely why you sent them out there."

"And what business is that of yours, Miss Macaid! We needed

to know what this man was doing down there, and this is all we have available to us."

"All right, this is all you have. I guess I can't debate that issue. But there is a difference between spying on someone to see how well he is liberating our people, as opposed to one who is getting in your way."

"Indeed," Thaelyn asserts. "If you were so curious, why not simply send a man for a polite chat. You do recall my offer to join forces in fighting this war, correct? Despite your supply shortages, you could still offer whatever meager support you could actually afford and make a fair showing that you appreciated my efforts. For all the benefits your city has been receiving, I think by now it should be clear that I am responsible, and therefore I might represent a positive influence."

"Your opinion," he huffs.

"Yes, mine, and all those farmers who are taking up renewed occupancy outside your walls, along with your smiths and other craftsmen who are receiving fresh supplies of materials, such as iron, to provide for their needs. It is my understanding your people were being heavily restricted due to your most unfortunate situation of war. My unexpected, and seemingly undesired arrival seems to have corrected that."

"Not to mention, Dean," Marelle adds. "Haran is my little brother, and he came to me after his meeting with you. That statement about keeping drunks off the streets came through our office over there, and neither I nor the Captain were very happy about it. We regard ourselves as soldiers and law enforcers with a duty to serve the people. And Dean, we're not anywhere as meek as you like your students to be. When we saw the opportunity to get any real work done, we jumped at it. Too bad you didn't see it the same way."

The Dean could see his argument on this matter was being thoroughly torn apart. He simply huffed and crossed his arms, then sat down as he tried to compose a rebuttal.

"As to our…resources…they are rather precious to us, and it's hard to trust someone who simply comes along with such a, eh…glamorous offer as what you were suggesting. When you're surrounded on all sides, you can't simply accept such statements."

"Oh, that's a good one," Tristeen rolls her eyes.

"Very well, Dean," Thaelyn offers. "So, it sounded too good to be true. Perhaps, in your long-standing disadvantage, you hold a point. Nevertheless, you and your Governor did seem rather entranced over my military and all of our…glamorous equipment. And yet, even after I mentioned I was the king of a full world, you still seemed offended that I was trespassing uninvited. Do you recall that demand for payment you made once?"

"That wasn't my decision," the Dean retorts. "My position is only the Dean of this academy. If you want to complain about that, you should speak to the Governor."

"I will leave it to you to lodge my complaint, as I am sure you will probably need to report to him after this is done. But I think it goes without saying, making demands of one who can transform a desert into woodlands, and further who is a king of a full world, with that same full world of resources and military power at his disposal, is not in the best taste, to say nothing of simply being unwise. I go to war with my enemies, Dean. And during those wars, I employ real military power to launch real attacks that yield real results. And all you have is one little city. Your walls are nothing to me, as I can simply fly over them, and then import several divisions of troops directly inside using portals."

"Divisions?" he muses hesitantly. "I'm not one who is very familiar with military terms."

"Very well. Back home, a division is a military unit consisting of roughly ten thousand soldiers. Therefore, I could overwhelm your full population with numbers before you know it."

"Great gods, you can move so many at once?"

"Indeed, it is a practice we have used on many occasions. Uniting a world, and covering so much space, demands efficiency. Therefore, portals are a common utility for us. We are well practiced at moving full armies this way. And in fact, we are currently using this technique on a full line, stretching for hundreds of miles and moving south against your local population of orcs."

The Dean grimaced at the implications as he tried to envision so many people moving through portals at one time.

"That's a very serious depiction," he mumbles.

"We even found one of their portals, and have a garrison waiting in place for any new arrivals. But anyway, proceeding forward, and regardless of your lack of confidence in any arriving body to represent a decisive element in a time of war, my achievements since then, assuming your…runners…were able to accurately inform of my movements, should speak for themselves."

"They couldn't tell where you were most of the time," he admits. "Your use of these portals denied us to track you. And if you're moving along so quickly overland, I doubt we could even keep up with you."

"At this point, perhaps not. Our rate of advance is intended to confuse and confound their ability to fight back. Maybe if I provide you with my own update. At this time, your orcs are on the run, currently many hundreds of miles away and diminishing fast. Our timing estimates, based on our experience back home, will probably depend more on their numbers, and perhaps the distance to travel, rather than their threat potential."

"From what I saw outside, I have no doubt. It also forces me to recall what your Captain said not long ago."

"Indeed. However, the Suuden-Aryku, for whatever reason, seem to be cowering behind their fortifications, and I would imagine the issue of the Flame Elves to be resolved fairly soon as well. Therefore, if you ever had any doubt of what a true military power, with true determination to actually fight, could provide for you and yours, just go for a little walk outside these walls and see the new world."

"You say the Suuden-Aryku are hiding? Are you launching against them, or holding back?"

"So far, I have held back, if only because they did not represent an immediate target for me, and certainly not outside offering defensive support for the Daanen-Aryku."

"And the Flame Elves?"

"Let us come to that in a moment, as we make our way around to it. I still have a few tricks to play against my own interpretation of the villains of the world, and I want them to know that I know who they are."

"I think that much is done by now, from what your priests told me the other day."

"Perhaps, but there is more to it, and here is where we are today. Your circle was not unknown to me, Dean. Therefore, I had to demonstrate to you how we do things back home."

"Wonderful..." he glares at Tristeen again.

"Dean," Thaelyn continues. "The message from my priests, as well as the message from my Captain, were intentional deliveries to hint of something you might not normally expect to see in a world like this. Today is what I might call a day of reckoning, if only due to your little accident outside. But to explain this, I feel we need to take a little walk down Memory Lane, if we can, as there is a curious bit of history that needs to be revealed to describe my meaning."

"Oh wonderful, another history lesson I couldn't care less about."

"You know, for a man who describes himself as an educator, you do not seem much interested in education. I suspect, at one time, just like so many others, you were once a young boy going to school where the previous Dean and those graduate students who became your teachers filled you with no less nonsense than what you are doing now."

"And just what do you mean by this?" he spurns. "If you're now going to complain that we intentionally..."

"Dean!" Marelle shouts. "Stuff it. We already know about you and the Governor trying to make up excuses for all your schemes. 'Oh, I can't be held responsible for all those who came before, except for upholding the same'..." she mocks. "We're a step ahead of you, Dean. We already took over that part. But you know, maybe, if you would go next door to our neighbors," she thumbs at Relissa, "rather than complain about their unholy this and that, you could ask to borrow from their library. They carry everything, all the way back to the beginning."

The Dean was instantly stifled by her outburst. He briefly felt a flicker of revulsion at the mention of someone holding more and better knowledge, and that he couldn't otherwise control it. But deep down, he also felt the old scar peeling open of the young boy who wanted to learn, but was summarily denied. He turned away and pouted.

Thaelyn watched, and he also used his Celestial senses to monitor the Dean for his reactions. He could feel the Dean's internal conflict, but he still had his own work to do.

"Nevertheless, Dean," he continues. "Whether or not you want to learn anything, I am sure your Governor would like to hear a report, and this is where it comes from, because it directly relates to something I know about him."

The Dean stiffened in his chair and glared at Thaelyn.

"What do you mean?"

"Let us bring a few pieces into conversation. We have the stories of the noble families and the conspiracy to take control of the city. We also have the history of the people of this world being immigrants from Tae'Eladar. But something we were recently associating, with the help of some old journals the elves maintained, is how you came to be here."

"I recall mention of a weird portal thing."

"Yes, but Dean, I carry a bit of privileged knowledge within me. Such a…weird portal thing…as that cannot be native to our society. By the descriptions we have, no one on Tae'Eladar would know how to build such a thing. Instead, it represents a device some would describe as a Door and uses what we call a Key. These terms may seem a bit simplistic, but the more enlightened the mind, sometimes is the greater need for simpler terms, as the knowledge now extends into reaches where the more complex terms soon become mundane. This becomes the standard, therefore the common terms."

"Interesting…but how high a society are we speaking of here?"

"Rather high, to be sure, and as such, this represents a unique form of knowledge which I would expect to be very old and not native to Tae'Eladar."

"Really!" he wonders curiously. "Then, where do you think it came from?"

"This is where the rest of it comes in. The stories speak of an individual who arrives with this inspirational tale of a mysterious device leading to new lands. At the same time, these journals also reflect on the first arrival of orcs in our world."

"I recall those priests mentioning this."

"Good, but here we have a paradox. Those orcs should not have been able to do this in the first place."

"Oh? Why is that?"

"To explain this, we need to afford ourselves a few definitions. First, Dean, are you familiar with the concept of a universe? My experience with some people around here tells me this word is not as commonplace."

"Actually, yes, I do know this word. The Governor also carries a bit of privileged knowledge, and explained it to me once, at least where the Suuden-Aryku are concerned."

"Very good, then let us move forward. Tae'Eladar is in another universe, and this would be yet another outside this one and the one the Suuden-Aryku come from."

"Really, how curious. And so, what of it? If the Suuden-Aryku are able to find their way around…hmm, well, is this to say these orcs are not as clever?" he chuckles. "It wouldn't surprise me, actually."

"This is true, they never represented themselves as being so highly adept in the magical arts, or anything else for that matter. So, they would clearly need help. But it is not that simple in our case. If you look up in the nighttime sky, you will see your local stars. Such beings as the Suuden-Aryku can travel between these in their ships. Not so in ours, as Tae'Eladar is encased in a huge shell to protect it from a turbulent outer environment. In our sky, all you see is the leftover storm that destroyed the rest."

"A storm that destroyed the rest?" he winces. "What kind of storm could cause that?"

"There was an ancient battle that occurred once in our space. Tae'Eladar is a survivor, and protected inside this shell now. But here is our paradox, or at least some portion of it. The only way in or out is by way of a portal. And for this, you need some rather privileged knowledge, or else special access simply to find it, to say nothing of actually opening a portal of any kind. This also holds true for departing the Shell. If it were not for your orcs and their portals leading me here, I might need to resort to other means to do this."

"Other means, like what? My impression here is this Shell of yours is impenetrable by common means, right?"

"Yes, one cannot simply pass through it. Even if such as the Suuden-Aryku could find their way into the local universe, they would be unable to access Tae'Eladar unless they could jump directly inside. As for me, well, I suppose I could simply ask the Estelar for help, as they are the ones who built it."

"Gah!" the Dean shrieks and jerks back in his chair. "This Shell was built by those gods of yours? But...but..."

"Dean, the Estelar are a society of beings nearly timeless in age and of such a level of development that people like you would describe them as gods by now. And yes, such a thing as this Shell, which covers our full star system, can be built by them. In fact, at this moment, I would think they are likely the only ones capable of building such a thing."

Tristeen gaped at Thaelyn for his depiction. She had been enjoying the conversation up until now, but suddenly she was asking herself just how closely related his people really were to these gods of theirs.

"But anyway," Thaelyn asserts. "We are digressing somewhat. Those orcs would need help, likely from the outside, and also likely from someone with direct access to Tae'Eladar. But for this, he would need to know of the simple existence of Tae'Eladar, or have such capacity as to move outside the cloud and peer into it in order to find it. This limits us to only a very few possibilities for what type of creature we are speaking of, and it is not a man."

"Not a man?" he whimpers.

"Yes, especially if you consider those orcs call Ruuki uy'Daan their home, and we know of them in the modern day to worship Sargeras as their god. Then we have this world, with all of you, and that inspirational figure leading you here, which would also require a special effort, and coincidentally with someone delivering orcs into our world. And then," he waves a finger for emphasis. "Here we are now, once again arriving on this world, as the result of more orcs assaulting us, and further to find Flame Elves and Suuden-Aryku, all of whom are following Sargeras, and your world is under siege up to the very last of you, and then it stops."

"Great gods above!" Tristeen shrieks. "Are you saying it was planned from the beginning? Someone built that portal, then led us here, also delivered the orcs, and then made this new trouble for you?"

"And who brought all of us into the condition where we see ourselves now. Yes. Very few types of creatures would hold the knowledge and the capacity to do all this, and the coincidences are simply too great by now. He would need to know of our world, with access to it by direct means, also with knowledge of this world, perhaps with access by direct means, likely access to Ruuki uy'Daan by direct means, and using all of this, he could link his portals to move bodies around. But the one responsible cannot be your ordinary sort, and the stories we have of Sargeras depict him as one such who could do this, as he is described as a very old and very powerful entity, and likely in possession of some fascinating skills. Therefore, we must point our finger at him, or perhaps someone closely associated with him, like an assistant with similar capacity."

"Oh, how grand!" she moans.

"Then, one day, he returns and takes the Flame Elves, as his slaves. This could be our link as to why you are here. He brought you here as part of a larger plan to use this world for some ulterior motive, which seems to be aiming at my home, or perhaps the general area, and you were essentially seeded here to be used as future servants, at least aside from the Suuden-Aryku."

"But why didn't he take all of us? Why only the Flame Elves?"

"We can suggest a number of reasons here, one being the Flame

Elves were all that he wanted at the time, or perhaps they were the easiest. Then, we might suggest he is holding the rest of you in reserve, therefore the reason you are pinned down so neatly inside your walls...at least until I came along and spoiled things for him," he smiles. "But he probably did not require this elaborate civilization you built during this time, instead desiring only a manageable few."

The Dean felt a sudden shiver rush through him. The meaning was clearly evident, if taken altogether. He instantly reflected on the Governor's constant references of Thaelyn as an unwelcome interference.

"And this is far too coincidental for my taste," Thaelyn concludes. "Especially when I factor in the Suuden-Aryku home world."

"Why?" Tristeen asks. "What does that have to do with anything?"

"According to the Daanen-Aryku, Sargeras first arrived there roughly ten millennia ago, which is very close to the same time as these other events on Tae'Eladar. Therefore, the timing is a little too convenient. He is becoming active with something and directing himself to some objective that is leading him in this direction, and I am not at all pleased by it."

The Dean's thoughts drifted in consideration of these statements. This story did actually hold some attraction to him as he reflected on a few of the accounts made by the Governor, even if by accident for his personal musings.

"Dean," Thaelyn continues. "Due to all this, I regard that recent invasion of orcs as an intended assault on my world. This is a clear act of war by whoever sent them. I have further learned they arrived as part of a mission. The collateral effect of them interfering in our world's affairs simply drew my attention to chase them back here."

"A mission?" he wonders. "How do you know this?"

"You are not the only one with spies, Dean, and I have the remainder of your societies on my world. This includes both humans as well as High Elves...the real name behind your Flame Elves. And clearly, we do not need invisibility cloaks to move around. Also, we may have our own desires to interact with the locals and ask questions, rather than simply spying on them. Therefore, I sent some into Kynesoth once to speak to a few Flame Elves. This was after we found an assassin entering our camp once. I was trying to hold off my interactions with them, but this act forced me to respond."

"Uh oh..."

"We learned a few things from them, one of these being this mission. Someone sent orcs into my world to serve some subversive purpose. Now you complain that I am responding. You dare to invade my world, and further dare to deny me the privilege of fighting back. Then you dare that I should come here to discover who sent them, and even worse, try to assassinate me as I am simply defending my home. I bury people for this, Dean. Be aware."

"All right, I get it." he implores. "But don't look at me. I don't interact with orcs or Flame Elves, and I didn't send anything your way."

"Granted, but someone did. I also learned the Flame Elves receive plentiful supplies of iron, along with the orcs out there, from the Suuden-Aryku. While this is surely to be expected, if they are in league with them, the supply is believed to be local, and so I have to wonder who is providing it. No one else in this world is conducting any mining ventures, except a group of dwarves I hear is operating up north."

"Um, dwarves, right."

"It is said they first appeared with this trade deal four centuries ago. Strangely, no one in this world knew they existed before this."

"Wait, no one knew they existed?" he winces. "So, is this to say they were hiding somewhere?"

"If you and the elves were the only immigrants to this world, they could not have been a part of it. We have them on Tae'Eladar, but ours is not their native home either. And we are aware they do have one...somewhere. However, this knowledge was lost to them after they arrived."

"All right, but this still demands one to ask where these examples came from."

"It does, and so conveniently at the start of this war. Nevertheless, I have learned your Governor holds a very exclusive agreement with them for your iron supply, but I also hear this does not come anywhere near to supplying your city's needs. While this is unfortunate, I also learned a few other things along the way."

"Oh grand, what other things?"

"In our early moments after our arrival, I made agreements with both the Night Elves and the Daanen-Aryku. They were both rather excited to find someone willing to help them in this war. We bolstered the Daanen-Aryku with some of our troops, but in order to keep a low profile, we made a deal with your Captain here for costumes to disguise our people as his, since your Guard is known to frequent that area on occasion."

"I actually heard something about this once."

"Good, but during one of our early patrols, they came under attack…a direct assault on our people, bypassing the Daanen-Aryku who were also out there. This seemed intentional, but it was also strange for the manner of equipment they were using."

"Why is that?" he leans forward onto the desk.

"They were not using their normal armor or weapons, instead using adamantium armor and swords."

"What?!" he shouts. "What are they doing with that out there?"

The Dean's outburst raises everyone's interest about his assertion. They all glared at him with curious amusement. He quickly realized his error and tried recomposing himself.

"I mean, uh," he flusters. "That stuff is something of a myth to us. How is it they might have it?"

"This is a very good question," Thaelyn accedes. "And for a number of reasons. The Suuden-Aryku, much like the Daanen-Aryku, should not be familiar with the practice of magic, as we believe they originate in a world where this is not a part of their background. This should also reflect on such materials as mithril and adamantium, as you need this same environment to produce this. Therefore, it is highly unlikely the Suuden-Aryku would know what to do with these metals, even if they did find some."

"Really! But this sounds like you just contradicted yourself."

"It would. Therefore, they must have a supplier somewhere. But this still does not follow politely if they were never seen using this before. And this one occasion stood out for another reason."

"Uh huh… Such as?"

"The Captain and his people tell us every…official…patrol you ever sent out came home safe. Ours was not sent by you, but how would the Suuden-Aryku know this, unless they have an informant inside these walls who knows of the official deployments."

"Oops."

"And this one example would certainly make a good demonstration for your Guard going against orders. Next, we hear no one in this city can recall, at least within their lifetime, any attacks on your walls. The Captain also mentions this for his father and his tenure. My spies have learned that the Flame Elves, probably also the orcs, all have orders not to attack your city. So, Dean, why do you think your enemies, that destroyed everything else out there, would stop at your walls. Further, that they have more iron than you, and your Governor, with his exclusive deal, does not seem to be living up to his promise for your city's needs."

"I think you are moving outside my scope of influence. My spies don't go that far out, and don't talk to Flame Elves. But if I'm interpreting this correctly, you're probably suggesting something like selling our iron for protection from our enemies out there, right? That's not my business. That's the Governor, so if you have an issue with it, you should talk to him."

"We also have the adamantium in this equation, and where it must be coming from. Therefore, how it fits in with people using it who should not otherwise be using it."

"I would not know how to answer that one."

"We also had that Flame Elf assassin enter our camp once, and also wearing adamantium."

"Really! Them as well? But wouldn't they at least know something about it? They are a magical group, from what I hear."

"This may be true, but this metal is nearly as much a mystery to them as it seems to be to the rest of you. Our spies tell us they do not carry the knowledge of how to forge it."

"Interesting…"

"This is further compounded by them telling us they receive their orders, as well as perhaps their equipment, from the Suuden-Aryku. So, we find ourselves coming right back to them."

"So it seems."

"We have further learned from the elves that you are being managed by someone. This no longer describes an informant, and it no longer describes a flawed trade deal. Your city is under enemy control. It is no wonder your Governor refused to join my crusade against the villains of the world. He is one of them!"

The Dean glared at Thaelyn as he leaned back in his chair. His ire was rising, at least as much defensively as it was for the accusations and the secrets being exposed. But at this point, there was probably nothing he could do about it. He reflected on the Governor, knowing he would surely want to hear about Thaelyn's conclusions.

Thaelyn continues, "This would then explain the story by the noble families, if he is the one causing so much mischief. Someone is controlling the Suuden-Aryku military out there, and it is not their native High Commander. We are told there is one who is in charge of this entire scenario with the name of Darumon. This is not the Suuden-Aryku High Commander, as his name is addressed as Geilv. We then did a little cross-referencing with Master Velen of the Daanen-Aryku, and he recalls that same name arriving alongside Sargeras on their ancestral home world of Azgarén. Therefore, to find him here is disturbing on multiple levels."

"But excuse me!" the Dean erupts sternly. "Are you pointing your finger at the Governor as being behind all this? I know the man, and he most certainly is a man…a human!"

"He may appear this way on the outside, Dean," Thaelyn asserts. "But there are such creatures out there that can change their form. They are called shapeshifters. And some of them may carry some rather elaborate qualities."

"Great gods," Tristeen wheezes. "So that's who he is? Oh, wonderful…there goes everything, or what's left of everything."

"And just how can you possibly justify that statement?" the Dean urges. "All I'm hearing out of this is a lot of wild supposition."

"We have a Daanen'kai officer among us who recalls this same man from their early arrival. This is enough. And for reference, this was three and a half centuries ago."

"Oh dear..." he moans.

"Let us now recall a few items," Thaelyn begins. "The Daanen-Aryku are chased from one world to another ever since leaving Azgarén over the course of thousands of years. If someone wanted them dead, I think they would be dead by now, as they do not have a proper military to defend them. But the Suuden-Aryku are known to use heavy force, enough to lay devastation behind them. During any of those occasions, a few carefully placed shots would be enough to destroy Velen's ship, denying him to escape again, and yet on no occasion did they actually do this. This means someone was toying with them, and according to our Flame Elf informant, the High Commander does not seem to hold any emotional content to take enjoyment out of games. Therefore, it has to be someone else, and likely above him."

"Um, yeah, I might have to agree, at least in theory."

"Furthermore, when jumping from one world to another, it is highly unlikely you can follow this sort of movement. Simply reflect on your own statement of following us using portals. It is generally the same. And yet, they were found each time. This tells us they were followed, but it had to be on the inside, not the outside. Next would be their mysterious arrival on Ruuki uy'Daan with the orcs, a species known to be owned by Sargeras and used previously to invade my world. So, whoever was directing their ship on that occasion did so intentionally, and with prior knowledge of the destination. I think Velen and his people would know if an alien creature was walking amongst them, and especially if he was sitting in such an obvious location as their navigation console. This means, whoever it was had to be impersonating one of them at the time."

"Uh oh... That does actually hold merit."

"Finally, to enable some or all of this, he would need to possess the ability to move about by jumping from location to location. This would be similar to using portals, but here we are speaking of an innate ability. I know there are beings out there with this capacity, such as the Estelar themselves, as well as a society of beings we call Celestials."

"I've heard that word before, Celestial, in a book I own. So, he would have to be something on the scale of one of those?"

"At the very least... These represent numerous coincidences that simply cannot be explained by anything other than a being capable of altering his form as desired and conducting any action he chooses. And if he arrived alongside Sargeras, he could be a servant creature of some sort."

"All right, fine. So this...Darumon...could be here with us, and you're claiming it to be the Governor by now. Despite what I saw out there with that demon, you're now speaking of something nearly on the scale of a god, right? And just what do you think you can do about it? You with your army and their adamantium armor."

"I will leave Darumon to those who govern the Seas of Creation. They are coming here to investigate this world, and what he and his false-god Master have done to the place."

"Oh, but of course," he chides. "Now you're going to bring the wrath of your gods down on us. I should've guessed as much. This now reminds me of your Captain and his story of how you have some kind of divine mandate to do this or that. So, you came to your world from somewhere because some god tells you to go out and conquer the place. From there, you take up a band of merry men and do exactly that."

Thaelyn glanced briefly at Relissa and the others around him. He could see they were all growing increasingly disturbed by the Dean's belligerence. But he kept his calm, as he still had a few tricks left to play.

"Actually," he responds smoothly. "She did not specifically tell me to go there and conquer it. She told me to go there because it might pose an interesting challenge to someone like me. It was not until later, when I learned of the divine mandate, that I was actually created for this purpose."

"Oh! Now there's a fine one!" he chortles. "So, you're saying these gods didn't even tell you what you were supposed to be doing until after you already did it?"

"Well, no, not precisely," he reflects nonchalantly. "Partway through, to encourage me to continue the process…yes, we could say that. After all, we are forgetting my merry men. I had to build that first from people who desired to follow me, rather than conquered slaves who did not otherwise care for my form of rule."

"Ah, but of course!" he laughs boldly. "How silly of me!"

Relissa and Marelle both giggled at his careful play. Tristeen glared at the two of them, and then looked into Thaelyn's eyes trying to judge his authenticity.

"Are you actually serious, or just playing with him now?"

Thaelyn smiled at her as he continued.

"Dean, in answer to your statement about gods coming here, I think you should temper yourself a bit. Your Governor may know more about this than you, at this point. If he and Sargeras hold any knowledge of who the Estelar are, they might know of their history. Such beings on this scale tend to learn a few things."

"Um…right…" he relents softly as he reflects on the Governor's reactions to that name.

"What is even worse is how they seem to be toying with me, and this is most certainly offensive. Given what the Suuden-Aryku are known for, as well as their capabilities, sending a simple assassin is nonsensical for them. Using adamantium is also implausible for their historical background. But someone who likes to toy with things, like the Daanen-Aryku, might also take pleasure out of a new arrival, and your Governor did threaten me on that first day of unknown dangers in this world."

"Yes, I recall that now."

"Therefore, despite this obvious play, if they knew who and what I truly was, they would not so quickly take this action. I am a very savvy opponent, one who plays on other people's unknowing and weak assumptions to give me an advantage. Haran reported back to me about his meeting in here, saying you regarded me as a simple man. I cannot blame you personally, as I had this on many occasions back home. But I will certainly thank you for reporting this to your Governor, as I am sure he was very pleased to see such a simple man and his merry men, dressed in adamantium, performing so expertly as to defeat his proud Suuden-Aryku military, as well as your demon outside."

"Yes, um, do be so kind as not to mention that," he begs. "My ears are still ringing from the last time he screamed at me."

"But of course, and yet, I suspect we are not finished. You still need to report back after we are done here."

"Yes, and I'm truly dreading this one."

"Well, with apologies, it gets worse. The assassin could be forgiven if you simply underestimated me. But that demon was pure recklessness. We knew about your circle, Dean, and my people are a bit more privileged in their studies to know what to expect out of it. Therefore, my demonstration out there was intended to tell you what my army is actually made of...merry men, adamantium, or otherwise."

"Yes, and it surely made a statement."

"And this was only a small handful. As I believe I once mentioned in the beginning, my full army consists of millions of such, each with a number of heavy enchantments, divine blessings, and a few other special qualities, making them especially robust as compared to the more common example. You probably took notice of how they were tossed around like rag dolls, but just stood up again and rejoined the fight, correct?"

"Yes, and that was very surprising. How did you do that?"

"My purpose was to conquer a world...and not take no for an answer. To do this would require more than just a few simple tricks of the trade. It would demand a very robust education system to develop our wisdom well beyond where it was when I first arrived. From this, among other things, we took benefit from much improved services and their associated inventions. Therefore, we can say our studies are much more advanced than yours, assuming you actually had any to compare with."

Tristeen let out a compulsive giggle at the suggestion. The Dean glared at her briefly for the outburst.

"Yeah," he sighs. "I'm starting to regret that now, and the Governor seemed a tad concerned over it."

"Good, then my point was made. But we still have another important issue to resolve before I can take my leave and give you the opportunity to resume your duties."

"Good, and then I can be rid of you," he sighs.

"For now, at least..." he smirks. "My Captain informed you that I am not native to Tae'Eladar. This means I am not part of that society, and subsequently not related to any of the various beings that live there, at least not in a direct sense."

"But you look human to me, so are you now going to tell me you are a shapeshifter?" he chuckles.

"No, I am not one of those. My appearance is similar, but not exact."

The Dean's face suddenly went from a humorous appeal to a concerned frown. He had long taken notice of Thaelyn's eye and hair color, but so far, he had been mostly ignoring it as a simple variation.

"Oh grand, then I suppose now you want to suggest that you are something on the scale of a god, like all these others, right?"

"Oh, come now, Dean," Thaelyn retorts sarcastically. "Surely, a man of your background would know better than that. After all, if you are so fervently denying my gods, such a statement as this would fail automatically."

Relissa and Marelle burst into another set of vigorous giggles, which again drew the attention of the others in the room. Tristeen studied them, and feeling a slight shiver run through her at the implications. The Dean also examined their reactions, and although he didn't want to admit to it openly, he felt a similar rush.

"Uh huh..." he moans. "Well, you certainly seem to have someone convinced."

"We're convinced, Dean," Marelle smiles, "because we've seen him in action. A bit like that demonstration of his men outside, he made a number of his own during this time."

"Simply grand…"

"This final argument is two-fold," Thaelyn continues. "But generally, it relates to a larger complaint. I think your Governor might be interested in hearing it."

"You think?" he raises his brow.

"Oh indeed. We will begin with an unfortunate event that took place back at the start of the alleged elven war."

"Alleged?!" he barks.

"I come from a society that studies and follows a principle we call the Measure of Balance. Perhaps you have heard of it?"

"Yes, actually, from your priests over there…at least in passing."

"Very good. The Estelar govern all of Creation, and that includes this universe and everything within. In fact, I am aware of only a very few places that might be excluded from this, and usually for some particular reason. The Measure of Balance is to be observed by any creature that might pretend to be a god, and if they cannot, they will be destroyed for their belligerence. The Estelar tend to be very strict on this point, and again, they have their reasons. When you reach such a prominent position, you cannot show leniency. Not when you hold the power to reshape Creation."

"Great gods…um…" Tristeen mumbles. "Well…yeah, I suppose."

"Indeed," he smiles at her. "And here we come to the violations of the elves. They once held their religion on this world, which was surely handed down by their ancestors. We have the same back home as well. And it was despoiled by what I believe to be that same agent that did so much harm elsewhere. He destroyed their holy Trees of Life, which are ancestral items that date back to the beginning of their kind. No ELF would do this, as their species depend on these things for their health and well-being. And yet, every city saw their local shrines desecrated, with evidence left behind to implicate the other side."

"No elf, because their species…depends on it?" the Dean winces. "What sort of species needs a tree to survive? Well, I mean…um…"

"Yes, this is perhaps a rather unique circumstance, to be sure. The trees bring a form of spiritual harmony to them, and everything else around them, as they come from a place where all life is closely tied to the natural world, more so than humans tend to be. And these particular trees are not your usual variety, as they serve as a type of bonding agent."

"Interesting," he muses thoughtfully. "And this was done by what you believe to be an agent. Are we speaking of him again?"

"It must be, as he would certainly not respect them or their religion, especially if you consider the Flame Elves were found offering their worship to Sargeras. This was after a type of forced servitude using telepathic mind control. Our spies learned they heard his voices enter their minds at a young age and not relent. Eventually, they succumbed to it and became his slaves."

The Dean grimaced at the depiction.

"And this happened when? Our history tells of them joining only after the Suuden-Aryku arrived."

"Your history, perhaps… But the Daanen-Aryku had their ship sabotaged by them on Ruuki uy'Daan, so this already refutes that claim, as they had to be involved prior to this."

"Yes, I suppose they would."

"This also occurred as the result of the death of their trees, which offered its own fulfillment, but Sargeras tried replacing it with his."

"Great gods… But evidence, you say? What kind?"

"We found bottles left behind on both sides and had the Daanen-Aryku conduct a little forensic study to see what was inside. It was a chemical compound of synthetic origin and could not be native to this world. Therefore, our only other suspect is the Suuden-Aryku producing it, and then someone delivering it. And the artisanry of the bottles pointed the elves at each other for the favor. This is now a conspiracy to start a war, and it reflects on Sargeras and his agents again."

"Well, bloody hell, that's a fine one!" he blurts. "So, what you're saying is they didn't actually start anything after all, at least not on their own."

"Correct."

Thaelyn paused a moment while he and the others studied the Dean as he unconsciously huffed and glanced around his desk, then briskly out the window. Thaelyn could feel a slight awakening within him stirring, but it was proving to be a steep climb out of its hole.

"Now..." Thaelyn resumes. "My arrival here has allowed the people of Solinaia to reunite with their kin on Tae'Eladar, and therefore their proper gods. My priests, who as you say snuck in under your noses, are doing the same with your people, as you should probably be made aware of who you are supposed to be worshiping, rather than that nonsense you had before."

"But just a moment," the Dean argues. "Do you actually think we would want that here?"

"At this moment, it is moot. As I said before, I am calling them here to investigate how all of you came to be here, and further in this condition, so badly abused by someone. Therefore, once they figure out who is responsible, and if this is also who you are worshiping, you are likely to lose it anyway."

"Ouch..."

"Furthermore, do you actually think I would want you to have this in the first place? We must recall these details... Your priests were committing murder. Your own Guard asked for my assistance. Therefore, I was invited in by the local legal authority. Your priests were also slandering everyone else. And since we are now speaking of my citizens in Solinaia, and good friends and allies at the Naarg uy'Sodrad, I take personal offence at this. I have been known to go to war for this much, to defend the honor of they who are wrongly treated."

This stifled the Dean, and he held back from any rebuttal. He briefly reflected on the words of the priests, and then the earlier statements of moving huge numbers of soldiers around using portals.

"In addition," Thaelyn continues. "We should remember who those priests worked for, and then who he works for, along with what I said about the Measure of Balance. And for this, I should reiterate, if this is your god, mine will have a few words for it, especially as

I believe we exist in a universe that is part of their jurisdictional domain. Mortal creatures such as you do not make these rules, Dean."

"Mortal creatures?" he mumbles softly.

Tristeen also caught the reference, and she reflexively looked up into Thaelyn's eyes. She followed this by glancing at Relissa and Marelle, neither of whom seemed affected by the statement.

Thaelyn continues, "The elves also had a number of holy symbols, the last few they still possessed after leaving Tae'Eladar. These were traded between the cities and last known to be in Kynesoth. They represent the elven gods, which means the Seldarine, and of course these are again members of the Estelar. And to be precise, these gods cover all the elves, not just those in that one city. However, they were stolen at the same time as these trees were killed."

"All right, so they were stolen," the Dean shrugs. "But this would again be back in the beginning, right? That's a long time passing to go around lodging complaints."

"Perhaps, and if it were not for a recent discovery, it might be a forgotten issue. But the discovery revives it, as we have learned where they were taken."

"Oh, this should be good. And are your gods going to groan about this as well?"

"I will tend to this one myself. Allow me to explain what these were. There are four of them, rather unique in their design. One is a crescent moon, another is a full moon with a halo, the third is an oak tree, and the fourth is a golden heart. And they are made from a metal that no one here seems to know how to work. Mithril."

As Thaelyn made his depiction, the Dean felt a cold shiver running down his back. And when the statement was complete, he felt a flutter inside as his mind shot to a cabinet across the room against the far wall.

"Dean," Thaelyn concludes. "I have information from multiple sources that you have four mithril artifacts in your possession, and by the descriptions, they appear exactly the same as these stolen holy symbols. I must wonder how they got here."

"And are you going to blame me for this?" he grumbles. "I wasn't even alive back then."

"Of course, Dean. After all, you are human. Clearly, it had to be that same person who killed the trees and brought the High Elves into such despair that his Master, Sargeras, could simply take over. I am sure whoever the Dean was at the time was a happy little fellow to have something shiny to look at. But that time is at an end now. The citizens of Solinaia have petitioned my government to retrieve them on behalf of their rightful owners."

"Citizens!" he blasts. "You would dare come in here and demand any such thing on behalf of those people?!" he points defiantly at Relissa.

Thaelyn's ire was suddenly rising. The Dean had been making a slow reckoning, but the roller-coaster ride of realization was hitting too many obstacles along the way, and this one was clearly a sensitive topic.

Relissa and Marelle could see in Thaelyn's eyes he was growing tired of the debate and the Dean's obstinacy. It was becoming clear by now a harsher approach might be necessary to drive the point home.

"Indeed, I would!" Thaelyn asserts sternly. "And further, as a political member of this world, I will also demand you and yours to stop debasing my citizens with your prejudices and unsavory ranting."

"A political member!" he shouts. "How can you possibly call yourself a political member? You invade our world, set up camp in that valley down there, and now you call yourself a political member?"

"Indeed, it is you who could learn a few things about politics, Dean, assuming you would ever make the attempt. By the merit that Solinaia has voluntarily joined my kingdom, I now hold political authority within this world. And as one who goes to war with those who offend my people, and with you holding such a paltry claim of any kind within this city, I would advise you to stay that waggling tongue of yours. I established that camp down there because someone here declared war on me! And that someone is further discovered to be in possession of former citizens of my domain."

"Huh? And just how do you explain that one?"

"You scoff at my notion of a divine mandate? Everyone here, save the Daanen-Aryku of course, were illegally stolen away from us by someone with ulterior motives of his own design. Even worse is the assault and torment he laid down upon you during this time, and all the other atrocities he committed. I will therefore grant myself the authority to cross the Seas of Creation to see this injustice corrected. And then, he and that infidel named Sargeras will be brought to justice by those who rule the Seas of Creation!"

The Dean found himself quickly backing down from his rant due to the strong reprisal.

"You can't be serious…can you?" he whines. "Would any such man, or whatever you claim yourself to be, go to such extremes?"

"We, Dean, most certainly would, as one universe is but a small slice of our domain."

"Yours…ours…erm, theirs…"

The Dean felt a new shiver run through him. This statement was hinting at something suddenly a lot bigger. The use of such words implied a decisive association of some sort.

"I choose to unite worlds, Dean," Thaelyn continues. "Not divide them. And I do not necessarily have to be limited to my own. That creature opened a door from Tae'Eladar to this place. Now, here I am, spreading my authority to farther reaches, and I will do no different here than I did there. And if he has anything else to say about it, I will hope it does not involve any more of his preposterous assassins."

"What about the Suuden-Aryku?" he whimpers.

"He controls them no different than anything else around here, using devices to govern their minds. They were perhaps his first victims, at least in recent history. I would choose not to go to war with them outright, as I am not a destroyer of worlds, and theirs would be a target under those conditions."

"Oh dear."

"And indeed, if they still hold any part of their ability to think independently, and if we say they are not such to recognize a true god, let us hope they at least recognize a power greater than their own, and choose to back away from it. But it would seem your Governor holds a very tight control over them. If he should try to unleash this, mine will unleash ours, and it will not be limited to this world."

The Dean pauses to consider the Governor's mention on multiple occasions of his so-called contacts and reports of things that should otherwise be outside his personal view. He also reflects on the deliveries in the basement, and the obvious relationship he apparently held, and then the tantrums he would sometimes have when things went wrong. The image was building up rather vividly by now.

"And here is where we need to tidy up our little parley," Thaelyn resumes. "I have relayed details of this place to my contacts amongst the Estelar. The Seldarine are especially upset to hear of a pretender who steals away their Children. At this time, we might even see some of them investigate personally. Their leader, one known as Corellon Larethian, otherwise known as the Protector, will likely want to learn of how the Flame Elves were stolen away, and who is responsible. Not only will he want to reclaim them, but he might also go in search of the heathens that did this."

"But...but..."

"The city of Solinaia is currently under watch, since they maintained their association, and my arrival has only strengthened it by now. Then we have this city. This religion you otherwise do not want could be the only thing that saves you from that creature across the way. Although, admittedly, the people here are not as attuned to it as yet. But we are working on it. Nevertheless, I want that thing you call a Governor to know this much. We are watching. I will demand all hostile actions by the Suuden-Aryku on this world to cease immediately. There shall be no further attempts at the Daanen-Aryku, no attempts at Solinaia, and none here. And especially none against me, or any of my people! Understood?"

"Yes, perfectly, but um..."

"What?" Thaelyn asserts firmly.

"Look, I'm not a man to take up in fisticuffs, but let's face it, this is a rather large load of...well... And if you're expecting me to bring this up to someone described as nearly a god..."

"Yes, I suppose it is a difficult concept. Then you should take with you a few precise terms that he will understand and recognize as something to run away from."

Thaelyn expected this would come eventually, as he had to make his personal demonstration. He formed a tiny smile as he mulled his direction.

Relissa and Marelle both watched. They knew Thaelyn's manners from his interrogation of the Flame Elves, and when they saw this curious sign on his face, they couldn't help but wonder what sort of plan he had in mind to finalize this tribunal.

"Recall the encounter outside," Thaelyn begins. "I was speaking to that glabrezu of yours in its native tongue."

"Glabrezu..." he wheezes. "You even know its name?"

"Did I not say we hold some privileged knowledge? But even more is that you and the Governor should have overheard this exchange, including the names being mentioned."

"Yes, we did hear yours at one time."

"And I called it by name as well...Navaatu."

"Right, I heard that one, too. It's a little scary, actually. How do you know its name? Do you call up demons over there?"

"No, this practice is actually outlawed in our society, same as with necromancy and a few others. I know of him, however, from personal experience. Do you see this sword on my back?" he thumbs over his shoulder. "I was once sent out to reclaim it...from him... as it was stolen property, and it fell to me to retrieve it. Later, it was awarded to me for my achievement. But along the way, I made something of a name for myself."

"Oh dear gods..."

"Yeah, Dean," Tristeen wheezes. "On this occasion, I might have to agree with you. Who sent you out there to retrieve it?"

"My Father..." Thaelyn admits. "But Dean, when my Captain told you I am not native to Tae'Eladar, this is to say I came from a place that would normally oppose such beings as that. I may not be a god, but I am the child of one."

Tristeen gasped and fell back a step. This reaction was not lost on the Dean, but the ludicrous nature of the suggestion, as well as his disdain for the young lady and what she represented, caused him to simply rebuke the notion.

"Oh! Really! The child of a god! Does this have anything to do with that divine mandate? Oh, I'm sure it must by now!"

"Dean," Thaelyn asserts. "I understand if you are not a religious man, and this is reasonable, as not everyone can be so enlightened. But for a man who can believe in demons, even to such extent that he tries calling one up, and who is in possession of a book of unknown origin, one he should not otherwise be in possession of, which details the flora and fauna of the Outer Planes, you should probably spend a little more time studying the beings found in the Upper Planes, not the Lower ones."

Tristeen stepped back even further, and was now covering her face and whimpering softly.

"Huh?" the Dean blurts unexpectedly. "How would you know about that?"

"My spies are everywhere, Dean, including under your nose!" he glances briefly at Tristeen. "You mentioned you knew the word, Celestial?"

By now, the Dean's face was flushing, first due to the mention of the book, and second to that word.

"Um…" he flusters.

"There are two flavors," Thaelyn interjects. "One is easy, the natural variety, which means to say a society of beings who have excelled in their development such that they no longer make their residence in a material universe like this one. The Estelar will commonly take them into apprenticeship to assist in their continued development until one day they evolve further to join with them proper."

"That's…strange…" he gasps.

"This is where such beings as they ultimately come from. And then there is the other kind, a hybrid form. But there is an important difference here, Dean, as Celestials do not need circles to conjure themselves into. We can travel as we please."

Thaelyn took a single step forward into the room and set his sights on the Dean's desk. He extended his hand with fingers outstretched and pointed assertively at the item of furniture.

The Dean glared at him for his odd behavior, and then he saw movement in front of him. The desk lurched off the floor and began levitating. Everyone in the room now followed the desk with their eyes as it rose up in front of the Dean's face.

"Oh dear…" he whines.

The Dean's eyes bulged as he observed the large piece of furniture hovering right in front of him. Thaelyn held it there, rolling it around while keeping the various papers, pens, and such in place as it turned upside down, then came around upright again. He then swiped his hand off to the side, sending the desk crashing through the wall into the next room.

"Great gods above!" Tristeen yelps as she cringes.

"My Father was Lord Tyr," Thaelyn asserts. "The former Lord of Justice before Torm took that role. I was created directly by his hand in human form. Mine is called Aasimar. My wife is another one, based on the elven frame, known as Eladrin. And when I say we hold a divine mandate, this is to say they put us there! And for such reasons as to bring all of you disobedient mortals into order! And Tae'Eladar was full of them at one time."

"Disobedient…?"

Now he gets serious. For added effect, he chose to energize himself with his divine power. He drew in a breath, and as he composed himself, an aura formed around his body, and his eyes radiated brightly. He then brought his other hand up and jabbed it at the Dean with an open palm. This gripped the Dean harshly in a telekinetic web, snatching him off the ground and reeling him in for a close encounter. At this point, Thaelyn further combined a reverberation effect into his voice.

The Dean wails in terror as he finds himself entirely helpless, hovering above the ground, and staring into the face of something he could barely comprehend.

"Look here, Dean," Thaelyn shouts. "Peer into the eyes of a

creature you would not wish to meet in a hostile contest. I am no mere mortal, and indeed mortal capacity is inferior to mine."

"Please, don't hurt me," he whimpers. "I didn't really mean anything truly bad."

"Not truly bad? The conjuration of a glabrezu with the intention to assault me is not truly bad?"

"Oh grand…" he sobs. "All right, it was reckless, like you said. I'll admit to this much. But it was that man…creature…him, the Governor. He wanted a way to defeat you, one you couldn't resist. And this simply fit the need."

"Very well, so be it. While your point is understood, the demonstration still needs to be made. Your refusal to admit to anything above your station is in need of correction. An assassin is no match for me. Orcs are no match for me. The Suuden-Aryku are no match for me. Even your demon is no match for me. My only true match would be that of the divine sort."

"That sounds wonderful, it does."

"As for Tae'Eladar, while it can be said I was convinced to follow my path there, it held a hidden purpose to it that I would only learn about later, when I was joined by others to take full possession of that world. And we did, despite the objections of those societies that felt much like you do. Tae'Eladar is a project for one of the Great Powers. It was filled with beings and destined for a future potential; one we are still pursuing. And I will not allow any foreign creature to interfere with it."

"Yes! Oh yes," the Dean titters nervously. "That's truly grand. I won't argue with it."

"But when those orcs rose up, we had to make a decision, one that my kind would find distasteful, to commit genocide upon them for the greater benefit of those who actually did wish to live in peace."

"Uh huh, I can surely see how that would come about."

"And then I find myself here, with all this blasphemy!" he waves at the window. "And worse is to see a pretender in the face of the True Powers harming the Children of Creation with his profanity.

I will not tolerate this, no matter what sort of creature he boasts himself to be."

"Wow," Tristeen mumbles timidly. "You people must be seriously determined."

"Indeed, we are, and for good reason. We govern the Seas of Creation. There is a history of those who came before who were put down for their errant deeds. And the Great Powers are always keen to watch for more. And here we have one."

"So, does this mean you want words with him yourself?" the Dean mutters tenderly.

"As I said, I will leave this to those in the appropriate positions. But if he is one that does not follow the Measure of Balance, he will meet with my family to correct this oversight. There are no other Powers before them, and only those who conform to their principles may follow after. As for me, he is not welcome here. Mine and his are not compatible, and I am not leaving. Instead, I hold in mind to reclaim these lost Children and restore them as they once were."

"I'm sure that's quite dandy…for those of us who may survive the affair."

"Now, Dean," Thaelyn concludes. "I will grace upon you the extraordinary occasion to perform at least one sensible act in your life. Where are those holy symbols that belong to the elves? They are regarded as stolen property, and we want them returned. It is due to this those High Elves suffered their tragedy. And it is due to that tragedy that I will cross any border to seek justice."

"Yes! Oh yes, I can see that now."

"Therefore, I will have you bring them out and give them to this young lady here," he directs at Relissa. "And do so with a smile on your face."

Tristeen felt a new giggle coming on as she watched the Dean squirming. Marelle and the others also grinned at the display. The Dean glanced around at the group, but at this point, he couldn't feel anything but weakness and dread for his obvious predicament.

Thaelyn lowered the man to the ground and returned his visage to normal again. The Dean stumbled back a step as he tried to put a little distance between them.

"Um, yes, but of course," he forces a broad smile through his distress.

The Dean reached into a vest pocket and pulled out a key. His hands were trembling as he pointed at a cabinet across the way and went to open it. He then stepped back to reveal the four mithril artifacts.

"Relissa," Thaelyn directs. "If you would be so kind..."

She confidently steps over and takes the items into her arms, then turns back to the Dean with a tidy smirk on her face.

"It's nice to have friends in high places, don't you think?"

"Apparently so," he laments. "But I suspect mine won't be so happy."

Thaelyn then turns and directs everyone out of the office.

"We shall take our leave of you now," he submits. "Tell your Governor I will be waiting for his next move with great anticipation. His little invasion of those orcs into my world brought back more than just an inconvenience to his games here. At the very least, I will demand him to leave this place. At most, he will deal with the Estelar."

Thaelyn begins to leave the room when a final thought hits him.

"And Dean," he adds. "This is for you alone. I may hold my privileged knowledge, but openly, if he is such a creature high enough to perform these deeds, I will reflect again that he should know who the Estelar are, at the very least by reference, if not also by personal encounters. As for you, be aware of him."

They now exit the room and proceed along the hall to the stairs. They descend to the first floor when Marelle turns to Thaelyn.

"Your Lordship, were you actually offering him advice, or was that last statement something else?"

"Recall what I said earlier today. Our games outside were playing with his mind, such that he might be weakening. I could see his emotions in there, and also his thoughts rising and falling. You already know I would not wish to bring intentional harm to one who might be just as ignorant as so many others. Some of his reactions were partly due to arrogance, some to bravado. I will attribute some portion of this to the influence of the Governor. But I also took notice on several occasions that he seemed genuinely interested in some of the lessons."

"I saw this too. I was trying to take note of those reactions, but then he fell right back to his bravado again."

"Yes, he is a man in turmoil. But this tells me he was not completely in the know. Therefore, if even he can be taught a lesson or two, I would not wish to ignore the possibility of opening his eyes to something bigger, as he could be every bit as much a servant as any other. I do not wish his ignorance to be his downfall."

"Gracious," Tristeen muses deeply. "You people must be exceptionally noble out there."

"The Celestial races follow in the path of the Estelar. We are as much parental figures as we are scholars and advisors. We do not throw people away, if it is at all possible. We encourage growth and self-improvement. I cannot guarantee anything where that man is concerned, but I sensed within him a tiny spark of a lost soul that was crying out in the shadow of a potent oppressive force. Therefore, I did what was becoming of my nature."

Tristeen gazed up into his eyes for a moment, as she reflected on all her own experiences with the Dean. She found it hard to believe the man could ever change, but to see someone who would even afford the opportunity was a humbling sight. Then she had another flash arrive. She turned to peer down the hallway.

"This reminds me. I want to see about that book. I don't want to leave it in his possession. If this is any part of his…corruption…I want to take it away."

She runs down the corridor and around the corner to the basement. She halts just in front of the door to examine it. The door, the framework, and part of the wall were thoroughly torn apart. The smell of sulfur and something charred wafted up out of the room. She stepped inside carefully.

The room was in disarray, like everything else. Tables were

upturned and smashed, broken lab equipment was strewn across the floor, and in the far corner she saw the circle with a portion of the runic glyphs smudged to provide a break in the warding barrier. She moved closer and found the remains of a body, badly scorched near the circle. It wore the robe of one of the instructors.

She could only shake her head and move forward to a table on the far side. There she saw the book. It was covered with a layer of ash, but otherwise undamaged. She grabbed it and ran out quickly to return to Thaelyn and the others who were still waiting for her.

"Here," she offers the book. "You take this. Get it out of here."

Thaelyn takes the book and examines it briefly as he continues leading them back outside. The book was professionally typeset on what seemed like pages made of plastic. Even though there seemed to be some heat damage from the demon's arrival, the material seemed to hold up well to it.

They arrived out in the plaza and began proceeding in the direction of the barracks. They halt just outside the gates and Thaelyn turns to the assembly again.

"Very well, everyone, listen carefully," he begins. "Miss Macaid, I would suggest you find shelter for yourself. The Dean may have been given the fear of God, but the Governor is another thing. We may need to act fast when he makes his departure, but he may also choose to leave behind a parting gift. Where are your two friends?"

"We were hiding in the park over there before all this happened. Willit tends to keep himself in the lower district at the Ten Eagles. I've made it a habit to stake out the park so I could watch things up here, and Jared sometimes makes runs around the city."

"At this moment, I might suggest you remove yourself from view. Perhaps you could go home and rest, or find some other occupation for yourself."

"All right, but what should I do if the Governor does that parting gift thing? And what sort of parting gift do you mean? I remember Willit speaking of a turning point, but with the demon gone, what's left?"

"I think, even with my warning, I would not wish to take anything for granted. He may run away, or he may try to play a trick on us behind our backs. More than anything, he may wish to punish those who are disobeying him in the city. My final statements in there were intended to discourage this, but his kind holds virtually no respect for life, unless that life holds some value for him, such as for utility or entertainment. And right now, your people serve neither of these."

"Wonderful. Do we know who he actually is and where he came from?"

"We believe so, but we must walk a fine line here. He and Sargeras have likely been in hiding for a long time, and if they feel themselves safe under their rock, I want them to stay there, not run again if the Estelar should come looking for them. For this, I must make the advance, as I will not stand out as much."

"But then what? Can you take him down yourself?"

"I may call in help, but timing and maneuvering are important here."

"All right, I get it, but gracious, what have we gotten ourselves into here? What will happen to our city and the people?"

"I have already made a promise to help your people, but we may need to evacuate them if he holds any interest in taking revenge. If we must, the city will be made sacrifice, if only to remove him from this world under the threat of the Estelar discovering who he really is and taking their own action."

"So, let me see if I understand this right. That threat was more of a bluff to get him to run away from you, back under that rock, so you can hunt him on your own terms. And also, this might reflect on those Suuden-Aryku he controls so carefully, and if they should do anything, bam! There goes their whole world, which you're trying to avoid."

"Very good, young lady," he smiles. "You hold a fair amount of deductive reasoning."

Tristeen smiles at the compliment.

"I swear...men," she shakes her head. "And it must run all the way up the ladder."

Thaelyn laughs softly at her dilemma.

"Yes, I suppose, but there are rules to such games as these, and they are not always limited to the male side."

"All right, I understand," she sighs. "This will be hard for a lot of people, but I'll do what I can."

"Good. We will try to inform you of what we learn once we have it."

Tristeen nods and turns to go home. She waves discreetly to the others, who are still in the park. They broke up, and each moved off in their own direction.

Thaelyn and his people make their final goodbyes. He orders a mage to use a portal rune to evacuate Relissa and her group while he and the rest take up on their gryphons again.

Chapter 13

ELUSIVE DUPLICITY

As the conversation took place inside the Dean's office, the Governor continued looking out the window, waiting for Thaelyn to emerge from the academy. He would not rest until he saw the man finally leave the city, only then to feel some relief for the events of the day. Time stretched out unbearably for him as the entrance of the academy still showed no signs of the visitors leaving.

He continued to stare down into the plaza. The pavement was in ruin from the pounding of the demon's immense weight, and the battle that took place. Citizens were just starting to reappear from their homes to examine the scene, and members of the Guard were moving out to investigate the damage.

When he finally saw Thaelyn and his entourage leave the building, he studied them carefully.

"What took you so long inside there?" he mumbles under his breath. "Did we have a pleasant little chat? What next do you think you can do to foil my labors? Maybe the Commander was right to begin with. I should've had you blasted off the planet for your troubles. But then, how could I know you would be so difficult to remove, and this assignment has been getting rather dull after four centuries of watching these peasants travelling in the same circles."

He continued to observe them parting their ways, with some using portal runes and others travelling off into the city.

"I will need to remember those who have been giving him so much assistance. They will demand something special once we finally do remove him."

Finally, he watched as Thaelyn and his people loaded up on their gryphons, and left the area.

"I must admit, however, those creatures are rather interesting. I wonder if one day I could breed them into something new."

Several moments later, a beleaguered Dean trudges into the Governor's office, having finally rid himself of Thaelyn and his troupe. He leans against the wall as the Governor turns away from the window. The man was pale and weary, and rubbing his cheeks and brow for all the wear he took.

"What happened in there, Dean?" the Governor urges. "Why did it take so long?"

"My Lord, if you will kindly indulge me a moment, I carry a number of statements to declare."

"I see. All right, this should be interesting."

"After a rather long and arduous discussion, and then I had to take a moment to change my pants, here I am to inform you of what was said."

"You what?" the Governor winces. "You had to change your pants. Why, did we have a little accident?" he muses wittily.

"Actually, yes, a minor one," he smiles tenderly. "But you might want to stay your teasing, because I suspect you'll be next."

"Oh! All right, perhaps I will retract my statement. What do we have this time?"

"First, if you thought he was hard to kill before, you don't know the half of it. Also, he's been learning all the little secrets of this world. To begin with, if you will recall those priests and what they said, well, more of the same here. Like we said once before, you wouldn't play nice with him in the beginning, and now he regards you, and me as well, as enemies. Initially, he was only interested in the orcs, although I suppose he would've turned to the others eventually. But when he caught that spy I sent, that marked us not simply as uncooperative, but as potential hostiles for spying on his efforts to free us from our alleged enemies."

"Oh really. And how did you respond to this accusation that we are simply trying to understand the workings of our world?"

"Poorly. It was easily shot down. His response in one statement was why couldn't we simply go down there and ask. It would've made for such a pleasant example of our willingness to participate in the world we are so concerned about."

"All right, point taken. This man is clearly more assertive than anyone else around here."

"Oh, indeed! Aside from that, he's not one to argue with. We need to recall he is a king of a full world, and with that full world of resources entirely at his disposal. And apparently, he doesn't skimp on anything, if we consider his military and their equipment. He sent his own spies out there to find out why, exactly, you won't play nice to him. And he found his answers."

The Governor went silent for a moment, suddenly feeling a sinking feeling for all his efforts.

"What did he say?"

"Like I said, if you will indulge me, he apparently wanted me to give you a full report of his findings, just so you know exactly how much he seems to know."

"Really! Very well, where do we begin?"

"Let's begin with that first invasion of orcs you apparently sent to Tae'Eladar roughly ten millennia ago. At the same time, that weird portal thing you apparently built to lead our ancestors to this world, and how this so nicely seems to coincide with you and Sargeras arriving on Azgarén and, as he says, apparently becoming active on some plan that is leading in this direction."

"Excuse me!" he shouts. "Where does all the 'me this' and 'me that' business come in?"

"Is your name Darumon? That's your answer. They remember you."

The Governor suddenly went very quiet. He felt a sting of

vulnerability as he glared at the Dean for a long moment before responding.

"When you say, they remember…who, and what is it they remember?"

"Well, first and foremost, apparently the Daanen-Aryku recall your name arriving next to Sargeras. He also learned from his spies speaking to the Flame Elves that you run the show around here, not the Suuden-Aryku military commander."

"What?!" he screeches. "He actually sent spies to talk to our precious little elves?"

"He apparently started sending out his own spies after catching that one I sent into his camp. That was a turning point for him to declare us as hostile. So, this might follow naturally."

"Yes, it would. Blast!"

"Also, his spies don't need invisibility cloaks, or at least don't use them as often. And he likes to learn things, not simply look at stuff for someone like me to toss away in the trash."

"Yes, as we have seen already. All right, what else does he know? For instance, does he know anything else about me personally?"

"I don't know precisely, but if he does, he probably wouldn't tell me about it, since he also likes keeping his secrets from people to use to his advantage."

"Oh really! Well, I suppose this is a fair enough expectation."

"Anyway, to continue… This man doesn't apparently forget, and neither does he forgive past deeds. So, we have the first arrival of those orcs from places and by means that should be outside their capacity. They're not that good at magic, and his home is in another universe entirely, which ought to deny them to know anything about it."

"Yes, this might stand out."

"Unless they had help, but that help would have to be special. Not only would it need to know Tae'Eladar exists, but also have the ability to find it and aim a portal to it. But here we have another issue. Apparently, it's hidden inside a huge shell to protect it from an outside maelstrom left behind by some ancient battle that destroyed their universe. Tae'Eladar is apparently a survivor."

"A survivor? Interesting. I would not think anything should have survived that."

The Dean glared at the Governor briefly as he pondered the unusual statement. But he kept silent for this point.

"Apparently," he continues. "This shell represents an impervious barrier, so the only way in or out is by way of a portal. In fact, he stated that if it were not for your orcs, he might need to consult the Estelar themselves for help to find a way out, since they're the ones who built it."

"Ah, so that's where it came from. Then I suppose it must be made of Imberium. That could explain it."

"And therefore, the need for someone special, with some very old and very privileged knowledge to find his way inside and build that weird portal thing, which by the way he calls a door that uses a key to activate."

"Really!" the Governor leans back in this chair. "So, he actually uses such terms?"

"He says there are those who do, and this represents that same sort of device they might build."

"I see. So his…privileged knowledge…must be rather extensive."

"It certainly seems so. I suppose this now leads to us here in this world, after so long a time, building up our local civilization, and then to have you come along and blast it to all the gods, leaving only these few remaining cities to enslave."

The Governor lurched forward at this obvious stab.

"Dean, do be mindful of your words here. If he explained so much, you might also know a little of what I am in all this, am I right?"

"At this point, Governor…or perhaps I should simply call you Darumon, as it would seem, the noble families were right. You blackmailed the old Council and took control illegally. But I think I do hold some minor right to admit I'm one of the citizens of this world, and I might take some small exception to you, or anyone else, blasting the rest of my people to oblivion simply to take control of whatever remained. This is only made worse by my compliance to serve you during this time. So, you are not my only problem. He mentioned burying people like us. Therefore, I think my fate, at the very least, is sealed, with or without your threats."

The Governor glared at the Dean as he pondered the statement. His ire was clearly ignited, but at the same time, he did have to admit to the Dean's argument. Regardless of this, his displeasure had to be tempered by his need for this information.

"Very well, Dean. I will grant you this little outburst. But I would still advise you to regulate your manners while in my presence."

"All right, so here we go with the rest of it. If to carry forward in some predictable manner for the timing, he believes you are also the one to kill the elven Trees of Life, and to steal those mithril holy symbols I had in my possession."

"Had?"

"Yes, he took them back on behalf of his citizens in Solinaia. They apparently filed a formal complaint that we are the ones who stole them, even though this was back four centuries ago. And since they joined his kingdom, he is now claiming official political authority in this world, including, but not limited to, demanding us to stop slandering them with our prejudices and whatnot."

"Well now, he certainly is a feisty one."

"Oh, I'm not even finished on that side of it. He says those Trees of Life are an ancestral holy thing from the ancient home of the elves, and are, as he describes it, necessary for their health and well-being. Therefore, no ELF would dare harm them. This had to be an outside job, and he apparently found bottles with elven artisanry laid as false evidence against each other, but containing some kind of poison that could not be of this world. This means the Suuden-Aryku, which must also mean you again."

"I see. And to demonstrate this, are we saying he has the ability to test this poison?"

"Yes, it's called the Daanen-Aryku."

"Blast, I would think by now they should not have the capacity in that rusting hulk of theirs to perform anything useful anymore."

"Now, moving forward, we have your orcs invading his world and making trouble, as we already know. This brought him here, where he found even more trouble. He was trying to avoid a fight on the side of the Flame Elves, at least up until you sent that assassin his way. And then we have that Suuden-Aryku patrol you were griping about once. All of which were apparently dressed in adamantium. You know, you should probably be more careful where you apply that stuff. It tends to stand out, especially for someone who knows what it is."

The Governor scowled softly, but realized the Dean was actually right.

"All right, this point is also taken. But I will temper this where that patrol is concerned, as we did not know it was him out there."

"Granted, but why would you use it directly inside his camp? Would it actually provide you with so much additional capacity in the middle of all his soldiers who are apparently so much better equipped?"

"I will admit, this might have been an error on my part. It was intended to provide the spy with a little extra protection, and maybe, if it was clever enough, a chance to evade without being shredded in the process."

"All right, I suppose this is fair. But in the end, this simply opened a number of questions on where the stuff is coming from."

"Did he mention anything relating to this?"

"No, not directly, other than to say the Suuden-Aryku are not expected to know how to use it themselves, not being magical in nature. And no one else in this world seems to know anything about it. But it does bring me to wonder about that mine up north. It occurs to me, whatever it is they're doing, it can't be for the Suuden-Aryku, and neither is it for any of us."

"Carefully, Dean…"

"I feel this is a perfectly reasonable statement. If we don't get any, and further, we don't even know what it is, and if they don't know what it is, but you do seem to know what it is, this doesn't leave too many options for the intended recipient, now does it?"

The Governor pauses in consideration. The logic was sound, even though it touched on something personal to him.

"Yes, Dean, you do hold a point, but do not ask me why, as I have my own reasons for it, and they are not for discussion with such as you."

"Yes, and I doubt I would understand those reasons, with you being something so much higher than I am, and with such knowledge that I probably couldn't fathom it to begin with. But on the other side of it, why does this crusade of yours seem to be leading towards Tae'Eladar, and that space where their universe got blasted by something? I might think there should be nothing out there for you to bother with by now."

"Yes, this is also a curious point. But again, for those of us in such positions where I am, I might find something even amongst all of that. By the way, if he is sending so many spies out there, does he know about the dwarves?"

"He mentioned knowing of them relating to your, as he calls it, flawed trade deal, where so much of their iron is going to our enemies. He related this to our Guard going out to the Daanen-Aryku and not seeing any action, and with no direct attacks on our walls, which might suggest you selling out to the others."

"Interesting, and this would certainly paint a bold picture. You once mentioned how those people were going out and rummaging through those refuse heaps. Surely, if he is taking any tallies, he might pay attention to what was in there."

"Yes, but I'm also sure he realizes this is simply a show by now. Our supply shortages are engineered while the others get most of it."

"Indeed, and what else does he have to say?"

"It became apparent, fairly quickly I suppose, maybe due to his relationship with the Guard, that the patrol came under attack on this occasion because you didn't send it. But how would the Suuden-Aryku know this, and especially to respond with this atypical armament they shouldn't otherwise have? Therefore, we must have an informant within our walls who knows when, where, how, and why the Guard goes outside. Also, the Flame Elves tell of someone on the inside who is managing us."

"Oh grand! Those blasted elves are becoming a burden for their lack of security."

"I suppose the topic is subjective if you think you're speaking to one of your own. After all, he has the rest of our populations on his world, and this is how he can send spies everywhere, and none of us would know the better for it."

"Yes, so it would seem. And one more liability, also one more error in judgment."

"They also informed on that orcish mission to Tae'Eladar. This naturally leads us to their point of origin, being Ruuki uy'Daan, then coming here, further going there, and using means they would need help to accomplish. Then to combine this, along with the Flame Elves, and the Suuden-Aryku, all under the name of Sargeras. This paints a rather bold picture of someone taking aim at his home. And as he said to me, and I quote: You would dare invade his home, and then you would dare deny him to defend himself, finally to send such as assassins at him to remove him from your troubles... This is where he promises to bury us."

"Oh! Does he now?" he balks. "But tell me, Dean. Let us make a small exercise. How might you justify that I actually am this person named Darumon. Do I not appear human to you?"

"Yes, actually, and such a nice resemblance. I'll bet, as a shapeshifter, and likely with your own portal ability, you made a fine Daanen-Aryku when you directed their ship at Ruuki uy'Daan, which I think would stand out to an outside observer with these missing details to put together, as well as whoever it was that poisoned all those Trees of Life out there. Each of us, within our own, might only see half the picture. This, combined with our native lack of communication around here. And then, here he comes, with our lack of control over his movements, allowing him to assemble it all together. This would also include one of those officers he has working alongside of him."

"One of the officers? Who, in this case?"

"I don't know the name, but maybe you do. It was the original Daanen-Aryku officer you apparently delt with three and a half centuries ago when they first arrived and made contact. You know, you should probably pay a little closer attention to our native lifespans. The original governor back then would be dead and buried by now. But he seems to remember you."

The Governor growls again softly, and then turns away.

"All right, Dean, another point in your favor. I will admit, when dealing with so many varied races, this minor detail can become problematic."

"I suppose it can. His spies also learned of that book. And also that circle. Do you recall how he and that demon out there were speaking to one another? Well, I have your answer. Might you be interested in a little wall-climbing?"

"Wall-climbing?" he hesitates. "What do you mean? What did he say about it? More privileged knowledge, perhaps?"

"Oh, absolutely! So privileged that his sword, which was once stolen property, was retrieved from that very same demon. They know each other."

"What?!" he shouts. "How is such a thing as that possible? And furthermore, how might he even be alive afterwards? You don't just walk around in places like those asking directions."

"Oh, I'm sure of it. From what that book was telling me, those places are simply nasty…unless you come from the other side, which seemed at least as nasty for their potential."

"Huh?" he blurts.

"He's a Celestial, Darumon. His family is the Estelar!"

"Aaarghh!"

The Governor shrieks and jumps out of his chair. He flings himself against the wall and slides away from the window, peeking outside as if waiting for something to appear in view.

"Yes, Darumon," the Dean asserts calmly. "Take a good look outside, as those Estelar are apparently very displeased with your work in this world. He informed me that he has been in conversation with this one they call Lord Torm, who, by the way, is the successor to his Father, one he called Tyr. Do you know this name?"

"Dean!" he screeches.

"I suppose that's a yes. He gave me a name, Aasimar. Do you know this word? His wife is also a Celestial. In her case, I think the name was Eladrin."

The Governor pauses to consider these words.

"I don't think I've heard of those, so they must be new...or at least very rare. They can't be natural, in this case. More likely a hybrid form with the locals...ugh!" he shudders.

"Yes, he used that word, hybrid. And I don't doubt he's every bit as dangerous as you might be, especially if you combine with his... simple woman out there. Yes, I think we both flubbed up grandly on this one. But then, as I suspect you might say, how could we possibly know...right?"

"Indeed, Dean! Even such as they ought to have a few standards. Why would they be there in the first place?"

"Oh, funny you should ask that. Apparently, Tae'Eladar is someone's garden, and you trespassed into it with your orcs. I guess he wasn't too happy about that. He was sent there to govern it, and you were interfering with that. Such a funny word. Interfering..."

"Dean! Are you deliberately trying to test my limited patience?"

"Darumon, you used that word on him so many times, I feel it's a bit ironic to see you were doing it over there. That's all. Maybe you didn't know, but then, I doubt he knew about you before arriving here."

The Governor was panting by this time. His rage was matched only by his shock. He glances around as he tries to reconcile that last statement.

"What is he doing now?" he asks urgently.

"Making demands of us...mostly you at the moment. I don't really have much play in this, beyond my collusion with your affairs."

"Demands...I see. What demands? Is he moving against anyone else out there...or us in here?"

"Ah, let's see. First, he's upset about you playing with him as a toy. He's not a toy, and I suppose as a Celestial, that speaks for itself. Second, he demands no action to be taken against Solinaia, or else these Seldarine will have something to say about it. Their association with his kingdom has brought direct support to watch over them. Then we have those Flame Elves. He gave me a name, but gods help me if I can recall it by now. I think he referred to him as the Protector. Does this hold any meaning to you?"

"Yes, he's their leader. What of him?"

"He's going down there to check on them, probably to reclaim them, and likely also to find out who is responsible for their corruption. This doesn't sound good for whoever it was that so unfortunately killed their tree, stole their holy symbols, and caused them to follow what he calls a false god."

"Really! Dean, do you recall my statement about monitoring yourself in here?"

"Yes, perfectly… But you want these answers, and as such, you'll need to keep me alive a little longer. And in actuality, I'm speaking indirectly here, not making any direct statements that you did it."

"Oh! Really! Well, actually, you do hold a point."

"Then we have the city here, and although he says the locals aren't quite as attached, he's working on it with those priests over there we don't otherwise want. Nevertheless, we're apparently also coming under watch of some sort. He also says those Suuden-Aryku will be watched. If you or they move in any direction he doesn't like, BOOM! All the way back to wherever you came from. This also includes the Daanen-Aryku out there, whom he refers to as his friends and allies. He's very protective, it seems. And this is how angry he is about you kidnapping citizens from his world and bringing us here to be tormented and butchered by your troops."

The Governor gasped at the allegation. His panting turned to wheezing. He once again peeked out the window, then closed the curtains, hoping to find a little privacy. He reaches out to take his chair, and stumbles into it.

"Does he say anything else about us specifically? For instance, these Estelar, do they have any of their own plans?"

"Other than taking this all the way back to Azgarén if you and your mind-controlled military try any more tricks out there, he simply wants you gone."

"Whoa, hold on… Mind-controlled?"

"He says you are apparently using devices of some kind. Does this sound familiar?"

"And how would he know this?" he demands nervously.

"I honestly wouldn't know, unless he got hold of some for a close inspection."

"Um, let's see. Well, yes, maybe…bodies left behind from all those attacks. If they brought any in for a study… Blast!"

"But anyway, worst case scenario, if any of this continues, the Estelar will get involved directly. And at this point, I think these old and otherwise obsolete religious practices will show themselves to be something else."

"Dean!" he blasts.

"Hey, you said it yourself when we spoke of that Night Elf delegation and those priests over there."

"Yes, I suppose I did," he huffs feebly.

"Beyond that, he's been avoiding a direct fight with anything other than what I suppose is his most immediate threat to his world… the orcs."

"Grand."

The Governor tried taking a few deep breaths to calm himself. His ire at the Dean's impudence was severely dampened by the sheer magnitude of the threat potential of the Estelar arriving on his doorstep.

"So…" the Dean wonders casually. "I have just one little question to ask if I may. What in all the bleedin' hells were you doing over there to begin with? You call him an unwanted intrusion, but you know, if you're so afraid of those gods, my first suggestion is to run back to wherever it is you came from and stay there, not play games in places you don't otherwise want to be."

"Dean," he grumbles. "Should I remind you, once again, of where you're standing right now?"

"Not in the least. Between you, Thaelyn, and the Guard over there, those priests once mentioned the stockade finding new occupants, but I don't think I would last long in there. When Thaelyn mentioned burying people, I think this is far more likely my outcome by now. So, kindly stay your own threats. At this point, it's all moot. My question still stands. Any village idiot can see the fallacy in this scenario. Maybe you didn't know Thaelyn was out there. All right, fine. But at the very least, if these Estelar own that space, why are you going there if you are so afraid of them finding you even here in this space? What was the point to all this, sending orcs there, bringing us here, and so on?"

"Very well, Dean," he relents tensely. "Perhaps you do hold a point. But knowledge of this sort can be dangerous. And considering where we stand together…" he sighs deeply. "I'm just not one to talk about this openly. We've been hiding for too long, and with them everywhere by now."

"The Estelar? He said they own everything. How does this relate to you and Sargeras?"

"Before I answer that, did he mention any words relating to who he thinks we are?"

"Only to say you and Sargeras are likely some sort of pretenders who don't care much for this thing they call the Measure of Balance."

"Pretenders! Bah! We were once a true Power. But, granted, this was a long time ago. As for their Measure of Balance, yes! You've got that much correct! Those overbearing blowhards with their self-righteous doctrines."

He sighs and glances around the room, surveying the arrangement of furniture, and then briefly reflects on the city outside and the world beyond that.

"So, he knows my name, does he? Very well, to those who address me out there, I go by the name of Marshal Darumon, although I might also admit the title is superfluous. My kind doesn't normally use titles. I'm the sole surviving attendant to my beloved Master, Sargeras. We are remnants of an ancient society that once occupied that space, and the last of a proud civilization that once governed all of Creation…at least until they arrived."

"Oh? What happened?"

"Disaster is all I can say. We were content in our rule, and that fold was the last bastion we could hold onto."

"A fold?"

"A term our kind uses to describe a dimensional body like a universe. Once you achieve a certain level, the terminology tends to change."

"Ah, yes. He did mention this with the terms Door and Key."

"Indeed. But anyway, then they found us, and demanded we conform to their policies of this preposterous notion of theirs, the Measure of Balance."

"Just for the sake of asking, what is it about this principle you disagree with?"

"First, it isn't ours. Second, it demands compliance under someone else, and we were OVER-seers, not underlings."

"Ah, I see. So, you felt offended that someone might hold themselves superior to you. This is rather curious for me, how one society of gods might wish to rise above another."

"It might be in your eyes, but our pride once held reason. And yet, our demise over so long a time was painful, and then they arose to replace us. Anyway, my Master and I are all that is left. But I am not finished, even with that Celestial out there. He complains that I like to play with toys? So be it. These were the only pleasures we had left to us. Simply look at the world around us, Dean, and judge for yourself. If I needed all this, do you think we would be sitting where we are now? Little things like these are toys to the likes of us. We once made a game of raising such creatures and competing them against each other. It is no different from you with some of your own sports, but those Estelar took exception to it. Now, unless you have any more questions, I will ask you to leave. I need to think of a way out of this."

"You can't just use a portal, or whatever it is you used to travel from place to place?"

"I could, but I'm not that easy to get rid of!"

"Of course not… Then, I suppose I should return to my office and sit on the floor for a while."

"Why sit on the floor?"

"Because he used some sort of mind power to fling my desk through the wall into the next room. It's not in a very operable condition at this time."

The Dean bows modestly and turns to leave. He exits the office and closes the door behind him. As he enters the hallway, he finds Leesa standing next to the door with her trans-com out recording the conversation. She looks up at him and smiles casually.

"Hello, Dean," she announces innocently. "Do you have any new errands for me to run today? That last one was fun."

He glares at her, then at her trans-com, and briskly glances at the door. He rolls his eyes at the audacity of the scene.

"And another one…" he moans softly.

He studies her briefly as she continues smiling at him. He again glances at the door before moving several steps away, waving at the girl to follow along.

"You're taking a really big risk standing here, young lady," he whispers urgently. "Just who are you really? Are you one of his people?"

"I'm from the lower district. My cousin works for the Guard."

"Uh huh, naturally. And the previous runner, what really happened to him?"

"He was feeling rather tired, so we gave him a leave of absence."

"Really. You people are truly insidious. But then, I suppose you're not nearly as bad as what is inside that room," he thumbs at the door. "Be careful, Leesa. I doubt he has anything good on his mind right now."

"You're actually taking concern for something?"

"Taking concern…" he sighs. "Were you listening to any part of that? What is this thing here?" he points at the device in her hand.

"It's called a trans-com. It's a communication and recording device borrowed from the Daanen-Aryku. I've been using it to record some of the recent meetings, so we know what that guy is doing in there. As for listening, yeah, I'd say you took a few risks back there, being reduced down to a puddle of goo for all your grousing. But I also heard you actually lodge a complaint about being a citizen of this fine world that was blasted to the gods. This tells me there's an actual fella inside who may just give a flaming wank about what happened to us. Bloody hell if I didn't expect that much."

"Right, for all the good it does now. Leesa, I may be many things, most of them not good, but I just had a face-to-face with the son of a god! You don't get any closer than that to meeting your maker. Not on this side of life."

He holds his statement as his words start to fail him. He glances at the door again, his face now puckering with despair.

"And now..." he whimpers as he begins losing his composure.

He gazes into Leesa's eyes again, and she can see his worry.

"Just be aware," he emits with a tremor.

He reaches out and pats the girl on her shoulder. He then turns and walks away, covering his mouth as he reaches out to find the handrail on the stairs before shambling down.

Leesa watches as he descends the stairs. She follows behind on her way back to her desk, taking notice of him exiting out the front door, rather than the rear as he used on his way in. She peeks out the window to see him standing there, apparently trying to decide what to do next.

He begins walking casually out into the plaza, trying to compose himself out in public, and surveying the activity of the people. He examined the damaged pave stones from the battle that took place a short while ago. He then observes the people attempting to resume their chores after the intense horror he let loose moments earlier.

"Pleasures..." he mumbles disdainfully to himself.

He turned to glance discreetly up at the Governor's window to see if he was paying any attention, but the curtains were still drawn.

"A full world of them," he continues. "Small things like us. And no doubt I played a fair role in it."

He turns towards the temple and proceeds across the plaza to the doors, entering inside and ushering slowly along the central aisle.

Priest Garrain takes notice of him as he arrives in view and steps forward to meet him.

"Dean?" he calls. "This is unexpected."

The Dean gazes at the priest with a budding air of gloom. He remains silent and continues ahead among the rows of pews, leaning on them for support as he goes along, but ultimately collapsing into one midway through. The priest follows behind, watching him mostly out of curiosity, and asking himself if the Dean was well, or if he needed help.

"Dean?" he utters again.

The Dean looks up at the man from his seat.

"What do you know about him?"

"Him?"

The Dean glances out the door in the general direction of the Governor's Manor. The priest studies him and takes his meaning implicitly.

"More than I'm allowed to say," he responds.

"Really, how delightful. And yet, you stand here, unafraid."

"I can do so because I know my gods will guide me, no matter what happens. We each serve our roles, and those roles transcend above us to a higher purpose."

"Your faith must be extremely powerful. But tell me, these Estelar, do they know who he is? What will they do to him?"

"If they were to come face-to-face, I would imagine they would destroy him. But we also have Sargeras out there, along with the Suuden-Aryku. This represents a complication."

"A complication?"

"The Suuden-Aryku are likely pawns, and we don't kill pawns."

"Oh really, unlike him," he chuckles ironically. "You know, he really hates those others for this thing you call the Measure of Balance. I suppose I need to ask this now. What exactly is it? How does it work? He said his kind would never submit themselves to it, so this makes me wonder why."

"Dean, if you really want to know, then let us share a pleasant little chat, and I'll educate you on the wisdom of a society that discovered a truly fascinating meaning of life."

✦✦✦

The Governor glared into the room after the Dean left. His mind shifted from one thought to another as he tried to reason his position and his next course of action.

"Evasion," he mutters. "This is all we have now. That man..." he frowns. "But then, how could I ever expect a Celestial to take up residence in that world. This isn't their normal habit. They shouldn't want to live in a place like that anymore than, well..."

He mulls the thought several moments longer.

"Someone's garden? When I was there that time, they were no more organized than Azgarén in those early days...multiple nations, some barely on speaking terms. Something happened over there since my last visit. Someone's garden...and it must've hit a threshold where it needed better governing. Yes, of course, just like that one time..." he drifts off.

He reflects on the Dean's report, and then finds himself recalling the conversation outside with Captain Hagmaert.

"Someone sent him. Yes, the owner, whoever it is. But I didn't think those Estelar played such games...well, not like ours, at least. So, he was sent there. This means someone selected him and began developing him as their leader. And not just one, but two of them... how quaint. A husband and wife of such high regard leading a bunch of peasants."

He sits back in his chair to think more about this.

"Well, I must admit, as distasteful as it is to me and my plans, they did seem to develop that world nicely, from what I've been hearing of it. This reminds me of our little pets we had once. They were such a fine creation. But this only means that whoever it was that placed him there may also be watching; now that those orcs called their attention to it. That man, and indeed his entire world, are simply too dangerous to approach in this condition. And I've already spent too much time on it. Now they're coming here, and I can't let them find me."

He reaches over to his drawer and pulls out his trans-com, then dials in a number and waits for the response.

"Commander Geilv, speaking..."

"Commander, we have a problem. I need you to listen carefully and do as I say, understood? First, I want to know about our evacuation. What is the situation down there in Kynesoth?"

"We are investigating the city. It appears to be empty."

"Commander," he issues warily. "When you say it appears empty, is this before or after the evacuation?"

"Before... Our convoy arrived, but the gates were closed and locked on the inside. There was no response from anyone within. The convoy hover-glided over the wall and down inside the city. We conducted a search, but the city appears to be abandoned."

"Commander, was there any sign of attack, or other clear reasoning?"

"None, but my conversations with the High Priestess and her assigns revealed an unusual anomaly."

"What sort of anomaly?"

"It began two days ago when she called into this station stating she heard songs that seemed unnatural. I do not understand the reference."

"Never mind that for now, Commander. I actually know her meaning in this case. What did she say about these songs?"

"They were inconsistent, as if being interrupted."

"Interrupted?!" he yelps. "And then what? This was two days ago?"

"Affirmative. I suggested she should find rest, believing she was ill. I called to follow up yesterday, and to relay your evacuation orders, and she sounded incoherent and delusional."

"Explain. Did she say why?"

"She spoke of these songs, now with harmony and spiritual fulfillment. And apparently all her people were feeling this sensation."

"Blast!" he shouts. "Those accursed Seldarine... What next?"

"This morning, I called to inform her that the convoy was in transit, but she was absent. Her First Deacon was also absent. I spoke to her Second Deacon, who was also delusional. She spoke of someone called the Protector calling up his Children, and then she ran away from the trans-com shouting she was here and to take her up. Again, I do not understand the meaning, but the full population appears to be missing."

The Governor stared into the trans-com panting from the implied meaning of the report. He appeared dazed and flustered. He turned over his shoulder towards the window, peeking through the curtain to study the sky above and the surrounding cityscape.

"Commander," he issues anxiously. "You must do exactly as I tell you now. Our larger opponents seem to have found us. Recall when I said we had a special plan waiting here for that man Thaelyn? Well, it failed miserably. He then made a meeting with my attendant to discover the cause of this occasion. We tried to play it down as an accident, to dissuade his attention, but he has apparently discovered many of our other operations. Furthermore, we've learned he belongs to this same opposing faction, which I wasn't expecting to find at this point. And now, he is calling on his friends to continue his investigation, and that means we need to withdraw before we are discovered. That incident in Kynesoth is clearly an example of this investigation."

"Acknowledged, what are your instructions?"

"He is granting us the most gracious opportunity to make the next move, under the warning that we will be watched closely for any aggressive actions in his direction, or any of those currently aligned with him. Here is where I need to make a careful play to ensure we escape without further interference. We will make our return at a later time when we can regain control of the situation. For now, I want you to make a false deployment along your side of that mountain range. Make it appear you are preparing for a large-scale engagement, defensive in nature, but seemingly aggressive.

This will turn his eyes away from my position just long enough for me to make a few of my own movements."

"Understood."

Thaelyn and Aerlie were just returning to the tactical office in Firstfall. Relissa and her group had returned a short time earlier, and Relissa travelled further on to Solinaia to deliver the holy symbols to her mother. Marelle chose to take time away to visit Bya'an Tamoranth and report to Haran, Sara, and Jon, who were acting as go-betweens with the students.

"General," Thaelyn announces. "We should prepare ourselves for a few contingencies."

"Very good, my Lord, what sort?"

"First and foremost, I believe the Governor, or perhaps I should instead call him the Marshal, if this is his proper title, will likely make one or more tactics against us. If my warnings serve any true value, he may not wish to attack us directly, or any of our friends, but he will surely wish to present an image of some kind. And since he is so well-known for his falsehoods, he will probably try some form of deception to fool us. Therefore, we shall begin by calling in more troops to reinforce our position. I want a full corps delivered to us as soon as possible, and oriented on our eastern border."

"Right away."

"I want scouts under cloaks to watch their lines day and night, each of them equipped with trans-coms to immediately report any movement. I want mages in position to conjure up elementals in case anyone sees them moving against us. And we will need as many shield mages as we can muster, regardless of what they do out there. Our people will likely need cover, to the best of our ability."

"Of course."

"Next, we need to ensure the safety of our friends, as best we can. We may need to evacuate some or all, depending on what they do and how they do it. Call in an assembly of mages with portal runes leading directly to Tae'Eladar, not here. If we come under attack here, this would be a poor evacuation point to use."

"Absolutely. I recall the Daanen-Aryku have that gateway node over there. Would this serve us, or do you think we should supplement it?"

Thaelyn turns to Padriyl across the table for his opinion.

"Lieutenant," he relates. "If given an evacuation order, how fast do you think your people could move through that gateway? It is situated at the rear of your ship, under that hillside, as I recall. So, if your primary concern is moving your people away from the forward section, what do you think?"

"As unfortunate as it may sound," he responds. "Our people have been conditioned by now to get their tails in motion when the sirens go off. The hull of the ship should be sturdy enough to take a few hits, so we might be able to evacuate the forward sections without any losses. We have an internal transit chute network that still functions, and this can move us to the rearward segments efficiently enough to serve our needs."

"Very good, then we shall focus ourselves on Solinaia for this point with our mages. Next would be Rolsklinde. This is my first guess for the Marshal to take any action, but as I said before, he will likely use deception in this game. General, if he should use bombardment, we need those people to basically run for their lives. I doubt even using shield mages would ensure any reasonable protection in this case, for the inherent blast effects those weapons would deliver. If he uses an aerial assault, I want our gryphons up there to see if we can engage his combat vessels in midair, but do so carefully, as we cannot use shields as effectively in this case."

"Your Lordship," Padriyl inquires. "Do you think your gryphons would actually be at all effective against gunships?"

"At this moment, Lieutenant, it is questionable, but we cannot simply sit here and watch. If we can pelt them with enough fireballs and lightning strikes, perhaps we can disable them and knock them out of the sky."

"That would be an interesting sight, and certainly one for the books," he chuckles faintly.

"But we should still prepare some form of evacuation, and in this case, if he chooses to attack them as the weak link in this equation, we could use our location for the endpoint."

"Then we should prepare a number of additional mages with runes arriving here," the General considers.

"Indeed, and as a little insurance, Aerlie and I have been working on a project together out there at the site of our new research base, trying to develop a new mage strike designed to hit and disable vehicles. So far, it is still experimental, and classified as an elite spell, but we may yet find a use for it."

"What sort is that?"

"It is based on a principle we would describe as an electromagnetic pulse. We already know how electricity can hold its utility value, and our society is slowly developing itself into a more robust industrial power. But this is a principle of physics we have not yet touched upon. There is a certain application that can create a type of shockwave that is severely harmful to electrically powered items. It can cause damage, perhaps even to detonate certain components if they hold a large current flow inside."

"Gracious! So, if this were to be used on one of their vehicles, it would essentially disable it, and maybe cause portions of it to explode. And if we are speaking of a flying vessel, I suppose this would simply cause it to fall out of the sky."

"Correct. We began this study sometime after we arrived and learned of the Suuden-Aryku. We expected we would eventually have to contend with them and their devices, and this is our answer thus far. We tested it on some donated Daanen'kai equipment in the Bahlaie testing zone, and it seems to work within our design constraints."

"Then, if our scouts should see anything moving our way, you and the Lady will need to be present to offer your support. May the Gods watch over us during this time."

<hr />

As the day progressed, Relissa and Marelle had returned back, and Padriyl was assembling a panel of operators with trans-coms requisitioned from the Naarg uy'Sodrad. A large quantity had been delivered and distributed to an army of scouts being prepared for their new duty. These would report to the operators, who would then take notes and summarize the reports for the officers in charge. By late in the day, the first reports were coming in.

"My Lord," the General begins. "We are seeing activity on our eastern line."

"What kind?"

"Several of our positions are showing a buildup of troops on the other side of that ridge. Temporary encampments are being established, and troop transports are arriving with garrisons."

"This would represent a response, but do they actually intend to attack, or simply decoy us from another target. Keep a close eye on them, General. I want to know if they make any movements."

"In the meantime, our people are also creating a forward line to our east. This is taking on the appearance of a kind of standoff between the two. They could be building up to oppose our buildup. Now the only concern is to see who will flinch first."

"I wonder if we could test that theory somehow. We already know our shields work well against them, and if such as simple bows and arrows are deadly to them, further if they hold any measure of self-preservation, they will wish to keep away from that."

"True, but I am also reminded of what the Med-tech mentioned of those implants affecting their higher thought processes. Do they have any actual control of themselves? Consider the dwarves for a moment and the control effect on them."

"Indeed, and if this Marshal is so desiring to control his minions with such affirmative action, we cannot be sure how much independent authority these Suuden-Aryku actually have. He might simply send them against us as an expense to distract us while he escapes.”

“Buggers to that guy,” Relissa mumbles under her breath. “He just uses everything and throws it away when he doesn’t want it anymore.”

“This was largely the argument the Estelar had in the beginning,” Thaelyn relents. “Now we are faced with it again.”

“Aye, and it hits a wee bit close to home for us.”

“One question…” Marelle inquires. “If he holds this folding space ability, why not simply go poof as his means of escape? Why set up a decoy while he tries sneaking off like a thief in the shadows?”

“Or use that conveyor in his basement,” Padriyl adds.

“Leesa filed a recording from the Dean’s final visit,” the General offers. “Apparently, the Marshal is holding to his defiant stance. We heard words from the Dean asking this same question, and the Marshal saying he’s not so easy to get rid of.”

“Oh great,” Marelle huffs. “Like I needed to hear that.”

“This largely confirms our suspicions of a final farewell,” Thaelyn submits. “Even with the knowledge of who I am and my association with the Estelar, and surely by this time a call to the Commander and learning of the Flame Elves, and everything else, if he is saying he is not going down quietly, we can and probably should expect something. The only real questions are what and where.”

“And when.”

“Yes, and for this, he will need time to make his preparations. So, as the General mentioned, we are in a standoff.”

“Wonderful, and we’re stuck out here waiting for him to finish packing his bags.”

“General, let us try a small experiment. Send a group of scouts out there under cloaks behind this new line they are forming. Find a safe location and make a long way-line of runes. Interspace them at wide distances, perhaps as a series of smaller rows per each new encampment you see.”

“An interesting thought, my Lord, but to what end? Are we planning on attacking them, even though we suspect this to be a false offensive?”

"Not a hostile one, but a quick hit-and-run nonlethal one," he grins. "Just to see how they respond."

"My Lord, what do you have on your mind at this time?" the General wonders curiously.

"We will make a fast run from their blind side using portals, but only mages at this point, and have them fire off a volley of stink clouds into those shiny new outposts of theirs. It would not be lethal, it would not follow up with a forward charge on our part, and we would allow them the opportunity to recover and make a new assessment of our capacity to hit without warning, and especially across a broad space."

"This is certainly a new tactic. All right, we'll see what we can accomplish."

⟡

The Dean had been sitting in his chair, staring into the open space of his office. If he thought he had so little work to do before, he had even less now for the absence of his desk, which lay partially splintered in the next room, along with a sizable amount of shattered wall fragments.

He sat there silently reflecting on the conversation he recently shared with the priest in the temple across the way, and further with the Governor earlier in the day during their last meeting.

"Pleasures..." he repeats sullenly in his thoughts.

He felt tempted to look out the window again, but the images of the scene outside shunned the ambition. His last memories in this office were the most vivid by now, how Thaelyn lifted his desk with the simple power of his mind, and hurled it through the wall with such force that it shook the building. Then, how the Dean himself was taken up and held in space, feeling as helpless as a mouse.

"What has that man...that creature...brought to this world?" he mulls. "And where did he come from? And why here...does he hold a grudge against them? He said they once owned that space, which means the Estelar took it away from them. Pleasures? Yes,

I can believe that. Creating such like we and using us as sport. And the Estelar found it just as intolerable as any other sane mind. No wonder he ran. And now he's trying to come back. The real question is what he hopes to accomplish if they're a full society and he's simply one individual."

He sits in his chair and rolls the idea around in his mind.

"He must be insane to return there. He's clearly afraid of them, so why go back. Does he hope to make trouble for them somehow? He's sneaking around under their noses, so it's clearly a subversive act."

He paused to recall Thaelyn's last words to him.

"He may hold his privileged knowledge…but…as for me, be aware. That was a message…to me!" he winces. "Gods above, and perhaps in a literal sense of it, he was actually warning me of something. Pleasures, yes, and Thaelyn must know something. His priests, too… They must both know something, but they're not allowed to say it openly."

He considers his words for another moment.

"Openly… But of course!" he lurches forward in his chair. "If they actually know who he is, they certainly wouldn't want to let on. That…Marshal…has been playing games on Thaelyn. Now Thaelyn is turning it back at him. This makes perfect sense. And right now, he wants him away from this world, probably to save what's left of us here. The Measure of Balance, where life is regarded as sacred, but it is so often pulled in both directions between the two sides. Those creatures, however, they simply don't care for it, as we're all toys to them."

He felt a moment of inspiration as he started pulling these pieces together. There was a mystery here, and deep down, he wanted to understand it.

"An educator…" he mumbles. "Yes, once, I did hold these aspirations. Then I became the Dean. Oh, how I recall those days…and now, how I loathe them."

He closed his eyes as he recalled his personal life. He sighed heavily.

"The only true mystery here is the adamantium. We don't permit anyone to acknowledge it openly, and the Suuden-Aryku probably can't use it themselves. So, what is he doing with it?"

He reflects again on Thaelyn's statements and the Governor's words from his past meetings.

"This must be part of his plan. He's using it for something. Thaelyn's men seem to be using it, and they've managed to chase away everything else out there. But then we have that one Suuden-Aryku patrol, and Thaelyn's men were able to defeat that as well. Not that it would surprise me now, for his demonstration outside," he raises his brow. "I doubt anything could defeat his men. Hmm..." he mulls his statement a bit longer. "Heavy enchantments, is it? This would make them dangerous to a lot of things, I might think, but what about gods? And yet, the Suuden-Aryku wouldn't likely know the first thing about this, so it cannot be for them, especially if he can cut them down so easily."

He glances around the room. It seemed eerily quiet without the sounds of classes echoing through the halls. He stood up and walked out of the office, then down the stairs. There he paused as he examined the hallway and the deep grooves carved into it by the demon as it clawed its way through to the outside.

"My precious academy..." he sighs. "My delight, my dream, and now my nightmare..."

He followed the corridor down to the corner, and then around to the basement door, which was completely smashed, and the framework splintered, ripping a large hole in the wall for the demon to emerge through. He descended the rickety remains of the stairs and halted at the scenery in front of him, focusing on the circle on the floor and the charred remains of the body.

"I did this," he murmurs remorsefully. "I'm a murderer now... or at least an accessory to one. Not that it matters much by now, as I'm at least partially responsible for a full city of them, if to consider the priests and what I knew of that. As for this...he was right, this was pure madness. I was simply lucky to get out at all. I suppose he was not."

He steps forward to take a closer look, observing the circle with the broken warding barrier, the body, and then the table against the wall. He frowns a moment as he tries to recollect his memories.

"That book. Where is it?"

He steps forward to search around the table, but he can't find it. However, he does take notice of a rectangular spot in the ash layer where something had been removed.

"It's gone… Fine!" he huffs. "Probably more of his spies, maybe Tristeen, she apparently knew of it. Good riddance, and to those mithril things as well. Now I'm free of it. But this still doesn't answer the part about the adamantium. If not even that creature could make a dent in them, then what?"

He ponders the significance of the metal, its properties, and further reflects on his conversation with Thaelyn again.

"Interference…toys… That Suuden-Aryku patrol was an obvious flub. We thought it was the Guard, but to use this instead of their normal gear? What was he up to? A demonstration to them for disobeying orders…maybe, and not a polite one at that. Does he so enjoy creating such carnage? He must, if this is his idea of sport. And then we have that assassin, also in adamantium…to ensure success, maybe also an escape? I would hardly think as much. He must've put a lot of faith in that individual if he thought they could actually plant a knife in someone's back and successfully run away before a score of soldiers pounced on them."

He pondered the scene as he tried to imagine how it appeared.

"If you were to ask me, I'd say that was a waste of a spy, also the adamantium, as I'm sure it wouldn't serve anything here, and clearly it would open up a new mystery, especially if the Flame Elves don't know what it is any more than we do. Sport? Oh yes, I hope he enjoyed that little show. And I'm sure it is more than enough reason for Thaelyn to investigate. He wants to know where this stuff is going as well."

He halts his thoughts briefly as he contemplates the suggestion.

"Or does he already know?" he wonders curiously. "Hmm, no, I suspect he doesn't! I remember his words. It's essentially coming from the Suuden-Aryku, as they're the ones picking up the supply from the dwarves! Yes! And no one can recall where they came from!"

He turns and charges back up the stairs into the hallway.

"They must be the only ones around here who know how to use it," he surmises. "But not in their condition. I recall them up there. Those deliveries for their farms…oh blast! That stuff I take up there, a dressing agent? Bah! 'We need to be sure they are still loyal to us…' he says. Loyal as obedient little toys doing his work!" he scorns. "Just like everything else around here!"

He makes his way back to the main hall, where he observes the wreckage of the bookshelves, the smashed remains of the tables, and the scattered books. He picks up one book that appeared partially burnt. He opens it to a random page to examine the contents, but then closes it and tosses it away.

"Rubbish…" he relents. "Just like he said. Nothing I ever did here will amount to anything, not that it was ever meant to."

He recalled Marelle's words on their school system, as well as the Governor's excuses.

"Yes… 'I'm just following a process. I can't be held responsible for that which came before…'. But I sure can be held responsible for what I did personally, which is already enough, and really no different from that which came before. We smear our history, and then we defame our neighbors, so we don't even go out to ask about their library to supplement our own. How convenient!" he grumbles. "He breaks us apart to isolate us, and then pins us down inside these walls, while he blasts the rest of our world away, and blames all the rest for it. He certainly does like to take care of his… pets," he condemns.

His mind now drifted to his shoulder, and he lifted a hand to pull away his collar. He then tried peering down at his scarring left behind from the removal of the implant.

"And then we have this, our fine gift of the Governor and his promises. Freedom from the Withering Death, power over the academy, a place of authority… Promises, promises…and all I needed to do was sell my soul to him, bit by bloody bit, along with everyone else in this city."

Now he was getting angry. He again reflected on his meeting with Thaelyn.

"A young boy…who once hoped to learn. Yes, Thaelyn, you are right. I was once that young boy. It didn't last long, though. My life…ruined."

He begins pacing around the room. He was growing determined to solve this riddle.

"Dwarves…also found on Tae'Eladar, but not native to it. And not a part of our migration, but with a home world of some kind. Oh grand, and no doubt, that fiend knows where it is. I've seen their dead bodies lying about on occasion, so this stuff must be poisonous after a while, and then new ones arrive to replace them. He has a supply somewhere. This could also explain where all that armor came from. But it still doesn't explain where the rest of the adamantium is going…and for so long…four centuries in that mine up there… hmm, maybe more elsewhere if he has a world full of them? Egads! That would represent an enormous volume. But for what reason? He wasn't going to tell me, and it likely has to do with his own level of privileged knowledge, something personal… Wait a minute!"

An idea slowly begins to form in his mind as he brings together several strange items of detail into one set.

"A battle… Oh dear gods! That's it! Blast him! He wants revenge on these Estelar! It must be! They found them once, destroyed them…even Thaelyn mentioned this. A history of others put down for errant deeds. It was them! This is what he doesn't dare let out openly. He knows who they are, and is probably surprised to see one still alive, I'll bet!"

He pauses in his steps and taps a finger on his chin.

"Something happened in that space to destroy all their native stars. Those Estelar built that shell to protect Tae'Eladar, as it was a survivor. And I recall a side mention by that Darumon… 'Oh, so that's where it came from…' Yes, naturally, he would know of it if he was there once. This means he was there at the time of that battle. It's no wonder he said there's no way Thaelyn could come from outside Tae'Eladar, because nothing else should exist out there. Oh, I'm sure of that! But how would he know if he wasn't there to see it, maybe even to cause it?"

He glances around the room vacantly as he considers this suggestion.

"This points to a weapon of some sort, and on the scale of gods. Indeed, and this would also explain how such a madman as he would go it alone, and so quietly. He's hoping to plant a knife in their backs now! Well, figuratively… And if Thaelyn is still searching for this…"

He turns around and hurriedly heads back down the halls, passing the door to the basement and continuing to the rear exit.

"He simply wants him off this world, maybe to save what's left of us. But if he actually knew the magnitude of this idea, I think he might take more assertive action to prevent it. This goes a little beyond this one world."

He leaves the building, but this time, rather than circling around to the Governor's Manor on the right, he instead turns left. He slows his pace briefly as he ponders his upcoming actions.

"I may find myself either in a prison or a hole in the ground, but I'm not there yet. I'll wager that creature wants to lay down another of the same. But if he's alone, this great volume of metal must be for something big enough to blast away another set of stars…and with it, the gods themselves, no doubt."

He picks up again and moves determinedly in the direction of the barracks.

He takes a circuitous route through the park and around the back of the building, coming up on the blind side from the view of the Governor's window, even though the curtains were still closed, but his paranoia was driving him by now. He then ducked inside the yard, where he searched for Captain Kholgard's office. As he arrives at the door, he hesitates momentarily, considering what sort of reaction he might find on the inside, and then knocks gently.

"Yes, come in," ushers the voice from inside.

The Dean slowly opens the door and steps inside, where he halts and gazes pensively at Captain Kholgard.

The Captain looked up from his desk to see the Dean…the last person he ever expected, or even desired to see in his office. He instantly frowned at the unexpected arrival.

"What are you doing here?" he announces bitterly.

"Captain, can we talk a moment without the arguing?"

"Talk? Why would I want to talk to you?"

"Because I'm here offering peace, not argument."

The Captain glared at the Dean, at least as much for the curious statement as the man's obvious posture.

"Peace? I don't think I can believe that…not out of you, and not after so many other things you did out there."

"Captain, I know you probably hate me, and I'm sure most of the city feels this way by now. So, allow me one small token to make amends. I want to apologize. I think my days are probably numbered by now, more so than anyone else in the city. So, will you afford me a small moment to explain my reasons for coming here? I wish to file a report with you to share with the others."

Captain Kholgard could clearly see in the man's eyes he was troubled, perhaps a lingering effect from their earlier confrontation. But then, he reflected briefly on Thaelyn's final words about giving him a chance for himself.

"A report? Gods be blessed, miracles do actually occur on occasion. What do you want to talk about? Did the Governor send you?"

"The Governor…" he huffs softly. "What a name… He's no Governor, Captain, and I think you know it. He doesn't know I'm here, nor do I want him to know. I'm quite sure that would simply accelerate things for me."

"All right, calm down. Let's just get through this. I'm assuming you made your report to him, so did he say something?"

"A number of things, actually…" he steps forward to the desk.

The Captain waves for him to sit down in the chair. He then takes out a piece of paper to write down his notes.

"He confirmed that name you gave. He actually called himself Marshal Darumon, though he also admitted his kind doesn't normally use titles, so this one is superfluous," he smirks tenderly.

"Really! That's interesting. What does he have to say about your report?"

"Other than I nearly got myself killed multiple times over by delivering it?" he chuckles morbidly. "Leesa was outside the door... listening. She's a daring young lady. She summed it up nicely that I was taking risks of being reduced to a puddle of goo."

The Captain let out a soft chuckle at the thought, although he was trying to hold it back, if only due to the serious nature of it. He studied the Dean's face, and he was clearly in a lot of emotional pain.

"Among other things," the Dean continues. "Darumon is the sole surviving attendant to Sargeras, the last of their kind, so it seems. He severely despises these Estelar and their Measure of Balance. His kind once represented a society of gods before them, but was apparently wiped out due to their vehement disagreement with these policies. Also, it seems they once occupied that space where I suppose we would find Tae'Eladar. He described it as their last bastion for what few remained after a long and painful demise."

The Captain frowned at the Dean. He mulled the idea privately for a moment before continuing.

"This sounds like a history with some background to it."

"Yes, he described his kind as overseers, not underlings to submit themselves to someone else. Therefore, I suppose, is their dismay at the Estelar arriving and demanding they conform to these new policies. I think I may need to admit to the understanding, at least in principle, which would bring us to where we stand now with him making a return. It's a revenge attack."

"Revenge! But him alone against all of them?"

"This is certainly the question, but he wouldn't reveal the rest of it. His final words, before sending me away, were that we are just little things for their pleasures. They once created such as we for some sort of sport. This now causes me to reflect on that Measure of Balance. I spoke to the priest over there for clarification, and I think I understand now. No wonder he hates it so. It takes away his fun time."

"Wonderful. But now, what about you? Where do you stand on all this, other than thinking you're on death's doorstep?"

"I started trying to piece together that conversation in my office, along with my memories of my past visits with the Governor, especially in more recent times. He sometimes talks to himself, even if I'm still in the room to overhear it. And I think I have an idea, though I'll admit I'm nervous just for sitting here. How do you tend to communicate with that man, Lord Thaelyn? Do you send runners?"

"Sometimes. Although recently, with his priests over there, and a mage using portals to send and receive notes, we don't need to make that long run anymore."

"They use portals even for that much?" he wonders curiously.

"Marelle tells me they use devices called gateways, which are basically portal devices to travel all across their world. They use this for people, as well as cargo, and even mail delivery."

"Incredible. That man must've worked hard with his people to bring them so far. I wonder where they'll go in the future."

"Personally, I'm just an old soldier. I can barely even imagine this much."

"I'm supposed to be…" he pauses briefly in thought, "…an educator. But I am a sorry excuse for one. And yet, here I am, looking at a society that clearly saw much better times. Captain, that meeting opened my eyes to something bigger than I could ever imagine. I was never a religious man, and I think it goes without saying, when you consider the priests we had before, I didn't have much incentive for it."

"You got that one right."

"Thaelyn mentioned something about a young boy trying to learn. I think this was a kind of message, hoping to remind me of something. Well, it worked. Blast him, that he can manipulate people like this. He's worse than the Governor," he chuckles giddily. "When I was a young man, I was a student in the academy, just like so many others. I caught on early how the system works, so I played into it as best I could, hoping my groveling would one day pay off. And it did. The Governor took notice of me, probably by the reports given by the former Dean, and I was offered the position after he retired. Then things started coming up that brought me deeper and deeper into his world. He shared secrets with me that I was expected to keep if I valued my most exalted position of authority, and all the perks that went along with it."

"And this is where it turned you into that creep we all came to know, right?"

"To put it very lightly, yes," he sighs. "He's a very powerful and influential figure, Captain. Be happy you weren't part of his Master Plan from the beginning. I doubt you would be the man you are today if that were so."

"Is this also why you look pale as a ghost?"

"Between your visit to my office and my visit in his, I would not be surprised by now. Since the time those priests began speaking of the Estelar, and I filed that one report relating to the plague and the implant devices, he began jumping like a frightened animal at the word. On this occasion, I simply went all out, no longer concerned for my own safety as I'm already expecting myself to find a final rest soon…in one or more pieces," he frowns gloomily.

"Dean…"

"Captain, I don't think it's in your hands at this time," he whimpers. "We have gods playing this game now, and I'm on the wrong side of it. But when Thaelyn told me to make…at least…one good deed in my life, I realized something has arrived in our world that overrules everything else out there. So, here I am, hoping to make one more. Maybe it'll serve a purpose, maybe not, and maybe someone will take notice, or maybe not. But I'll be damned if I'll let that creature over there have his way of it!" his face now puckers heavily in despair.

The Captain had never seen the Dean in such a fragile condition, not that he ever had an occasion to speak with him personally before. But at the same time, he couldn't recall seeing any man in such a condition as this.

"Therefore," the Dean continues. "I began thinking of how to explain the mystery of this adamantium. It must be going somewhere. I've been to that dwarven mine up there many times, and seen them lying dead on several occasions, and then later they're replaced. So, he must have a supply, and it must be that world Thaelyn spoke of that is their home. This cannot be good...for them, at least."

"No, it isn't."

"But Captain, were you aware they mine this metal up there?"

"Yes, actually. His Lordship's men already investigated, and found out what's happening up there, and that the Suuden-Aryku are the ones picking it up."

"Of course, I should expect no less out of him by now. But here is our mystery. If the Suuden-Aryku are no good at using it, and the dwarves are simply more pawns in this game, as the priest likes to say...who is using the metal? I asked him, hoping maybe to understand something about why he would go to so much trouble with all this," he waves his hands around figuratively at the city. "But he told me it's personal and I'm not one to know. Not that I might understand it to begin with if he's nearly a godlike figure. His knowledge must therefore be much higher. But this then triggered a thought. That ancient battle, the destruction of those stars, and thus the storm outside their Shell, and then Thaelyn mentioning a history of someone who came before, and was destroyed out there. It had to be them. Darumon said they once owned that space."

"Yes, and I do know of a story like this from what Thaelyn shared with us once. But this is a very private story, so far."

"Oh, I have no doubt. If Darumon were to see them catching on to him, I'm sure he'd run far away, not simply back to that place, Azgarén. But he's moving like a thief here. He's afraid of them, but still pushing into their space. Why? Unless we say he's mad, which may be the case regardless, but he's got to be planning something, and I'll bet it involves a weapon based on his godlike knowledge."

"Gods' pity, if that's the case."

"And this simply brings me back to the metal. He's mining up vast quantities of it here, and maybe more if he owns the dwarven world. I don't know what is required to see this through, but what if it relates to another of the same that blasted all those stars?"

"Great gods!" he lurches back. "I can only barely understand what you're talking about, and already it sounds bad! You know, you should probably take this directly to His Lordship."

"Oh no, I don't think I dare come face to face with him again. Of all the people in this world, I think he hates me the most by now."

"Dean, he's actually a very reasonable man, just determined to get the job done. His kind doesn't seem to take no for an answer," he chuckles.

"Well, all right," he smiles tenderly. "But maybe I'll pass for now."

"As you say, but I'll put your name on this, just to let them know where it came from."

"I thank you, Captain. That is most gracious," the Dean lowers his head and sighs heavily. "Perhaps, if this one small contribution can hold value, I won't be condemned to the deepest layers of the Abyss."

"Dean, if you feel yourself in such danger, you should probably leave the city."

"And go where, to their camp down there? I think if that Darumon wants me dead, I doubt he'll let even those Estelar get in his way. Even though I already sold my soul to him once, that doesn't mean he might not want to collect on it, especially after all this. No, I think I should stay here and pretend all is normal. It might keep him calm, within reason. Although, I think this is subjective, as he said he's not so easy to get rid of."

"Oh wonderful. But it's up to you, and I want you to know, I'm here if you need me."

The Dean gazes wistfully at the Captain for the statement.

"That actually means a lot to me, Captain," he mourns. "Um, since we're on the topic, I do have one small request."

"What's that?"

"It seems I had a little, um, accident in my office recently. My desk, as it seems, found its way into the next room, and is not in a very operable condition. Perhaps, if you would allow me a piece of paper and a pen, I would like to send off a note to someone."

The Captain grins and reaches over to a box on a side table to take a sheet of paper. He sets it down along with a pen and an ink well for the Dean to use.

"Who is this for?" the Captain asks.

"A man I had a most unfortunate argument with. I want to apologize to him especially. He was right and I was wrong, and I want to make peace with at least a few individuals before anything else happens. This reminds me, I would also like to speak with that young lady, Tristeen Macaid. Do you happen to know where she might be at this time?"

"I saw her going home after our meeting."

"Do you know the address? I've never actually travelled up that way before."

"Yeah, Number Nine, Veradin Way, in the Upper Ward."

"Thank you. Now as for this note…"

The Dean pauses to collect his thoughts, and then writes down several lines on the paper. He reviews his work, taking a moment to check his wording, and finishes it with his signature.

"Here you go…" he folds the paper and hands it across. "This needs to go to Haran Carronel, but I have no idea where he is at the moment. I can only suggest forwarding it to his sister, that young lady who was with you in my office. She should know where he is. Maybe she can pass it along for me."

"Of course, I'll get this out right away."

"Now, Captain, if you will excuse me, I think I would like to take a little walk in the Upper Ward. I hear they have a most extraordinary bazaar up there."

The Dean smiles gently as he gets up from his seat. He bows humbly and leaves the office.

He moves through the yard towards the gate, eyeing the Governor's Manor across the plaza, and trying to see if there is anything in the window. The curtains were still closed, so he quickly ducked around the side and through the park. He then passed through the gates into the Upper Ward district, where he began to follow the neatly paved streets past the large manor homes and their manicured gardens.

He strolled along the roads until he found Veradin Way, and followed the street numbers to a post with the number nine on it, the Macaid home. He stood there on the street as he looked up at the elegant stone manor house with the slate tile roof. He began towards it, passing through an ornate wrought-iron gate and up the walkway to the front door.

He felt nervous even for standing here, worse than with the Captain's office. He reaches up and knocks tenderly on the door. After a few moments, a mature woman answers.

"Yes?" she responds as she studies the man. "Can I help you?"

"I, um…" he tries in vain to clear the lump in his throat. "I am here to make a small meeting if I may. My…my name is, um…" his voice begins trembling, "…is, um, Dean Alin Malorn. I was told I might find Tristeen Macaid here. Is she available for speaking?"

The woman instantly frowned at the name.

"The Dean of the mage academy…here? Dear Sir, I'm not entirely sure if my daughter would wish to speak with you after what happened out there today."

"I suspect the same. But I do beg for even a tiny moment, and if you could be so…" his voice is now faltering, "…could be so kind as to pass the word that I wish to offer…an apology. Perhaps, she might afford me this much. It's actually rather important, as I feel… um…" he pauses to pull out his kerchief. "My pardons…" he turns away briefly to wipe his eyes, then to return again. "I… I would really like to make my peace."

The woman could see he was disturbed, and now becoming emotional. The Dean was unable to hold his posture by now, becoming deeply despondent.

"All right, wait here, please."

While he waited, the Dean felt himself losing control. He turned away to dab his eyes again, feeling very vulnerable and alone by now. He stepped away a few paces, hoping to find enough strength to continue the effort.

Tristeen arrived at the door to see him hunched over and sobbing. She studied him for a moment, trying to understand what she saw. She turned to meet the eyes of both her parents, who were hiding behind the door and peeking around.

"Dean?"

The man jerked partway around to peer over his shoulder at the girl, trying desperately to contain himself. He raised a finger in pause as he wiped his face again and pulled himself back upright, as best he could.

"Yes, um…" he stammers and turns forward again, almost unable to meet her eye-to-eye. "Please excuse my appearance. I don't mean to disturb your lovely home, but I had to do this. I was hoping, perhaps… Maybe… You could afford me a few words."

"What happened?"

"Never mind, I don't want to disturb you with my troubles. I simply hoped to seek your most gracious forgiveness for my actions. I realize they probably cannot be forgiven, but I wanted to at least present myself."

"Dean, I can't actually believe what I'm looking at right now. What happened in the Governor's office? I'm assuming you went over there, right?"

"Well, yes, I did, and I reported on our meeting. I had to…you know. It's expected of me."

"And what did he say? And why are you standing here looking such a wreck?"

"Oh, this…" he attempts a chuckle, but it doesn't work. "Yes, um, just like young Leesa was saying on my way out, I'll probably find myself as a puddle of goo before I know it."

"It's that bad?"

"Tristeen, I'm scared!" he sobs. "We're just little things to him. Little things for his pleasure, and I probably just dug my own grave. But before anything else, I went to the Captain. I shared a few thoughts I had with him. I don't know if it'll matter, but it's all I could do. Now I'm here hoping to make my peace with you and the other students. I doubt I'll be able to find them all, or if they would even want to speak to me, but if you could relay the message…"

"You won't find them in the city anymore. After we walked out, I evacuated them with the help of the people inside the temple, and sent them to Tae'Eladar for shelter."

"You're a very clever young lady, Miss Macaid," he nods. "That was very wise of you."

"May I ask a question while we're here? Do you know exactly what was inside that fancy new elixir you were going to feed us?"

"No. He told me it was simply to tame some of your wilder ambitions from asking so many questions about our recent work. I was supposed to have you perform a number of simple exercises in the basement to allow it time. This is all he said to me. What did you finally do with it?"

"I sent it with my two friends, Sara and Jon, to His Lordship. But now, do you want to know, or…"

"At this moment, I don't think so. I can already guess it was one of his toys to remove something unpleasant in his eyes. He seems to like doing this, and doing so in such ways that it amuses him. That's our purpose in life if we don't hold any other value. This is why I suspect those Estelar are so displeased with him."

"But Dean, I feel I should at least ask this question. Even if you did know, and if to say it was some kind of poison or whatever, would you have done it?"

The Dean stood there pondering the question and reflecting on his former devotion to his service under the Governor.

"Miss Macaid, I would never have imagined myself able to commit such a thing as murder, certainly not directly. But at the same time, I think you should know, he is a very powerful figure, very demanding of compliance, very authoritative, and I suppose I should also say, very influential. He corrupts things. He considers us as simple tools to affect his revenge."

"Revenge?" Josef asks as he emerges into view. "What sort of revenge?"

"Against these Estelar, his kind hates them for their, as he says, overbearing and self-righteous policies. He's a creature that I suspect shouldn't even exist right now. He told me, once I started asking questions, that he and Sargeras are the last of their kind, a god society that came before, and apparently didn't like being pushed out."

"Oh grand!"

"Yeah, Dad," Tristeen moans. "I'll bet that's what His Lordship meant when he said he had to be careful of his words out there. If this guy learns we're on to him, he could run, hide again, and gods' pity what he does to the next world he finds."

"And so," the Dean offers. "He wants to play some of these games back at him, right? So be it, and good luck to him."

"But what about you, you're a wreck."

"Yes, I suppose so…" he glances at himself. "My life is coming full circle on me now. I didn't start out this way, you know. I was much like you and Haran, in many ways. I climbed a very difficult ladder to reach my position. You think you had it bad, well," he chuckles feebly. "I went through the same once. I kissed every backside presented to me until one day I won the prize. I was so proud of myself. The prestige of holding that office felt so good, and I had hoped to use it to repair so much other damage I saw around me. Then he started sharing all his little secrets, one by one drawing me into his world. After a while, I started sharing his same attitudes and perspectives. I became just like him."

He turned away to catch his breath, grimacing at his own image.

"He poisoned you with his venom for everything else out there," Josef muses.

"Yes. Reflecting on those priests…the original ones. I knew of them, of course. Did I do anything about it? No. Although, I doubt it would've mattered, even if I did. The only difference being I probably wouldn't be here talking about it now."

"Yes, probably so. He'd just find someone else, and here we go again."

"Indeed, and then, as for that elixir. Tristeen, I don't know if I could give you a proper answer to that. Would my conscience finally slap me on the face to wake me up from this delirium, or would I simply follow as I did so often, like feeding those dwarves up there that…stuff…they used in their farms. I didn't ask these questions. I couldn't, and certainly not under his rule."

"All right, Dean," she responds thoughtfully. "I suppose I can accept that, within reason. You're a tormented man, perhaps as much, if not more so than anyone else. But, what about that man in the basement?"

He turns to look at her concernedly.

"You went down there?"

"I went looking for that strange book of yours. I wasn't going to let you try this again."

"As if I actually would…" he shakes his head delicately. "That book, by the way, as far as I understand it, is originally from the Governor. I think it was handed down through at least a few deans before me. As for the man, my instructions were to smudge the warding circle to let the creature out, then run as fast as my feet could carry me. I barely had time to catch my breath before it was bursting free. There were two instructors down there with me, one was already on his way out, but the other was not as quick on his feet. That's all I can say. I know I'm at least partly responsible for this act, so I will blame myself for this foolishness. It was my lust, maybe my curiosity to try something unique, something forbidden. But I will admit this much. The Governor liked the idea. His assassin failed him, and he wanted something big to overwhelm any support Thaelyn might have to back him up. This seemed like a viable solution."

"Viable, but a little excessive, don't you think?"

"I suppose this is subjective. It would reflect on that aspect of trying something forbidden. That book represented knowledge we're not otherwise supposed to have, and I was curious to see it for myself. Well, I did…" he turns his gaze down in horror.

"Yes! This much I can certainly agree on. Are you sure you couldn't have found a bigger one?" she chuckles ironically. "All right, I can clearly see you learned something, but at the same time, this probably cost you dearly. I learned a few of my own lessons from

His Lordship, so I will offer you my forgiveness, and I'll share this with the others once I see them again."

"I am so very thankful, Miss Macaid," he bows deeply. "Then I should return to my office...what's left of it. I can't imagine he would want me for anything else at this point, but I should probably keep myself in view, just for appearances."

"Dean, maybe you shouldn't do that."

"Tristeen, I already had this argument with the Captain. If Darumon should get any ideas of his favorite little pet going off and doing something I'm not supposed to be doing, I think my last day will occur sooner rather than later."

"But you're still suggesting your last day is coming because of him."

"Yes, but better me than the rest of you. Although, I would expect he might have plans for you as well. He mentioned a few things during this time...special efforts to bring things back into alignment. And now, with this new threat, he stated he's not so easy to get rid of. I don't like the sound of that. But Tristeen, do take care. At the very least, he knows your name."

He ducks is head, turns, and shambles away.

"Jared," Willit whispers quietly at their table in the Ten Eagles. "The people down south are talking about an evacuation of the city. They don't know exactly what the Governor may do next, but Marelle called a while ago and said the Suuden-Aryku are building up a large number of forces on the other side of that eastern ridge down there. It might be a bluff, or it might not."

"But that's in the valley, not up here."

"Right, but if it's a bluff, it's for distracting them from up here. If Lord Thaelyn and his message to the Dean actually did anything, the Governor wouldn't dare actually attack them. Now, let's say it's a bluff, which is what Marelle thinks is most likely. It's not a sure thing, but a good bet. That means they might try something in the city.

The question is, will it be by land or by air, or will it be something she calls bombardment, which means those bloody bastards with their ships out there in the Great Beyond pelt us from above."

"Buggers to that! How do you fight something like that?"

"Well, unless you've got another of the same, I think you don't. And what's worse, we don't stand a chance against something like this. They're just taking advantage of doing the deed, and we have no possibility of fighting back."

"Bloody wicked, that is."

"That's basically what I said, but she cautioned me about something, which doesn't really help my nerves."

"What was that?"

"It's not really the Suuden-Aryku at fault, since His Lordship believes they're being used just like everything else around here."

"So, what then? We blame the Governor, or whatever he is, for all this bloodshed?"

"He's really the one doing it. Without him, life would be a grand sight better for all of us. But she's suggesting we should quietly start spreading the word. They'll send mages up here with their portals to bring us out, but we'll need to go halfway to meet them. The city is just too big for them to run door-to-door with it."

"All right, got it, but where do we go?"

"That's a hard one to say, and it depends largely on how they attack us. If by land, we need to run the other way. If by air, they'll see if they can hit their air vessels and knock them down, but we still need to go somewhere, so she's thinking maybe out the south gate into the fields."

"All right, fair enough. Let's hope we can use that as a pick-up point."

The two of them break up and leave the establishment into the city, splitting up to start spreading the word.

Willit heads over to one of the nearby schools. At this moment, the class was out, and the instructors were simply tidying up after a busy day.

"Excuse me," he calls to the headmaster.

The man turned to Willit's address, recognizing him after a previous visit, and through instructions by Marelle with her incentives to take over the education system. He steps over for a conference.

"Yes, Mister Sarens. Do we have new instructions today?"

"I need you to assist in spreading a new message to the people. His Lordship has delivered an ultimatum to the Governor, by way of the Dean, that he needs to leave. Our problem is the Governor is one who doesn't like being told what to do. Even with the threat of his old enemies at his back door, he's not likely to go quietly, and that means trouble for us."

"Grand, but what sort of trouble?"

"The sort that could burn our fair city to the ground. Therefore, we need the people to know how to react, rather than just running in circles waiting for the end to hit them."

"You must be joking..." he sighs and glances around the room. "Right, then what are our instructions?"

"If they make a ground assault, our people need to run out whichever gate is farthest from the noise, either north or south."

"What if they hit from both sides just to foil that?" he grins shyly.

"Bloody hell, I wish you didn't just say that!" he smiles and shakes his head. "Favorites would be to use the south gate, I suppose. They might also try by air or something else, so turning south is the choice in those cases. They'll be sending mages up here to use portals on us, and so far, they're planning on the south side."

"All right, I'll tell the parents as they come in, and have my people spread this to the other schools."

Willit pats the man on the shoulder as he turns to leave.

It was late in the day, and the Governor was making another call on his trans-com.

"Commander, I have some instructions for you. I believe we need to cover ourselves for one or more liabilities that could backfire against us. If we leave any loose ends, our opponents could potentially follow us, and we cannot allow this. We need to keep this on our side, do you understand?"

"What are your instructions?"

"First, I will have you make a few special requisitions. I need plasma mortars. I believe three hundred will suffice."

"Three hundred? For what purpose?"

"We are going to create a distraction, and at the same time remove one or more of those liabilities I spoke of. I also need you to contact Morndindor base, and call for a special requisition of armor suits. Keep it simple, with chest pieces, plus arm and leg guards."

"What physical specifications?"

"The locals probably have something on hand, they often do. If not, have them make up a standard design to their personal liking. But it needs to be quick. Nothing fancy, just functional. Next, I need a small atomic device and a timed remote detonator."

"An atomic device?"

"Yes, we do not want them to discover our mining operation. This might give them a few ideas of what we've been doing here."

"Understood."

"And finally, I want you to configure the reactor downstairs to disable the safety protocols. I need to clean up after myself, and this is a convenient way of doing it."

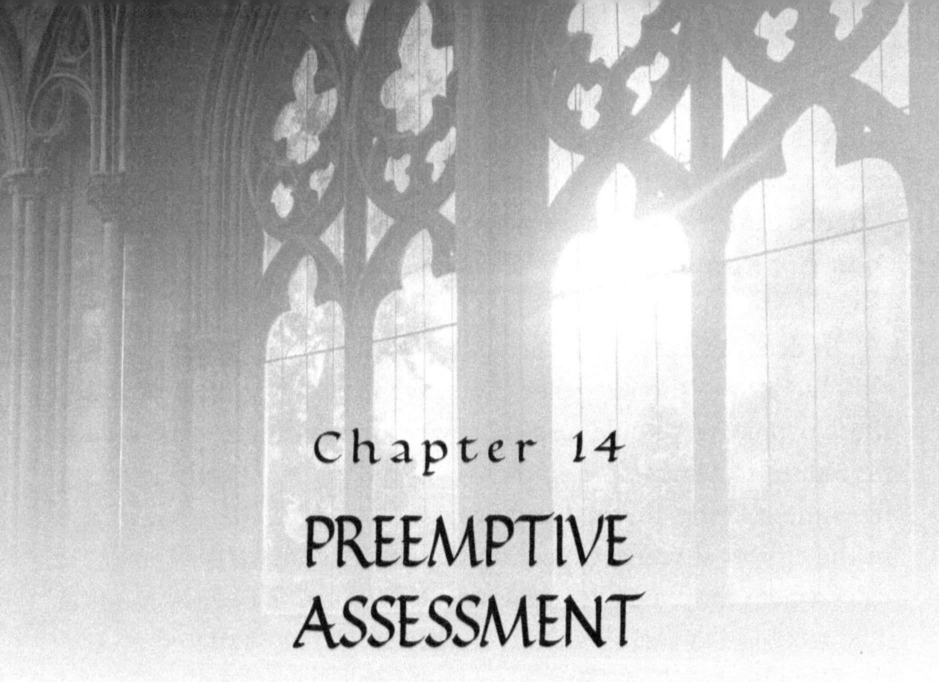

Chapter 14
PREEMPTIVE ASSESSMENT

Thaelyn was in a morning conference on his trans-com with Med-tech Tad'vaal discussing the implants used on the people of Rolsklinde.

"The virus contained inside the reservoir makes for an interesting case study," she relates. "The genetic coding of the strain seems to be very exact, meaning it will only seek out and attack cellular tissue of a specific pattern, in this case human neural membranes."

"That sounds like a rather remarkable design. Could it be a threat to anyone else?"

"I suppose it could affect other races with a closely related pattern, but this cannot be a naturally occurring strain. I ran a careful scan on it trying to sequence the coding, and although I'm getting an anomaly in my scans, which I'm having trouble isolating, in my professional opinion, it had to be specifically created for this purpose. In its present state, the coding matches human genetic patterns very precisely."

"An anomaly... What sort?"

"I'm not sure yet, the computer registers it as some sort of contamination. I ran the scan twice so far, and it's coming up the same. Maybe my equipment isn't calibrated properly, or maybe the sample I was using is imperfect. I may have to take one out and put it under a microscope to see what it is, but I'll save that for another time. The greatest priority should be removing them as soon as possible."

"Indeed, this is a clear certainty."

"But now," she suggests. "If you're planning on evacuating those people, we should also see if we can coordinate some kind of procedure to remove the implants. We don't want anyone to slip by without being checked and processed, and it's either we do this in the city, or if you're expecting the city to be destroyed, may the cu'Nar help those people, then we need to plan for a field hospital. The trouble I'm seeing already is they might be scattered all over the place by then."

"Yes, I would agree," he relents. "And so far, the biggest variable is the Marshal and what he has in mind. Right now, all we have is a buildup of troops on the other side of the ridge to the east, but they are not moving in this direction, or anywhere else that we can determine."

"I don't want to be in your place right now. That scares the curl out of my horns just thinking of it," she chuckles.

"Indeed, and fortunately I do not have any horns to worry about, but I certainly understand the sentiment. However, if we do make an evacuation, we will likely have a few casualties, so a field hospital would be a fine idea. See if you can put something together to have on call if we need it."

"All right, I can do that, and you let us know what happens."

"Excellent, Med-tech, until then…"

They end the link and Thaelyn returns to their morning review.

"General," he begins. "What do we have on those scouts we sent out yesterday?"

"We have a collection of runes available for that series of new staging posts they created on the other side of those mountains. These open up just behind them in a blind gully within some local vegetation."

"Good, and this offers us a vantage point to launch a secret strike with our new tactic."

"Yes, it does. But you know," the General considers. "Despite the suggestion of the Marshal supposedly creating a more militaristic body out of them, they do not strike me as very clever in their organization. They set down a garrison in plain view with only rudimentary fortification against a ground assault. And even though we are on this side of the mountain, and they must surely realize by now we tend to use portals, they are not covering their backs at all."

"One might suggest if your opponent uses portals, how do you offer a proper defense against that? But then again, a circular fortification would surely make more sense. We should also consider they are more accustomed to using ranged assaults rather than close melee engagements, especially if you consider their inherent vulnerability to injury."

"True, and if they are not trained for close combat, and in fact should not even engage in it to begin with, they might not otherwise train for this as a proper army would."

"Ah! Wait. Here we might have an important clue…an army. Theirs is a spaceborne military…a navy."

"But of course! So, ground maneuvers would be less commonly practiced in this case. They would more likely engage in ship-to-ship combat, or using combat vessels of some sort."

"Indeed, so if this is their normal tradition, what we are seeing out there is a bluff to fool us. They should know better after their experience in front of the Naarg uy'Sodrad that any ground movement is going to result in a lot of casualties for them."

"Then what would be their true intentions?"

"I feel that whatever plan the Marshal makes either has yet to be conceived, or has already been conceived and needs preparation. Therefore, this is a mere stall tactic."

"Very well, let us say we are looking at a stall tactic," the General ponders. "That line out there is a front being held in place simply for show. My first question is for how long. Then, what can we expect to be his final play? According to Leesa's last report, he stated he was not going to be so easily pushed out."

"Correct, and if we also consider my message to the Marshal about the Estelar and any repercussions of an attack on our position or that of our obvious friends, he should not wish to tempt fate if he desires to find any true escape for himself. Therefore, under these conditions, we should not expect one here, Solinaia, and I would hope, the Naarg uy'Sodrad."

"And this simply returns us to Rolsklinde again, and his most immediate subjects who are disobeying him. But if the Suuden-Aryku are not as effective at a ground offensive, I might think even the Allegiance Guard would be dangerous to them. For that matter, a common innkeeper with a broken bottle would be dangerous," he chuckles.

"This may be true," Thaelyn grins. "And if we also suggest the Suuden-Aryku may be something of a favorite minion society for him, being perhaps his first, and further if we consider Sargeras is stationing himself on their home world, then he might not wish to spend them this way. And I somehow doubt he has any more adamantium suits for his people, as this would take time to prepare. You often need to fit them to the individual, and we only saw that one example during this time."

"Either way, if that one rogue example is any indication, with or without adamantium, a ground offensive would not work well, not in comparison to ours using magic and such. It would be too exposed for us to see, and he doesn't have cloaks as far as we know."

"Perhaps, although let us not forget, the city has two gates to it. And they have large carriers, some of which surely would be able to drop off troops behind the lines."

"Yes," the General nods. "If to use the south gate, which is the closest and perhaps the most convenient, this would backfire on them, as we can see this one easily. Therefore, the north gate would make for a handy covert action. But I think I must still maintain that the use of common troops is not a wise course. Regardless of where they deploy, ours can counter and cut them down no different in the city than outside the Naarg uy'Sodrad. Further is to say it is too visible, especially if we suggest the Estelar are watching, and those repercussions you mentioned. He might wish to avoid calling attention to anything that could return back to him. Or at least, so immediately to return."

"This is reasonable. And if he had anything else in mind, like this bombardment tactic, we might already see it in action, I suppose."

"Maybe. It could be a simple call, make a hit, perhaps a brief engagement, and then depart immediately thereafter. But so far, he is holding out for something."

"And this has to be as a result of this stall tactic. He is preparing something…another of his little games, no doubt."

Thaelyn leans back in his chair and pauses to contemplate the idea.

"Games…to toy with something…" he muses. "Yes, he seems to like that. General, he wanted those students out of his way for making noise over his plans with that conjuring. Did he choose a simple method of silencing them? No, he thought up a solution using an obscure medicinal agent that might bring about a rather gruesome result. Also, if we consider that rogue Suuden'kai patrol wearing adamantium launched against what might be a common Guard deployment, again for visual effect. He enjoys using elaborate methods of removing his obstacles."

"So it would seem, and again with Leesa's report, he described all things as toys for his pleasures. This naturally reflects back on the Primordials, and what has been said about them using small creatures in elaborate games of intrigue and conquest. It yields more entertainment value."

"Indeed. Therefore, we could say he would not wish to use his people on the ground for the obvious repercussions, and an air assault might be amusing, but it may also be too straightforward. As such, what entertainment value would it offer? He will more likely set something in motion and let it go, and at this moment, he might further wish to clean up a few loose ends along the way."

"Oh good gracious, of course, a cascading effect. This reminds me of that reactor. Why attack something at all if you can set that to blow up?"

"Absolutely. And furthermore, why not, as they say, kill two birds with one stone. We still have those dwarves. If they are so expendable that he literally works them to death, what will become of them?"

"Blast," the General curses silently. "Then, I would suggest we send a scout or two up there to peek in on them."

"Agreed, see to it, and send word to Leesa to have her pay close attention to the Governor in case he should decide to take a leave of absence for any reason. We need to know as soon as he is out of that building, so we can make an attempt at that basement."

◆◆◆◆

"An evacuation, is it?" Tristeen mutters. "Our entire city, the only thing we have left in this world, all because of that fiend up there."

"His Lordship promises to help us rebuild…" Willit affirms.

"Bloody hell," Jared moans. "The whole city? At that point, he might as well own us for all the trouble we'll be causing him," he chuckles weakly.

"Maybe. The Night Elves have already joined up, and the High Elves might actually follow suit. So, why not make it a full set. His world is a fine place to live. I don't see anything wrong with the idea."

"Aye, but I think that's not my place to say."

"The noble families once held the authority of rule," Tristeen reflects. "They don't anymore, of course, all because of that Governor, but perhaps they could offer some influence. For all these new stories going around, I think the people will need some help to consolidate the idea."

"Are you thinking of getting up on a soapbox now, Tris?" Jared grins.

"Don't give me any ideas," she smiles playfully.

"Well, one thing I think I can say for it," Willit admits. "He'll probably turn us around for it well enough. After all, Haran sure seems to like it over there."

Tristeen jerks around at the blatant mention of the name, and grabs Willit's arm for his attention. The sudden change in her manner shocked him.

"What?!" she urges strongly. "Haran is on their world now?!"

Willit was jolted by her reaction, and Jared propped up in his chair as he watched the exchange.

"Well, yeah," Willit admits gently. "You didn't know?"

"Nope, she didn't," Jared grins. "That flaming fool is in for it now, I'll bet. You know how the two of them are, don't you?"

"I, uh… Well, I've heard a few whispers in the back rooms, but criminy, Tris!"

"What is he doing over there?" she charges. "And why didn't he tell me about it?"

"Well, as I hear it, he took refuge after that bout with the Dean. He told me he didn't dare go back, and didn't care much for the other choices he had around here. And they have that mage academy over there that simply staggers you for all you can learn. He couldn't pass that up."

"All right, fine. But what about the part of not writing…at least a little note…"

Her face softens as she reflects on their last meeting. She recalls the argument Haran had with the Dean, his expulsion, and how he simply walked out of the academy, never to be seen again. She lowers her head and sighs heavily.

"Dammit… But he's right."

"Tristeen?"

"Our last conversation… I'm a noble and he's not, and we would probably never have a future together."

"Buggers to that, Tristeen!" Jared retorts. "It's your life. You should put your foot down on how you want to live it, despite what your parents might say to it."

"He's right, Tris," Willit affirms. "This city will be going to all the hells soon. So whatever it is you think might be holding you back, it won't be there much longer. You should take what you can get, and play it for all it's worth."

"You think so?" she looks up at him shyly.

"Darned right, I do. Nobody will hold it against you, not for all you've been through. People are still people. And besides, if your parents are so fidgety about him being a simple nobody, he told me he wants to take his lessons as high as he can get them, just out of spite for what the Dean did up there. When I asked him what that might lead to, he said it could put him in a position of authority over how they make the bloody things!"

"Really?" she exalts. "They have something like a regulatory committee over there?"

"Aye, and you don't get any better than that for notability."

"All right," she smiles and drifts off. "I suppose that could pass a little smoother."

Their meeting came to a close as each of them had to return to their other objectives.

Tristeen went home to consider her next course of action. She entered the family room in deep thought and quietly sat down. Her parents were both present and trying to find something to occupy their time, but in the end, all they could do was dwell on the previous day's events and wait for whatever might come next.

Her father was reading a book, but only half involved with it, while her mother tried relaxing herself with some knitting. The whole family was tense. In time, Tristeen's extended lull after sitting down worked into their minds, as she was the one most involved with the resistance efforts. She simply sat there with her hands clasped and elbows resting on the arms of the chair while she mulled her thoughts. Finally, her father decided to speak up to see if something might be wrong.

"Tristeen, you've been very quiet ever since that activity out in the plaza yesterday."

"Yeah, it left a heavy mark on me, plus the visit to his office afterwards."

"Did you want to tell us anything more about what was said?"

"There wasn't much else, other than His Lordship laying down his charges against the Dean and the Governor for their combined wrongdoings. The trouble is the Governor isn't the kind of person to just get up and leave."

"Based on what was said yesterday," he sighs. "That would be my impression as well."

"But it goes deeper than that, Dad. I didn't tell you who, or for that matter what he actually is."

Josef pulls forward in his chair to place more focus on his daughter. His wife does the same in her chair, lowering her knitting needles to listen in more intently.

"What do you mean?" he inquires tenderly. "I heard the words spoken by the Dean yesterday...Darumon, is that his real name?"

"Yeah, and according to what the Captain told me when I went to visit him later, he's actually known as Marshal Darumon, the one in charge of all these invasion forces."

"Grand, just grand... But when you say 'what' he is, how do you mean that? Did we finally learn something about him?"

"His Lordship learned something, and apparently, it's really bad for all of us. He's a servant creature of some kind to Sargeras, and likely to be nearly godlike as compared to all the rest."

"Great gods, Tristeen!" he gasps. "What would something like that be doing here?"

"Like the Dean said, looking for revenge against his old enemies, these Estelar everyone is talking about lately, and using us as tools along the way, for all the good we serve. We're all immigrants from Tae'Eladar...us humans, the elves, and apparently according to some plan where he must've visited Tae'Eladar once, built a strange portal device, led our ancestors here, along with sending a bunch of orcs over there to make trouble for them. The timing stood out, however, once they found all the pieces to it. Then, here we are on this world, the war, then Thaelyn arriving due to more orcs, and everything with the name Sargeras written all over it."

"Indeed! And this represents a rather complex plan with a long timing sequence to it. I can certainly see how a godlike creature might do this if he's patient enough. And what sort of trouble is it His Lordship thinks he has in mind?"

"His Lordship is suggesting Darumon will probably want to punish all those who are disobeying him, which would probably mean everyone in the city by now. But then, I'm thinking of the Dean and what he said here at the door. And this is causing me to worry a little."

"About what?"

"Dad, I think we're in trouble, more than anything else right now."

"What sort of trouble, Tristeen?" he asks urgently.

"I apparently got on his list with all my rabble-rousing in the academy. Of course, even though I knew this might cause trouble with him, and perhaps the Suuden-Aryku, what I did not know was who he is in reality, or his true manners."

"At the time you were doing this…" he surmises. "Very well, this simply cannot be avoided. You did what you had to do to preserve lives. What next?"

"Now I'm thinking of something new and trying to pull together a few thoughts. During this time, we had to let it out that the noble families kept all those old records of our history. So, it's known that WE, collectively, are also responsible for doing something he was trying to bury with the help of his cronies in the academy."

"Grand! And here we come back to him trying to pressure us under his thumb. But again, I guess this was unavoidable. And this would likely involve all the noble families simply for the merit that we were trouble once before during the days of the old Council, and even now with our determination to keep our heritage intact."

"Exactly. Therefore, I think we'll be on top of the list by now, all of us."

"Dear," Tristeen's mother urges. "What are we supposed to do about this? I mean, how do we protect ourselves from something like this? It seems so barbaric that we're only trying to provide for our people, and this beast wants to use us like animals."

"Margo," Josef admits. "This beast, and that's probably the best way to describe him, clearly has no interest in what we want. To him, we are animals."

"I just got back from a meeting with Willit," Tristeen offers. "He says they're expecting we may need to evacuate the city. The Governor may want to raze it to the ground, and at this moment, in order to preserve lives and get him to actually leave our world, we may have to sacrifice that much."

"Sacrifice our entire city?" Josef balks. "Can't they do something to prevent this?"

"It gets complicated, Dad. If they kill him outright, the Suuden-Aryku may go haywire without his control effect. And apparently, he controls them with devices that make them behave almost like machines to do his bidding. If this is the case, they won't stop until we're completely destroyed. However, this is where the Estelar may get involved, and in this case, it goes back to the Suuden-Aryku until they are destroyed, perhaps every last one of them. This is also unacceptable, as they're also regarded as victims."

"Victims… Does he think he can rescue them somehow?"

"That's his hope."

"All right, so we need to sacrifice our city in the hopes to save what could be a world full of people. Gods be blessed, what have we found here? So, what then? Where does this actually leave us?"

"According to His Lordship, we need him to leave. Simple, and by whatever means will actually get him out of here. And then, I suppose, His Lordship and these Estelar will go after him later, but under their terms, not that monster's."

"I'm trying to imagine this," Margo ponders feebly. "A battle of such proportions that it involves these godlike beings, and right here in our world."

"It seems incredible," Josef relents. "But then, I guess it's just our great misfortune to be in the wrong place at the wrong time for it. But now, Tristeen, you say he might have it in for us especially? How do we protect ourselves? Does His Lordship offer any ideas?”

“For one thing, he’s made a promise to help our people, whatever the case. This apparently includes helping us to rebuild.”

“Indeed! Well, that will surely go a long way.”

“As for the evacuation, this is where it gets hairy. We don’t know what the Governor has in mind, and probably won’t until he actually drops it on us. So, it’s a waiting game, and it gets problematic if we should want to evacuate early, because if he sees a mass movement, he might just do this in the quickest manner possible to keep us from getting very far.”

“Oh, and that’s an even grander snag. If we don’t run, he hits us at his leisure. If we do run, he simply hits us harder and faster.”

“His Lordship will send people up here to help, but we shouldn’t provoke something by making a big scene. This is as much a waiting game as it is a guessing game. I’d say, leave it to those who know how to play it best. They’ll tell us if they learn anything new.”

She pulls out a device from her dress pocket and holds it up for display.

“Do you see this? Willit gave this to me this morning. It’s from the Daanen-Aryku, called a trans-com. They’re using these down there to communicate with each other out in the field.”

Both of her parents lean in to examine the strange item as she shows it off from all sides.

“I’m able to punch in a special sequence here and make contact with someone. Willit showed me how to do it. I’m able to call him or His Lordship directly, if I must, and tell them if I see anything. I’m going to keep this on me until this whole thing finishes.”

“How interesting,” Josef considers. “So, in a way, you’re serving a bit like a Civil Watch officer.”

“Right. Now, my biggest concern is with the noble families. We could be a prime target, so I think we need to escape now while we still can.”

“Escape...” he mulls the thought. “But to where? Run to His Lordship’s side, I presume?”

"Yes. We should order up a number of coaches, and pack them with whatever we can carry…"

She pauses a moment to survey the room, and rolls her eyes around as she tries to envision her home and family estate for so many generations. She closes her eyes in memoriam of her life here, and that of her entire family.

"We're going to lose this," she mutters softly. "I know it."

Josef and Margo follow her as she recalls her lifetime memories. They glance at each other, and then back at her as she prepares to finish.

"Mom, Dad, I need your help, and even though you may not want to do this, we must. We need to gather up the other families, spread the word, pack whatever we can carry, and leave under the cover of darkness."

"Tristeen," Josef ushers cautiously. "That sounds almost like we're trying to sneak away."

"We're trying to save ourselves from a monster that wants us dead. That's not sneaking, that's trying to avoid him seeing us slip away from him. Assuming he actually sleeps at night, we'll use this to our advantage, but we're not just sneaking off. You're going to organize yourselves with His Lordship, and help our people on the other side, while I do so here."

"What?!" Margo yelps. "You're not coming with us?"

"Mom, I have work to do, and I'm not running out on these people. You, however, can be a great help after the rest of them have to escape. We're going to have a lot of broken lives, so it's up to us to put it back together."

Relissa, Marelle, and Padriyl were once again arriving in the tactical office from their language lessons. This last month of study seemed to be dragging on, if only due to the recent excitement up north. They each take up their usual chairs at the table, and Marelle reaches over to her box to check for any mail. This would be the first time since yesterday's activities when she would pick up on her work again.

"My Lord," Relissa wonders. "Do we have anything new with the Suuden-Aryku out there?"

"So far," he relates. "It seems like a standoff between the two of us, but we are fairly sure this is some sort of stall tactic for the Marshal and his latest plans. And we are now thinking he will want to close up a few loose ends, one of which might involve those dwarves."

"Oh grand, so how do we help those buggers if the Suuden-Aryku are likely keeping a close eye on them?"

"We sent a couple of scouts up there earlier to check on them, but so far nothing new is occurring."

Marelle was examining her mail. She opens one note that was sealed with the classic wax stamp of the Allegiance Guard and pulls out a second note tucked away inside, also closed and sealed. She holds it up to examine it, frowning perplexedly as she reads the address.

"Huh?" she mutters softly. "Why is he sending a note to him?"

Relissa notices her private mention and turns to check on her friend.

"What do you mean?"

"The Captain sent this, and it has Haran's name on it."

"The Captain sent it?"

"Well, wait a moment. Let me read this other one."

Marelle begins to read the cover letter. As she progresses through it, her frown deepens significantly.

"Gods above," she wheezes silently.

Relissa leans in and gently taps Marelle's arm with her hand.

Thaelyn also took notice of the strange reaction.

"Marelle," he remarks. "I am sensing a strong emotional burst from you. What is it? Is this a personal issue, or something else?"

"Your Lordship, I'm...um..." she pauses uncertainly.

She studies the letter again and then turns to the next one. It appeared as a common letter, but also addressed to her, and apparently passed through the Captain. But the paper didn't appear as something typical of the fashion from the lower district, which would be the only place she might expect to receive mail from. This one involved delicate scrollwork around the borders, and was also sealed with a wax stamp.

"Who in all the hells do we know with paper like this?" she blurts. "I never got one this nice before. The letter M, this must be from the Macaid house…Tristeen."

She opens it and begins to read. After several long moments, she clamped a hand over her mouth, and her face began to show worry and distress. Thaelyn and the others in the room wait patiently for her to finish. When she was done, she turned to look at them with troubled eyes.

"I'm actually sorry now that I took so much pleasure watching that man squirm yesterday."

"Marelle," Relissa nudges her arm. "What is it?"

"Here, read this, both of them," she pushes the two letters across the table.

Relissa takes the two letters and begins to read. As she finishes, she also appears affected.

"Jiggers, that ties it for sure," she whispers.

"Eh, Marelle, or Relissa," Thaelyn asserts gently. "Would one or the other of you desire to share this? Clearly this seems very distressing, but is it a personal issue, or related to our concerns with the city, perhaps?"

"Your Lordship," Marelle sighs deeply. "I think we need to reconsider a small issue here. The Dean is frightened for his life."

Thaelyn pulls back from the table into his chair, gazing at her concernedly and contemplating the sensations he is feeling from the two of them.

"In what way?" he inquires.

"I'm recalling your message to him yesterday, and then what you said downstairs. Gods above if you didn't hit the mark. I have two letters here. One is from the Captain, the other is from Tristeen. The Dean apparently visited both of them yesterday, and it must've been sometime after our meeting, and after his meeting with the

Governor. The Captain says he came in and offered an apology! An actual apology for his actions!"

"Indeed!" he leans in again.

"He also shared a few thoughts, which I'll get to in a moment, and he wanted to send a special note to Haran," she holds up the second sealed letter. "He wanted to apologize to him for the argument they had once."

"He's feeling his last days on him," Relissa mutters solemnly. "He's trying to make his final peace now."

"He also went to Tristeen's house," Marelle continues. "She writes that he was falling to pieces on her doorstep, as he again made another apology, and tried to explain his actions, saying how the Governor holds so much power and influence, that he simply got caught in a whirlpool of intrigue and nearly drowned in it."

"Dear Powers," Thaelyn emits quietly. "I did not wish to shock him quite to this extreme. It was necessary for us to lay down a demonstration, to provide evidence, something tangible to see, and even to touch, but this…"

"We were probably leading up to it, regardless," Marelle suggests. "All those other demonstrations and his reactions, some of which made it seem like he was being driven mad by all his work being made public. If he was being driven by the Governor, and Tristeen says he told her he once held such high hopes for a career as the Dean, kissing up no different from anyone else, then the Governor started pulling him in with all these little secret plays of his. That's what got him."

"And now he feels his last moments, likely due to his encounter with the Governor after our play with that demon, and then his office. And I suppose this small revelation would probably mark him in the Governor's eyes, as he likes to keep himself hidden from his toys. Do we have anything else?"

"They each mention notes here about the Governor's attitude towards the Estelar. In fact, according to the Captain, the Dean tells us the title of Marshal is actually, um," she grins cutely, "superfluous, as the Dean has word that his kind doesn't normally use titles."

"Oh, is that so? Then I shall reconsider my use of it."

"Anyway, he further tells us of Darumon describing himself as the last survivor of Sargeras's attendants. He also said they were the last group holding out in that space after a long period of decline."

"This makes it sound as if they were simply fading from existence, or perhaps being hunted into extinction by the Estelar."

"Maybe both, but surely the latter," Marelle suggests. "He says they were once a god society that apparently ruled before the Estelar."

"Indeed!" Thaelyn states firmly. "I recall mention of an older race, though admittedly the stories tend to run a bit thin on the details. There was this rivalry between them, and ultimately the Estelar purging them from Creation. Here is where we have some number of these Celestial Wars, with the last of them, to my knowledge, being in our space."

"And naturally, they absolutely hate each other, with these Primordials of yours holding themselves as overseers, not underlings giving themselves to someone else's rule."

"Uh huh, this would follow quite nicely with their manners. It might also explain a few things from my side of it. My experience with the Estelar is they do not wish to discuss this history by now. This might also coincide with the name Primordial so often being applied as a derogatory term."

"Wow, they actually use bad language up there?" she giggles gently. "Yeah, he says they describe them as self-righteous and overbearing with their policies."

"How quaint."

"But here is where he and the Captain had a little talk. Roddy says the Dean believes Darumon is out for a revenge attack."

"Revenge!" the General blasts. "That would be preposterous, to say nothing of suicidal. But how does the Dean suggest this? Surely, even if Darumon is a last survivor, he would not have made so many extended plans with so much wanton disregard for himself or his Master."

"Yeah, he had an idea, and it reflects on the huge amount of adamantium, which may not be limited to this world. Darumon must have another one, and it likely involves those dwarves."

"All right, this is bad for the numbers. What is this idea?"

"You're not going to like this. He figures it can't be for people to wear as armor, not if no one around here even knows what it is or how to use it. He said it was something personal to Darumon, apparently because Darumon admitted to something, but he's not saying what. But the Dean feels it must be something on the scale of a god, for the knowledge content alone."

"I suppose this is fair."

"So, the Dean had this crazy idea, and it's crazy alright...for Darumon. He suspects it must be a weapon, since he's generally alone, and he's moving around like a thief. But this weapon, and I think I would use the term loosely here, is to bring another of the same as that battle you told us about that blew up your universe. He might have been present during the first one."

"Jiggers!" Relissa yips. "You mean the old Celestial War?"

"Great Powers above!" Thaelyn shouts. "Yes! This would be absolutely insane, as well as devious and pure maliciousness."

The suggestion sent a chill into Thaelyn, as well as the rest of them at the table, at least insofar as they could comprehend the scenario. Thaelyn leaned back anxiously to consider this statement.

"I am going to need to make a consultation on this to see if we can associate just what sort of weapon we are referring to here. If we really are speaking of the same as what caused the first destruction of our universe, this would need to be deployed elsewhere, as our local space is already destroyed. If he wants to launch his revenge directly against the Estelar, this will have to be delivered into those places where they normally make their homes."

"That sounds really bad," Marelle moans.

"Worse is to ask how far along he is, and how to prevent it. But it also fits with his mentality. If he cannot have it for himself, destroy it completely. And if he is the last of his kind, what does he need with the rest of Creation."

"Oh gee, thank you so much."

"I understand, Marelle. I feel the same for this point."

Thaelyn takes a deep breath, hoping to calm himself and now reflects on the Dean for his extraordinary contribution.

"I was right, it would seem…that lost soul calling out."

"The Dean? Yeah, you hit that one dead on."

"My Lord," Relissa wonders. "I can't say I ever held much care for the guy, but this turns it around a wee bit for me. Can we do something for him?"

"Yes," he affirms. "General, inform Master Dastien up there to keep an eye on the Dean. I think that man just bought himself a ticket to redemption."

✦✦✦✦✦✦

The meeting in the tactical office had adjourned with the General seeking rest at a small café in the village square in Firstfall. Relissa and Padriyl both joined for some tea and a bit of pleasant conversation, while Thaelyn and Marelle returned to Tae'Eladar.

Marelle diverted to the guildhall to visit Haran. She met with him in one of the study halls where he had been taking up temporary employment with one of the Masters until his language studies were complete.

"Haran," she sings. "You have mail."

"Huh? Me?" he responds curiously. "From whom?"

"Someone you know, but probably would never expect to receive a letter from. Here…" she hands it across.

He studies it carefully for the paper and the wax stamp.

"This is the Allegiance Guard here."

"Yeah, well, I guess he had to borrow a piece of paper from them. His desk was probably not in very good condition by now," she smiles.

"His desk…but who are we talking about?"

"Just open it and read it. And if you don't mind, may I have a peek? I'm curious to see what it says."

"Really!" he smirks. "So, my big sister now wants to sniff around my mail?"

"Hey, I need to keep a close eye on my little brother. You never know what sort of trouble he'll get into."

He eyes her suspiciously as he opens the letter. He then begins to read.

"Haran,

At this moment in time, I have little else in my life but to make amends to all those I so deeply offended during my time in my office. I was once like you, although I knew the way to the top was to behave exactly as I was expected, no matter how demeaning it felt. When I finally found myself in the most prestigious position of Dean of the Academy, I felt like the world would turn to my every beckoning. I would change everything and make it right again. That was before he began to share all his intimate plans with me, slowly devouring me in the process. It was devious, and before I knew it, I was carrying more burdens than was healthy for a man.

That day you came in with your report, you reminded me of that man I should have been, what I wanted to be. But the Governor got there first. All I had left by then was a burnt-out soul. You were right, and I was wrong, but I couldn't admit to it. All I could do was follow in the tracks laid down for me by that thing who would dare call itself a Governor for our people.

Carry forward for us, Haran. Wherever you are at this time, seek that which you feel is the worthiest cause, and make right all that the rest of us failed at so miserably.

Dean Alin Malorn"

Haran and Marelle both read the note. Haran felt faint, and had to seek a nearby chair, nearly falling into it. Marelle wrapped her arms around him to comfort him.

"Dear gods, Sis," he wheezes. "How could I ever possibly know this? He never spoke of it, or behaved in any way to give even the slightest hint."

"I got a note from Tristeen. She said he came to her house to offer an apology, and was coming apart at the seams. The Captain also wrote he made an apology in his office, and even offered a hint or two on what he thinks the Governor is doing with all his adamantium. He's trying to make up for his errors, but he's also behaving as if his last days are upon him, which they probably are by now with the Governor getting tired of him and everyone else."

"We have to do something. Does His Lordship know about this?"

"He does, though not this specific letter, but the others I got today, and he's giving instructions for Master Dastien to keep an eye on things, but that doesn't really offer any special guarantees."

"Can I do anything?"

"I don't know what, at this time. We're in a waiting game, all of us, it seems."

"All right," he sighs. "But tell me what happens as soon as you can."

She nods and they hug, then she turns to leave the room.

Thaelyn was on his way to the temple to meet with Aerlie and give a report to his contact among the Estelar with this latest revelation about Darumon and his apparent intentions. On his arrival through the gateway, Aerlie could feel his presence and came out of her office to join him. They met on the dais inside the temple.

"Thaelyn, what's wrong?" she asks. "You seem unusually tense."

"We think we have learned what Darumon has in mind, and it is just as much sacrilege as what his kind is best known for."

"Darumon?" she muses. "Simply Darumon?"

"Yes, we got a recent word that titles are, ahem, superfluous with his kind," he smirks.

"Oh, my goodness, how unfortunate! So, can you tell me what's on his mind this time?"

"Marelle received a couple of notes from her Captain today, and she related that the Dean, if you can actually believe it, has turned over a rather substantial leaf for himself. He came to the Captain, and also that young lady, Tristeen Macaid, with apologies for his actions, and explanations that he had his own troubles during his lifetime. He also shared a thought that Darumon desires revenge on the Estelar for their actions, likely dating back to the days of the old Celestial War."

"Dear gods, he must be insane if he thinks he could assault them now."

"Not simply that..." he sighs. "He affirmed his kind was a precursor to the Estelar, once having ruled Creation, and later being destroyed for their conflicting beliefs. And their passionate rivalry relates to the Measure of Balance, and how the Primordials were likely a supremacist authority that did not care to give themselves to any others."

"Very nice!" she huffs.

"Indeed. But the Dean also speculated on the reason for the adamantium, and it might be to create a weapon comparable to the one used during that same moment, the one responsible for our skies up there."

"You must be kidding me!" she shouts. "The Rending, as they call it? Can he actually do such a thing?"

"This is what I need to check on. I need to discover what the weapon actually was, and if it can be produced in such a manner."

Aerlie listened to his statement and pondered it briefly, only to be interrupted by movement coming in through the doors on the other side of the room. She turned her attention to it, rolled her eyes briskly, and patted him on the shoulder to gain his attention as well.

Sauntering along the central aisle was a tall female fully in silver hues. She wore a long silver gown, had silver skin, and long silver hair. Her face was uniquely contoured, slim and sharply angled. And she had silver catlike eyes.

The two nobles, along with the rest of the priesthood on the platform, and the few visitors who were in attendance at this time, all bowed as she made her approach.

"Adalon," Thaelyn calls to her. "What brings you here at this moment, as if I could not guess by your traditional manners," he grins.

"Naturally, I have... A reputation... And surely... I cannot allow it... To go ssslack," she chuckles demurely.

"Indeed, and I would not expect anything less from you. So, what is the special occasion?"

"You have a quessstion. I have the anssswer. And at thisss time... I think it bessst... We do not disssturb... The Essstelar..."

"Why is that?"

"Even they would be afraid... Of what you... Have jussst learned. We cannot allow them... To interfere... With these plansss..."

"Not allow them to interfere? Should they not know of this?"

"They will... But we do not... Want them... To jump ahead... Before we can corner... Our prey..."

"Ah, I see, and in so doing, possibly cause our prey to attempt another escape, correct?"

"Yesss... And I am sure... The Maker... Would desire... To keep thisss... Contained. We will inform them... But with termsss... That we will attend to thisss... And they mussst hold back. I believe... We can demonsssstrate... Sssufficient qualificationsss... To sssee thisss through... Sssuccessfully..."

"Very well; if you feel this is possible. Then what do you have to offer us on this occasion?"

"I have been keeping... Myssself aware... Of your dealingsss... On that world. I knew thisss... Would come out... Eventually... And that you mussst... Undersssstand... The purposssse he holdsss... For his ancient rivalsss. But you are right. By himsssself... He is of no concern... To the Essstelar... Unlesss he can provide... A way to ssstrike... From the shadowsss... And desssstroy them. For thisss... He needsss a weapon... Unlike any used... Sssince the Celesssstial War..."

"Do we know the nature of this weapon and how it can be made? We know he has been harvesting large quantities of adamantium."

"Indeed… But it is not… The metal… He desiresss. Thisss is a form… Of knowledge… Known only to those… Of a sssupreme level… Of development… And ethereal in nature. Material bodiesss… Would not be as privy to it…"

"Which means such like the Estelar, and perhaps also the Primordials in their day?"

"Yesss. In itsss puressst form… It would be derived… From the dynamisssstic flowsss. But he does not have… Sssuch easy accessss… Nor does he hold… The full potential… To create thisss himsssself. Therefore… He musssst use… Lesssser grade materialsss… And ssstruggle with lower yieldsss… Until he sssucceeds…"

"And so, this would explain the large quantities we are seeing. And such a waste it is for its other utilitarian values."

"Indeed. Both adamantium… And mithril… Possessss sssmall quantitiesss… Of the arcanic energiesss. Thisss would need… To be extracted… And concentrated… Condensssed… As a missst condensssses to water… And then to ice…"

"That sounds like a very potent derivative," Aerlie considers. "How would this appear as an end product?"

"It would carry… Qualitiesss… Of a fragile… Crysssstalline geometry… But not fully sssolid. Inssstead… Vaguely amorphousss… And extremely volatile…"

"Gracious! So, the slightest touch, and boom?"

"On a ssscale… You would not want… To imagine… As it would erupt… In a cataclysssmic… Chain reaction… Of the entire arcanic cloud… Consssuming everything… Along with it…"

"Dear Powers," Thaelyn relents. "He must be mad."

"He would have to be," Aerlie admits. "But I guess no more so than the others were in the Celestial War. And if they used it once, what's to stop them from trying again?"

"Indeed, and if we further consider he makes his home in a universe without this cloud, he might consider himself safe from the blast effect. And for this, we might have the reason for those orcs invading our space. They were looking for a portal of some kind. But such a portal as this would have to be…of…oh dear…"

"Thaelyn?"

"I am willing to bet this is more of his work. If he made that one to lead those immigrants away, could he have made a second one to another location?"

"Uh oh..."

"Adalon, can you answer this for us?"

"I will anssswer... Yesss..." she affirms. "It is the sssame... But with two... Dessstinations..."

"Two! How interesting. But where is it?"

Adalon smiles demurely.

"You will know... When the time is right..."

"Why am I not surprised at that answer," Aerlie smirks.

"I swear, Aerlie..." Thaelyn shakes his head. "Very well, and thank you, Adalon. By the way, what is this substance called?"

"Sssuch as the Essstelar... Would dessscribe thisss... As the Agent of Unmaking. But for those of usss... Of a more material bassse... We might use the name... Arcanicium..."

"How interesting, and I also find myself wondering how you would know all this," he eyes her suspiciously.

"I recall my hissstory..." she grins shyly.

"Of course..." he smiles warily. "Is there anything else you would wish to share?"

"Thisss is enough... For one day..."

She bows her head and turns to leave.

"Jiggers," Relissa moans. "So this is it, ay? That's what he's up to with all this bloody adamantium? Buggers to that, I say!"

"Indeed, Relissa," Thaelyn affirms. "This is a surprising one if only for the daring. But this leads us to a few new objectives. Adalon suggests we can do this on our own without the direct involvement of the Estelar, and I trust her opinion. Although I will admit, there are a number of uncertainties ahead of us yet to be resolved, not the least of which is to find where he is producing this material."

"Would it be found here somewhere?" Marelle wonders.

"If I apply a bit of interpretation, I might suggest he would not dare try producing this in a universe with the flows. If for no other reason than to prevent accidents that could destroy that universe and everything involved, and perhaps even himself, if he is present at the time."

"Aw, that would be such an awful thing if he blew himself up. But yeah, I think I would agree. So, if I'm guessing this right, it would have to be a universe without the flows, maybe a bit like that one the Suuden-Aryku came out of."

"That would be a viable option. Furthermore, I might suggest he would use a storage depot located in another area, far from the production facility, to prevent the destruction of his supply in case the facility producing it has an accident."

"Great, this now means there are two places for us to find, neither of them on this world, instead both likely to be in a completely different universe, and us without any means of travelling in space. Yeah, I love these little paradoxes," she giggles.

"Indeed, Marelle, I agree with you fully, but we will follow our course and see what opportunities present themselves. Adalon has a long history of prophecy behind her, and she seems to be remarkably accurate, if also extremely cryptic. This suggests we will find our way, and this might also imply answers to multiple other concerns where the rest of it goes. We simply need to be prudent in our actions."

"Lovely. All right, so our first concern has to be getting this guy off our world, and running home to crawl back under his rock. What do we have next on our list?"

"This next morning, we will be preparing a hit-and-run strike on that new row of garrisons over there. We will inform our people outside to prepare for a charge against us, in case they respond to the aggression, but I suspect if ours is not lethal, they might resist making any movements. And I think I could also use this later, if I should ever have the opportunity to speak with that High Commander of theirs."

"You would want to speak with him?" she winces. "Oh grand, but what would you say?"

"For one thing, if he holds any potential to think for himself, I will point out the fact that we hold the power to make such surprise hits, but on this particular occasion we chose a non-lethal strike as a kind of message that we do not necessarily want them dead simply for their existence. I would also combine this with their presence on a world already devastated by their own activities. There can be no justifiable cause to destroy a world full of technologically inferior societies, other than to commit murder on a grand scale. I want to see how he feels on this matter, with or without his implants controlling him."

"Interesting, but this is assuming you actually have a way to talk to him without being face to face, and likely fighting each other."

"True, so we shall see where this takes us."

The day was bustling in the Upper Ward. The noble families were hurriedly employing a small army of assistants, and nearly every available wagon in the city to convene in the area, and they were packing everything they could carry that held any special value.

"Margo, look here," Josef directs. "I've collected all our pedigree files in this box. This is our full family history; in case anyone should ask."

"Do you honestly think this will serve us with a society on a completely different world?"

"I can't be sure of that, but I feel we shouldn't be without it, at least to carry our family history."

"All right. Now let's see, I've packed as many of our heirlooms as I can find, and the attendants have filled at least two wagons by now. We have our dishes, family keepsakes, clothing and linens... my goodness, I've never had to pack a house before, and with so much we simply cannot bring. It's so distressful."

"Yes, and to do so in one day while under so much duress," he nods. "But according to Tristeen, we should not delay ourselves. That creature in the Governor's Manor could unleash his vile plans at any moment. We simply must be ready for it on the other side to help our people."

"Are you sure we can actually do this? We'll be in at least as much need as any other."

"Granted, but with His Lordship's aid, I hope to gain a small foothold before the deluge breaks free."

The stream of people continued to pack the wagons at each of the noble houses, hoping to be finished by sunset. By the time the sun was on the horizon, each of them had several wagons forming a long caravan ready to roll out, along with drivers and other handlers still in their employ to aid in the unpacking at their destination.

Josef and his friends surveyed the scene to make their final plans.

"Now listen," he begins. "Tristeen says we need to launch out after dark, but we can't be sure if that fiend even sleeps at night, or where he might be at the time when we go rumbling through the plaza down there."

"If he's actually in the Manor at all," Abraim mentions. "Maybe he sneaks off for his own evening somewhere."

"If that's the case," Seth considers. "We would have less to worry about, but personally, I wouldn't wish to take the chance."

"All right, then how do we plan this?"

"I would say to stagger our wagons at intervals, so it doesn't make as much noise going through there."

"Sounds fair enough," he nods. "Then, once on the other side, heading into the lower district, it shouldn't be as bad."

"Good," Josef agrees. "But the part that troubles me is moving through the open fields and finding our way in the dark, especially over that mountain. I hear that pass is a bit rundown by now."

"That could be a problem," Seth muses. "We'll need to take it very slow, maybe to have a man out front with a lantern to guide us."

"Fine enough, so long as we get there in one piece."

They watch the sunset, and line themselves up in the streets. Tristeen joins her family for one last farewell before they head out.

"I called them down there, and told them to expect you," she asserts. "My understanding is the journey, at least in the daytime, and under good conditions, would be no more than a half a day trot by horse. But at night, well, just be careful, no matter how long it takes. The General said he would send out a bunch of their scouts to assist in crossing the mountain pass."

"That sounds quite comforting," Josef accedes. "All right, my dear," he reaches out to hug her. "I feel like we're making some sort of pilgrimage journey here, a bit like some of the old tales handed down to us of our ancestors from long ago."

"In a few ways, we are, and don't worry about me. I'll stay close to those people in the temple."

She reaches up to hug her mother, and then steps back as they begin forward.

The wagon train slowly pulls ahead along the lanes of the Upper Ward until it approaches the junction opening up into the plaza. They slowed to give themselves time to peek at the local structures, focusing on the Governor's Manor at the far end. The windows seemed to be clear and there was no light shining through.

One by one, they begin parading out, giving a generous delay between them to allow one to pass through the area before the next pulled out. In time, they reassembled on the avenues leading into the lower district until they approached the south gate. The guards at the gate had been informed of their departure, as part of a plan to remove them from the most immediate harmful intent by the Governor, so the gate was held open for them.

The convoy emerged outside the city, where the broad fields represented an exposed and vulnerable sensation for them, since none of them had ever travelled outside before. There were no more walls, just open space in all directions.

They travelled to the south, trying to follow the old vestiges of the roadway that once led between the cities. In time, they came upon the southern watch tower, and in the distance, they could just make out the mountain range in the dim moonlight.

"Somewhere along there," Josef strains to peer ahead. "There must be a road leading up. The trouble is finding it, and then following it successfully."

"I wonder where those scouts are that Tristeen mentioned," Margo remarks.

"They must be further ahead. Let's keep going."

They continued along the old road until they were able to make out a cut in the ridgeline representing the pass. Then they saw movement. A man jumped into view, shining a strange light from his palm, and waving at them.

"There!" Josef points. "But what in all the hells is he holding up? Is that a lantern?"

"It doesn't look like one to me," Margo offers. "Too small, and it seems to be directly inside his grip."

Additional men formed up along the rising pathway leading partway up the hillside, forming a chain of lights. They directed the caravan to pull around and line up with the incline, which would lead to the difficult climb.

As Josef and his wife passed by the first of these, they could see better the man holding a pure orb of light in his hand…not a lantern or anything else recognizable. It was simply a glowing orb, and quite bright, illuminating the roadway under him, and allowing them to find their way past.

"That's got to be magical," Josef muses softly. "There's no other word for it."

"But are we saying these are mages?" Margo wonders. "I thought Tristeen said to expect scouts."

"Who knows…they're probably a little of both."

Several of the scouts, and other troops that had assembled to assist the wagons, began to lead the caravans up the hill, taking the reins of the horses to help guide them on the narrow slope. The night passed slowly as they continued uphill, taking well longer than it would even on foot, and finally cresting over the top.

Josef and his wife peered out from the small mesa into the valley below. It seemed to stretch out as far as the eye could see and was covered with wooded glens and open meadows.

"Is that what they call the Badlands?" Margo mutters.

"Indeed, it certainly appears much different from how I learned of it as a boy."

They proceeded down the other side, once again taking it slow and easy to find their footing. The troops continued to lead the way, drawing the horses along steadily until they at last reached the bottom. There, they waited for the full assembly to reunite.

Josef stepped down to check the other wagons, as well as his friends.

"Fine work, everyone," he ushers as he surveys the procession.

He turns to find one of the scouts and offers his hand.

"Thank you, my friend," he nods with a smile.

The scout smiles back, and then directs him towards the south, speaking in a foreign tongue relative to Josef and his people. Josef realized by this time, as he could hear them speaking along the way, that they used a different language. He simply turned to examine the journey ahead and nodded again, then climbed back up onto his wagon.

"Now to find His Lordship's people," he notes. "Tristeen said to simply head south, we can't miss it," he chuckles.

They moved forward again, now as a grouping of wagons, rather than a single-file line. They continued past clusters of trees, and through open terrain, passing by a number of small farms in the northernmost region, and soon to catch a glimpse of something coming into view ahead of them. The moonlight just barely lit the scene enough for them to find their way, but a substantial glow was beginning to dominate the area.

"That must be them," Josef affirms. "No wonder she said we can't miss it, and I'm sure the Suuden-Aryku couldn't either, if they had such a desire."

Coming into view was a surprisingly large village setting surrounded by a wall that gave off most of the local light. But much to Josef's surprise, the wall didn't seem like a solid fortification. Instead, it was a series of pylons emitting a barely visible barrier between them.

"Great gods, Margo," he mutters. "These people look nearly as mystical as those Daanen-Aryku are said to be."

The northern gate of the settlement came to life as the guards saw the approaching caravan. They waved at them to come through the gate, and directed the wagons to circle around in the village center. As Josef and his wife came to a halt and began climbing down off the wagon, two men appeared out of the tactical office to greet them.

The elder nobleman tried in vain to straighten his attire for a better presentation, but the rush to pack earlier in the day, along with his general state of distress, still left its mark. He stepped forward, soon joined by his two friends, to meet with their hosts.

"Good greetings, friends," announces the first of the two officers. "And welcome to what we might describe as a hamlet thus far, called Firstfall. My name is Master Cydulean, and this here is Priest Sumisal."

"A hamlet?" Josef ponders. "Gracious, and here I thought you were maintaining a simple military camp," he chuckles. "My name is Josef Macaid. And this is my wife, Margo, and then we have some of our close friends, Abraim and Jenna Whitcord, and Seth and Helene Farlind. We represent the surviving noble houses of Rolsklinde, such as we are."

"Very good. I believe it was your daughter who informed us of this preemptive effort to preserve you, in case that individual who would presume himself to be your Governor should get any nasty ideas up there. Our Lord is currently in bed at this time, but he hopes to attend a formal meeting on the morrow at your leisure. In the meantime, I suspect you are quite weary. Did you suffer any incidents along the way?"

"No incidents, but travelling over that mountain was rather strenuous, to say the least. I thank the gods for your men offering their help."

"Most excellent. I am aware we are making plans with some of our people back home to see if we can improve some of your local roadways between our various destinations. This will likely take some time, but in the future, we hope this will improve matters."

"Good gods, you people…" he smiles and shakes his head. "You come in, fight our wars, solve our mysteries, dismantle our criminal government, and give our people a chance at freedom again, and you also rebuild our roads, and according to Tristeen, you're offering to help with the city in general. Just how can you afford all this?"

"We are a prosperous people with many resources to spare, and our Lord teaches us the generosity and compassion of his Father and the other Estelar."

"Eh…" Josef hesitates. "One moment… Did I interpret that correctly? You said his Father, and the other Estelar? Is this supposed to mean…"

"Indeed," he smiles. "His Father was one of them. Lord Thaelyn belongs to a unique selection of races we call the hybridized Celestials. This, in contrast to the more natural ones."

"What's the difference…as if I think I can take it at this time?"

"The natural ones are societies that have developed over such a long period of time that they are nearly on their own doorstep to godhood. The hybridized varieties are special cases, born half of the mortal races and half of the Estelar themselves. They are usually created to serve as an intermediate form between them and us. This gives them a number of very curious qualities, not the least of which is one that can unite worlds and bring about such moments as what we have seen during our history back home."

Josef felt stunned by this suggestion, and he gazed blankly at his wife and friends.

"No wonder the Dean was collapsing into a puddle of his own despair on our doorstep."

"Yes, I think to meet with one in such manner as that would surely leave a mark. But now, I'm sure you must be very weary, so we have instructions to lead you to Tae'Eladar, to our capital city of Bya'an Tamoranth, where we have arranged accommodations at some of our local inns," he scans the full assembly of people for their general count. "We have a fair number of people here, so we may need to divide you into groupings."

"And what about our wagons?"

"We will have some of our people move them off to the side and place them under watch until later. You may return as you need to retrieve your personal effects, but in the longer term, we will need to find a more appropriate solution, especially if that Marshal Darumon should get any funny ideas about your homes."

"Yes, and then we have him. That sounds like a military title, am I right?"

"It is, although it also came out recently that his kind doesn't seem to use titles, so we are debating if we even want to bestow upon him the honor of it."

Cydulean begins directing the wayfarers, assigning some escorts to give aid, and sending them through the gateway into the city, where they branch off to their different destinations to find a room and some sleep.

+ ✦ ✦ ✦ + +

The next morning, several squads of mages were assembling in the settlement. Another row was lining up with runes leading to the garrisons on the Suuden-Aryku side of the eastern mountains. The sun was rising, and they were preparing to make a quick strike in fast sequence.

Thaelyn and the General observed the assembly and counted down the timing, then gave the word to begin. The way-line mages opened up the portal apertures and the squads jumped through.

They arrived in a gully behind the Suuden-Aryku lines nestled within some local shrubs to conceal their presence. The garrison camps were just coming to life with only a few guards standing around appearing to be on watch. The full complement of troops in each camp counted less than a hundred, and they had no idea they were being watched.

The mages crept forward to within range of their magic attacks. One held back with a return rune ready to go. The command sounded out, although quietly, and the mages popped into view, immediately casting a ball of sickly green condensed gas. A line of them sent these out to spread across each camp, filling the local area with a choking stink cloud that would invoke coughing and gagging, but no physical harm. At most, it might cause a person to go unconscious for a period, although this particular formulation was a lighter version designed to debilitate rather than fully incapacitate.

The balls fly out and strike in a diffuse pattern around the camp, instantly blinding the occupants of anything beyond their immediate surroundings, and obscuring the area with a green smoky cloud. The mage with the return rune opens a portal, and the team dashes back across, departing the area as quickly as they had arrived.

The full line of garrisons now showed the same green clouds permeating the area. The Suuden'kai soldiers choked and coughed as they stumbled around groping for their weapons, and searching for their equipment to make any kind of response. One of them fumbled for the communications station to report in.

"Base Prime," he coughs. "This is Garrison Post G03, we have come under attack."

He coughs several more times, but seems to be holding his own against it.

"Post G03," ushers the reply. "What is your status? Are you taking losses?"

"Indeterminate. I cannot see far enough through the smoke to locate any casualties."

"What do you mean? Are they using a smoke screen?"

"They hit us with some kind of malodorous smoke cloud. Stand by."

He gets up and shouts into the cloud.

"I need a report out there! Does anyone see anything?"

"Negative!" shouts a reply. "I cannot see anything for the cloud."

"Try moving outside the cloud. I need a sighting."

"Sir!" echoes another voice. "I have found the outer edge of the cloud. I am on the south side, but I see no invaders here."

"Circle around, but be on your guard."

"Sir!" issues another one. "I am on the north edge, and no sightings. The area is clear. I can see Post G02, and they also got hit."

"Do you see any invaders on their front?"

"Negative, no sign of anything other than our own people trying to escape the cloud."

"This does not make sense," he returns to his com-link. "Base Prime, we are unable to locate any hostiles in the local area, and we can see Post G02 in the same condition."

"Acknowledged, G03, what is the condition of your complement? Are you injured? Do you need medical assistance?"

"Negative, the An'gamu seeds seem to be filtering the effect."

"Understood, stay on alert and keep us advised."

On the ridgeline, the scouts used scopes to survey the activity of the Suuden'kai garrisons. They could see people moving in and out of the clouds, which would normally be enough to cause a fair amount of suffering for most people, but the Suuden-Aryku seemed only lightly affected.

"That's a fine one!" mutters one scout.

"Aye, they're walking about with barely a slouch. We need to call this one in. Non-lethal or otherwise, this is a curious result."

✦✦◆✦✦

A tonal ring ushers out of the Governor's desk. He picks it up to answer the call.

"Yes, Commander, what is it?"

"We have taken an attack."

"Ah, have they pushed themselves across our lines to test us?"

"Uncertain. This did not involve the troops on their front line. This appeared as a stealth attack and did not cause any casualties."

"Excuse me, Commander," he urges. "How can someone launch a stealth attack that does not involve any casualties? What sort of attack was it?"

"I do not know how to describe this as anything other than a test. We believe they arrived behind our lines and launched a series of smoke cloud attacks on our positions. They hit all our garrison outposts simultaneously. The smoke appeared harmless, and the An'gamu seeds filtered the effect."

"Ha!" he shouts. "Count one victory for us, Commander. They were probably hoping to incapacitate our troops, but that lovely little gift of our technology has proven its value. I'll bet when they saw your people still walking around, they had to pull back to reconsider."

"What are your instructions? Do we launch a reprisal, or hold our stations?"

"I am still of the mind that their larger friends will involve themselves if we launch, and if this was indeed a test, or simply a failed exercise, and their forward line has not moved, we should not press ourselves yet. What is the status of my last requisition?"

"Morndindor base reports it has collected samples of existing armor from the local population sufficient to fill our order. It is currently in transit. The plasma mortars are in our loading docks, and the engineers are running their final diagnostics on the atomic device."

"That atomic, where did we pull it out from, one of our planetary assault launchers?"

"Affirmative, and then reconfigured to link with a remote detonator."

"Good, we'll set the timer once the other components are in place and our last details are in motion. Then I will be leaving my post here to rejoin you. What about that reactor downstairs?"

"The safety protocols are disabled, but you will need to set the control rods manually for the overload effect to occur."

"Fine, that shouldn't be a problem. And one final thing, Commander. I would have you call in one of our heavy cruisers and park it in orbit overhead. We will keep this on hand as a little insurance. And let me know when those last pieces are in place."

"Understood, Base Prime out..."

A gentle knocking comes at the Dean's door. The door was standing open at this point, as he no longer cared to close it for privacy. He was sitting on the floor examining a number of papers from his former workload. Even though it seemed pointless, as his cherished academy was shut down by now. He had no students and all the instructors had been sent home. Now he was alone in the building.

"Dean?" ushers a voice from the guest as he peeks inside.

The Dean looked up to meet his visitor. He stares at the man, trying to identify the face.

"Acolyte Sarens?"

The Dean straightens his posture as he studies the unexpected caller.

Willit smiled and entered the room, observing the mess left behind from Thaelyn's visit, including the gaping hole in the wall.

"I heard about that," he points at the wall. "Good gods, if a man can hold that much power inside his noggin, I wouldn't want to be on the wrong side of it."

"Indeed, and fortunately you weren't. I was..." he chuckles lightly. "I'm surprised to see you here. You were the one captured in his camp. My apologies for that..."

"It's alright, Dean. In a way, it was probably the best thing that could've happened to me. It set a few things in motion for us to take charge of the situation, at least within reason. I'm actually sorry it hit you so hard. I never would've expected you to fall apart on us like you did."

The Dean sighed deeply as he glanced at his papers again.

"Perhaps this is what I needed. I only wish it could've happened sooner so I would not have made as many mistakes. But then, when you consider who was governing those mistakes, I must ask myself if it would actually matter."

"Probably not, as he could always find someone else."

"Yes, he probably could at that. Those priests, for instance. He certainly had them wrapped around his finger. I wonder, where do you go to find people like that? But now, why are you here? Do you have some special word for me? And what have you been up to since that day, or would you actually wish to tell me?" he smiles delicately.

"I'm one of his spies now," he chuckles mischievously. "However, he's working to help our people, and now he wants to help you. But you're in a bad place, so we need to be careful."

"No. Tell him not to spend his time on me," he sighs.

"Dean, my word is your actions may have bought you a special ticket to redemption, and as I understand it, the Estelar specialize in this. Now listen up. We understand you have access to the Governor's basement, is this correct?"

"Yes, I have a key for it. Here…" he reaches inside a pocket under his vest. "Do you want it?"

"No, you keep it. You can help us. Consider yourself on our pay wagon now. But the bigger issue is another door inside the basement. Have you seen it?"

"Yes!" he nods eagerly. "I've often wondered what was inside. I recall once asking about it, but the Governor simply said it's an old vault with some historical treasures left behind from a time before the war."

"Oh really!" he laughs. "That's a fine one, and so typical of him, too."

"Yes, I suppose so. It surely doesn't look like any door I've ever seen before. And it sits near some odd looking…thing…which I never could understand. I've mostly come to the opinion it was once a base for a statue, as it seems to hold a cavity for something."

"Not a bad guess, but way off the mark."

"Eh, and just how would you know?" he grins warily. "Have you somehow managed to get down there?"

"Not me…Leesa. She's our spy in that office."

"Oh dear…right, I recall now she followed me a couple of times to help with a few things. Blast, she's good, but she's so young! How old is she?"

"She's Marelle's cousin, and only seventeen. But she's got talent, and Marelle gave her some special coaching, along with Lady Aerlie, Thaelyn's wife."

"Indeed. So, what is that thing in the corner down there?"

"A piece of Suuden-Aryku technology called a conveyor. It's a bit like a portal device for them."

"Really! So, that must be how he receives his deliveries down there. They bring it in through that device, and probably leave it on the floor, then depart. Very clever. And that door, do we know anything about that?"

"We have a good idea for it, but it's bad for the city. The conveyor requires a lot of power to work, and for this, we think he has something behind that door called a reactor. It's probably managed remotely by the Suuden-Aryku at their main headquarters. But if they should decide to dispose of the city, that'd be a good way to do it. They can set it to explode, and we're talking about a boom big enough to remove at least half the city, maybe all of it."

"Gracious!" he comes to attention at the prospect. "Then we need to find a way to disable it or something. And this is why you're asking about the key…yes! Then, how are we planning this?"

"One thing we still need is a way through the other door. There's a small panel next to it with a series of buttons on it. Do you know anything about how to use it?"

"No. I've seen it, so I know what you're talking about, but that one is a mystery to me."

"All right, we need to find a way inside, and this means either to discover the key to unlock the door, or simply blast a hole in it. Either way, keep yourself handy. And stay close to the temple. Our people will watch over you."

Willit smiles and waves politely, and then turns and makes his exit. The Dean felt a mote of comfort that he had friends somewhere watching over him, although he was still uncertain as to the final outcome.

✦✦✦✦✦

"This is indeed curious," Thaelyn admits. "And it leads me to wonder something."

"What is that, my Lord?" the General asks.

"Lieutenant," he directs to the Daanen'kai officer. "When speaking of this stink cloud attack, and the Suuden-Aryku apparently resisting the effects, if you will forgive my wording a moment, does your species hold any innate resistance to such noxious fumes or other debilitating gases?"

Thaelyn and his officers, including Padriyl and the others, were in session for the early afternoon meeting. The most immediate topic was the morning hit on the Suuden-Aryku garrison outposts.

"While I can't say for certain how we might react to the exact contents of this cloud," he considers. "If I'm interpreting this correctly, any common lifeform like ours, that is to say an oxygen-breathing lifeform, would likely feel the same effects as you would. For instance, we would feel the same suffocating effect from common smoke, carbon dioxide, carbon monoxide, hydrocarbons, and similar gases."

"Very well, so how would we describe this result? I recall your Med-tech mentioning something about those biotech seeds as an old science project with the premise of augmenting your bodies to support nonstandard capabilities. Could this be one of those?"

"That's a very different line of study from mine, but I could certainly pass it along and see what she has to say about it."

"Good. In the meantime, our scouts are reporting no outward activity from the Suuden-Aryku, which means they must be in a standby condition more than anything else. This suggests Darumon is preparing something to be delivered behind our backs, and this most likely involves the city. General, do we have anything new on those dwarves?"

"Nothing as yet," he advises. "Not even a visitation by the Suuden-Aryku to check on them or to collect the metal again. Although I must admit, I am unsure of their schedule for this. The last time coincided with a large stockpile of the metal lying in wait."

"Enough to fill one of their heavy transports," Padriyl suggests. "This could be when they come for it, to make the trip more efficient."

"Perhaps, and with that, ahem, orcish raid they suffered recently," he grins. "They may not be as eager to risk losing another of those."

"It's bad enough they're having so much trouble with the first one," Marelle adds. "Those nasty orcs and all their raids, it's enough to make you pull your horns out," she giggles.

"You know, Marelle," Padriyl smiles. "I think you're taking too much enjoyment out of our language now."

"Very well," Thaelyn considers. "When we do see something, we must be ready to move quickly to resolve it in our favor. The only true wildcard is that basement and whether we can gain control of it efficiently enough. If we lose that, we could lose a great many lives all at once."

A knocking comes at the door of the tactical office from Captain Hagmaert. The assembly turns their attention as he enters the room with Josef, Abraim, and Seth, all of whom were hoping to make their meeting after spending much of the day trying to settle their personal effects, and a place to stay temporarily on Tae'Eladar.

"Ah, are you the representatives we received last eve?" Thaelyn announces.

The three men made a humble approach and bowed reverently, then Abraim took notice of Thaelyn's eyes.

"Gracious, are those gold?" he whispers softly.

Thaelyn simply smiled, as this was a common reaction by newcomers.

"Eh..." Josef steps forward for his introduction. "Your most gracious Lordship, I am Josef Macaid, and this is Abraim Whitcord and Seth Farlind. We wish to submit ourselves to you and your hospitality during this troubling time, and at the same moment, we would also wish to offer whatever meager services we can provide to give aid to what we are expecting to be a great many more to follow, if my daughter is correct for the future of our once great city."

"Indeed, and for as much as I would offer my welcome and appreciation of your offer, it is also to my own sorrow regarding your city, but I must follow a tender path here where that creature is concerned. Cities can be rebuilt, and I will surely give aid to you and yours. As for Darumon, I wish to turn this more to my own favor, and at present he still holds too much on his side, other than for my threats of the Estelar. We have innocents in our way, and he has some rather potent firepower, as well as the unpredictability to use it. I would instead wish to turn him away from this world entirely, and then pursue him on my own terms."

"And so, our city may need to be sacrificed, if only to give him his leave. Tristeen mentioned to me about his authority over the Suuden-Aryku. That certainly throws an unpleasant twist into this debacle."

"It does, but if I can pursue him, perhaps to approach in such a manner that does not involve his military again, at least not directly, I may find myself able to preserve many more lives along the way."

"It would seem that's becoming your greatest labor in this war, preserving the lives of people you never knew existed."

"The great Seas of Creation are filled with such. I may never know most of them, and they may come and go without even a proper memorial. But for those we can touch, we will do what we can to see them through."

"You clearly hold a much greater perspective than any of us. I would be happy simply to serve that role which I feel I may be best suited for. As representatives of the noble families of Rolsklinde, we would wish to offer ourselves to give aid in organizing the others, once they are evacuated, and to help coordinate with you as we move along to restore our homes."

"This is a fine course of action. Then we should discuss these issues as we move forward, and see what we have to work with."

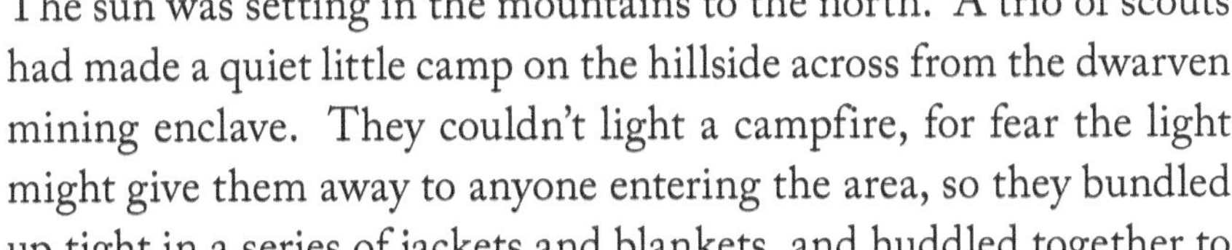

The sun was setting in the mountains to the north. A trio of scouts had made a quiet little camp on the hillside across from the dwarven mining enclave. They couldn't light a campfire, for fear the light might give them away to anyone entering the area, so they bundled up tight in a series of jackets and blankets, and huddled together to conserve their body heat.

In the skies overhead, they saw a set of lights approaching from above. They included several red and white lights, some steady while others were flashing, and a set of large softly glowing oblong pods on the sides, representing the engine nacelles.

"Hey now, lads," whispers one scout. "Look what we've got here!"

"Right, here they come at last," responds the second one. "Now for the fun part. What are they doing, and how does it relate to anything else?"

They watched the large transport settle down neatly into the box-like cove in front of the enclave entrance. Then a ramp drops down in the rear, and a large number of armed troops emerge. They quickly take up positions around the area.

"Oi, look at that now," the third scout ushers. "Looks like they're not taking any chances on this run."

"Aye," the first one responds. "Fully armed for war, they are. No bloody orc would dare try a go with that spread."

"To say nothing of anyone else," the second scout accedes. "But this only means they're doing something grand in there."

They continued to watch as the Suuden-Aryku troopers began unloading a series of containers into the enclave. One by one, they made a long convoy of couriers, some with large boxes, and others with elongated crates carried by two men each.

"Whatever it is, this is serious," the first scout relates. "I don't see them carrying anything out, only a lot of goods going in."

"We need to get inside there and see where they're going with it," the second one admits.

"Right," the third one relents. "Where they're going and what they're doing with it. Are they simply delivering something? Are they putting something together inside there? Are we talking about redecorating with festive wall hangings? What can you do with dwarves that barely know up from down?"

"Not a lot, if you ask me, but who knows with these blokes."

They watched the caravan as it continued for many long minutes. Finally, after a long series of smaller boxes and crates had been unloaded, a team began wheeling out a large cargo platform carrying a similarly large spherical object enclosed in a box-like framework. The framework was centered on a pallet which seemed to hover above the wheeled base, to afford a cushion to the bumpy ride the base might otherwise suffer.

"That one doesn't look at all happy," the first scout observes.

"Right to that," the second one affirms. "All right, one of us needs to go in. Make it quick and report back smartly. Just a peek at first so we can get an idea, then we'll decide from there."

Chapter 15

INDIGNANT REPRISAL

"My Lord!" the General announces. "We have something." It was early morning in the tactical office in Firstfall, earlier than usual, and the General and Thaelyn had both been called in for an urgent meeting with one of the scouts from the dwarven mines.

"Good," he responds tentatively. "Or at least, it is good that we have something, not that it might be good in itself."

Thaelyn arrives at the table to see the scout with his trans-com showing a series of photos.

"My Lord," the scout begins. "My apologies for raising you out of bed so early, but we felt this was important. The Suuden-Aryku have spent the greater part of the night inside the enclave unloading and setting up the dwarves with a bundle of new toys. I have here a series of pictures we took while under our cloaks. It's a bloody good thing these trans-coms can work while cloaked. Not being mechanical in any way surely makes a fine addition to our toolset."

"Indeed, I am pleased. But now, what do we have?"

"The Suuden-Aryku must've raided someone's old closet. They delivered chest, arm, and leg pieces of adamantium armor to each of the dwarves. They seem to be setting them up nice and neat for some kind of action. And then we have this…" he pulls up one of his photos. "I don't know what you might call these bloody bastards, but I wouldn't want to be on the wrong side of it. They look a wee bit like those rifles the Suuden-Aryku were using, but these are bigger. And the Suuden-Aryku were apparently trying to teach the dwarves how to use them."

"And this is while those dwarves are still under that drug influence?"

"Aye, they still looked like zombies, but now dressed in adamantium and hoisting up shoulder-mounted cannons."

"This is not at all pleasant to hear. If those dwarves behave the same as they did in the mines, we will not be able to stop them unless we physically tackle them. But with weapons of this sort, simply making the approach could be suicidal."

"We should call Lieutenant Lapäli to the attention of these weapons," the General suggests. "He might hold a better understanding of what they are. But my concern is by the time he normally arrives, we might already see them in action."

"We will deliver this to him before he goes to his classroom study. This should not take long to identify. But then, we need to know when they will launch against us, and in this case, I am quite sure they will go to the city. This actually fits with our earlier suggestion of an attack from the north, opposite the side we might normally be watching. Even if Darumon might think we know about the dwarves being under his influence, he might also consider they are a non-military target, and the least likely to make an attack."

"That's simply sinister," the General admits. "And them in such a condition as this."

"This also places them inside the city, potentially with that reactor going off."

"Killing two birds with one stone, just like you said. Perfect mentality…"

"My Lord," the scout interjects. "Just in case this wasn't disturbing enough, we have one more problem. Take a gander at this…" he pulls up another photo.

Both Thaelyn and the General look down at the image of the large spherical object nesting inside the dwarven feasting hall, and another photo of a box on one of the tables.

"This box here looks like some sort of control mechanism," the scout offers. "They unloaded both of them together, and set them down in their main hall. This other bugger, I don't have a bloody clue what it is, but it doesn't look like a feasting cart."

"Not at all," Thaelyn mutters. "This looks like it might be a weapon, and likely a bomb, with a remote detonator. See here…" he points at the photo of the controller. "We have a switch which seems like for power, and a small display monitor, and this red cap with a button underneath. This configuration is generally used for something sensitive."

"Aye, it sure looks like it. So, if this is a bomb, it would have to be a grand one for the size of it."

Thaelyn returns to the photo of the bomb. He studies it carefully.

"This is a perfect sphere, enclosed in a framework to give it stability on the ground. And this general image is very disturbing for the implications. If we were simply speaking of a conventional weapon, this would be a rather potent one for the size alone. But if we are speaking of an atomic… Scout, you should show these to Lieutenant Lapäli at once and get his opinion. You might also wish to confer with the Daanen'kai Chief Technician. She would probably be at home at this time in the Naarg uy'Sodrad. See if you can find her and get her opinion as will."

"Aye!" he nods and dashes off.

"My Lord," the General offers. "How would we try to disarm this weapon? If it uses a remote detonator device, could it be as simple as turning it off?"

"Assuming there are no fail-safes to prevent that, maybe. But at this point, if the control unit does indeed link to the bomb, my first suggestion is to use a portal rune on the box to send it away out of reach. If it cannot link with the weapon, the weapon, hopefully, will not detonate. But I would still recommend we evacuate the area, once the controller is removed, just in case the bomb itself holds an activation device. We can return later to see if the area is still safe."

"Good enough, and may the gods guide us on this one."

"Indeed, this is one of those technologies I would personally disagree with, and exactly the sort I might expect out of Darumon. That detonator has a display on it, so we might be speaking of one with a timer, enough for someone to activate it, and then run. Therefore, we need to know precisely when they will do this, and then pray we can intercept it before the timer runs out."

✦✦✦✦✦✦

"Marshal, your requisition is ready."

"Excellent, Commander, now listen carefully. First, send word to have them begin marching out. We will have them make our disturbance for us, and once they arrive, I will have you call a full retreat. You should begin with the nonessential troop staging points and supply depots now, leaving the garrisons for last."

"Acknowledged."

"As for the atomic, we want to be sure our distraction is out of range before it goes off. With it buried under that mountain, the blast effect should be contained somewhat, but I want our distraction to arrive in the city to draw their attention, rather than any mushroom clouds over the mountains. Now, if given their average walking speed, and the fact that they need to wander along the roads a bit, we should look to midday. Set the timer appropriately and be sure you close and lock those doors when you leave."

"Affirmative."

"Have that ship overhead monitor their progress carefully. Tell them to scan the area and measure their timing. I want a precise assessment of their arrival time for the next step."

"Understood, but for what purpose?"

"I am going to have them launch a preemptive strike to open a hole for the ground team to enter unabated. There is one segment in the northern quarter that has been particularly disruptive to our efforts. I want to ensure they are removed from the equation above all else. The rest will follow as our distraction progresses forward.

I will remain here until then to observe the results, and then set the reactor. I'll join you once that's done."

"Acknowledged."

The Governor ended the link and returned his trans-com to his desk drawer. He then turned to gaze out the window at the plaza below. It was sunrise, and the people were just starting to come out to conduct their daily business.

"That's right, you little peons," he mutters to himself. "Go about your trivial deeds as you must, and before this day is out, you will have yourselves a first-hand opportunity to meet with your new gods. Such a delight that should be," he chuckles wickedly.

In Firstfall, Leesa and Willit were both in a meeting in the tactical office.

"Mister Sarens," Thaelyn begins. "We will have you direct your friend Jared to station himself outside the north gate. He has a trans-com on him, correct?"

"Yes, I gave one to him, and another to Tristeen."

"Good. Contact both of them with these latest details. Jared's first duty will be to keep watch for anything approaching from the north, then to instruct the guards to report to Captain Kholgard and begin an evacuation of the city. Be aware of the Governor, in the event he is still in his office at this time. We cannot be precisely sure when he will leave."

"This is where I come in, I suppose," Leesa interjects anxiously. "I need to play my best role on this one. So far, I don't think he suspects anything about me, even though I don't usually interact with him directly very often."

"Yes, but on this occasion, you need to see if you can follow him into the basement, assuming he goes down there to interact with that door, and then the reactor."

"Am I expected to undo whatever he does with that, or just concentrate on how he opens the door?"

"The door is the most important. I somehow suspect he will not want any observers inside the room, but if you can distract him with some light conversation while he operates the door, this might be just enough to afford you an opportunity. Just remember your training where your thoughts are concerned."

"Right, daisies and rainbows dancing in my head, like a good little empty-headed nitwit."

"I don't know how you're able to get any work done like that," Willit winces. "To say nothing of spying on someone who could probably read your thoughts."

"Well, Lady Aerlie gave me a few lessons, and a bit of testing to see if I got it right. I think my age, as much as I hate to say it, can actually be a boon if I play into it as the naïve little girl from a sheltered upbringing."

"Just be careful on this one."

"The difficult part here," Thaelyn resumes. "Is trying to determine when the Governor is actually departing. I have a number of thoughts on this, ranging from simply exiting through a door to using that conveyor of his one last time. Therefore, I am at something of a loss on how to suggest you discover this, except to play it by ear."

"All right," Leesa affirms. "I'll do my best, and then call you with the details. And if I can't get in there myself, I'll need to get the Dean with his key, and you need to send someone up there to work those controls. My concern is that we were thinking of using Lieutenant Lapäli for this. What if he's not available?"

"From what we are currently observing up north, our scouts just recently called in with a report that the Suuden-Aryku are sending the dwarves on their way. The time and distance involved suggests they might be arriving at around midday, and if the Governor is waiting for their arrival, I think the Lieutenant will be back by then. But if he takes a different schedule on us, we will make the appropriate adjustments."

"Good, then hopefully we can take care of that before anything really bad happens."

"Indeed. In the meantime, the Suuden-Aryku were also making their final adjustments on that control unit inside their enclave. I am going to make an assumption here that the timing delay will need to afford the dwarves enough distance before it goes off, especially if their primary purpose is to assault the city. If it detonates too early, it will likely take them along with the mountain."

"Ouch! How can people build such nasty bombs?"

"It is an unfortunate side effect of the development of certain sciences that allows one to discover ways of using materials for weapons of mass destruction."

"Do your people have anything like this?"

"So far, no, and although we might one day study this, I would not otherwise permit the production of such things for such casual application."

"Good."

"Anyway, with the Suuden-Aryku making these final preparations, I gave instructions for one of our scouts to station himself under a cloak inside the enclave with a rune returning directly to Tae'Eladar. We will use this on the box, and have him depart immediately thereafter. We will return to investigate the area later to see if all is well."

The meeting adjourned, with Leesa and Willit taking a rune transit up to the temple in the city. Leesa would take up her station in the secretary's office in the Governor's Manor, while Willit would travel to the Ten Eagles to make his contacts.

⟡

Tristeen was waking up and trying to refresh herself inside the temple. She was camping out in one of the priest's quarters, rather than her own bed at home. Although she longed to feel the comfort of her home, she felt safer being with the priests at this time. She noticed the passage of Leesa and Willit as they arrived and proceeded to their own objectives, and delivering their message along the way.

"So, he's doing it…" she mutters quietly. "That bastard is actually doing it. And worse, by using those innocent dwarves, sending them to their deaths along with the rest of us."

Master Dastien and the local priests were all on high alert today, after receiving their orders.

"We need to start spreading the word," he mentions. "At least to those here in the upper district. Maybe we could have them begin a movement to the lower district as a means of distancing them from the area."

"Agreed," Priest Garrain affirms. "We'll tell the people who come in this morning to slowly vacate the area. Nothing dramatic, however, as it might give that man ideas of what we're doing."

"We also need to prepare a series of shield mages to act as a wall to guard the rest when they start to run."

"Shield mages?" Tristeen asks.

"These are mages who are trained to use a special shield, like the one used during our Lord's visit to fight that demon. We can form up a wall as a barrier to these weapons, hopefully to hold back the dwarves long enough for the people to escape, and then pull back through the city as we evacuate the rest."

"Hopefully," she smirks feebly. "Well, good luck with it."

Jared had moved forward to the north gate, and was speaking to the guards stationed outside.

"Dwarves, is it?" ushers one guard. "Supposed to be marching down here with Suuden-Aryku weapons on their shoulders? Egads! Aye then... Corporal Gannit," he directs to one of his men. "Go tell the Captain. Let him know to be expecting company soon."

"Aye!" the younger man salutes and returns inside.

Leesa was sitting down at her desk in the Governor's Manor. She was clearly tense this morning, and the secretary took notice of her fidgeting with her trans-com and repeatedly checking the door.

"Leesa, what's wrong?" he asks.

"Expect trouble today."

Of the two remaining scouts stationed near the dwarven enclave, one had repositioned himself inside and under a cloak to observe the Suuden-Aryku making their final adjustments to the timer on the control box. When they appeared to have finished, they picked up the last of their equipment and proceeded out of the room.

He followed them to see where they were going. For instance, were they simply making another run to their transport, or were they actually leaving. When he saw them halting at the front entrance, he stopped some distance back to study them. They appeared to be closing and locking the door.

The scout on the outside also took notice of the Suuden'kai team exiting the tunnel and closing the door. He then watched as they loaded up into their transport one last time and the vessel began to lift off. He paused a few moments until it was out of sight before he emerged from his hiding spot and pulled out his trans-com, dialing up a number.

"This is Thaelyn," ushers the voice on the unit.

"My Lord, the Suuden-Aryku just left the area in their transport and closed the door behind them. Scout Lynsen is inside. I bloody well hope he can solve our problem for us and get out before anything bad happens."

"Indeed. I imagine he will be attending to that shortly. Meanwhile, how far along are those dwarves from your position?"

"Out of sight around the bend to the south."

"I see. Very well, I will have you return to us here. I think your work is done for now."

"Aye!"

The scout inside the tunnels was now returning to the feasting hall. He knew his instructions, and that was to use a rune on the control box to remove it from the local area in the hopes of breaking the link with the bomb.

He arrived in the large chamber and carefully approached the unit located on one of the tables. The bomb sat in the middle of the room, seemingly inert, but ominous simply for its appearance. He pulled out a rune from a slot in his belt. This one led directly to Tae'Eladar, arriving in an open space near the new research center, where it could be collected for study.

He gazed briefly at the item in his hand, and then glanced at the bomb again. Then he pulled out his return rune to keep it readily available, just in case. He enchanted the removal rune first, and the traditional ring formed around it in his hand. He then reached out gently, holding it over the control box and cautiously touching it to the side. The box was enveloped in a quick glow, and then swallowed up in the vortex to send it away.

He anxiously glanced at the bomb again. It didn't seem affected in any way, so he pocketed the first rune and picked up the second. He hastily enchanted it and clamped his free hand down on it, sending himself back to camp. On his arrival, he breathed a quick sigh of relief as he promptly reported to the office.

"My Lord, it's done…that is, as best it can be for what we have to work with. The box is away, and the bomb is just sitting there, nice and quiet."

"Good. We will keep the area under quarantine for now, and return at a later moment to investigate the situation. If the mountain still exists at all, we can say we were successful at resolving that dilemma."

"Blast, when you put it that way…" he chuckles. "Right, then, what else do we have?"

"Our next greatest concern is the city, and whether Darumon has anything else planned for us. We will need constant updates on his front line out there, including the forward staging posts against the Daanen-Aryku, and anything new that may arrive."

A short while later, the third scout of the group returns from the Naarg uy'Sodrad with his trans-com images on the new dwarven equipment.

"My Lord!" he pants. "I have a few words from Chief Technician Lapäli."

"Ah, and what does she say about those devices?"

"Firstly, she agrees the big one looks like a bomb, and likely atomic, but she suggests it's not a standalone item. Instead, it looks like it was pulled out of something and repurposed."

"Pulled out of something… Did she specify?"

"Best guess is likely a delivery system, like a missile package."

"This would make sense. So, they have atomic-capped missiles over there. One more thing to take into consideration…" he sighs.

"The other item is that weapon. She says she doesn't recognize it straight off, so it must be part of their new development after Darumon took over. She tried comparing it to what she can recall of their antique technologies, and her best guess is it looks like a siege weapon, for the size of it. Therefore, if based on the same technology, she's giving it the name plasma mortar."

"That, in itself, sounds bad enough."

"I must agree," the General admits. "A mortar weapon is dangerous enough, if only to use black powder and a projectile. But if this is derived from their plasma technology…gracious, we will need to be wary of that one."

"Indeed, and if we are speaking of a siege weapon, this makes sense if they are turning it on the city. We may need to place ourselves between them and the citizenry, if only to provide an escape."

✦✦✦✦✦

It was near to midday. The army of dwarves made a steady pace along the roads out of the mountains and into the foothills to the south. In orbit high above, a Suuden-Aryku heavy cruiser had positioned itself with a clear view to scan the surface. They were watching closely the progress of the army as it marched along. When they saw it come into near proximity, they contacted the High Commander to report in.

"Commander Geilv, we are observing the troop movement, and it is approaching within sighting range of the northern fortification. What are your instructions?"

"Stand by," he replies. "I will connect you directly to the Marshal."

The com-station officer patches the link through to the Governor's trans-com in his office. He picks it up, anxiously waiting for this moment to finalize his plans for the city.

"Yes, Commander?"

"The Captain of the cruiser in orbit has a report for you."

"Good, what is it?"

"Marshal," emits the voice. "We are observing the troop movement nearing its target. What are your orders?"

"Do you have the schematics for the city layout in your targeting computer, Captain?"

"Yes, Marshal."

"Bring up the section known locally as the Upper Ward. This is your target. Make it precise, as I want to open a hole for our troops to enter and finish the rest for us. Leave nothing standing, Captain. I want the whole area reduced to blast craters."

"Affirmative. What about your position, is it secure?"

"So long as you hit your target, my position is secure. Make it a limited engagement, only that one section, and then depart the area immediately thereafter."

"Understood."

They end the link, and he turns to look out the window to watch the show.

Tristeen sat in the last row of pews near the door, listening to the sounds coming from outside. At this time, it was mostly just people passing along through the plaza.

Leesa sat at her desk, unable to focus on any work, and generally realizing it didn't matter, anyway.

Captain Kholgard also sat at his desk in the barracks. He and his guardsmen had stationed a number of horses in the yard, all saddled up and ready so they could ride out and start herding the people out of the city.

The Dean was once again sitting on the floor in his office perusing a number of papers and considering if he should bother assigning laborers to any repair duties. He was not fully inside the circle of information, like the others, to know about the dwarves. This was partially to protect him in case the Governor should desire to peek in and see if his favorite pet was misbehaving.

Thaelyn and the General were attending to their reviews of the war against the orcs, which was still ongoing, despite the affairs in the city. Relissa and the others were still in their classes at this time.

Josef and his group were sitting at a table in a local café in Firstfall in deep discussion of their plans, and how things might appear if anything should happen to Rolsklinde.

And then it happened. The first of them came.

Somewhere in the far northern section of the city, a brief flash streaked downward, followed by a titanic boom as it made impact. A cloud of fire rose up, accompanied by smoke and debris. It shook walls, rattled windows, and rumbled the ground underfoot. A series of additional shots followed behind in quick succession.

Tristeen lurched out of her seat and ducked for cover. Master Dastien and the priests all jumped at the first shockwave, and then dashed to the door to look outside. Tristeen followed close behind. To the north, in the area of the Upper Ward, they saw huge blast clouds reaching up, with additional bright flashes raining down from above.

Leesa dodged out of her seat to the floor at the first rumble, as did the secretary. Captain Kholgard did likewise in his office, as did the Dean in his, although he could only cower from the sound, as he was already on the floor.

"Great gods!" Tristeen mutters urgently. "What in all the hells is that?"

Master Dastien had his trans-com out by now and was dialing a number.

"This is Thaelyn…"

"My Lord!" he screeches. "Dastien here, we're under attack! We need shield mages up here at once!"

"Understood! General," he redirects. "Get our people up there now."

The General rushes outside with a mage and passes the order. The mage opens a portal to the temple directly, and a number of other mages who had been grouping together all file through. The sudden rise in tension quickly brought the full settlement to an alert condition.

"Master Dastien," Thaelyn issues. "What is happening up there?"

"My Lord, we're watching the whole of the Upper Ward district being blasted sky high. I can't be sure, but I believe I'm seeing fire coming down from above…maybe that bombardment we spoke of once."

"Bombardment! Master Dastien, your position is very vulnerable under those conditions. Have those shield mages provide cover for you and anyone else you can gather up into a tight circle."

"Aye!"

Tristeen peeked out the door to watch the scene, trying to imagine her home, as with the rest of the neighborhood, now being reduced to dust. She reflexively turned to look at the Governor's Manor, and there she saw a face peeking out the window upstairs.

"That horrid little creep!" she scorns.

She pounds on Master Dastien to get his attention and points.

"My Lord," he ushers into his trans-com. "I'm looking at the Governor's window now, and I can see him watching the sights from up there. That bloody monster is playing this like a night at the theater!"

"Is he now! As much as I might share your sentiment, at least this offers us an idea of where he is presently. If he is ordering a strike on the city, it is likely a localized one, perhaps specific to the noble families for their part. Surely, he would not involve a location where he is situated personally. But keep on alert in case the situation changes."

"Right!"

The shield mages arrived inside the temple, along with a number of others with transit runes to Firstfall. The scene in the plaza was now chaos as people were screaming and running in all directions, but mostly southward. Master Dastien contemplated how to employ the mages, but with the destruction seemingly located in the Upper Ward, his concern might need to focus on the people in the plaza. Then he recalled the dwarves. They must be nearby at this time. He rushes outside, calling the priests and the mages to follow.

"Tristeen, you stay inside," he orders. "If he's got it in so badly for your people, you need to be out of sight."

"But I can't just stay here!"

"For now, until he pulls back from that window, you must. He's apparently trying to exterminate your noble families up there. Let's not give him cause to think he missed one."

"Oh grand…" she mumbles under her breath.

Jared and the guards at the north gate all jolted when the first of the hits shook the air around them. They turned to see the smoke clouds billowing up and hurried back inside the gates. But just as he turned to go inside, Jared glimpsed a mass of bodies coming over a small rise from the north. It was the dwarves.

"Bloody hell, and now they come."

He turns and dashes back inside to make his way towards the temple.

Captain Kholgard rushed outside to see the destruction occurring up north. He starts issuing orders to his men, and together they mount up on their horses.

"Lieutenant, start moving these people south and out of the city!"

The yard Lieutenant rushes off, along with several others, to start directing the people out of the plaza. The Captain rides over to speak with Master Dastien.

"What is that up there?" he shouts.

"We think that cretin is using bombardment tactics on the noble houses," he points at the Governor's window to show him viewing the spectacle.

"I can't believe I'm actually watching him watch all of this," the Captain grumbles.

He then rides off to start moving the people.

In the tactical office, Thaelyn is giving his own orders.

"General, send someone to the guildhall, now!" he commands. "Tell them to cancel the remainder of that language class and order those people into attendance…all of them."

"Right away!"

The General calls a page from outside to pass the order. The man then runs off through the gateway to the city.

Thaelyn continues, "We need Lieutenant Lapäli, at the very least, for his role concerning that reactor. The rest can be useful in other areas, particularly the local language to instruct these people."

"Aye!"

"We need our evacuation team up there, those shield mages and such with their runes to the field outside. Send them in to arrive south of the city. Let us also mount up some mages on gryphons to offer aerial support, in case anyone needs it, and send them off. And call Aerlie into attendance."

The General gave out additional instructions, some to Captain Hagmaert, and more to other pages and officers.

Leesa and the secretary were peeking out the window at the destruction and madness now rushing through the streets.

"Sir..." she issues. "You'd better start running. Get out of here and go south."

"What about you?"

"I have to stay here. I have one last chore ahead of me, and I need to get it right."

"You're a very courageous young lady, Leesa. May these new gods watch over you."

He returns to his desk to grab a bag of his personal items and hurries outside. Leesa stays at the window, still watching the smoke clouds, and now taking notice of Master Dastien and the others coming into view.

"You're not running away yet," she notes to herself. "So, you must know something. Good, let's hope you're right."

The Dean was halfway down the stairs by now, trying to steady himself as the building shook from the blasting outside. He hurried out the door into the plaza and jerked around to find the disturbance, then to set his eyes on the Upper Ward.

"Dear gods above, Tristeen, I hope you aren't up there right now, nor anyone else for that matter, though it's probably a vain hope."

He turned to find Master Dastien and his people coming outside, and he further turned to see the Governor peeking through his window. The Governor peered down into the street to see the Dean looking back up at him.

"Yes, Dean," he mumbles to himself. "You and your wretched ilk are on your last days. Go ahead, try to use your pitiful magic to save them, if you can. You're no better with it than your undereducated students," he laughs harshly.

Tristeen continued to peek outside from behind the temple door, intermittently ducking away from the dust and rubble that was now pelting the plaza and the nearby buildings. She watched as the people panicked and ran off in different directions through the streets. Several moments later, the blasting stopped, and the sky was now choked with smoke, and raining debris.

Now that the show was over, the Governor withdrew from his window. He returned to his desk and began collecting himself for his final departure. Tristeen observed from the doorway that he was no longer peering outside, so she decided to emerge into view.

"Master Dastien!" she shouts. "He's gone from sight, so I'm guessing he's getting ready to leave. Those dwarves can't be too far behind."

The Dean scrambled over to meet with the priests, and he caught notice of Tristeen among them.

"Tristeen, thank the gods you're alive…but, what about the rest?" he turns to glance over his shoulder at the Upper Ward.

"They're all evacuated by now," she replies. "I sent them away a couple of nights ago to the valley."

"Oh, you're a credit to your breeding, Miss Macaid," he coos. "This much is certain. But how did you know he would do this?" he turns to examine the priests for an answer.

"We didn't," Master Dastien admits. "This was a surprise hit. However, it's only the beginning. There's an army of dwarves heading our way now."

"Dwarves! He's sending them at us? But those poor sods couldn't possibly be so much of a bother, could they?"

"He gave them Suuden-Aryku weapons, and these are apparently big ones. So, they're regarded as a serious threat under these conditions."

"Blast that creature. Pleasures, indeed!"

Captain Kholgard rode up to the group on his horse again. His men were moving through the upper district by now, collecting the people and redirecting them south.

"Master Dastien," he shouts. "What's the word so far?"

"Run, would be the first one in my mind. Get these people out of here and through the south gate."

"Right you are!"

"And be aware of an army of dwarves bearing up shoulder-mounted cannons!"

"Blazes of the infernal," he mumbles under his breath and rides off again.

+·+·+·◆·+·+·+

"My Lord!" Relissa blurts as she and the others rush into the room. "We got the word. What's happening right now?"

"Master Dastien tells us they used bombardment to destroy the Upper Ward district. This is likely a personal issue aimed at the noble families. Now, the dwarves are set to make their arrival at any moment."

"My Lord," Haran asserts. "I want to offer my help. Is it possible you can send me up there to confer with the Master?"

"I could, but the area is likely to become very dangerous, very quickly."

"So be it."

"And Lieutenant, we need you to go up there and assist with that reactor, but hold back inside the temple until we can be sure that creature has departed."

"Understood..." Padriyl responds.

Thaelyn now directs them to a mage with a rune to send them along.

"Marelle and Relissa," he continues. "You can be of service to us out in the fields coordinating the evacuation. Find Mister Sarens, and if possible, Acolyte Galwen, and bring them together to help. We will be sending a group of mages up there shortly with portal runes."

"Right away," Marelle responds and heads outside to find another mage.

The commotion stirring up in the settlement brought the immediate attention of Josef and his group. He strides over to the tactical office and peeks inside to see if he can get some information on what was happening.

671

"Eh, Your Lordship, my pardons, but can we assume something is happening up north?"

"Indeed, that heathenish Darumon is laying down his parting farewell."

"I see, and what does that mean, exactly?"

"So far, he used a bombardment tactic to blast away your fine Upper Ward, and we are now waiting for the next volley to arrive."

"Blast him," Abraim spurns. "A small part of me was hoping to one day return home to at least some part of my former holdings, but now what? It's just a big hole in the ground?"

"Stay with us and we will take care of you, but right now, your service can be of great value in the fields outside the north gate. We will be pulling people out to accumulate in that area."

"All right," he nods. "Josef, Seth, we have work to do."

The three of them return to the village square to make their plans.

✦

Leesa studied the scene from the window and took notice of the lull from the bombardment. She surmised the next part must still be coming, but she was uncertain if the Governor was upstairs watching, or somewhere else. So, she decided to make a preemptive effort to discover his activities. She pulled back and began up the stairs to check his office.

The Governor was just getting up from his desk. He glanced around one last time to survey his former post.

"Four hundred years," he murmurs. "Sitting here and directing these tiny creatures around their pitiful lives, and all washed away due to those filthy orcs and their mindless rampaging. Well, may that man have his way with them, this much I'll grant him. In fact, perhaps I'll have the Commander send his people to give one final order to make sure those beasts meet with a proper end. As for the rest..." he briskly glances out the window at the city.

He turns to pull out the drawer with his trans-com, but rather than picking it up to take along, he just stares at it.

"Bah, for all the trouble this place has caused me, I don't want any souvenirs. Let it stay here and be destroyed with everything else when the reactor goes off."

He turns and begins to leave the room.

Leesa arrived at his door and paused. She was just about ready to knock when he opened it and began his way out.

"Oh, Governor!" she yips anxiously. "I was just coming to check on you. Did you see what happened outside? My goodness! Something big is going on out there. I saw all these big clouds, and heard these horrible noises…"

"Young lady, can you actually be…" he halts his wording to study her a moment. "Yes, of course, I saw it from my window. It would seem we had a terrible series of, eh, well, it's difficult to say without going up there personally."

"But how could something like that happen? I mean, gracious, all that smoke and those big noises."

"Big noises? Yes, they certainly were big. Eh, surely you must realize that was in the Upper Ward, correct?"

"Oh my, yes! But wow! The only time I hear stuff like that is in a really bad storm or something."

The Governor studied her for her obvious dimwitted reaction. But he had his own objectives now, so he proceeded towards the stairs.

"Yes! You might hear such as that during a storm."

"And I think I saw flashes. Could it be some kind of lightning hitting the ground? I've never seen anything like that up close."

"Oh, really? Indeed, and you can be sure it can cause a bit of a disturbance."

"I'm also wondering about the people up there right now. Isn't that stuff dangerous if you get too close?"

"Oh, I think only if it hits something delicate. But I'm sure the Guard will take care of it. It's their duty, after all."

"But you know, I didn't see any clouds up there today. Do you think this could be some kind of attack? Maybe it was the Flame Elves. Or wait! Oh! Could it be the Suuden-Aryku? I hear people sometimes talk about them. Can they do something like this?"

Leesa begins following him as he descends the stairs, tagging along like a young child pestering a convenient adult.

"Sending lightning down?" he muses distantly. "Well, I suppose, if you consider the strange things they're said to be capable of. Have you heard any of that new talk lately? I'm aware there have been a number of interesting developments, if you only consider the events just outside in the plaza. You did take notice of that, did you not?"

"Oh, well, yes," she responds casually. "Sitting in this office, I had a chance to see people walking around. And I heard a lot of shouting and bells ringing, and so on. But my mother never really let me out much to talk to the common folk. You know, she always said that the noble families and the common people don't consort with each other. It's so unbecoming, or some such."

"Really," he considers. "So, you spent most of your time in the comfort of your precious estate home, did you?"

"Well that, or at this one nice little bazaar we have down the way. Ooh! Did you know they have some fabulous art displays up there? In fact, I recall the last time I was visiting, and I saw this darling little sculpture..."

The Governor proceeded down the stairs and around the corner to a hall where he would find the basement door. Leesa continued rambling idiotically about the niceties of the local cultural venues. She watched as he pulled out his key and opened the door, then stepped inside. She continued to follow just behind, but her persistence and continual jabbering was wearing on him by now.

"Eh, Miss... What was your name again?"

"Me? But, my goodness, I thought we did that already. Leesa, that's me!"

"Yes, Leesa, I have some important work to do in here and..."

"Oh, don't mind me. Wait... Oh dear, that's right. That terrible noise outside! Hey! I'll bet you're down here to cast one of your big spells that protects the city, right? My mother once said something about how you hold this great power to protect us from that awful curse. Is that right? Ooh! Can I watch?"

"Important work? Oh, indeed, but eh..."

"I promise I won't get in the way, but I always wondered what the Great and Powerful Governor had in his secret room. Everybody says you have a secret room with all your magical things to fight those nasty Flame Elves."

Leesa begins peering around the room inquisitively until she sets her eyes on the alien door. The Governor didn't care for her insistent intrusion, but her obvious display of puerile innocence, combined with her whimsical conversation intrigued him to find a convenient solution.

"Rainbows and flowers," he whispers to himself. "That's the only thing inside your head. How lovely. Such a fine example of a lesser creature."

He turns to find the keypad control for the door and steps forward to interact with it. He passes a glance over his shoulder again to see Leesa gazing curiously at him.

"Eh, this requires a private moment, if you please. Perhaps if you simply turn around briefly..."

"Oh, sure... Is this your secret room?"

"This here..." he examines the door again, and then the conveyor unit in the corner. "This is more like...a storage room, yes. I need to arrange something in here, and then I need to travel off to my secret chamber to conduct my, ahem, powerful magic."

"Oh, wow! All right, I'll turn around."

She turns her back and peeks over her shoulder with an innocent smile to make sure he is happy. As she turns away, she secretly slips her hand into the hidden pocket to pull out her trans-com, then brings up the video recording mode and holds it up to peek around her while he punches his code into the keypad.

The Governor oriented himself to allow the limited lighting from the nearby wall sconce to highlight the keypad, while he selected a series of buttons on the panel. He then waits for a button on the bottom row to light up, and then presses that to open the door.

Leesa listens to the sounds of the door opening and turns to see him going inside.

"Wow, is that some kind of a magic door that just opens on command?"

"Yes, many of my special items are like that. Now, just wait out here a moment while I attend to this."

He steps up to a console and begins operating a series of controls, pressing buttons and arranging sliders, until a set of status lights come on to indicate a pending overload condition.

"And this will take care of the rest," he muses silently.

He leaves the room and presses another button to close the door, then begins moving in the direction of his conveyor.

"Now, Leesa, I need to go to my...secret chamber. But perhaps... yes, I could have you just wait right here. Don't bother yourself with any new noises you might hear outside, it's just my, eh, powerful magic doing its work. We don't want to offend your delicate eyes with anything unpleasant, now do we?" he grins mischievously.

"Oh, whatever you say. Just wait right here in the basement?"

"Yes, this should be fine, and in time, everything will be made right again."

He steps over to the conveyor and positions himself on the circular pad. He takes one final look around, observing Leesa watching him and glancing around the room as if waiting for something.

"Yes, just like that..." he mutters.

He activates a control on the unit and a soft electrical whirring starts up. A moment later, the unit begins to glow, enveloping him in a bubble of light and whisking him away.

Leesa studies the action, realizing it resembled a portal, like what Thaelyn's people used.

"And good riddance, you horrid creature," she groans.

She pulls out her trans-com, hoping she got a good shot at what he was doing. She replays the video and studies it carefully, then steps up to the keypad to try her guess.

"Center on top," she mumbles to herself. "Center on the right, then this one on the left, and another on the bottom, and last is smack in the middle. How cute."

She watched as a button on the bottom lit up. She pressed it and the door opened to reveal the control room inside. She breathed a quick sigh of relief at her success, but now she had very little time to react. She turned and made a mad dash out of the room, down the hall and through the foyer, then out the front door.

She ran across the plaza to the temple, where Master Dastien was coordinating the shield mages to form up a defensive line.

"He's gone!" she shouts. "He just did his thing in that room, and left in some kind of portal."

"What about that door?"

"It's open! I played the total idiot and followed him down there. He told me to sit and wait for something big to happen, so I guess he thinks I'm not worth more than to be blasted to bits. I recorded him as he used that keypad, and I got the door open. Where's the Lieutenant? I need him right now."

Master Dastien nods as he turns to peer back inside the temple.

"Lieutenant Lapäli, front and center," he shouts.

Padriyl jumps through the door and rushes up to meet them. Leesa beckons him to follow her, and together they run back to the Governor's Manor. She leads him through to the basement and the control room door. Once inside, he quickly studies the console to discover what it was doing.

"Right, just as we thought," he remarks. "He set these controls to overload. I could probably reset them, but according to my mother, it would be best to simply shut it down completely. This would prevent anyone from linking back to this station with the conveyor, and I should also disable the links to their central monitoring station, to make it appear as if this unit has gone silent."

"Silent, meaning what…gone, destroyed?"

"Exactly. If he wants this city destroyed, and we're assuming he's not actually watching it from somewhere, this will make it appear that way on their monitoring station."

"All right, whatever you think, just do it."

He first turns to a communications panel with the remote monitoring linkage. He examines the status indicators of the overload condition, hoping to time the event to make it appear the reactor was approaching a critical containment condition. He would turn off the com-links just before that moment, in order to make it appear the reactor actually did explode. This meant he might need to delay for a while in case anyone was watching.

✦✦✦

Haran had been holding back inside the temple, same as Padriyl, after they arrived. When Padriyl was called out, he followed and joined with the others. Tristeen took immediate notice of him coming outside.

"Haran!" she shouts and rushes up to begin scolding him. "Why didn't you tell me you left the city?! I was worried sick about you for I don't know how long. You didn't write, and you didn't even bother to pass any word through anyone else, including your sister or Willit, or...anyone!"

"Tristeen, I..."

"Don't 'Tristeen, I' me, Mister Mage Academy Dropout. And then, I finally learn, if only by accident, that not only did you leave the city, but you left, well, everything...our whole world, and went over to that other one! Ooh!"

"Tristeen, wait a minute," he begs. "First, do you really think this is the right time or place for this? I hear we're about to come under attack. Maybe you'd like to scream at me later, after we get out of this?"

"That would be my suggestion, as well," Master Dastien admits.

"Right. And besides, after being kicked out of the academy, there wasn't really anything else for me to do here. And you know how I felt after that argument with the Dean."

"All right, fine," Tristeen wags a finger at him. "But a simple note wouldn't have killed you. So, to remind you who's in charge here..."

Now she flings herself at him and wraps her arms around for a tight hug and a kiss.

Master Dastien and the priests all grinned, and shook their heads at the scene.

By this time, the dwarven army was just arriving inside the remains of the Upper Ward, having crossed the rubble left behind from the north wall. They brought their weapons to bear, preparing to destroy everything else in the city. And as they caught sight of the next line of buildings near the plaza, they opened fire, sending off a volley of pulse energy blasts that slammed into the walls, exploding the stone and wooden architecture into fragments.

This newest ruckus sent another wave of panic through the people. Master Dastien and the priests all jerked around to follow the disturbance, only to see another series of explosions and debris clouds.

"And here they come!" he shouts. "Shield mages, form up and make a wall."

Tristeen and Haran both ducked down behind the others as the shield mages began casting their chants to create a barrier in front of them.

The Dean had moved off to another section beyond the north gate, trying to assist in ordering the people to evacuate. He had already checked a stable near the gate itself, but the area was clear by now, so he continued among a series of workshops, peeking through doors and shouting for people to run. He had just finished one circuit when these newest explosions echoed through the streets. He halted and turned to find another blast cloud rising up, so he doubled back to check on the others, circling around behind the Governor's Manor.

"What's going on with that reactor?" Master Dastien shouts through the blasting.

"Should I go check on it?" Haran asks.

"Yes, do so, but be quick about it."

Haran hurries across to the Governor's Manor and ducks inside. He searches the foyer to find the hallway leading to the basement door.

"Where is everyone?" he shouts.

Leesa hears the call and rushes out of the basement to meet him.

"Haran! The Lieutenant is downstairs. He's working with that reactor."

"Why is it taking so long?"

"He says they might be watching it somewhere, so he wants to make it look good, like it actually blew up before he turns it off."

"That's taking time I don't think we have. The dwarves are outside."

"Great. All right, you go talk to him. I'll check outside."

Haran proceeds to the basement while Leesa rushes up to the window to observe the activity. The dwarves were just emerging through a dust cloud that used to be a row of shops on the other side of the plaza. But from her vantage, she couldn't see them very clearly, so a thought came to go upstairs and use the office window for a better view.

She runs up the stairs and dashes through the Governor's office door, briskly trotting up to the window to get a bird's eye view of the plaza. She could now see the mages with their shield wall, a line of dwarves starting to enter the plaza, and the last few people trying to get away.

Satisfied with what she saw, she turned to leave, but quickly took notice of the Governor's desk with the drawer pulled open. She looked inside and saw a strange device, so she reached in and grabbed it.

"This looks like a trans-com, and I'll bet it's his, what he used to talk to those people."

She takes it and runs back downstairs into the basement again.

Padriyl was just getting ready to hit the shutdown switch. The reactor was near to going critical. The reaction inside the chamber was getting out of control and causing the room to shudder. The heat was becoming unbearable.

"Padriyl," Haran cautions. "I think it's now or never!"

He nods and turns to the com-station, then begins cutting the links, shutting down the carrier signal and disabling the feed. He then hits a large red button that was clearly marked inside a striped outline box. This causes the reactor to begin a shutdown sequence. A series of control rods engage, and the reaction process begins to wind down, cutting off the fuel supply and venting the surplus plasma through an underground exhaust chute. The roaring of the flames down the exhaust tunnel rumbled the floor and walls of the basement.

"I don't know where that goes," he mentions. "But I wouldn't want to be on the other side of it."

He waited several moments longer to ensure the reactor was shutting down successfully before directing the others outside again.

The plaza was in turmoil by now. The dwarves were swarming through the area, with many of them attempting to take down the shield mages and their barrier. Master Dastien was directing the group to pull away from the temple towards the Governor's Manor to pick up the people inside, and together they would withdraw down the avenue.

The Dean was just emerging from around the upper corner of the Manor, coming into view of the plaza and the new devastation that was occurring. He halted as he rounded the corner of the building, trying to judge his best course of action, and choosing to return the other way, now circling around the Manor and hoping to come up behind the mages.

Master Dastien was making another call on his trans-com to report in.

"My Lord, the dwarves are advancing through the plaza now. Most of the buildings are gone, and we're pulling a tight circle with the mages. We need to pull back."

"Understood. What about the reactor?"

Master Dastien studied the door to the building and then saw movement. Haran and the others were just now arriving in view.

"My Lord, they're coming out now. One moment..."

He jerks up and shouts through the chaos.

"Haran, what's the situation down there?"

"We got it! Let's go!"

"My Lord," he returns to the trans-com. "I believe the reactor is taken care of."

"Good, now what about the people?"

"The upper district seems clear by now. There's a mad rush behind us. Last word from Captain Kholgard said he was going into the western boroughs while his men would direct the people through the south gate. Tristeen is already moving forward to catch any stragglers, but I haven't heard from either Willit or Jared, so I'm assuming they are somewhere behind us."

"Let us hope so. Very well, pull back and vacate the area."

"Aye! Let's go men."

The team now begins a full withdrawal, pulling away from the area. They begin backing down the avenue, with several dwarves advancing on them.

"We might have those few chasing us all the way through the city," Haran notes. "We need to stall them so we can pull back safely."

"Aye, but I don't want to bring any actual harm to them."

Master Dastien mulls over a few ideas, and then turns to the gryphon riders in the sky overhead. A thought comes to him, so he raises a hand and calls a cantrip to create a bright flash of light. He repeats this several times to attract their attention. Several riders descend and circle low overhead. He then issues a series of hand signals and points to the row of dwarves who were making the assault on their shield barrier.

The Dean was just now coming around the south side of the Governor's Manor, but much to his chagrin, the line of shield mages had already receded further down the road. There were no other alleys for him to navigate at this point. His only choice was to make a run for it on the street. So, he jumped into the open and took off as fast as he could.

Master Dastien and the others saw the man making a desperate dash along the side, hoping to avoid the dwarves advancing on their line. But at this point, he would need to pass right by them to reach their defense.

"Hold fast, men, open a lane."

He looks up at the gryphon riders and urgently points at the dwarves.

From above, the mages on the gryphons cast a sheet of ice on the ground, freezing the roadway and partially encasing the dwarves in a shell to restrict their movement.

The Dean hurries past the front line to join the others, but before he can reach it, one of the dwarves finds just enough freedom to pull the trigger.

An energy blast rockets out and strikes a nearby building, exploding the wall and sending shards of rock and splinters of wood across the street. The blast effect catches the Dean and tosses him aside.

"Dammit!" Master Dastien growls. "Men, push forward and cover him. Pull him in!"

The line makes an assertive thrust to advance up to the Dean. A pair of priests grabs his arms and drags him back. But as they reel him in, they notice a large splinter of wood impaled in his side.

"Dean! Hold on, man."

Priest Garrain examines the injury, only to see the stick piercing almost completely through the Dean's flank.

"This is bad," he offers. "Right through the kidney…"

Haran leans in to try to comfort the Dean. He could see in his eyes he was fading.

"Dean! Can you hear me?"

The Dean turned to the voice. His breathing was raspy, and he appeared to be going into shock.

"Haran?" he whispers faintly. "You came back?"

"Yes, Dean, I'm here."

"You got my letter?"

"Yes, I did."

"I'm so grateful. I needed to do this."

Tristeen was returning to check on the line. She took immediate notice of someone on the ground. She rushed up to investigate.

"Dean!" she shrieks. "What happened?"

"He was late in returning to us," Master Dastien relents. "He tried to reach us, but the dwarves hit that building, and he got caught in it."

"He looks bad. Dean?" she bends over him to study his face. "Can you hear me?" She looks up at the priest. "You have to do something!"

"Master Dastien," Priest Garrain asserts. "We need to call an EMT immediately and evacuate this man to Firstfall. Send word, now."

The Master pulls out his trans-com and makes another call.

"Hold on, Dean," Tristeen begs.

The row of dwarves was starting to emerge out of their icy prison, and the shield mages found themselves again in the line of fire. Elsewhere, the rest of the army marched forward, with buildings exploding and more plumes of smoke rising up. The group found themselves being hit by occasional debris and rained on by dust and ash. By now, many fires had broken out, and anything that wasn't blown to bits was now burning.

"We need to escape from here," Haran notes urgently. "If any more of them come this way, we could find ourselves surrounded very quickly."

The priest looks up at the dwarves coming to life again, and then turns to the gryphon riders overhead. He makes a new series of hand signals, giving instructions to lay down another round of suppressive fire.

"We need to pull back! Quickly now, before we get caught in this volley."

The group pulled back to a new position, still dragging the Dean as the priests continued their efforts to stabilize his condition.

The mages on the gryphons cast a new volley, this time stink clouds to stifle and confound the dwarven line. This would hopefully hold them long enough for the priests to prepare the Dean for transport.

"We have an EMT in transit to Firstfall," Master Dastien affirms. "We just need to send him off."

Haran and Tristeen both leaned over the Dean, holding his hands, and patting him on the shoulder to keep his focus.

"We'll get you out of here," Haran comforts. "Marelle told me you earned a special favor. Thaelyn doesn't let people slip away like that."

"Haran, I can't...feel... Don't trouble...with..."

The Dean's voice trailed off and his body sank.

"Dean!"

The priests examined him again and checked for a pulse. Priest Garrain pulls back, sighs deeply, and looks around.

"No..." Tristeen moans. "He doesn't deserve this. He had it bad from the start."

Haran stared at the Dean's body lying on the ground, then made a pass around the group.

"She's right, he deserved better."

"I agree," Priest Garrain nods solemnly.

He glances at Master Dastien, and then the others as he recalls the last several days.

"A ticket to redemption…that's what he promised. And this…" he ponders for another moment. "No, not this time…" he announces determinedly. "That monster has taken too many in all this."

He reaches into his vest and searches among his holy symbols. He pulls one out resembling a pair of bound hands. He holds it tight and raises it up.

"Ilmater, hear me, your humble servant…"

He bows his head and closes his eyes as he mumbles a silent but urgent prayer to the one known as the Crying God.

"Haran," Tristeen mutters privately. "What's he doing?"

"Calling a little divine aid, I think."

The priest continues his chant, whispering a series of depictions, as if haggling at a merchant's desk. Finally, he smiles and nods as the holy symbol begins to glow softly.

"Gracious," she gasps. "Is that…?"

The priest opens his eyes and begins giving a new set of orders.

"We are taking authoritative action!" he orders. "Open him up, pull his clothes away. Get that stick out and put a field closure on it. Be ready with a sleep trance."

The others unbutton the Dean's vest and shirt to expose his chest. The lead priest lays the still-glowing holy symbol on him and prepares for another chant.

"Master Dastien, where's that rune?"

"Here…" he pulls out a return rune to the settlement. "But is this really a good time and place for this?"

"Just keep those dwarves off me for another few moments. I don't care how."

"Right."

The priest begins a chant, raising his hands up and folding them together, while the Master gets up and considers a new plan. Time was short, as the dwarves were still trying to shake off the effects of the stink cloud.

"Part a hole," he orders of the shield mages.

He steps forward and casts a new spell, sending off another smoke cloud. He then begins a long-casting chant. Tristeen and Haran both watched as he built up a potent arcanic charge.

"I don't know what that is," Haran mentions. "But it's big."

Master Dastien carried his chant to a climax and directed himself forward. He lifted one foot, making ready to stomp down. He made fists in both hands, raised them up, and then yanked them down as he stamped his foot hard on the ground.

A shockwave erupted in the ground as a potent earthquake rumbled away from him. The rippling effect sent the line of dwarves tumbling back along the road, disorienting them, and keeping them off-balance to prevent any new attacks. He then began another chant, this time to call up an earth elemental. He summoned the creature from the ground, and gave it life on the surface right in front of him.

"I've never seen anything like that before," Tristeen whimpers.

Master Dastien then began issuing a series of strange commands in a mystical language. The creature seemed to acknowledge its instructions and lurched forward towards the dwarves. It burrowed underground and began tussling with them under their feet, not to inflict harm, but simply to occupy them by keeping them distracted.

"You've got a brief moment, Priest. Let's go."

Priest Garrain had charged himself with the divine power of the god Ilmater. His hands were now glowing, and he brought them back down. He set one over the Dean's heart and the other on his forehead, transferring the glow into the Dean's body.

From within the Dean's chest, his heart began beating again, slowly at first, but rapidly increasing to a steady rhythm. Haran and Tristeen looked on as his chest began to rise, seemingly mechanical in its motion, causing his lungs to draw in a deep breath, then to release it and repeat.

The other priests monitored his condition, peering inside with their Healer's Sight to observe the reaction. One of them placed a sleep chant on him, with his fingers making a clockwise circle over the face.

Master Dastien returned to the group and took out his rune. He enchanted it to make it ready.

Priest Garrain continued until he had spent his divine charge, and then pulled back. The Dean now seemed to be in a stable condition, well enough for transport.

"Send him off. We'll let the EMT take it from here."

"What's an EMT?" Tristeen asks.

"Over the last couple of centuries, Lady Aerlie has shown us ways to improve our medical services. It became apparent, once we had our gateway network established, that we could use this, or at least a derivative of it, to send out what we call Emergency Medical Teams to give aid to our people. This became a necessity after the Spellplague demonstrated the great need to deliver medical aid to the far reaches of the kingdom. We use special teams travelling through portals to reach out and return victims of injury to the nearest Healer's Ward for rapid treatment. In this way, the normal wait time due to travel becomes negligible. Normally, the team would arrive with a stretcher to pick up the injured, but we're in a bad place here, so we'll send him to Firstfall for the occasion."

Master Dastien touched his rune to the Dean, sending him off in a ball of light.

"Now, we need to go," he issues firmly. "Let's get out of here before the rest of these dwarves find us."

The group once again begins their retreat, with the only people in mind to watch being those further along.

Chapter 16

A TENDER VICTORY

The population of Rolsklinde had been pouring through the south gates. A row of shield mages had lined up, forming another wall out in the field, and behind that was a line of mages with runes to evacuate the people from the area.

Relissa and Marelle, along with Willit and Jared, had teamed up to direct the flow through the portals. Many of the people had to be strongly encouraged to jump through, as none of them knew how to use a portal. On the other side, Thaelyn had a small army of soldiers pulling the people away from the arrival zones to keep the way clear for more.

The dwarves continued to rampage through the streets, blasting every building they came across. Haran, Tristeen, Leesa, and Padriyl hurried ahead with Master Dastien and the rest close behind until they had receded out of range of the dwarves who had been directing their focus on the shield mages and their wall.

Somewhere still within the city was Captain Kholgard on horseback. As Master Dastien and his group found their way outside, they took up near the portal mages to assist in directing people through, anxiously watching the last few stragglers as they stumbled out the gates, followed by the Captain and his remaining men.

The Captain rode up to the Mage Master to report in. He was covered in soot and dust from the smoky barrage inside the city.

"That's the last of them, as best I can tell. I don't think anything else could survive up there. I just wish we could've known about that damned fool's plans to help those poor people in the Upper Ward."

"Captain," Tristeen comes forward. "Don't worry about them. I secretly evacuated them a couple of days ago. I was expecting something special out of that beast when the Dean came to my house and warned me."

"Really! Well, that's a new one. Between that and my office, maybe he's not such a porker after all. All right, we should get ourselves out of here before anything else happens."

He looked over his shoulder at his former home. Great plumes of smoke filled the air as the city burned. The last home of the human population in this world turned into rubble and ash, but the evacuation saved many lives.

Clustered around Firstfall, the citizens were in turmoil, confused and shaken, and now huddled in tight groups in the fields north of the settlement. There were many injuries, though none were very severe, and Aerlie was busy with an army of priests called in to assist those in need. Med-tech Tad'vaal of the Daanen-Aryku also arranged a field hospital, and a multitude of Night Elves and High Elves lent a hand to assist the people in interacting with Thaelyn's citizens.

Word had been sent to the people of Tae'Eladar to offer volunteer aid in the form of food, blankets, and other materials to set up temporary camps for the refugees. And now, with the most immediate threat of the city behind them, Thaelyn and his officers reconvened in the tactical office.

"My Lord," the General reports. "Our scouts on the eastern ridgeline are reporting a large-scale withdrawal of the Suuden-Aryku to the southeast. They look to be leaving us now."

"This is both good and bad, as we cannot be sure if we will be able to follow them. I find it highly unlikely they will allow us to locate and make use of whatever means they have to depart this world."

"If you were to ask me," Padriyl offers. "I might suggest they're retreating to a base compound with a nether-space conveyor facility. This would seem the most likely solution since they've been occupying this world for a long enough time, so they should've built a few conveniences for themselves by now."

"That would be a fine catch, but I think they would not allow us to come anywhere near to it, to say nothing of capturing it. Still, we should try locating it, if only to observe and ensure they do actually leave this world. General, send out some gryphons, but tell them to be extremely cautious. Travel at high altitude, to keep out of sight, and perhaps also their weapons range. And let us hope they do not have any anti-aircraft weapons. Then, have them report back if they find anything."

"What about the dwarves?" Marelle wonders. "What are they doing right now?"

"According to our scouts, those we still have on the gryphons circling the city, they report the dwarves seem to be in a confused condition up there. Now that the major portion of the work is done, that being the destruction of the buildings, many are simply standing around or moving in small circles. We suspect they have finished their last instruction and with nothing else to come after."

"So, the Suuden-Aryku, or maybe simply Darumon, didn't expect them to live long enough to actually finish anything, not with that reactor going off like they were hoping. Now, they have nothing else to do and no new instructions."

"Yes, but the concern we have now is if we were to go in and attempt to capture them, they might turn on us as new targets found within sight. They do not seem to be returning home, not that I would expect them to know where home is in this world, so we are in a condition of wait and see. For instance, if we should see them drop their weapons, that might be an indication that they are returning to a settled state. If this is the case, I will authorize a careful approach to manhandle them and take them down."

"Where will we put them after this?"

"This is a good question," he sighs. "We cannot regard them as enemies, or even proper prisoners. But at the same time, whatever reaction they might have, if they should ever wake up from their delirium, is unknown, so we will surely need a strong security force."

"Perhaps if we create a holding pen arrangement," the General suggests. "We could make a circle of shield walls, like those we have around us here, but turned inward to create an enclosure. Then post a number of guards to contain them."

"Very good," Thaelyn ponders briefly trying to envision the scene. "And perhaps we could go one better. We do not know what sort of reaction they will have to us, so let us try to ease them into it. What if we offer some decoration, a bit like a disguise or camouflage, and the guards should all be dwarven. If they wake up in a setting surrounded by faces that are more likely to fit their expectations, they might hold a better response to us."

"Excellent, my Lord, we'll see to it."

"And we should also have the Med-tech take a close look at them to see how badly they might be suffering from these heavy metals."

"Of course."

Leesa had been surveying the scene outside and trying to locate her family. But in the confusion of the masses, with so many people calling out to each other, her efforts seemed futile. Then she recalled the trans-com she found in the Governor's desk in his office. She reached into her pocket to pull it out and studied it briefly before turning to find the tactical office to report in.

"Your Lordship?" she calls into the room.

"Leesa, yes, what do we have out there?"

"Well, out there is a mess, if you really must know. It's going to take a long time just to bring our families back together. Right now, I'm worried for my mom and dad, and my two brothers and sister. But that's another thing, so far. Instead, I found this…"

She sets the trans-com on the desk and pushes it across to him.

"I found this in the Governor's desk. I was up there looking through his window when the dwarves attacked, and this was in a drawer."

"Interesting," he mutters as he takes the item to study it. "I wonder why he did not take it with him."

"The drawer was open, like he was going to do something with it, but then he didn't."

"Very well, so be it, it is ours now, and this offers a curious little twist. I wonder if we could use this for ourselves, if only briefly for a little farewell chat," he grins.

"Oh buggers," Relissa moans. "And what kind of chat would you like to share with him?"

"I recall once I was hoping at some moment to share a word or two with that High Commander, if only to see if I could impress upon him the errors of his ways where this world is concerned. Not that it might actually achieve anything, but if to leave a mention somewhere within that artificially controlled mind of his, perhaps at some later moment, he might recall it."

"Aye, that's a good one."

"As for Darumon himself," he muses. "We suspect we know what he is up to, but perhaps if I play dumb and fish around, I wonder if I could invoke a hint of one kind or another that could provide us with something for later."

"Your Lordship," Padriyl submits. "If you have in mind to do this, I think you would need to find his base first. I doubt that unit would have the range to reach him from here, especially if he's pulling up all his outposts with their repeater stations."

"Very well, then we shall see if our gryphons are successful at locating him. Then, see if we can get a rune to the local area in time for our chat."

"What about the mine up north?" Marelle asks. "Are we going to do anything with it?"

"We will, assuming it is still there when we go check on it. I will regard this as a low priority thus far. We can check on it after they are gone from this world, and we have some freedom to ourselves."

"Jiggers, that's a fine one to think of," Relissa wonders. "Freedom, something I didn't ever think I'd see in this world. I was born in this war, and fully expected to die in it."

"While we might congratulate ourselves for a tender victory on this world, this war is not truly over until we find Sargeras. But for now, you are right. We will find our freedom, within reason, and we will use this to prepare ourselves for the next one."

Tristeen and Haran walked amongst the refugees outside the north gate of the settlement. They were eventually joined by Willit and Jared, as the group reassembled near the gate to assess the situation.

"Bloody hell, if ever I could see the day," Jared relents. "And this is where we stand now."

"Aye," Willit admits. "But we're alive. That's the good news. Not that being alive and homeless is any good, but His Lordship promises to help us rebuild."

"That's good to know, but it leaves a bitter taste in you. Everything we ever had, not that it was ever much, is gone now. Even for the nobles. What does that do to a person?"

"It levels the field, I guess," Tristeen replies thoughtfully. "Even though we managed to pack up a lot of things to bring with us, a lot had to be left behind. So, when speaking of a bitter taste, we all have to bite into it."

"Everyone except Haran," Willit smirks faintly as he passes his gaze around.

"I'm not any better than the rest," Haran reassures. "The only real difference with me is I left mine voluntarily. But I'm still starting over on Tae'Eladar."

"What about the rest of your family?"

"Marelle will have to start over, but she might have it a little better than some, if she stays with His Lordship. Our parents are both gone by now, taken by the Plague. Leesa and her family will have it hard, especially with three young children. But the school system they have on Tae'Eladar is excellent, so if they can enroll in that, or whatever they set up for us here, they should at least get a good education this time."

"By the way," Jared interjects. "What about the other students from the academy?"

"I met with them. Sara and Jon came to me over at the guildhall, much to my surprise at seeing their faces. Sara was all googly-eyed by the time she entered the study hall where I was working on my apprenticeship. I have no doubt she's got her mind set on something already, and I would imagine her brother will need to push himself hard to keep up with her."

"Aye!" Willit affirms jovially. "Those two always were inseparable in their class studies."

"It's good that they stick together," Tristeen admits. "They need each other, and especially during such times as these."

The group turns to pass through the gates into the settlement. They started moving in the direction of the village square where they hoped to find a café to sit and relax for a moment before considering their next move. Tristeen spots her parents and family friends already at a table, and leads the group to join them.

"Ah, Tristeen!" Josef calls. "Thank goodness you're alright. From what we were hearing during this time, and then to see all that outside there, we were frightfully worried for you. Are you well? You look fair enough, though I can see in your eyes the terror you must've been through."

"Yes, Dad," she responds wearily. "We're all doing fine, within reason. But you can be sure we went through at least six of the nine hells on our way out of there."

"Good gracious," he shakes his head morosely. "I heard about the bombardment. Egads, to think that any creature could treat another living soul with such manners."

"Worse! I saw him peeking out his window watching it like it was some sort of stage performance."

"You're kidding me!"

"That man," Abraim relents. "Or whatever we might call him."

"I would hardly call him a man," Seth retorts. "I think any man would hold better moral values than that."

"Well, whatever the case," Tristeen continues. "The whole Upper Ward is nothing more than a big hole in the ground now. We'll need to work hard just to bring ourselves back to even a modest position."

"Very well, Tristeen," Josef concedes. "We've been sitting here debating how we might go about this, but for now I think we will be very dependent on His Lordship's support until we can better organize ourselves. I believe he will wish to meet with us soon, once he has a proper moment, to discuss these issues in more detail."

"Good. By the way, while we're here, let me introduce you to a few of my friends from the academy. This is Willit Sarens and Jared Galwen," she gestures. "These are those two spies I mentioned once who would come home with their stories on occasion."

"Ah, very good. It would seem the three of you made a fine team working together for us up there."

"Thank you, Sire Macaid," Jared smiles. "But I think a lot of credit needs to go to Tristeen for her creativity and determination. She saved a lot of lives in all this."

"Aye," Willit affirms. "She's a clever one, and I think I know where she gets it. The only thing now is to see where she can take it from here, especially when you look outside the gate up there."

"Indeed," Josef agrees. "And surely, she is not the only one. We will all have our work ahead of us for the foreseeable future."

"I just hope we don't have any new surprises in the meantime," Jared offers. "It's not completely over until that monster leaves us fully alone."

"Right," Willit replies. "And then we have the cleanup, the rebuilding…I wonder how long this might actually take. How long does it take to rebuild a full city?"

"Gods above, Willit, I can't even imagine it."

"Well, I have my bets on Tristeen taking a big role somehow. You know how she was with all those group study sessions at the academy."

"Right to that! She made something of a name for herself in that regard. I wouldn't be surprised to see her as our new Governor one day."

"Maybe. I just hope she doesn't go and trod a bunch of dwarves with shoulder cannons through the streets."

The group shares a laugh together as they imagine the scene.

"But in truth," Willit continues. "She's got a level head and a cool temper…well, most of the time."

"Most of the time?" Josef inquires curiously.

"Well, yeah. She's great with keeping her details straight. But you don't want to go and try playing any word games with her. Right Jared?" he grins.

"Word games…" he muses.

"Aye. We sure wouldn't want to tell her folks about that occasion at the Ten Eagles when I was bringing in that initial report to recruit you into service."

"Oh! Yes, that. Absolutely! We surely wouldn't want to tell them how she stormed around the place spewing every curse word she could imagine for herself all across the lower district. Nope, never that…"

The two of them sat back and beamed while Tristeen glared at them over the obvious revue.

"Ahem!" she blasts emphatically. "Are the two of you quite finished?"

The group shared another laugh while Tristeen continued.

"I swear…but then that's what friends are for, I guess."

"Swearing?" Margo ushers amusedly.

"No, Mom…although I'll admit, I did let myself go on that occasion, and for good reason. But I mean sharing moments like this. No amount of tea parties can replace some of the experiences I've had with my friends."

"Very well, Dear, I suppose I can't argue with you, as you clearly did develop some fine relations. I just wish one of them might lead to a future for you."

"Yeah, um, this actually brings me to…um…him," she coughs and thumbs at Haran.

"Uh oh," Jared mumbles. "I think I know what's coming next."

"Aye," Willit agrees. "I wonder if the dust has settled up in the city yet, because it's just about to be raised here."

"You're not helping!" Tristeen chides playfully. "Mom, Dad, this is Haran Carronel, another friend of mine from the academy."

"Indeed," Margo leans forward. "And why is it you're introducing him independently, and these other two appear like they're ready to leap out of their seats and run off?"

"I think I have an idea," Josef suggests. "Might this be the one you mentioned who got into the argument with the Dean, and then expelled?"

"Yes, he is," Tristeen responds.

"Josef?" Margo wonders. "Do you know about him?"

"She mentioned this mostly in passing, but my impression is she holds a special interest."

"I see, and therefore the insinuations," she grins. "Well, of course, I simply cannot allow this to pass without a proper evaluation. After all, if my little girl has any manner of interest in a gentleman caller, it must pass my approval."

"Oh great," Tristeen grumbles. "Here it comes."

Margo gets out of her chair and circles around the table to make an inspection. Haran feels an instinctive compulsion to stand up and present himself.

"Just go gently for my appearance," he mentions. "After all, we did just come out of a disaster zone with the city."

"Very well, so be it. Tristeen, dear…"

Now Tristeen stands up next to him.

"Hmm…" Margo pauses to study them together. "So, Tristeen," she follows with her highbrow decorum. "Does he come from a noble family? Does he carry any sort of station?"

"Oh come now…" the girl retorts softly. "No, he doesn't. He's from the lower district, originally."

"Very well, but then does he hold any manner of esteemed title?"

"Not yet, but maybe…one day…perhaps?"

"I see. Might he bear any wealth or fame?"

"Wealth…from the lower district?" she coughs emphatically. "Fame…well, he got into a furious argument with the Dean once. That sort of became famous, at least inside the academy."

"Really! How interesting," she grins.

Margo briefly casts her eyes to meet with her husband before returning to the couple.

"Do you love him?" she finishes with a gentle smile.

"Yes, Mom, I do."

"Um…" Haran gestures with a finger. "Do I have any sort of potential to speak in this matter?"

"Certainly," Margo affirms pleasantly. "What do you have to say for yourself, Mister Carronel?"

"Well, as far as wealth goes, I basically had to abandon everything I owned in the city while trying to escape from the Dean's wrath, not that I had that much to begin with. But then again, when looking at this mess outside here," he thumbs towards the gate. "I think most of the city is like that now. So, even if I did have something, it's all dust and ashes by now."

"Yes, of course, you are right, so I must rescind that portion."

"But this doesn't necessarily deny me from accumulating more, if I work hard enough."

"Naturally."

"Title, fame, status… On Tae'Eladar, these things can be earned as much as inherited, and they actually hold a higher regard if to demonstrate your worth to society for your deeds. And I do hope to achieve some portion of this during my studies."

"Oh? And how would this apply?"

"I hold a strong interest in continuing my mage studies, and the courses they have over there are fabulous. For them, magic is as much a part of their local culture as any other craft or art form. It represents a major industry, and everybody learns it. But this also demands careful regulation and licensing. If one were to carry this to its upper levels of study, they could become a scholar in their universities, a researcher in their laboratories, and even a legislator in their government to present new policies and licensing practices. So, the prestige of simply holding that position is automatically regarded very highly."

"Really!" she muses. "That's actually very interesting. Then I would regard this as a fair alternative. But I will require you to fulfill some portion of this before you take my daughter's hand. After all, I want to make sure she is well taken care of," she grins brightly.

"Oh, absolutely," he smiles.

⁘

"So, this is how it looks now," Marelle mourns. "All our work, all our suffering, and although I understand the reasons, this is where it brings us."

"Yes," the General affirms solemnly. "These photos just came in from some of our scouts still circling over the city. We had them take these to show us the progression of the dwarves, and then the aftermath. We feel the need to record this as an important moment in our history."

"Yours or ours? Technically, you're from another world."

"Well, yes, of course, but our policies demand us to record our actions here, as it might prove valuable for future generations. It is still a moment of history, regardless of who it belongs to or who actually records it."

"Right, naturally, I understand. I just don't care much for it being my history, and I'm still living through it. That's my life under that heap of dust."

"I know, Marelle, and it pains me just as much to see this when I think of all those people outside."

"I need to find my Captain and talk to him about this. As a member of the Guard, I have to ask myself what's left for me when our city is wiped off the map. I don't have a home, no place of work, and other than for Haran and my aunt and her family, I'm basically alone now."

"Marelle," Thaelyn asserts. "You should know that we will stand by you. No doubt, your full generation will feel the impact of this moment, and all those leading up to it. And it will likely carry for a long time. However, the battle is not won until we defeat Sargeras, and you may still play a role in that."

"Aye, Marelle," Relissa affirms as she reaches out to pat her friend on the shoulder. "I'm with you, and you know the rest are with you as well. Besides, um…" she coughs gently as a reminder. "You told me once about that, um, thing that was on your mind. If it's still bouncing between your ears, now would be a fine time to think about it again."

"Thing…" she mulls briefly. "Yeah, that's right, but wow," she sighs. "That seems like a while ago now, and then we got so busy chasing down all these conspiracies. But you know, you're actually right. We got a lot of work done together, more than anyone ever did up in the city, and it felt good. And then to think of all the things we learned along the way, it was so exhilarating."

"Aye, and that's the part that bamboozles me the most. I always hated my old schooling."

"If it weren't for Haran and some of his stories from his spy runs, I would probably be like most everyone else, not knowing hardly anything of what's going on around us. I might even behave more like my Aunt Tania for her attitudes."

Marelle leans back to consider her feelings. She then excuses herself from the meeting and goes outside, where she strolls up to the gate to peer out into the fields at the huddled masses. There she sees Leesa again, in conversation with several people about the situation, and elsewhere she sees several guardsmen on horseback, including Captain Kholgard. She rushes out to catch his attention.

"Roddy!" she shouts.

He turns to the address to see her running up to him from the settlement.

"Yes, Marelle?"

"Can you come down here a moment, we need to talk."

"What about?" he asks as he bends low in his saddle.

"Roddy, this is personal."

The Captain knew that when she started addressing him by his first name, this was special. So, he glanced discreetly around the area one last time before dismounting and approaching her for a private discussion.

"All right, Marelle, what's on your mind?"

"They were showing off a series of pictures they were recording of the city up there from those gryphons."

"Oh? How does it look?"

"Like a complete wreck. I've never seen what a real warzone looks like, but this would pass for the worst kind."

"Great," he sighs. "Well, you know what His Lordship promised, right?"

"Right, and they're all telling me to stay strong, that we'll get through this."

"Good, so what's troubling you?"

"Roddy, I'm feeling a little confused and bothered. My home, my life, everything I had up there…what we all had, is basically a pile of splinters and broken rock. It was bad enough to be told we might need to let it go, if only to get that demon out of that building and away from us. But to actually see it in these photos really hits home."

"I think I know your meaning. I was inside there trying to round up the last few neighborhoods and dodging half of it as it was coming down around me. My home is buried somewhere in that heap as well, Marelle."

"I know, but where does that leave us…you, me, everyone else? So what if we rebuild the city. My home, as it used to be, is gone, along with everything I own, probably. And, so what if I get a new house built for me, as I'll be starting out fresh regardless."

"All right, but what is it you're actually trying to suggest here?"

"Roddy, when we finally had a chance to do some real work, it felt good. We were solving problems, helping people, and making a difference. And it was all because of His Lordship. He led us through it, and supported us with the means to get it done. Compare that to anything we had before this."

"What we had before this was what caused it in the first place," he chuckles.

"Well, yes, it was. But with or without the Governor letting us out long enough to actually do any work, we weren't doing any actual work. Look at the Night Elves. They didn't have the Governor hovering over them, and still, they couldn't get any appreciable work done. Four hundred years, Roddy. We might have had it bad, but they at least remembered their history, and held some amount of purpose. And yet, they were still stifled. And technically, we're not even done, not while Sargeras is still out there."

"All right."

"According to Relissa, she's told me they're making all sorts of plans for redeveloping Solinaia according to Tae'Eladaran standards. And I know what this means because I've seen Tae'Eladar and what they have over there. Now we need to essentially rebuild Rolsklinde from scratch. So, why not simply do the same?"

"The same...meaning to say you think we should join up, like they did? Marelle, I wouldn't be opposed to it, but I'm just an old soldier. I don't really have that level of authority."

"I doubt anyone has that level of authority by now. But at the same time, being in the service of His Lordship, even as an agent working for the Guard..." she sighs deeply and glances around the area.

The Captain studies her and recognizes this mood, as he would sometimes see it in her office.

"You know, Marelle, you were never really happy in your old service. I know this, but it's all we had to offer. Then we have these reports you filed for all these recent investigations and running around, and you sounded like a schoolkid with a new toy. Now look at you... You look like the candles on your birthday cake are all burned out. Maybe you'd like to go work for him instead?"

"Roddy, the idea has gone around inside my head several times already, but I always felt like I had so much work to do for our side."

"Yeah, but our side is a big pile of rubble now."

"Right, and our work still isn't done. But now, it's going to take us to other worlds, I think."

"I can barely even imagine what that means."

"Same here, but one thing I know is I want to be a part of it, and I also think I know how, but it scares me a little to leave you in that office alone."

"Should I remind you my office is also a big pile of rubble?" he smirks.

She grins and slaps him on the shoulder.

"When they build you a new one, silly!" she retorts. "We won't be able to see each other as much."

He smiles softly at her minor outburst, and glances around the gathering to see if anyone was paying any special attention.

"Marelle, unless they send you off to that new world alone, and you lose your way back, I think we can work with it."

✦✦✦✦✦

The day was progressing to late afternoon. Volunteers were moving amongst the refugees, arranging them into groups around large campfires, and passing out blankets. The crying and moaning had settled somewhat, and a series of makeshift kitchens had been assembled, with several wagons full of food arriving to prepare an evening meal.

In the tactical office, the General was reviewing a series of reports that were arriving at intervals from the gryphon scouts following the Suuden-Aryku retreat.

"My Lord," he declares. "We're getting some word back from a few of our forward gryphons. They have to make runs out and back again into the range of their trans-coms, but at least they're making some progress."

"Good, General. What do they have to report?"

"The Suuden-Aryku have been pulling back in a generally south to southeast direction, a long line of them. It would appear, from the volume, that they must have been uprooting a fair number of outposts, and not only those we were aware of on the front lines."

"They must have had a lot of supplementary stations. I wonder why, if their only purpose here was to harass the Daanen-Aryku and oppress the others. They could have done this with fewer troops. Perhaps these were supply stations, or could they be for some other purpose?"

"By the reports I'm receiving here, I doubt this could be a simple series of supply stations. These appear too heavily laden, with many large vehicles and a sizable amount of equipment and troops. The composition reminds me more of a convoy, like what you would see of a large-scale troop movement, along with their gear, perhaps from a series of training exercises into mock battlefields."

"Interesting, like what we might use for the Cormyr training fields. Then, could we be speaking of training exercises and staging posts? But again, for what reason? Not for the locals. It would need to be in preparation for something else, and the only thing that comes to my mind would be a future engagement against their greater foes, that revenge aspect again."

"Perhaps, but to use such as this against the Estelar? Surely, any mortal race used as a weapon against such as they would be inadequate, would it not?"

"Ultimately it would, unless you are using it as a distraction, and based on how Darumon has been behaving of late, this is surely a possibility."

"So, he would spend even his Suuden-Aryku troops on some folly. His ire against the Estelar must be great if to spend everything he has acquired in this time against them."

"If it drives him to such extremes to make any effort at all of returning, I might further suggest he would stop at almost nothing to accomplish his goal. And this means any race he uses along the way is expendable in the end."

"He can always find more, I suppose," the General shakes his head morosely. "But anyway, we have a report here, finally. One of our scouts has spotted a large installation on the horizon, and this convoy seems to be making straight for it."

"Good, but it is still bittersweet. Have them approach it very carefully. Keep at a distance and find a landing site to mark a rune."

"Yes, my Lord."

"With this many troops and firepower in the area, it would be nigh impossible to launch against a target like that. And even if we did, I find it highly unlikely they would permit us to take it before destroying it. Darumon could employ another atomic, or perhaps if they have another reactor onsite, he could use that instead, and we might have no other choice but to withdraw."

"Then what can we do, except to allow him to leave. What comes after that?"

"This is a question I have been pondering for a while now. One thought that comes to mind is I want to pursue him on our terms, not his, and to simply follow him through his own conveyor would be inappropriate. We would likely come out right in the center of a military camp on his side."

"Buggers!" Relissa yips. "That wouldn't be much fun."

"Indeed, and not simply for the trouble we would find on our arrival. Rather, I would wish to make a quiet incursion, not only to surprise him in his lair, but also in the hopes of preserving innocent lives on their side."

"Aye, I'm with you, if such a thing is actually possible."

"But the paradox is we cannot know where or how to find Azgarén. My understanding of the Naarg uy'Sodrad is the navigation systems were damaged during the sabotage event, right Lieutenant?"

"Yes," Padriyl replies. "And the ship is in a completely inoperable condition, other than as a shelter for us on the ground."

"Then we are locked here unless something special comes our way. Hmm..."

Thaelyn leans back in his chair to ponder his options.

"We have those orcs on Ruuki uy'Daan, and Kaliya might provide us with a curious potential to correct that. This could allow us access if we can work it in our favor. But it still locks us, if only to that one additional world."

"We also need to think about those dwarves," Relissa offers. "How do you think we can help them, or can we, if we don't know where they're coming from?"

"It is another paradox, but once we are able to procure those dwarves in the city... General, what is the situation up there? Have they settled any more by now?"

"Let me check with our scouts," he replies, and then turns to a row of operators handling the trans-coms.

"But anyway," Thaelyn continues. "From Ruuki uy'Daan, we may also be locked. But if we could somehow find access to that world of dwarves, there may be a possibility. I would imagine the Suuden-Aryku ought to have a facility on that world if they have such a need for adamantium and are so capable of drawing out mining crews. A resident outpost would be almost mandatory under those conditions."

"Aye," Relissa nods. "Sounds fair enough, but how do we find it, that's the part we need the most."

"Sehnisavain mentioned something about orcs being used once to invade that world. I wonder..."

Relissa and the others at the table study him as a thought arrives, and he suddenly frowns in contemplation.

"Portals..." he mumbles distantly. "Could it be?"

"Portals, my Lord?" the General inquires gently.

"...And then the elves. But wait, Sehnisavain said something about the Suuden-Aryku coming to take large numbers of them away somewhere."

"Yes, I recall this now, using their transport vessels."

"But are we speaking of delivering them directly to that world, or is it another covert maneuver. They used portals to invade Tae'Eladar, and covert moves everywhere else."

"If we say he is trying to hide his actions, perhaps from any profoundly overt displays in front of the Estelar, and if this universe has the flows, then it stands to reason there ought to be some here. Therefore, to use portals as an indirect means might be preferable."

"Yes! But this still does not follow logically. If he wants to use the elves as an invasion force, why not simply give them the same portal teachings as he did the orcs."

"Maybe he's trying to keep them under better management," Relissa offers. "He spent a lot of them here, and more over there with no word on the result. Now he's down to the last. He used orcs with portals to go to Tae'Eladar, and apparently elves to follow behind them on that mission. What that says to me, although not nicely, is the orcs are expendable, but the elves are not."

"Indeed, and this is also evident if you consider that evacuation they were planning in Kynesoth."

"Of course," the General asserts. "So, he sends a measured number of them at the dwarves, but he wishes to keep the rest under control."

"This is an interesting perspective," Thaelyn admits. "And perhaps you have a point. We might also say the orcs on Ruuki uy'Daan are using portals to arrive here, so they already have the means to use them, therefore, the elves do not require this. Here is where we need to ask why, however. He sent orcs at one time, but I seriously doubt orcs would pose much of a threat to dwarves. They are a stout folk, and very sturdy in battle, especially if you equip them with the proper accessories."

"Perhaps as a test, either to test their portal magic, or to test the dwarves for their nature against a known enemy force."

"Or both, maybe?" he muses. "And then, once they have their results, they know better how to use it with their later targets. For instance, this world, once it was put into service."

"And then, later, they came back with the elves," Relissa suggests. "But if he didn't teach them portal magic, and instead took them up in their transports, um, maybe they went to those same orcs with their portals since they already have it by now. And here's your covert move."

"Yes, this makes good sense. Here we have a potential means. But as the General said, it was a measured amount. We must be speaking of a full world here, and any sort of measured amount would not serve to conquer all that. So, it had to be a localized event, maybe to establish a foothold. But it still does not follow politely, as elves versus dwarves would not make a good match hand-to-hand, especially if you factor in the adamantium they no doubt must have over there."

"Right, but what then? They supposedly got it anyway."

"Could it be a limited occupation?" Padriyl wonders. "Maybe a remote or difficult to reach location they could easily defend?"

"While this is a fine suggestion," Thaelyn surmises. "I am dreading the prospects, no matter the means. Just look at this world for your answer. They used lies, deception, and other distractions to delude the people into thinking their woes were completely unrelated. Could it be this was just a distraction to turn their eyes long enough for some other covert move?"

"Buggers!" Relissa scorns softly. "So, they use elves that probably can't stand up to a proper fight against peeps with better goods. The only thing left is how the Suuden-Aryku finally took it."

"If he applied such methods as what we saw here, he might have simplified his efforts, and then placed the rest under management. Powers help us, what might we find if we should ever reach it?"

"Aye, it won't be a pretty sight."

"The only question to ask now is if those orcs still recall the methods used to find it in the first place. If they maintained any records, or whatever it was they used back then, this could provide us with our link."

"Aye, and this could give us another step to follow, with a Suuden'kai base at the end. But it's a big 'if', my Lord."

"Indeed it is, but it might be the only 'if' we have at this point. We may need to depend on luck again, and this is so very problematic."

A member of the communications team was handing a report back to the General on the scouts and their observations. He reads it a moment before drawing the attention.

"My Lord," he begins. "The scouts are reporting a slowing effect up there. Many of the dwarves have set down their weapons by now, likely due to weariness, or perhaps boredom, assuming you can feel such a thing while under the effect of that drug. Some have sat down with apparently nothing else to do, while others are still walking in slow circles."

"All right, we need to take action, as it does not seem to be improving much beyond this point. Call for a rough head count of our quarry, and then prepare at least double that number of troops to manhandle those dwarves and restrain them. We need to ensure we disarm them and hold them firm until we can properly remove them. We will have mages cast invisibility cloaks on the full assembly and sneak up on them, and then have our gryphon scouts send a signal for a mass charge to take everything at once."

"Jiggers!" Relissa winces. "That would be a bugaboo of a surprise attack."

"It may be our best option to ensure our own safety against any further use of those weapons. Then we will restrain them with shackles and prepare them for transport. And General, send word to rush that holding pen."

"Yes, my Lord," he replies.

Several hundred miles away, in the Suuden-Aryku command base, High Commander Geilv and his officers oversaw the evacuation process, where the troops and their vehicles were busy loading up on supercarriers which were designed to transport large masses to and from the field through the nether-space conveyor.

The headquarters facility was the regional staging point for their military advance, used as a forward position on their move to seek out their final goal. It consisted of tactical and command buildings, a barracks and mess hall, a communications center, munitions and vehicle stockyards, and maintenance facilities.

The conveyor, which was the most prominent feature of the base, was a large, fixed installation consisting of a raised platform with four tall, arced spires arranged in an oblique cross configuration. The spires each projected powerful focus beams at a central point above the platform, creating a dimensional rift aperture. The facility was further surrounded by a containment field maintained as a shell around the platform to keep the rift from expanding uncontrollably. A control building and an independent reactor were located off to the side to maintain the field and the conduit within the rift.

The massive withdrawal of the Suuden'kai forces from around

the region had collected near the base, creating a morass of vehicles and personnel flooding the area. These were being systematically loaded up on the supercarriers, which would lift off, circle around, and then pass through the rift.

High above and on approach were several of Thaelyn's gryphon scouts entering the region. Although they were at altitude and still at distance, the base scanners picked them up and sounded an alert to the operator.

"Sir, I am picking up inbound objects," the officer reports.

"What kind?" the Commander responds in his flat monotone.

"I am unable to determine a clear signature or other characteristic of the objects. But our scans indicate they entered the region at supersonic velocity. They are travelling at only moderate altitude and appear to be following our retreating forces."

"Likely, they are scouts. Scan for their composition."

"Yes, Sir."

The officer configures a new scan to determine the structural composition of the inbound bodies. In a moment, a result displays on the monitor.

"Sir, this is very strange. They do not match any recognizable form of powered vessel. They appear to be surrounded in a spatial envelope of abnormal energy, and my scans indicate something of a biological nature inside."

"Understood. We have seen these before. They come from the intruders' outpost. We do not understand how they are able to travel in this manner, but they are apparently a form of flying animal the intruders employ as a mount."

"A flying animal that can travel supersonic?"

"It uses their abnormal practice. Our science does not understand this method."

"As you say, Sir, but do we know if they are dangerous?"

"We have observed them on several occasions from orbit as they enter and leave the outpost. They appear to be used mostly for surveillance, not for attack."

"Understood, so how should we respond to this?"

The Commander mulls the idea a moment as he studies the scope.

"Our orders are not to engage the intruders, or else we may invoke our greater foes. If these are only scouts, they are likely here to ensure we are evacuating this planet. We will not engage unless they attack first."

"Yes, Sir."

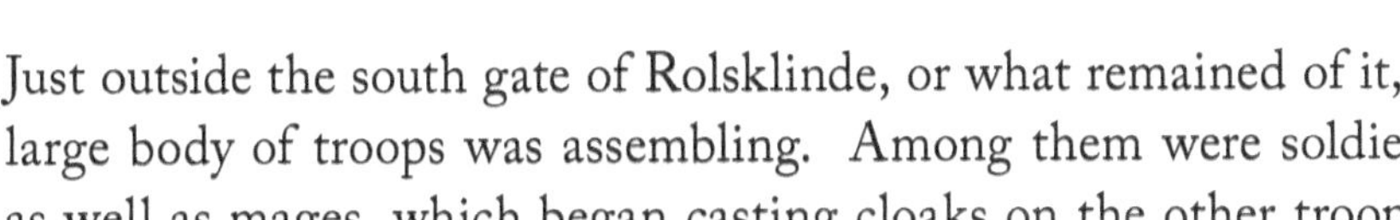

Just outside the south gate of Rolsklinde, or what remained of it, a large body of troops was assembling. Among them were soldiers as well as mages, which began casting cloaks on the other troops. The mass slowly vanished from sight, and then the invisible army snuck into the city and along the roadways to seek out their dwarven opponents.

The gryphon scouts circled overhead, offering directions to locate the clusters of dwarves scattered around the city. The hidden soldiers took up positions near each of them, ready for a signal from above to invoke the full assembly to lurch forward at once, thus disallowing any individual dwarf from reacting to any others being attacked. Once they were in position, the gryphon riders gave their signal with a bold flash of light erupting from their hands. In rapid succession, the troops jumped at their dwarven adversaries, grabbing them as they exited their cloaking auras and wrestling them to the ground.

The dwarves never knew what hit them, and not simply for the mind-dulling effect of the drug. Not one sound or harsh word came out of them on their way down, and they offered virtually no resistance other than to try returning to an upright posture, as if to continue moving around as they were before this. Their hands and feet were shackled as mages swarmed around the area, preparing to transport them away. They removed their armor, confiscated their weapons, and sent them to the Bahlaie Research Center for study. The dwarves, now reduced to their common work clothes, were then relocated to Tae'Eladar and detained within a temporary enclosure, pending the completion of the holding pen.

Now it was simply a case of wait-and-see, wondering what would happen if they should wake up from their stupor, and then what sort of reaction they might have to their predicament.

⊹ ◆ ⊹

A page from outside had just finished delivering some items to the General. He made a quick review and was now ready to make a report to the officers at the table. By this time, Marelle had returned, and sat quietly as she contemplated her earlier discussion with her Captain.

"My Lord," the General declares. "We have word from one of our scouts out near the Suuden-Aryku command base."

"I hope we have some good news on this occasion," he responds. "What is it?"

"He does report something favorable. He says he found a nook where his team came down behind a knoll covered in a layer of foliage. They apparently flew in very low to the ground for cover and came down not far from the base, within easy sighting range."

"Excellent. Can they tell what is out there?"

"So far, he reports a lot of vehicles, people, a fairly large arrangement of structures, and he sent in one of their trans-coms with some images included, along with a rune to his location."

The General brings around a trans-com and a rune received along with the note. They studied the images together, which included the base, the structures, the vehicles, and the people.

"This here, Your Lordship," Padriyl points to one of the images. "This would be the conveyor I spoke of. And these vessels here look like they're custom made to move large volumes of materials in bulk."

"So it would seem," Thaelyn nods. "They appear to be nicely outfitted to conduct their military operations on foreign worlds. Then, we could suggest we are right, and this was an effort at some kind of large-scale operation, like training or a staging post for something big."

"I might have to agree, which only makes matters worse on our side, as we were not the primary focus, but just a side attraction along the way. And now they're loading up and going home."

"And we can't follow," Marelle moans.

"Not on this occasion," Thaelyn notes. "But we will not let this stop us. We will find another way. For now..." he picks up the rune and studies it. "I think a fond farewell is in order."

"Um, I'm still wondering what sort of...farewell...you have in mind."

"I have a few thoughts, but I will likely need to improvise in the hopes of nudging loose some small detail or another. Much of what we know about him still seems a little superficial. We are guessing his plan is for the Estelar, but this is based mostly on circumstance. I wonder if he actually has anything to say for himself."

"Well, just make sure he doesn't say it with his atomics," she chuckles.

"Thank you, Marelle, for your kind consideration," he returns with a smile.

Thaelyn picks up the trans-com from the Governor's office, which was sitting on the table next to him. Between this and the rune, he makes one last review of the people in the room.

"General, although we might suggest Darumon is feeling restraint from my earlier threat with the Estelar, we should consider if he still holds any final intentions. I will flash you if I feel anything of great importance, but the most immediate would be an evacuation of these people out of the local area. Send them to Tae'Eladar, if you can, but if he should wish to use any more bombardment, we must prepare ourselves to move quickly."

"Yes, my Lord, although I surely hope he doesn't make any more surprises."

"I think at this moment, he would wish more to preserve himself. By this time, he ought to feel the pressure after what he did to Rolsklinde. If he did not make any moves on the others due to my threats, he should surely expect something for this by now."

"Do you think he would still be around?" Marelle asks. "Maybe he's already gone."

"This is a good question. But there is only one way to find out. General, I need a mage to handle this rune."

"Yes, my Lord."

The General calls in a mage to take the rune, and Thaelyn leads them outside, where the mage enchants the item for Thaelyn to make his journey.

He arrives nestled within a small cluster of tall shrubs on a gentle hillside. Nearby was a pair of scouts and their gryphon. The scouts involved a human and an Avariel, but unlike Aerlie, this one's wings were a pale gray mottled with dark spots.

"My Lord!" calls the first scout in a hushed voice. "What a pleasant surprise. As you can see there, we have their base in sight. We've been watching them for a bit now, and they just keep picking up more of their men and machines onto those big birds and taking them through the gate."

"Indeed, and so very efficient," he admits. "Have you seen any of them depart the area travelling elsewhere?"

"No, my Lord, they all seem quite set on going through that portal."

"What I'm wondering is why we have so many of them out there," the Avariel scout mentions. "I can see plenty of soldiers, but some look more like utility or support."

"We were discussing this back at the base," Thaelyn offers. "And our thoughts suggest this might be a training or staging post operation, possibly to prepare for some future campaign."

"That would make good sense to me. From what I'm looking at, they have enough to build a small town down there."

"So, what's next on the list today?" the first scout asks.

"The only thing remaining for us at this time is to say our goodbyes. I have this here..." he pulls out the trans-com, "...which came to us from the Governor's desk in the city."

"So, that one belongs to him, does it? That's a fine one. But I don't know if I'd want to be the one making the call," he chuckles.

"Indeed, but I wish to see if I can draw out a few final words from him. Nevertheless, depending on their reaction, I want you to make yourselves ready if we should have a sudden need to vacate the area."

"Aye!"

Thaelyn examines the alien communicator and begins stepping through the menu system to review a dialing directory and call history. Only one number was listed.

"I think I would also like to record this, at least as much for posterity, as well as perhaps a later review."

He switches to another menu and engages the recording mode before dialing the number. He took a deep breath to compose himself and waited. In a moment, a flat monotone voice answered.

"Commander Geilv, speaking…"

"Ah…" Thaelyn begins jovially. "So, here we have the famous High Commander Geilv of the Suuden-Aryku military. Such a pleasure to make this occasion."

"Famous?" he responds curiously. "Who is this?"

"I am your humble opponent in this game, although much to my disappointment, I have heard references describing me as little more than an inconvenience to your operations."

"You are Thaelyn?"

"So, you actually do know my name. Very well, I will take this as a minor consolation. For a while, I thought you had no actual interest in me."

"We had an interest in you since we first detected your arrival."

"You did not seem much in the way of demonstrating it, not even after we began laying into your compatriots, the orcs."

"Our orders were to hold back in order to study your methods."

"I see, and this would be a very wise strategy…from a tactical perspective. After all, I am an unknown, as undesirable as I may have been. And considering who I actually am, as I am fairly certain you must have been informed by now, it would do you well to maintain that position."

"How are you able to link to this station?"

"The Governor of Rolsklinde left in such a hurry that he seems to have forgotten his trans-com device. We found it."

"You were in the city? I do not understand. The city should be destroyed by now."

"Oh, it is, I can assure you of that. Those dwarves you sent did a fine job of it. I have photos to prove it."

"That is not what I mean. What I mean is…"

"What you mean is probably the reactor in the Governor's basement. Yes, that would have represented a problem, had my spies not informed me of it so we could go in and shut it down. Thank you for your concern, Commander, but yours is not the only society in this world with enough cognitive capacity to understand such things."

"You discovered it, but our indicators here monitored a severe overload, nearly to a critical capacity."

"That was the plan of one of my operatives, to allow it to appear that way in order to convince you to keep your distance from us. We shut it down just in time before it actually went critical."

"You are very clever."

"I am attempting to save lives here, Commander. Clever is not the only thing I am, as I am also rather upset. Would you like to know my reasoning?"

"Your reasoning is likely due to the suggestion you just made."

"Very good, but it goes much deeper than that. Commander, with whatever proper respect is due to your military rank, I regard you as a monster. This world, as it was described to me, was fully populated and apparently at peace with itself, at least until you arrived. Now look at it. Most of that population is in ruins, and what remains is a shambles. And for what reason, Commander, can you tell me?"

"They were described as being associated with our opponents and needed to be contained as we move forward in the service of our benefactor."

"Such a fascinating definition… Listen to yourself a moment. Your benefactor; let us first examine that statement. You are a society representing itself as a rather highly adept and scientifically advanced variety. To describe anything as a benefactor to you would automatically suggest it to be of a higher form in order to offer any benefit. Might this be a reasonable suggestion, Commander?"

"Yes."

"And who are these people here? Are they so high, in and of themselves, that they could be described as any manner of proper opponent to such as your society, to say nothing of that which might be even higher? They are not a technologically advanced society. They do not hold any space travel technologies, and likely knew nothing of any world or society outside their own. To describe them as an opponent to anything other than their own kind is therefore preposterous, as not only could they not reach you, but they could not oppose you with their inferior technology. Would this definition also hold merit to your mind, Commander?"

"It would, but this is not how they were defined. They were defined as holding association to another opponent of a higher form and needed containment."

"I understand, but where is this opponent of a higher form? Is it found on this world, perhaps?"

"We do not see evidence of it occupying this world."

"Then why would you even bother with such an inferior form as this if your true opponents are not to be found here. Based on what I am seeing out here, you brought with you a lot of people simply to contain the few remains of an inferior society. This looks more like you had something else in mind. Very well, but why bring it here if you only needed space for a staging operation? Surely, you could find some other world for that, preferably one that was unoccupied, could you not? Instead, you came to this one, robbing it away from its owners and leaving mass death and destruction in your wake."

The link is silent as the Commander does not have an immediate answer.

Inside the command base, Commander Geilv stood stoically near the com-station while he listened to the exchange. The other officers in the room also listened, and several of them were now looking at him to see his response. Although he was clearly under the influence of a potent control effect, he stared at the com-station unflinchingly until a sudden tick formed at the corner of his mouth.

"Commander," Thaelyn continues assertively. "You do not necessarily need to answer this question, as I already know you and your people are under some form of influence. Our victories outside the Naarg uy'Sodrad allowed the medical teams of the Daanen-Aryku to examine a few bodies and conduct autopsies, hoping to understand how and why you hold this odd appearance you have now."

"They do not know?"

"Velen's people? Why? Should they know? It is my understanding they fled shortly after the arrival of Sargeras to your home world. After that, you apparently hunted them like animals across many worlds, and finally to this one. Previously, before these studies, they regarded you as mutated cold-blooded killers. I have even heard a few to use such words as fiends and demons."

"Fiends and demons?" the Commander emits softly.

"Even worse, I have heard some of their leadership say how they regard their once fine civilization to be in ruins based on your representation, all due to your devotion to this benefactor of yours."

"Oh no..." he moans quietly, and with another tick flinching across his cheek.

"And so, they ran, trying to escape from you. But you came after them, persistently and relentlessly."

"They were described as having taken sides against us."

"Against you, or that benefactor of yours? We should probably clarify this point, especially if they see you as the monsters by now... because of him."

"Yes, I see your point."

"But as the result of these studies, we have come to understand you have, among other things, an artificial, perhaps even a parasitic lifeform you impose upon yourselves, which they describe as a biotech seed, correct?"

"Yes, we call it the An'gamu Seed."

"And they describe this seed, which they say was once part of some ancient research project no one appreciated, as providing some function or capacity that might not normally be inherent to your species, correct?"

"Yes, it is intended to provide us with increased survivability in hostile environments."

"Interesting. This might provide us with an answer to our test on your false front line."

"False front line? You knew it was false?"

"Well, it was certainly a reasonable expectation, if you were to heed any part of my warning. I expected the one you call Marshal Darumon to play some manner of backhanded trick on me. This seems to be his style in this world."

"You know of him?"

"I heard the name secondhand from some of my spies trying to understand why you do not seem to be the one in control around here. According to Velen's people, the position of the High Commander should be second only to your native government authority. But here you are taking orders from someone else, and seemingly not even a native resident. Even worse, your actions relating to my arrival do not follow properly for a military commander who might not otherwise desire me to be here. Then I learn of him, and that he seems to be related to this Sargeras of yours."

"Yes, he is the one who leads us in his campaign. But if you do not know of him personally..."

"I did not know of any of you before your orcs invaded my home and drew my attention to places outside my immediate view. Nevertheless, relating to that false front of yours, my play, which was designed to be non-lethal, was simply to test your reactions, to see if you would make your own advance. You did not, which means you were in a standby condition, and a rather strict one at that, waiting for something else to occur. And as we saw, it involved that city up there."

"Under the circumstances, I must admit you are correct."

"We also found you have one or more artificial implants within your neural tissues, and in such locations as they might interfere with, or otherwise influence, your cognitive functions, correct?"

The Commander stalls his reply, but soon provides his answer.

"I suppose I must admit to this as well. There are two primary implants. One of these is to provide a solution to a medical concern, and it inhibits emotional output as a collateral effect. The other is a military grade implant to..." he stalls briefly, "...to govern our compliance."

"A medical implant. I believe these were being found in each of those bodies. Is this something affecting a greater population back home?"

"Yes, it became a Council mandate for our full population as a precautionary procedure."

"I see, and this is unfortunate. And so, I suppose the mention of the emotion dampening effect might account for the lack of compassion you demonstrated on so many occasions. But on the other hand, if speaking of Velen's people, we might also ask ourselves if they ever once demonstrated such extraordinary military potential as to warrant this long chase or your continued assaults. However, for this I might suggest this other device, as this one might actually offer a clue. Commander, did you just now listen to your own words? To govern your compliance... This is to say, you are given an order, and you must comply, regardless of what that order might suggest. Now, let us associate this with these actions, maybe also your earlier statement. You hunt people who apparently never fight back. You assault worlds of inferior societies and fleeing refugees, hitting them repeatedly, and then pursuing them to their next destination."

"But..."

"One moment, Commander. Whatever excuse you have is not likely sufficient for the crimes committed. Then we find ourselves here. Relating to this world, how would you describe your actions here in a world that does not directly hold your opponents, and where your efforts to contain an otherwise technologically inferior society, with virtually no capacity to oppose you anywhere except on this world, has resulted in the near extinction of their kind. Further would be Velen and his people, who could not even come outside to smell the fresh air without you shooting at them. This goes beyond containment. This is criminal harassment."

The Commander again stood silently with the ticking still occurring in his face, but this time becoming stronger.

"And even further," Thaelyn asserts. "If you now include your statement of them turning against you. Oh yes! I would do the same if someone like you behaved this way."

"Yes, I would agree…" he grunts through another hard tick on his cheek.

"It is therefore well within reason, Commander," Thaelyn concludes. "That you and yours are best described as monsters for your actions, regardless of whatever purpose you may serve to this benefactor. Be warned, for there are other societies of a very high level of esteem that take great offence to this manner of conduct, and you have just angered one. We are a society of laws, and those laws carry weight. The next time you go out and destroy a world, you might find yourselves receiving the same in kind. Do you understand, Commander?"

"I understand, and I also recognize your complaint. I will not argue with you. But I must ask, what are your intentions, especially after that city?"

"We evacuated the populace, and allowed those dwarves to have their way with the city proper. I will take responsibility for it from here. As for you, I want you and your people to depart from this world. I will grant you the luxury of a full and complete evacuation, and you are forbidden to return."

"I thank you. This is a generous offer."

"As for your leader, the one you call Marshal Darumon, I hold a number of grudges against him and his treatment of the people of Rolsklinde, at the very least. My studies of his activities there lead me to believe he was treating them no better than livestock. Commander, the society I come from holds some rather prestigious morals where life is concerned. His actions go well beyond any easily definable crime."

"I am not personally familiar with his activities in that city, other than a form of management of the populace for containment reasons."

"I see. My investigation of this world, and the various societies he seemed to be controlling, suggests he does not commonly give out anything you do not need to know beyond serving your immediate function. So, perhaps he did not share anything with you because it was not your concern to know of it. This is unfortunate, as you might actually hold an opinion…but then, this is probably the point."

"I…" he holds as yet another tick flinches his cheek. He continues tensely, "…do not have anything to say on that at this time."

"But you are the highest-ranking officer in your military, are you not? Does this not demand you to be in the know, regardless of anything else?"

Inside the command center, the operator at the com-station, and others in the room, watched and listened to the conversation. They looked up at the Commander to see his face showing stress, and several more ticks erupted and flashed through his cheek.

"It should," he accedes disconcertedly. "I will admit he does keep many secrets. I have interpreted these to be personal information."

"Very well, so he has personal information, but again, you are the High Commander of the Suuden-Aryku military, based on Azgarén, and yet you are apparently under the authority of an alien creature. How does your government respond to this?"

"They…" he pauses in consideration, "…accepted his plea for aid, they granted him authority to modify our military, and since only he knows his true enemies, we are asked to follow his lead."

"And so it is. And I suppose this might seem reasonable, at least on the surface. But again, here we are. If this is his lead, I do not care for the results."

"He did claim you to be a part of this opposing faction, but my impression is he did not recognize you immediately. Can you explain?"

"Without a specific reference to who he is opposing, it is difficult to say. What I can say is this. I am the king of the world we call Tae'Eladar. Tae'Eladar is owned by someone who refurbished a dead world and seeded it with new life. Later, they installed me to govern it. Therefore, if his claim involves this, or anything similar, I believe he must be in error, as I am familiar with a long history of that space, and this history tells of a completely different body to be in the governing position. But this now leads us to him sending a secret mission of orcs into my world, clearly for subversive purposes, and they started a war with my people."

"He did mention this action with his agents."

"Very good, and I am here for the sole reason of protecting my home and my people. Prior to this, I did not know of you, him, Velen, or the existence of this world. Ours is in a completely different universe, Commander. So, whatever it is he is claiming to be opposing, either you made a wrong turn somewhere, or these others must span a rather broad space. Although, at this point, I might also suggest, if he is truly opposing anyone who might span a dimensional bound into this space, if I were you, I would be very careful of angering them."

"Granted...although at this moment, it would seem we have anyway."

"Yes, for the merit of this one world alone."

The comms officer now turns to the Commander.

"Sir, if what he says is true, could we have made an error in this operation?"

"According to the Marshal," the Commander reflects. "This occurred sometime prior to his arrival on Azgarén. His statements suggest this other body to be his opponents, but he does not specify who they are by name."

He turns again to the com-link.

"Thaelyn, when you say this body owns your world, for how long?"

"Our archeological history informs us that someone restored it from an ancient ice age around thirty millennia ago or so. I came into it fairly recently, by comparison, but only after the local lifeforms had progressed to the point where it was warranted."

"Understood, and this precedes any reasonable claims. What about this other body? He claims you are a part of it."

"Again, without a proper name, and if he never even gave you a name, the answer to this becomes problematic. On a side note, I would imagine this Marshal of yours is not physically present with you in that room, correct? Otherwise, I think he might have something of his own to say by now."

"This is correct, he is currently in his office."

"Very well. When we are finished, I would like to share a word or two with him directly. But for now, this is exclusively for you and your men, in the event that one day you might realize an opportunity to pull these details together. This benefactor of yours, I am assuming the one called Sargeras, if he and the Marshal are pursuing any such opponents as the society I am associated with, you should know that the Estelar, as they are called, govern the greater part of Creation, which involves virtually anything and everything of interest out there. They are a governing body that is not limited to any one universe. They are a society of laws, policies, and practices that serve to protect all forms of life. If we look at this world, this is a clear violation of that. And as I said, if this is the direction he is leading you on, followed by invading my world, this will land you in a lot of trouble."

"I understand, but at the same time, he told us he once occupied that space, and it was taken from him."

"All right, let us examine this a moment. If we say he invaded my world with orcs as part of a clandestine operation aimed elsewhere, and it was only those orcs who made trouble, and I know orcs can be difficult to get along with, we could then excuse the Marshal for this, if this was not his original intention. But then, we must ask this. My spies say they were looking for a path of some kind. This suggests he is trying to locate an endpoint. But why would he need them for this purpose? They are not native to my world, nor would they hold any knowledge of it, or anything beyond that. They are not even as advanced as the local races, to say nothing of yours. And if he came from my local space, presumably hoping to find his way back into it, I would imagine he could simply program your ship's navigation system to find it directly."

The comms officer pats the Commander on the arm to draw his attention again.

"Commander, I must admit, he has a point. This does not follow logically."

"Yes, actually…unless we say our technology and his would not be compatible for programming a jump drive."

"Um, Commander, he spent a rather long time improving our technology up to a level to serve his needs. Do you think by now he could improvise the coordinates?"

"All right, this is rational. And this would follow logically."

"That is a very well-made deduction," Thaelyn considers. "But now, what about this. If we say my world is located in another universe entirely, why would he come here to this one with any such claims, regardless of ownership or allegiance, if his real opponents are located elsewhere? You surely needed coordinates in your jump drive for this one, so who programmed that?"

"In all the nether-space, of course. But, um, we were also following...um..."

"Velen? Maybe so, but why chase him all the way over here if your true goal is some opponent to Sargeras? Is Velen an opponent on such a scale to drive you to this extreme? He is not even military enough to defend his own position."

"Yes, I think I must agree. But he found his way here..."

"Commander, according to his people, that was due to a wild jump action to escape from you and your murderous aggression."

"A wild jump?" he surges, and then grunts from another tight flinch of the cheek. "That would be nearly suicidal," he whines softly.

"It might, but they seem to have hit a mote of good fortune on that one. And strangely, you found them...again...and this in itself might seem very odd. Can you actually track someone after a jump like this?"

"After a wild jump? Such a thing would be technically impossible. But our station received a report of an energy signature believed to be a tracking probe that followed behind them."

"Interesting. And it also seems that world is the source of these orcs. Very well..." Thaelyn feigns to close the topic. "But this would also lead me to one last point. Why would the Marshal go in search of you for help? As you are also from another universe. Therefore, we must be speaking of someone making some rather profound claims of ownership, and further with little or no regard for any lifeforms he crosses paths with along the way. This is already a bad sign."

"Yes, I must agree."

"Even worse is if he simply wiped them out of existence to make way for your staging outposts. This is simply despicable."

The Commander ducked his head and sighed, and again his face was flinching hard, now causing him to emit soft whimpering sounds.

"Agreed," he accedes softly. "I suppose we could say it was his authority that crossed the boundary, but this does not explain our actions in this world to…" he whines softly as he experiences another tick on his face, "…contain…these people."

"Commander!" the comms officer notes. "You are experiencing feedback. We should call a med-tech up here."

"Commander, or someone," Thaelyn asserts. "What is occurring over there that he seems to be groaning?"

"The Commander is experiencing feedback from the Suppressor chip. This is the one that also interferes with emotion, as it has a feedback component to enforce the, um…medical effect."

"This does not sound at all pleasant, especially from what I am hearing on this side. Is he well?"

"Thaelyn," the Commander resumes. "This is nothing new for me. I will survive, and I thank you for your concern. I will admit to your perspective. I will also apologize for my actions. I do not hold the appropriate level of background knowledge to interpret these suggestions, and the Marshal is very…reserved…at providing additional details."

"Very well, Commander," Thaelyn offers. "Then simply keep this in mind. I do not wish to place you at any undue discomfort for your chips, and further, if we consider the Marshal's treatment of others, let us not make matters worse if he is pursuing objectives that may turn around on us. Still, it is important for me to say that although I may not personally wish to destroy whole civilizations simply for their existence, the Estelar may find it necessary to take such action if those same civilizations are threatening others."

"I understand."

"Life is sacred, Commander…all of it. However, we must give our greater interest to the greater numbers. Do this again, and yours may fall out of favor. This…benefactor…of yours, if this is his traditional manner, may be leading you on a dangerous path."

"Acknowledged."

"Now, if you would kindly call his attention, I will share a few words with him directly."

"One moment…"

The Commander places the com-link on pause while he prepares to call Darumon on a local line. But before he makes the call, his comms officer pipes up again.

"Commander, wait. I am concerned about the implications here. How do we correct ourselves for this? If we made an error on this world…or if he made the error…" he glances out a nearby door.

"I do not have a response for that at this time. But it does remind me of words spoken by another."

"Another?"

"An old friend of mine, he shared several private conversations with me concerning some of his…opinions…"

As he makes his statement, another hard tick flinches across his face.

"Commander, perhaps you should see a med-tech about your interface."

"Negative. I am intentionally allowing it to fail."

"Intentionally? Commander, I do not think that is a wise course of action."

"Neither is it being in active mode for half an eternity."

He continued to the com-station to make his call.

"Marshal, your presence is requested in the control room."

"What do we have, Commander?" issues a raspy voice from the speaker.

"Thaelyn has contacted us and desires to speak with you. He called you by name."

"What?!" he shrieks into the com-link. "How could that abominable creature know where to find us?"

"We detected some of his scouts arriving in the local area. They

likely pinpointed our location, and I presume he used one of his…
portals…to find a way here.”

“All right, fine, if he feels himself so bold. But how can it be
possible for him to contact us? Even if he uses a Daanen’kai trans-
com, they shouldn’t have access to our channels or security encoding.”

“He claims to have found one of ours in the city.”

“In the city!” he screeches. “That’s not supposed to be possible.
Argh!” he screams. “Blast it! Where could he have found…oh wait.
Blast those insipid spies of his! Is it mine?”

“He says he found it in your office.”

“Naturally! All right, but what does he actually want? Knowing
him, he probably wants to rub his perceived victory in my face.”

“I cannot be sure, but I suspect to issue a warning.”

“Oh, but of course, why didn’t I think of that. Well, perhaps we
could listen to his little tirade for a moment. A parting word or two
between old adversaries…”

They end the link, and the Commander waits several moments
for Darumon to arrive. On entering the room, the Marshal steps
up to the com-station and waves for the officer to reengage the link.

“Well, Thaelyn, so you found us, it would seem. How do you
like my little command base?”

“Not a bad arrangement,” he muses. “I am standing out here
observing your people moving to-and-fro, and it gives the appearance
of a well-organized affair.”

“I am so pleased to hear it. We do pride ourselves on our efficiency.
But I hope you are not holding any aspirations of acquiring it for
yourself. I think it goes without saying we would not wish to see
you take possession of such an extravagant facility as this.”

“Such a pity, but I suspected as much. The results of what you
did in the city, even what you seemed intent on further north, leave
me to suggest you would do the same here.”

“Absolutely! So unless you would like to meet with these gods of
yours personally, I might actually suggest you refrain from any such
ambitions. But now, what is it you actually want. Did you come all

this way simply for a parting farewell? Perhaps you would wish to share a friendly cup of tea?"

"My dear Marshal, such a generous offer, but unfortunately, I am simply not in the right sorts for it today. No, I have too much on my mind, especially after what you did to that city up there."

"Ah, did you happen to hear about the most unfortunate disturbance that occurred? Yes, I just barely took notice of it before I had to make a hasty departure to meet with a prior engagement."

"So, you did not happen to notice what occurred after?"

"Not directly, but word tends to filter down after a while."

The Commander watched and listened to the interaction, as did the other officers, each of them reflecting on the conversation that came before. They were careful at this time to study the Marshal for his wording.

"Well, Marshal," Thaelyn reflects. "Indeed, it was rather unfortunate to see that level of destruction brought to a full city. My people communicated with me about that bombardment of the Upper Ward district. That was surprising."

"Oh, that. Yes, well, it would seem we had a minor issue to attend on our way out."

"I also received a report about dwarves marching on the city."

"Dwarves?" he feigns. "My goodness, did they finally decide to come out to play? I don't think I ever recall them making such a long journey before."

"Perhaps, but on this occasion, they must have been rather motivated. Nevertheless, between them and that bombardment, the city is a wreck. Fortunately, we managed to evacuate the people in time for it."

"Huh?" he blurts. "What people? There shouldn't be any more after all that!"

"I will admit, the noble families would surely be in a bad way had they stayed in their homes during this time."

The Marshal gawked at the com-station. He then roared at the outrage of those people apparently having escaped. His outburst shook most of the people in the room, causing many of them to flinch.

"As for the rest," Thaelyn continues nonchalantly. "Well, I had some of my people up there trying to hold back your plasma mortar equipped army with my shield mages. Do you recall that demon attack? This is the one. Just ask the Commander there, as he might be able to advise you on its effectiveness by the Naarg uy'Sodrad. It held up to these as well."

"Impossible! And intolerable! Just where did you find that thing?"

"We invented it to counter the blast effect I laid down in the Badlands valley. If it can hold up to that, I think it can hold up to a lot of things."

"Blast effect...and what about, um..."

"...Your fusion reactor in the basement? Oh, that. Yes, we had to shut that down. It would seem it was in a very unstable condition by the time we got inside that room."

The Marshal glared at the com-station and screamed again. The startling reaction was causing some of the officers to move away from the local area.

"Marshal," Thaelyn asserts concernedly. "I assume the Dean told you about my spies, correct? Well, I had one right under your nose. You might know the one, if you ever tried peeking into her thoughts...flowers and rainbows, if I am not mistaken."

The Marshal screeched again and pounded hard on the console.

"And just how are you able to describe such an imbecilic young lady as that to be a spy?"

"By teaching her how to present a false image to foil a telepathic intrusion...as well as play a role. We Celestials know how to do this, you know."

"Argh! You would actually teach...and then she did it! Successfully!"

"Indeed, she is a talented young lady...quick thinking and good at improvisation. I may need to employ her officially in something, like an anti-espionage service. Now, the city may be a loss, largely due to those dwarves having their way, but I find it interesting to see them with such extraordinary weapons in their possession. I wonder where they found those. Could it be that military transport we observed delivering some specialized equipment into their hands?"

"Celestial! Are you actually trying to taunt me now? And what else do you know about them up there?"

"Well, surely you should realize, at the very least, we would hear about them, for all the talk going around."

"Yes, of course."

"And if I was sending out diplomatic invitations after my arrival, they would be included, would they not?"

"But of course, the noble king and his politics."

"But they did not show much interest at the time. In fact, they did not even show enough interest to offer a simple hello. How rude of them…"

"Oh, my goodness," he feigns. "However, I cannot be accountable for their manners. They are dwarves, after all."

"I suppose so. However, we did find it interesting that they were said to be supplying the city with iron, and yet the city was not receiving a fair share of it."

"Oh, yes, I recall this from the Dean and his report. So, I suppose you were trying to investigate where the rest of it was going?"

"Indeed, it did become something of an interest, as well as the adamantium they were mining deeper down."

The Marshal growled coarsely into the com-link.

"Marshal, you should probably attend to that throat of yours. It sounds rather harsh. But anyway, we were curious as to the adamantium, as no one in this world even knew they had it. Therefore, we were wondering if you might hold any knowledge of it. After all, some of your people were wearing it."

"Yes, I suppose that was an unfortunate miscalculation on my part. The Dean told me about that little incident. You were clever to disguise your people, and we let loose a minor detail as a result. But not to worry, I do not actually hold such desires as to waste it on such frivolous exercises. It holds far too much value for other purposes."

"Other purposes? My knowledge of the material would suggest to me the Suuden-Aryku might not hold the native capacity to use it at all. How do you plan to apply this with such people who cannot use it?"

"Do not try to fool me, Celestial," the Marshal charges. "I think you are wiser than that to know there can be other desirable uses for it. But how I apply it, and with whom, is my own concern."

"Other uses…with whom to apply it…" Thaelyn allows his voice to surge, hoping to force a response. "Marshal, as a Celestial, I can imagine a few desirable uses, but most of those might be industrial. And yet, my impression of your activities thus far does not grant me to believe you hold such interests, not when you devastate entire worlds for it."

"You insolent little crossbreed!" the Marshal shouts. "Those of us from the higher echelons hold greater knowledge than one of your caliber should ever be given. Do not question me, as mine is above you."

"Keep in mind, Marshal, this insolent crossbreed holds some very close associations with those he is crossbred with. Do not tout yourself so boldly. Your actions saw you cross my doorstep with those orcs. This alone is tantamount to an interest in my home with your so-called desirable uses. If all you wanted was to conduct a mining exercise, this world alone, or any other in this universe, would have been sufficient. You should not have a need to cross into mine."

"I will admit as much with those orcs, and at this time I am truly sorry those bestial lumps disturbed your little paradise and drew you to us. That was another miscalculation, but one I suppose could not have been anticipated. The last time I peered into that space, it was not nearly as organized."

"Yes, you peered into it, suggesting an interest in our affairs. Be advised, Marshal, if you hold any such intentions for my world as what you did here, I will pursue you all the way back to Azgarén to exact my vengeance. And I will not be alone."

This quickly stifled the Marshal for any further outbursts, causing him to back down a step.

"Very well, Celestial," he responds with tenuous restraint. "I will have you know I do not have any direct interest in your world. It was mostly curiosity to investigate that place, among others. I had, eh, a bit of spare time on my hands and did some travelling. Yes! Surely, as one who understands the grander nature of Creation, there is more to see than just the local affairs."

"That was carefully played, Marshal. Keep it in mind. And would this have anything to do with a book the Dean had in his possession?"

The Marshal halts with his eyes bulging at the obvious implications of that statement. This represented something delicate.

"What book would that be?" he asks tenderly.

"It was curious. One of his students mentioned noticing it during some moment when he had it out for study. When he stepped outside for a brief rest, she apparently took the initiative to peek into it. What she saw was truly fascinating."

"Oh really! And what extraordinary details did this one reveal?"

"It spoke of strange creatures and unfamiliar places, most of which she could not interpret, but where someone like me, or perhaps even you, might be more aware of. I wonder where the Dean found it."

"Yes, how curious…I must wonder this, myself. They apparently had some strange old tomes on those shelves. You and your spies seem to be very thorough, even to know of this much. It took me four centuries to arrange this world…"

"In the modern day, perhaps," Thaelyn asserts. "And then, how many millennia before that just to seed the populations? Let us not forget that Door on my world with the abnormal origins that led them away, and then the arrival of orcs from places unknown, and by means impossible for them to achieve by themselves."

"Oh, yes, let us not forget that little detail…"

The Commander and his local officers all glared at the Marshal from behind his back as he countered this recent accusation. It was clear he wasn't denying it, and further pointed to a plan that seemed to involve this world as an expendable target, and from a much earlier point in time.

The Marshal continues, "…and then you tore down my efforts in barely a flicker of that time."

"By the time I arrived, this world was already on the brink of collapse. I had my work cut out for me simply to stop the destruction of what remained. As for your efforts, a simple exchange of information amongst the local populace was enough to do that."

"Nevertheless!" the Marshal shouts. "This is all the more reason to curse those repugnant mounds of primordial ooze, the orcs."

"For this much, I suppose you carry a valid point. Although, at the same time, I must ask myself why you would keep them as long as you did, even from before the time Velen and his people made that so-called wild jump to arrive at their home world. Surely, by then, you might realize the potential, or perhaps the lack thereof, they might pose to these grander plans of yours."

"Yes, but at the same time, they did offer a small amount of opportunity."

Again, the Commander glared at the Marshal for this response, as did the other officers who were listening to this cleverly concealed clue, which now suggested that 'wild jump' was not so wild. This further refuted the Commander's earlier claim of a probe leading the way, as this now represented personal knowledge pinpointing that world for ulterior motives.

Thaelyn continues, "This might also be why you so often described me as an inconvenience to your plans. I suppose it is reasonable enough, as you were not likely expecting one such as me on that world to begin with."

"No, I was not. My understanding is that one such as you would not find it worthy."

"While I might not put it into precisely those terms, you are right in a certain context, as we do tend to restrict ourselves to that which holds sufficient potential. However, I am something of an exception to this rule, as I went looking for something new."

"Oh, how delightful. I just wish you could have stayed there. But this can be just as easily corrected here in this world. From what we have observed of you, your society does not seem to hold any capacity to travel across space, is this correct? I certainly would not wish to see you on any other world we might visit."

"Indeed, Marshal, in our present day, we do not, although I should temper this statement with emphasis on the present day, as we are surely not finished exploring the sciences. I must thank you, however, for providing us with an escape from that shell. That was indeed most thoughtful."

The Marshal grumbled again, letting out a harsh snarl into the link.

"Celestial! Are you trying to deliberately mock me?"

"Actually, I would regard this as proper thanks. After all, I had long pondered how to teach our people the means of finding their own way out once we reached that point. And you so conveniently gave us the answer."

"Really! Very well, I shall consider this as another of my miscalculations. I probably had to drop those orcs over there by other means, and then simply let them rot after their work was done. But now, unless you have anything else to torment me with, I would wish to be on my way. I have better things to do than play this game of idle banter with you."

"Yes, to be on your way," Thaelyn's voice turns more serious. "Marshal, it goes without saying that you would be best on your way...far away, and you stay there. I care not for your presence in this place, nor what you did to these hapless people. And I care even less for your incursion into my home and whatever plans you truly held there. Actions carry consequences, Marshal, this much you can be certain of."

"You would now dare suggest that I cannot have my pleasures? You and your over-righteous kin are no different than last I recalled them. Raise this precious little world of yours as you desire, but one day we will return, and we will be a Power once more!"

The Marshal ends the link and storms out of the room.

The other officers in the room all glanced around at each other, and then to the Commander, who continued to hold his stoic poise through the full conversation. The only indication of his impression was that flinching tick in his cheek, which was repeating itself by now.

"Sir," offers the com-station officer. "You do not look well."

"I am adequate."

"Understood. But now, do you have any instructions? Maybe also impressions?"

"Impressions?" he muses distantly.

The Commander stood there a few moments longer as he pondered his thoughts.

"He called them over-righteous and denying him his pleasures."

"Yes, I heard that. Now I am reminded of the earlier conversation. Sir, among other things was that statement of the wild jump. Did you hear it?"

"I did, and this now represents a contradiction. Perhaps also premeditation."

"It does. I must ask myself who was programming that wild jump to a world with orcs on it, which themselves were apparently part of this from a much earlier moment in time. Also, some of those statements suggested a form of familiarity, but not necessarily recent familiarity."

"Meaning something historic, or perhaps ancestral?"

"I do not know if I could comment on this directly. The words 'last he could recall' might suggest something from a distant past, and then becoming something…again. A return to something he apparently desires. Also, that man did not claim to know the name Sargeras directly, but what if it is an indirect reference, as if to say something associated, but not him specifically."

"Perhaps to mean others of his kind?" Geilv muses softly. "Over-righteous kin… This could describe an association of one body with another…"

"And not a friendly one."

"Agreed. And then the word crossbreed, and who he might be related to. This might suggest something. Another body, a larger one. Someone owns something, and the Marshal seems to detest them. He claims he once owned the same, but now they own it."

"Something he and his kind once owned, but now taken away by someone else?" the younger officer winces.

"The Marshal did tell us about something stolen. And this

is where he might claim these associations of bodies to the larger opponents, therefore, our need to…contain them.”

“Stolen, yes. But Sir, by people described as a form of law enforcement? And then to reflect on this world and what we did to it. To contain… If this is his pattern, or even if it was a mistake, this might contradict the term stolen. Confiscated would be a better one.”

“Yes. The global destruction of a potentially innocent, perhaps unrelated world…”

The Commander pondered these suggestions, and the ticking of his cheek continued.

“Sir,” the younger officer continues. “Much like you, without the finer details, I would hesitate to comment further. If the Marshal likes to keep so many of his secrets, I doubt we will discover anything else here. And we are apparently under watch by these others to vacate with all due haste.”

“You are correct, Ensign.”

“Therefore, I think we should take his advice and not expose ourselves with our interpretations. Anything on a scale that owns entire universes would be dangerous.”

“Affirmative. Continue the evacuation. Make haste, and then set the reactor.”

Outside on the knoll, the two scouts watched and listened to Thaelyn on his trans-com. And even though they didn’t understand the Suuden-Aryku language, they could tell by the inflections that he was playing his usual interrogational games. But the finale certainly left an impression, no matter what the interpretation. They studied his face.

Thaelyn paused at the close of the link, allowing those final words to sink in for their implied meaning. He frowned gently as he pondered the various permutations of the suggestion.

“They will be a Power once more?” he whispers to himself. “They who? The two of them could not possibly hope to be any sort of Power together.”

“My Lord?” mutters the first scout. “What do you mean?”

“His last words, they will return and be a Power once more.”

"Didn't I hear tell they had it in for the Estelar?"

"Yes, the Dean suggested how Darumon might wish to create a weapon out of all that adamantium, and Adalon revealed what form it might take, but just the two of them…"

His voice halted abruptly as he spoke these words. The two scouts watched and waited, almost feeling a sense of doom descending upon them.

"He could not possibly mean…" his voice surges.

"My Lord?" the scout whimpers uncertainly.

"Men, pack up and go…now! He says once they are finished here, they will destroy the base, and I should think it would involve either an atomic, or their local reactor. I want you removed far from here to observe and verify, then to return back."

He scans the surrounding area for a suitable vantage.

"There, those mountains off to the north. Go there, quickly. Find a nook and crawl into it. And do take care to keep out of the blast effect."

"Aye!"

The scouts scramble to their feet and hop back onto the gryphon, latching themselves down with the restraints. The driver calls the animal to begin sprinting back up the knoll and take off. As soon as it's off the ground, he begins enchanting the transport sphere and it flashes away at blinding speed, reaching supersonic velocity in a mere instant.

With the scouts safely away, Thaelyn pulls out a rune from a pouch at his beltline. He enchants the object and brings his hand over it. He takes one last look at the conveyor and then claps down on the rune sending him back to the settlement. He then briskly makes his way back to the tactical office.

"General," he issues firmly. "Order all our people out of that region as soon as possible. We may have a small amount of time for them to finish evacuating, but they promise to destroy that base soon after. I gave instructions for that one team to observe and report back to confirm."

"Right away, my Lord. What about Darumon?"

Thaelyn approached the table and took his seat. He was mumbling to himself along the way.

"He must be mad if he thinks he and his Master could ever be a Power again."

"Excuse me?"

"Firstly, he does seem to hold an interest in using the metal for something elaborate and tried pulling rank on me for his perceived station of superiority, claiming one such as I should not possess such fabulous wisdom. In a certain manner of speaking, he is technically right, but this is beside the point."

"Of course...I think."

"This would also corroborate with Adalon's ideas, so we can assume this to be the case, and I would not wish to discount the potential, regardless."

"Naturally, my Lord."

"But then, he dared to suggest that 'they', whoever 'they' might be in his mind, will return and be a Power once more."

"Your Lordship," Marelle inquires. "Do we have any idea who 'they' are supposed to be that it would get you so upset?"

"I have one idea, which is just as maddening as all the rest. We spoke of his incursion into our space, and he admitted to peeking in on us. This is a clear indication of an interest in our local affairs, especially if you consider the Dean's reference book. He was investigating the various flora and fauna of the Outer Planes. But I cannot accept this to be for a tour guide, so it has to be for something else, and this might also involve their massive buildup on this world."

"A large-scale invasion of some kind?"

"But not of Tae'Eladar, as I did at least get him to admit he has no...direct...interest in our world, so it must be the rest of it. And if we factor in the Estelar, this will certainly correlate the idea. He also berated them for depriving him of his pleasures, and me and my kind for our, ahem, hybridized nature."

"Jiggers," Relissa mutters. "I guess he really doesn't like you peeps."

"I would hardly expect him to, at this point. Lastly, was his statement about becoming a Power again. Again…this is the word, as they once were a Power…the Primordials. And from what I understand of it, we still have a few in that old prison plane."

"Buggers and bamboozlers, ten times over!" Relissa yelps. "Are you saying he wants to bust the others out of that prison?"

"That would be a problem," Marelle moans.

"But to do so," Thaelyn affirms. "He would need to clear the way, and therefore his weapon."

"And that's an even bigger problem. Well, Your Lordship, I guess there's only one thing to do…"

Marelle gets up from her seat and steps over to her lockbox. She opens the lid and pulls out a smallish trinket she had been hoarding away in there. Relissa watches her, with a gentle smile slowly curling its way upwards. Marelle closes her box and returns to the table. But rather than sit down again, she stands at attention.

"Your Lordship, after a long and careful consideration, and a little encouragement from Rod…" she coughs subtly. "Well, Roddy…"

"Roddy, your Captain again," he smiles.

"Yeah. Anyway, he said I should do this, and with nothing holding me to my former post, which is a big pile of rubble at the moment, and never was much fun to begin with, I want to submit myself to your military service and join your most illustrious Order of Tyr. I'm already approved."

Now she affixes her Spirit test badge to her lapel for presentation and waits for his reply.

Thaelyn studies her for a moment, and reflects on their experiences together, and further on where they might end up going before this is done.

"Marelle," he announces thoughtfully. "I suspected a long time ago you might hold such an interest. Even from that first moment, when you so eagerly offered yourself to us as an agent for your Captain. And though I regret the condition of your former post, and for that matter the rest of the city, I must consider our time together and the work we achieved. I would be greatly honored for your service to our cause, and I will look forward to more of the same in the years to come."

"Thank you…my Lord!" she grins. "So, when are you going to teach me how to fly?" she winks as she beams a smile at the rest of the room.

Thaelyn rolls his eyes at the scene.

"General, do you recall my list?"

"Yes, my Lord."

"Keep it handy."

TO BE CONTINUED